I0578479

A Fiery Farewell

PAUL CUDE

Copyright © 2020 Paul Cude

This edition revised 2021

All rights reserved

Cover design by Damonza

ISBN-13: 978-1916352445

GRAB A FREE 'WHITE DRAGON SAGA' STORY

FREE STORY: As new friends face ruthless enemies that have designs on not only their bodies, but their minds as well, will an ancient mantra come to their rescue? Treachery, intrigue and a bare faced lie lead to gruesome negotiations. Will a cold hearted, duplicitous, double-crossing dragon fire the opening salvo in a wicked and unwarranted war, or can virtue and the moral high ground turn things around at the very last moment?

A Selfless Sacrifice is available for free when you join Paul Cude's newsletter at www.paulcude.com.

CONTENTS

1 DIPLOMATIC INTERVENTION

"Which of them do you think we should kill first, my love?" enquired Manson, every word dripping with evil.

"Funny, that's exactly what I was thinking," echoed a much softer and kinder voice from behind a huge swathe of the dark dragon and naga forces, some way off.

Instantly every being there, but two, turned in that direction. Telepathically, Manson gave the order for his troops to part, so that he could face head on whatever new surprise Fate had tossed his way. Immediately they did so, forming a corridor littered with huge chunks of rubble and numerous dead dragon and naga bodies from the battle that, up until a few moments ago, had been raging for some time.

From the shadows and debris at the far end of what they could all see, out strolled a short haired, well built human, hands casually held behind his back, looking as cool as a cucumber, pretty much without a care in the world.

'TANK!' thought those light-sided heroes that knew him, simultaneously, delighted to see their friend despite the precarious nature of the situation they all found themselves in.

'The rugby player,' thought Manson, instantaneously recognising him from their encounter at the Salisbridge sports club. Manson, along with his enemies, all wondered the same thing. 'Where has he been all this time?'

"Don't forget what I told you... I won't murder them outright!" a soft melody whispered within the rugby playing dragon's head.

"I haven't forgotten," he replied, also telepathically, already picking out targets, but not the ones you'd expect... Richie, Peter, Flash, the king, Fredric, Yoyo, the group of young dragons and all of the haggard King's Guard, essentially all of those here he was allied with, except of course the humans, Janice and Hook. Sights firmly fixed upon them, he knew that in but a moment, he could carry out what he had planned. First though, he had to deal out a little diplomacy.

Thanks to the unexpected interlude, nobody, including her love, had noticed what had happened, with even her mind struggling to deal with the fact that she'd frozen entirely, apart from the snakes writhing about on top of her head. Perhaps deep down within her very DNA, a distant part of her realised that the shock of the moment had all but rendered her temporarily useless.

'It can't be, can it?' she thought, trying to arrange the pieces of the puzzle together within her mind. 'Surely Fate can't be that cruel.' But she knew better than that. The markings on his body matched those on the outside of the egg just perfectly. Even after all this time, it was still ingrained firmly in her memory. It would also explain HIS savagery, and the way he'd fought, if of course what she saw before her was true. There and then though, her mind refused to accept the reality of what her body could see only a little way out in front of her.

Of all the king's allies, he'd been the only one not to turn away when the mysterious voice had spoken out of nowhere, his eyes locked only on HER. Despite the lack of magic, his blood boiled as everything left inside him rallied against their situation, determined to have his revenge, not only for his sake and the others that she'd killed, maimed and harmed along the way, but for the sake of the boy. Nobody deserved a mother like that, nobody. As far as he was concerned, it was time to put an end to it, and deep within his mind he vowed to do just that, at the earliest available opportunity. With everyone else turned to face the newcomer, it was then that he noticed her gaze was locked on an entirely different target, one only a few steps away from him... PETER!

Delighted to see Tank, and still shielding the love of his life with his relatively ordinary prehistoric body, the young hockey playing dragon couldn't help but wonder what was going on and just what would happen next. Events were as bizarre as it was possible for them to be. Just where the hell was this all going? It was then that he turned away from the dragon he thought of as his brother, as a feeling of being watched pricked at him like someone stabbing a needle into his arm. Arching his neck ninety degrees, he locked eyes with her, the embodiment of evil that had not only scared the hell out of him already today, but had tried, in vain it might be said, to kill him. There she was, glaring in his direction, eyes firmly fixed on only him. Terror, starting in his toes, wormed its way up through his ancient genes, almost paralysing him in fear... but not quite. The soft touch of a human hand brushing gently against the membranes of his wings dispelled the doubt, causing what little courage he possessed to return en masse. Swallowing nervously, he twisted his face into a scowl in one last effort of defiance against Manson's malevolent queen.

Surprised to see his friend, Tank, appear out of nowhere, it had been the catalyst that had staved off Flash's out of control spiral. For him, having his magic ripped away like that had been a violation like no other, leaving him an empty shell, a husk of what he'd truly been. But to see his rugby playing pal emerge seemingly from nothing, gave him the one thing that he'd lacked only moments ago, the one thing that had disappeared along with the power he was born with... HOPE! Something else must be going on, every atom in his body screamed. What? He had no idea. What he did know though, was that Tank wouldn't have shown himself if he didn't have a plan, and so the cool, calculating part of him, without his magic, set his mind in motion as to just how he could help his buddy.

They'd been so close to relative safety, at least that's what she'd thought as the energy barrier from the others had encompassed them all, buying them a brief respite, but now this! With her magic stripped away, she fought the panic and fear rising inside her, falling back on her decades of military training and the discipline it had instilled within her. However, nothing had prepared her for something like this... how could it? In all of her time and studies, she'd never ever come across even a rumour that anything like this could be possible. How it had been done, she had no idea, all that she knew was that she had to protect her king. After all, that was what she'd signed up to do, and he'd got them this far. So, shuffling sideways through some of the other beings around her, Amelia Battlehard made her way ever closer to the still reigning dragon monarch.

Through a haze of thoughts and against the backdrop of incredible pain radiating out from both hands that had been clutching the dagger, giving her all to channel the magic, the sound of one of her two best friends' voices drifted throughout her mind. Eyes closed, she assumed it was a dream, because Tank hadn't been seen since the very start of the raging battle that had ravaged everything around them in the fiercest way possible. It certainly sounded like him, her mind agreed, but either because of the pain or the shock of having the entirety of her supernatural power violently stripped from her, all the lacrosse playing dragon could do was remain huddled on the floor, her hopes and aspirations crushed, her consciousness cursing everything that she'd been through to get to this point.

Standing next to his friend, almost able to feel the pent up frustration and rage at the hopelessness of their situation exuding out of him, he was well aware of where all that anger was directed... his daughter, no doubt. Mindboggling didn't begin to cover it, and for the life of him he couldn't understand what she was doing here and now, allying herself with this Manson chump, or just what had gone on between them that would cause this sort of hatred, although he might be able to make an educated guess. It was one thing to have a family falling out, but quite something else for father and daughter to each want to kill the other. Fleeting thoughts of all this were quickly thrust to one side for George, because in the dire situation they found themselves in, there were of course much more pressing matters, mainly the one that had just walked out in front of them, the one that might have taken death off the table, if of course, as he suspected, he'd done virtually the impossible. It was inconceivable, unattainable... almost. Monarchs throughout time had taken weeks, months even, in an effort to bond with the enigmatic piece of enchanted jewellery that had been handed down across the ages. He'd read about it, seen their firsthand accounts of just how stubborn and unforgiving the ring had been. For anyone to have accomplished getting the consciousness it contained onside in under a couple of hours, least of all not the rightful king but a young and inexperienced mantra expert, was nothing short of miraculous. If, of course, that was the case. There were no guarantees, and the young man's hands remained firmly clasped behind his back. Wondering what other surprises lay in store, George urged the rugby playing dragon on, knowing that they were now well and truly in the last chance saloon.

It was a kick in the teeth, that's for sure, and one that had frightened the very life out of him. Across his many years, he'd never once heard of anything that could do this... strip a dragon, or any other being for that matter, of their divine supernatural abilities. But here they were, right on the other end of it, evidence that it was indeed possible. The scholar in him was strangely intrigued at the technicalities of it all, but his alarm at the dire predicament they all found themselves in wouldn't allow Yoyo to focus on that. More pressing matters willed him on, in particular his young charges and what, if anything, he could do to keep them safe. And then Tank had shown up, completely out of nowhere. What this meant he just couldn't say but it was something, totally out of nothing, when they'd needed it most. Inside, he just hoped it would be enough, and that the master mantra maker's constant companion had learned a trick or two from his boss, that would finally see them safely out of this mess.

Turning back to his love, having almost totally enclosed her beautiful, broken body on just about all sides with his wings, gently he ran the edge of one of his fingers across her right cheek, horrified at seeing her this way, hoping to snap her out of unconsciousness, desperate to wake her up. It did not have the desired effect, provoking no response at all. Glancing across at Yoyo, Peter wondered briefly if the dragon healer would be able to help. It was then that their situation bit him on the ass once again, reminding him that their entire group lacked any conceivable magic, reinforcing that he was well and truly on his own with Janice. Continuing to monitor his soul mate, for that's very much how he now regarded her, he hoped with all his heart that Tank had some way for them all to get out of here, and soon.

"It's nice that you've finally plucked up the courage to join us," ventured Manson in Tank's direction. "It doesn't surprise me that your default position is cowering in the shadows, leaving others to do the real work. In that regard, it probably mirrors how you play that stupid sport of yours on the surface."

Fully understanding that the devious dark dragon leader was trying to get a rise out of him, Tank was far too smart and switched on to react, that is until he mentioned rugby. That irked him more than a little, something that the enigmatic band found amusing. Concentrating on what needed to be done, particularly in light of the alarming circumstances his friends found themselves in, he put on his best poker face, and using everything he'd learned from his mentor, tried his hand at some diplomacy.

"You've had your fun and games. I think now might be time to consider the big picture in all of this. There's no way you're placed to rule the entire planet. And even if you were, what good would it do you? Insignificant pockets of dragons and humans in the most outlying places are no good to you at all. They would mean absolutely nothing, and there is simply no way you could or would control every living being on earth, making sure there would always be resistance, always be fighting. Surely even you can't want to spend your entire tenure on this world at war? There'll be no respite, no time to even catch your breath. It will go on and on like this forever. You really don't seem to have thought it through. Perhaps now is the time to come to an understanding, one in which a shared world would benefit us all. There are enough resources to go round if used wisely, and you wouldn't have to kowtow to any kind of dragon justice or interference. A bright dragon such as yourself must surely see the benefits an agreement like this can offer."

Reactions to the gentle giant's words differed greatly across the silence of the cavern.

For Peter, it was unnerving hearing his friend speak like this. Proud of the way in which he carried himself and his exceptional attempt at diplomacy, a huge part of him really hoped he wasn't trying to cut any sort of deal with Manson, because undoubtedly he would be betrayed big time at some point, the cost of which would be phenomenal.

Drifting in and out of reality, Richie barely registered anything her friend had said. It was a good job too. It was hardly likely she'd agree with any of it.

Amelia Battlehard digested everything the re-emerging young dragon had said, pondering whether or not he was sincere. It certainly seemed like it, because she'd sensed no duplicity at all. And she considered herself a great judge of character in matters like these. All she knew was that the member of their tight knit group who was unknown to her, very much held their lives by a thread, and was currently dangling that strand directly in front of the most vicious and evil monster that roamed the planet. Everything within her screamed that it was a disaster in the making, and that prolonging the inevitable was all that was happening.

Dragging his new, unfamiliar and truly astounding prehistoric shape up off the floor, all under the watchful guidance of the surrounding naga and dark dragon army,

Flash pondered his friend's words, searching desperately for any hidden meaning or clue as to where this whole thing was going. Nothing stood out... no outright lie, no hint of any plan. For all intents and purposes, it seemed completely genuine, a peace offering, an olive branch from one side to the other.

'How odd,' was his underlying thought.

The words could have been bellowed directly into their faces from about a centimetre away, it would have made no difference. For varying reasons, George, Earth, Fredric, Vasuki and Janice had no recollection of what had been said. The founder of the Crimson Guards stood consumed by anger, his logical and brilliant mind searching for ways in which he could end his daughter, in an all consuming trance.

Earth herself was stranded in the past, where she had stood outside a particular nursery ring in the middle of the night, about to hand over her egg. Thoughts and feelings from that exact moment inundated her mind, with a particular focus on the strange markings on the shell, ones that were now mirrored on a dragon she'd already terrorised and tried to kill, one only a short distance away. Contemplating what her deceased husband would think of the situation she now found herself in, provided very little in the way of solace.

Janice's mind lay broken, like her body, both still flabbergasted that Fu-ts'ang had been destroyed, and at the manner in which it had happened. From an internal perspective, part of her very being had been shattered into oblivion, never to be seen again.

Lying on the crushed, burnt and scorched remains of what had been a magnificent masterpiece of a floor, Vasuki's curled up snake-like body resembled something dragged from the ocean and left to rot by uncaring fishermen. He looked like a giant slippery eel at the end of its life.

'You're good,' thought George. 'The master mantra maker's taught you exceedingly well. Keep on giving him what he wants. Make sure he senses no deception in you, and we might just get out of this in one piece.' Now you might think those last two suggestions were reserved for that especially dastardly picture of evil, Manson. But not so.

And speaking of the all encompassing evil that resided in charge of proceedings...

Briefly he was reminded of the last conversation he'd had with the naga king in the middle of the pitched battle, the one in which he'd tried desperately to play for time. Of course it had worked, and whatever primordial magic had been in play had resulted in that gigantic silver dragon springing up in mere moments, almost at the cost of his own life. He had to admit though, that something about this sounded a little bit more... authentic, and although he had absolutely no intention of handing back even a smidgen of the power and authority he now thought of as his own, he did at least vow to hear the rugby playing idiot out. Madness by its very nature comes and goes, and right at this very moment, for good or for bad, it was nowhere to be seen.

"What makes you think you're in any position to propose anything? Your friends have been stripped of their power and are totally at my mercy. That just leaves you, and while I don't doubt you regard yourself as something of a warrior, I think these odds might be too long for even you."

Tank smiled, inside at least, determined to keep things on track and as professional as possible, not wanting to give any part of the game away.

"As you're well aware, surprises, unwarranted and otherwise, come in all shapes and sizes. A being of your experience knows that and I very much doubt would want to risk losing everything when it's still possible to take away so much. Let's sit down, negotiate, bargain, compromise... an agreement can be reached that satisfies both sides."

Not one of the conscious light sided heroes grouped together some way off Tank's position thought this was even vaguely possible, with each wondering in their own inimitable way whether the young dragon was at all in his right mind. Of course he was. There were just rules to follow, that is, if he wanted his plan to succeed.

"Are you being frank and open about all of this?"

"You tell me? Aren't you the one inside my head, able to see each and every one of my thoughts? That's what you told me you could do. And I believed you with all that I had when we struck the deal. It would be incredibly stupid of me to renege on it now, wouldn't it?"

"I was just checking... call it keeping you honest, if you like."

"If that's what you have to do. You at least implied that you had more power and more of a grip on things. It would be nice if we could just get on with it. I'm keen to be reunited with my friends."

"At any cost?"

"No! Not at any cost. I want the killing to stop, to end for good. Too many beings have died, both here and on the surface. It's time for that to end. I thought we agreed on that."

"We did... I mean we do. It's just that..."

"It's just that what?"

"It's nothing. Never mind. As agreed, my power will course through your veins should this all go wrong. I hope it doesn't."

"So do I."

Words across the residence resounded just out of reach, their syllables sounding more like static than anything else as the heartbreak of the past gobbled up all of her memories. Bentwhistle... she supposed it made sense now looking across at the markings. At the time, they hadn't known what to make of them, both wondering what he'd be called later on in life, not really able to see anything in the pattern themselves, and also not knowing whether or not it would correspond to anything on his or her scales. And it wasn't as if they were ever likely to find out, not without revealing themselves for the crimes they'd committed. And that wasn't going to happen. No! Both of them loved their new found life in Swanage so much, that there was never any chance of them giving it up, even for a child. And so it was on that fateful night, after completing all the paperwork, and making sure that her interfering father couldn't get within any real distance of their offspring, they turned on their heels and left. To this day, it was the hardest thing she'd ever done and felt as though someone had twisted a knife through her heart, something she was reliving right at this very moment. Closing her eyes and shaking her head, she cursed herself for not putting things together when Manson had brought forth this whelp in his human guise. BENTWHISTLE! It should have at least occurred to her to take a look, get him to transform back. But it didn't, and now here they were. If she was correct, and she was pretty sure she was, then her long lost child was standing only a short way away, opposite her, amongst a group of beings she'd vowed to destroy in an effort to become this new world's joint ruler. Things were never easy, never straightforward.

Watching in stunned silence, George, the rightful heir to this kingdom and the entire planet, wondered exactly what the rugby playing dragon before them had agreed to in an effort to gain the ring's trust. Knowing firsthand just how stubborn and dupl... no! Not duplicitous, more arrogant and conceited. He knew just how arrogant and conceited it was, which offered more of a challenge than anything else. Whatever it was he knew only too well that he'd have agreed to practically anything to save his friends, they all would have in fact. He just hoped it didn't come back to bite him in the back end of the trouser department much later on.

After some consideration, Manson replied.

"How about I give you all Australia, and you can live out

your precious little lives there, alongside their population of humans? Can't say fairer than that."

"That's a little unrealistic, don't you think?"

"Seems like the perfect plan. A colony full of criminals getting a new influx. Sounds ideal."

Deep, deep within himself, he wondered if the doubts had started, whether or not the consciousness he was now bound to could see exactly where this was going, and if any so called 'red lines' had already been crossed, or would be shortly. It was a roundabout way to get where they were going, that's for sure. But if it got them there, then that's all that mattered.

Amongst Yoyo's band of misfits, doubts and fear started to reverberate. They'd all, as much as was dragonly possible, recovered from having their primeval powers so brutally stripped away, and were now listening intently to the conversation echoing throughout the arena where the mammoth battle had only recently taken place, all the time sharing their thoughts telepathically, which they were still able to do, despite the attack.

"Our boy can't really be serious about doing a deal, can he?" asked Monty.

"It's not the craziest thing that's happened today," declared Wiz.

"There's no way in hell that he'll honour it," observed Hillier. *"He must be the least trustworthy being on the entire planet, politicians included."*

"Agreed," reflected Trayrin.

"So why do it?" mused Zebediah.

"It's got to be a ruse," put in Tina.

"To what end?" ventured Wiz.

"Buying some time for something," ventured Monty. *"Must be."*

"Or," added Yoyo, surprising them all, *"the dragon in question has a plan to save us all, something that wouldn't surprise me in the least. So cut the chatter and get ready. We might still get out of*

this yet."

Suitably chastised, the connection went silent while they all waited to see what would happen.

Regulating his breathing in an effort to stave off the darkness of having no magic, the tiniest glint of light out of the corner of his eye forced him to take his eyes off his demonic daughter for the first time since the dreadful deed had been done. Wishing nothing more than to be able to arm himself, to his utter surprise the distraction proved something of a stroke of luck. There, not three metres away, alone and discarded on the floor, next to a naga corpse dripping in blood, lay Aviva's laminium dagger, the one he'd inherited on that unofficial mission all that time ago, just willing to be picked up. Knowing that now was not the time to make any sudden or rash moves, especially as the eyes of the dread force of nagas and dark dragons were upon them all, he carefully mapped out in his mind, the very first actions he would take when things once again went to hell. He was certain they would, and equally sure that in the blink of an eye he'd be reunited with that weapon, and even without its vast reserves of magical energy, he would at least have a fighting chance.

Wings tucked in, standing there patiently, almost subservient, Flash tried to look as unthreatening as possible, mighty difficult in the magnificently fierce dragon visage that he maintained, all the time using his well developed vision to take in what his allies were doing, trying to get an overview of the circumstances they all found themselves in. Fredric, he could see, was eyeing Richie's stunning looking dagger on the floor only a short way in front of him, no doubt ready for one last stand... a dragon after his own heart. The young lacrosse player was still curled up on the marble, on the exact spot she'd last been seen when powering the shield, whimpering quietly, nursing her badly burned hands. His heart went out to her, but he knew that now was not the time. Peter's cute little dragon form that could very easily have nestled underneath one of his wings stood curled around Janice, who he could just make out lying prone on the floor. Momentarily he wondered what effect the destruction of the weapon Fu-ts'ang had had on her mind. No doubt some kind of psychic feedback had rendered her all but out of the fight. Internally he wished her well, knowing that if not for the courage and strength she'd shown during her time down here, then almost certainly none of them would have gotten this far. Yoyo's band of resilient renegades appeared to have stumbled back to their feet, no doubt feeling the effects of being without their supernatural gift. If their out of the box thinking could come to the fore even now, without all their dragon given magic, then they might yet have a part to play. Yoyo, standing ready, defiant and angry, gave him a sly wink as their eyes briefly met. Returning the gesture, he knew that the Australian healer would give his all in an effort to protect everyone here, particularly his young charges. The impressive looking female dragon that had led the king's force gave him a surreptitious nod when he looked in her direction. In his mind's eye, Flash knew she'd be up for the fight, ready no doubt to die for her king, in very much the same way he was. And that left George, the being that he was responsible for, and the one he would protect up to and including his dying breath. Strangely, thought Flash, the rightful king of this world for how much longer, who knew, looked remarkably calm and at ease. Almost as if he knew something most didn't, which in fact he did. Licking his humungous dragon lips and rolling his giant prehistoric head all the way around his shoulders, Flash readied the anger and injustice within him, prepared to let it flood his body when the time came, hoping that it would be a suitable substitute for the supernatural power that was not only missing, but that he craved.

"So... what do you think, are we at that tipping point you talked about yet?" asked Tank's consciousness.

"While I would agree that things aren't going quite the way I'd hoped, it's not all doom and gloom. He's at least considering a compromise of sorts, even if it is quite some way off reasonable terms."

"You really think negotiations can bring us closer together?"

"You don't?"

"I didn't say that. It's certainly worth a try," Tank continued, *"but you have to see where this is going. I don't trust a word coming out of his mouth. Even if we signed up for every dragon left to be held captive in Australia, I still very much doubt that would be enough for him and we'd be betrayed the moment we turned our backs. Is that not as obvious to you as it is to me? Please tell me you can see that."*

"*What would you have me do?*" replied the enigmatic band's awareness, thinking that his dragon partner would want to attack straight away, more than a little surprised by his answer.

"Be ready if this goes south in a hurry."

"I like to think that I'm always ready."

"I'm sure you are, but I think there might be a little something we can do in advance to make us MORE ready."

"And just what would that be?"

Tank told him, and it nearly blew his mind. And so while part of each of them remained in the here and now, smaller sub sections of their minds disappeared off on a mission to right a huge wrong.

It was something of a standoff, at least within her mind. Good and bad, light versus dark, fought for supremacy in a battle that at the very least mirrored what had gone on in this sanctum for the last couple of hours. Spiteful hatred for her father writhed and coiled around the edge of every thought she had. All encompassing clouds of darkness bubbled up within her mind, washing over everything, touching each memory, putting a twisted and demonic tint on them. Despite all this, one beacon of bright, pure, good shone through, washing away huge swathes of shadows, albeit momentarily. And that's what it kept coming back to... her child. Bentwhistle! Imagine that. She was the mother of a dragon called Bentwhistle. It hardly seemed real. In her trance-like state she pondered all the things she'd missed out on. Watching him hatch... some dragon parents like to do that, taking their youngling to the nursery ring straight afterwards. Others get called in, just when the *tors*, the dragon guardians and teachers, think it's about to happen, sharing in the special day. Missing out on his first words, usually around the time they break out of the shell, and of course the rest of his education. It didn't have to be like that. Some dragons opt to home school their offspring, much as some do in the human world above ground. It's rare, but it does happen. They still take their exams at the end of each year beyond year five, and the authorities closely monitor the magic used when learning about mantras. Apart from that though, there is little distinction, having their parents tutoring them aside of some unfamiliar *tors*. Arguments about which form of education offers the most benefits have been raging for centuries throughout the dragon domain, and are unlikely to be settled anytime soon, particularly with the planet about to change hands. Missing out on all these opportunities hurt her like hell, right here, right now. Seeing him standing there broke her heart, or what little of it remained. Memories of her missing (presumed dead) husband flooded her consciousness, consuming her with grief at what she considered a double loss. They could have had it all... a family life, happy and full of joy... but for him. Again her thoughts turned towards the being only a matter of metres from her son... her father, Fredric! Brilliant black gorged on her intestines, grappling with her insides, winding around her organs, embedding itself within each of her cells, reducing the pure, bright good to but a pinprick of distant white light. Deep within, she was losing her own personal battle... BIG TIME!

Mustered at the back of the array of different species that it regarded as its troops, one of the leaders, shaped very much like a unicorn but with one noticeable difference, reared up on its hind legs unexpectedly, startling all those around it. Ordering them through their psychic link to calm down, the head ra-hoon reined in his magical abilities, both shocked and delighted at what he'd just discovered. You see the mythical ra-hoon have a very particular set of skills when it comes to magic. They can't be harmed by it, but can be enhanced by it. They also like to feed off it, something that might be described as their primary purpose. At this point in proceedings, they were about to go after all the supernatural just outside the council building and were currently taking refuge and formulating their last minute plan, during which something had caught the attention of their principle, something almost unbelievable. Despite any outward appearance, the ra-hoon contingent were nearly in a frenzy at the amount of sheer supernatural power lurking in the beings in and around the chamber on the other side of the bridge. It was almost overwhelming, ecstasy, pleasure personified. But just a moment ago, their leader had gotten a sniff of something else. Only briefly of course, but whatever it was it made all the other magic in and around where they were, pale into comparison. As supernatural sources go, it was vast, and easily the biggest he'd ever sensed. Almost as soon as it had shown up on his magical radar, it had gone, but it was here, and going nowhere any time soon. Vowing to personally hunt this one down, he gave a little nneeeeiiigh, and shook his mane vigorously, both horns on the top of his head reflecting the dull light of the room around the vast array of different creatures gathered here. Against the backdrop of pincers clacking, nifoloa buzzing, scaled apes beating their chests, snakes hissing, tiny jets of flame roaring, two-headed eagles ripping through the air and dark brown lizards scuttling along the wall, spitting out vicious bolts of dark green lightning, orders were issued. The time to cut down their enemies was close at hand, and surprise would play a monumental part.

Earth's Surface. The Black Forest, Germany.
Sunbeams dispersed in every direction through the cool, low hanging, thinly veiled mist that had collected across the surface of Lake Titisee, the densely packed tree line barely visible. A beautiful sight to be sure, one that contained a carefully hidden secret on the secluded banks surrounding the stunning expanse of water.

Before they could get started on their main objective, there was work to be done of the magical kind. They and their mission had to remain undetected and so with that in mind, a perimeter three kilometres out from the main camp was set and lined with a series of magical traps that were all interconnected and would tell them should anything bigger than a rabbit start to head their way. Given the circumstances and what they were about to attempt, their solitude and anonymity needed to be protected. After that, a supernatural bubble one kilometre in diameter around where they would operate was created, tested, and retested. It needed to be perfect and it was, excluding all extraneous light and sound, blocking and nullifying it totally, making sure nothing gave away their position or indeed their ultimate goal.

With a few hours of sleep gathered by all, and the sun poking through the clouds, reflecting off the water, the contingent of nagas and dark dragons, all in human guise, very professionally, got to work.

Avoiding using magic near the vault because of what it contained, combining all their might, they just about managed to lift it out of the electric Mercedes truck and place it at the centre of the clearing. Non-descript in the main, a dull, matt black, all of them knew it was imperative that they break into the lead lined box surrounded by a carbon fibre and titanium monofilament wall, to get hold of the valuables inside. It wouldn't be easy, and there would have to be magic involved, but orders were orders and the being that had sent them down was not one to be trifled with, on that they were all agreed.

It was decided that the nagas would use their supernatural abilities to try and break into the vault because, it was assumed, their very unusual and different type of magic was far less likely to react with the laminium inside than that of the dark dragons who were guarding and patrolling the perimeter. The nagas started a series of careful scans, wisps of purple and blue ethereal energy flickering across the huge cube for hours at a time, those in charge writing down calculations as it did so, knowing that time was of the essence, also aware that their priority was to get the precious metal out in one piece, no matter how long it took. It was a balancing act and a precarious one at that, but no matter. If it took days, it took days. If it took weeks, it took weeks. The most important thing was doing it correctly, and that's where all of their endeavour was fully focused.

2 A WAYWARD DESTINATION

A dull, hazy grey surrounded everything on all sides, much like a river enclosed in mist on a wet winter's day. Depressing didn't begin to cover it. There was a good reason for that. Of all the places in the cosmos, this was like no other, and one that any being rarely chose to venture to... mainly because those that knew of its existence tended to keep themselves to themselves, and once having arrived there, seldom returned to the realms of life. It didn't really have a name, although most of those passing through tended to refer to it as 'the gloom'. More a mid-way point than anything else, it offered little in the way of comfort, only encouraging those that travelled through it to move on at the fastest rate possible. A mid-way point to what, I hear you ask? Specifics were hard to come by, given its very nature, but it was what passed for existence somewhere between life and death, carrying the souls that once were, to their very final resting place. Not so much a ghostly gathering, more a departure lounge for the departed. Once your number was called, that was it. Time was up. Few ever made it back, though that's not to say it hasn't happened. Luckily for Tank, his soul was currently intertwined with one that had visited briefly once, only to be saved by a dragon monarch long, long ago.

Feeling the depressing dreariness close in all around them allowed the memories to come flooding back in droves. His true name all but forgotten, given just how long he'd been away, For'son was startled as his time in the land of Ahrensburg returned. It had been a favour for the pal he'd fought beside many times, and one he was glad to repay. Their friendship had flourished beyond being comrades in arms, almost to the point of brothers, at least in his eyes. Inheriting a smooth and orderly domain, one issue and one issue only kept things from being perfect... the outlying region of Ahrensburg. Weekly reports inundated the monarch's desk about the undeniable levels of poverty amongst the dragons, the sickening brutality with which the humans were treated and the cruel and vicious way in which every being was kept in line. It was all his councillors talked about, and it needed to be sorted out in a hurry, not just for those in what is now known as Scandinavia, but for the sake of the whole world. Reaching out through more military channels than diplomatic, it was indeed an unexpected surprise when a proposition to talk about a treaty was thrust in their direction. Too good an offer to pass up, the king needed to act in a hurry as a time limit had been placed on their participation. Also needing somebody he could trust one hundred percent, that led him to believe there was just one person for the job. That's right, you've guessed it... For'son! With a small entourage of trained diplomats, he left in an effort to bring peace to the planet, hopeful that they could convince the savage ruler to become one with the parts of the world currently under a single banner. It was all a ruse however, designed to kick back against the military might which constantly watched that ruler's kingdom, much to his displeasure. Once there, it appeared on the surface that things were going swimmingly in the way of most diplomatic efforts. Not so. For'son and his allies were poisoned, with the king's friend the only being to survive into the following day. Having watched the others amongst their party die a slow, agonising death, with little he could do about it because of how debilitated he was, the mighty warrior's huge prehistoric body filled with rage, anger and dismay. The savage leader sent back a message to the incumbent dragon king in the form of the bodies of the poisoned dragons, informing him that he still had For'son. Knowing exactly what he was doing, this opened the floodgates for a full scale, wild and unruly war that lasted over two decades. During the very start, For'son was tortured violently, in a manner that no being should ever endure. In the end, many months later, he died in terrible pain, broken and half the dragon he once was. And so after the despicable ruler of Ahrensburg was finally defeated, and his land brought alongside the rest of the planet, For'son's body was recovered. Remarkably, it was still intact, but that wasn't the best part. During his final day alive, a serving dragon that the monarch's friend had looked kindly on at the start of negotiations, had tried in vain to free the sorry prisoner. Strange and powerful magic had negated any rescue, but the subjugated servant had one last surprise left in her. In one final thank you, she cast a little used, and almost unheard of spell across the unconscious body of the, by now, dying For'son. In doing so, it effectively kept a tether on his soul, keeping him linked to this world, no matter what happened to his body. This spell and this spell alone kept the brave and fearless dragon in 'the gloom' for over two decades, forcing him to roam the depressing and cheerless realm all on his own, that is, until the king came up with the idea of having part of his solidified heart crafted into the famed ring.

Remembering very little until he awoke, bound to the band, it was as much of a surprise to the monarch as it was to For'son for them to both be able to communicate with one another. The consciousness has often thought that a side effect of whatever magic was used, whether in the crafting of the ring or by that poor servant dragon, was behind his ability to wield so much magic, and provide an almost limitless amount of mana. It's never been proved, but that's at least what he thinks.

Breaking through the misery and wretchedness, here and there vague shapes pierced the shadows. Dragon forms mainly, occasionally human, with the odd one or two so twisted and skewed it was hard to make out, each and every one of them heading in the same direction. So the two bound souls followed, tethered together via the ring, all the time on the lookout for the hero of the day, hoping they might once again get him to commit to the fight.

Back in the chamber, the politics of tiptoeing around the real issue continued.

"If you gave us Australia, you'd just be wasting a great deal of the earth's resources," continued Tank. "There's no way you and your force could make use of the rest of the planet. So much of it would go to waste. What would be the point in that? Surely there must be another way to divide things up, one that would benefit us both?"

On some level it sounded incredibly rational, even to Manson's twisted and warped psyche, and that was saying something. Beneath the surface though, duplicity, mistrust and the torrent of rage at having to live out such a big part of his life in that icy hellhole combined to muddy the waters of his mind. From moment to moment, you never really knew what you'd get from the deranged dark dragon, none more so than right now.

"I'm not sure what hole you've crawled out of today, or what you've been doing all this time, but I do believe you're trying to mislead me into thinking that your pitiful offer is real."

Across the distance separating them, Tank shook his head, his neutral face giving absolutely nothing away.

"No tricks, no traps. Just a genuine offer to end all the unnecessary violence and return the world back to some semblance of normality," offered up the rugby playing dragon.

"What makes you think you even have the authority to make such an offer? After all, the reigning monarch is over here, defenceless and about to be crushed like the insignificant bug that he is. Why should I deal with you, when I'm on the edge of having it all for myself?"

'A good question,' thought Tank. And one whose answer he was really going to have to consider carefully.

Back in 'the gloom', the clouds of grey, misty haze had retreated somewhat, leaving just an overall sense of defeat and acceptance as a steady stream of broken, dark souls travelled alongside each other on their way to the departure gate. Frantically, Tank and For'son scanned the crowded contingents for who they were looking for.

"There..." announced Tank, gazing off into the distance.

Following his stare, the enigmatic band had trouble picking out a target.

"What did you see?"

"A blend of two different shapes, one dragon, the other... sword-like."

"That has to be him. We have to move."

And with that, their combined consciousness took off, whistling through dark dense clouds, zipping in and out of other souls, carelessly on occasion travelling right through them, all in an effort to catch up with the one that they needed.

Time had little meaning here, with small concentrated pockets of it dotted about, as well as large swathes of it stretched to the maximum. Minutes might have been days, weeks could well have been seconds. After what seemed like about an hour, but could in fact have been anything at all, the pair of them caught up with their target. Almost impossible to distinguish particular individuals because in the main what remained of the beings was only visible as a shadow, in this instance it was made easier by what he'd become, long ago.

Although only a tiny speck of him had ventured off into the ether, the feeling of the wind rushing across his body as their psyches chased down their quarry made the hairs on Tank's arms stand to attention, despite still being stood in the private residence. It was exhilarating, daredevilish and as downright dangerous as it gets, because the only thing stopping them both from joining these tortuous souls, was the magic of the ring hidden behind his back, acting as a tether to the real world, anchoring their souls in no small way. Hopefully that would be enough to keep them safe for at least a little while longer.

Wrapped up in the pain from her blistered and burnt hands, everything that had happened since she'd put on the ring at the Indian restaurant in Salisbridge played out scene by scene in her mind as she lay curled up on the floor. As the memories assaulted her, threatening to crush what little of her remained, her conscious will rose up... just a little, in an effort to fight them off. About to be swallowed up because of her lack of magic, the lacrosse player in her had just risen to the fore, ready to fight, once again, for all that she and her friends stood for.

Blinkered, focused solely on one thing and one thing alone, the young hockey player who through no fault of his own had been dragged into this unruly disaster right from the beginning, was starting to get worried. Not about the dire circumstances that had stripped away their magic, held defenceless against a murderous tyrant who was determined to not only destroy all of them, but rule the earth with an iron fist, much to the detriment of its population. No! His concern was for the woman he loved, who remained unconscious below him. So far, he'd tried everything he could in an effort to wake her, but to no avail. He'd even gone as far as probing her with what remained of his telepathy, all to no effect. If he'd had any magic left, he would have showered her with it, that's how desperate he'd become. Ignoring the much larger picture, he concentrated solely on his love.

Back in the realm of the leeching light, unusually, something very British had happened... a queue had gathered. Writhing shapes in one form or another waited patiently to, quite literally, have their tickets punched. Towards the back, For'son and Tank's entangled entity glided to a halt next to the most curious silhouette there. Looking on, the two watched transfixed at the constantly transforming, graceful, drawn out Chinese dragon that seemed to be the dominant personality of the two, staying in flux for a little longer than its much more familiar counterpart. While intricate details were obscured by the fully encompassing darkness of its shadows, both were captivated by its obvious beauty. Few dragons like this existed in this day and age. And then it happened, something they'd spotted a couple of dozen times during their manic chase in and out of all the other souls... the change! Like a frightened, trapped animal trying to flee any which way possible, the ever present black wriggled, squirmed and twisted, each part of it trying to head off in opposite directions. Fascinated, Tank and For'son had decided to wait until its alter ego made an appearance, before announcing their presence. It was the right thing to do. Finally breaking the confines of the dragon guise, painfully, the dark squeezed and pushed, eventually bundling itself up into something far more familiar to the two of them, something ever present from the battle that had been raging on between Manson and the light-sided heroes. A weapon! One instantly recognisable... Fu-ts'ang!

Sidling up to the ghostly shape of what had been Janice's constant companion, until it had been blasted into smithereens by the vicious and evil Manson, it was Tank that started to do the talking.

"Fu-ts'ang," he ventured with a soft whisper, not wanting to attract any unwarranted attention from those all around.

Standing vertically, with the tip of his blade pointing straight down, (at least it appeared straight down, but up and down, left and right were an unknown concept, much like time, in this strange and awkward realm) the charismatic weapon turned on its axis, almost as if to face them.

"That was once my name..." came a garbled reply.

"We know, and we're sorry for what happened to you," added Tank, softly.

A short pause interrupted proceedings, almost as if the blade was pondering his response.

"YOU! I fought with you outside... the big building. What was it called?"

"Outside the council building."

"That's right... the council building. I suppose you're here having also been dispatched by that... evil fellow and his mate. I can't for the life of me remember their names. Sorry!"

Tank could completely relate to what he was saying about not remembering. Everything here seemed to muddy the mind, confuse and confound. Basic thinking became something of a difficult chore.

"Manson and Earth," he replied.

"That's it, that's it. Manson and Earth."

"But I'm not here because of them," said the rugby player in a soft voice.

That got Fu-ts'ang's attention, his hilt leaning ever closer to the consciousnesses of For'son and Tank.

"If not that, then what?"

"We're here to offer you another chance to rejoin the effort, wreak vengeance and finish the fight that you started."

"IMPOSSIBLE!"

"Not so," bragged For'son.

"What you say cannot be done."

"I believe it can."

"And just who are you?"

"A being more ancient than even yourself and one that visited this place long ago."

Again more silence, until finally...

"Even if what you say is true, I believe my time has come to an end. My expiry date is well overdue. I should have travelled through here thousands of years ago."

Tank was incredulous.

"You're being offered another chance. To go back, right an injustice, fight for good against the pervasive evil you know to be wrong, the wickedness that tore your physical form into a thousand pieces, and that's about to plunder the planet and decimate its denizens. You have

to come back!"

"I don't HAVE to do anything! Don't you see? The end, for me, is well and truly here. I've lived on borrowed time for centuries, sealed inside an inanimate object of great power, coveted by almost everyone. Granted, this place is as depressing as hell, and a more morose confinement is hard to imagine. But in some ways it's a relief after being trapped for so long. I appreciate what you're trying to do, but my steadfast answer is NO! And there's nothing you can say to change my mind."

Although not in his physical body, Tank's heart sank, knowing just what a difference the mighty weapon might make to the fight, if such a thing should ever come around again.

Subtly, well kind of, Amelia Battlehard edged up to the king's side, facing out across the void at the huge army there to destroy them.

"Captain," whispered George, glad to see his fighting partner.

"Majesty," she replied.

"What have I told you?"

"I know... it's just that I have a hard time of thinking of you as anything but our leader. You are and always will be my king."

"It's kind of you to say so my dear, it really is, but I think a true monarch wouldn't have found themselves in this mess to start with."

"I don't think that's the case at all, and I'm pretty sure you know it. Everything that's come about has been decades, if not longer, in the planning. There's no way you could have foreseen all of this, let alone intervened before now. And don't forget the betrayals, of which I'm convinced there have been many. Duplicitous double dealing dragons are almost as hard to root out as they are to say."

This made him smile.

"I appreciate the words my dear, I really do, but in my heart of hearts I still feel that I've let everyone down. And the only way for me to rectify that is to defeat all of this evil, although how that's supposed to happen is a little beyond me at the moment. Our young diplomatic friend over there might be the answer though."

"Do you truly believe that si... George?"

"I think you'll find he has a little something... hidden away, let's just say, that if used correctly, might just turn things around."

Hearing this brightened up the captain no end.

"Can I ask you a question?"

"Shoot!" uttered the king.

"Do you believe Tim was THE White Dragon? Or is it just possible that the Rump girl over there is the real thing?"

'Wow,' thought the king. 'Don't pull any punches, or hold anything back, will you.'

Already having had this talk inside his head with only himself for company, and knowing that now was not the time for games, the king answered the questions with total and utter honesty.

"From the first time I clapped eyes on Tim in his totally white dragon form, I was convinced beyond doubt that he was what the prophecy had referred to all along. It was a surprise indeed that it had come about on my watch, but there it was. I checked, double checked and then after that, rechecked. Everything about him, down to the tiniest detail, fitted exactly with what the prophecy talked about. That he derived from a human though, was something of a puzzle. Nowhere did it mention anything about that, or even hint in its direction. Personally, I would have thought it would have, if that had been truly the case, which is why I'm more inclined to back young Peter's claim that Miss Rump over there is indeed The White Dragon."

"Really?"

"Yes, I'm pretty sure. The markings on her back aren't a coincidence, at least not in my mind. And given everything that's happened, for her to appear here at exactly the right time to drop down from that vent, slay Troydenn and then perform as admirably as she did in keeping us all safe, leaves me in no doubt whatsoever that she's the one. Don't tell her I said that though."

This time it was Amelia Battlehard's turn to smile.

"Also, Peter said that the master mantra maker, Gee Tee, had agreed with his prognosis. While some might think that does little to argue the case," right at this point he gave a sly glance over to his newly returned best friend, "I believe this to be all the confirmation we need. I'd trust the old shopkeeper with my life, indeed he's already saved it at least a dozen times over."

This pricked up the captain's scaled ears.

"So you think there's still hope?"

"I do Amelia, I really do."

"If she really is The White Dragon," Captain Battlehard said, nodding in Richie's direction, "what do we do now? She looks a long way short of providing any help or any answers at the moment?"

"A good question my dear, a very good question."

"We have to go, get back," urged For'son, tugging at Tank's psyche.

Stubbornly, he refused.

"Hang on a minute I'm not quite done yet."

"What more is there left to say? You'll never change his mind."

Tank however, had other ideas.

"Fu-ts'ang!" he positively shouted through the darkness.

The bladed hero, having turned away, wriggled round to face his former comrade in arms.

"I've already told you, my answer is NO!"

Focusing fully, and like any professional gambler worth his salt, Tank laid his cards on the table, figuring that he had a winning hand.

"WHAT ABOUT JANICE?"

Although nothing of any real physical substance existed in this shadowy, drab realm, Fu-ts'ang felt very much as though he'd been dealt a knockout punch, only now remembering the shining beacon of light in the darkness that had kept him on the path of good, even when it had been easier for him to relinquish everything. Memories of his friend and all her hopes and dreams came flooding back in one flap of a hummingbird's wings. Once dead set on following the queue and ending it all, now real, unbridled conflict swirled around inside what remained of the fierce warrior and loyal friend.

Tank could almost witness the contradiction between the blade's two ethereal forms, a struggle trying to quell the dispute deep within. Deep down he hoped mentioning her name had been the right thing to do.

Hundreds of dark, dastardly beings looked on, some starting to lose their patience, others, mainly the nagas, magically enthralled by Manson's underlings, waiting with no fixed goal in mind, eager to follow any command issued, paying no attention to their king, the being they'd fought and sold themselves for, lying on the cold marble floor, off in the distance, free at last, and maybe forever.

Back at the department for the insane, deep inside Manson's malicious and malignant brain, thoughts about events going on around him were taking a new and twisted turn. Of the voices in his head, and there were many, one above all others stood out, constantly babbling that he was being played, and that this was nothing but a ruse. Others wanted to know - but to what end? Most didn't care, keen for it to be over, eager to be ruling the world and making all their perverse pleasures come true. Amongst the wreckage of an epic battle, was another epic battle playing out deep within his mind. Disturbing didn't really cover it.

Slowly, the remaining contingent of King's Guards started to come around, the assault that had rendered all of their magic useless having knocked at least a few of them unconscious, the rest of which had been shocked into submission. For each and every one of them, it was a harrowing experience, like no other.

3 LITTLE WHITE LIE

Things were falling apart faster than a self-build wardrobe without the accompanying screws. A thin vein of reliance had turned into suspicion. Suspicion had turned into mistrust, with mistrust certainly now edging towards downright rebellion.

'Damn,' he thought. 'It's not supposed to be this hard.'

"Lead a team," she'd said. "They'll all follow you," she'd said. "Oh he's a genius," she'd said, or at least implied. But she and they hadn't counted on this. None of them had. An hour had passed since he'd last had to lie... that's right, LIE, to his second in command as to what he thought was going on inside the compound, and exactly what they should do next. Three times now he'd been rather economical with the truth, and he could sense it was about to come back and bite him on his rather large and scaly derriere. Originally, he'd thought he was helping the situation, keeping up the confidence of those under him, leaving them with less to worry about, because goodness knows there was enough of that. Something very much akin to the fibs a parent might tell their child... monsters under the bed, about the tooth fairy paying out money for their teeth (everyone, even dragons know, that she's merely a broker until the teeth can be moved on), or Santa coming down the chimney into the house (that's most certainly not how it happens). By his thinking, truth was subjective to say the least. I mean if he'd wanted to be totally and utterly honest, he'd have told them all that the young woman they'd been briefly led by, was in fact the much discussed and maligned figure straight out of history, The White Dragon herself. Of course he hadn't mentioned it, purely because he'd assumed it would have been too much for each of them to handle, and he'd probably have been right. That in itself was one hell of a 'WHITE' lie. Looking back on it now though, he did wonder whether or not he should have. It might have at least bought him a little more good grace, which would have helped out right at this very moment.

Hidden in the darkness, concealed by a wall of slaughtered dragon cadavers, their meagre force a shadow of its former self in the midst of the senseless killing and destruction, an overwhelming feeling of doom and gloom threatened to overcome them all. Sensing their anxiety, and with the building housing the Fleet Street crystal node in sight, he let out a long, smooth breath, closed his eyes, and opened himself up to all of his primeval supernatural power, determined to be as subtle as possible. Instantly he caught the attention of all those under his command.

"Gentledragons... rest easy, it's me, your leader, Gee Tee."

Through the touch of his mind, he could feel the mental barriers from each member of his force relax just the tiniest little bit. Bolstered by that feeling, he soldiered on.

"I understand the discontentment you've all felt over the last few hours, and know I've played my part in that. As you're all probably now aware, I've not been as honest and forthcoming as I should have been with you. There were no malicious intentions on my part, I had just hoped to lessen the worry and fret, in the hope that I could relieve you somewhat of the burden we all carry at this moment. I now realise that was wrong on so many levels, and that I should have been totally honest and forthright with you from the beginning. I hope you can forgive an old dragon shopkeeper very much stuck in his ways."

Briefly a ripple of surprise echoed throughout the invisible connection at their leader's frank admission.

"From now on, I intend to be nothing but upfront and truthful about what we face, and just how we fight back. With that in mind, there's something I think you all need to know."

Sitting silently in the middle of the tiny dragon force, four humans all kept their thoughts to themselves, their minds ravaged by memories of their friends and families, wondering whether or not they would ever see them again and just how worried they were about their disappearance.

"Something's gone wrong, of that much we can be sure," continued the master mantra maker, sharing his worst fears,

having long since realised the trouble they were in and the failure of what was supposed to have been one of his most cunning schemes. Now was not the time to dwell on that. Action had to be taken.

"Steel should have set off the mantra some time ago now. Why he hasn't is anyone's guess, but I think it's safe to assume he, along with the other two with him, are in the hands of the enemy. If that's the case, then with every passing second, the chances of us as a force being discovered increase exponentially."

This time more of a gasp undulated across the dragon only connection.

"I have a..." Gee Tee stopped dead momentarily, his new found honesty giving him pause for thought. *"I was going to say plan, but on consideration, suggestion would be more like it, as what I have in mind involves each and every one of you."*

An irresistible feeling of not only surprise but anticipation as well grasped their minds.

Arms shackled to the wall high above his head, huge metal bolts having been hammered through the carpus and metacarpus of his wings to hold them in place, the heroic, reborn, laminium ball player looked quite the sorry sight as his torturous terror continued at the hands of the being Jar Man thought of as just 'Red'.

For quite some time the two friends, Jar Man and DomCon had stood transfixed in the darkened inner sanctum, surrounded by wicked, slithering nagas, too afraid to move even an inch, unable to turn away from the twisted reality unfolding directly in front of them. What was happening to their friend broke their hearts, devoured any hope that had been residing inside them, tore at their very souls. But they could do nothing, so perilous was the position they found themselves in. Severely outnumbered, without the mantra Gee Tee had taught their brother in arms, any thought of fighting had to be dismissed. It would have been instant suicide, both of them knew. In the latest fiendish twist, and having pulled off about fifty of the newly formed scales around Steel's genitals, one by one with a ferocious looking pair of wickedly sharp pliers, Red, enjoying every second of what was playing out, now tormented her prisoner by sending sickly bolts of crackling electricity into the extremely thin layer of bright red flesh that was now revealed to the world. The laminium ball captain's howls of writhing agony echoed throughout the building, much to the delight of the dark force holding him.

4 WISHES AND DREAMS

Huge oak trees disappeared off into the distance for as far as the eye could see on both sides of the road, towering over perfect paving stones, offering shelter to those top of the range vehicles that had not been parked in the oh so sumptuous drives. Garages, no doubt used as workshops, man caves and hobbyist hideaways sat next to each of the homes atop said drives, adjacent to stunning four and five bedroom houses. Perfection it wasn't, more of a kind of dreamy, hopeful bliss. Suddenly a stunning light wood coloured front door clicked open, the sound of a couple's laughter echoing out from within. Loving whispered words accompanied a brief struggle, as the pushchair was very carefully manoeuvred across the threshold. Giggling followed by a brief kiss preceded the lovers heading down the drive, past their cars and out towards the road, all the time wheeling their precious cargo.

'Odd,' was his only thought as the images continued to play out. Blinking, or at least that's what he thought he was doing, something that was all but impossible given his non-corporeal form, the former dragon, long lost weapon and now ghostly visage tried to shake his visions away. Unfortunately for him, they continued on their own steady course.

A tiny squeak from a misaligned wheel on the pushchair punctuated the birdsong resonating from the magnificent specimens lining the street all around them. With the male steering, his female partner wove her arm around his waist, in this scene of harmonious contentment. Slowly the figures crept forwards, both their faces obscured due to them facing each other, occasionally kissing, but mostly gazing happily into each other's eyes.

All thoughts of shaking the pictures gone from his head, an everlasting impression of warmth, fulfilment and joy radiated out, fully encompassing his current cold, dark form.

With the inquisitiveness and wonder of a young child, the former killer and master weapon smith watched in awe to see what would play out next.

Almost reaching the road, the couple with the pushchair stopped momentarily, swung the buggy around, and in that instant their faces became apparent. Sucking in what should have been a deep breath, an involuntary cold shiver ran across his ethereal form, for he knew both of those in front of him. The male was the dragon who'd almost been the first to die at the hands of Manson's queen when the battle from hell had first kicked off. Somehow though, the young dragon in the form of a man had escaped, much to his relief and that of his partner. Speaking of which, the cherub-like female face whose eyes he found himself gazing into, belonged to only her... JANICE! A sudden rush of emotions immediately flooded all that was left of him. Oh Janice! Instantly he yearned for their link to be returned, the one that would make him whole and allow him to wallow in her emotions, dreams and of course wishes. But it wasn't there, having been so rudely and abruptly severed by that brute Manson, at what for him had become the end of a very tragic and personal fight. Back in 'the gloom', his ethereal visage faltered, forcing other essences behind him in the queue to adjust their courses and skirt around him. Directly by his side, fragments of For'son's and Tank's minds looked on, ever alert.

Compartmentalising everything, from watching Manson and his queen plot and scheme, all of Tank's light-sided hero friends bereft of their magic, to watching Fu-ts'ang's shadowy presence stopping abruptly, being here now caused not only a shudder of fear to run through him, but made him feel lost and alone, due in no small part he assumed, to his time spent in this place, all those years ago.

It was understandably bizarre, at least, that's what he told himself. One moment he was conducting negotiations, the next, all of those in his retinue were dead, and he'd been poisoned, all by that crazed and outlandish dragon from far in the north. There'd been no clue, no hint of betrayal, everything had seemed fine, well... kind of. And then out of nowhere... THIS! Vaguely he could remember the effect of whatever toxin he'd been dosed with. Every sinew of his body hurt with the most abominable pain. Movement was impossible. Drinking was torture, and of course they kept him hydrated, wanting no doubt to keep him alive as a bargaining chip, or as some sort of trophy to display to those under him. But he'd wanted to die, that's how bad it had been. In what he knew to be his final day, a servant dragon had approached him out of nowhere and before he could ask, had cast some sort of unfamiliar magic upon him. After that, the memories were all but gone, with him only really able to remember snippets of dragons in front of his vision, some hoping to keep him alive, others angry and outraged. After that, he found himself here, in what almost every being that passed through it referred to as 'the gloom'.

Instinctively on arrival, his essence followed all the others there, figuring they must all know what they were doing. Strangely, he seemed to only be able to move much slower than those all around him, with many tens of thousands racing past him over the course of his journey. Traversing one hell of a space over what seemed like many days, but could in fact have been weeks or even months, eventually he arrived at what appeared to be a funnelling point, with all of the ghostly apparitions bunching up closer together, effectively queuing if you like. Floating in a sea of fog, occasionally the beings in front would move forward, at something of the pace of a snail. A mindboggling amount of time later, out of 'the gloom', a gigantic fiery crack started to appear, cut into the fabric of whatever lay before them, spewing ominous lava-like material in all directions. Only then was their destination evident. Neither scared nor concerned, he continued to move along slowly behind all the other visages, gliding ever closer to the ominous fissure that looked very much like the entrance to hell itself, having already accepted what Fate had in store for him. It was at that exact moment that something unseen exerted a powerful force on him, stopping him dead in his tracks. Unsure of what to do, and slightly taken aback, it wasn't until a loud voice started resounding around what was left of his mind, that he had any clue something was wrong.

"YOU CANNOT PASS! TURN AROUND AT ONCE!"

Suddenly filled with dread and fear at the thought of having done something wrong, his ethereal spirit started to panic and tried to sidestep whatever it was that held him in place and surge forward. Again the voice rang out deep within him.

"REMOVE YOUR TETHER TO THE PAST. AFTER THAT YOU MAY PROCEED."

'Tether to the past, what the hell does that mean?' was all that he could think. Spinning this way and that, the wispy form of what remained of him looked out of control, clearly attracting the attention of those all around him. Only then did For'son get the help he so desperately needed. From alongside him in one of the many queues that drifted off into the distance, a wraithlike darkness in the shape of a very fat dragon wandered over in his direction. Assuming whatever it was would stop when it got close, it scared the living daylights out of him when the thing flew straight into whatever he now was. If he'd thought his head was spinning before, it most certainly was now, seemingly mixed up with someone or something else entirely.

"Calm yourself," came a soft voice across the void of his thoughts. *"I mean you no harm."*

Slowly, he regained what little composure he could, and with as much confidence as he was able to muster, projected back,

"Who are you? What's going on?"

Amusement of some sort was the first thing he got back, quickly followed by a reply.

"It matters not who I am, only what I know. You're on the threshold of the afterlife, a place from which there is no return. Not all magical beings make it this far. It would seem you had great power, courage or a combination of both. That is the only reason you're here."

"Uhhhh... is that a good thing?"

"Who's to know? Certainly not me, that's for sure. But the only way to find out is to go through the 'Devil's Eye' up there."

Metaphorically, For'son gulped.

"I appear to be held in place by some invisible force that won't let me go any further. It keeps on rambling on about some sort of tether."

"Extraordinary!" exclaimed the interloper.

"Do you know what it's on about?"

Almost visibly grappling with his mind, the newcomer racked what little was left of his brains before answering.

"Legends abound with tales of magic that can keep a dragon's soul stuck fast in the physical realm. Old, dangerous magic that be... no doubt somebody thinking they're doing you a favour."

"So what do I do?" enquired For'son nervously.

"The only thing you can. Head back the way you came, and look for a way out."

"Is there one?"

"Not that I know of, but that's not to say it doesn't exist. This place is all but infinitesimal, so who knows exactly what is present here."

And with that, the fat old dragon's essence curled up in multiple directions at once and in an instant was gone, having skipped eight lines over and returned to his original place in the queue.

What remained of For'son's mind was blown, well and truly. Reluctantly turning away from what he now knew was called the Devil's Eye, a warm feeling coalesced across his molecules as he was once again allowed to move freely. Without hesitation, he soared back in the direction that he'd come from, or at least that's what he thought... who actually knew? Space, time, direction... it was all a clumsy mess here, with absolutely none of it making any sense at all, almost as if the apprentice had thrown this place together during the coffee break on his very first day. So with at least a purpose now, gradually weaving in and out of all the souls travelling in the other direction, he headed on back, all the time keeping an eye out for something that would take him home.

Time passed. Sometimes minutes, sometimes seconds, sometimes years. No sense could be made from any of it. All he knew was that he'd remained in 'the gloom' for what could be considered a very long time. Little did he know just how long.

Infinitesimally big would be about right. Over time, he attempted to map what he could, and given that the concept of time itself kept changing, it was difficult for his brain to understand exactly the scale of what he was dealing with. Just when he thought he'd come to an outer edge, boundaries warped and changed, writhing and wriggling, sometimes only a small amount, on other occasions a great deal. The one thing he had correctly surmised during all of what he thought of as his incarceration, was that the Devil's Eye was located in a far off corner, where two edges of the miserable existence met at a tangent, creating a huge funnel of epic proportions to filter those passing through this place directly into its path. Not having been back quite as far as when he'd been caught in the grip of the invisible presence again, he had however observed the Eye from a distance on many an occasion. Each time it scared the wits out of whatever remained of him.

And so it was that on one particular day, night, goodness knows what, as the all encompassing gloom never changes, something unusual tugged at his conscious will. Not so much weary, but more mentally fatigued, the disturbance within him was enough to put him immediately on guard. Having his wits about him did little to prepare him for what would happen next. From floating at a leisurely pace in the direction of what he hoped would be another outer edge of the incomprehensible dimension he currently found himself in, he was abruptly hauled off in the opposite direction at ten times the speed of anything he'd travelled at since arriving here. For the first time in he didn't know how long, discernible fear and terror gnawed at his insides. All but a blur, he crashed through hundreds, if not thousands of what remained of other beings as they entered this place and casually headed off in the direction calling them, scattering the wisps of their fine dark particles into what little breeze existed.

Dread freezing his mind, and thinking it couldn't possibly get any worse, just then, right there, it did, big time.

Approaching rapidly, a light sucking, perfectly round hole appeared out of nowhere on what looked like the floor, but knowing this place, could have been either a wall or the roof. Spewing out more of the glum gloom than he'd seen on any of his travels here, the anomaly, as that's how he thought of it, radiated the light it appeared to be sucking in around its rim. Almost on top of it now, he had no last thoughts, no time to think of any last words or even wonder what was about to happen next. In an instant... it gobbled him up.

And SPAT him out. Or at least that's how it felt. But not him or his previous physical form, but his mind only. Feeling defenceless, full of fear and worst of all... physically sick, it took his conscious will an age to get orientated. Eventually it did, and if he'd had a face, his surprise would have been palpable.

Not able to actually see as such, the experience was difficult to describe. He could understand his surroundings, know what they were down to the finest detail, recognise the beings within them, comprehend all of the senses, from sound and movement to magic and the supernatural. Best of all though, was the fact that he was back in the realm of the physical, something he thought he'd never see again. But just where, that was the question.

Casting out tiny tentacles of awareness, it didn't take his mind long to form a picture. A relatively large space, one that seemed vaguely familiar, one in which sat many small tables, with a much larger one at what would be described as the front of the room, around which crowded a group of very pleased with themselves dragons. And so they should be after ten months of constant work.

"Magnificent," stated one.

"Totally and utterly majestic," chipped in another.

"Perfect," added yet one more.

And so it continued until they'd all had a say.

A sense of familiarity washed through him as one of the sensory tendrils soared up high in an attempt to get an aerial view of what they were all talking about. Drifting over their heads, looking down directly from above, it was only when one of the dragons rose up to his full height, that he spotted it. When he did, each and every one of the words that had been spoken by the group finally made sense. What was he gazing down upon, I hear you ask? It was the most amazing, the most stunning and marvellous looking piece of jewellery he'd ever seen. As you've probably guessed, it was a ring, and one that would go down in history as one of the most famous ones ever to have been crafted. What For'son didn't know at that exact point, was that his presence resided within the crystalline structure that sat embedded into the fabulous piece of jewellery. The blue of the gemstones was part of his crystallised heart. It wouldn't, however, take him long to find out. Only a matter of hours in fact, as later that day the ring would be presented to the king, at a ceremony, as a token of the dragon domain's appreciation for finally winning the war with his adversary from the north two decades on, and to remember the friend who'd been lost trying to conduct the diplomatic efforts at the very start of things.

Peculiar couldn't begin to describe sitting in the middle of a plumped up purple cushion and escorted by all the craftsdragons along a twisting maze of corridors to the waiting dignitaries in the throne room, all the time looking down on yourself from above. That and the fact that instead of having a physical body, your spirit was now well and truly embedded in an exquisite piece of jewellery... surreal didn't begin to cover it as far as For'son was concerned.

Doors opened, trumpeters trumpeted, as a fanfare to end all fanfares buried the room in noise. It was a scene like no other and in all honesty rather a fitting reception for the being trapped inside the ring, not that anyone there knew such a thing had even happened.

Days passed, with For'son accompanying the king everywhere... well, what choice did he have? He was, after all, very firmly stuck on one of the monarch's long, spindly fingers. During all this time, all For'son could think about was whether or not he should try and make contact with the being he still regarded as his friend. Caught in a quandary, he fretted for days before reaching the conclusion that it could do no harm. So one evening, after all of the officialdom had finished for the day and his friend, the king, was relaxing in his own private residence, the presence trapped in the enigmatic band whispered a warm greeting to his long lost pal, having chosen a specific moment when the monarch wasn't holding anything he could drop and of course when he was sitting down. Surprised couldn't do justice to the king's reaction. At first he thought he was hallucinating, but after For'son had explained and told him some things that only he could know, they sat and chatted for hours, catching up on everything that had happened over the two lost decades, both apologising profusely for what had happened, the monarch for sending him there in the first place, his friend for not spotting the assassination attempts as they were happening. It was a touching reunion, made slightly more bizarre because there was only one living and breathing body in the room. Over the course of the coming months, in a time of peace, with the war won and no other challenges on the horizon, wondrous discoveries were made by both as they travelled the land, using not only diplomacy and tact, but sometimes outright threats and aggression where needed. For'son's thirst for knowledge, something that his dragon persona from decades ago was renowned for, knew no bounds, with his magical gift strangely increasing and updating by the day. As they traversed the globe, it was almost as if the information from tomes and magical artefacts contained in libraries, both private and public, was sucked up into him as they passed. He didn't even have to be particularly close. His record for this was over twenty kilometres. For his part, the king unearthed all sorts of new powers. Almost immediately the amount of mana he had access to appeared to have grown exponentially, and continued to do so for some time. Spells, hexes, mantras and all sorts of unusual magic constantly popped into his head, most shared by his friend, the enigmatic band on his finger, though some were just out of the blue. Learning to imbue magic with a limited self awareness was just one of many new discoveries, a skill that he taught George and which had saved George's life on many an occasion, including during the battle they now stood in the middle of. It was a match made in heaven, if such a place even existed.

As life continued like this over the course of decades, there was a corresponding downside, well... for For'son anyway. As their powers and magical knowledge increased, so did the king's age, and whilst not considered young at the time he gained the monarchy, the supposed loss of his friend and the course of the vicious and bloody war had taken its toll on both his body and mind. As the years passed, the friend confined in the band worried for his brother in arms and for what lay ahead after he departed this world.

And so it was that a conversation was had, whilst the ruler still fully commanded all his mental attributes. There and then they decided between the two of them, much to For'son's relief, that he, and of course the ring, one and the same, would be passed down from monarch to monarch, with a view to using his wealth of magical knowledge, power and vast experience to benefit whatever dragon sat on the throne throughout their reign, ensuring a legacy from one, for the other. Immediately afterwards, what they'd agreed was enshrined in law.

And there you have it. The story of the ring... For'son, his history, how he ended up in 'the gloom', became one of the few to ever escape it, and just some of the memories that were now circling around his consciousness as he drifted next to Tank, both wondering what the renowned weapon Fu-ts'ang would decide.

Slowly, the inky black form of the former cold-enshrouded weapon turned to face the two of them, images from the mind of its former partner having finished playing out. Abruptly it spoke up.

"I'd do anything to help her. But what you ask just isn't possible."

About to respond, Tank was beaten to it by his new partner in crime.

"I have a wealth of magic available to me from across the ages, the likes of which the planet has rarely seen, and I say it is possible for me to restore you to what you once were."

"Oh I believe that part's possible. But I think you'll find there's a significant flaw in your plan."

"And what would that be?" asked the young rugby playing dragon, just dying to get in on the action.

"The young woman... Janice, she's been damaged, and looks as though she may never wake again."

Back in the king's private residence, Tank's face turned to a picture of horror on hearing the news about his best friend's lover.

Momentarily, For'son's consciousness wriggled off in the direction of a different reality, the one in which Tank's face had just changed for the worse. Almost instantly he returned.

"You appear to be correct."

"Can't you do something?" pleaded Tank, to both entities.

As all three of their wriggling, writhing, twisting shadow energies flitted around 'the gloom', the most powerful of them, For'son, suddenly came alive.

"*I may have something,*" he announced.

"*You can bring her back?*" enquired Tank.

"*No... not that... something else that just may do the trick.*"

"Really?" he whispered in his friend's ear. "And just how many of them do you think you can take out with the dagger before they take you down?"

"It's a very special dagger," replied Fredric to the king's question.

"I know."

"How so?"

"Your grandson showed it to me."

"Did he now?"

"You think that unwise?"

"Maybe."

"I would never have taken it from him. You do know that, don't you?"

"Of course."

"Then what's the issue?"

"Nothing really. I guess I'm just finding it hard to get my head around the fact that he's been confiding in you, when it should have been me."

"That it should, and your anxiety is understandable, old friend. May I suggest though, that we focus solely on the problem in front of us."

"Agreed. After you've told me how many you thought you were going to take out with the dagger," said the king, smiling just a little despite the precarious situation they all found themselves in.

"Just the one, just the one," answered Fredric, his eyes glancing over to where his disowned daughter stood, some way off, next to the psychotic Manson.

Lost to the world, barely registering her new king and

other half standing right beside her, Earth's thoughts, mirroring For'son's first time in 'the gloom', lay tethered to the past.

Visions of other dragons living peacefully in the domain, all that time ago, regularly visiting their offspring at the nursery ring, attending graduations, recitals, shows and performances...

'What bliss it would have been,' she thought, wondering how very differently her and her husband's lives might have turned out, if not for their rebellious leanings that had led them to falling in with not only the Nazis, but the nagas as well. Instead of facing off with the dragon that she'd birthed all those decades ago, maybe right now they'd be standing side by side, ready to defeat evil together. It could, and in her mind, should, have been oh so different.

Neurons and atoms colliding at a skyrocketing rate did little to interrupt the madness fluxing throughout his mind as he stood gallantly next to his new bride, the future queen of this newly reborn planet. At least that's how he saw it. What had played out over the last few days had little effect on his view, with it being in his mind, very much like 'fake' news, even though he'd taken part in a great deal of it himself. As always though, impatience was steadily eating away at him, constantly gnawing at his consciousness. Bruised, weary and generally bored, he just wanted to get things over with and celebrate his win. All that was happening at the moment, as far as he was concerned, was that they were delaying his celebration, an event that he'd been planning in his mind for decades at least. And his want, no need... his need to be at the victory party, knocking back drinks, telling jokes, rallying his troops (all of which really didn't sound like him at all) constantly niggled at his psyche, battering his brain and chomping on his intellect. All in all, his mind painted a much more confusing picture now than it ever had, something that on its own should be a grave cause for concern.

'Australia,' he thought, 'hhmphf.' It sounded kind of sincere, but almost as if someone was pretending to be sincere for some other reason, although right at this very moment, for the life of him, he couldn't think what that would be.

'It does sound a little tempting... keep them all alive and corralled on one big island for all to see, for the rest of eternity, all the time watching and viewing. No doubt there'd be infighting, squabbling, vies for power, betrayal, treachery, double dealing. Perhaps we could televise it,' he briefly thought. But his underlying instinct fought back, overriding almost everything. And his underlying instinct was to kill... everything in his path. In a split second of clarity, or perhaps sanity, he turned to his queen, not noticing the faraway look in her eyes, and asked her,

"What do you think my love? Do we grant them their wish? Do we give them a second chance and let them live out the remainder of their lives in Australia?"

Garbled sounds, no... noises reverberated around outside her head, desperately trying to infiltrate the sanctuary of her mind. It was an interruption and an unwelcome one at that, so she tried to bat them away, ignore them. Still though, they floated through, seductive, tempting, all with an air of familiarity. It was then that she recognised them for what they were... WORDS! And just who they belonged to.

Realising right now that something wasn't quite right, the hot tempered leader of the dark force repeated the question he'd just put to his queen, paying close attention to her response.

"Should we, my love?"

Understanding what was being asked of her, the purple lines crisscrossing her face, covering up her own form of madness, took on a look of careful consideration, buying her at least a few more moments.

Throughout all her long, vicious and violent life, not once had she ever felt so conflicted. Her son was over there, almost within arm's reach (in fact he had been, and she'd nearly killed him on multiple occasions within the last few days). She was remembering back to that night, the one where they'd taken the egg to the Purbeck Peninsula nursery ring, extraordinarily late, in the hope that it would minimise the scrutiny they'd come under. Of course it had worked, but it almost broke her heart. Barely able to keep her magic contained, at that singular moment she'd have done just about anything to keep hold of her egg, and the tiny being inside it. But it wasn't to be and the love of her life, her husband, had made compelling arguments for doing what had to be done. And so they'd left, there and then, a tiny sliver of her heart remaining behind, forever bound with the being that she'd given birth to. And of all the things... here they were today, on opposite sides of the chasm. Despair and chaos remained unchecked, with fate, as far as she was concerned, once again dealing her a busted flush.

Unlike her human friend whose petite blonde frame lay hidden beneath Peter's squat little dragon body, the heroic leader of this whole sorry bunch of light-sided heroes started to regain consciousness, her mind reliving every sordid detail of the sorry debacle that had led to them being relieved of their magic. Letting out a ragged breath whilst still lying face down, flat on the floor, out of the corner of her eye, a gold glint caught her attention... AVIVA'S DAGGER! But then it came back to her... how all the magic had been siphoned from it, leaving it but an empty husk. Ignoring it for now, and fighting back against the pain from the throbbing in her head and the agonising stinging in her palms, very gently she stood, a wretched nausea and a sensation of spinning violently, her reward. Glancing around, she acknowledged her friends with the tiniest of nods or winks, all except Peter, who was too busy caring for Janice's prone body. For a split second she wished them both well, before turning her attention towards her other best friend, the one who'd appeared out of nowhere, having for some reason missed out on just about all of the battle.

'Where has he been? What has he been doing? More importantly, what is he up to now? And just what does he hope to achieve?' were all questions that zigzagged in and out of the monstrous pain that laid constant assault to her head, right behind her eyes.

Not giving a damn about anything else going on around them, the young, naive, inexperienced and utterly in love dragon, Peter Bentwhistle, only had eyes for his soul mate currently seeking refuge through no choice of her own in the shadow of his wings.

"Wake up... please," he whispered gently in her ear, hoping against hope that she'd recognise his voice and immediately snap out of it. She did no such thing. Searching for any last semblance of supernatural power within himself in the hope of sprinkling her with it, all he was rewarded with was a crushing defeat. Just like his allies, he had nothing... not even a drop of his dragon born abilities. It was then that he felt it, the cold grip of evil attempting to crush him in its fist. All the time cowering over Janice's inert body, his small scaly neck turned around, glancing right back over his shoulder and wings. Instantly they locked eyes, mother and son, one knowing the truth, the other as usual not having a clue. In that moment she felt nothing but unrequited love, a first for her in so many ways. On the exact opposite end of the scale, a bone chilling, frozen to the core, cobweb of terrified started to entangle him from head to toe, filling him with dread and a horror too tortuous to explain. In that one moment, his heart nearly stopped. So did hers, but for entirely different reasons. With the family reunion from hell still playing out, Manson got his answer.

"I think we should at least hear them out, my love," gushed Earth, as sincerely as possible. "Who knows, there might just be some added advantages."

Back in 'the gloom', For'son's indiscriminate shadowy shape turned ever so slightly to look at Tank.

"Did you hear that? The crazed one, she's advised him to think about the offer. Perhaps bloodshed can be avoided. Your negotiating skills may yet save the day. Well done."

He certainly couldn't say it, and probably shouldn't even think it, but the one resounding feeling flickering through Tank's molecules right at this very moment, in both of his guises was... 'GREAT!' very much sarcastically, as if you couldn't guess.

"So what is it you think you can do?" wondered the great Fu-ts'ang.

Thoughts of diplomacy still on the table and fighting on hold at least for the time being, the most powerful being there, and the king's former ring-bound ally replied.

"Not only can I bring you back, but I can return to you that which you so desire. I can make your will your own, and let you have full autonomy. You will no longer need to be linked to anyone. You'll be able to do your own bidding. How does that sound?"

Pausing momentarily, busy taking in every last word, Fu-ts'ang could hardly believe what he was hearing. Everything he'd ever wanted since being confined in weapon form wrapped up with a huge bow on top. As choices go... there really wasn't one.

Earth's Surface. Salisbridge, United Kingdom.
Throughout the course of his many years on this planet, he'd never known anything like it. To him, it felt as though the earth were in disarray. Watching the beloved cathedral explode had torn him apart from the inside out. Up until now it had stood for centuries, a beacon in the night sky, offering hope, refuge and solace to all... but not any more. The loss of life had been staggering, well into three figures, and that didn't even include all those hurt and injured.

Surrounding buildings had been decimated, with the city shops and the ancient Close that the cathedral had sat in undisturbed for all that time, both taking the brunt of things. Momentarily he wondered who would commit such malevolence? He supposed it was the same beings that were perpetrating wicked and evil deeds across the world. Berating himself for getting sucked into the darkness, Al Garrett shuffled the papers from the file on his desk, wondering just what the hell it all meant. Through a combination of his carefully nurtured contacts, some well placed bribes and goodness knows what else... he didn't like to ask the more nefarious characters that undertook the shadier side of things for him, almost every infinitesimal speck of information on the missing residents from across the city had been gathered and collated. It made unusual reading to say the least, with the local constabulary's conclusions lacking any real or definitive answers. What it did come up with was a starting point, one that just maybe with all of the means at his disposal he might be able to use to find some kind of breadcrumb trail that would lead to what happened and where his two valued colleagues actually were now. Their situations constantly played on his mind, not just for them, but the other missing individuals as well. Finally reaching the only conclusion possible, and with employees from across the company mortified by what had happened to their city, a powerful thirst for revenge threatening to consume him and a desire to find out exactly what had happened to two of his most up and coming staff, who'd been missing for days now, there and then he vowed to plough every resource he had into finding out some answers, and so lifting the phone, he depressed a bright green button with #5 marked clearly across it in white.

"Ahhh... Dr Island. It's good to hear your voice. Please could you join me in my office at your earliest convenience?"

5 IN THE BLINK OF AN EYE

It most certainly wasn't the answer he'd been expecting, that's for sure, figuring that she'd want them all dead as quickly as possible, finishing things off, so they could all then move on to the next phase of their lives. Because it was her though, he actually paused to give it some thought... Australia! Could it work? Would it even be possible? It was an outlandish idea and proposal, that's for sure. Logistically, he supposed, anything COULD be done, but the question was, SHOULD it be done? Amongst the madness and the dark, deadly thoughts, Manson's mind tossed a coin and through the misery, rage, stoked anger and eternal thoughts of vengeance, waited to see which side would land face up.

Back in the king's private residence, hundreds of dark dragons and nagas looked on dispassionately as the events to crown a new ruler for this unruly planet continued with a brief lull in proceedings. Despite the calm and quiet, a rippling wave of anticipation spread out across their ranks, keeping them on their toes (more like tails and talons), readying them for what was to come. Inside, to a beast, they knew the time was close at hand, and the limited resistance right in front of them was living very much on borrowed time. The end was nigh.

Locking eyes on Tank, vague words lost in the wind from only a short time ago came back to her, announcing his arrival on the scene. Deep within, questions about where he'd been and just what he thought he was doing now held a desperate need to be answered, filling her with urgency. But as she gazed fondly across at him, a feeling of emptiness was all that crept over her. It felt as though he was here, but not here. What the hell did that mean? Slowly regaining her strength, and her courage, the young lacrosse playing dragon stood facing the hordes of hell, almost ready to make them pay with their lives, well... some of them anyway. Even without her magic, she was still a formidable adversary, something every one of her lacrosse playing opponents could attest to.

Part of her mind questioned what she'd done, whilst the fragment that was thrilled to be reunited with her son across the way delighted at what had been said to her king. If she could play for time, then just maybe it would be possible to separate Bentwhistle from the others, hopefully presenting her with an opportunity to explain. Within her, words fought for dominance as sentences formed, some with potential, most instantly discarded. What she said needed to be perfect, of that she was certain, because she'd only get one shot with him.

Poised, slick, shiny muscles bulging, ready to be unleashed, Fredric calmed his mind and slowed his breathing. Still as a statue, hoping against the odds to have one last opportunity to kill his daughter, vowing to take it with everything he had, despite his lack of magic, should it present itself, the founder of the Crimson Guards had one eye on his devilish offspring and was exceptionally disappointed to see that her focus was still maintained on his grandson... PETER!

'She must have figured it out,' was all that he could think. 'Perhaps his dragon markings gave it away.' That kind of made sense, he knew. If the 'bent whistle' markings had been visible on the outside of the egg, which sometimes they were, when the evil couple (he'd subsequently found out that they'd dropped the egg off together) left it at the Purbeck Peninsula nursery ring all those years ago, then the penny may well just have dropped. If indeed it had, what were her plans for the boy? Death, a forced adoption of some sort, or a tortuous end to his time on the planet? Of course she'd already tried to kill him at least once that he knew of, perhaps even more than that during his detainment by Manson's huge force. Whatever she had in mind, he'd give everything he had in an effort to thwart it. There and then he promised himself that she would get her hands on Peter, over his dead body.

"Well... what do you say?" asked For'son, watched eagerly by Tank.

Without any sort of doubt or hesitation, Fu-ts'ang's flimsy dark fluctuating form answered.

"I'll do it. What do you need of me?"

"Not a thing. Just be ready."

"I will be."

Tank was delighted, only of course on the inside. Outwardly he still had to appear as if he wanted diplomacy, and a life contained in Australia, to win. Something of course he very much didn't.

"I've put a bind on Fu-ts'ang's soul with my magic. Let's return to the physical plane and see what's unfolding. Hopefully he won't be needed."

Nodding his head very sombrely, Tank braced himself for the return journey and hoped that it would only be half as bad as getting here. Inside, he knew that he'd done everything he could to give them all a fighting chance. What he needed now was some treachery and a double cross. If only he knew someone who could provide both of those things. Oh hang on... he did. As the fragment of him that had been in 'the gloom' was sucked back into reality, a small smile blossomed out across his vaporous face.

Cutting through the air as it spun, the gleaming silver coin hit the floor with a CLINK, wobbling precariously at first, before sitting stock still, the tails side of it facing up. Inside what passed for Manson's consciousness, a decision was made, with no going back.

Turning to face his queen with something of a disappointed look ingrained into the features of his bruised and battered face, Manson let out a small sigh before he spoke.

"For once, my love, I think your judgement may be compromised and misguided. While I value your opinion beyond belief, I truly believe in my heart of hearts that it's time to finish things off, move on to the next stage of our lives and start moulding the planet to our desires."

These words instantly snapped Earth back to the here and now, a new kind of fear stalking her body and mind, not for herself for once, but for another... her son!

Manson's words echoed around their shared link, just as they returned to the physical plane, Tank showing absolutely no reaction to them.

"Damn!" exclaimed For'son angrily, *"I was convinced it was going to work."*

Wanting to respond and say that's how the madness worked, Tank remained more than a little wary of the enigmatic band he wore on one of the hands that were hidden behind his back. For that reason he remained silent, choosing to focus instead on the plight of his friends, ready in every aspect to put his plan to the test.

Racking her mind for another way to extend the uncertainty, delay her lover's plan, buy every being there just a little more time, finally the hammer dropped for each and every one of them.

"I've made my decision RUGBY PLAYER," spat Manson, making the words 'rugby player' feel dirty, tainted and like an insult.

Tank stood tall, prepared for any eventuality, at least he thought he was. Much depended on the inscrutable presence trapped within the band he wore. If he went back on his word, or the agreement they'd reached, then this would all be for nothing and he'd die here today with his friends, something that might happen anyway, even if his plan was successful. Keeping the unkempt and battered features of his face as neutral as possible, he replied as diplomatically as he knew how, only able to do so because of everything he'd ever been taught by his friend, the master mantra maker. For but a split second, he wondered how the old devil of a dragon was doing.

"And just what have you decided?"

Glaring intently at the human shape he stood addressing, the leader of this dark force probed and prodded using faint trickles of magic designed to detect any underlying scent of deception. It found none. Strange!

"I will not give you Australia or anywhere else come to think of it."

"You're making a mistake," replied Tank. "It is possible for all of us to coexist. Please, let's just try and make it work?"

For'son watched with pride, pleased that the young dragon had stuck to his word and was giving everything he had in attempting to find a non-violent solution to the problem.

As for the light-sided heroes, they could hardly believe what they were hearing. Tank, almost begging Manson to let the remaining dragons alive, live cooped up in Australia.

'How on earth has he sunk so low?' wondered Richie. But as quickly as that one thought appeared, another superseded it. 'Never! That's when he would beg that despicable, evil and downright deadly murderer for their release. There's something else going on, that's for sure. But what, that's the question.' Knowing that her friend was up to something, no doubt in an effort to save their lives, she immediately gave him the benefit of the doubt, doubled her resolve and once again prepared to get stuck into the aftermath of negotiations.

From Yoyo to Peter, Flash, Captain Battlehard, all of the Australian's band of young renegade dragons, Richie,

Fredric, the singular remaining councillor and what was left of the King's Guards, to a dragon they all hoped with everything they had that the young dragon disguised as a human, referred to as a 'rugby player' whatever that was, had some sort of plan. And if he didn't, and if it wasn't absolutely the most amazing, most astounding, most cunning and audacious plan of all time, then they all knew that they'd be dead within a matter of moments. Watch and learn.

One being knew. George! Not exactly the details, but he had a pretty fair idea about the perceived diplomacy, the neutral facial features and the sincerity radiating off him like heat from the sun. For'son! It just had to be. And that was the only thing about this diabolical situation that gave them hope. Spoilt, petulant, stubborn and conceited at times, could all describe the arcane presence contained within the ring, but, and it was a BIG but, very much like the ones in Sir Mix-A-Lot's hit song, if any one being here could turn the tide of the malevolence, wickedness and disgustingly vile evil that threatened to take over the planet from top to bottom, then it was almost certainly the mind behind the magic in that fantastical piece of jewellery. And although they'd had their differences, and boy had they, George the king still regarded the unfathomable spirit as a friend, confidant and protector of the dragon way of life. In short, all of their eggs had been put into one basket... For'son's. Inside his head, the king wished both the rugby player and the legend good luck in whatever it was they had planned.

The time had come to make a decision, and make it he did. In truth, there'd been no other real choice, not ever, even before the battle had started, with everything that Tank had said in that mentally shared space proving to be true. With no small fuss, For'son, warrior, diplomat, magician and almighty supernatural god, acted.

Using the breadth of a split second, the powerful entity that he was carved some words together, spliced in some magic, added his own unique touch and with only a thought, released what he'd created off along the mental tether towards what remained of the weapon smith Fu-ts'ang, not one hundred percent certain it would work, but sure enough. In essence, all that he'd done was take a dash of intelligence from the mantra he'd taught the king all that time ago, the one which added a little self awareness to some of his offensive spells, combined it with a drop of his own finesse, and after tasting it to make sure it was sublime, added just a splash of free will. No other being on this planet or any other could have achieved any of this, or even come close. But his depth of knowledge was second to none, something that was about to be tested more than ever amongst the deceitful evil that he found himself in the middle of. After that, and with their connection blossoming all the time, he handed himself fully over to his newfound caretaker and opened up all his magic, hoping it would be enough.

Ecstasy didn't begin to do it justice. How he remained motionless and straight faced was a mystery, even to him. But he did, a tiny little portion of his mind listening to Manson droning on, "I will not give you Australia or anywhere else come to think of it." Dull, dull, dull, dull! Every fibre of his being cried out to do it now. This was the time, the exact second. But he knew, in his wise, experienced and ever calculating brain, that to give his friends the best chance in the world he had to wait, just a few more moments, for For'son's magic to kick in. When it did, he would strike like lightning. After that, it would be up to them. Mentally wishing them luck, he let the ethereal feel of everything exotic take him, and prepared himself for what he'd have to do.

"It's strange," announced Manson with a keen interest flickering in his eyes. "You seem so sincere, and yet somehow I can't seem to possibly believe you. Perhaps you'd like to clue me in, before I have you killed. I'd very much like to know."

As Fate and Destiny strolled hand in hand across a ropy old bridge, high over a bottomless cavern, not a care in the world, every being in the king's residence looked on, each desperate for some indication of a winning outcome for their side. Finally For'son's power delivered its magic, and so with all eyes on the discussion between Tank and Manson... it restarted!

From nowhere the air between the two of them hissed, crackled and rustled, instantly becoming thick, cloudy, statically charged and full of magic. Manson's first reaction was that his queen had cast one of her unusual spells. One look was all it took to confirm that very much wasn't the case.

'If not that, then what?' he just about managed to ask himself.

Similarly puzzled, all of the light-sided heroes, without their supernatural birthright, and that's just how heroic they were, readied themselves to fight. Think of everything that's gone on, the magical battle of a lifetime, and these beings, each and every one of them, were about to give their all, knowing that they'd be dead in only a few seconds if that. Bravery of the highest order, with each a credit to the dragon, and human (in Hook and Janice's case) race. Would they last longer than a few seconds? We're about to find out.

As the miniature clouds between them tugged and pulled, wriggled and jiggled, an almighty BOOM from within exploded out, knocking every last being in the arena off their feet. Stunned momentarily, it took less than a couple of seconds for all of them to get upright. As they did so, much to Peter's astonishment, his love, and soul mate, Janice, let out a long, deep satisfied breath. HER FRIEND WAS BACK!

There, where the clouds, static and thick magically infused air had been, hovering in mid-air, majestic in all his glory, setting a chill in those hundreds of beings there that opposed him, was the weapon to die for, the frost-enshrouded destroyer, something almost every being there coveted. Gleaming from impossible angles, a shinier example of metal it would have been hard to find. The blade looked stunning, not quite the length of a sword, but considerably longer than a knife. Of course you can guess its most eye-catching feature... that's right, the continuous circling magical moving frost that shimmered occasionally as it gave off an eerie light blue glow, all the while spluttering and hissing. As one, the dark dragons and nagas gasped. Manson and Earth both took two steps back. All the light-sided heroes had exactly the same thought simultaneously...

'What the ****?'

Nothing hung in the balance, there were no decisions to be made, it had already been determined at some moment before. What happened next was inevitable, with both Fate and Destiny agreeing on that, something unusual for them, as normally they argued like tired, stubborn toddlers fighting over the same toy.

Manson and Earth ignited their magic. The force of nagas and dark dragons followed suit. For all intents and purposes the light-sided heroes looked done for, if not for two of their kind... Tank and For'son.

As Fu-ts'ang batted away the first of Manson and Earth's magical mischief, deflecting it off into the ether, a cleverly designed ball of poison from the latter and a high intensity bolt of bright pink lightning from the former, Tank, formidable warrior, master mantra maker (THAT'S RIGHT!) and beast of a rugby player, closed his eyes, merged his mind with that of For'son and in one hell of a feat of the supernatural, using a fraction of the ring's force, as one filled all of his friends and their allies with magic. When I say filled, oh I don't mean he'd trickled a few drops into them to get them going. I mean he topped them all up in an instant, so much so that they were nearly all overflowing. And that includes Aviva's, or more appropriately, Fredric's laminium dagger, Richie's necklace and Yoyo's purloined ring. With the lacrosse playing dragon's mind the quickest of them all to react, up sprang the shield that they'd had stripped away from them, now much more powerful than ever. It was on. They were back in the game. GET READY!

The restoration of their magic was the biggest bombshell of the day and given everything that had gone on so far, that was saying something. Yoyo's young band of dragons and most of the King's Guards took a few moments to absorb what had happened, feeling the joy of being reunited with that which they'd thought had been lost forever. Not so everyone else.

Yoyo, noticing the young human warrior and other half to the stunning eclectic floating weapon, come round, turned back to Vasuki in an effort to heal the king of the nagas, knowing just how important he might be in coming events.

With a flick of his finger and a splash of his willpower, the laminium dagger that lay discarded on the burnt marble floor shivered for a moment and then, hilt first, shot through the air, smoothly landing in Fredric's powerful grip. Legendary, both of them, the gleaming metallic blade maybe a little more so, the combination was as deadly a team as Janice and Fu-ts'ang on their day. Speaking of which...

Opening her eyes, the sight that greeted her came as something of a shock, causing her to wriggle backwards at speed whilst letting out a stifled gasp. Only then did she remember that none of it had been a dream, only reality playing out far underground.

"Easy sweetheart," drifted his soft words into her ears.

"PETER!" she cried, wrapping her arms around his massive prehistoric skull, before laying her head against his.

"I'm so glad you're okay. What happened?"

Her delicate sweet skin nestled against the strong leathery scales of his face, thinking back, she tried to remember. Trapped... they were all trapped behind the shield. Something was going on with the two dreaded leaders of the dark force opposing them. He was going to try and stop it... stop them. And then out of nowhere... BOOM! He was gone, shattered into a thousand pieces, their link, their memories, their regard and love for one another destroyed in the blink of an eye. It was all too much. After that, darkness consumed her, up until now anyway. And then she realised, he was there, restored back to what he'd been only a short time ago. But something was wrong... she couldn't feel him, couldn't feel his presence buzzing amongst the background noise of her mind. They'd been totally and utterly separated. Racking her brain, she wondered what had happened. Was he bonded to someone else? To see him there outside the shield, which had magically sprung up after having been taken away, was something of a surprise. How was it possible for him to survive, batting away attacks, cutting through the hazy air, striking at enemies, left, right and centre, all without her? He must have bonded with someone else, was all that she could think.

"I can say with a reasonable amount of certainty that nobody could replace you, not even the mighty Flash."

"FU-TS'ANG!" she cried across their link. Only it wasn't.

"Hello gorgeous girl. How the devil are you? Did you miss me?"

"How are you even here?" she started out, rambling just a touch.

"That's a very long story, that I'll gladly share with you some other time. More importantly, how are you? When I reappeared, you looked damaged beyond repair. Are you okay?"

Thinking for a moment, still hugging Peter's gigantic dragon head, the young bar worker considered her friend's question.

"I... I... I... I was knocked out I think, the very instant that you were destroyed. There was a loud noise that increased dramatically in pitch before BAM, that was it, I was gone. And then I woke up, only a matter of seconds ago."

"Some sort of feedback from our link no doubt. I'm delighted that you're okay. I only came back because of you."

"REALLY?"

"Of course my child, of course. You are the most wondrous being I've ever bonded with and I'd do anything to keep you safe."

Janice's stomach rolled, goose bumps raced up her arms as a warm shiver ran down her back. In that instant she knew she felt the same way. Not so much love, as a friendship that knew no bounds, one that extended beyond the physical and into every other plane of existence. There and then, it was written that their familiarity and companionship would stretch until the end of time. It was a done deal.

"If not me, then who are you linked to?" Janice whispered politely.

"No one. For the first time in millennia I have control over my own destiny, and need nobody else to steer or guide me. When this is all over, I will tell you how it has all come about."

As the warmth and happiness she felt for her friend's new found freedom spread across their shared camaraderie, mighty magical explosions of supernatural power in every imaginable colour bombarded the shield they all sheltered behind.

"Good luck and stay safe during the battle," ventured Fu-ts'ang.

"You too my friend," she replied, watching through the transparent barrier as he skewered the hearts of the first two approaching dark dragons. Mischief, magic and mayhem had begun.

Amelia Battlehard, more than a little taken aback at the return of her ethereal power, watched open mouthed as the glinting laminium dagger soared past her leader about knee height, into the outstretched palm of his newly found best friend. Not knowing the details of their relationship, all that she could ascertain was that she'd never seen the king happier than in the company of this newcomer. Friends clearly didn't do their association justice, with it being obvious even to her, that there was so much more going on.

"Bravo my boy, bravo," whispered the monarch to no

one in particular, congratulating Tank on a job well done, knowing that he'd achieved what no other king in history ever had... to join with the ring in a matter of hours, rather than days, weeks or months. A glorious feat to be sure and one that had bought them time to regroup and given them one last chance to save the world... There and then, he vowed to himself not to let it slip out of his hands this time.

Flash couldn't remember a time when he'd been more proud. Not of anything he'd accomplished, or even witnessed, that was how startling and utterly dramatic and brilliant what his friend (yes FRIEND, he was friends with THIS dragon) had achieved. How he'd done it, he just didn't know, but he didn't care either. Full to the brim with magic, and back in THE most majestic dragon form, it was time to finish this once and for all. With that in mind, he let out the greatest "ROAR" the world had ever known, attracting the attention of every being there, and then sought to be released from the shield to give these bastards exactly what they deserved.

Watching Fredric's laminium dagger whizz past her in something of a blur, Richie marvelled at what had just happened, how much power she had at her disposal and considered exactly how it had been done. Although knowing nothing of the ring swapping antics from before the battle had started, deep down inside herself, she knew that her friend Tank had been involved somehow.

'He never fails to surprise me,' she mused, all the time letting her magic hold the brilliant defensive shield in place. Suddenly a cacophony of voices vied for attention somewhere within her mind.

"I need to be free of this shield," demanded Fredric sternly.

"You need to release me, Rich," pleaded Flash in his deep dragon voice.

"The need for me to face this horde is overwhelming. Let me out from behind the barrier, my young warrior. You've been a credit to everything dragon and human today and I'm proud to have been part of your force, but the best way to defend my king is to get out there and

take these scum down," declared Amelia Battlehard, telepathic cheers from the remaining King's Guards resounding around her words.

"*Hear me now,*" exclaimed Richie, pushing her voice out with magic to every light-sided being there. "*Some of us will remain securely encased behind this shield, providing refuge and respite for the rest. Our jobs will be to spot danger, heal and target whatever we can offensively. Coordination will be down to all of Yoyo's young dragons. You've more than proved your worth today, and I can think of no other force I'd rather have been fighting with than the one I'm with right here, right now. So those of you that are going beyond the barrier to join our friend, the mighty and fearsome Fu-ts'ang, prepare yourselves. I'm about to let you out. Not that it needs pointing out, but the entire planet's depending on our actions here and now. Give your all, and we'll be together again on the other side. Steel yourselves!*"

For the dark dragon and naga force, the unbelievable events playing out before them took a lot longer to register than for the light-sided heroes. Because there were so many of them, and because they were so far away, and some of them had been magically enthralled and were just waiting for their next command, a confused sense of not knowing what to do next hung in the air. Until that is, their wits returned, and the burning desire inside them to protect and fight for their new king and queen asserted itself with a vengeance. With a roar twenty times louder than the one Flash had just let out, the whole force as one, nagas and dark dragons together, all surged forward, most of the dragons leaping into the air as the nagas slithered across the debris strewn floor. DING, ROUND TWO!

After swatting away the evil pair's decisively dark and deadly magic, the master weapon smith, in the form of the ice enshrouded blade, imagined the hilt that he was trapped in rising, and then levelling out the shining fearsome blade, in an inspired move he skewered the closest two dark dragons heading towards him at speed, straight through their hearts. Backing out instantly, he watched with a mixture of satisfaction and awe at what he'd just accomplished. 'Two down, many hundreds to go,' he thought.

Out of sight, lurking in the shadows, just inside the council building, the ra-hoon, lethal mythical beasts, unicorn shaped apart from their two horns instead of one, took a moment away from rallying their troops to savour the taste of the magic that had once again presented itself from out of nowhere. It felt delicious, all encompassing and vaguely familiar. How? They weren't sure, but there was something about it that set alarm bells ringing deep inside their heads. Back to the task at hand, and having all agreed what needed to be done, they forced the minds of their subjects open, and gave them one singular order, that was to be obeyed above all else...

"*ATTACK!*"

Some compelled to do so through magic, others due to their mental weakness and yet more because they were scared of the consequences of not conforming, the mob of mythical creatures streamed out of the exit and onto something that had come to be regarded as a landing pad, the dark dragons taking off from that point after having left the council building. Now filled full of powerful serpent-like nagas, the lines at the back of Manson's force were about to take a battering, one none of them could have predicted. Camaheutos bounded along walls, their razor sharp clawed feet easily finding grip, flicking their tongues out as the ever buzzing nifoloa zipped past them, taunting them with that poison-laced tooth the size of a man's finger, as they did so. Fire breathing gnats accompanied their winged associates, having learnt over the past few hours not to attack them. Scorpion men stopped clacking their pincers and vied for position as blue maned asena and the giant were-jaguars leapt up and over their shoulders, eager to meet the enemy. As monstrous bright red and brilliant green gaki raced side by side with the scaled apes to see who could get out in the open first, the primates swinging from anything that would get them up in the air, a devilish anticipation of what was to come gripped the ra-hoon, stirring up their pleasure receptors, teasing their magic, leaving them writhing in ecstasy. This was what they'd always dreamed of.

It felt as though he were a genie, having just granted a wish. That was the only way to explain it. Through his link with the ring, sorry... For'son, he could sense the reactions of each and every one of his friends as their magic had returned. All of them felt some surprise, after that, they were very different. Peter, for example, only had eyes for Janice, wanting nothing more than to shower her in his primordial power in an effort to heal her wounds both mental and physical. But just as he'd been about to do that, she'd come around of her own accord, very much awake and back in the land of the living. Richie's thoughts weren't about individuals, but about how she could make up for losing the shield and leaving them all in this precarious position even though no one else blamed her. Indeed, how could they? It couldn't possibly be her fault. That's not how the young lacrosse playing superstar dragon saw it, especially as she'd pretty much been declared their leader, almost with royal assent. So an instant before anyone else and with her chosen sport having honed her reactions beyond anything magical, she'd been able to materialise another, much more significant and stronger shield, out of thin air. Smiling despite everything, he was proud to have her as his friend.

Flash did what his Crimson Guard training had taught him... he prepared to attack. And by that, I mean that when the unexpected magic arrived, he used it to reinforce every physical part of the wondrous natural dragon he'd become. A wisp of magic zinged and zipped across the outer edges of his scales, tinting the gunmetal grey with just the tiniest hint of purple. Snippets of supernatural power ricocheted between his jaws, lighting up his teeth, providing them with a deadlier edge than normal. For all intents and purposes he looked like the fiercest protector of the lot.

Amelia Battlehard was difficult not to admire. A fraction of a second behind the others, her dedication to her duty was second to none and something all of us should aspire to, thought Tank, his mind ablaze with magic and possibilities. The instant her mana returned, she readied a terrific defensive shield, not to protect herself, but to wrap around the king whom she'd pledged her life to die trying to protect.

Yoyo prepared to heal, whilst maintaining his focus on Vasuki, as his dragon charges forged a connection telepathically before reacting as only they could, with one of the females amongst them delegating tasks, making sure they were all as ready as they could be for what was on its way... much in the same way the dragon councillor and the remaining King's Guards had, although there was a little more disagreement in that multitude of minds.

And that left George and Fredric. Both had different things at the forefront of their thoughts. For the king of the dragon realm and the leader of the planet itself, it was all about rescuing the earth from a fate worse than utter decimation. With his steely will and his power returned, apart from that of For'son, George was utterly determined to do anything and everything to stop Manson and the evil going on here today. He would, without a doubt, give his life freely to do just that. And that left Fredric, Peter's grandfather and founder of the renowned Crimson Guards. Although they'd never met and been introduced, the rugby playing dragon had heard all about him from both Flash and Peter and had already formed a high regard from just those conversations. Any being that could endure the kind of torture and suffering that he had, in those temperatures, was a tough son of bitch. Right now, even without that information, it would have been perfectly evident to anyone looking at his harsh, dangerous and hard-hitting human form. He should have come with warning signs and a list of possible side effects:

Sneak up: suffer the consequences.

Attempt to harm my friends and family: instant death.

Catch my attention: severe diarrhoea.

This made Tank smile, even in these most unusual and dangerous circumstances. What had puzzled him though, was Fredric's reaction when his magic returned. The first thing he did was telekinetically call the dagger to him from across the floor. That Tank understood, after all Richie had told him about what they had thought was Peter's dagger, left to him by his grandfather, Fredric. So it was his weapon, and he wanted it back for the power it offered up. That was understandable. But his response after that was a little left of centre. Not at all focused on how he could help the team, his grandson or even his long lost best friend the monarch, the highly skilled and trained founder of the Crimson Guards' sole intent was centred on one being and one being only: the wicked and evil queen that was Manson's other half. Okay... so you want to get into the fight, take out the most powerful beings there as quickly as possible to make everyone on your side that bit safer... understandable really. But that wasn't it, Tank was sure. During his time at the Mantra Emporium, he'd studied enough magic, been turned into enough damn things and taken part in all sorts of the most goofy, downright stupid and dangerous magical incidents, all mainly due to the master mantra maker, the dragon he loved like a father. And all that experience told him something different, something more was going on with Fredric. It wasn't so much picking out an enemy, as forging an obsession. There and then, he vowed to himself to keep an eye on what was going on. And so back to the present, with those all around coming to terms with the newly reformed shield and presence of magic.

As the horde of dark dragons roared and hissed, all surging forward to aid their leader and bring these usurpers to their knees, Tank knew what he needed to do. With all eyes on him, in particular Manson's, he brought both arms around in front of his body, lifted his right hand up to his mouth and planted a huge kiss on the ring that monarchs had passed down for generations. Manson's face was a picture of shock, wrath and singular annoyance on realising just what the young rugby playing dragon had there. Whirling around to unleash some of his most devastating and debilitating magic, the dark force's leader backed out of the release of his supernatural power because, surprisingly, Tank wasn't in the same spot that he had been only a moment ago. In fact, he was nowhere to be seen.

Wanting to buy his friends a little time in the hope that they might just be able to finish things off, and knowing that he'd be protected by the ring, at least in the short term, with Manson gathering up his magic in an attempt to strike at him, the master mantra maker's apparent equal assembled all of his courage and power, bent his knees ever so slightly and, enhanced by everything supernatural, his huge muscled frame bounded over the head of the first assault wave of monsters, landing directly in the middle of the massive swathe of beasts, being immediately set upon. In the blink of an eye, any sign of him had disappeared from view as nagas and dragons alike piled in.

6 A RISKY RESOLUTION

Unanimously, all the dragons under his command agreed to the plan, no... suggestion he'd put forward, even after he'd been totally honest with them about just how much risk it involved. Credit to them, they still wanted to go ahead, with no other options apparent. Hidden amongst dragon corpses and scattered burnt and bloody body parts, the dragon contingent of this small outlandish force all, as one, unveiled their minds, looking for one guiding beacon full of magic, ready to welcome them with open arms. It wasn't particularly hard, especially given their close physical proximity, nevertheless the psyche was unmistakably that of the sometimes cranky old shopkeeper.

One by one they added their mental resilience, much to his pleasure. It felt not only comforting, but nice to have more than his usual reserves to draw upon, that and being able to hear their whispered thoughts. Most of them he hadn't known, not really, not before being crafted into a group, one in which he'd had command thrust upon him. Here and now though, deep within the recesses of his huge intellect, to hear their concerns, their wishes to see loved ones again, and to feel the resolve and passion with which they were desperate to rid their domain and planet of the pervading darkness that had started to spread over it, indeed offered more than a crumb of comfort, something without knowing it, he needed now more than ever. Despite his outwardly calm and professional facade, emotionally, he was a mess. Thoughts drifted through his mind of his young charge Tank, and the others, off doing goodness knows what, as well as the ex-Crimson Guard Flash who'd been sent off back to Antarctica, somewhere he no doubt didn't want to go, a being he held in exceptionally high regard. Now though was not the time to worry, but the time to act. Composing himself as best he could under the watchful eyes of the rest of those in his force he ran through what they were about to do. Essentially, he was going to extend his mind out into the confines of the building with the crystal node and of course Steel, DomCon and Jar Man, with a view to finding out exactly what was going on. It was dangerous beyond belief, and that was on a good day with no magical traps or defences waiting for them. It didn't help that he was tired, crotchety and that age had caught up with him, its firm grip filling him with fatigue, aches and pains as well as installing a huge element of doubt in his mind. Hopefully, and in theory, being able to draw on the strength of the other dragons all around him should make up for his shortcomings. If it didn't, then they were well and truly in the mire with no way out. Regulating his breathing, a deep breath in through his nose, ignoring the sickly scent of death, letting tiny licks of flame tickle his nostrils, he felt his lungs fill from the bottom upwards, before expelling out through his mouth, enjoying the sensation of the air washing over his prehistoric tongue the size of a man's arm. After thirty seconds or so of this and with his eyes closed, his spindly old arms moved down towards his waist, fingers delving into the hidden pouches that circled his belly.

'Now where is it?' he thought to himself, having a good old rummage. 'There,' he mused, pleased at having found the hidden treasure he'd been searching for. Slowly he retrieved a small, clear glass vial filled to the brim with sparkling brown dust, a pale coloured cork stopper keeping everything contained. Holding it up to the light, he opened his eyes just long enough to marvel at his discovery. Through the darkened haze and the cloying smoke, he could just make out random sparkles of gold effervescing inside the sturdy looking tube. With the others having no clue at all as to what was going on, the wily old shopkeeper removed the cork with the delicacy of a mother lion picking up one of her cubs, and then astonishingly poured the contents into one of his hands. Tossing the glass tube to the floor, Gee Tee then rubbed both hands together, before wiping them firmly across his face, making sure to smear the dust into every nook and cranny of his weathered and beaten skull. War paint was what it looked like, although it was something far more cunning and magical.

Beneath the heart of the Himalayas, one of the most difficult places on the planet for a dragon to get to, there is a river system so remote and untouched that only a handful of beings during the course of history have ever seen it in person. Clear, fresh meltwater from the mountains above dribbles through some of the cracks of civilisation down into what should be part of the dragon domain, but is so impossibly hard to reach that it has never really been regarded as such. During an outrageous expedition in some of his more formative years, the master mantra maker, out on his own as per usual, completely by chance stumbled onto a route that led him into this rare and magical masterpiece. A uniquely monstrous valley eighty kilometres long with huge, grey monoliths rising up on either side, some nearly a kilometre into the air, looking like lines of soldiers saluting, ran off into the distance. From the slick slate grey slopes that the monoliths planted their feet in, rivers of brilliant bright red, boiling hot lava spluttered and rumbled, fizzled and drizzled alongside ice cold streams of chillingly cold water from the snow fields up above, merging in the form of two majestic river systems in the heart of the valley below. A cloudy haze hovered over the surface of both, one of ice cold, perfectly transparent water, the other of roiling magma, a mass of steaming molten liquid flowing at very much a snail's pace. Continuing on their journey side by side, the old shopkeeper had spent days following the course of each, marvelling at how close the two came to intersecting, but never actually touching. Even when looking back on the memory of the secluded spot, the only way he could think of it was as one of the great wonders of the world, one that hadn't as far as he knew ever been documented, and one that probably never would be.

Following the course of the monumental valley, sometimes in the air, occasionally plodding on by the side of the molten meandering river of lava, eventually he reached what can only be described as the conclusion of his journey, when the valley turned into a gorge, before after a kilometre or so, opening out into a giant basin, surrounded on all sides by huge craggy overhangs that disappeared off into the insides of the mountains from the surface up above. It was stunning and more than a little surreal, even for him, and that was saying something. The most eye catching thing of all was the fact that both tributaries opened out into lakes, each merging into the other. In the middle, where the two met, hissing plumes of super hot steam rose into the air, forming wicked looking pockets of cloud along the boundary, inside which a constant bombardment of nefarious lightning strikes constantly cut through the atoms and molecules, setting the air on fire, filling it with static. As the master mantra maker looked at this cul-de-sac of chaos and the impossible, to the left bubbled the molten magma, slowly twirling, writhing and sparking, all the time throwing tiny chunks of debris up into the sky, the sound of falling rock and stone an eerie reminder of the danger this beautiful place represented. On the right a placid, still lake of calm mirrored the mayhem of the margin and what lay beyond. It was both spectacular, frightening and mind blowing. In between the rumble and the clinking of rubble falling to the floor, Gee Tee noticed with his enhanced dragon hearing that just occasionally a very gentle 'tick tock', could be heard. Intrigued, the stubborn and inquisitive old shopkeeper pressed on, gradually going beyond what was safe to do so, ignoring the tiny stone fragments peppering his body, shielding his head with his wings when he needed to. Throwing caution to the wind, he purposefully strode across to the edge of the lake where both the water and lava met, using his vast array of knowledge to erect a magical shield that should in theory protect him from the statically charged lightning strikes and the ever increasing salvo of falling debris. Kneeling down, homing in on the 'tick tock' sound, it was then that the shopkeeper noticed just a wriggle of silver movement beneath the water's slick surface. Cruising along close to the bottom, a fish with a shiny metallic finish and rippling rainbow colours shimmering across its scale covered body glided this way and that, looking for the whole world as though it were investigating the solid wall which had been thrown up in its way as the lava hardened on meeting the ice cold water. Gee Tee looked on fascinated, wondering if the species was in any danger from the frequent lightning strikes that littered the place. Just then, the fish, almost appearing to sense something untoward, puffed out its cheeks and dispelled a little bubble of brown sludge that in a type of inverted atomic cloud started to get ever smaller the closer it floated to the surface. Through the perfectly still water, tiny golden sparks flickered on and off throughout the sludge, just before it reached the surface and pooled out over the fish. Accompanied by a harsh crackle, an energy packed bolt of fluorescent blue appeared out of nowhere, slicing the air in two, proceeding to strike the water at the exact point where the sludge spread out. Unwittingly, or so he thought at first, the mass of electrical energy was totally and utterly absorbed by whatever the fish had ejected.

'What an amazing coincidence,' thought the ever watchful dragon, well... at first anyway. But it didn't take long to put that right. That species of fish, and the only one down there from what he could tell, side slipped their way through the crystal clear water along the entire part of the lake where both elements met, and more astoundingly, each individual had the same trick up its sleeve as the first one, with a view to avoid being struck by the numerous lightning bolts that appeared at random every minute or so. It was a revelation to the curious dragon and one that he just couldn't let go of. So, having enough remaining supplies for a few more days yet, he set about trying to learn more, fathom out what was happening and answer just a few of the questions burning at the front of his mind. How did they know when the strikes would arrive, and at which point? What was the sludge? Was it purely organic and if so, was it infused with magic or something else?

Over the next few days, Gee Tee did all he could to learn about the remarkable species of fish and when not doing so, spent his time exploring everything else within the basin beneath the mountains. Of all the solo adventures that he'd had, this one easily made his top ten, and boy some of those would make your hair curl. With a sad heart he awoke from a brief slumber on his final day, already having extended twenty four hours longer than he'd brought supplies for. Doing the one thing he'd promised himself he wouldn't do, he dived in at the deep end so to speak. Casting multiple mantras to protect him from the icy liquid, something even he wasn't sure would work as they were derived from a long since unused form of Inuit, he plunged into the wickedly ice cold water side of the mighty lake, his mighty prehistoric form creating a huge swell that rocked the entire lagoon, sending the fishes into a frenzy, most of them scarpering from view immediately. One or two stayed where they were, picking at scraps of blackened lava from the barricade beneath the water. Surrounded by magic, the cold unable to nibble at his heat loving scales, the master mantra maker dived down, settling beside one of the fish, waiting patiently to see what would happen. It didn't take long. Once again the same thing occurred, although this time, whether because of his close proximity or something else, Gee Tee could feel the nearby taint of magic. Whatever was going on, as he suspected, the supernatural was involved and this spurred him ever forward in an effort to find out more. After that lightning strike had passed and been absorbed by the brown sludge, he found another of the aquatic species and started to wait, his senses on alert for the merest hint of ethereal power. After an hour or so, his vigilance paid off. As the fish expelled the occasionally sparking goo, the master mantra maker whipped out a glass beaker and in one fell swoop, collected all of it. Only then, as the creature eyed him nervously, with more than a hint of intellect did he realise what he'd done. If the lightning hit the water without being absorbed, it would probably kill the whole shoal, and maybe even him. DAMN! Quick as a flash, out of nowhere he conjured up an oversized fully metal trident, something the Romans occasionally used to fight with, and stabbed it into the bank of the lake, letting it hang out close to where the fish was swimming. Before taking to the air with one giant flap of his wings, he scooped up the creature with one hand and tumbled out of the way. Sure enough, the lightning strike appeared exactly where predicted, but instead of zigzagging into the water, got grounded through the metal in the trident.

'PHEW,' he thought, 'that was a close one.' After returning his friend back to its rightful environment, much to its indignation, he set about studying his highly valued, and hard won prize.

Obviously it didn't happen there, he had to take it back to the Emporium, but over the course of four or five years, when some free time presented itself, he did indeed use everything at his disposal to study and ascertain what magical effects the unusual substance had. Quite remarkably, it did something no other concoction he knew about did... when either ingested (it tasted ironically like rotten fish eyes, or at least how he imagined them) or preferably massaged into the skin, it gave your consciousness a little nudge in the right direction, or a tiny advance warning of what was to come, or sometimes both. Also, it offset how much magic was needed to leave a physical body, allowing someone to travel for not only longer, but further. Intriguing and utterly unique couldn't do it justice. It was something he'd been back to collect more of on numerous occasions, but not for many decades now, due to just how harsh it was to trek to the secretive entrance of that valley. Here and now, outside the Fleet Street building containing the crystal node, he hoped that whatever small advantage it might provide would be the difference between winning and losing, life and death.

Spread out along the line of Gee Tee's dragons, all four of the human contingent fingered their remaining grenades nervously, each frightened, more so for being separated. What they were attempting had been explained to them and although difficult to comprehend, they did at least have a rudimentary understanding. And so now they stood guard, watchful for anything out of the ordinary. At the first sign of trouble, they were to alert the others in the hope that they wouldn't be too distracted to fight. In an unfamiliar world of death and destruction, the humans were now well and truly playing their part.

7 SEARCHING AMONGST THE MISERY

Earth's Surface. Salisbridge, United Kingdom.
Twenty four hours earlier.

With the terror, extraordinary loss of life and misery still fresh in everyone's minds, it was a shock for those stunned few who felt the need to venture into what remained of the renowned historic city centre to see huge metallic screens surrounding one of its most famous and still standing monuments, the CCTV camera watching over it on the long blue pole, the one Richie had so recently shimmied up, covered over with a black plastic bag. Nondescript, unmarked vans surrounded the site as numerous men and women, most in white lab coats, entered through a curtained off hole in one side. Something hugely unusual was going on and, very slowly, it was drawing a crowd.

Back in his plush Cropptech office, the head of the company, the kind and caring Al Garrett, sat pensively at his desk, unable to decide what to do. Rarely if at all had he ever found himself in the predicament he now faced, with waiting really the only option. It had taken all of his favours to get his scientists on site, particularly in the aftermath of the cathedral's destruction. But alongside the odd greased palm or two, it had happened relatively quickly. After that it had just been a case of explaining to Dr Island exactly what they'd be looking for. And since he didn't know, that particular conversation was more than a little awkward. In the end he'd had to rely on the truth, hoping that the aforementioned doctor would feel so indebted to Peter, for after all it was he that had saved not only her job, but had prevented a rather longwinded death for himself and ultimately the company. He'd explained to her in this very office that Peter, Richie and a whole host of their friends had disappeared. Of course she'd read about it in the local papers, who hadn't? But when he'd gone into the details of the evidence the authorities had and how it all led back to the Poultry Cross, not only did she appear eager to help find the missing hockey player, but was intrigued by the puzzle the whole thing threw up. There and then she vowed that her team would do everything they could to help solve the mysterious disappearances. Pleased with the way things had gone, Garrett had told her in no uncertain terms that she had access to every resource the company had, and if it wasn't available here, then he would personally procure it from somewhere else. Money, he'd said, was of no consequence. Whatever the cost, they just had to get it done. That was five hours and two updates ago. Knowing the team he'd sent had been on site for some time now, he wished them luck and hoped they would find something, anything, that would help figure out just what the hell had happened. Tapping his fingers to a rhythmic beat on the dark wood of his desk, he wondered if he was leading them all on a wild goose chase, and whether or not he was just wasting time and money in having Dr Island's group of scientists look into what had happened at the Poultry Cross. With the police unable to find any link or even the most remote clue even after all their forensic specialists had spent over a day at one of the city's most recognisable features, it did seem unlikely that his group would be able to turn something up. But with the world around them being upended with almost every minute that passed, long shots were all that they had. And so he waited, wound tighter than a ball of wool on a diet, wondering where the missing Salisbridge residents were and what harm had befallen them, if any.

Long, slightly curled, black hair cascaded down past her shoulders, offsetting her beautiful, dark complexion as she studied everything going on, making sure the team she was in charge of were on top of things and not missing anything out of the ordinary, no matter how big or small. Bowled over at standing beneath the stunning stone arches that had seen so much history, she wondered what sights the momentous monument had witnessed, what secrets it kept hidden and just what had happened to Peter and the rest of his friends. At the mere mention of his name, her thoughts returned to the reign of that devilish fiend Major Manson, the weasel that had attempted to harm Garrett her boss and steal the much valued laminium. Losing her job like that had been a devastating blow, the likes of which she'd never felt before. During the days afterwards, and with no explanation or word from her boss, she'd felt not only depressed, but nearly suicidal. Thoughts of turning to drink in an attempt to ease the pain plagued her constantly, but she'd seen some of her friends' lives spiral out of control that way, and so with a determined sense of purpose, just about managed to avoid making the same mistakes. Luckily for her, the young Peter Bentwhistle had thwarted the entire devious plot, almost at the cost of his own life, and sent Manson packing never to be seen again, which meant her livelihood had been restored. Occasionally, he still haunted her nightmares, showing up out of the blue, picking up from where he left off. The very thought of this sent a shiver down her spine, even though she knew it was illogical. Fortunately as time moved on, the nightmares become ever more infrequent.

"Be careful with that, Thomas," she ordered, much more harshly than she intended to.

"Sorry Ma'am," he replied.

"That portable lidar machine is one of a kind, built to order and probably costs more than all of our houses combined. If you drop it, you pay for it... that's the deal. Got it?"

"Uhhhh..." stammered Thomas.

"I'm kidding, of course. And I'm sorry to be so stern, but we all need to be on our A game today. What we're doing here is important, more so than maybe anything else we've done. Chop, chop... come on crew, let's get down to it."

And with that, the small group of scientists went about

their business as only they could, slow but methodical, looking for anything remotely out of place and unusual.

Full of nervous energy, the head of Cropptech now paced around his office, wondering whether or not he'd taken things a step too far in the last few minutes. Three phone calls was all he'd made, with the main one delegating the task at hand. In this day and age and in particular, in this country, receiving a delivery of the most hi-tech weapons available on the planet would be more than frowned upon and could well end up landing him in jail. But right at this moment, it seemed like a small price to pay if it got him closer to the truth and found out the fate of the young man that had not only saved his company, but truth be told, himself as well. So he'd done it and the shipment was on its way, under the guise of the highest security he had, known only to the most trusted individuals under his command. The weapons would be kept here under lock and key, only to be used as a last resort, and that was still dependant on Dr Island finding something, however small, to point them in the right direction.

Their breaths freezing in the cold, lab coats fluttering in the breeze atop assorted coloured base layers to keep them warm, the scientists investigating the ancient monument located in the heart of the city pursued their goal with the utmost dedication and professionalism. Unlike their leader, Dr Island, they hadn't been told the reason for what they were doing, only that it was vitally important to not only their city, but to their fellow employees and of course to Al Garrett. That was enough for them to get their heads down and work as diligently as possible.

Having acquired technology from across the vast Cropptech site which included ground penetrating radar, resistivity meters, X-ray guns and the jewel in their crown, the portable lidar machine, currently two of their kind patiently used an X-ray gun each, working their way around the entire structure anticlockwise, identifying the chemical makeup by measuring wavelengths and the intensity of the emitted radiation. It was slow and quiet going.

Less than a hundred metres away, three men watched through a huge pane of glass, wondering what the hell was going on behind the gigantic, all encompassing screens.

"What do you think they're doing?" asked one.

"Who knows? From what I've seen though, the men and women all look like scientists."

"What does that mean?"

"Nothing good I would think."

"It's got to be related to the disappearances, hasn't it?"

"Shuuuush..."

"What?" whispered the youngest of the three.

"His father will hear you. Do you want to upset him even more?"

"Uhhhh... not really, no."

"Then quieten your tongue. The boy's father has been through more than enough and deserves to catch up on the sleep that he's lost out on over the last few days."

"Sorry."

"Don't be sorry, just think before you speak. This family tragedy is something that affects us all. Now go and see just how close the chefs are to being set up. We open in less than ten minutes."

"Of course," and with that he scuttled off in the direction of the kitchen, eager to get away from all of the speculation, hoping that at least a handful of customers would turn up today to make opening up at this dreadful time, at least slightly worthwhile.

The remaining two returned their gazes to what was happening outside, each wondering if events would lead to their young friend and colleague, Taibul, being returned to them safely. If only they knew where the young man really was, and exactly what he was facing.

With the X-ray guns a bust, those under Dr Island's leadership had now turned to ground penetrating radar, using the high-tech pieces of equipment to bounce high frequency radio waves off every part of the Poultry Cross, measuring the reflected signals received in the hope of some good news. After two hours more, that clearly wasn't to be. Only then did they break out the big gun... the portable lidar machine. Unique and extravagantly expensive, the scientists spent over an hour calibrating the machine that used a combination of light and radar to scan its surroundings. Once done, and under the watchful eye of their boss, they began.

Three quarters of an hour later, they had something.

"Uhhh... boss, you might want to come over here and take a look," ventured Thomas, a little sceptically.

"What have you got?" demanded Dr Island, strolling over, grateful to give the muscles in her weary legs a little work out.

"It's not much, but there's a slight anomaly in the centuries old stone above the circular seat that runs around the base of the monument."

"What sort of anomaly?"

"That's just it, we don't know. The equipment doesn't recognise what it is, only that it stands out from the background."

"How big is it?" asked the intrigued Dr Island.

"Miniscule at best," replied Thomas. "But you did ask us to look for anything, no matter how small."

'I did,' she thought to no one but herself. 'Could this be it, what we're looking for?' Pausing for a moment to consider their next move, briefly she wondered whether or not she should call Garrett. No... it was too early, and they really didn't have anything to go on just yet.

"What else have we got left to try?" she asked, showering her colleagues with a proud smile, a reward for all of their great work.

"The only thing we haven't tried is the magnetometers," piped up one of the other scientists.

"Okay," answered Dr Island. "Try those, and focus on the anomaly that the lidar found. Let me know when you have something."

"Will do," they replied, before heading out of their secluded workspace, back to the nearest van to put the lidar safely away, and pick up the magnetometers. The rush to find the treasure was on.

Ninety minutes later, just as the portable electric lights had been set up to illuminate everything, and darkness was falling, they had something.

"Dr Island, come over here please."

Without having to be told twice, their boss arrived on the scene, eager to see what they had.

"Well...?" she asked.

"Look for yourself," commented Thomas, handing her the magnetometer and moving out of the way.

Standing on the circular, ancient stone seat, careful not to damage it, she held the device up to the area her colleague had just been scanning. Sure enough, behind an indentation that looked like an upside down tankard and a finger sized groove, there appeared to be a smattering of something metallic and wholly unidentifiable. Instinctively, and without a second thought, the brilliant, unconventional and dedicated leader of the scientists ran one finger along the groove whilst handing off the magnetometer, and put the tip of one of the fingers from her other hand into the indentation. For all intents and purposes, nothing happened. That is until one of her colleagues abruptly shouted,

"OH MY GOD!" Gobsmacked by the absolute unprofessionalism, she turned around about to give him the telling off of a lifetime, when all of a sudden she noticed what had caused his unlikely outburst. Like the rest of them, she was stunned into silence, for a moment anyway.

Just as he started to head out of his office to the toilet, having drunk enough tea to fill a swimming pool, the shrill sound of his phone ringing returned him to his desk.

"Garrett," he answered.

"It's Dr Island sir. I think you'd better come on down here."

Turning full circle at a mind numbing speed, one of the greatest heroes of them all threw himself headlong into the attacking mass to devastating effect. Limbs, wings, tails, heads and legs were all separated from bodies, spewing brightly coloured blood and body parts up the wall, leaving the floor slick with visceral thick fluid. Fu-ts'ang, having gained his independence, was having the time of his life, almost singlehandedly decimating the enemy force. After batting away the original two strikes of magic by the malevolent would-be rulers of this shadowy new world, the fear of being struck down by whatever dark magic they had previously employed encouraged him to run for cover, knowing full well there'd be a whole host of takers to engage the wicked couple. He couldn't have been more right.

His former other half though, peeked out from beyond the relative safety of Peter's pert little wings, feeling more than a little redundant and at a loss as to how to help.

"What can I do?" she shouted out to her soul mate, determined to find something to keep her occupied.

Peter's honesty surprised her.

"I don't really know. To be honest, my magical ability is not on par with everybody else here. I can use the odd enchantment and mantra here and there to affect what goes on out behind the barrier, but apart from that, not much else. The only thing I can suggest you do is look out through the chaos, keeping an eye out for anything untoward or sneaky, something that our allies might have missed. With your experience guiding Fu-ts'ang, just maybe you'll spot something unusual, which could mean the difference between life or death for one of us."

Knowing that it wasn't much, the young bar worker was at least relieved to be doing something and so with all her determination, turned her focus to what was happening all around her.

"Steel yourself," echoed around the link from the perfectly formed mind of the lacrosse playing dragon.

As it did, George, the king of the dragon domain, whose monarchy hung by a thread, one that all the beings here fighting beside him represented, made a conscious decision... to, at least for the moment, remain inside the shield and ply his magic from here. It made sense on a number of fronts, but mainly because it allowed others amongst their small band to go fully on the attack, and not waste their attention on whether or not he was safe. So as the front of the shield facing the monstrous attacking horde of demonic creatures dematerialised, he stayed put, feet planted firmly on the ruined marble floor, hands and fingers moving at a blur, working in perfect unison with the magic being cast by his mind.

Every atom in Fredric's taut muscled body exploded into action the second the supernatural barrier in front of him disappeared. For a dragon so old, missing his natural form, he put Flash to shame with just how fast he moved. Blur could not do justice to the speed with which he travelled. Ploughing straight into the first three nagas to race forward, the protective spell he'd cast around his body before he'd taken off worked a treat, scattering the despicable beasts widely across the floor. That all took place in less than a tenth of a second, as you've already probably guessed, on the way to his main objective, ready to resume the family feud that had already been playing out today.

Shiny, bright silver scales accentuated by a stunning sea of Nordic sky blue whistled through the air mere centimetres above his comrades' heads as Flash lurched forward, eager to be free of his confinement, determined to put his new found prehistoric form to good use and finish this once and for all. Offering both Peter and Janice a wink from one of his gigantic scaled gun metal grey eyelids as he zipped past, the ex-Crimson Guard, much like Fredric before him, had his sights firmly set on one target, and one alone... MANSON!

Watching the front of the shield disappear entirely, a primal and deep rooted urge took hold of Captain Battlehard, something that screamed vengeance and revenge for all of those that she'd lost under her command today. Acknowledging her king's desire to stay behind with the others, a fulfilling wave of freedom washed over her as the shackles to which she felt she'd been bound crumbled into ashes. There would be no escape today for these dastardly creatures, no free passes, no forgiveness, not from her at least. They would pay, each and every one of them, for what they and their brethren had done. And once all of those here had been destroyed, she would personally hunt down the rest of them and kill them one by one until the planet itself had been cleansed of the evil their shadow had cast. Zipping forward in Flash's huge wake, she spat fireball after fireball off to each side, watching with great satisfaction as huge swathes of the enemy caught alight, revelling in particular at the suffering of the partial to the cold nagas.

"Remember to keep your guard up at all times. Always work as a team. You're all so much stronger that way." Yoyo's wise words abounded through their telepathic link, encouraging them all, spurring them all on to greater things. As a unit, each indelibly linked, they cast their unique and unusual mantras out beyond the shield, creating mischief and mayhem by tripping, ripping, tearing, shredding and just downright destroying as many of their adversaries as possible. Although they downed many, it was still only a drop in the ocean as far as Manson's dark force was concerned.

Redeploying the centre of his attention, abruptly all he felt was... COLD! And not just any cold, but an all knowing, all seeing cold, one that might capture a dragon forever, death's tortuous grasp the only form of escape. It was a conundrum and one most beings might just shy away from. Not Yoyo, not here, not now. Pondering what to do about Vasuki, the stillness of his heart and the underlying frostiness emitting from where his conscious will should have been, the experienced healer fought to hold back his power momentarily, for fear of using the wrong kind of magic. Would any sort of heat harm his body? Or would it warm his soul just enough to reignite his elegant mind and bring him back to the land of the living? Two of the many questions he found himself asking as he watched proceedings all around him once again go straight to hell.

With hundreds of nagas queuing to slither across the rebuilt magical bridge, and the air around it full to bursting with monstrous dark dragons, barely any of it free, Manson's dread force all had but the same compulsion... get to what would now be considered the front, attack the enemy, and save their leader. Spurred on by magic, fear, and in some cases thoughts of rewards once the planet had well and truly changed hands, all the diabolical beasts surged forward, concentrating on everything in front of them as well they should, not even one giving a single thought to anything going on behind them. That might just be their undoing.

A naga as far back as it was possible to be was the first to be made aware that something out of the ordinary was going on as abruptly, a searing pain from about halfway down her tail caused her sensory receptors to nearly overload. Using all her strength of will to keep from crying out, snaking around one hundred and eighty degrees, she attempted to check exactly what had caused her such agony, feeling as though something were dreadfully wrong. Perched atop the fine dark scales of her tail, was what looked like a very large bee, seemingly doing nothing exactly where the pain was located. Baring her needle sharp fangs, her cobra-like head swaying around all over the place, she darted forward in an effort to get a better look. As she did so, the nifoloa pulled what looked like a giant tooth out of her tail and proceeded to fly up into the air. Too stunned by the impossibility of what she'd just seen, the shocked naga realised she'd missed her opportunity to exact revenge on the little devil as it had flown up and very much out of her range. Still reeling from whatever it was that had breached not only the scales but the skin as well, she wriggled around to take a better look. Sure enough, around the sides of the entry wound a thick layer of slimy, green mucus was enough to set off alarm bells inside her head. Just as she'd suspected, she'd been poisoned. That was the bad news. The good news was the fact that nagas, as a race, were immune to almost every toxin on the planet. Occasionally there might be one that instead of killing produces an array of various inconvenient side effects, but to her knowledge not one of her kind had ever died from any kind of venom. This buoyed her spirits, despite the resentment she harboured at being bitten and caught out by such a creature. Pleased at the thought of having survived when most other beings wouldn't, and considering whether or not her immediate concern should be to wash out the gaping wound, her attention was suddenly captured by streaking bolts of bright blue forked lightning, lighting up the wall beside her. Wondering what the hell was going on now, she died instantly as a lightly spotted, silky smooth conaima jumped down from above, and in one swift move, fastened its razor sharp jaws around her neck, clamping them tight, eliciting a stifled gurgle that was easily drowned out by the impatience of the dark force desperate to throw themselves at their adversaries. With their first kill of this particular phase under their belt and a ringing confidence echoing across their telepathic connection, the mythical creatures rejoiced as they charged into the fray, devouring any and every being out there in front of them.

Grotesque gaki bounded into the crowd of despicable dark creatures, a haze of distorted bright red and neon green movement, bulging bellies wobbling like jelly on a bouncy castle, sharp talons, horns and bony protrusions carving bone, scale, muscle, sinew and occasionally brain in two, the whirlwinds that their bodies had become acting very much like rotary razor blades.

Two-headed eagles, weaving in and out of the hovering dragons dive bombed the nagas, pecking at eyes and gills, causing a great deal of harm from deep within what were supposed to be their own defences.

Mighty scaled apes swung in from the air using whatever handholds were available, targeting necks and heads, ripping, tearing and gouging wherever possible, their incredible strength causing no end of damage.

Flying pixiu, essentially winged lions, zipped in and around the crowded mass of dark dragons waiting in a holding pattern on the council side of the bridge, slicing their wings in two, piercing tails. On the ground, one or two echeneis slithered into the multitude of nagas all around them, the twelve centimetre long serpents putting their freezing breath to good use.

Scorpion men skittered this way and that, the stingers on their tails stabbing, always looking to pierce the hearts and gills of the slippery serpent-like creatures before them, constantly using their giant pincers to deflect any and all magic heading their way.

Snarling and chomping blue maned asena hunted in packs, mostly targeting the nagas' tails, sometimes unpredictably leaping up for a go at their necks, the brilliant blue fur around their throats standing to attention every time they killed. Fighting over food was usually the norm, but not here, not now. There was plenty of it to go around, something that pleased them all. Tonight, their stomachs would be full and the blood lust that was part of their very DNA would be sated.

Swarms of fire breathing gnats infiltrated the mayhem in an effort to help their fellow mythical creatures, under specific instruction from the ra-hoon, only to target eyes and then move away as quickly as possible. This they did, as only they could, by leaving a trail of distraught and disabled creatures in their wake for the others to finish off. It was elegant, coordinated misery of the very finest order.

Garrett arrived within fifteen minutes. Walking past the guards designed to deter unintentional visitors and would-be nosy parkers, the 'bald eagle' as his staff liked to call him was surprised to see all the scientists just sitting on the cold, hard stone of the Poultry Cross, waiting for him.

"Dr Island, you said you had something. Perhaps you'd care to enlighten me."

Without a word, all the time trying to curtail the rather large smile that was attempting to escape her calm and controlled demeanour, the good doctor turned, stood up on the seat she'd previously been sitting on, and repeated what she'd already done ten times in a row, hoping against hope that once again it happened. Of course, there was no reason that it shouldn't, but with the unexplained you never really knew, that was the whole point. Having stuck one finger in the indentation, whilst running another along the groove, she turned around, jumped to the ground, and along with all of her colleagues, continuously stared at a completely dull piece of the stone floor.

About to ask them what the hell was going on, and thinking that their little road trip had driven them quite insane, Garrett watched with absolute amazement as a section of the perfectly ordinary piece of stone on the ground that they'd all been gazing at, in total silence, dropped down, slid out of sight, revealing a set of worn curved stone steps disappearing down into the darkness.

"Oh my..." gasped Garrett.

"Indeed," responded Dr Island.

Taking a few seconds to regain his composure, he just had to ask.

"Where does it go?"

Surrounded by her group of scientists, all wanting to go down the steps into the depths, their leader answered.

"We don't know where, only that it's quite some way

down. Having done what you've asked of us, we thought we'd leave it at that for now."

Looking on utterly mesmerised, about twenty or so seconds after it had appeared, the triangular piece of flooring soundlessly slipped back into place. Amazing! Scratching his chin with a faraway look in his eyes, Dr Island's words had little effect on Garrett's thought process. It took him only a matter of moments to figure out his next move, for which a phone call was required. Turning to address all the scientists, calmly he composed his words.

"I'd like to thank you all for your outstanding commitment and professionalism here today. To unearth all this is nothing short of extraordinary. I'm sure each of you have questions about where the passage leads, and about its ultimate purpose. Right now, I'm in no position to answer them I'm afraid. But I'm duty bound to find out, and intend on doing exactly that. Once I know, you'll all know. But for now, I'd ask that you pack all your equipment away, quickly and quietly, and not utter even a word to anyone else about this, not until I've told you that you can. As always, I appreciate your efforts and value all your work. Thanks, you can start clearing up."

Leaving Dr Island and her team to it, Garrett disappeared outside and pulling out his specially encrypted mobile phone, dialled one particular number. After two rings, someone picked up. Before they had a chance to speak, the head of Cropptech beat them to it.

"Bring everyone and everything down to the Poultry Cross. We're going on the hunt."

Very little light and sound punctuated the stillness behind the gigantic barriers Garrett sat within. Darkness had fallen some time ago, leaving a cold chill in the air, allowing his breath to freeze every time he exhaled, forcing him to constantly rub his hands together to speed up his circulation. None of that mattered though, not now he'd been shown how to uncover the secret entrance that seemed to have been part of this treasured monument for a very long time. So many thoughts brushed his mind, something that had no doubt happened to each of the scientists. With their work over, they'd long since shot off back to Cropptech to return all the sensitive equipment they'd been using throughout the day. But he was still here, curious beyond belief, thoughts centred on this incredible journey, ruminating about what could or should happen next. Ultimately it was his decision to make, but the lack of information about what lay beneath them did little to quell the fear running down his back. That terror though, was evenly balanced by his inquisitive nature and the strong desire to find those missing people, Peter and Richie included. So as he waited for backup, he pondered just what his orders should be, one or two very fanciful and bizarre ideas reaching the top of the pile. Putting emotion to one side, and using all his valuable life experience, there and then, he made up his mind.

A short while later Owen Brown, deputy head of security at the Salisbridge Cropptech site and Peter's second in command hurled his huge frame through the curtain covering the entrance, proffering out his hand to Garrett as he did so. The 'bald eagle' shook the outstretched appendage, glad to see its owner and the rest of the people he'd brought with him.

"Do you have everything you need?" he asked.

"We do," replied the burly Owen. "Where is it we're headed boss?"

Repeating Dr Island's action, Garrett showed them the secret entrance, which blew each and every one of their minds. And then he told them. They weren't afraid... surprised maybe, certainly not afraid. Then they became concerned, not for themselves, but because their boss, Garrett, announced very firmly and precisely that he himself was coming with them. What on earth were they supposed to do with that?

As stealthily as possible, Owen and the five others with him carried the huge metal cases through the curtain that covered the only entrance into the sealed off Poultry Cross, as Garrett held the huge sheet to one side for them. Using a key only he had, Owen unlocked each case, before laying it on its side on the cold stone floor. After they were all done, each of the men and women chose a case and opened it up. Their contents were all identical, as well as being highly prized not only because of their extortionate cost, but because these specific items weren't and wouldn't be available anywhere else, for at least another couple of years, with the United States military having supposed first 'dibs' once they were manufactured in bulk. Knowing just how potentially bad this search might be, once again Garrett had called in a whole host of favours as well as spending eye watering amounts of cash to get hold of the best that money could buy. And he had. Inside the cases, protected fully by highly specialised foam, sat the latest, most terrifying (depending on which way you looked at it) automatic assault rifles available on the planet. Next Generation Squad Automatic Rifles, or NGSAR for short, the weapons were nothing short of fantastic, able to fire their ammunition at a pressure equivalent to that of a tank, easily penetrating any known body armour from up to six hundred metres away. Not only that, but they were considerably lighter than anything else on the market, making them much easier to carry over long distances. As well as the rifles, a great deal of specialised ammunition and a handful of explosives had been provided. Slipping on their Kevlar vests and protective helmets, they were almost ready to go. The tiny force could well, if it wanted to, start a very large war.

With all of them armed and ready, Owen knew that now was his last chance.

"Are you sure sir?" he asked. "There's no need to come along. Why not stay here and monitor things? If we discover anything pertinent, we'll communicate it straight away."

But that was not what Garrett, now their acting commander-in-chief, had in mind. NO! He fully intended to go with them, determined to find out at any cost exactly what had happened. So explaining this in no uncertain terms to all of them, he promised that they would be unusually well compensated for their actions, and that the importance of finding the missing Salisbridge residents was of the utmost priority. In his mind, Owen whispered to his friend Peter, that he was on his way, and to hang on just a little bit longer.

Fastened into his own bullet proof vest that looked more than a little odd poking out from underneath his suit jacket, also wearing one of the specialist helmets, the 'bald eagle' opened the secret entrance for the very last time, and with Owen at the front, two of the others behind him, Garrett in the middle, and the last three at the back, without a sound, the small squad activated their head torches and stepped into the darkness, each one of them wondering what the hell they were getting themselves into.

10 BREACHING THE BARRICADES

Leaving everything worldly behind, the master mantra maker let the magical essence of his mind slowly drift out in front of him, his floating consciousness tethered to all those under his command as he did so. Not only did the link provide him with a way to bolster his energy and supernatural power should he need to, but it also offered him some well needed reassurance. It wasn't often that he could admit it, but he felt lonely and lost without his friends. Mainly his young appren... Tank. Not apprentice, NO! Now he was a fully qualified master mantra maker in his own right, if such a thing existed. His experiences and adventures over the last couple of years alone had earned him the right to be called that. A slight wisp of regret washed over his detached mind.

"If only I'd told him back at the Hampton Court nursery ring," he worried, *"I really should have."*

Soft velvety voices whispered across their shared link,

"It's alright, you'll get your chance to tell him once this is all over." But would he? Would they both still be alive at the end of all this?

Soaring around pairs of naga guards in the midst of the choking dark smoke, Gee Tee's intellect, wary of the individual presences in and around him, made for the main entrance with as much haste as he dared, all the time alert for anything magical that might be a trap. Reaching the first entrance unhindered, with only two inert dragon guards standing either side not really paying much attention, some of those outside, joined to him by the supernatural, gave a little *"whoop whoop,"* celebrating just how easy passing that stage had been. Immediately the shopkeeper admonished them, promising there'd be more difficult challenges to come. Suitably berated, the others remained quiet, determined to be there for the old shopkeeper when called upon.

Rubbing his finger across the switch of the grenade he held in his left hand, the young boy (as that's all he really was) and waiter wondered what the dragons all around him, who he was supposed to be looking out for trouble on behalf of, were doing right at this very moment. Describing it as a journey to the centre of the installation with only their minds, Taibul pondered the possibilities. Imagine being able to send your thoughts off somewhere else while your body stayed in another place entirely. Were you able to program it to do things while your thoughts were away? If so, surely you could just get your body to go to work, and send your psyche off anywhere you like, only to return at the end of your shift. Wouldn't that be fabulous? As well, you could just lie in bed at home and send your conscious will off to explore the entire planet. How fast did a mind travel, he wondered. Was there a limit to how far it could go on its own and could the body be sustained of its own accord while its intelligence was away? So many unanswered questions rattled around inside his head. Once this was all over, he was determined to find out the answers to all of these and more.

Passing the first three checkpoints with little or no trouble, even the cantankerous old shopkeeper was beginning to think that this would be easy and felt a modicum of regret for the telling off he'd given to his more optimistic companions. Zipping along now, the sensation of speed almost tangible, the joined awareness swooped above and below huge wooden rafters, watching intently as birds scattered in their wake, hugging the relative safety of the shadows, all the time searching for one of the three beings that had headed in here of their own accord, quite some time ago. So far, there'd been no sign of them. Hopefully that would change soon.

11 NO GUTS, NO GLORY

Sweeping through the twisted rubble at speeds no other bladed weapon had ever achieved, Fu-ts'ang cut the knees from under one murderous dark dragon before sweeping up and over, slicing another's right wing straight off and then sensing a terrifying array of dastardly foes up in the air, shot straight up vertically, skewering the beast directly above him right up his asshole, piercing his heart on the way through. Caught in the act of coughing up a massive fireball, the life in his eyes extinguished before his magic could be brought forth. Zooming out in the form of the fastest U-turn in history, the mighty blade watched in fascination as the monster's cadaver tumbled to the naga filled floor, before exploding on impact, the fireball too far down the line to just disappear back off into the ether. Pleased with his work, but missing the constant touch of the young bar worker, like a giant, deadly game of chess, he started thinking three or four moves ahead, picking his targets, and set off desperate to help the heroes of this piece win a well deserved victory.

Shy, timid and more than a little self conscious, Peter Bentwhistle was most certainly not the dragon for this, or even most occasions. Of that, he was only too aware. But just like growing up in the Purbeck Peninsula nursery ring alongside his friends, Tank and Richie, he just kept plodding away, using what he had and what he knew to the best of his ability, trying not to worry too much about what others thought... a continuing trend amongst the middle of the chaos. Sheltering behind Richie's fabulous defensive shield, he'd so far tried all sorts of fancy magic, to little or no effect. It was only after having gone back to basics that he made any real impact.

In their fifteenth year, less than a third of the way through their schooling, all of the young dragonlings spent nearly a month learning the history of, and how to conjure and successfully use, deflecting spells. Not pretty, clever or complicated, they were for the most part functional and plain, but were an essential part of any dragon's defence in a fight. And so it was that Janice's soul mate, quite by accident, had, here and now, learnt how to put the knowledge from all those decades ago to great use.

Shrugging his wings, rolling his prehistoric head this way and that, trying pitifully to make sense of all the chaos outside the shield, Peter watched enemy combatants for the first signs of them attempting to cast anything magical.

'There!' he thought, a dark dragon dropping down from the sky, looked as though he had the blur that Fredric currently was, racing off in the direction of Manson and his queen, firmly in his sights, clearly about to cast something dark and gruesome. With the mantra one word away from being complete, the hockey player watched eagle eyed, ready to reinforce the supernatural with all his willpower. Sure enough, a twisting, twirling vortex of poison spores appeared between both of the dragon's fragile little hands, meant entirely for the grandfather that he loved dearly. In that instant Janice's soul mate cast the deflecting spell between the homicidal looking dragon and the founder of the Crimson Guards. Hoping he'd done enough, the young hockey player mentally patted himself on the back as he watched the assailant physically throw the wicked ball of raging toxins off in the direction of Fredric, only for it to redirect into a group of dark dragons circling in the air above, exploding on impact, taking at least three of them out of the fight. The best bit of all though, was the look on the face of the beast who'd cast the magic. It was priceless, with him wondering what the hell had happened, how on earth he'd just taken down three of his comrades, and whether or not he should shy away from using any more of the ethereal power he'd been blessed with. Looking for another target, Peter continued in exactly the same vein.

Using just one word deep inside his head, George, the current king and ruler of this magnificent planet, crushed the spine of a particularly evil looking dragon heading down at speed to intercept his long lost best friend, watching contentedly as it plunged straight to the ground, smashing down in the middle of a pack of nagas, its broken body doing plenty of damage. Switching his attention to the next one, he cast another mantra, and then another and then another. Non-stop supernatural mayhem surged from both his hands, powered by a conscious and sturdy will, adamant he would take what he considered his last chance to not only save his friends, but the planet he felt responsible for. As far as he was concerned, he carried the weight of every being firmly on his shoulders. Up until his dying breath, he was determined not to let them down.

The one remaining councillor and the rest of the King's Guards lined one side of the inside of Richie's shield, each picking off individuals, not having to worry about the defensive side of things thanks to the relative safety they found themselves amongst. It was a great relief to them all, particularly after the harrowing time they'd had during the first phase of the battle. Now at least they could visit some real pain on the enemy, and they did, each destroying at least one of their opponents every second. At this rate the end could well be in sight. But it couldn't be that easy, could it?

Yoyo's band of young dragons had all decided to sit down cross legged on the cool marble that had clearly seen better days. It looked odd, especially in the midst of what was going on, but this was mainly how they spent their time practising magical arts with the enigmatic Australian healer when he had occasion to seek them out, something that seemed to happen less and less these days. With their psyches opened up to each other, sharing new possibilities and ideas, together they knew they could achieve almost anything if they set their minds to it, easily stronger than the sum of their parts. Wiz and Hillier, each knowing what the other had planned, both set off concussive supernatural charges, below knee height, about twenty metres apart. The sound tearing across the private residence was singularly epic, bursting eardrums close by and disorientating beings over one hundred metres away. That wasn't all though. Discharged in the midst of the throng of viciously wicked beings, the dark dragons and nagas in the immediate vicinity of the blasts had everything below the knees destroyed, with maimed dragons toppling to the floor like a set of well used dominoes, while their naga cohorts' tails were for the most part disintegrated. Chaos ensued, with what remained of the bodies of both nagas and dragons writhing around in agony, wailing and howling, their ear piercing screams echoing around the chamber for many minutes to come.

Using a light touch, Yoyo gently ran his hands along Vasuki's cold, alien body imbuing it with just a tiny trickle of heat, starting at his tail, working up to his head. It wasn't fancy, bold or possibly even the right thing to do, but it was all that he could think of to bring the king of the nagas around.

In a distorted, fast moving blur, Captain Battlehard launched herself into the melee, striking against the enthralled nagas with superheated arcs of roaring red, yellow, orange and blue tinged flame, melting their faces, chests and tails, none of them getting even close to launching an attack. For her, it was a relief to go on the offensive at last, knowing that the ruler was as safe as he could be, down here in this, the most dire of situations. With the slain corpses of all the nagas at her feet, the king's most valiant protector turned her attention to the sky and started dealing out all sorts of magical mayhem. Impossible icicles rained down from above, piercing and puncturing dark dragon wings, causing monstrous howls of the most agonising kind to garner attention from all around, whilst tiny tornados manufactured harsh, unpredictable winds that threw the denizens of the air off course, sometimes crashing into each other, occasionally bumping into something solid, incurring devastating injuries. In short, the highest ranking member of the King's Guard left there alive was a credit to the uniform, easily becoming one of the biggest thorns in the sorry little side of Manson's force.

In a frenzied panic, Tank kicked, punched and head butted an assortment of creatures, which were so tightly packed that he was unable to identify naga from dragon; all he really knew was that the enemy had scales. Still they kept coming at him, relentless in their onslaught. For'son helped, boosting his mana, providing a protective shield that absorbed the worst of it, filling his head with bold and audacious new spells, pointing out trouble and occasionally updating him with an overview of how his friends were doing. For Tank, even with his strange, intelligent adaptable dragon mind, very much used to multitasking, it was still a lot to take in.

Soaring in behind Fredric, only a couple of metres off the ground, Flash in his superb new dragon guise cut through the air like a knife through butter, legs tucked firmly up against his body, head down, teeth bared, a ferocious snarl stamped into his dinosaur-like face, ecstatic from the thrill of battle and getting a surprising second chance. Not having a clue what his rugby playing friend was up to, but knowing he had something cunning in mind, being topped up with as much magic as possible was a total and utter shock, one that was surpassed only moments later when about to leave the solace of the shield, Flash spotted something wrapped around one of Tank's fingers, looking as though it had always belonged there.

'The king's ring! How in the name of all that's dragonly possible has he got his hands on that? Not only how, but when?' As far as Flash could tell, since arriving Manson had been parading the ring, although it hadn't seemed to work for him. Tank must have somehow fooled the idiotic would-be leader of this world into thinking his was the genuine article, when all along the rugby playing dragon had the real one. But where had he been all this time, and why only show his face now? Two questions very much on his mind, but they would have to wait, for now at least. Because a split second later, in a thunderous roar, he crashed heftily at great speed, straight into the bully and tormentor that was... MANSON!

An electrical tingling sensation lit up the fingers of his right hand, only in a good way as the feeling of the power from the laminium dagger that had once belonged to the famed dragon Aviva became one with the cells of his body. That supernatural tickle, the one that felt like nothing else in the world, instantly recognisable even after all his time incarcerated below the Antarctic, once again took his breath away whilst at the same time forcing the hairs up and down his arms to stand to attention. If not for the seriousness of the situation it would have been unwarranted bliss, a moment to be savoured and delighted in. Here and now though, there was just too much at stake to get caught up in any of that, and so with a sense of purpose that eclipsed all of the others on the battlefield that day, he ploughed into his runt of a daughter, not for the first time, catching her briefly off guard and unaware, both of them tumbling head over heels, each wrestling for some kind of advantage, both bringing forth their magic in an attempt to counteract the other's power.

Still too caught up in what had happened and just what she was doing to fully comprehend exactly what one of her best friends, Tank, had done, she too savoured the feeling the laminium in the necklace that Flash had procured for her, as its radiant supernatural power bolstered her own, making her feel almighty and invincible. Knowing that wasn't quite the case, Richie allowed a little of the magic to seep into her head, clearing fully the muzzy sensation from before, after being shocked at having what was rightfully hers stolen. Briefly she wondered how Manson had achieved the all but impossible, and on such an epic scale. Doing it to one individual was some achievement, but to a group of highly trained and gifted dragons, some of the most commanding and influential in the domain, was something else entirely. Realising that it didn't matter, and understanding just how grateful she was to have a second chance, out of the corner of one eye, the two halves of Tim's broken, all-white body swam into view. Only then did she understand the trauma his death had caused her, only at that point did she recognise what they'd had, and just how happy she'd been. There and then she vowed to apply all her considerable conscious will to ending this today, and taking back the planet both above and below ground.

Furious flaming fireballs exploded against the magical barrier held in place by Richie's strong will and newly restored magic, shaking the air itself, the noise almost deafening.

Crouched behind Peter, standing next to Janice, Hook, the powerhouse of a rugby player, had to shout to make himself heard.

"Peter, look, our friend there, I'm sorry I don't know her name, is about to be attacked by both of those slithering beasts off to either side."

Stopping what he was doing with the deflecting mantras for but a moment, the young hockey playing dragon followed the direction Hook had been pointing in. Sure enough, two sickly dark nagas, brilliant matt black bastard swords held over their heads, looked as though they were about to outflank Amelia Battlehard whose focus was very much directed skyward at that moment. With a glistening drop of sweat from concentrating so hard dribbling down his prehistoric chin and continuing further onto his chest, leaving a gleaming trail across his scales as it did so, Peter reached out within the awkward telepathic link that they'd all cobbled together and agreed to be a part of, and straight away shouted,

"They're coming for you on the ground. Take the one to your left. I'll take the one on the right."

Launching a barrage of wickedly green lightning at two dragons closing in on her from the air, side by side, the adaptable leader and King's Guardian somersaulted back on herself twice before coming to a standstill, facing the would-be attacker on the left, hoping that whoever had sent her the message would fulfil their part.

Aggrieved that one of their own was about to be ambushed, Peter found one of the worst mantras he'd been taught, and screwing his face up in concentration, focused all his will on the brutal serpent-like beast trying to sneak in from behind. Slithering in and around the carcasses, trying to stay in the female dragon's blind spot, making virtually no noise at all, the naga knew that he was almost in range to strike, sure that nothing would stop him now. There was simply no way in hell she'd be able to react in time, especially as she'd just started to engage another. With the jaw dropping realisation of magic, not so much washing over him, but more... running inside him, he dropped the heavy sword on the ground, it managing to avoid all the cadavers, instead choosing to hit the hard marble floor with an almighty CLUNK. Instinctively the urge to flee overcame him, but it was quickly dispelled by the magical enthrallment that bound him to the brute Manson. Being instructed to fight, no matter what the situation, it was at that precise point that every single one of the naga's bones turned to mush, his goo and gelatinous filled body plopping to the floor like a beanbag full of jelly. To his absolute horror, he could do nothing at all about it, unable to move, his mind just trapped in an unforgiving excuse of a hot water bottle. Dispatching her opponent easily with a phantom blade that took the monster's head straight off, Captain Battlehard was only too aware of what had happened. Offering up a quick salute in Peter, Janice and Hook's direction, she sliced open the boneless sack on the floor behind her with a razor sharp talon from her left foot, letting all of the sloppy innards run out across the cold white marble, before once again turning her thoughts to those attackers in the air.

As they tumbled across the private residence, locked together, nagas and dragons scattered out of their way, the odd one or two too slow, immediately paying the price for their sloth-like attitude. Bouncing upright, Manson drilled a venomous bolt of pure forked poison into his adversary's stomach. The new and improved silver scales barely felt a scratch as Flash went on the attack. Lashing out with his right wing, the very tip slicing through the air caught the maniac Manson fully in the throat, tossing him twenty or so metres skywards, an awkward and hard landing in some loose rubble the reward. Instantly four nagas threw themselves at Flash, a pair on each leg, all having but one thought... to bite and inject their debilitating and deadly poison. Aware of what they were about to do, for a split second the ex-Crimson Guard's mind rewound to his first trip to Antarctica, and the vicious wound that had almost ended his life. Memories of the pain filled his veins with anger. There was no way in hell that was happening again. One flap of his mighty wings later and all five of them found themselves hovering high up, much to the slippery serpents' surprise. Tensing the gigantic muscles in his thighs, Flash slammed his legs together as hard as he could, rewarded with two of the four falling straight to the ground, both landing with a sickly crunch. Wondering what to do about the other two before they injected their agonising venom into him, a soft and familiar female voice floated through his head.

"Just a little bit higher, and I can deal with them."
"RICHIE?!"

Not sure whether or not he should be taking help from someone whose mind should be fully focused on keeping the main part of their force safe, especially the monarch, without hesitation he flapped his colossal wings twice more in quick succession, gaining another ten or so metres straight up. With the wriggling nagas resembling worms on a fishing hook, two laser-like bolts of fire shot up from the direction of the shield, each one intersecting a naga, causing them both to spontaneously burst into flames. For a brief instant Flash relished the surge of heat from their fiery deaths, before remembering his original objective. Sending a heartfelt thank you in the direction of his friend, he whipped around, hitting upon the main cause of his ire... the leader of this would-be world superpower. As Manson stumbled to his feet, wiping himself down, Flash gave everything he had, moving much faster than a speeding bullet, bearing down in no time at all on the darkest being in the room. Well, darkest but one, perhaps.

They hit with the force of two atoms colliding, at least that's what it felt like to her, anyway. Winded, unable to pull in a breath, her nemesis and of course father continued to press his advantage, delivering a meaty uppercut to the bottom of her chin, enhanced by magic, instantly breaking her jaw in a ground quake of a sickening CRUNCH! Eyes wide with surprise, she dropped to the floor with a THUD, tiny particles of marble dust spraying into the air as she did so. Through all the madness coursing around her mind, a tiny voice sought to escape, wanting nothing more than to explain, to give in, to reconcile in an effort to save, and ultimately get to know her son. But there was a problem, a not insignificant one. With that one devastating punch, he'd broken her jaw, without which she couldn't speak or make herself known. And as she threw up her defensive shield in absolute terror against her snarling father's next offensive blitz, there wasn't a drop of spare supernatural power to divert to healing. She wouldn't be talking any time soon, and likely even if she could, something deep inside her screamed that he'd never listen. Caught in a conundrum, wrapped in a riddle, mired in a mystery, she fell back on the one thing she knew only too well, the one thing she was born to do. Letting out the mother of all psychic screams, bringing those close by to their knees, she fought back.

Unexpectedly, a sliver of frozen air escaped Vasuki's blue tinged lips, accompanied by the flicking of a bright red forked tongue, startling Yoyo more than a little. Slowly the healer recoiled in an attempt to give the king of the nagas slightly more personal space. Scaled eyelids fluttered open moments later, the realisation of where he was, yet to take hold.

"Easy, Your Majesty," ventured Yoyo with all the diplomacy he could muster.

"Uhhh... wwwhaaaat haaappppened? Wheeere aaam I?"

"You're safe for the moment, tucked away behind the defensive barrier with the rest of our force. Whatever you did was a great success and bought Flash enough time to get you over to us. We're all very grateful."

Shaking his snake-like head and swallowing hard, Vasuki tried in vain to sit up, without, it had to be said, much success.

"I feeeel terrrrribbble. Whaaat haaaappened tooo meee?" he asked.

"If I had to guess, and that's all it would be, I'd say you used up every last drop of your power in some kind of magical explosion. It certainly made an impact, decimating a great deal of the dragon force and I'm afraid, many of your kind."

"DAAAAAAMN!" uttered the naga king on hearing this.

Sensing the frustration at having had to pick a side and battle his own brethren, Yoyo just had to ask,

"Is there nothing you can do to turn back the tide and get them on side? I was under the impression that they're doing all of this for you."

"I thiiinnk yooouu'rrrre riiiight and thaaat theeey arrrre, buut it wooould appeeear thaaat soomewheere aloonng the liiine, magiiic haass beeeecoome invoollved. I've triieed tooo reaaach ouuut tooo theem, caallll theeem baack too mee iffff yoooou liike, all tooo nooo aavvvvaiiilll. Whatttever's haaappeeened, theey seeeeem tooo a beeeing, welllll and trulllly captivaaated by thaaat dreeeadful fellllow and hissss cooohorttts. If I cooouuld, I'd giiiive my liiiife tooo undooo whaaat haaass happeeened."

Yoyo didn't doubt it for a second.

Crouched next to Janice, tucked away behind Peter's

cute little (relatively speaking) dragon body, it was only now that Hook realised how things had turned around, and exactly how much safety they were afforded by the supernatural shield encompassing them all. Still keeping an eye out for anything underhand and dangerous beyond the barrier, he decided to take a little stroll. Slipping away from his two friends, he hurriedly marched across to what would have been considered the front of the shield.

"Alright Tiny?" quipped Richie, hands and arms outstretched, without of course the dagger this time, using up a tiny smidgen of the power contained within the necklace.

'Tiny?' thought Hook, smiling at the very notion, because of course he dwarfed her... well, in her human form. He supposed that if she could or would turn into a dragon, then that would be that, but he was far from the smallest of all the humans here, below ground in the dragon domain. Luckily, he recognised the playfulness in her tone of voice instantly, thinking much more of the lacrosse playing dragon, seeing that she could joke around when there was so much at stake.

"How are you doing?" he asked softly.

"Me?" she enquired. "I'm fine... how about yourself tough guy?"

'More ribbing,' he mused, absolutely fine with it, because of course that's what happens in a team, there's lots and lots of... banter.

"Tough would be good about now. At least that way I could get out there and help, head off and find Tank, because he sure looks like he could do with some."

Listening to the melancholy in his voice, Richie changed tack somewhat.

"Although I was giving you a hard time, just because I could, does not mean you should take me seriously. You rugby players should learn to lighten up."

"You may be right," he replied, but the seriousness of the situation has me at a loss about what to do. I feel utterly helpless. You're all fighting and casting your magic about, leaving Janice and I to just look on, able to do very little, almost as if we're just here for the ride."

Glancing across to one side at the strapping rugby player, she could almost feel the pain etched across the bold and handsome features of his face.

"Don't say that," she urged with a smile. "During everything that's happened here, the bravest feat I've seen is you in the middle of the magical mayhem, dragging Flash's body with the laminium chains across the floor towards Yoyo. Not once did you falter, not once did you think of yourself. You're easily braver than fifty dragons twice your size. In the future, songs will be sung of your bravery. That is, of course, if we go on to prevail."

"Hmmm... somehow I think not."

Beaming that classic Richie grin, she thought carefully about her next words.

"It could be called, Hook the rugby player, not only that, but he's a dragon slayer," she joked, making them both laugh, something the young human needed dearly.

"I knew I could count on you to say the right thing and cheer me up."

"You're welcome," she announced, still grinning.

"Is there anything I can do?"

"Apart from massage my aching back, no... I don't think so."

Slipping in behind her, he started to use his huge hands and sausage-like fingers to firmly manipulate the muscles in her shoulder and back.

"I was joking, you know," she declared, feeling the knots in her muscles disappear instantly.

"I know, but since I'm a sports masseur and movement coach in the real world, whatever that might look like now, then I'm probably the best man for the job. And I do have a little free time on my hands."

"You really don't have to... ahhhhh..." she started, but what he was doing just felt too good, and so she shut up, let him do his thing, and thought that under different circumstances perhaps the two of them could have become very close indeed.

12 A VERY BIG SURPRISE

It was slow going, due to the confined space, the darkness, Al Garrett's age, all the protection they wore, but mainly because of the intensely stifling heat. Sweat gathered across their foreheads, swamped their necks and dribbled down their backs and legs, attempting to undermine their concentration. It didn't work. They were, after all, consummate professionals.

Keeping one hand on their valuable new weapons, the lights from their helmets directed at the floor so they could see where the next tightly wound stone step was, they continued into the depths, that is, until they could go no further.

"Why have we stopped?" whispered Garrett, his voice reverberating around the enclosed space.

"We've reached a dead end," Owen answered softly.

"What does it look like?" Garrett put in.

"The steps go straight into a wall. It just stops, and that's it."

Silence surrounded them for a few moments as Owen re-examined the space in front of him, with the man that had dragged them all down there pondering their predicament. Sure there was absolutely no way of going any further, and about to voice his concerns Owen was beaten to it by his boss.

"It's got to be like the entrance," observed Garrett from slightly further up, the narrowness of the circling stone staircase making any movement other than backwards and forwards all but impossible. "There must be a hidden switch of some kind. Use your fingers to scour every possible surface. We have to get through. We've come too far to give up."

Feeling an unwarranted amount of pressure, and with what felt like gallons of sweat positively running down his face, Owen very slowly and very carefully ran the palms of his open hands across the rocky surface in front of him, using the torch from his helmet to light the way, making sure to put his fingers in as many of the irregularities as he could.

Wiping moisture from their brows, the others waited patiently in the relative darkness, occasionally wondering what they were doing here, and whether or not the pay would be worth whatever it was they were getting themselves into. As for the 'bald eagle' himself, his thoughts and attention were very much focused on the whereabouts of Peter, Richie and the other missing Salisbridge residents.

Abruptly the contemplation was interrupted as the tiny movement of metal on metal somewhere in the background was accompanied by brilliant bright light shining upon them. And if they'd thought the heat was bad before, this felt like a sauna adjacent to the sun. Temperature wise, things had been ramped up a few more levels.

Carefully, and with his NGASR aimed out in front of him, Owen stepped through the gap that had appeared without warning and strode out into the light. His first thought at what he was seeing went something like...

'This is unreal and just can't be possible.'

Slowly the others joined him, one by one, spreading out in a tactical formation just as they'd been taught, Garrett in the middle, stripping off his suit jacket before throwing it to the floor to leave him in just a shirt and body armour. To a person, they were all completely dumbstruck. In front of them, and stretching off into the distance, were rounded houses, flats and businesses from the look of things, here underground. And although a surprise, that wasn't the jaw dropping part. The fact that the buildings were built for beings at least three times their size and carved very specifically into the rock, was more than enough to send a chill down all their spines.

'Who on earth lives here? What are they? And where are they now?' These were questions that all raised their ugly heads.

In the middle of it all, Garrett opened up the top two buttons of his shirt, turning around three hundred and sixty degrees as he did so, taking in the solid stone wall from which they'd exited, which had to be well over three hundred metres tall. Following it up as far as he could with his eyes, it was difficult to see the ceiling of the... cavern, if that was even the right word for what they were standing in.

After letting it all sink in for a while, Owen piped up.

"What's the plan, boss?"

Wiping sweat from his right cheek, while taking a swig of water from a bottle a young woman called Judith had passed to him, he swallowed thirstily before composing himself, all the time trying to believe the reality of what they found themselves in.

"I think we should move out and explore, with of course extreme caution. Whatever lives here is clearly considerably larger than we are, by the looks of things. Whether it's giants or monsters, it doesn't really matter. We will probably have the firepower to overcome them, if it gets to that point. But we should be cautious. I don't want anyone opening fire, not unless it's a life threatening situation, and certainly not until we've tried negotiations. Do you all understand?"

Simultaneously the word 'yes' echoed throughout their little group. After each of them had taken a little drink, and with more trepidation than he liked to give away, Owen led the close knit squad off down the nearest road, or at least that's what it felt like to him, but he supposed that judging from the size of everything else, it was only really a footpath. Scared and intrigued in equal amounts, as a group they moved silently towards the settlement's centre.

13 TRAPS, TRICKERY AND SLEIGHT OF HAND

Two outer layers of security had been passed relatively easily, leaving the multilayered collection of dragon consciousnesses feeling ever more confident with every step closer they got towards their goal of the crystal node. Swooping up a long, twisting hallway, the ethereal assemblage of minds stuck to the shadows in the rooftops, ducking and diving around obstacles, staying well clear of any beings walking around down below.

Despite the use of the magical fish goo, as he liked to think of it, leaving his body and travelling this far away was a taxing effort for the master mantra maker and clearly taking its toll. If anyone had bothered to look at his physical body, which only the humans guarding it were capable of doing right at this very moment, they would have found that his glasses had fallen to the floor, a slick coating of perspiration covered almost all his scales, whilst his hands shook and he panted like a dog. All in all, not a very good position to be in. Still though, they ploughed on, desperately in search of three minds amidst hundreds, each of the dragons on that crazy journey looking out for Steel, Jar Man and DomCon, in the hope that they were still alive.

Hovering in the air all of a flutter, the gathering of conscious wills stopped to spy on the next entrance through which they had to travel. While the others had been a breeze, this one looked like a different level altogether, with writhing tentacles of dark, grizzly magic scouring the air around all sides of the gateway.

Abruptly a feeling of overwhelming happiness echoed throughout the link. One of the dragon minds had found what they were looking for, at least not what, but who... Jar Man and DomCon. Briefly Gee Tee rejoiced, that is until he realised there was no sign of Steel's intellect. Sensing that their friends were located much deeper in the building and concerned for the laminium ball captain's whereabouts, all that they could do was push on, hoping that by getting further into the building, Steel's psyche would become apparent, because in all honesty he was probably the only one that could save them all now.

Deep within the same building the master mantra maker's mind sought to travel further into, howls and blood curdling screams rebounded throughout the shadows as Red continued with her despicable monstrosities, constantly torturing the newly reborn dragon whose body and mind lay in tatters for all to see, especially his friends, Jar Man and DomCon.

'Surely there's nothing left of him,' thought DomCon, frightened for not only what remained of his friend, but for his own life as well, knowing that if the torturers gained access to Steel's mind, then the ruse itself, and more importantly, their disguises would be revealed, leading to nothing but a deeply unpleasant death for all of them. But what could he do? Nothing sprang to mind, and so looking on, wishing with all his might for it to be over, he stared off into obscurity and waited for the inevitable to happen.

For Jar Man, a more glass half full kind of dragon, his thoughts and prayers were only with Steel, encouraging the superstar laminium ball captain to hang in there, sure that the master mantra maker would have, by now, realised that something was wrong, and right at this very minute would be enacting a plan to come and rescue them. How? He had no idea, but it was the only comforting thought he could come up with in this absolute nightmare they all found themselves caught up in.

'Hang in there Steel, hang in there,' he thought somewhere back in the dark recesses of his rather terrified mind. 'They're on their way, of that I'm totally sure.'

Shattered like a damaged mirror, that's how his mind

felt, with tiny fragments threatening to break off and scatter in all directions at any moment. During the entirety of his whole life, he'd never felt so much pain, never even thought it could be possible... but it was, and he was on the end of it right at this very moment. Knowing that they wanted access to his thoughts, after recovering from the shock of the first mental onslaught, he did the only thing open to him... he hid in his past, well... sort of. What he'd really done was use the best memories from his laminium matches to keep his physical self strong, what remained of his mind, focused, and stop the miniscule splinters of what was left of his intelligence from shooting off in all directions, which would have let them win for sure. Instinctively he screamed in absolute terror, the kind of scream known only to a few, most on the verge of death, the mind bending pain from what was being done to him almost too much to take. But because his physical body had become separate from the rest of him, it almost carried on of its own accord, leaving the best part of him locked away in the past, protected to some degree, but for how long, who knew?

Their invisible collective of consciousnesses had got closer to the entrance through which they needed to travel, almost within touching distance of the shadowy black feelers that wriggled and squirmed around most of the outer circumference. Without warning, Gee Tee felt an overwhelming sense of danger threaten their position. Nothing looked wrong, and they did at least seem to be out of reach, but his gut feeling rolled with it, and so being the one in control of where they went, he quickly pulled back away from the doorway, just in time to avoid one of the black tendrils of magic striking the exact position they'd been in only a moment before. Collectively the others shuddered, their fear almost palpable through the shared link. It was a close call, that's for sure and what would have happened had they been caught was anybody's guess, but nothing good, on that they could all agree.

"We should return to our bodies," argued one.

"I concur wholeheartedly," agreed another. *"We need to find our friends. They need our help and are the only ones capable of turning this thing around. Don't you remember what the stakes are?"*

And that was just the start of the arguing. For his part, Gee Tee remained silent, multitasking... listening to them squabbling like kids, knowing that what they thought was pretty much irrelevant as he controlled the combined group of minds and it was HIS decision and HIS alone as to whether or not they would go back. All the time though, he worked the problem of just how they could get through this next barrier. Watching the deadly looking magic twist and turn, not taking up the same space for longer than a second or so at any given time, the wise old shopkeeper magnified his vision using the magic within him and focused in, hoping to gain any sort of insight into exactly what they were facing. Thirty seconds later... he had it.

Above the sound of the continuing arguments, the master mantra maker raised his voice and shouted,

"ENOUGH!"

Immediately they all stopped, most unhappy at being interrupted mid rant, their feelings of displeasure very much showing through the link they shared.

"We need to change our form from that of a large fluffy cloud, to a superfine, super small, elongated cylinder... NOW!"

"But, but, but... why?" asked one.

"Because," announced the shopkeeper, *"I know how to get us past, and we're going in."*

"I... I... I... think we should return," announced one of them again.

"NO!" screamed Gee Tee in their heads. *"There's one leader here, and that's me. And I tell you now, we're going in. You've got exactly ten seconds to do as I've asked. If you don't, then almost certainly we'll fail. One way or another, we're going through that door."*

Terrified and cowed by the Emporium's owner, instantly they all did as he'd suggested, each of their consciousnesses squeezing against the next, forming what would have looked like, if it were visible, a very small and very long straw, with the master mantra maker's mind at the front.

With them all in position, he led them forward, slowly at first, lining up on one part of the circumference, holding back just out of reach. All clung together for dear life, each of the others wondering exactly what was happening and how their leader would keep them safe.

Like most things over the past few days, it was a gamble, but a calculated one, something that at the moment he could live with. You see there were gaps in the defences around the entrance. It was just that the haphazard nature of the self-protective magic made it impossible to see them for any length of time, behind the supernatural evil that looked like a massive ink blot with a life of its own. But if he relied on the side effects of the magical fish goo that he'd smeared himself with, he knew with absolute certainty it would guide them to the right place at exactly the right time, allowing them to find one of these diminutive slits and voyage through it. Giving himself fully over to the magic, he pushed the invisible straw of intellects towards its target, increasing his speed as much as he could. Lost in the sixth sense enhanced by the goo, the old shopkeeper motored ever forward, heading straight for an eclectic pattern of magic, almost certain to be detected. Like the maverick he'd always been, he held his nerve, convinced it was the right thing to do. At the very last instant, the slivers of ethereal energy disentangled, changing shape completely, letting them pass unscathed and slip undetected through a tiny fissure that was already there. Not having a physical body, not there anyway, the entire dragon contingent, with the exception of Gee Tee, all reopened their eyes, not realising that they'd closed them, each breathing a sigh of relief. They were through, at least this one anyway. For the master mantra maker, it was a different story. On breaching the latest barrier, a spark of recognition had ignited inside him, momentarily revealing the essence of the laminium ball captain alongside his two friends. Joy instantaneously turned to despair on reaching out and trying to make contact with Steel because from a distance, his mind felt as though it had been decimated, flayed within an inch of its life. Hope vanished there and then, replaced simply by a dreadful despair and an almost physical pain at having let down all of those that had travelled with him, as well as those he loved... his friends. For the first time in as long as he could remember, he was out of answers, bereft of solutions, with nothing up his sleeve that could save them. As the others rejoiced at sneaking through the gateway to get this far, Gee Tee couldn't bear to tell them the bad news.

As the snakes in and around her head nipped at his eyes, Earth, though pinned to the floor, expelled a long, deep breath into her father's face. Poison spores erupted, instantly recognisable because of the green tint that accompanied the lungful of air heading his way. Fredric, mighty dragon warrior and founder of the Crimson Guards, held his breath before conjuring up a harsh winter's breeze that enveloped both of them, whipping his long matted hair in every direction and giving the snakes something more to think about. Raging with disappointment at having her cunning strike countermanded, the murderous and bordering on insane soon-to-be-queen struck out with her heel, digging it into his shin before slamming it down onto his foot. It was all a ploy really. That particular move would not set her free from his weight on top of hers, it was only ever intended to get him to move just a little. Reacting to it, he did, and that gave her the opportunity she'd been hoping for. Ready and waiting, she brought her knee up as harshly as she could, rewarded instantly by a lessening of his strong grip on both hands and a very stunned look across the entirety of his ragged and weatherworn face. Slipping out from his grasp, she pummelled his nose, causing brilliant red blood to splatter them both. Ignoring the build up of her father's rage, she spat in his face, a huge globule of white foamy discharge landing square across his left cheek. Just as he should, he ignored it, focusing fully on getting back the advantage and delivering a killing blow. It should have been easy. It was anything but.

Struggling to break free with everything she had, thoughts of her son, somewhere close by, just wouldn't leave her alone. What they could have had, what potentially was still there for them. During his incarceration at her hands, she now regretted not having got to know him when she had the chance. Of course, that wasn't the way to do it, but the madness twisted reality and events within it. Would Peter really have responded favourably when chained back to back with Tim and told for the first time that she was his mother? You can bet your life he wouldn't have. In her mind though, things played out differently, with them able to reconcile and reconnect. They could have been a family once again, especially with her father out of the way. But he'd only gone and appeared, putting a gigantic spanner in the works. Boiling with anger and rage at having been denied that last gasp opportunity, her mind returned to the here and now, vowing to defeat him and see what remained. Perhaps the boy could be turned and would join them in the brave new world her partner and king was on the verge of creating. Doubling down, she head butted the tiresome old man fully in the chest, causing him to release her completely. Before he'd even had time to realise what had happened, she rolled out from underneath him, backflipped to her feet and ignited magic in both hands, radiant streams of ethereal dark power twitching across her fingertips, ready to be expelled. Without hesitation she did, all in his direction.

The pounding in his face felt like a lumberjack sawing away at a tree; the pain could only really be described as exquisite. Always one to respect an enemy's handiwork, so long as he lived and prevailed, a tiny fragment of him admired her ferocity, her cunning and guile, the way she feinted one way and then struck the other. She would have been a formidable dragon warrior and one he would have been proud to fight alongside, if only 'IT' hadn't happened. Things might, no, WOULD have turned out differently, and just maybe the world wouldn't now be standing on the precipice that it found itself on. Pushing away the thoughts of happy families and knowing that currently she had him at a huge disadvantage, he feinted right and then rolled left with all the power and speed he could muster, the ground beneath where he'd previously been scorched by dazzling bolts of sickly, dark, shadowy magic. Bounding to his feet, something didn't seem right. Ethereal energy flowed through him, energising his cells, filling him with power the likes of which he hadn't known in decades, if ever. But the pain in his face hadn't receded, in fact if anything it had gotten worse. Turning to face her, a searing ball of superhot flame readied in his right hand, it was then that he noticed the wicked grin spread out across her magically mad features, those that made her face look like the web of a particularly exotic spider. She'd done something, something bad, and breached his defences. But what, that was the question.

With the top speed of a Ferrari and the agility of a gymnast, the giant silver, grey and blue prehistoric monster cut through the air with ease, about to hit its objective, ready to end this whole encounter and return the planet back to its rightful status. Certain of slicing right through his target with razor sharp talons, at the very last second the menace that was Manson ducked to one side, avoiding having his head parted from his body by a gnat's... ear. We'll go with ear, though that's probably not what I mean. But Flash was Flash and named that way with a clear sense of purpose. Manson might have avoided his head being taken off, but the ex-Crimson Guard was nothing if not adaptable, his mind a calculating and scheming resource, one that could, if used right, offset any difference in supernatural power and magic. As the would-be king of all this dipped out of the way of one set of talons, those on the other foot adjusted themselves in an amount of time barely measurable, plunging deep into his shoulder, embedding themselves there, before lifting him off the ground, carrying him skywards, all the time screeching out in pain, unable to bring forth the malevolent evil magic that was his trademark. Barrel rolling off to the right to avoid colliding with two dark dragons, themselves taken totally by surprise, Flash inverted as he cornered, very pleased to hear the fearful screams of the despicable wriggling creature beneath him. Glancing down at the battlefield, briefly able to see Tank inundated by a horde of slippery nagas, the ex-Crimson Guard looked for somewhere to put Manson down so that he might finish him off once and for all.

Thrashing about in absolute agony, Earth's other half had similar ideas, well, at least about getting back down to the ground. Struggling in vain, the pain ramping up with each and every turn and drop, there was simply no way he could conjure up even the simplest of spells to help him break free. As they pulled another tight turn, the G-force from which nearly made him pass out, he glanced down at his shoulder and on witnessing the bone, muscle, sinew and skin all flapping about, did his best not to throw up. Now was not the time.

Scanning every last part of the King's private residence from the air, dodging fireballs and scything dark bastard swords being waved around in despair, Flash suddenly noticed something unbelievably odd, more than a little concerning, but just maybe something that would help all of them in the long term. Back towards the entrance to the council building, a cloud of massing nagas was being taken down from what looked like behind. Not sure how that was possible, or who the slippery serpents were brawling, even with his enhanced magical vision, his concerns returned to the present as a pair of dark dragons working in unison tried to ram him from opposite sides. Slamming the brakes on and using the overflow of magic within him to transform his weight into that of a heavy base metal, he dropped straight down like a stone, avoiding their attack, watching in delight as they both smashed into each other with a sickeningly bone crunching sound. Approaching a group of nagas and their cohorts the dark dragons, on the ground at speed, Flash flapped his powerful wings in an effort to gain some height. As he did so, an intense pain from his talons forced him to cry out, alerting those all around him to his presence.

During his unintentional flight, Manson, finding a way

through the debilitating pain, had reached out telepathically to any and all of his force fighting thereabouts. It wasn't fancy, clever or even very king-like, but he knew he was in trouble and it was all he could think of. And so it was that two of the nagas on the ground, slithering amongst the throng of their kind, eager to get to the shield and throw all the magic that they had at it, stopped for but a moment, the magical enthrallment guiding them in a different direction. Raising their serpent-like bodies almost over upon themselves, looking to the air, they suddenly found their magical master, the being whose life commanded theirs. You might think that ideas of letting him die and freeing themselves from his corrupted spell might have entered their heads. But not so, not even a single glimmer, because the supernatural power that bound them wouldn't allow it. The only thoughts they had were of rescue and how best to help him. Both watching the dragon whose talons had pierced their commander's shoulder drop like a stone towards them, they immediately knew this was their chance and so working in tandem, set their magic free. Plunging toward the ground at speed, Manson attempted to shake his shoulder free from the talon that had carved right through it. The pain though was just too great and impossible to overcome. Nearly blacking out from the attempt, abruptly the tingle of familiar naga magic tickled his being.

'They're answering my call,' he thought. 'Thank God for that.'

As one of the slippery serpents cut two of Flash's talons off with the precision of a laser scalpel using a fine blade of impenetrable ice, the other used his vast experience to heal Manson's wounds, knitting bone, sinew and skin back together, all as he fell through the air. It was complicated, even for two of them at once, and required a vast amount of concentration and mana, and although their outrageous attempt worked spectacularly, the one thing they couldn't do was either catch him or break his fall.

Plummeting to the ground, the familiar feeling of

ethereal energy washed over his shoulder, dampening the pain, allowing all of his supernatural power to rise to the surface, a dreamy smile crossing his harsh, human face. Without warning or any drama at all, he thundered into the floor, or more accurately, into the nagas below him.

Letting out a long slow breath, whilst healing the minor injuries he'd sustained in flight, Manson sneered at the dead beasts that had unsuspectingly broken his fall. If not for them, then his injuries would have been much, much worse. Off to one side, two nagas, one dark green, the other dark brown, sidled up towards him, with what passed for a grin etched onto their scaly faces.

"We're so glad you're okay," they stated with great satisfaction. "It was us that saved you from that flying monster."

"Was it indeed?"

"Yes sire," they both responded simultaneously.

With the human shape that they'd just rescued glancing away from them momentarily, the two nagas gave each other a nod of satisfaction at a job well done, about ready to rejoin the fight. Once again though, the madness had reared its ugly head.

Turning around in a blur, the insanity captured in human form blasted roaring cones of fire at each of them, reducing their bodies almost instantly to charred, roasted blobs.

Brushing himself down, before shaking his head, he turned towards their remains and in the middle of the pitched battle playing out all around him shouted,

"You should have got to me quicker. You'll know for next time."

A crazed smile lighting up his face, he wandered back off in the direction of his beloved, determined to fight side by side with her until this was all over.

Streaming a bright burst of brilliant warmth down into his leg to rid him of any after effects from the freezing cold magic that had sliced off one of his talons, Flash, still dishing out offensive magic to those that showed too much of an interest in him, allowed a small trickle of ethereal energy into the same area and in his mind, started to rebuild that which had been taken.

Pivoting at speed on one of her giant dragon feet, Captain Battlehard turned through one hundred and eighty degrees and, straightening her other leg, put the talons of her foot right through the gills of an onrushing naga, killing him straight away. No time for celebrations, the adaptable young warrior threw out a long line of fluorescent orange magic, casting it in a circle as the nagas closed in on her position. As the beasts moved forward, all tangled up in the swathe of orange, in her mind she shouted the accompanying words, reinforcing them with all her will, eager to see the results. Instantly the line of ethereal energy ignited, furious magic resistant flames leaping out in all directions, burning, scorching and engulfing those on the ground. Serpent-like enemies hissed and screamed, melting from the bottom up as some of their cleverer comrades attempted to douse the flames with their supernatural gift. But it wasn't to be, something they learned just a little too late. The side effects of that particular spell rendered the fire impervious to magic for whatever reason. Mana intensive and not something she'd normally choose in a fight, it was only because she was so full of magic that the thought to bring it forth had come to her at all. There was, however, no time to dally, as yet another wave of the deadly monsters approached, all intent on having her head, all ready to give their lives thanks to the powerful enchantment that had them in its grip.

Foot fully repaired on the hoof, Flash used the momentum from a tight turn to double back on himself, kicking an approaching dark dragon straight in the teeth as he opened his jaws wide, about to release an explosive fireball. Ducking out of the way of an onrushing thick, deadly tail, with one flick of his fingers and only two words the ex-Crimson Guard let a crackling pulse of electricity shoot from his fingertips, destroying one wing of the creature, sending it spinning off towards the ground. Hovering in the only free air space of the whole chamber, quickly he used his well trained senses to take stock of the entire battlefield, still wondering what on earth was going on back towards the council building itself. Enemies toppled like dominoes, which of course was great, but he'd hoped to see a rescue party of dragons coming to save the king... something he didn't, and that he knew just might be an issue. A fleeting look towards the ground showed him that one of his own might well have taken on more than they bargained for, and so in that split second he decided that's where he needed to be.

Scorching hot flame screaming from her mouth, igniting the air in shades of yellow, orange, red and blue, Amelia Battlehard, wings spread out, circled for all she was worth, destroying anything that dared to come towards her. Unfortunately, she could see no end to the mass of slithering nagas and that presented a problem in itself. At some point only moments away she would need to draw breath, and when she did they'd be on her, something they all seemed to instinctively know. While her personal shield surrounded her right now, there was no way it could block that number of enemies. Thoughts of taking to the air abounded in her head just as a loud BOOM echoed out from directly behind. Afraid that one of the dark dragons had breached her defences, she whirled halfway around to greet whatever darkness had targeted her. Luckily for her, she had the sense of mind to stop her flame throwing act.

"Thought you might need a hand," offered up the

staggeringly handsome silver, gun metal grey, white and blue dragon that had crashed to the ground at her back, all the time dispensing fireball after fireball in the direction of the enemies on the ground. "I don't think we've been properly introduced. I'm Flash and I've been working for the king for some time now."

"I... I... I... I know who you are," stuttered Captain Battlehard, slightly in awe of the prehistoric form before her.

"And you would be...?"

Pulling in a huge lungful of air, avoiding using anything either poison or cold, knowing about the nagas' limited resistances to those particular elements, she scattered a huge arc of electricity out from behind her back, blue and white zigzagging lines of deathly voltage burning holes in the front of those that had thought to catch her off guard. Flash was impressed. No easy feat.

"Captain Battlehard."

"A pleasure," replied the ex-Crimson Guard with all the sophistication he could muster.

"But you can call me Amelia."

"Good to know, Amelia. Now, shall we show them that we mean business?"

"Let's do it!"

And with that, the two mighty warriors started fighting back to back, their shields melding into one, a greater understanding of coordination and battle tactics it would have been harder to find throughout the course of the day. After only a matter of moments, it was as if they'd been fighting together all of their long lives. A fantastical partnership had been formed. Manson's dread force had better watch out.

Sheltered by the magical barrier from Richie's ongoing exploits, and with Peter using the odd deflection mantra here and there to do what he could in the raging battle outside, he was very much able to compartmentalise everything that was going on. Right at this moment, he had to have the answers to questions that had been burning in his mind since the very second she stepped back into his life, and unbelievably, the dragon domain.

"You came for me," he whispered, keen for none of the other dragons behind the shield to hear.

"Of course," Janice replied nonchalantly.

"But why and how?" he asked.

Staring up into his huge prehistoric eyes, whilst stroking the scales running along his jaw line, the young bar worker thought about the question before answering.

"When I realised you'd gone missing and that something was wrong, alongside Richie over there, I started to panic. And only at that point did the scale of my feelings for you become clear. I'd have done anything to have you back, to feel the warmth of one of your hugs, to feel your soft lips..." ironic really, given right at this very moment she was running her index finger over his harsh, monstrous lips, "...melding with mine, the warmth of your breath sending shivers down my neck and the touch of your soft skin intertwined with mine. I've never felt this way before, about anyone."

Mind totally and utterly blown, it was all he could do not to transform back into his human guise and throw himself at her. Given that he'd potentially be naked if he did so, he knew it wasn't either the time or place, much to his disappointment, and so he listened as his soul mate continued.

"When Richie recovered her memories, we all came with her, down here, on this most fantastical of adventures. To find out there were dragons below ground was just unbelievable, but when that old dragon with the glasses, what was his name... ah that's right, Gee Tee. When he confirmed my suspicions that you were a dragon, and that you loved me very much, well... let's just say I had a decision to make. As it turned out, it wasn't much of one. Whether you're a dragon, a human or anything else, I love you and that, as far as I'm concerned, is all that it boils down to."

Having forgotten all about deflecting spells, what they were fighting for and just how much danger they were in, Peter, eyes fixed on the one he loved, whispered very, very quietly,

"I love you too." If he could have, he would have kissed her, but there was no way that was going to go well. Apart from the risk of setting her head alight, his razor sharp teeth could well be considered a health and safety risk.

And that was that. Both knowing what they were now fighting for, a life together on the surface with all that it entailed, something that would hopefully spur them onto greater deeds, making the outcome of the battle all but a foregone conclusion. But would it be so? Could they overcome the obstacles in their way? I'm not just talking about winning this battle. Dragons and humans have been kept apart for centuries, for a reason. Not only would they have to change destiny, but they'd have to thwart history as well. No mean feat on either front.

A short way out from the shield, in the midst of hundreds of dark dragons and slippery nagas, ten or so of the serpents had all gotten together after one of them had conceived a plan to breach the supernatural barrier that prevented any sort of concerted attack on the light-sided heroes' position. As one, and avoiding stray missiles, fireballs and shimmering particle beams of frost, they formed a circle, their cobra-like bodies on guard on the outside, the tips of their tails touching at the centre, a formation almost identical to the one their comrades had used when rebuilding the magical bridge at Earth's command, what seemed like a lifetime ago. Slowly, and with each of them swaying either backwards and forwards or from side to side, magic with a fishy taint was shared and chanting started. Working together for the greater good as they saw it, was about to make them more powerful than the sum of their parts. The light side had better watch out, because their barrier was under scrutiny from a group that would do anything to take it down.

Snaking unobserved from debris pile to debris pile, avoiding stray bolts of magic, ignoring its serpent-like brothers and the dastardly dark dragons crushing and crowding, trying desperately to get to any one of the enemies that lay outside the protective barrier and almost within reach, Earth's familiar, its two giant serpent heads working in perfect unison, slithered this way and that, occasionally pausing when cover presented itself, all the time its sights set on one particular target, one that it thought might make the difference between winning and losing the battle. It had detected the unique whiff of very powerful healing magic and had followed it back to the source, knowing that if it could remove whoever or whatever was dishing that out in huge amounts, it might save its mistress a whole world of pain and gain her and her side the advantage they were looking for. From some distance away, through naga tails bigger than its whole body, dancing feet and wings of dangerous dark dragons and magic in every shade of the rainbow exploding in and about, it could just make out Yoyo, his hands distorted, so fast were they moving, weaving and working his magic, reinforcing here, deflecting there, doing his very best to keep those outside safe, whilst keeping those inside focused. Little did he know that death was coming for him.

Buried beneath a heap of dragon and naga bodies, all scrunching, punching, and munching, each one in its own way trying to incapacitate, maim or even kill him, Tank's shield enhanced by For'son's magic, experience and exquisite will fluttered and fluctuated, shimmered and sparkled from the weight of the bodies crushed against it and the sheer overwhelming force of the magic cast in its direction. Things, it had to be said, were not going well. As a hand sized part of the personal protective barricade sizzled into nothingness, jagged, needle sharp teeth gnashed away, trying to get to the flesh revealed beneath. Spewing out spell after spell with For'son as his guide, it was an instant too late that the young rugby playing dragon realised he was in trouble, and vulnerable to attack. As the first set of incisors readied themselves for a taste of blood, moving in like a hungry T-Rex on a freshly killed hunk of prey, mysteriously the missing part of the shield reappeared, without any help from Tank or For'son, patched up and as strong as ever. An exotic howl of epic proportions rocked the human shaped dragon and his ally the ring, as the naga in question's teeth cracked and crumbled, coming into contact with a most immovable magical object.

Back with his band of young renegades, Yoyo hoped that what he'd just done was enough to help keep Tank safe for at least a little while. Able to heal at that range with relative ease, throwing out something offensive at that distance was little more than a shot in the dark. And so he decided not to, conserving his energy, watching out for Fredric, Flash and Captain Battlehard, sure that with the ring's help, the young rugby playing dragon could come to little or no harm.

Punching one naga in what he considered the throat, watching it slink off, Tank head butted another, the supernatural power encasing him knocking the beast immediately unconscious, while all the time he tried to shrug off three more, sitting on his shoulders, effectively pinning him to the ground. Trying to think several moves ahead, much like a game of snooker, this particular strategy was not paying dividends because there were too many of them, all moving too unpredictably. A change in tactics was required.

And so it was that For'son, his memory banks scoured, shared with his newfound partner some wisdom from the late 12th century, a speciality mantra, one that he'd picked up a long time ago from a crypt beneath a cathedral of all places, there for all to see, had you known exactly what to look out for. Surprised at the consciousness's apparent recklessness, Tank let the ethereal energy of the spell wash over him, wondering if he'd feel any different. He did a little, mainly his senses seeming more heightened, which given how much greater they were already when compared with a human, was quite something indeed. With For'son having explained that he needed to start off slow and build up some momentum, the young rugby playing dragon did just that, punching and kicking, seizing every opportunity to inflict damage of any sort, major or minor, it didn't matter as long as there was some. Gradually, the weight of those trying to tear him apart subsided as the blows he dished out contacted with more precision, each one now doing significant damage, maiming, rendering unconscious, some even killing blows. And with every enemy he became free of, the more lethal his attacks were, his muscled arms and huge solid fists becoming a whirring blur, nagas and dragons now flying back from his position, so well executed had the berserker spell become. But at a cost though, with For'son's well of inexplicable mana draining considerably, just as it had when Tank had restored all of the light-sided heroes' magic. On only a handful of occasions during the course of his long life had his magical capacity been allowed to get this low, all of those being reckless gambles, something they both hoped this wasn't. So with Tank in full swing, hurling nagas and dragons out in a circle, with just the two of them at the centre, slowly the number of enemies within the king's residence started to drop.

From above, looking down at the whole of the private residence, impromptu battlefield for the fate of the planet, the freshly recharged heroes and the mythical creatures were having a devastating effect on Manson's dread force of evil.

From the looks of things, the army which had stood so strong when the would-be king and his witch of a queen had taken down the shield with whatever unusual magic they possessed had been culled by about a quarter, a significant amount I think you can agree. How things would play out from here on in was anyone's guess.

Watching him from high up, striding purposefully through his troops, kicking and punching them out of the way on some occasions, using dark, deadly naga magic to carve himself a path, a tiny fragment of Fu-ts'ang actually admired and in some sick sense respected the brute and sadistic murderer that was Manson. Whilst his attacks lacked the grace, coordination and sophistication of those he regarded as the best throughout history, the raw savagery, outstanding power and sheer dominance of will he exerted was impressive to say the least. If only he'd been using it for the good of others and the planet at large, then he might have had a chance at being a superstar, falling into the category of legend after his demise. Not so though, not here, not now and probably not even if his new order came to pass, sensed the master weapon smith's soul, buried deep beneath the blade he now thought of as his outer shell. No, there would be nothing left to remember him by, not even a footnote in the garbled scribbling of history.

Weary enough after what had caused him to die once already, the chilling dragon killing blade knew to give the monster in human form a particularly wide berth, but became concerned on noticing the trajectory of the path he was carving. Without compunction and cutting the most direct route possible, Manson was heading directly for his queen. This was not good, not good at all.

"Pure and innocent one, you need to hear me," rang out throughout her mind.

"Fu-ts'ang?"

"Of course, who else?"

"Are you okay?"

"I am, but it's not me that you need to concern yourself with. The boy's grandfather, currently fighting that demonic witch, is about to have some company in the form of her other half. I think he might be more than a little outmatched when that happens."

"What should I do?"

"I would suggest you tell the king... George. And I would hurry if I were you."

Much to Peter's surprise, Janice tore out from underneath his wing, and shot off in the direction of the current king of this land. Deep in the middle of tripping enemies, deflecting harmful magic and keeping an eye out for anything unusual, the young hockey playing dragon put all his trust in his other half, and let her do what she had to.

Sliding to a halt on the scorched marble floor that was slick with blood, Janice pulled up next to George, surprising the hell out of him as she did so. Taking a break from magically exterminating the enemy force, his grey haired head turned to face the newcomer.

"Youngster, what can I do for you? You've interrupted me at a most inappropriate time."

"Your friend, Peter's grandfather... he's in trouble," she blurted, her tongue twisted more than a little in awe of the most powerful being the world had to offer.

Smiling a serene and confident smile, the king brushed away her concerns.

"He's more than capable of looking after himself, young lady, and was once one of the mightiest dragon warriors to roam the planet. I doubt very much whether he's lost those instincts, so I shouldn't worry unduly if I were you. Even now I can see that he's well on top of the personal battle that he's fighting."

"Uhhh... it's not that, um, Majesty. It's the fact that their leader, that murderous Manson fellow is on his way, and almost upon them. I thought I should let you know at once."

Immediately this changed the king's complexion and view of the whole battlefield.

"Are you sure?" he asked fearfully.

"I am, Majesty. What I've told you comes straight from Fu-ts'ang himself."

"Who?"

"Our flying ally, the chilly mystical blade that saved your life before."

"Fu-ts'ang!" murmured the king, thoughts of what to do next consuming him. "Well done for letting me know, little one. Your efforts are nothing short of exemplary. And you're a credit to your race. You'll have to excuse me now though, I have to get out there and help my brother."

For him, brother meant both in arms, and quite figuratively, thinking of his missing friend as the sibling he never had. Sprinting over to Richie, nervous energy threatening to consume him, once he'd got her attention, he didn't ask nicely. No! He did what he hadn't done in what seemed like an age. And although now he, like most of the others believed her to be The White Dragon from the ancient prophecy, unable to worry about that, he issued a command, something that couldn't be mistaken.

"I need to be the other side of the shield, NOW!"

15 FIRST CONTACT

Owen leading the way, with the others following in the same order that they'd come down the secretive staircase in, slowly and very unsurely they traversed the eerily deserted gigantic town, following the main thoroughfare, mouths open at the stunning scenery surrounding them all.

Reaching a crossroads, after much whispering, a decision was reached to go straight on, deeper into the heart of the urban sprawl, in the hope that they would find the answers they were so desperately looking for. Hugging the walls of front yards for cover, the stifling heat causing them all to sweat profusely, they marvelled at the gates that were above head height for them, but clearly meant to be only waist height for whoever lived here. Fear and inquisitiveness gripped them all to some degree, but Garrett, well for him it was the epic culmination of a lifetime's worth of experience, so he was only slightly afraid, more full of wonder.

'Whatever we've stumbled across has clearly existed for an awfully long time,' he thought. 'And most certainly we weren't supposed to find it. This all reminds me of an old story I heard when I was a kid, about bumbling giant ogres stomping around with massive wooden clubs hanging across their shoulders. Could that be what they are?'

Crouching down with the rest of the team, Garrett wiped huge droplets of moisture from his brow as they continued on, the sound of dozens of chickens in a nearby coop making them feel uneasy, the smell from the birds assaulting their olfactory senses. Overwhelming and chaotic, the thoughts of the missing Salisbridge residents spurred them all on. Step by step, they pressed forward.

Six of them had been left behind on the command of their new leader. The decision at the time had been unanimous, with her seeming to be not only the best choice, but the most logical. But they hadn't liked being ordered to stay behind, each having wanted to fight to save their monarch, or at least die trying. But they couldn't argue with her reasoning. "Keep an eye on what was left of the city," she'd said. "Watch out for any more of the enemy or a rescue force of dragons from elsewhere that could join them and bolster their ranks." It seemed unlikely that more of their kind would come, but you never really knew. Perhaps there was a flaw in Manson's planning, and sometimes Fate had a way of turning things around. Reluctantly, they'd stayed, waved their brothers and sisters off as they launched themselves into the darkness of the flying tunnels of old, and wished them good luck on their missions to retake Fleet Street and rescue the king.

After they'd gone, it had been an odd few moments, with all six of them wondering what on earth they should do next. The answer lay on the soft floating breeze as the smell of death bombarded their sensitive nostrils. The dead! They should attend to them. But it wasn't that easy. The bazaar was exposed and out in the open, leaving the possibility of an attack. And so they decided that three of them should hide in the shadows on the outer edges of the city, still within telepathic range, guarding against intruders of one sort or another, whilst the remaining three tended to the dead. With the decision made, they very quietly got on with their tasks, all the time wondering how their friends, neighbours and relatives would fare once they got to London.

Gripping their NGSARs for all they were worth, their helmets and Kevlar body armour feeling restrictive, especially in the cloying humid air, they crept down what they figured was an alley, but in effect was actually about the size of a normal human road. Two storey dwellings on either side, it was an awesome sight, especially the construction of the residences, which were for the most part made from rock, the likes of which could be seen far off in the distance in the form of massive walls and huge cliff faces. It was a staggering achievement for whoever had built it. Only now did it start to dawn on them that whoever they were actually dealing with, they must be hugely advanced and well ahead of them. Whether that boded well or not would be the key question, one that might get answered in the not too distant future.

"My friends... we have visitors," whispered a voice across a very short range telepathic connection.

Instantly the other five became alert, augmenting their senses with magic, on the lookout for any kind of treachery.

"Can you tell who they are?" one thought to ask.

"I can, and you'll be surprised to say the least."

"After what's already gone on over the last couple of days?"

"Oh yes. A little bit like buses, you wait ages for one surprise to come along, and then a few more show up."

"You're fully aware of just how little knowledge of the human world I have," urged one, *"having never visited myself, so don't start using some of their things as an example."*

Confused, worn down by the sickly smell of death and at having been collecting and covering dragon bodies now for over twenty four hours, they really only wanted to know one thing, and it wasn't about transport.

"Friend or foe?"

The answer almost made them laugh.

After nearly ninety minutes, the small band of intrepid human explorers arrived at the periphery of a huge cobbled market place. Glancing out from their hiding place, trying not to gag from the most disgusting of smells that wouldn't have been out of place from one of the challenges on 'I'm A Celebrity', Owen their leader suddenly caught sight of the slightest movement some way across the bazaar. It was hard to tell from here exactly what it was because it was obscured by a huge grotesque pyre, made up of all sorts of dead bodies. Swallowing back the bile that threatened to rise up and shame him, the big burly second in command security officer explained to his boss exactly what was out there.

"We have to go and see," whispered Garrett.

"We'll be totally exposed," piped up one young lady.

"I know," replied the 'bald eagle', "but all this sneaking around is going to get us nowhere. As well, there's a good chance they might already know that we're here."

"Why do you say that?" asked Owen curiously.

Mouth immobile, eyes wide, all their superior could do was raise his arm and point in a direction over their shoulders. Immediately they all turned around to follow his gaze. There, in the middle of the alley behind them, was an almighty yellow and red shaded dragon, easily four times the size of Owen, who was the biggest of them all. As a group they all froze, all apart from Peter's friend and understudy who brought his NGSAR to bear, pointing it straight at the prehistoric beast.

"Easy, young ones," echoed a voice from behind them.

Instinctively they all glanced back, apart from Owen who was intent on keeping his weapon trained on the one in front.

There, standing wings stretched out wide, was yet another mythical monster, dappled brown, orange and green colouring his body, while a hint of dull white outlined the features of his primeval head. It was a sight to behold, but not for the humans, not yet at least.

"Whoa... youngsters. Take it easy. We're not your enemy, we're friends... allies."

Regaining hold of his senses, Garrett quickly evaluated the situation.

"How can we be sure of that? All of this is as much of a surprise to us as it is a secret. Can you explain all of that?"

Letting out a deep breath, wisps of scorching flame flickering from his nostrils, the huge ancient beast wondered where to begin. And then it hit him. Perhaps there was no such thing as a coincidence.

"If you can tell me why you're here, then just maybe I can answer some of your questions," his husky voice resonated.

Momentarily the 'bald eagle' wondered what harm it could do to tell them. Not able to come up with anything, he fell back on pure and brutal honesty.

"We've lost some people... friends. They went missing from a particular part up above and have been gone for quite some while now. After conducting a thorough search, all roads led to an ancient monument in the middle of the city..."

"Ah... the Poultry Cross!"

"You know of it?" declared Garrett astounded.

"Of course, of course," announced the dragon.

"But..."

"It's a long story and one I'd be happy to explain at greater lengths a little later. But let's deal with the matter at hand first. The people you say have gone missing they wouldn't be led by a Richie Rump, would they?"

"Yes, yes... that's it, she's one of them."

"Accompanied by three other females and three males?"

"Yes... that's who we're looking for," said the 'bald eagle' realising they were short of one male.

Both dragons shared a look, something that Garrett was quick to pick up on.

"What is it?" he asked.

"They were here, but they've moved on."

"Moved on? Are they alright? Why are they down here? Don't they know the chaos they're causing on the surface?"

"Slow down, slow down," stressed the brightly coloured beast, the one not covered by Owen's weapon, speaking of which...

"Little ones, we need to talk. Perhaps you'd be kind enough to put away your weapons so that we can sit down and discuss what has happened. If you can do that, I'll be as honest and open as I can about exactly what's going on. It affects us all, including you and your brethren."

In the most bizarre and surreal situation he could ever remember facing, Garrett, responsible for the wellbeing of all of them, made the only decision really open to him.

"Lower your gun Owen. Keep your weapons out of the way... all of you. We need to listen to what they have to say."

"A very wise evaluation my friend. I'm Tyro and this," he stated "is Nexus. It's a pleasure to meet you all. It's just unfortunate that it's under these circumstances. If you'd like to follow me, we'll find somewhere a little less out in the open to chat."

And with that the small gang of humans trudged off in the wake of the dragon that had just spoken to them, his colleague all the time bringing up the rear, each of them wondering what the hell they'd all got themselves into.

16 PUZZLED

Fragments scattered in the wind, tiny slivers of memories in each, effectively broken beyond repair, but for the threadlike strand of unbelievable resolve that held on for dear life. That was the current state of Steel's tortured mind, about the same as his crushed and broken body.

It was sickening, the things she'd already done to him. Bones had been broken, nails removed from every single one of his talons with a vicious set of rusty pliers, eliciting the most horrendous screams ever heard, his right hamstring had been brutally severed, stopping him from putting any weight on it at all, a hammer had been taken to both his kneecaps and his wings had been punctured in a plethora of places with an array of jagged instruments. How he'd survived any of it was a mystery, as much so as the fact that his body still breathed. But it did, and it was a testament to his character and strength of purpose.

Helplessly looking on, Jar Man and DomCon sucked down the nausea that threatened to give them away. If they were sick here and now, the evil surrounding them would realise their ruse. So in sticking with their disguises, they smiled and played along, wondering what would happen next and whether anything could save what was left of their friend. For all intents and purposes though, any hope they'd been holding onto had long since died. For them, it was only a matter of when they were found out, not if.

Their hounding voices startled him from his self pity party, eager to know exactly what they were supposed to do next. Deflated, feeling very sorry for himself and oh so tired, all the master mantra maker wanted to do was to ignore all of them and just let the ether take him. It felt as though his over-extended life had caught up with him all at once. Death right at this very moment would be a blessing, a way out, the only method to forget what was happening here and now and the very sorry state his friends were probably in. Again, the voices rang through his head, pestering him, not willing to leave him be. Most of him tried to ignore them, but the spark of brilliance with which he'd led most of his life refused, urging him to listen, go back, and make a difference. It was hard to pull himself out of the spiral of despair that had taken him, though, slowly, he did, his consciousness returning to the others.

"Shopkeeper... what's wrong?"

"Uh... nothing!"

"You're keeping stuff from us, we can all feel it. I thought this was supposed to be about honesty... no more lies. I thought we were all in this together."

Of course they were right, but he didn't have any answers for them and that made him feel like a failure.

"I briefly touched what was left of Steel."

"What was left of him?"

"That's right. He seems broken, shredded almost, at least that's how it felt."

"Are you sure?"

"As sure as I can be... I've never felt anything like it. His mind and body have been tortured simultaneously in dastardly deeds that must have been absolutely horrific."

"Is he still alive?"

"As far as I can tell, yes."

"Surely then we must save him. There must be something we can do?"

"I've racked my brain and can think of absolutely nothing, no spells, mantras, hexes or enchantments that would help heal him," uttered Gee Tee.

Silence abounded across their link which had become shrouded in sadness.

Moments later, one of the dragons spoke up.

"Can we not just go ahead with what we had planned?"

"What do you mean?" enquired the old shopkeeper, tetchily.

"We send him all the magic we can muster. Transfer it through our conscious wills, after all that was the idea wasn't it?"

"It was, but didn't you listen. He's broken, almost dead, hanging on by a thread. I can't think of anything or anyone that could possibly come back from that. Death, right now for him, would be a kindness."

"What if we did it anyway? What's the worst that could happen? We can't attack as we are, we'll be slaughtered. Clearly Jar Man and DomCon aren't able to act, otherwise they would have already. If we send him over everything we have, just maybe he can do something with it. After all, it's not the first time he's come back from the dead."

This gave Gee Tee pause for thought. Would it be worth the risk? They'd be using up a great deal of their magic, with little residing back in their own physical bodies, left outside with the humans. With all of them having come round to the idea and urging him on through their telepathic union, the wily old shopkeeper decided there and then to roll the dice one last time.

Explaining to the others what would happen, that once the mantra had been cast their minds should automatically be reunited with their bodies on the outside, he failed to mention the risks the magical traps around the doors that they'd already traversed presented, knowing that in some way shape or form it could interfere with the process.

Continuing to urge him on, silently he sent a blessing off in the direction of his friends... Richie, Peter, Yoyo, George, the humans outside guarding their bodies, the beautiful Janice, the tough as nails Hook and of course the young dragon who he thought of as his son... TANK!

With that done, and his mind fully focused on the moment at hand, he gathered all of the conscious wills together, using his mighty and forceful presence, and holding them in place, he started to chant the words, all the time giving everything he had. Tiredness had been replaced by strength, certain defeat by just a smidgen of hope. As the words grew louder and the other minds joined in, magic crackled, sizzled, zipped, zapped and shone, from nowhere, lighting up the darkness of the shadowy corridor they all found themselves floating in. And then suddenly, BOOM, it was done, and the combination of minds were forcibly dragged back through the building at one hell of a speed, the overwhelming feeling of cold air brushing their faces and extremities, almost causing sensory overload.

Somewhere close by, a tiny spark in a cold dark, lonely space gurgled, a feeling of recognition resurrected albeit momentarily. And then a dam burst, and the ethereal raging river of supernatural power flooded out across time, space and more importantly, that tiny little thread. Could the odds be defeated and the impossible achieved once more? For the sake of the entire planet, let's hope so.

17 JUST LIKE OLD TIMES

Already feeling the pressure from having to maintain the magical barrier that constantly kept them all safe, a request, no... order from George the king to set him free only added to the weight on her delicate young shoulders, as the battle raged all around them... it was a good job Hook was still kneading her tired and worn muscles, she thought. With refusal not an option, she came up with a plan.

"Head at speed in the direction of your choice and I'll drop a king sized hole in the shield for a split second," she urged telepathically.

"Can you time it so perfectly?" he asked, eager to get out to his friend, a tinge of concern for everyone safely tucked away evident in his voice.

"Inundated with this much magic, I believe I can. Whenever you're ready, Your Majesty," she ventured. *"Save Fredric and give 'em hell!"*

Smiling at the superstar lacrosse player's words, he turned to face the direction of where his friend was struggling crazily with his daughter, closed his eyes, applied all of his magic and bringing up his own personal shield... set off.

The humans there would have seen nothing. Well maybe not nothing exactly, perhaps it would have been the king there one moment and then gone the next. For Richie, letting her supernatural power flow through her, time slowed, her reactions sped up and her brilliant brain worked on a thousand different calculations. Regulating the shield, not only its size, but the width of the magic involved, thinning it out in some places, whilst thickening it in others, tempering it just enough to keep the evil out, all the time trying to take in everything going on inside with her and as much as she could outside. The most advanced super computer in the world would have struggled. And now this! Watching him take the very first step, her mind's eye calculated his trajectory and just how much shield she would need to bring down, as she now took account of his blinding speed, attempting to work out the exact point at which he'd reach the barrier.

Bounding forward, propelled by the supernatural power that had been his since birth, he pumped his arms and legs with all that he had, his long, unkempt grey hair flowing back over his shoulders, approaching the still raised barrier at an alarming rate. All he could think was,

'I hope she's got this right.'

Judging it to perfection, just as she'd promised, a hole the size of the king appeared in the shield a millionth of a second before he should have bounced off it, letting him pass through safely. Before their enemy even had a chance to realise what had happened, the gap disappeared, along with the monarch into the fray, the barricade returning to normal.

Protected by impervious ethereal energy, nagas and dragons alike bounced off him as he cut a path towards his friend. Concentrating on only one thing, he just hoped he'd be in time to save his brother.

Readying a swirling ball of molten flame in two hands, about to dispatch it in his foul daughter's direction, an ever increasing pain from his face suddenly overwhelmed Fredric, instantly dropping him to his knees, the fireball disintegrating into nothing. Struggling to cut through the fog of the agony in his mind, he tried desperately to work out what was going on, with a view to rectifying it immediately. But for the life of him, he just couldn't think, that's how bad the fiery pain was.

Deeply amused at her father's plight, preparing her next attack, she strode forward ready to finish him off, particularly pleased that her little trick had worked so well. There was no way in hell he was getting out of this.

Scrabbling around on the floor, eyes closed in torment, he could feel her closing in, sense her despicable magic about to be unleashed. Fear took him, that is until one of his flailing hands bumped into something instantly familiar: Aviva's laminium dagger which he'd previously dropped in their struggle. Gripping it for all he was worth, cloaking it behind his hand and body, he waited until she got into range, all the time fighting against the agonising pangs from the front of his head. It was at that point that it came to him... a clear and present memory from only minutes before, of his vile daughter spitting in his face. That's what was causing the suffering. No doubt the despicable wretch had somehow laced it with magic, infecting and infesting. Heart racing now, the urgency with which he needed to buy some time nagging away at him, with one humungous effort he cleared the pain, rolled across the scorched marble and in one swift motion, threw the laminium dagger with all the strength he could muster, all the time wondering if it was the right move, because if she could capture it and use its power, things would probably all be over.

Distracted by the thought of finishing him off once and for all, she never saw the dagger coming and was unable to move out of its way. Zipping through the air towards her head, the angle at which Fredric had thrown it took it away from the centre of her face, striking more upwards than that, cutting a wicked swathe through the wriggling and writhing snakes that sat where her hair had once been. WHOOOOSH, cut the famed blade through the air, almost scything the atoms in two, slashing three snake heads from their brightly coloured scaled bodies, causing the she witch to shriek and wail in absolute misery, the weapon clanging to the floor somewhere in the distance. Foregoing a hold on her supernatural birthright, it was her turn to drop to her knees, all thoughts of finishing off her father forgotten.

Time of the essence, and figuring what she'd spat at him had been imbued with a poison of some sort, gripping his magic, Fredric, ignoring the chaos going on in and around him, produced a shield around his face and instantly flooded it with water. The relief was instant as what was actually acid and not poison became diluted to the point that it no longer did any harm. Repeating this twice more in a mere matter of moments, and with no lasting effects or pain, Fredric reconstructed that part of his face with just a tiny dribble of ethereal energy, before gingerly getting up on his feet.

Excruciating pain from feeling the death of her serpents fanned the flames of madness coursing through Earth, a seething mass of anger, resentment, determination and revenge pumping through her veins, watching in absolute disgust as the being she hated most on this loathsome planet staggered to his feet.

'He will pay, and he will pay now,' was all she could think.

Bounding and leaping towards each other at great speed, the two met in the air, a resounding rumble the result of their collision. Tangled up once again, both blood relatives went at it hammer and tongs.

Stomping past all his magically enthralled troops, smashing some of them out of his way, batting away stray bolts of magic here, the occasional fireball or icy blast there, Manson had his sights set on only one person... his queen! Relieved to have escaped unscathed from that gigantic silver, grey, blue and white dragon, he knew he'd been more than a little lucky, something that disappointed him no end. This never should have been allowed to happen. They should both be ruling the planet by now, enforcing their will on others, slaughtering the innocent, decimating the dragon domain whilst rounding up the pet humans on the surface for indiscriminate fun and games. But here they were, fighting for their very lives, events turning on their heads, all because that bloody rugby player had turned up, wearing what he assumed was the king's real ring. Oh yes, it didn't go unnoticed when things kicked off. That was why the ring he'd been given didn't work, wouldn't respond. It was a dud, a fake, nothing but a falsehood. And he'd tried for so long to bend it to his will. No matter. They wouldn't succeed, he vowed there and then, kicking one of his dark dragons out of the way as he strode past.

'Either I will be ruler of this world, or it will be destroyed, there will be no other outcome,' he thought.

Fighting off the one handed choke hold around her neck, struggling to breathe, it was difficult to focus enough to bring forth her deathly, dark and destructive magic, especially as black spots had started to appear on the outskirts of her vision. Slapping his face as hard as she could gave little respite. In the end, she settled for piercing the muscle of his right bicep with one of her long, sharp purple fingernails, an elicited howl and the slackening of his grip the reward. Seizing the opportunity, she snapped the wrist on his other arm, a bone breaking CRUNCH giving rise to a deep seated satisfaction within her.

Ignoring the vicious pain snaking up his arm, he just about managed to punch her in the face with his good hand before she squirmed free and somersaulted back out of range of any physical attack. As she conjured up a bank of twenty pink projectiles all heading towards him, Fredric, about to cartwheel out of the way, suddenly realised his wrist wouldn't stand for it, and that there was no time to heal it before her dastardly magic would be upon him. Exhausted and addled, momentarily he was confused as to what he should do next, all the time the pink death closing in on his position. Before he had chance to even think or deflect them away, a blur of grey and white gathered him up at breakneck speed and whisked him off, leaving the deadly magic to explode without finding its target.

More than a little miffed at once again having been defeated, she watched as the blur that had snatched up her father unveiled itself off to the side.

'Damn!' she thought, recognising... the KING! Furious and about to erupt, a soft, warm hand found its way onto the skin of her exposed shoulder. Instantaneously she whirled around, ready to fight for her life, only to find...

HER LOVE!

"It looks as though they're trying to team up on you, gorgeous. Would you like some help?"

"I would be very grateful," she purred, leaning in, planting a soft kiss on his warm cheek.

"Let's do it then," announced Manson, itching for a fight.

Skidding to a halt, Fredric wasn't sure what the hell was going on; it was only when George released him that he understood what had happened.

"Thanks for the save," he murmured, healing his broken wrist and the deep hole in his bicep, the thick red blood retreating quickly back into the wound.

"No problem my friend... I should have been here sooner."

"This one's not your fight. Concentrate on everything else," Fredric cautioned, back to being battle ready.

"I know how much this must hurt you. Let me help, please? It would be an honour to take some of the burden," urged the king.

Simultaneously the two watched Manson appear out from behind three dreaded nagas, put his hand on his would-be queen's shoulder and settle for a kiss.

"It looks as though you have evil of your own to defeat. Good luck my friend," whispered the founder of the Crimson Guards, "it seems you're going to need it."

Feigning dormancy every now and then, Earth's familiar, the two-headed massive serpent, meandered around thick muscular naga tails, slithered in and out of huge dragon feet and the razor sharp talons that adorned them, all the time getting closer to the defenders' magical barrier that supposedly kept them all safe. Desperate to taste and test the ethereal energy that held it in place, thoughts of breaking through it and striking the most prominent healer were at the front of its mind, knowing that because of its unusual makeup, it might well be the only being here capable of doing just that. Sneaking ever nearer, careful not to catch the attention of any of the enemy, in particular the flying, frost shrouded blade that continued to wreak devastation, both heads agreed on a particular strategy, much to their delight.

Unnoticed due to the sound of multiple explosions and impacts almost every second, the circle of ten nagas, their tails all touching at the centre, had started to chant louder, all now swaying in unison as if the words echoing from their deadly jaws offered an irresistible beat, one which they were drawn to. As dark dragons swooped over them and their kind slithered around their little group, compelled to attack the mighty supernatural barrier and those behind it, magic merged, thoughts became one, a clear and singular purpose forming in their minds. Across their slippery bodies, sparks of ethereal energy flickered into being. Crisscrossing lines of power rippled up their torsos, engulfing their snake-like heads, occasionally jumping across to the next naga in the circle. It was a standout act of defiance, cunning and naga ingenuity and would surprise the hell out of the enemy in short order.

Within the safety zone, Yoyo's band of intrepid and fearless dragons were putting their unconventional training to good use, each conjuring up a different form of magic to outwit those outside that would look to end their lives.

Wiz, in an effort to emulate a superhero she'd seen on the television only quite recently, had developed a sensational conjunction of magic in the form of a lasso outside the shield and was currently grabbing dragons and nagas by the head, before swinging them around into their allies and in a couple of cases totally decapitating them. Brutal but ultimately effective, it was what worked for her.

Monty had chosen to rain down icicles from the ceiling much further back into the dense dark dreadnaught force, figuring that he'd do more damage because they were so tightly packed and it would help them out later, with there being less enemies alive to face and was specifically targeting any of the dark dragons on the ground. Beautiful, intricately carved, thin shards of sparkling white ice tumbled down from high above in the shadows, skewering some, rendering others unconscious and damaging yet more. Using this across random parts of the battlefield to great effect, the young dragon was rightly proud of his ingenuity, especially since it was starting to cause mass panic in the midst of the enemy.

Tina, meanwhile, had been creating brilliant tracks of scorching orange and yellow flame that ran the length of one side of the shield, setting alight the nagas trying to break through, forcing them to retreat and take stock, leaving them wary of getting too close.

Assisting with any healing and defensive mantras, Trayrin had a knack for exactly that, just like her mentor and saviour, Yoyo. During her time in his care, she'd often pester him for new mantras and insight into how to heal better and although he loved them all equally, she was most often his star pupil.

Hillier, standing some way off from the others rained down fireballs, watching in grim satisfaction as they exploded out into great pools of superheated terror, melting naga tails, peppering the surrounding area with blisteringly hot shrapnel. Killing and maiming seemed to have become his speciality.

Zebediah focused in on the air, attempting to freeze as many dragon extremities as he could, a ploy that so far was working well. Rigid tails hindered their ability to steer, forcing them to crash into either each other or the outer structure, while frozen wings sent them spiralling out of control, crashing aimlessly into groups of their comrades on the ground. Together, the youngsters were making a huge dent in a force that still substantially outnumbered them. In tandem with the efforts of the other light-sided heroes, it went a long way to making a big difference.

Feeling the tension disappear in her back was a huge relief, and she wondered if the giant rugby player Hook had any idea just how marvellous his hands and sausage-like fingers actually were. Putting that to the back of her mind for the time being, she promised herself that she'd watch out for George from afar, knowing that Captain Battlehard, the king's singular protector, was busy fighting back to back with Flash. The young lacrosse dragon superstar found she almost enjoyed using the shield to deter their adversaries. It was both challenging and rewarding at the same time. If it hadn't involved copious amounts of maths, she'd probably have been revelling in it. Not her strong point as a subject, and although she'd received high grades during her time at the nursery ring, it wasn't something she enjoyed even in the slightest, preferring instead subjects that she could stamp her own mark on and express her inner self.

Abruptly, out of absolutely nowhere, a fantastic POP echoed outside the shield high up in the residence. Dragons took flight as a magical, twenty five metre long, black metallic cylinder, a metre in diameter, burst into existence, just hanging there in the air. On the ground beneath, nagas scattered in all directions, desperate to get out from under its shadow, thinking it yet another one of their enemy's cruel and vicious attacks. But not so, you see this was the culmination of the circle of ten nagas' bizarre and supernatural chanting. And it was up there with everything fantastical that had happened already that day.

'What the...?' thought Richie, unsure of the object's nature, attempting to study it closely.

"Rich, what the hell is that thing?" whispered Hook in

her ear.

About to reply, she stopped when the huge tube pulled back a little. That was when she got it.

'Oh crap,' she thought. 'It's a magical battering ram.' In the blink of an eye, powered by the ethereal energy of the ten nagas, the huge battering ram surged forward, hammering against the magical barrier held in place mainly by the lacrosse superstar's will. BOOM! A thunderous roar rocketed around the king's private residence, toppling nagas to the ground on their side of the shield, knocking Richie off her feet, with the assault feeling as though somebody had hit her over the head with a club. A testament to her resolve was the fact that the shield still remained in place, despite her mind and the magic within her taking an absolute pummelling. It helped that Hook had caught her before she crashed fully to the floor, something that might have affected the barrier's integrity.

"You okay, Rich?" he asked.

Shaking off the ringing in her ears, watching wide-eyed as the hope destroying battering ram pulled back for another strike, she braced herself and reinforced the barrier with everything she had. Would it be enough though, that was the question.

'Oh,' it thought, 'that would make things much easier,' as it watched the gigantic battering ram pull back for another strike. 'Perhaps I'll get into position and wait for it to destroy the barrier, that way lessens the risk and gives me more of a chance to succeed.' With that, the slithering two-headed serpent slinked off into the melee, all the time using the cover of cadavers and debris to disguise itself as it closed in on its target.

Peter in his dragon form remained upright, using his wing to stop Janice from landing with a bump, who'd returned immediately after telling the king the news about his best friend. Yoyo and his youngsters were caught much more unaware, with most crashing to the floor, whilst Hillier was thrown some way by the concussive force. Stumbling to their feet, they all watched agog as the battering ram drew back for yet another go.

'Oh crap, oh crap, oh crap,' thought Richie, screwing up her eyes, mentally bracing herself for the next big hit. BOOM! It struck with the explosive force of something fired by a tank, the point of impact sending out circular waves across that side of the barely visible barrier. Hook had wrapped his huge arms around Richie, something she initially felt troubled by, but instantly became glad of straight after it had happened.

"Thanks," she whispered in his ear, still confused and momentarily stunned by not only what had happened, but by the effect it was having on her magic. When it had struck, a shock wave of sorts had rippled back through the link to her supernatural power, right to her very core, physically hurting her in the process. It felt very much like a punch to the gut, and the only reason she was still standing up was because of her rugby playing friend.

Opening up telepathic communication with everyone behind the shield, the superstar lacrosse playing dragon quickly got her point over.

'I can't take much more of this. You either have to find the source of the magic and destroy it, or we have to take the shield down. All of you stop what you're doing and concentrate on this!"

And they did, straight away, with one or two taking to the air as much as they could within the confined space, hoping to look over the heads of the mass of dragons and nagas still assaulting their position, still throwing everything they had at it.

Breathing shallow now, sweat pouring down her brow, Richie, holding tight to Hook, could do little to affect things, with her main focus on keeping them all safe. However, she knew there was little chance she could take much more, a couple of hits at best if they were all like the previous ones. As her mind swam, ignoring the pain in her stomach, she tried to plan out what would happen if the worst came to the worst. It didn't look good.

Driven by extreme anxiety, the group of King's Guards, Yoyo and his young dragon charges all attempted to find whoever had conjured up the giant battering ram, but it was an almost impossible task. Although the group of ten nagas in a circle weren't actually that far away, the enemy swarm was so vast and so compacted that there was simply no way to see them.

Desperation led Yoyo to send out a telepathic shout for help to any of their allies outside the shield. Unfortunately for him, they were all busy with their own battles, and had no time at all to give any aid.

Fighting back to back, holding off aerial foes peppering them with fireballs, the devastating collateral damage to their comrades the nagas of little or no concern to the dark dragons, Captain Battlehard and the ex-Crimson Guard moved as one, like poetry in motion, almost as if they were joined at the hip. Deflecting, scratching, clawing, punching, kicking and using the vast array of their knowledge to conjure up incredible mantras that killed multiple beings in an instant, it was a savage riposte to the overwhelming numbers that were looking to tear them both in two, and even if they'd taken note of Yoyo's call for help, which they hadn't, there would have been very little they could have done about it.

Giving his friend a knowing look, one that they'd shared many hundreds of times over the centuries, Fredric turned to face his daughter and Manson, knowing that things were now more out of control than they had been at any other point in the battle with the fighting raging around them.

Ignoring the fleeting touch of a telepathic contact, knowing that he needed all his wits about him, especially now, facing off against what he considered the two biggest threats the planet faced, he wondered just who was going to kick things off once again. If he'd been a betting man, he would have said the thuggish clown Manson. For the moment, he'd have been wrong.

Earth, queen of dread, taker of lives, would-be joint ruler of this world, Manson's bride, Fredric's daughter and of course Peter's mother, unbeknown to him, spoke up over the mayhem, shocking them all.

"Perhaps there is a compromise to be made," she declared.

Manson, surprised at the words coming out of his queen's mouth, covered his tracks and played along for the time being, wondering where this was going and just how she would ambush them.

"I don't think so, WITCH!" growled Fredric furiously, magic sparking off him on all sides, itching to be released.

"Calm down, my friend," urged George gently. "Think of the bigger picture. Perhaps this would be in everyone's interests. Remember the siege at Tintagel all that time ago? Negotiations and compromise by all involved were the only thing that saved us there, and look how that turned out."

Blowing out a long, deep, resigned breath, Fredric's mind was suddenly cast back decades to a much more primitive time, thinking about his friend's words. And he was right, the standoff at Tintagel was only ever going to get resolved one way... but it had been a bluff, something clearly his newly rediscovered friend was trying to tell him. All was not lost or as it seemed. The king was about as taken in by these false promises as he was.

Seeing his friend too easily cowed into submission by just the mention of Tintagel, he knew that Fredric had understood his message and so continued on with the charade.

"What sort of compromise?" he asked.

Astounded to see her father concede defeat so quickly, briefly she wondered what had happened in the past at the place called Tintagel. No doubt one of their crazy adventures as knights, something that meant nothing to her as a youngster when he'd tried to recount stories from times gone by.

'A long lost world that nobody's bothered about, least of all now,' was all that she thought. 'Two old timers reliving past glories... who on earth cares about all of that in this day and age.'

Having expected to still be fighting, the lull in proceedings had taken her aback, because she was making this up as she went along. She just had to work out a way to get to Bentwhistle. If she could somehow come up with a solution to stop the chaos, just for a while, then maybe a reunion with her estranged son might be possible. After all, they still held the upper hand.

BOOM! In it came, the next blow to the shield from the mystical battering ram controlled by the group of ten nagas, hiding somewhere in plain sight. More powerful this time, it took everyone off their feet, including Richie and Hook who landed in a heap together, the strapping rugby player cushioning the fall of the fresh faced lacrosse wizard. For a moment, they had a moment. If Time and Fate had been kinder, it could well have transpired into something more. Crawling to her feet, head spinning, looking absolutely spent, once again she sent out a message to everyone hiding behind the massive barrier she was responsible for.

"I'm sorry, I've had enough. One more hit will probably finish me off. I'm going to take down the shield just before it strikes again. Get ready, and good luck!"

With that, she cut off communication, glancing over her shoulder at Peter. Nothing needed to be said, because for years now they'd been able to communicate with just a look, no matter where they were. Through a room of crowded people, out in the open or even flying side by side in their dragon guises, it was something special and unique to them. Through that look, she told him to take care of Janice and that she would see them on the other side. He wished her and Hook good luck. Smiling back, she said they wouldn't need it. And then it was over.

Turning around to face the strapping rugby playing human, all the time maintaining the barrier and aware of the battering ram slowly pulling itself back in an attempt to have another crack at things, she unclasped the laminium necklace that Flash had found for her from somewhere in the middle of the first part of the battle, and placed it around Hook's huge, tree trunk-like neck.

"Uhhh... this is so, unexpected," he quipped, a huge smile bored into his face.

"You're hilarious," she replied, fixing the clasp at the back so that it would stay on.

"I have to say I normally like to be treated to dinner a couple of times before a woman gives me jewellery. It makes me feel a bit cheap otherwise."

"Oh ha ha."

"What's going on Rich?"

"In a matter of moments, the shield is coming down and we get to fight."

Hook swallowed nervously, his giant neck moving the necklace ever so slightly.

"I think I'm gonna be in trouble," he stuttered looking out at all the nagas and dragons baying for their blood.

"Right, stand still!" she ordered.

He did so. Well, you would, wouldn't you? For her especially.

Closing her eyes, she ran her fingers a full circuit around the necklace, whispering so quietly under her breath that the mighty rugby player couldn't make out any of the words. And then it was done. Taking a step back, the lacrosse playing young dragon pointed one finger in his direction and shouted,

"SIC FACIUNT!" which roughly translated meant, "Make it so!"

Abruptly a shimmering, tingling golden light surrounded Hook, startling him as it did so. Before he could speak, she explained.

"It's a personal shield, one powered by the necklace that should keep you safe out there. All I will say is, stick with me, don't take any super heavy blows and I'll do my best to protect you." And as the battering ram swung back towards the shield once again, she shouted at him over the cacophony. "Get ready!"

They'd all heard her... the King's Guard and the remaining councillor, Yoyo and those under his care and of course Peter. But not his soul mate, so he explained to her exactly what was about to happen. Instantly mortified, in her mind she called out to her friend, the weapon smith, Futs'ang hoping to catch his attention. Not taking it as a slight on his abilities, especially knowing she was probably right and backup in the form of the frost shrouded blade would most certainly be welcome, Peter took one last look over his shoulder at Yoyo and the dragons surrounding him, sure that they had a plan.

"What is it, youngster? I'm busy slaughtering the enemy." Futs'ang enquired formally.

"The... the... the barrier, it's about to come down."

"You can't possibly know that," he replied. *"It could well take a few more hits before it fails,"* said the bladed weapon having been keeping an eye on it ever since it blinked into existence.

"No, I don't think you understand. Richie can't take any more. Before it strikes again, she's going to remove the shield. Can you help us please? They'll be on us in moments."

For the master weapon smith, there wasn't even a choice to make, that's how fond of his former partner he was. After hacking off a brute of a dark dragon's tail, before swivelling around and decapitating a sneaky looking, magic filled naga, he spoke the words that she was utterly desperate to hear.

"On my way, little one, hang in there."

Gathered in close, using the private telepathic connection that only they had access to, Yoyo laid out what he wanted them to do. Form a circle, very much like the one the King's Guard and Amelia Battlehard had previously, and use their own defences to hold off the onslaught that would be headed their way, while dishing out as much destructive magic as they could. Yoyo assured them he would keep them all healed, as well as do his part in an attacking sense. But they were to use all the tricks and talents they had, no matter how unusual or vile they may have seemed. They had one chance to get this right, one opportunity to battle through a now diminished force, one possibility to end this and vanquish evil for good. Lifted by their mentor's passionate words, each of them agreed to give their all for the sake of themselves, each other and of course the planet. Shoulder to shoulder, they stood ready.

Pinned to the floor, underneath one severed tail, hidden by another, two forked tongues tasted the smoky magic that filled the air, inhaling the exoticism, savouring the flavour as it wafted in between their needle sharp teeth, rolling firmly through their gaping mouths. Mere metres separated them now from the objective that they'd had their eye on for quite some time. They were, they knew, within striking range, and could get through the supernatural barricade to him right now if they so desired. But they'd agreed to wait and see if this next strike by the battering ram which had the scent of naga all over it, would once and for all bring down the shield for good. If it did, their work was made much easier, and who knew, they might even be able to take a few of the others out, if they could get close enough without being seen. Biding their time from their prone position on the cold marble, they gazed up and across, begging the naga magic to work.

Traversing the war zone at lightning speed, frosty tip first, Fu-ts'ang angled for the magical barrier that he knew was about to flit out of existence, ready and willing to protect one of the few beings he'd ever really had true feelings for. And that included all of the time his physical form roamed the planet millennia ago. Cutting through the air in a smooth arc, it was at that point with one eye on his partner's precarious position, that he spotted a suicidal dark dragon heading straight down from the depths of the shadows of what should have been the ceiling, but it was hard to know exactly with so much of it having crashed to the floor. Noting the beast's position, it then dawned on him exactly what he was about to do... come crashing down straight on top of Flash and Amelia Battlehard. Not wanting to be late to Janice's 'invasion party', he could see that the ex-Crimson Guard and his partner had absolutely no idea what was headed their way. Although the bond between himself and Flash had only been brief, each recognised the other as a kindred soul. In the spirit of friendship, and knowing that they all needed these two to survive and continue fighting, the chilling blade made a slight alteration to his course, angling upwards and with perfect precision, cut through the joint where the monster's left wing attached itself to its gigantic prehistoric body, sending it sprawling off in a totally different direction altogether. Doubling back to get to the angelic young human he recognised the faint touch of the ex-Crimson Guard, no doubt offering up a *"Thank you."* Giving a mental nod back, he continued on course to rescue his friend.

Drawn back as far as it would go, the battering ram started moving forward, gaining momentum, looking to smash into the magical barrier one more time. For those hidden behind it, time slowed, every second seeming like a minute, each of them knowing that the madness was about to begin, each afraid of what would happen once the shield fell. Slipping ever closer to the supernatural barricade, the ten nagas controlling it had no idea that there would be nothing for the battering ram to hit.

Watching closely, waiting until the very last instant, Richie had already run through in her mind just what would happen next. Of course, there were a few possibilities, but in many ways they were pretty much the same. All she had to do was fight, keep an eye on her friends including this one, Hook, now at least with half a chance given that he had some limited magical protection, and stay alive long enough to taste the sweet smell of victory... easy really.

Apprehension and misdirection hung in the air as the battering ram sped up, almost at the point of contact. With the exception of the smaller battles going on outside the shield, every being there waited to see what the next hammer blow would do, to see if the magical defences that had kept them at bay for so long would fall.

Timing it to perfection, the young lacrosse playing dragon and de facto leader of this small band of rebels withdrew her magic and let the barrier drop, watching as the ethereal battering ram continued on its journey unhindered, the vaguely transparent outline of the barricade fizzling into nothing. Time stopped. A frozen moment in which every being there had decisions to make.

The King's Guard all banded together, reunited as before. Peter stepped out between Janice and the approaching mass of enemies, igniting a blue tinted oval of supernatural energy in front of them both. Yoyo's band of intrepid youngsters, for really, the very first time, given just how long the sanctuary of the shield had provided them with safety, felt the tinge of fear running through them, slowing their reactions, keeping them locked in place. Richie's mind filled with possibilities, all the time knowing that she had a duty to look after her private masseur and friend. A primal surge of murderous adrenaline combined with a need to do their leader's bidding surged through the naga and dark dragon force, compelling them on, urging each and every one of them forward. The tiny little hand on Fate's clock skipped ahead and time resumed. Chaos collided with confusion as anarchy and pandemonium rushed forward in the form of an army of nagas and dragons, all firing magic at the vulnerable heroes. Death and destruction were on their way.

A rainbow litany of different coloured magic flooded out in front of the opposing force in almost every different variety. Furious flaming fireballs burned through the air from the mouths of brutal dark dragons intent on inflicting the most damage, determined to earn their leader's favour. Missiles with long arcing tails in blue, green and white spun out from the hands of the slippery serpents, sending poison, ice and acid hurtling towards their opponents. It was a 'stuck in the car headlights' moment, one in which it would have been easier to stay still and die, rather than react. But heroes they were, to a man, woman and dragon. And react they did.

Stepping out in front of Hook, Richie harnessed the anger and rage of Tim's cruel death, channelling it into her well of ethereal energy, allowing it to focus her mind and bring forth the words she needed to decimate and destroy those that would do them harm. Lips barely moving, the words appeared in the forefront of her imagination, and so reinforcing them with all her will, she unleashed the mantra she'd had ready for a few moments now.

A kinetic blast wave of epic proportions exploded out in a huge semicircle in front of her, scything through bodies, scattering shredded limbs, knocking those that survived off their feet, sending some tens of metres into the air, devastating at least the first four rows of the enemy trying to get to them. Still they came though, jumping, sliding and slithering over their dead comrades, pushed on by the magical compunction, nothing else mattering, not even their own safety and wellbeing.

Pleased for but a second at her handiwork, whilst swatting away an array of destructive magic with just the flick of a finger, deep inside her hope had been permanently dented at just how many of them there still were. Letting pure instinct take her, and pulling Hook along in her wake, she did the last thing her adversaries would expect. She charged forward.

Marvelling at his friend's mantra and the devastation that it had caused, only then did it occur to him to let loose all his offensive magic, which to be honest was pretty pathetic, compared with all the others around him anyway. Hoping that Janice's partner in crime would arrive sometime soon to give them some much needed support, with a giant roar, Peter spat out two enormous balls of blue, red, yellow and orange tinged flame, one after the other, and set about casting the only offensive mantras he knew in the hope that it would be enough. With the air exploding all around them, covering them in supernatural shrapnel, his expectations weren't too high.

Across their telepathic link, Yoyo urged his charges to pull themselves together, to gather up their knowledge and put it to good use. Unfortunately, the situation had become more than a little overwhelming, rampant fear petrifying nearly all of them.

Sizzling out of existence with a smoky hiss, the barrier disappeared, much to the simultaneous delight of two identical minds. In total and utter agreement, Earth's familiar raised both of its evil looking heads, keeping its forked tongues firmly tucked away inside its mouths, sensing the air and everything around it with its nostrils, taking in not just what was in front of it, but the big picture as well. A deep seated delight at not being noticed rolled through its entire body causing its scales to expand and contract in pleasure, both heads eyeing up the prey in front of them. Only five or so metres away, concentrating solely on the other dragons around him, the healer's back was exposed and there for the taking. Knowing that this wouldn't be easy because he was surrounded by his comrades, both minds agreed that they had to get it done. This could very well be the key to unlocking all of it, winning the battle and saving their mistress. Even if it meant sacrificing themselves, they just had to do it. There would be no messing around, no taking a leg each, no nipping away at arms, fingers or toes. They would go straight for the head, determined to do as much irreversible damage as they could before they'd even been discovered. That way, there would be no return for the healer, and in the long run their enemy would be done for. Coiled up, muscles burning ferociously with all of their magic, tiny drops of deadly toxin dripping from the overloaded injectors inside their teeth, momentarily they dropped into a dreamy trance. It didn't last long though because they soon opened their eyes, one goal and one goal only firmly in their sights, knowing that nothing could stop them now. In a whirling blur of supernatural speed, as one, they powered on with all the wickedness, malevolence and cruelty of their mistress. Sweeping through the air, their twin heads side by side, jaws wide open, teeth bared, they homed in on Yoyo's scaled head, as the thick muscular coils of their tail uncurled on the ground.

18 DEATH IS JUST THE BEGINNING

Crushed by darkness and cold, the loneliness closed in all around him as Steel's will finally conceded defeat, having suffered as much punishment and pain as it could take. Itching for the final release of death that was now so tangible he could almost taste it, frightened beyond belief and lacking everything supernatural, his physical body exhaled one final time as the torture continued unopposed.

Back in the darkened chamber, adjacent to the room containing the highly prized crystal node, the relic so relied upon to broadcast information across the entirety of the dragon domain, the body of the laminium ball captain slumped lifelessly out in front of him for the very last time, much to the satisfaction of those watching, all but two, anyway.

"Ahhh... seems he wasn't so tough after all. Who'd have thought? Pretty boys all of these laminium ball players, no steel, excuse the pun. Oh well. Onwards and upwards," announced Red, very matter-of-factly.

It was all Jar Man could do not to be sick, the bile doing everything it could to race up his throat. No nausea for DomCon, just the red mist of revenge clouding everything in his mind, wanting nothing more than to strike the savage Red down to the ground and end her life in an instant. All fully achievable as far as he was concerned, it would of course come at the cost of his and his friend's lives, as there were simply too many of them to take on alone. Watching the nefarious female tormentor kick Steel's lifeless husk of a body, both friends fought down the same desire to just attack her, hoping that they could still get out of this in one piece. Could they? Only if a miracle presented itself.

The thin thread that held what remained of his mind together started to fray. Memories of laminium ball heroics drifted off into the ether. Friends' names disappeared, hopes and dreams vanished. It was over. What remained was an eternity of alone. Except it wasn't, because at exactly that point, a dam bursting rush of the supernatural flooded over him, personalities that he recognised standing out, offering up hope and the support he needed to refuse to give up. A dragon face swam through the obscurity, hard to make out at first, that is until the huge, square, plastic glasses flickered into view. Gee Tee! And then there was the familiar warm touch of compassion and admiration that he immediately associated with one of the nurses who had not only helped restore him to good health, but had played a major part in defeating the nagas. Ahhh... Nurse Conscience as she'd become known. It was their magic being given freely in the hope that it could once again bring him back to life. Struggle, didn't do it justice. It was a choice and one that was still there to be made. To come back from the brink, to be reborn and utilise the supernatural power and magic that was being offered up, would mean more pain and sorrow, of that he was well aware. But this time he wouldn't be facing it alone... the others, whose ethereal energy they had loaned to him, would be there in essence and spirit. Knowing nothing other than to fight, the decision was made almost without him being aware. Instantly the ropy looking thread turned into metal wire, some of its strands uncurling, reaching out into the darkness, retrieving memories, names, hopes and of course dreams, pulling them in tight, one by one, piecing his mind back together, until it became what it once was: sharp, bright, cunning and fearless. He was back, in all but his physical form. But here's the thing. Dragon bodies can easily last for over an hour without air, something that helps them hunt successfully underwater, with one huge breath being all that's needed. Here and now, Steel's physical frame was preserved, albeit in quite a state thanks to Red's nasty skill set. All he had to do was make sure it remained that way for a little while longer. Empowered by as much magic as he could handle, the laminium ball captain knew there was no choice in what he had to do next. And so hoping he wouldn't scare the hell out of the two of them, gently he sought out their minds in an effort to convince them they could still win.

"Don't show any outer signs that you can hear me," he sighed softly in their heads.

Jar Man was knocked for six. DomCon nearly peed his pants. Neither spoke, each figuring it was a trap of some sort.

"Although it doesn't look it, I'm alive. I don't know how, but I think it has something to do with Gee Tee and the others stationed outside. Just as I started to fade away, they came for me. I could see the master mantra maker's face and recognised one of the nurses that helped heal me back in the medical centre. They've passed on their magic to me. I'm getting stronger with every second that passes."

Still both friends looked unblinkingly, front and centre, determined that nothing would give away their ruse, unable to reply.

"I know you can hear me, even if you daren't respond. I want to thank you for your support during all this. Without both of you here, I wouldn't have got this far, lasted this long. I know it can't have been easy on either of you. We shall remain friends forever."

It was DomCon's turn to struggle now, the words from the laminium ball captain almost forcing him to tear up, but not quite.

"We're going to try this all again, but this time I will not have my mind ripped apart and I will enact Gee Tee's mantra. Get ready boys, for the fight of your lives."

Inside, both friends rejoiced.

They landed with a THUD, if that were at all possible, back in their own bodies, each feeling as if their minds had been thick, gooey icing, their journey back the piping bag constricted by an angry chef, their arrival akin to being squirted out on top of a cupcake. A venture none of them wished to repeat ever again.

Simultaneously letting out long, husky breaths, their arrival startled the humans guarding their prehistoric bodies.

"Wow!" exclaimed Angela.

"Wow indeed, little one," mumbled the old shopkeeper, more than a little parched.

Noticing his discomfort, the young human lacrosse player passed him a two litre bottle of water from one of the discarded packs on the floor, watching intently as he downed it in one.

Shaking his head whilst licking his lips at the same time, droplets of water splashed out everywhere, like a dog shaking himself dry.

"Thank you, little one, that was much needed. Did anything happen while we were gone?"

"Not that we could tell. On a couple of occasions we heard approaching footsteps, but nothing ever appeared. We were ready to do our best and take them on, should they have though."

Chuckling softly to himself, the master mantra maker replied,

"I don't doubt for a minute that you were. Well done. Well done."

All around the other dragons drank their fill, all dehydrated and on the verge of exhaustion, their mana dangerously low, having passed on most of their magic to Steel in the hope of some kind of miracle. Little did they know, that's what they were about to get.

It was an awe inspiring feeling, the magic of others replenishing your own as well as bolstering your life force, thought Steel, slightly disturbed that he could almost smell each individual's own supernatural power and recognise them by scent. How on earth did that work? Anyway, it didn't matter. Becoming more formidable by the second, something tickled the back of his mind. There was something he had to do... two things in fact. One... he had to remember the mantra that the old shopkeeper had taught him. VENTOSUS FUROR! That was it, he recalled, wondering what the other thing was. Oh, that's right... find out where the crystal node was so that he could set the arc of the destructive concussive wave, making sure not to destroy either the node or his friends. Filled with magic, there and then his mind wandered off, all but repaired, seeking to end this as soon as possible. Passing through doors and walls as easily as if they weren't there, he quickly found what he was looking for and with maths more advanced than anything prevalent in humans, calculated everything that he needed to know. Before he returned to his body, he had one last job.

"You each need to take three steps to your left and then stay put so that I can unleash the mantra and give us all a fighting chance. If you understand, move the index finger on your left hands down just a touch."

Slowly, aware of being surrounded by an array of deadly beasts, both friends did as Steel asked, each confirming that they understood his instructions.

"Quick as you can then. Try not to get made though. Good luck."

And with that, the sound of his voice was gone.

Sweat flooding off their falsehood forms, gradually, almost millimetre by millimetre, the friends started shuffling to their left, having already chosen a spot to aim for, all the time hoping nobody would pick them up on it.

Out of nowhere, vicious magenta magic sizzled into being, sparking off the walls, lighting up shadows, magnifying the terrifying rage strewn across Red's face. Holding out her arms, her body depicting a cross, the supernatural energy still arcing from her fingers, the sadistic woman who was no doubt really something else, arched her neck to face the ceiling and let out an almighty yell.

"AAAARRRRGGGGHHHHH!"

Around the room, nagas slithered back as far as they could, common sense telling them to stay away. Recognising a gift dragon in the mouth when they saw one, making it look as though they were stumbling out of the way in fear, which was more than partly true, both friends shuffled over to their assigned positions, ready to end this farce and take back Fleet Street for the world.

"Nothing of any use from him... DAMN!" she screamed in frustration, forcing the nagas to cover their ears.

Without warning, the lifeless shell exhaled and raised its head. Completely flabbergasted, Red took two steps back, astonished at how this could be possible.

It was then that he did it. No... not use the mantra as instructed. He smiled at his torturer, and then gave her a knowing wink. And only then, as the infuriating rage started to spread out across her face, did he use it.

"VENTOSUS FUROR!" he yelled inside his mind, adding all his considerable willpower.

19 FLANKED AND SPANKED

The element of surprise had long since disappeared at the rear of Manson's dreaded attack force with their numbers diminishing with every second that passed, at first because of sneak attacks from some of the tiniest creatures in their ranks such as the nifoloa or the fire breathing gnats and then the shape shifting venomous snakes that proved difficult to lock down and get a grip on. Finally though, the mythical creatures under the telepathic guidance from the ra-hoon went crazy in an all-out assault, determined to put their stamp, (quite literally in some cases) on the enemy.

As nagas tried to ignore their enthralled orders to help their leader, and instead defend themselves against these troublesome newcomers, a colossal part of the council building's wall blasted out from a mighty explosion, sending giant scraps of metallic shrapnel shooting off in all directions. So loud was the percussive sound and so big the opening, that momentarily all those battling it out at the back turned to face the commotion, wondering what could have caused such damage, hoping for maybe another ally. Through the dust filled smoke cloud that had accompanied the destruction, out stomped the giant, hideous rock demon, the asag, moss and lichen dangling precariously off its body, fists the size of a car waving around angrily, its evil purple gaze casting about for something to attack. Luckily, it was in the right place. There was no shortage of targets.

Rearing up on their hind legs, whinnying in worry, the two horns on their heads bobbing about frantically because of the newcomer's arrival, the ra-hoon were concerned and not just a bit, purely because they'd already seen what the asag could do, and like them, just how impervious it was to most forms of magic. Commanding their force of every size of mythical creature to attack the crowded naga and dragon contingent in an effort to keep out in front of the mammoth rock demon, a familiar inkling of recognition tickled their minds. MAGIC! There it was again, somewhere in the midst of these dark, despicable creatures... a huge source of supernatural power, one that outshone anything they'd ever been aware of. To charge into the dragons and nagas now made more sense than ever for the ra-hoon, not only to escape the asag's attention but to find the source of THAT power. Once they did, it would be shaped to their will, ordered to do their bidding, and then there would be no stopping them.

In the midst of a berserker rampage the likes of which the world hadn't seen for decades, Tank's muscular and enhanced body whirled through the air, kicking, punching, head butting, gouging, biting, elbowing and stamping, using all his physicality to its upmost ability, occasionally adding a twinkle of magic into the mix, always at For'son's command. A whirlwind of death and destruction, the nagas in particular had no answer to the bedlam that he continued to cause in the middle of their ranks.

Only having nudged the young rugby playing dragon here and there to use a particular supernatural spell, for the most part the enigmatic band circling Tank's finger had chosen to remain almost silent during this stage of the battle, eager to test the limits of his new found partner's strengths and abilities. So it came as something of a shock when For'son, the conscience within the ring suddenly shouted out in the midst of it all.

"DAMN!" he swore.

Dishing out a powerful uppercut, smashing a naga's nose back up, straight through its skull, Tank turned on a sixpence, deflecting away a frosty wave of ice with the other hand before elbowing another of the beasts straight in the eye, a sickly squelch and a howling roar the instant reward for all his efforts.

"What is it?" he questioned, worried that one of his friends might be in trouble.

"Uhhhh... they've found us I'm afraid."

"THEY?"

Taking a long, deep breath which, granted, was an odd thing for an inanimate object to do, the unfathomable loop continued.

"Deep within the basement of the council building, there is a facility used to house exotic mythical and magical creatures that have been captured over the centuries. A vast amount of magical power is required to keep it running, one only readily available from me."

"Really?" exclaimed Tank curiously, all the time continuing on with his swirling, unstoppable assaults.

"That's right. Anyway, when the king, I mean George, was cornered back here, a short while ago, he ordered me to stop using my magic to contain them, not wanting to let Manson get his hands on them for obvious reasons. Some of those beings are rarer than rare and would provide him with the ingredients to some of the most despicable spells ever recorded. And so the decision was made to free them, hoping they would escape and maybe even hinder the enemy."

"And has it?"

"Well... they've escaped, and they're certainly hindering the enemy."

"That's great!" exclaimed the big man.

"Ummm... there's only one problem though."

"And what might that be?"

"There are ra-hoon and they seem to be in charge, having co-opted the rest of the creatures there."

"I've never heard of the ra-hoon. What's so bad about that?"

"Not only are they one of the most cunning and crafty races to ever grace the earth, but they feed off magic and are immune to its touch."

"I could see how that might be something of a problem, but surely not more of one than the issue we're dealing with right now."

"You don't understand. They're continually hungry... it's what drives them on, always on the lookout for their next meal. And they and those under them now know that I'm here, having sensed my presence. We're their next target, and they might just make Manson's force look like a playful group of pussycats."

"Oh..." puffed Tank, more than a little taken aback.

"And that's pretty much where we find ourselves right now," huffed one of the three dragons sitting at a humungous table in one of the buildings that skirted the bazaar in the dragon domain's version of Salisbridge.

"Wow!" commented Owen.

"Amazing," added Garrett.

"Unreal," stated another member of their team.

"And, just to be clear, one more time... dragons have been living below us for millennia?" asked the 'bald eagle', not for the first time.

"Oh yes," replied one of the other remaining dragons. "We've looked to maintain a level of secrecy in the hope that we can coexist peacefully and just get on with our lives."

"But you've already mentioned that you disguise yourself as humans in an effort to guide and protect us. Why not just reveal yourself and come out in the open?" suggested Owen.

"That's a good question, my friend, one I'm afraid I don't have the answer to. I would suggest it all boils down to what the king and the dragon council think. Us ordinary citizens aren't privy to the inner workings of the bureaucracy."

Guns lowered, minds blown, the human contingent sat back in chairs that made them look like babies, each wondering if they were dreaming or had suffered a major blow to the head, none more so than Garrett himself, who despite having the most life experience of them all, was still trying to bend his mind around the strange turn of events they'd got themselves caught up in. From what little he could tell though, that wasn't the most important thing going on below ground right now.

"And you say that Miss Rump, having taken up the leadership of this force, went..."

"Up to London in an effort to rescue the king and retake Fleet Street so that contact could be re-established with the rest of the world."

"I see," observed the human leader, barely able to keep up.

"Also, I think she was hoping to rescue her friend... what was his name?"

"Bentwhistle," answered one of the other dragons.

"BENTWHISTLE?!" babbled Garrett. "That's one of the missing humans and one of my employees. Of course she's gone to rescue him, they're as thick as thieves those two."

"Both he and a friend were taken earlier, before Miss Rump's stunning rescue."

"Taken earlier?" asked Owen. "Taken by who?"

"From what little we know, part of the main force, principally the leadership we think, came through here on their way up to London. They kicked things off, killing all the residents, some of us only just surviving by the skin of our teeth. While a small contingent of them stayed behind, most of them headed off up to the capital, taking the captured Bentwhistle and his friend with them. Their leader, Manson seemed to have some kind of history with the boy."

"MANSON!" exclaimed Owen and Garrett simultaneously.

"Whoa, little ones," announced a pink and purple hued female, who up until this point had just sat and watched the whole bizarre situation play out. "You recognise the name?"

"Was he human shaped?" Owen urged.

"He was."

"Can you describe him for us?"

"Ummm... let me see. Unnaturally dark eyes I would say for that form. I struggle with how tall humans are, they all look the same in that regard to me. But I would say he was almost exactly the same height as your friend. Stocky, with a square clean shaven jaw, what little of the hair on his head he had left was both brown and straight."

Rubbing his eyes, shaking his head and ignoring the sweat dripping off his brow, Garrett let out a sigh as Owen put a firm hand on his shoulder.

"It's alright, we'll deal with him when the time comes," affirmed Peter's co-worker and friend, in an effort to reassure his boss after all he'd been through at the hands of the despicable being.

"It's not me I'm worried for, Owen, but Peter. Whatever went on at Cropptech, clearly our young friend put a huge spanner in the works. And it sounds like this Manson fellow is out to exact revenge."

"We'll find Peter and bring Manson to justice, I promise," declared the burly security chief.

"It's the same being then... you're sure?"

"The description fits him perfectly," murmured Garrett.

"You do realise that he's not human?"

"You mean HE'S a dragon too?"

There was a pause, while their newfound friends thought for a moment.

"I was some way off, hiding in one of the upper floors of a deserted building and so even with my enhanced senses it was difficult to see. The overriding feeling I had on seeing him was of not being able to sense his true identity. He might have been a dragon, or maybe even something else. All I do know is that he has an aura of evil about him, and after seeing some of the things he's capable of, I wouldn't want to get anywhere near him, that's for sure. You do so at your own volition, little ones. Don't say you haven't been warned."

Turning to face Owen, Garrett pushed away the fear he felt from the memories of what Manson had tried to do to him. That particular time in his life was the worst he could remember, having suffered terrible things, ones that he never would have done if not for being under the influence of whatever it was that dastardly Major had been peddling. Just the very thought of him made his blood boil, but also brought him out in a cold sweat. All he wanted to do was wipe his name from his memory forever... clearly though, that wasn't going to be possible. And even if it was, would it have been the right thing to do with Peter's life at risk? He already knew the answer before the question had even been asked.

"Owen, I think we need to somehow find Peter and Miss Rump. What do you say?"

"Even though it would appear to be way more dangerous than what we signed up for, I think you're right boss."

Looking around at all of those under him, immediately he received barely perceptible nods from the others.

"We're all in. How should we proceed?"

Slipping down off his high chair, landing on the dusty wooden floor with a bump, Garrett wandered over to the pink and purple dragon, admiring her stunning scales and exotic radiance.

"Can you give us directions on how we travel through your domain to London please? It's important that we find our missing friends."

Superior intellect shining through her twinkling brown eyes, wonderment at the humans' courage, regard for their friends and exactly what they had planned poked and prodded her mind, stirring up ancient primal feelings, the taste of battle almost on the tip of her tongue. Not taking her eyes off the humans for one moment, she opened up a telepathic link with the five other dragons left behind here.

"*They've got balls... you have to give them that much,*" she said.

"*Not all of them,*" scoffed one of the dragons sitting across the room.

"*You know what I mean.*"

"*Indeed.*"

"*What they're attempting is utter madness. I think we should try wiping their minds and send them back to the surface,*" suggested one of their kind, called Lotty, still on guard duty on the outer edges of Salisbridge, listening to everything telepathically.

"*What do you think, Polo?*" asked another on guard duty, on the opposite side of the city.

Polo was the pink and purple dragon and although no one individual had been delegated as being in charge, it had in fact fallen to her, due mainly to her seniority, because long ago she had once been a scientist tasked to the dragon council itself. So while they didn't have to take orders from her, her opinion really did matter. After much consideration, she told them all what she thought.

"*I don't think we should give them directions to London,*" she said across the link, leaving Lotty ecstatic.

"*But...*" started one of the others.

"*I don't think we should give them directions,*" continued Polo. "*I think we should take them there ourselves. I for one am sick and tired of shifting dead bodies. I think it's time to find our friends and see if they need any reinforcements.*"

"*You're absolutely mad,*" exclaimed Lotty.

"*What happens if any reinforcements show up here from somewhere else? How will they know where we've gone?*"

'A good point,' thought Polo, conceding defeat on that one. If only there was some way to leave them a message.

Rounding a pile of debris the size of a football pitch and 200 metres high, the human contingent, trying to remain focused, gasped at what lay before them. Carved through the sheer cliff face directly in front of them, lying almost in the centre of the underground city, a tunnel that would easily incorporate two of the world's biggest passenger planes side by side, sat there gaping for all to see, the darkness beyond the entrance all encompassing, the massive mountain of rubble excavated in an effort to reopen it not so long ago.

"The flying tunnels of old," announced an old timer by the name of Vion, watching the humans' gaping gazes.

"This will take us up to London," asked Owen.

"It will."

"How will it do that?" asked Garrett sceptically.

"We're going to fly you there," announced Lotty, having thrown her lot in with everybody else, not wanting to be left behind on her own.

"Really?" remarked Caren, one of only two females on the team of intrepid human explorers.

"REALLY!" all of the dragons replied at once.

"Shall we?" gestured Polo with one of her wings, towards the sweltering heat of the darkness and shadows.

Terrified and awestruck, Owen and his troops trudged around what was left of the debris and made their way towards the entrance of the tunnel, some of the dragons following them.

"Are you okay?" asked Polo softly, to a sombre Garrett who remained firmly entrenched in place.

Scratching his stubbly chin, blowing out a long hot breath, wondering how it must have felt for the dragons to do such a thing, his mind was very much still focused on what had happened at the bazaar. No, not the battle in which Richie and her allies had saved the day, something that had been described to them in a stunning amount of detail, an event they almost wished they'd been there to see. Almost! But what had happened after they left the house? Unbeknown to them, the six dragons remaining in Salisbridge had all made a decision, one to accompany the humans to London. Needing to leave a message for any potential reinforcements coming through here, they gathered on the cobbled market square and, in unison, began shooting huge fiery streaks of blue, red, yellow and orange flame into the ground. Puzzled, the humans couldn't figure out what the hell was going on. Perhaps it was some kind of ritual for the dead, something they were surrounded by, Owen thought, whilst Garrett wondered if they were just letting off steam (quite literally) in a bid to get rid of an excess of adrenaline. Both were wrong. Once the prehistoric beasts had finished, proud of their work, all the humans were beckoned over to take a look, all marvelling at what had really happened. Concerned about not leaving a message, the dragons had only gone and scorched one into the cobbles of the bazaar, one that could not be missed from the air. Huge, black, still smoking and flaming letters read:

KING AND DOMAIN IN SERIOUS TROUBLE. HEAD UP TO LONDON QUICKLY. REINFORCEMENTS DESPERATELY NEEDED!

Gazing intently into the gorgeous beast's eyes, the 'bald eagle' swallowed nervously before asking,

"Do you think it's possible to find them? Please, tell me the truth."

Flattening herself out to get as low as possible, putting her giant face level with his, Polo tried to give an honest answer.

"Truthfully, I don't know. It will be dangerous, that much I can guarantee. But we'll head off to the council building, their last known destination, and see what we can find. And if need be, we'll die fighting by your side. We're all sick and tired of caring for the dead. It's time we gave some thought to the living. Let's go!"

Side by side, they headed off to join the others, Polo's huge footsteps shaking the rubble on the pile, Garrett falling in time beside her. Just when they thought Fate couldn't throw anything else at the humans, they had to climb aboard their prehistoric allies. Owen and his boss jumped atop Polo, while the rest chose a dragon each, much to the amusement of the prehistoric monsters. With one almighty roar, they charged off into the darkness, not knowing what the hell to expect.

21 A SENSE OF DANGER

Shaken to the ground by the last big hit of the battering ram, magic dispelled, Hillier staggered to his feet, looking around for his next target, aware that the shield was about to come down and that he was supposed to group up with his friends. But there was still time, time to take down a few more of them before the ram tried to strike and Richie removed their protective barrier. At that exact moment, the tiny little voice that he relied upon to keep him safe, the one that was his constant companion, the only company he'd had for years, that is until Yoyo had found him and given him a home and a purpose, screamed out in absolute terror that something was dreadfully wrong. Scales across his body shivered, tiny spurts of flame snorted from his nose as a million possibilities played out in his mind. Immediately he checked the battlefield, watching Flash and Captain Battlehard fight back to back, slaughtering the enemy all around them. Moving on, his gaze homed in on Fredric and George, standing side by side, about to face the would-be king and queen of this world. Nothing appeared out of place with them. Somewhere much further in the scuffling melee of nagas and dragons, the youngster who he didn't know, but who had returned all of their magic, fought valiantly if not a little crazily, with tens of beings at the same time. No danger was evident there either. Bentwhistle, the humans, Janice and Hook all appeared okay, and that just left Richie, who looked well in control of the situation. Then what? Swivelling around to face his pals, who'd all just got together, leaving one space specifically for him and one for Yoyo who was currently healing some of their allies outside the shield, he tried desperately to ascertain the threat. Nothing there screamed out at him. Noticing the battering ram high above him swinging ever closer to the shield, and realising they were about to be overrun, a tiny flicker of movement caught his eye. It shouldn't have been anything, and if not for his nagging internal sense then it would have passed him straight by. But it was something alright, something serpent-like. At first he'd thought it another dismembered naga tail, goodness knows there were enough of those strewn about the king's private residence, or what remained of it. But the scales were different to that on any naga he'd met today. As well, the way it moved was odd, not so much meandering like a river as very covertly wriggling side to side. And then he spotted the head, a giant python like thing, dark red tongue flickering in and out, razor sharp teeth reflecting the colours of the explosive magic going off all around it. About to shout a warning to Yoyo and his friends, it was then that destiny reared its ugly head in the shape of, yes you've guessed it... another head, mirroring exactly the first python he'd spotted. Blinking frantically, doing the mother of all double takes, that tiny voice inside him for the very first time in its life roared at him to do something. Barrier still in place for now, magic wasn't the answer because that stood between him and the beast. Judging the exact moment that it struck would be almost impossible and rely wholly on luck, which he was reluctant to do. Splashing himself from his restored well of invigorating supernatural power, he put one foot in front of the other, powered his arms and hands in time and sprinted for all he was worth in the direction of the two-headed monster.

Uncurling like the chain from an anchor being dropped off a huge cargo ship, the demon snake's body cut through the air, mouths opened wide, fangs bared, its vertical slanted eyes locked on Yoyo's back, the healer not standing a chance of seeing it coming.

On the move, faster than he'd ever travelled before, soaking up all the ethereal energy he had, the thought of a warning crossed his mind, but he knew that would only be a distraction, giving the Australian little or no time to react. It was down to HIM and him alone.

Forming their own circle, leaving room for Yoyo and

that slacker Hillier, the young group of dragons were in the middle of sharing ideas on how best to decimate the enemy force when a dragon sized speeding blur caught their attention. About to berate Hillier for being tardy in joining the rest of them, confusion ran amok as he shot straight past the hole he was supposed to slide right into. Necks craning around simultaneously, it was then that they zeroed in on their mentor and the trouble he was about to be in.

One moment changed everything. In that one instant, Richie's barrier came down and the fear-provoking two-headed serpent broke through, now only a couple of metres away from attacking Yoyo. Pushing himself to the max, Hillier flooded his body with all the mana he could, using some of it to encase his dragon form in a solid outer shell, the rest powering his speed, all the time getting closer and closer. Not having a plan as such, all he could think to do was get between the threat and his mentor and then see what happened, sure that the ethereal energy protecting his body would be enough to keep him safe.

Sensing something behind him, Yoyo started to turn, a fraction of a second too late to react and bring up any kind of defence. Wide eyed at two giant snake heads closing in on him, for the first time in a very long time the healer knew not what to do as thoughts of his wife and the young charges who'd fought valiantly alongside him over the last couple of days flickered through his mind. Paralysed in absolute terror, the Australian healer kept his eyes open, determined to meet Fate head on. As the twin heads, jaws wide open, needle sharp teeth ready to inject venom, closed within half a metre of his face, a miracle presented itself from out of nowhere. Hillier came flying past Yoyo's stunned expression, his whole form crashing into the monster of a serpent, slamming it off to one side in a mighty meeting of bodies.

Ignoring the fact that the shield was down and hundreds of slithering nagas on the ground and dark dragons in the air were headed their way, Yoyo and the rest of his charges all headed in Hillier's direction, having watching him land with a BUMP, entangled around the slippery serpent.

"HILLIER!" screamed Wiz, the first to approach.

"STAY BACK!" commanded Yoyo, streaks of rippling blue lightning arcing from his fingertips.

All of them skidded to a halt a few metres away from the entwined bodies, watching in horror as the slippery form of the snake tightened its grip on Hillier's inert body which was face down.

"Find its heads and destroy them!" shouted their mentor.

Not needing to be told twice, the young dragon contingent quickly circled the bodies, sure to remain out of striking distance from the devilish reptile. As the charge of attackers from the main battle started to flood up towards them, Yoyo ordered half of the youngsters to form a line to stop them getting this far. It was done almost as quickly as it had been said, with the charges throwing as much magic as they could at the fast approaching marauding monsters.

About to zap the serpent's body with the lightning tickling his fingertips, from underneath Hillier's armpit out shot both heads, venom injecting teeth bared, ready to bite down, forcing the healer to stumble as the backward facing teeth tried to sink into his scales. About to release the lightning he'd readied, the need to do so disappeared as two blazing beams of heat closed in on each of the terrifying heads, burning away the scales, splintering bone, melting brain. In the blink of an eye it was done. The double-headed snake was dead. And as its charred remains collapsed to the marble, Yoyo and a few others tried to free Hillier.

Across the way, standing next to her husband, her thoughts directed at finding a solution to the problem that was her son, or as the others knew him... Bentwhistle, all she wanted to do was arrange a temporary truce so that she might gain a chance to meet with him. With the situation resting on a knife edge and the lucidity that gripped her in charge of everything, the only thing that mattered was halting proceedings and convincing her son to come with her. Maybe they could just leave this place and all the beings here and go live a life together just the two of them. One of the thoughts running through her merry consciousness at the moment, the madness just being kept at bay by memories of her previous life, the husband that she'd lost so tragically and the son she was so desperate to be reunited with. Still thinking it possible despite the terrifying, hellish circumstances in which they'd been thrown together, perhaps coming over to the side of good was a distinct possibility, despite the simmering hatred of her father. Faster than a speeding bullet, things went straight to hell.

Intrinsically linked to her psyche, her familiar was made up from a small shard of not only her magic, but her physical being as well and no matter the distance between the two of them, she could, in the background, always feel whatever it was experiencing. Pleasure, pain, the thrill of the hunt, satisfaction of a job well done or disappointment at not apprehending its target, were all sensations shared by the two of them. Right here, right now though, a very strange and different sentiment crossed the bond between them.

Clasping her hands over her ears, the remaining snakes writhing around on her head ducking back out of the way, instantly she dropped to her knees in agonising pain.

"Arrrrrrgggghhhhhhh!!!" she screamed to the heavens.

Immediately Manson readied his power, a huge swirling fireball appearing from nothing in between both of his hands.

"What have you done to her?" he demanded of Fredric and George.

Both allies turned to face each other, astounded, each with just one look knowing that whatever was afflicting the tormented woman, neither of them had caused it.

"It's not us. We've done nothing," announced the king.

Battle raging all around them, supernatural explosions filling the air, Earth on her knees, a decision needed to be made. Soon it would be.

As quickly as was possible given the circumstances, Yoyo and his young dragon charges pulled the remainder of the snake's body off Hillier and rolled him over onto his front, as what was left of his magical shield flickered and stuttered against the backdrop of the ethereal explosions bombarding their position.

Gasps of shock and pain rang out from the small group the instant they finished turning him over. He was DEAD! Two gigantic bite marks on either side of his neck exposed corrupted tissue filled with a dark green and white pus, the veins around his neck and face having already turned a deadly black. A ripple of despair passed through the telepathic link they all shared that remained constantly open, the young dragons mourning the loss of one of their own, never having known anything like it. Death would have been instantaneous, Yoyo knew, something that was little consolation right at this very moment. Heart well and truly crushed like an old car at a scrap yard, not only was Hillier one of the longest serving of his charges, but probably the brightest character of the lot. For all their sakes the Australian healer knew that he had to snap out of it and rally them in an effort to continue the battle. All was not lost, and although a valuable friend had died, things could still be turned around on this, the darkest of days.

"ENOUGH!" he yelled across the private telepathic link only they shared, startling each and every one of them. *"He's dead, and that's unforgiveable. But so will we all be if we don't buckle up and concentrate on the here and now. Hillier, wonderful soul that he was, gave his life saving mine. Words right now can't do him justice, but they will do at some point in the future. But only if we make that future happen! And right now, that means fighting with everything we have against these evil sons of bitches. Fight for Hillier! Fight for your*

friends! Fight for everybody else here! Fight for the planet! More importantly, fight for the future these bastards are trying to deprive you all of. Remember your training. Let's go!"

Powerful enough to stir them from their grief, tears streaming from their eyes, as a unit they bounded into action, slipping into gaps in the line their friends had created, dishing out disaster to the enemy, some powered by thoughts of rage and revenge for their fallen friend, others inspired to throw everything they could at it by the strength of Yoyo's words. They were back in the game, and more pissed off than ever.

Clouds filled her vision. A visceral hatred crept through her bones as the false human form of a body shook of its own accord. Something in the recesses of her mind screamed at her to be remembered, something about the sun or something. But it had become background noise, static to be ignored, with her feelings taking control, the madness once again flowing through her. Death has a way of consuming even the best of us, something she most certainly wasn't to begin with. In her case though, the brutality of having her familiar ripped away from this world was akin to any of us losing a limb or an eye. Impossible to come to terms with in an instant, an all consuming rage at the injustice of it overwhelming every thought, every instinct, it was no surprise to anyone that the lunacy, her default setting, had returned with a vengeance.

Climbing back to her feet, through tear filled eyes the very first thing she saw was the being on this planet she hated the most, standing there gawping at her. An ever pervasive darkness took hold of mind and body, wiping away the past and any ideas of the future. Negotiations were ancient history, with thoughts of her deceased husband and son all but permanently erased. Howling like a deranged wolf with its foot stuck in a bear trap, magic sprang to life in the form of a beach ball sized sphere of crackling electricity, the light from which lit up the remaining snakes wriggling around the top of her head. As visions went, very few could have been scarier. Even George and Fredric felt fear course through their veins at the thought of facing this. But for the sake of the planet and all its residents above and below ground, they knew they must.

Standing stoically beside her, Manson smiled. With the decision made, there was no turning back, and as Earth bared her teeth, Fredric and George both took a deep breath and let the divine will of their supernatural power take them. Simultaneously, the four of them charged towards each other.

Surging forward at speed with one ear-splitting cry that sounded very much like a fish gargling glass, the murderous mob of slippery, slithering nagas swarmed into the hero's safe space, spitting furious cold and poison spells, gnashing at anything that got in their way.

Looking on, deeply appalled by their actions, Vasuki, naga king and leader of this most ancient of races, once again sent out a rallying cry, telepathically of course, in the hope that it could and would change his subjects' attitude and indeed their allegiance but, not for the first time, it failed spectacularly. Not knowing what else to do, and lacking most of his powerful magic, he slipped around Yoyo and his gang of young dragons, who he could see were mortified at having lost one of their own, and met his kin head on, determined to fight with his allies until the bitter end.

Taking one step forward, Peter opened up his wings as far as they'd go in an effort to intimidate the hundreds of nightmarish beasts heading his way, sucked in a deep breath, and with just a little dribble of his unique ethereal energy, started blowing out the biggest stream of flame he could manage, turning his head in an arc, forming a cone of superheated fire that melted pretty much everything in front of him. It was impressive, for such a small dragon anyway, and something he'd given himself over to, not knowing what else to do. As the thrill of the heat whistling down his nostrils, up his throat and over his tongue satisfied his base cravings like a dragon of old, memories of the evening he'd spent with the master mantra maker back in the Emporium, the one in which they'd shared the 'Peruvian Mantra Ink' and he'd melted the filing cabinet into slag, rushed over him. Thoughts turning to the old shopkeeper and the team he was leading in an effort to take back Fleet Street and restore communications planet wide, he hoped they were safe and having more success than he and his fellow comrades. Almost running out of fiery breath, knowing that he'd have to take another during which there would be an almost insignificant gap in what he could do, thoughts of being overrun sent a shiver of fear up his spine, not for him, but for his soul mate who currently sheltered behind his diminutive (as dragons go) frame. Anything he could do to protect her, he would. And that included laying down his life in a heartbeat.

Refreshed and replenished by the mana that For'son had shared with them, the single councillor and the remainder of the King's Guards had returned to their previous stance by forming a circle and coalescing all of their personal shields together once again. It was effective and the only way they knew how to fight such a superior (in numbers, anyway) force. Working together and using cutting edge tactics from their training allowed them to slice huge swathes of the enemy down in the blink of an eye. Fire seemed best suited to destroying the nagas, something they'd learnt the hard way from their previous exertions before Richie and Yoyo's dragons had rescued them by walking the shield over to their very exposed position. Spitting violent bursts of flame through gaps in their defensive barricade, as well as conjuring up storms of raging fireballs, the nagas stood little chance, their magic vulnerable to everything heat related. And although massively outnumbered, there really was only one victor in this one-sided fight. Up until now that is.

What had happened below hadn't gone unnoticed from the air and so as the shadowy dark dragons circled around the area where the shield had been only moments before, they hatched a plan to take out the experienced enemy group that were currently slaughtering their naga cohorts on the ground.

Through their shared dastardly dark magic, the prehistoric beasts in the sky decided to blitz the circular group of enemies on the ground in a series of attacking runs, focusing on the top of their shield, hoping to find a weak spot to pummel and pound relentlessly. Taking the lead, a dark brown beast with tiny blotches of outstanding purple banked around tightly before lining himself up with his adversaries. Air buffeting his wings, much to his delight, he stretched them out, now gliding towards his target, wondering how best to go on the offensive. Quickly deciding to see if the cold would have an effect, he readied the mantra in his mind that would summon up a massive ball of ice and prepared to add all his willpower to it. Closing his eyes, focused absolutely on what he was doing, exactly as he should have been, excruciating pain from his outstretched left wing brought him back to reality with an almighty scream. Opening his eyes, he just had time to see the white blur of a sword shape cut through the air beneath him, leaving a trail of sparkling white cold in its wake. Concentration shattered, the gaping hole in his wing leaving him with little in the way of control, ungainly and unbalanced, he spiralled to the ground, crashing head first into a multitude of nagas, the force of the crash killing half a dozen in an instant, his efforts helping along those that he fought against.

Not so much a smile, more... smug satisfaction at having taken out another one of the enemy, one that clearly thought he was going to surprise the group of allies fighting in the sphere down below, Fu-ts'ang doubled back on himself in the tightest of turns, slicing through the air as he did so, on a mission to protect his former partner and friend.

Exhaling every last molecule of flame, the burnt smell of

roasted fish ravaging his olfactory senses, Peter swallowed nervously before sucking in the biggest breath he could, all the time readying the supernatural fire in his belly, preparing to go again. Unfortunately for him, one or two of the nagas, having watched their brethren die in the most hideous of ways, had taken stock of what the young dragon was doing, and waited patiently for him to pull in another breath. This was their chance, and they were determined to use it to destroy him once and for all.

In the kind of coordination only magic users could really appreciate, three nagas, yellow, green and brown in colour respectively, rushed forward out of nowhere, their speed enhanced by the ethereal energy coursing through them, magic in all shapes, potencies and colours splayed out before them, their target the young hockey playing dragon.

Poking out from behind one of his wings, long blonde hair tangled down both sides of her beautiful face, Janice tried to get a handle on what was going on around her, having gained a lifetime's worth of battle insight during her partnership with Fu-ts'ang earlier in the day. Filled with nervous energy, she looked on in dread as Peter replenished the fire within his prehistoric body. Shocked to see the gaudy serpents heading their way, a dizzying array of magic shooting out in front of them, an utter sense of helplessness froze the young woman in place, even stopping her from crying out, something she was desperate to do. As Peter picked up on his soul mate's concern, almost choking on his magic as he did so, a rescue in the form of a friend made a very timely intervention.

Swooping in from behind the two lovers, Fu-ts'ang darted out in front of them, batting away the deadly magic that was meant to maim and kill in but an instant. Immediate threat dispensed with, turning on his horizontal axis, the master weapon smith ploughed forward, slicing the head off the green naga in the blink of an eye, stabbing the brown beast straight through the heart, before skewering the yellow snake-like monster straight through its cobra-like head. In all but a heartbeat, the pair had been spared a brutal and sadistic death.

Zipping back around, their comrade the blade, a circling coating of frost constantly shifting around him, pulled up by their sides.

"Uhhh... thanks," exclaimed Janice, pleased to see her friend unharmed, despite the thick coating of blood that dripped from its shining edge.

"You're very welcome young one. Might I say that it's great to see you once again," replied the mystical weapon.

Suddenly coming alive, Janice just had to ask.

"H... h... how on earth did you survive? I'm sure you were shattered into a million pieces, at least that's what it felt like."

"It will take too long to explain I'm afraid," replied Fu-ts'ang to both Peter and his lover. *"I can tell you though, that your friend Tank had a great deal to do with it. You have him to thank."*

'Of course,' thought Peter. 'Who else?' The admiration, love and respect he had for one of his two best pals shone through, making him stand taller, puffing out his chest, filling him with the courage to take on all comers, of which...

"I think it's time you got back to your little party trick," urged Fu-ts'ang, his hilt gently nudging in the direction of the ever approaching horde of nagas and dark dragons. *"I'll attempt to cover the air. See what you can do about those on the ground."*

Peter nodded to the weapon, which at first he thought a little odd, but the more he dwelt on it, the more it seemed like the right thing to do, because if nothing else he'd come to regard the master weapon smith as an intrinsic part of their team. Pulling in one long breath, he flooding it with magic and exhaled with all the force he could.

Shielded from the heat and the light by her love's scaled wings, Janice watched in awe as a thick cone of brilliant blue, orange, yellow and red flame spewed out in front of them, instantly dissolving the next wave of the vicious serpents. Survival, for now at least, was becoming more and more manageable.

And so it was that where Richie's magical barrier had stood resolute not long ago, three different stands were being made simultaneously by three groups of light-sided heroes. Yoyo and his young dragon charges fuelled by anger, despair and thoughts of revenge for Hillier's death battled without fear, dishing out a drubbing, using all their creativity and cunning, aligning it with their supernatural abilities in an effort to destroy as many of the enemy as possible.

A short way along from them, the councillor and King's Guard contingent were doing almost exactly the same thing, with about the same success, wilfully dispensing their ethereal energy in the form of fire on the ground, knowing how much damage it did to the slippery nagas, whilst all the time employing other tactics against the dragons in the air. It was masterful, a sight to behold and instilled hope into those that had already taken a walk with death.

And in the middle of those two groups, Peter, with the most powerful flame he could muster, continued to annihilate nagas by the dozen, his love and soul mate pointing out gaps in their defences, their friend and ally Fu-ts'ang providing air support, carving open the dark prehistoric monsters above, causing dragon body parts to rain down from the sky like the most powerful of winter storms. As turnarounds go, it was one of epic proportions.

A tempestuous tornado in human form, Tank's heroics continued as he thumped, pummelled and clouted his way through the naga mob that surrounded him, something that must have been at least twenty deep in every direction. And that didn't include the attention he'd attracted from above in the form of many a dark dragon. Whirling, swirling and hurling attack after attack, he was ably complemented by his partner in crime, For'son, who sliced, diced and severed using his extraordinary array of offensive magical mantras. Wings were pierced, tails disintegrated, stomachs shattered and skulls crushed as ethereal energy zipped through the smoke choked air, a laser light show that would have matched any celebration on the surface. Despite the catastrophic death toll, there was still no let up by their adversaries' dread force. Still the monsters kept coming and coming, not perturbed by the slain bodies of their comrades, compelled ever onwards by the magic cast over them by the evil and monstrous Manson.

"*I don't want to worry you,*" exclaimed For'son across the telepathic bond that they shared, "*but they're getting closer and closer. At this rate, they'll be upon us in only a matter of minutes.*"

"*BUSY!*" screamed Tank, blocking one attack with his weaker arm, whilst kicking out at another naga's gills after pirouetting admirably given his substantial bulk.

"*YOU NEED TO LISTEN TO ME!*" yelled For'son.

"*I am,*" replied Tank. "*But if I stop for even one moment, we'll be overwhelmed. What do you want me to do?*"

In their minds, silence abounded. Outside their heads, it was a very different case. The torturous sounds of bones snapping, agonising pain inflicted at every turn, the wet THWUMP of damaged gills pumping furiously and the death knells sounded of both dragons and nagas. A sensory overload of noise surrounded them both.

"*I'm sorry,*" mumbled For'son, only just audible over everything else, despite being hooked up directly to Tank's brain.

Not for one moment faltering in his berserk rampage, Tank replied as only he could in the situation.

"*It's okay. I understand. You're scared, and so am I.*"

"*SCARED! Do you have any idea who you're talking to?*"

Despite being almost overrun with nagas, dastardly dragons and magic, the young rugby playing dragon managed a smile.

"*Do you know who YOU'RE talking to? Someone who shares a*

common bond with you, a bond that extends both ways. You might know everything about me, something you've already proved, but I have a far greater insight into you than almost anyone else that's ever worn that ring. So there's absolutely no use in denying you're scared. Let's move on from that and face those fears together. We can accomplish more working as a team than we ever could as individuals."

"*You truly believe that,*" observed the rather startled presence of the ring.

"*If you can see inside me, then you'll know emphatically that I do, more than ever.*"

"*Interesting.*"

Using one naga's head to crush another's skull with both hands, Tank continued fighting for all he was worth, kicking another so hard in what he assumed was the stomach, that his boot smashed right through its skin, leaving him but a moment to pull it out and avoid getting stuck and overwhelmed.

"*What's rugby?*" asked the inscrutable band from out of nowhere.

"*What?*"

"*You heard me.*"

"*We really don't have time for this.*"

"*I know. But whenever I sense your thoughts about working together, that one word always pops back up... RUGBY!*"

"*It's a sport, alright! Something I play on the surface in the guise I'm currently in.*"

"*REALLY!*" exclaimed For'son, never having heard anything like it.

"*REALLY!*"

"*Why would you want to do that?*"

"*You're kidding me right? You want to have this conversation... NOW?*"

"*Well...*"

"*NO! Not now. If we ever get out of this, I'll take you to see a rugby match. Until then, we focus on what needs to be done, not just for us, but for everyone else here and the planet at large.*"

"*Agreed,*" asserted the mighty magical presence,

reluctantly.

"*How close are they?*" solicited Tank.

"*Very close, and by the way they're chomping through the enemy, they'll be upon us in no time at all.*"

"*What can we do?*"

"*Assess the nature of the beings acting as the ra-hoon's forward line. As per usual the cowardly beasts are skulking at the back somewhere, no doubt letting their infantry do all the work, waiting until they can stroll in, finish us off and feast on all of our magic. If we can grasp the nature of those under their command, we might just be able to hold out a little longer, buying us some more time.*"

"*Sounds like a plan.*"

Less than twenty minutes, that's all it took to reach the outskirts of the capital, all six dragons and their riders halted by the same rocky barricade that had prevented Richie and her heroic group from going any further, sometime earlier. Just like their predecessors, the impromptu band of dragons and humans led by Polo immediately headed up the service tunnel and out into the ravaged urban sprawl that was thought of as Greater London.

Following all but the same path as those before them, eventually the tiny contingent rocked up at the entrance to the Hampton Court nursery ring, only to be greeted by a huge, dull matt yellow coloured dragon known as Watcher who in fact was one of the *tors*.

"More of their kind down here," he announced haughtily, on noticing the humans travelling with the dragons in charge, clearly looking down his long scaled snout at them.

"May we come in please?" asked Polo politely.

"I'm afraid not," replied the frightened and stuck up *tor*.

"We're just looking for a little respite and information."

"Those things," declared Watcher, pointing at the humans with his left hand, "are nothing but trouble."

"Why would you say that?" asked Polo softly, brutally aware of their savage surroundings, the fires and thick black smoke.

"The last lot to visit us took not only nine of our elder pupils with them, but convinced one of the other *tors* to join their rash and hopeless cause. We won't be making that mistake again."

"We're not here to pilfer any of your dragons. We'd just like to come in off the street and rest a little. If you could tell us what happened to the others that would be great."

"NO!" bellowed the agitated *tor*. "You're not coming in. I have young pupils to protect and think of. Conspiring with all of you will do them no good at all."

About to interrupt and chastise the exceptionally rude and unpatriotic dragon, Watcher shut her down before she even had half a chance.

"I will, however, tell you where the others went."

Realising that this was all she was going to get, Polo remained silent, hoping to gain some useful insight.

"The young human shaped girl... the former dragon, she was leading them. After resting here briefly, she split them up into two groups. One, led by the famed shopkeeper, was to head to Fleet Street and take back the crystal node so that worldwide communications could be restored. The other was to head to the council building in an effort to rescue the king, and somebody called... Peter!"

"PETER!" exclaimed Garrett from a little way back in the shadows, revealing himself for the first time to the snooty dragon *tor.*

"That's right. Do you know him?" asked Watcher.

"I do, and he's one of the reasons we're here. Please, if you can tell us anything else, we would be most grateful."

Rolling his eyes and shaking his head, against his better judgement, the *tor* continued.

"Their leader, the human shaped girl was convinced that this Peter was being held at the council building, that's all I know. Oh, and the other thing I forgot to mention, was that they split into three before they left."

"Three?" mused Polo.

"Three," confirmed Watcher. "The shopkeeper and his band took off towards Fleet Street. His colleague, I think called Tank, led the group to the council building, while the young leader... Richie, headed out on her own somewhere. Where? I don't know because she wouldn't tell anybody."

"Is that it?" urged Polo.

"That's everything," confirmed the *tor.* "Now... leave and don't come back. You'll get no more help from any of us."

And with that, he slammed the gigantic silver door back into place, locking it firmly behind him.

Scratching her head whilst turning to face the others, Polo pondered what they'd been told.

"Why would the young girl go off on her own?"

"That would be Miss Rump I assume?" asked Garrett.

"It would certainly seem that way."

"We don't know where she's gone though."

"No," answered Polo.

"So we need to focus on what the rest of them were doing... off to some council building in an effort to rescue the king and Peter," urged the 'bald eagle'.

"It's THE council building, and given the state of everything around us, I can't think of anywhere more dangerous. You still want to pursue this, little one?"

Inside, Garrett smiled at being addressed that way, remembering that one or two of them had also referred to him as 'young one'. 'Only in my wildest dreams should I ever be called that,' he thought, suppressing the madness of it all.

Addressing them, not just Polo, there and then he made up his mind to follow through on what they'd all started.

"We came down here to find our missing friends, only to find new ones in the process. Who would have thought such a thing existed?" he said, whirling three hundred and sixty degrees, arms outstretched. "I can't ask any of you to follow in my footsteps, because as the very charismatic and beautiful Polo has just pointed out, the dangers seem to be rife and overly abundant. But I feel a pressing need to push on in the vain hope that something can be done to rescue those that we've been searching for. I won't hold it against any of you if you'd like to return from whence we came."

Without hesitation and almost before the old man had finished, Owen piped up,

"I'm in."

It was swiftly followed by six more, "me too's."

Chuckling softly, the dragon contingent shook their huge prehistoric heads in unison, marvelling at the courage and of course stupidity of their human counterparts.

Having discussed it momentarily, telepathically, the leader of their new found comrades announced their decision.

"All of us are in. We'll lead you to the council building."

So there it was... settled. Not faltering for a moment, the group trekked off in one long line, into the devastated ruins of the below ground capital, a mixture of fear, uncertainty and excitement running through them all.

In all her life, not once had any of her victims ever had the courage or stupidity to wink at her, or for that matter, come back from the dead. No one in their right mind would. Fear, terror, pain and a job well done on her part would make it all but impossible. But in an instant this one had been reborn and had done just that. Red, as Jar Man and DomCon had named her, was as surprised as she'd ever been, the anger inside her exploding out into every molecule of her being at the outrageous turn of events. However, she was a professional and had been trained for many decades in the magical dark arts as well as torture and suffering. And so, unlike the slippery serpents surrounding her, the practiced assassin in her reacted as only it could, and brought up all her magical defences, despite every atom in her body wanting to attack, as magical words left the mysterious dragon's mind.

In a surge of green and blue ethereal energy, with Steel at its very centre, Gee Tee's mantra exploded out with the force of a jet fighter, in a horizontal arc that ripped through everything, everything that is apart from the crystal node and Jar Man and DomCon. Nagas throughout the facility were sliced in two around the waist, dying instantaneously, not even having time for one last scream at the injustice of it all.

Red, despite the magical defences that had instinctively been erected around her, was tossed through the nearest wall at not far off the speed of sound, into a darkened, far flung part of the room containing the crystal node itself, bones broken, organs shattered, for all appearances dead, just like her cohorts. The ground shook, the building rattled, dust and the supernatural filled the air, that and the smell of rotting fish and of course... DEATH!

Over in but an instant, the three dragon friends stood, absolutely gobsmacked, words failing each of them, at least for a few moments. And then reality and what had happened kicked in.

"Oh my God! That was amazing," DomCon raved.

Jar Man was more concerned with his friend's health.

"I'm sorry for what they did to you and that we could only stand by and watch. Are you okay?"

Contemplating everything that had happened, including the agonising pain and his mind nearly being torn apart, the selfless laminium ball captain thought long and hard before replying, what he'd been through, almost too much.

"I thought I'd died for good. My previous brush with death was nothing compared with that. Alone, lost and afraid, I admit to giving up all hope and all desire to live. I would have welcomed the end of it all with open arms for much of that time."

Enough to nearly bring tears to the two friends' eyes, they needed to know more about what had provoked such a change in circumstances.

"What happened then?" asked Jar Man sympathetically.

"From out of nowhere, just as I seemed to be drifting away, suddenly I could hear the old shopkeeper's voice. At the time, it felt like a goodbye almost, or a welcome into the afterlife. But it wasn't, it was real. Joined with the others from outside, their presences under the command of the master mantra maker guided me back, restored my faith, my hope and everything within me. In truth, I've never felt so glad to be alive."

Rushing forward, both DomCon and Jar Man clasped Steel's hand, each hugging him firmly, both delighted that their friend had succeeded in his mission.

"I just hope we're in time to restore that optimism and faith to others across the world," uttered Jar Man.

"Amen to that," added DomCon.

Thirstily gulping down gallons of water, their huge prehistoric bodies shrouded by the thick choking smog given off by the burning dragon cadavers, Gee Tee's force attempted to reconcile what had just happened during their out of body experience. However, time waited for no dragon, and so suddenly, without any warning, a tumultuous green and blue shaded supernatural explosion tore outwards from the building in front of them, forcing the ground to quake, shattering stonework in its way, destroying entrances and exits, decimating those would-be imposters intent on keeping the prize for themselves.

At once, they all had the same thought...

'STEEL!'

And although parched, despite the water they'd all knocked back, instantly the meagre dragon force became reinvigorated, because that's what the ignition of hope, courage and belief can do to an individual. Full of absolute joy and buoyed more than a little, instead of using their telepathic link, Gee Tee shouted the word at the top of his voice sure the humans would want to hear exactly what he had to say.

"CHARGE!"

Each knowing that their daring and outrageous ploy had given them all a second chance and not needing to be told twice, the dragons, with the exception of the shopkeeper, bounded into the air, all flying straight towards the now unguarded opening, eager to find their three comrades. Hot on their heels, the master mantra maker ran alongside the humans, who all fingered their grenades nervously, hoping that everything had gone to plan and that whatever this thing called the 'crystal node' was, that it was still intact and those on the inside were safe. Survival was the name of the game for all of them. None had come this far only to die now. How the fickle fortune of Fate felt about that though, was anybody's guess.

25 READY TO RUMBLE

Four human forms taking up the exact same space... it was never going to be pretty or for that matter anything but explosively violent, but the simple raw aggression with which Fredric, George, Manson and Earth met exceeded anything else that had gone on previously that day, by nothing short of a great deal. Fredric and Earth, father and daughter, like star crossed lovers, only had eyes for each other. Manson, ignorant of the family connection, knew little of the underlying machinations playing out and so hadn't really chosen a target when he'd bounced up to meet his adversaries next to the woman that he loved and considered his newly crowned queen, happy to take on either or both of them, depending on how events unfolded. George, wanting not only to give the friend he thought of as a brother the best chance of erasing all his family demons, but to savour the sweet taste of revenge for what had gone on after he'd surrendered to the malevolent Earth, crashed Manson's party, bombarding him with enough ethereal energy to power a small city. Ignoring the deranged woman he thought of as his, Troydenn's son and successor immediately realised the gravity of his situation, and leaving his other half to fight her own personal battle, ramped up his defences and turned his attention to his deceased father's nemesis.

Opening out his palms, the would-be leader of this planet excreted a series of crimson tentacles in the current dragon king's direction as he tumbled head over heels high above his dreaded naga force. Deflecting them away with an almost dismissive gesture, George tucked himself in and rolled off back to the ground, all the time keeping his shield in place. Leaping up to a standing position, attempting to mentally probe Manson's dark and malicious mind in an effort to finish things once and for all, the slashing, hacking, crashing and clashing sounds of magic on magic off to one side of him diverted some of the king's attention away, wanting to make sure that his newly returned friend remained on top of his private battle. Currently, he was doing just that.

Almost tearing right through each other, but for their defensive mantras, the venom between the pair was laid out bare for every being there to see, had they bothered to look. Of course they hadn't because each and every one there had nothing on their mind other than their own individual battles. Through a cloud of splintered supernatural fragments and the grey foggy residue of spent magic, father and daughter clashed, Fredric's gleaming muscles tensing as he tried to get a grip on any part of his relation, Earth throwing his way the most deadly and evil hexes and enchantments that she knew, both intent on one thing and one thing only... the death of the other. Wielding righteous dragon magic of old, the founder of the Crimson Guards unleashed a surge of white hot brilliance from almost point blank range at the barrier that encased his misbegotten spawn, certain it would cause untold damage. Almost as if she could visualise her father's next move, Earth countered with a blanket of cold, visceral, evil dark magic, the two ethereal opposites producing an explosion that split the air, the thunderous concussive force tossing them both high up towards the shadowy ceiling, enemies on the ground hurled in all directions, scorched forked black trails zigzagging across what remained of the white marble occasionally wounding the odd naga or dark dragon.

Furiously flinging flurries of multicoloured bolts of lethal magic at each other from no more than ten metres away, the detonation triggered by their cohorts had both Manson and George tumbling head over heels on the ground, bumping them into the remainder of the naga force, much to the disappointment of them both.

Climbing unsteadily to his feet, Manson turned to face the nearest naga, one that he'd crashed into and that had cushioned the blow. Ignoring the gormless look on its face, and with no compunction not to, he drilled a superheated dart of sizzling fire straight into its head, a warm satisfaction flowing through him as he watched its features melt like wax running down the side of a candle.

Harmlessly deflecting away a few stray arrows of poison with the wave of one hand, the dragon king rose to his feet, watching in disgust as his nemesis and the being responsible for all of this carnage and so many needless deaths, in cold blood (of course it was, that's how the nagas were designed) killed one of his own.

Turning to face his father's pathetic long time adversary, Manson's mouth turned into a sick twisted smile on noting the disgust etched across the dragon's human face.

"What's the matter? Haven't you seen discipline dealt out on a battlefield before?"

"I agree that discipline is indeed needed at times like this," replied George, almost sick to his stomach, "but you and I have very different views on how that should look. Wasting lives on a whim is a fool's errand. Very much like using magic to bind others to your will. It just goes to prove that you don't have the leadership qualities necessary to inspire loyalty and devotion. No good or sane leader would take it upon his or herself to do such a thing. It's time you were stopped once and for all."

"And you think you're the being to take me down, old dragon."

"You think you know me, through the vengeance your father sought for all those years. You think you have a special insight into everything about me. Well... how about we see how that plays out for you?"

And with that, George, the reigning dragon king threw a tirade of the supernatural in Manson's direction, leading with a frosty cold cloud that closed in on the murderously deranged dark dragon, followed swiftly by a crackling hail of unpredictable lightning that forked out in all directions while at the same time assaulting his mental defences, probing his mind for any weakness at all, determined to find some way through. In many ways, it was an all or nothing kind of strike.

Overly confident as always, the deluge of ethereal energy heading his way out of nowhere for once had him backing away, and as afraid as he could remember. Somewhere his psyche screamed that this being was the dragon king, and wouldn't have been chosen to occupy that role for no apparent reason. Stretching out his arm, instantaneously he melted away the cold with a flaming surge of heat that he knew would counteract the very obvious attack, whilst at the same time using his mind to pull a huge chunk of rubble from off to one side in between him and the lightning, constantly aware of the pressure surrounding his mind from his opponent's mental queries. Erecting a firewall that he knew could not be breached, the psychopath in him, now angrier than ever, was ready to go back on the attack.

Controlling his descent as best he could in the shape that he'd been stuck in for so many decades now, thoughts of changing back to his original form tickled his mind, prompting him to at least consider it. But he'd already thought about it on coming through the wormhole from Antarctica, encased in the laminium chains that had provided so much of an advantage. Then, it had seemed that sticking to the familiar form, drawing so much power from the magically enhancing base metal made total sense. That and the fact that he wasn't one hundred percent sure the bonds inside him would obey the command they hadn't heard in so many decades, meant he'd chosen to remain as he was. Now though... should he change, or at least try to? It might make it easier to take her down... destroy the daughter he'd loved with every essence of his being, rid the planet of a disease that was capable of destroying it. What it boiled down to was that he didn't know, and that self doubt, that hesitation, was something he was all too aware could kill him here and now in the heart of the mother of all battles. So landing with a THUMP, taking the impact on his knees before rolling off to one side onto his shoulder and leaping back up to his feet, he immediately felled one naga that tried in vain to surge forward and bite his left leg, then putting a hole right through one of its comrades with a beam of laser-like light straight from the index finger on his right hand. Buying himself a fraction of a second, he stretched out with all his senses, wondering just where the hell his dreaded descendant had got to.

Toppling head over heels whilst plummeting at quite a rate, she'd caught the brunt of the explosion, or at least her overcharged protective shield had, tossing her up almost as high as the ceiling that was practically invisible from below. Passing the apex of her journey, Fredric's daughter found herself plunging towards the floor, something that for her, with all of her special abilities, really wasn't a problem. In fact, right at this very moment, it was proving to be a boon, because unbeknown to her father she was speeding down head first, straight on top of him.

Lining up some of the deadliest magic that he knew, Earth's other half sprinted through his army of nagas, crisscrossing individuals, trying to put at least a little distance between him and the dragon king. Unfortunately it wasn't working nearly as effectively as he'd hoped.

Chasing after Manson was on its own a perilous risk that he knew could well cost him his life, but one he felt worth taking given the consequences of what they were doing down here in the first place. Having always had broad shoulders he'd been able to easily carry the burden placed upon him by any of the roles and positions that had come his way across his long life. On achieving the rank of king, things had changed very little. Of course his horizons and responsibilities had vastly increased, and he'd had to constantly readjust his thinking to include not just the dragon domain into his future plans, but the human world above. It took some time for him to wrap his head around it all... many months in fact. But once he did, it didn't seem like a burden or a weight to carry at all. More of a privilege was how he thought of it. Guiding, protecting, nurturing the promising spark all the humans possessed was how he thought his tenure as king should be defined. It was, however, never going to be that easy. And so it proved. Council members played games... more interested in their own welfare and those dragon communities which they represented than the rest of the world, and in particular the humans on the surface. Passing laws and decrees that benefitted mankind was difficult at best, all but impossible at worst. The long standing arrangement passed down from the prophecy all that time ago mattered less and less with the more time that passed. Slowly, over the decades, George took it on himself to do the right thing, to make sure the individuals on the surface got a fair shout when it came to matters of importance regarding the planet's future. It was a big ask, particularly as it didn't have to be done; he could, like most of the other dragons, just forget about the prophecy and ignore the problem altogether, concentrating only on the below ground domain. But he couldn't do it, because that wasn't him. So the weight of the burden had ever so steadily increased over the years, leaving him with much to worry about and do. Never in all that time though, had he ignored his responsibilities regarding the humans, always giving their rights equal shares with the dragons under him. At that very moment he was fighting for them, as much as for his brethren, and it could be going so much better.

Hot on Manson's heels, George skidded across one of the few intact pieces of white marble flooring, dancing out of the way of a myriad of magical attacks all meant to destroy him at the same time. Leaping over a swishing naga tail that looked to take his feet out from under him, Fredric's best friend spun, let rip with a palm strike to the solar plexus of the nearest snake-like beast, and was off again in pursuit of his prey before the CRACK that had to be the breaking of bones had finished resonating.

Pushing his way through his ground force of dreaded nagas, Manson, for all but a split second had become disorientated, forgetting whereabouts in the king's residence he actually was, which was easy to do given that there were still probably a thousand nagas on the ground, with about half as many again dark dragons in the air above them all. It was however, a schoolboy error from the being that would seek to hold the reins of power to the planet, one that he might well come to regret.

Fighting off the blind panic that threatened to take him, the would-be dark king of this new world searched up high for any recognisable feature so that he could get his bearings and figure out exactly where he was. It was then that the hairs on the back of his neck pricked up, sending his danger sense into overdrive, forcing his heart into his mouth and a surge of adrenaline across the whole of his body.

Two nagas who'd been side by side only a moment before were abruptly hurled back through the air, their writhing, twisting bodies wriggling uncontrollably in terror as they both smashed into the underside of a dark dragon, forcing him into a sharp dive, which ended with them all splattered across an array of naga cadavers. Standing in the gap that had just been made, George the dragon king had his eyes focused solely on just one target... MANSON!

Through the pandemonium of all the fighting and craziness that still continued, the two kings glared across at each other, both thinking that they had the high ground and the moral right to rid the world of the other. One would be wrong. One would be right. Which one it would be was anybody's guess.

Steaming down at him headfirst from above, she thought about launching all of her magic. But that didn't seem quite as delicious as the alternative, which of course was to plummet straight onto him, breach his defences and strangle him with her bare hands. As the distance between them closed immeasurably, the tiniest of smiles sneaked across her purpled lined face at the thought of finally having her revenge.

Scanning through the crowd of nagas and dark dragons, whilst turning three hundred and sixty degrees in a circle, a sense of puzzlement nibbled at Fredric's mind at not being able to locate his insane offspring. Knowing that she should be here somewhere, briefly he wondered if she was using one of the other beings in the vicinity to shield her from his gaze. Hurling a half dozen tennis ball sized fireballs at two nagas attempting to out flank and surprise him, an instinctive sense of self preservation flooded his body. Even after all his time incarcerated, he recognised it for what it was, and despite not being able to distinguish the source of the danger, his gut feeling urged him to move, and so he did, diving off to one side, hitting a small pile of rubble hard, tearing open his right shoulder and breaking one of his fingers in the process. About to curse his stupidity and the blind faith he put in relying solely on what he'd come to regard as some sort of sixth sense, a monumental blast from where he'd previously been standing tossed marble and dust up into the air like a sandstorm in the desert, temporarily blinding him.

'DAMN!' She cursed on contact, not feeling the cushioning impact of his soft skin or the satisfaction of breaking bones beneath her fall. Earth was unable to believe her father's luck and the fact that he'd jumped out of the way a split second before she would have hit him with the full force of a runaway train. She knew that it wasn't over, and that the very fortunate bastard had only bought himself a few more seconds of life.

Springing up, one foot planted firmly in front of the other, facing the spot of the collision, the founder of the Crimson Guards erected a shield all around him and readied all of his supernatural power, knowing only one thing could have caused such mayhem and destruction. Sure enough, strolling out through the dirty air, the daughter he'd long since come to think of as his nemesis, oozing magic from every part of her body, headed directly for him.

Simultaneously, each king thrust out both their hands and unleashed their most diabolical spells, neither willing to settle for anything less than the other's agonising death. Fire sizzled from George's palms, igniting every molecule of air in front of him, huge raging, bellowing flames warding off any nagas in the immediate vicinity, the slippery serpents slithering away in the opposite direction despite their enthrallment's calling.

Nightmarish strands of black leeched out from Manson's palms, dark inky wisps seeping out from each of his fingers, forging a path forward towards their enemy, gathering up into one huge, unbreakable mass, dangling in mid air halfway between the two of them. Ethereal opposites met in a clash of the Titans battle, neither having the power or attitude to overcome the other, both cancelling each other out right there and then. Standing on opposite divides of the fire and darkness, both beings gave all they had in an effort to push the other back, willing their own particular brand of supernatural to succeed. It looked now as though all it would come down to was which one of them had the most mana. If George had kept hold of For'son then winning would have been a certainty. As it was though, victory for him looked elusive.

26 CLOSING IN ON THEIR GOAL

Leaving the Hampton Court nursery ring, the small band of dragons and humans had chosen a circuitous route towards the council building in the Buckingham district of London. Avoiding taking to the air, instead hugging burnt out buildings and rubble strewn piles of debris higher than most human houses, only once had fighting become the only option. And even then, it was left to the dragons in the group, as the humans had been told not to fire their NGSARs unless it was an absolute last resort because the sound would attract more enemies than it was possible for them to defeat, even with the suppressors on their weapons.

Skulking in the shadows on the ground floor of an overcooked high rise, dragons at the head and rear of their line, abruptly the prehistoric monster at the front dropped to one knee, his right hand held up high as he did so, clenched into a fist. Instantaneously every one stopped, apart from their heads that continued on a swivel, desperate to seek out the supposed danger. This wasn't the first time this had happened on their relatively short journey, quite the opposite, with it becoming almost commonplace every few minutes or so. Complacency hadn't quite taken over, but for the humans anyway, the whole stop/start nature of their journey had begun to take its toll, with their concentration levels waning somewhat. That all changed when the sound of rubble cracking against rubble echoed from around the corner they stood against. Breaths were held, nobody moved as the tension mounted. Dragons within the line of sight of the human contingent waggled their index fingers, implying that their guns should not be discharged. It was a scary moment for them all not least those from up above who'd already caught glimpses of their so-called enemy from a distance on their roundabout journey to avoid them. As the faint sound got increasingly louder, they all readied themselves.

Sliding effortlessly along, side by side, occasionally moving tiny chunks of debris accidentally with their undersides, both of the rather overconfident nagas patrolled the route that they'd been assigned with little fear or trepidation, knowing that most of the city's denizens had already been removed one way or the other and that the miniscule amount still alive were no doubt cowering away in hiding, somewhere far, far away. Ignoring the thick, choking black smog and staying as far away as possible from the tiny little fires that still littered the landscape, both continued without a care in the world. Imagine their shock then, when they glided around the corner and bumped straight into a huge dark brown wall of scales.

They were on them in an instant. Blowing iridescent mouthfuls of flame into their eyes, pummelling their bodies with vengeful magic, springing from thoughts of what had been done to them and their loved ones back in Salisbridge, as well as physically assaulting them with talons and teeth, it was more than just a one-sided fight. In essence, the two unwitting snake-like monsters hadn't stood a chance, and that was the way in which it had gone down... quickly and quietly.

Sneaking back into the shadows, all the humans shaking profusely at the viciousness of the violence they'd just seen, Polo tried to whisper an apology.

"I'm sorry my friends... but it had to be done. Despite what you think and what you've just witnessed, we are not a violent civilisation or given to acts of aggression easily, quite the opposite in fact. We always try and resolve things peacefully, whether that's a potential war, or two individuals making a stand against one another. What you have to understand though, is that what happened to us back in the market place in Salisbridge came out of nowhere, with absolutely no provocation and no warning. The savagery was like nothing any of us here has ever heard of, with the death toll too high to count. We all lost dragons we knew and loved there, something that may not justify what you've just experienced, but might go some way to explaining why it happened."

Ever the leader, always looking at things from another's point of view, and despite nearly losing his stomach contents, it was Garrett that responded.

"We understand, we really do... and once again, we're sorry for your loss, all of you. Although I'm sure you must think the human world full of brutality and bloodshed, I assure you that all of us here, and those in our city, would only fight very much as a last resort. We're grateful for your company and your support in trying to get our people back."

'Wise words indeed,' thought Polo, more impressed by the minute with the manner and demeanour of the ape shapes from above, under her command.

"I think it's time to hot foot it out of here, just in case anybody realises that they," she inclined her head towards what remained of the two nagas, "are missing. We don't want to be discovered that way. The good news is that the council building is only two kilometres away now. With a little bit of luck, we should be there soon. However, there's no telling what we might find when we get there. Hundreds or even thousands of guards might be waiting right outside. If that's the case, then it will be impossible to go any further. Do you understand?"

The humans nodded their heads in agreement, at the same time staving off their terror at the thought of thousands of the beings they'd just seen torn apart, waiting for them. Aside from Garrett, they all started reconsidering their career paths, wondering if perhaps an office job might actually be the thing for them.

Devastation on a phenomenal scale didn't begin to do it justice. Those slippery nagas that hadn't been cleaved in two lay shocked and dazed, the magic from Gee Tee's mantra, cast to perfection by Steel, having hurled them into the air, slamming them either into the floor, a wall or sometimes one of their own. And as the master mantra maker's rowdy rabble came storming through the building, any naga opposition was easy pickings. Not so much the dark dragons though. While some had been sliced apart, others had survived either intact or with just minor damage, having been on the move either in the air or slightly above where the supernatural wave of energy had been discharged.

So as nagas were easily dispatched, roaming in groups of two or three, dark dragons did their best to hinder the all-out assault by the light-sided heroes, lying in wait, lurking in shadows, setting magical traps and ambushes for the unconventional force. And that had taken its toll on their numbers, with four of their kind dying during the first few minutes after they had blindly raced in. Now those that had rushed ahead, obeying without question Gee Tee's order to "CHARGE," waited in silence at a locked doorway, looking much the worse for wear, forlorn expressions sewn across their brows, sorry that their recklessness had resulted in the deaths of some of their brothers and sisters. From back the way they'd come in, soft, plodding footsteps accompanied by much lighter footfalls resonated down the protracted, ancient hallway, long before the makers of the noise could be seen, the silent mantra that had accompanied them halfway across the capital having disappeared once they'd headed out on their mind bending mission to let their consciousnesses infiltrate the building they were now in. Suddenly though, they appeared from out of the shadows, a look of absolute thunder chiselled into the scaled prehistoric features of the old shopkeeper's face.

"REPORT!" he commanded.

"Uhhh..." mumbled the first one.

"Ummmm..." murmured the second.

"WE WERE SUPPOSED TO STICK TOGETHER!" he bellowed, the plastic glasses on his face jumping about like a bare footed child walking over hot coals.

"WHAT IN THE HELL HAPPENED?" he

demanded.

"W... w... w... we... we just got caught up in the moment, I suppose," stammered another of them.

"CAUGHT UP IN THE MOMENT?!" the old shopkeeper yelled. "YOUR COMRADES ARE DEAD BECAUSE YOU'VE GOT CAUGHT UP IN THE MOMENT! EVEN THESE YOUNGSTERS," he declared, whirling around to point at the group of humans, "HAVE MORE INTELLIGENCE THAN TO GO OFF HALF COCKED INTO A BUILDING FULL OF MURDEROUS CREATURES. HAVE YOU NO COMMON SENSE?"

Looking thoroughly ashamed as a group, despite the dire circumstances they found themselves in, the dragons all remained steadfastly staring at the floor, something that seemed like not only the right thing, but the only thing to do with Gee Tee's wrath bearing down on them all.

Shaking his head, removing his glasses with one hand while massaging his nose and eyelids with the other, the master mantra maker for once looked older than his reputed nearly six hundred years, seemingly having aged centuries in the last few moments. Time and the burden of leadership had finally caught up with him.

"I never thought it would be easy," he uttered to no one but himself, "but to get this far and then suffer these losses is just heartbreaking. How on earth can that be just?"

Bleak... just about summed up their situation, with the old shopkeeper overcome with sorrow, about to implode by the looks of things, the other dragons in the group full of regret and remorse, barely able to move under his watchful and judging gaze. There was still a job to be done here, and it didn't look as though things could go any further, that is until one of the most unlikely of them stepped forward.

"I only have to look at the alien features of your unfamiliar faces to see how much each of you mourns the loss of those that have fallen," volunteered Taibul softly. "But I wonder if it's the time and the place to be having this conversation. Right now, there are quite literally millions of lives depending on the actions that WE take... something you've continually emphasised throughout our journey here. As upset, scared, disappointed and afraid as we are, shouldn't we put aside all of our differences and finish what we came here to do? To get so close and fail would be an utter tragedy and one that would be an insult to those that have already laid down their lives. Excuse me for being so blunt and rude, and forgive me because I'm aware that it's probably not my place either, but I can't help thinking that all of you need just a little nudge in the right direction. PLEASE... let's just finish this off."

'WOW!' thought Angela, 'where on earth did that come from?'

'I knew there was more to him than sheer good looks, but that was something else,' mused Sam.

All Emma could think was just how brave her friend had been, voicing his fears in front of every being there, and what would happen next.

Slipping his glasses back up his nose into place, the master mantra maker turned his attention to the young human waiter and stomped right over to him. Frozen in place, it was all Taibul could do not to shy away from the gigantic prehistoric jaw that leaned in close. Both Emma and Angela closed their eyes. Sam stepped up beside his friend, his legs almost giving way from under him in fear. Balanced on a knife edge, not even the rest of the dragons could predict what would happen next.

Monstrously sharp teeth only a matter of centimetres away from his comparatively small head Taibul, understandably, started to shake uncontrollably under the shopkeeper's withering gaze, wondering if the bravest thing he'd ever done had turned out to be the most stupid. Of course, he needn't have been concerned.

"YOU, my young friend, are wise beyond your years. The songs that will be sung about you in future generations to come will reflect that, I'm sure."

Every being there, with the exception of Gee Tee, let out a breath, most not having realised that they'd been holding one in.

Giving Taibul and all the other humans a knowing wink, the master mantra maker turned to face the rest of the dragon contingent.

"You heard the young man... now is not the time to mourn or have any regrets. We have to get to Steel, Jar Man, DomCon and more importantly, the crystal node. It's imperative that we do so with great haste, not only to restore communications, but there's something else I have to do, something that will benefit everything going on across the planet, especially in the council building. But we need to be more careful. I want no more lives lost. Slow and steady wins the race, and that's how it's going to be for us. UNDERSTOOD?"

A muted array of yes's echoed around their immediate vicinity, all of them determined to do better, to be more on guard and to see off the despicable and murderous dark dragons while avoiding any more losses. Without further ado, three of the dragons turned towards the locked door and started applying all their magical knowhow in an effort to bring it down. It wouldn't be long now.

Deeper into the facility, lights flickered and consoles sparked in the shadowy dark, against the backdrop of footsteps crunching across a myriad of broken glass.

"Are there any left?" asked DomCon quietly.

"Probably," ventured Jar Man, erring on the side of caution.

"He's right," whispered Steel. "There's far too many of them for all to have died. Stay sharp."

Turning a darkened corner, stepping over the bleeding bodies of half a dozen ravaged nagas, an eerie green light started to illuminate their path. Their goal, the crystal node, still amazingly intact, swam into view. Looking majestic, the faintly pulsing light it gave off was kind of hypnotic. The three friends admired it in all its glory, keenly aware of not only how important it was in dragon society as a whole, but just how valuable it was here and now.

For all intents and purposes death had taken her... only it hadn't, not quite, her steely will staving it off for the time being at least. Covered in debris, dust and blood, shrouded by shadows, little of her magic remaining, one thing became quite clear to Red as she lay on the cold, hard floor in absolute agony, only a stone's throw from the pulsing green monument that controlled communications worldwide, barely able to focus, let alone move. Right here, right now, she'd do anything to stop them from gaining access to the crystal node and calling up reinforcements, including giving her last breath and what remained of her magic. It wasn't over, not yet, not so long as the tiniest spark of life remained within her.

27 IN THE HEAT OF THE MOMENT

It turned his stomach, it really did, and that says all you need to know, for nagas never normally experience nausea. Vasuki, naga king and long time Antarctic captive, having failed with yet another telepathic call to arms to the rest of his race, ordering them to desist and fall in behind him, was doing the one thing he'd vowed only a short time ago, not to do... fight against his own kind. That's what things had come down to. It broke his heart, mirroring the conflict between his cell mate, Fredric, and his daughter, Earth. Both were doing what each felt was totally and utterly RIGHT, despite the dreaded consequences, each fighting against their very nature and fundamental values. They would pay a heavy price at some point in the future, if indeed they survived.

Low on his unique and interesting magic, the naga king had fallen back on the physical training he'd received many, many decades ago, long before the humans of this world had created the motor car or taken flight.

Charged by two of his own, each baring needle sharp teeth, very calmly Vasuki used all his momentum and, to the surprise of the attackers, rolled forward towards them, bringing his huge cylindrical tail up and over his body, clubbing them both over the head with it simultaneously. The last thing they saw before they lost consciousness was a swathe of concentric shades of blue, right before their eyes. With no time to relax, the serpent monarch whipped around to deal with yet another of his kind that was about to sink his poison filled teeth into his tail. Rolling his whole being off in the opposite direction, leaving his opponent biting air, Vasuki rose up to his full height and head butted the crazed beast right between the eyes, watching with contentment as his adversary fell dazed to the floor. Not having finished off the other two because he knew they'd be out cold for quite some time, the leader of the nagas pondered what to do next. This one would be back up and fighting in no time at all, of that there was no doubt. Ever the pragmatist as king, he knew that there really was no choice, not if he wanted to help his dragon allies and vanquish evil from this planet once and for all. It might only be one member of his race, but it could be the one that rejoins the fight and causes unmentionable harm to one of his other allies. Decision all but made, stomach churning in anger and disgust, the naga king's cobra-like head shot forward and, clamping his needle sharp teeth in a vice-like grip around the monster's neck, he bit down with all he had, a single tear streaming down his face as he did so.

Not a stone's throw away, an example of the kind of coordination that would normally take decades to realise was relentlessly playing out in the form of Flash and Amelia Battlehard, battling back to back, the King's Guard captain having recently reacquired one of the huge black bastard swords, now wielding it with all the expertise of a master in the art, scything down nagas, slicing through dark dragons, piercing anything that moved that wasn't her partner in a devastating display of death dealing. She was on fire, and Flash was bowled over.

Heart hammering, the ex-Crimson Guard and master of almost anything used every mantra he knew to deflect away the constant bombardment of dark and unsavoury magic that continued to be directed at them by the superior number of opponents they both faced, whilst his partner brandished her sword against others of the same kind, in an outlandish, musketeers style do over.

Sidestepping a shadowy matt black blade thrust straight at her stomach, Captain Battlehard wheeled around on the spot and using the pent-up fury within her, struck with surgical precision, delivering a basic vertical cut that sliced through the dragon from his left shoulder straight down to the inside of his left leg. Shrieking in terror, the beast's body split in two, bright green blood spitting everywhere as the CLANG of his weapon hitting the ground resounded above the chaos of all the fighting. Ticking yet one more enemy off in her mind, the brave, centred and talented captain knew there was no time to rest on her laurels and so parrying yet another blow that was aimed at her head, used the leverage of Flash's back and with all the speed and strength she could mobilise, rotated her sword around that of her attacker, instantly disarming her. Without hesitation and with all the poise of the cool warrior that she was, she delivered the fatal blow with no nonsense style, decapitating the dragon's head from its body, the stunned look on its face barely noticeable as it tumbled off into the pandemonium of the battle.

Attempting to keep an eye on everything in a three hundred and sixty degree radius, Flash in his almighty new dragon form, despite the seriousness of the circumstances they all found themselves in, was having the time of his life. For him to be fighting back in his natural guise was a dream come true, particularly since he'd been stuck in human form for what seemed like an age. Obviously it wasn't that long, it just felt that way, but not to have had access to his prehistoric body had been a blow that he'd struggled to come to terms with, despite all outwardly appearances. Here and now, fighting tooth and claw with dastardly adversaries whose primary purpose was to rip him apart, felt like pure unadulterated bliss, even though danger surrounded them and death was but a moment away. For the first time in what seemed like forever, he felt well and truly alive. Was it just because he'd been reincarnated as a stunning, gigantic prehistoric beast, or was it something to do with his fighting partner? Only time would tell.

Batting away one of the dark dragon's fireballs meant for his partner with an invisible hand, Flash used his mind to snap three crucial bones in the left wing of the circling beast, not bothering to watch it spiral out of control into the throng of nagas off to his left, more concerned with a trio of slippery serpents who'd almost broken through their defences on the ground. So many threats to watch out for, so little time to do something about them. Things were getting crazier than ever, that was for sure. Using an incantation that would grant him momentary magnetic control, the ex-Crimson Guard ripped the hilt of a huge bastard sword out of the hands of the naga nearest to his partner, slammed it up against its scaled chin and then, reversing the blade, plunged it straight through its chest, the grisly CRUNCH of bones shattering scant reward. One down, two to go.

The previous mantra having long since disappeared, Flash whispered three words inside his mind, adding a great deal of willpower to them, watching as an invisible grip grasped the naga by the neck, forcing air out of its gills and throat, effectively choking the monster. It was then that he felt the first tendrils of a powerful mental assault, one that could only be coming from the fiendish, snake-like brute, because of the desperate nature of the attack. Holding on for dear life, the ex-Crimson Guard did his best to swat away the multi-pronged onslaught on his mind. But with so much going on, one of the unusual wisps struck home and breached the ramparts of his intellect. Dazed and dazzled, head swimming as if trapped in some bad dream in which zero gravity rollercoasters were the norm, Flash held onto the invisible grip for all he was worth, knowing that in mere moments it would be over. But his opponent had other ideas, invading his thoughts, using his fondest memories against him, targeting every emotion, hoping to gain some traction in an effort to distract the dragon enough to break free from the near death, vice-like grip. But the link that had been forged worked both ways, and as the snake-like beast sieved through Flash's psyche hoping to find a recollection powerful enough to disrupt the spell, a glimpse of the naga's previous life infested the newly embodied dragon's psyche. Images of a family, cresting the waves of cool, blue ocean water together ran riot across the bond, much to the monster's despair. Teaching offspring to hunt and an immense feeling of pride caused Flash to falter momentarily, relinquishing his grip ever so slightly. Feeling the impetus going his way, the naga struggled to break free, all the time ransacking the ex-Crimson Guard's mind. It was an unseen battle of epic proportions on a very personal scale, giving Flash cause for concern, until that is an image of a being he knew very well popped into his head from his foe's thoughts. VASUKI! It was the naga king looking royal and regal, curled up on a throne made of brightly coloured, orange, red, green and blue coral, somewhere deep beneath the surface, looking out at hundreds of his kind, all hanging on his every word. Heart threatening to leap out of his chest, Flash couldn't help but hold on to the reminiscence, wondering where it would lead. And then things got a whole lot odder. Although not able to understand the garbled language through the tinted green undersea waters, it appeared to the ex-Crimson Guard as though this was some kind of significant ceremony, one in which the beings there were being honoured. One by one strange serpents swam up, each anointed by the king, until it was the turn of the being whose mind and life was wholly wrapped up in Flash's thoughts. Swimming up to Vasuki, a feeling of contentment, pride at a job well done and loyalty washed through the connection.

'This one's special,' Flash thought, 'he's part of the naga king's inner circle.' That thought, and that alone, forced him to relinquish the grip he'd had on the naga's throat, a fatal mistake, one the professional killing machine inside him chided himself for. Reinforcing his mental defences, severing the link immediately, he returned to the heat of battle only to find his adversary about to unleash a deathly combination of unrecognisable magic at him. That is, until the timely blade of a matt black sword burst out of the naga's dark brown chest, quelling the magic, shedding blood and guts everywhere. The surprise jolting Flash back to their situation, he whispered a heartfelt, "thank you," to his partner and in a brutal show of force, vaporised the head of the last of the three nagas with but a flick of his fingers, wastefully using up far too much mana to take out just one being. Cursing his recklessness, his mind returned to the cool, calculating persona that it had nearly always been, casting away thoughts of Vasuki's friends and lieutenants, for now at least.

Lashing out, Tank caught one naga in the throat with his elbow, whilst planting the sole of his right foot straight through the gills of another, in a death defying display of agility that even the legendary Bruce Lee would have been proud of. But there was no rest for the wicked, or those fighting them, and so pitching forward, he poked yet another firmly in the eye with the tip of his index finger, feeling the soft squelch as his nail pierced the dense, fibrous nerve tissue, semi blinding the beast. Dodging the tip of a tail the size of a human thigh meant to catch him full on in the throat, the young rugby playing dragon lunged forward and karate chopped that one right in the windpipe, knowing full well that it wasn't recovering from that any time soon.

"They're nearby," whispered a voice deep inside his head.

"Okay... tell me when," he replied, ducking out of the way of a slashing blade meant to cleave him in two, his errant reply streaks of furious fire lancing out from his fingertips, piercing the monster right through in at least half a dozen places, all performed instinctively under the guidance of his partner For'son. As a torrent of rubble dropped from the air onto the battlefield strewn with bodies, clearly hoping to add his to the tally, he gracefully backflipped twice, before assuming a crouch and letting out a scintillating wave of energy in every direction. Nagas exploded like fish being hunted with dynamite, dragons tumbled from above, huge black lines of fire scorched the, by now, well worn marble flooring. For a split second he had a chance to breathe and take in everything that was going on around him. And then with a little nudge from his partner, he spotted the first of them.

'That's impossible,' he thought only to himself. Of course it wasn't. On the contrary, it was totally possible.

"*Underestimate them at your peril,*" was the reply from the enigmatic band. Unable not to watch in some sickly, horrified kind of way, the two of them looked on as a swarm of more than a dozen flying insects dived straight through the skin of dark dragons and nagas alike, easily puncturing scales and sinew with their one massive out of proportion sharp tooth the size of a man's finger.

"*Those, my friend, are called nifoloa and are quite deadly. One drop of their poison and you'll be taking a one way trip from which there's no return.*"

Swallowing hard, Tank gathered up all his magic.

"*Avoid using poison of any sort on them. They're immune to most forms of it.*"

"*Thanks,*" he replied, readying a haze of frost for them.

Dropping the last of the nagas between them and their intended target, the buzzing grew infinitely louder as the swarm set their sights on Tank, and more importantly, the ancient band that smelt of magic.

Pulling in a deep breath through his nose and exhaling out of his mouth in an attempt to calm himself down, without a sound he whispered the words that had appeared at the front of his mind and applied a little of his ethereal energy to them.

Swooping through the air as a squadron, the tiny mythical creatures vectored around before darting forward with a great deal of speed, screaming through the space towards Tank and For'son. Taking their velocity into account, the magic that the young rugby playing dragon had cast materialised in the form of a huge, icy glass plate, directly in front of him. Unable to alter their trajectory, the demon insects flew straight into a whole world of wicked cold, instantly regretting their decision to attack, falling to the floor as one, their flimsy wings frozen in place, their deadly weapon proving to be a weighty burden. Lying there helplessly, twitching uncontrollably, For'son urged Tank to finish them off with a ball of flame. Unsure at first, the sense of overwhelming urgency and danger through their bond quickly changed his mind. Opening out the palms of both hands, the young dragon discharged two blistering balls of intense fire that instantly incinerated everything lying on the floor. Turning to face the direction from which the nifoloa had come from, Tank's heart sank at what he spotted in the distance. Huge scorpion men with bodies the size of cars and the torso, head and arms of a human, were indiscriminately ripping open nagas, the stinger on their tails puncturing the scales of low flying dragons, causing utter carnage in their wake. And that wasn't even the most scary part. A pack of blue maned wolves fought over the remains of two nagas, gorging on intestines, fighting over the limbs and tails, shaking innards and organs everywhere. Scaled apes used their differing number of arms to beat a downed dragon to death, ripping off parts of its wings, stamping on its head, pulling out its teeth to keep as trophies. Heart stopping as these events should have been on their own, unbelievably there were more. Two-headed eagles dive bombed the slippery serpents on the surface, taking out eyes and gills with little fuss or bother, while in the end the feared pixiu, winged lions of sorts, tore apart unsuspecting dark dragons, having little knowledge or experience of how to fight off this new and exotic enemy. Filling the space up above, huge clouds of fire breathing gnats whipped through the air, squirting flame at anything that moved, including those on their own side. It had been absolute bedlam up there before, now though, a new word was needed to describe the total turmoil and anarchy.

'Things', Tank thought, 'can't possibly get any worse.' That's when the giant asag reared up to its full height, some way off in the distance, the huge, hideous rock demon scouring the battlefield with its purple vision, pummelling targets into the ground with its gigantic fists, sending beings of every sort skittering into the air. From out of nowhere a flash of colour caught the young dragon's eye. Barely able to avert his gaze from the asag, Tank focused in on the bright blood red and brilliantly neon green that had attracted his attention.

'What in the...' he thought, having never seen anything like it. There in front of him were human bodies with bulbous, bulging bellies and the heads of cattle. Each had three eyes, with sharp talons, horns and bony protrusions littering their monstrous forms, something they put to good use by spinning viciously, cutting open everything around them with the efficiency of one hundred razor blades. It was bone chillingly scary.

"*Ah... the gaki. Monstrous legends of the Far East,*" added For'son. "*Rumour has it that they feed off the souls of evil men and women.*"

"*Great!*" replied Tank sarcastically. "*Are there any other surprises out there that I should know about?*"

"*You've spotted most of the really dangerous ones. There are a few others, but they're of little consequence. Only the ra-hoon present a greater threat than those you've seen and they, from what I can tell, seem to be lurking in the crowd somewhere towards the back near the very disappointed rock demon. Resembling a unicorn, only with two horns instead of the usual one, if you stumble across a ra-hoon, you need to run for your life. Under no circumstances should you try and engage it. IF YOU DO YOU WILL DIE!*"

"*Understood,*" replied Tank, shaking his head.

"*Heads up,*" declared For'son. "*INCOMING!*"

Briefly he thought she was on fire, but it only took him a split second to realise that every part of her being was leaching supernatural power, ethereal sparks igniting randomly across her entire body, lighting up the shadowy darkness created by slippery nagas battling all around. Impressed at how his daughter carried herself, a part of him knowing they would have made great allies under different circumstances, Fredric, after his near miss only a few seconds earlier, swallowed away his fear and remembering all the terrible deeds she'd been responsible for, brought forth everything he knew. Fate smiled, watching with interest.

A sparkling, ivory salvo of magical darts sprayed out from his right hand in a horizontal arc, each tearing through the air on course with his dreaded offspring.

She almost laughed, that's how pathetic she found the attack he'd just launched at her. Tossing up whether or not to get out of the way, the tiniest motion with her index finger and six choice words from thousands, combining a naga and dragon spell, abruptly opened a hole directly beneath her father. Watching with a great deal of satisfaction, knowing exactly what was coming next, she hoped he'd pass on her regards to those that she'd committed to the afterlife.

Eminently surprised as the floor gave way underneath him, something about her attack didn't ring true as he fell. Bouncing off the sides of the hole, a fear the likes of which he'd never really known, even during all those years held captive in Antarctica, started to gnaw away at him.

'There has to be more,' he thought, all the time knowing that he had to get out.

So utterly joyous at watching her dad's haggard old body drop out of sight in front of her, aware of what was to come, she'd barely given a thought to the magic he'd sent heading her way, thinking that she could just swat it to one side when it arrived. Attempting to do so, her first touch triggered a series of devastating explosions from the supernatural ivory barbs, shrapnel ripping into her, the blast waves splitting her skin, cutting her face, arms and legs, throwing her back almost twenty metres, a pile of dead bodies cushioning her fall.

'Surprise!' thought her father, or at least he would have, had he not been dealing with his own magical downfall.

Managing to halt his descent down the huge, dark hole that had suddenly appeared out of nowhere beneath him, looking up, he could see he was about fifty metres below the main floor of the king's private residence. With no room to turn into his prehistoric alter ego, he knew that he was going to have to climb, and do it fast, because one thing that he was certain of was that there was more to this attack than met the eye. And he was right. Starting as a small, ground shaking rumble, a pinprick of bright orange light some way below him was the first clue as to just how much trouble he was in. Looking aloft, he knew within himself that he'd never climb back up in time. Harnessing all of his magic, he used it to throw himself up and across to the opposite wall, and then the same again, and again, gaining five or six metres in height at a time. But with whatever it was rushing up to meet him at quite a rate, it didn't look as though he'd taste freedom before it found him.

Head pounding, body bleeding, and deeply pissed off at not recognising her father's attack for what it was, she did at least feel grateful for not suffering more damage, having managed to shield her face with her hands at the very last instance, and for having some naga cadavers break her fall. Diverting a small amount of her power from sparking on the outside to healing herself on the inside, groggily she stumbled to her feet, determined to witness what should be one hell of a spectacle firsthand.

Heart thumping in his ears, now feeling the heat and power from whatever was chasing its way up the cylindrical hole, Fredric pumped all his magic into throwing himself as fast as he could at the different sides of the chasm in an effort to gain some height and escape, doing inexplicable amounts of damage to his human form as he did so, despite his personal shield. Everything shaking violently, the founder of the Crimson Guards got within eight or so metres of the surface before a superheated, utterly ferocious column of scorching hot flame caught up with him, the skin on his falsehood form roasted in an instant, his blood boiling, all of him cooked like a chicken for Sunday lunch, his supernatural protection vanquished in an instant. Excruciating pain overwhelmed him, his magic of absolutely no use at all.

Unsteady on her feet, it took her a moment to figure out that now it wasn't because of her injuries, but because the ground was actually trembling violently. Planting one foot firmly in front of the other, ignoring stray bolts of magic pinging all around her, Earth watched the result of her demonic spell with excited anticipation, hoping that she would finally be rid of that bastard forever.

Luck is indebted to no one. Never has been, never will be. Not once in his cruel incarceration deep in the bowels of the Antarctic did Peter's grandfather ever receive even the tiniest smidgen of luck. It just didn't happen. Even on escaping, things still hadn't really gone his way. Of course he'd just about managed to get a fingertip on the laminium chains that had enhanced the power of his birthright and had saved Flash's life and killed that sadistic jailer, but that was more his rescuer's doing than anything to do with luck. But here and now, things might well have changed, and although it didn't look it from the outside, chance could indeed have just become his best friend. Because he was so close to the top of the hole when the seething column of jet fighter-like flame came steaming up from down below, zooming up towards the cavernous ceiling for all to see, it threw Fredric's scorched, burnt and cooked body up, out and over the side, leaving what was left of him a bloody mess on the ground, his toasted flesh still sizzling.

Pleasure personified wrapped her up in its soft embrace, washing away all her fears and doubts, kicking out all the shadows, bringing her into the light, making her feel not only special but vindicated by her actions. Watching the remains of her father's smoking body get tossed over the side of the abyss from which the massive column of flame had shot out of, gave her a sense of wellbeing that she hadn't felt in decades. Smiling epically, her neck arched allowing her head to face the sky. Starting off as a dim chuckle, it got louder and louder, the booming laughter soon becoming hysterical. She'd only gone and done it!

Luminous, luxuriant fire and flame clashed against a bulging mass of spectral black shade as the two kings unfurled their magic, both giving everything they had in an effort to kill the other. George was powered on by the unwavering belief that it would end things once and for all and nullify any more threats to the earth, Manson motivated by thoughts of instilling his will across the planet and creating a brave new world. Both were truly inspired, both believing themselves to be right.

For the current dragon king, it had become something of a struggle, his magic waning ever so slightly, the reserves of mana deep within his body, starting to become dangerously low. Thoughts of his rift with the ring and its presence, For'son, threatened to consume him. If only he hadn't been so stubborn, if only they'd gotten on better, then perhaps the legacy of all the other dragon monarchs before him wouldn't now be in so much danger. Presently though, he could do little to change that, with the master mantra maker's partner off somewhere else in the room, no doubt battling for survival, the enigmatic band guiding his every move. With his formidable fiery flame being pushed back ever more in his direction, inch by inch, George had a choice to make, one that he wished to avoid at all costs.

Gloating on the inside, Manson's warped mind revelled in his tormentor's turmoil, more than happy about how things were going, feeling his magic gain ground with every second that passed, knowing he was winning and that nothing could stop him from taking the life of the imposter that called himself king.

Stretching every sinew, drawing power from every molecule of his body, he concentrated his mind in the hope that he could strengthen the resolve of the ethereal energy that had always been his, trying to recover in his battle, overwhelm and destroy the pervading evil that he now knew had been infiltrating HIS planet for many, many decades.

But it was no use. The more of himself that he gave over, the more he tried, the more ground Manson gained, as their two very different types of magic argued amongst themselves. There and then, hope died, with the inevitable consequences of what would happen playing out in his mind. Ultimately his death would lead to a lack of confidence and inspiration. Individuals on his side would seek revenge and to redress the wrong, leading to chaos, confusion and a distinct lack of cohesion. It would almost certainly lose them the battle, and the planet. Not one to blow his own trumpet or big himself up in any way, shape or form, his thoughts on the matter at hand merely told the story of the facts as he saw them, in the most dispassionate way possible. Right there and then, he sought any sort of solution that wouldn't let his enemies win. There was one, and it might just work, but it would mean sacrificing himself, something he was more than willing to do. First though, he had to get closer to his adversary... much, much closer.

'Unbelievable! Still they're coming,' thought Peter, exhaling another long fiery breath out in front of him, the raw exhilaration of his magic tinged breath rushing up his throat, zipping in and out of his teeth, tickling the underside of his tongue, making it tingle ever so slightly as the deliciously hot streak of smoking flame roared out from between his huge prehistoric jaws, incinerating anything in its path. Whilst the act itself was repellent and stomach churning, killing other beings en masse, even if they were trying to murder every single one of his friends and a whole lot more, he had, for the most part, gotten reasonably good at predicting how long to hold back and then just where to shoot his flame. Between himself on the ground doing that and shielding his beloved Janice, and the prodigious Fu-ts'ang in and around the air, they pretty much had things covered.

At the end of his outward breath, he inhaled with all his might, letting the oxygen in his lungs combine with the sprinkling of magic needed to ignite the flame within him. As the fire and smoke cleared from in front of him, off in the distance he could just make out the one being on the planet that he hated the most, battling furiously with George in his old man guise, long straggly grey and white hair flowing out behind him, his feet barely able to maintain grip. In short, the king was losing his personal battle and Peter knew there and then that he had to do something about it, not just for him, but for the sake of everyone.

About to ask Fu-ts'ang to intervene, thinking that he could keep himself and Janice safe from both the ground and the air in the meantime, and the wicked weapon could reach the king in but an instant, if not killing Manson directly, then at least providing enough of a distraction to allow George to flee, right at that very moment a wall of noise battered the private residence, scattering beings left, right and centre as a humungous brightly lit column of fire and hateful rage erupted from somewhere in the middle of the room, blasting its way straight up to the shadow soaked ceiling. Every being there trained their eyes on what had happened, including the young hockey playing dragon. What he witnessed made him tremble with terror. There, spat out from one side of the volcano-like flare-up, a smouldering, human shaped body that despite being shrivelled, burnt, scorched and thoroughly cooked, Peter recognised in an instant. It was... HIS GRANDFATHER!

Watching the murderous witch that had almost ended his life as the battle had started all that time ago raise her head to the sky and cackle uncontrollably, the young hockey playing dragon had the choice of his life to make: attempt to save George the king, leader of the dragons, caretaker of the planet, a being who'd done so much for him in the past and shown him great love and attention when he'd needed it most, or go all-out in an effort to get to the grandfather that he barely knew but loved beyond belief, in the hope that they might still have a future together. If Fate had been a gambler, she'd have struggled to call this one.

"HANG ON!" shouted Richie over all the din of the fighting, her words aimed at the rugby playing giant Hook.

"What am I supposed to do?" he yelled back.

"You'll be fine. The barrier powered by the necklace will protect you. Just use your momentum to do as much damage as possible. Don't stop moving."

Having hurled him, and the oval shaped sparkling shield that he was cocooned inside, around three times already with her magic, a small glint of a smile on her face covered just a little more ground as she bowled him through the throng of slithering serpents, knocking down a great number, almost as if they were pins at the end of a bowling alley. It was a glimmer of light on a very dark day. Diving off in the opposite direction to the one in which she'd just thrown her friend, she came up, whirled around and pulling her knee in tight to her body, let go with the mother of all kicks, straight into the gills of a fast moving naga, causing it to crumple without a sound. Igniting the air in front of another, temporarily blinding it, as it wriggled out of control, spitting green flecks of poison in every direction, its needle sharp teeth chomping and chewing on nothing but air, the lacrosse playing superstar picked up a discarded sword from a fetid pile of corpses and in one swift stroke, took its head off. Satisfied, but not at all complacent, and keeping hold of the weapon, Richie spent a moment thinking about where she could best be of use next.

Rolling head over heels, the magic surrounding him preventing any damage at all, apart from what felt like the dismemberment to the insides of his stomach, Hook ground to a halt at the end of a trail of flattened nagas, delighted that their ploy had worked, wondering what he should do next. And then, through a tangle of tails, a mass of debris and a rainbow litany of every different kind of magic exploding all around, he spotted it, the unmistakeable golden colour drawing his attention like a magnet. Instantly he recognised it as the blade that Richie had been powering the shield with when she'd been protecting them all. Wondering what on earth it was doing out here all alone in the middle of the combat, the resilient rugby player figured it must be of great value, given everything he'd seen. Bounding off as delicately as a ballet dancer, nagas bouncing off the protective magic keeping him safe on all sides, he headed straight for the unique and much coveted weapon, determined to lay his hands on it before anyone else.

There was no choice, there really wasn't, and he was sorry it had to be this way. After all, he loved George the king with all of his heart. But the planet versus the only family he had left? There was a compelling argument for each, but not for him... not here, not now. Mind made up, and with a steely determination that had never reared its ugly head within him before, he looked to the sky, eager for some attention.

"FU-TS'ANG!" he screamed.

Instantaneously, the frost shrouded blade pulled up, almost as if looking around.

"Get Janice to Yoyo and his friends. She'll be safe there."

'What the...?' thought the master weapon smith's soul trapped inside the weapon, burning to ask some questions. But it was too late because the young hockey playing dragon had already turned away.

"What's going..."

Before the young bar worker had a chance to even finish the question, Peter's giant prehistoric frame enveloped her in one great big hug, before he let go and put his huge scaled face next to hers.

"I love you," he declared, a shiver of excitement traversing the whole of his body.

"I..."

She didn't even have a chance to tell him that she loved him too, that's how quickly he moved, turning, throwing himself up into the air, swooping a few metres up above the nagas' heads, attempting to stay clear of all the carnage, all the time heading for his grandfather's broken body.

Watching him leave with a mixture of fascination, awe, shock and an overwhelming feeling of love, in but a split second all of that was forgotten as the first swathe of nagas closed in on her position, determined to take the young, defenceless human down. Backing away ever so slightly, the look of murderous intent on their faces, up so close and personal now, threatened to stop her in her tracks. As it was, she needn't have worried. While one partner deserted her, another arrived just in the nick of time.

An icy, white trail of sparkling frost in his wake, Fu-ts'ang dashed down from the sky, stabbing two of the beasts before Janice had even realised what had happened, spearing two more, and skewering a fifth before she'd even had time to take a breath. As saves go, it was awe inspiring and especially timely.

"*Thanks,*" she exclaimed through that part of her mind she knew was linked to his.

"*You're of course very welcome, little one. I do think, however, that it's time to make a move.*"

"*What about Peter?*"

"*I'm pretty sure he has his own agenda right now. If you want to do something for him, then stay safe, that'll be a weight off his mind. He loves you a great deal you know.*"

"*How can you possibly be aware of that?*"

"*Having lived hundreds of lives, you pick up a thing or two. I haven't always been imprisoned deep underground or trapped within this fantastical body.*"

"*Good to know,*" she replied blushing ever so slightly.

"*Do you know why he had to leave?*" she asked, not sure if she wanted to know the answer.

"*The one thing on the whole of the planet that could tear him away from you... his only surviving family member."*

Letting out a small gasp, the young bar worker understood what had happened. Being reunited with a relative thought long gone and then almost having it all taken away was enough to drive anyone crazy, and the fact that the first thing he did was ask... no, order... Fu-ts'ang to keep her safe, made her heart leap. As her partner, the dragon killing blade from another time attempted to guide her to safety, murdering those that would do her harm in an instant, she wished Peter well, hoping that he could not only save his grandfather, but meet up with her on the other side of the ferocious battle they both found themselves caught up in.

That one singular moment that she'd bought herself might very well prove to be vital in not only their cause, but that of the planet itself. Ignoring the raw nastiness coursing through the hilt of the matt black, two handed bastard sword that she held by her side, instinctively and with a keen eye, she took in everything playing out around her. Scores of nagas ran riot on the ground, attacking Yoyo and his companions, threatening to overrun the contingent of King's Guards and the one remaining councillor, attempting to swarm their own king, a being she'd heard referred to as Vasuki, and keeping Captain Battlehard and Flash on their toes at all times. It was absolute bedlam, but her mind was kind of able to make sense of it all and see it for what it was. And although still hugely outnumbered, they were as a force, making a considerable dent in the enemy numbers, with her cohorts pretty much on top of everything going on. At that exact moment, the ground shook uncontrollably, almost toppling her to the floor, but for her excellent sense of balance. Turning to face the source of the quake, she jumped back just slightly as an almighty pillar of superheated flame came shooting up out of a hole that she hadn't noticed before, pulling a scorched and burnt shell of a body with it. Skin crispy black and roasted red, still sizzling and smoking, even in that condition she could still identify who it was... FREDRIC!

Knowing that's exactly where she needed to be, through a maze of wings and a jumble of tails and scales, she spotted something that suddenly made the choice less obvious... the king, struggling against that brute Manson, looking as though he was in real trouble. Not George's biggest fan by any means, especially as he'd let the priesthood wipe her mind and banish her to the surface, knowing the seriousness of the situation, and with the experiences of everything that had happened since she'd left the Indian restaurant in Salisbridge, what seemed like a lifetime ago, she put all of that behind her, and very much like her best friend Peter, made the only decision she could.

Battering the dark, slippery beasts out of the way, wondering why the hell they smelt so badly of fish as he did so, amused by their looks of confusion at not being able to harm him with either their magic or physicality, Hook, in amongst all the confusion and congestion sprinted towards the point on the floor where he'd last seen the glinting dagger. However, it wasn't quite as straightforward as that. Although he couldn't be harmed, he could be knocked off course and off balance, something the nagas were particularly good at, swiping him with their scaled tails, bumping him with their overtly muscled chests. He felt as though he'd become the ball inside a pinball machine. On one occasion he'd got so 'disappointed off' (see what I did there) that he'd kicked out with his powerful right leg, regretting it immediately, thinking himself in danger. What he'd found though, was instead of his leg breaching the barrier and being exposed for all to get at, the shield itself extended out around his limb and foot, keeping the whole of him safe, as well as adding a little more brute force to his attack. AMAZING!

With this in mind, the courageous rugby player, having re-established his bearings, now knowing exactly where the dagger was, started kicking, punching and head butting his way through the crowd to great effect.

'If only Richie had told me earlier,' he thought, 'then I'd have been able to do much more damage.' Soon though, damage wouldn't be a problem.

Readjusting his height, making sure the slippery serpents couldn't hit him with their tails as he skimmed over their heads, a brief sense of enjoyment at the air tickling his wings almost made him smile. ALMOST! But now was not the time or place for that because he had to give his all in one concerted effort to save his grandfather. Now was the time to step up. Pumping his wings furiously, he dodged a trio of fireballs meant for him, picked the most expedient path and barrel rolling between two dark dragons, both of them trying to take a bite out of him as he zipped past, headed directly for his grandfather's broken body, determined to save him.

Dancing forward, her procured matt black blade whirling faster than an overworked fan in the height of summer, Richie lunged and cut, pierced and smote, all the time focused on moving in one direction... that of the king. Slashing, hacking and parrying, constantly deflecting dreadful magic with her free hand, it was an exercise in poise and calm, saying much about not just her fighting ability, but her character as well. Scrambling over the dead and patches of uneven floor, she snorted with contempt as yet another naga came at her, teeth bared, tiny droplets of deadly green poison dripping from his incisors. Running out of time, she finished the monster off with a sickening head butt, before shoving the hilt of her weapon through its ever expanding and contracting gills, a nauseating gurgle the reward for her effort. After sending another four to meet their maker in all but a moment, finally she found herself within spitting distance of the one-sided magical onslaught that her king was very clearly losing. But what to do, that was the question?

Sweat pouring off him, not for the first time today he felt afraid. Not for himself, you understand, but for everyone else, the entire planet in fact, as he slipped ever further back along the rivers of slick blood that meandered across what had been a pristine white marble floor. Batting away a flurry of bright purple magical bolts, clearly meant for him, or to distract him, George dug deep in an effort to give every last ounce of magic that he had, hoping that the smug Manson who he could just make out through the inky blackness where their supernatural powers met, would falter or better still, run dry. Unfortunately, there was simply no way that was going to happen, something that despite his vain hopes, stared him straight in the face as the despicable dark magic loomed closer and closer.

Salty wet tears of laughter traversed rivers of crisscrossing purple on their journey to the drop off, as howls of echoing hilarity pierced the battlefield above the blazing noise of the gigantic column of flame that had almost burnt itself out, having not only destroyed the being she hated the most, but also slain or injured many of the nagas in the immediate vicinity, something she couldn't have cared less about. Wiping away what remained of the watery droplets with the scarred back of her hand, the taste of victory sweeter than anything she could ever have imagined, her dark, devious and dangerous thoughts turned back to her nemesis, something screaming out inside her to check what remained of his body, finish him off if need be. With that in mind, she stepped forward.

Inverting and rolling out, he banked sharply in an effort to avoid being boxed in. Despite his squat body not really being designed for these kind of aerial acrobatics, his audacious move worked, much to his surprise, buying him little in the way of respite. It didn't matter though, because he'd almost reached his goal, and if he was any judge, not a moment too soon.

Jinking out of the way of a desperate line of fire from some far away unseen naga, he picked his spot, just in front of his grandfather's body, brought his tail as far up as it would go, opened out his wings vertically, using every last millimetre of them to sheer off as much speed as he could, and like an out of control plummeting stone, headed for the ground.

Two steps in, she realised something was wrong. Unable to see what, she scouted about, glancing in and around her slithering allies, fearing some kind of sneak attack from behind or amongst them.

BOOM! An ungainly dragon lump of twisted scales and wings hit the ground with all the force of a meteor, concentric cracks in what was left of the marble echoing out from his point of impact. Straight away Earth took two steps back, nearly slipping on the river of tears she'd discharged onto the ground.

Through a haze of smoke, marble dust and thunderous magic, the dragon in question rose to its feet to face her... BENTWHISTLE!

Among pilots on the surface, they say that any landing you can walk away from is a good one. Right at that very moment, Peter felt that nothing could be further from the truth. Staggering to his feet, turning to face the monstrous witch who'd already attempted to kill him what seemed like only a short time ago, he started to wonder whether or not he'd done the right thing, and just how the hell he was going to face her in one to one combat. Swallowing nervously, he watched in utter horror as a clown-like smile worked its way across the terrifying purple of her face. If he hadn't known he was in trouble before, he most certainly did now.

Giving him only a few more moments at best before his magic succumbed to the cloying dark demonic force of whatever it was Manson was countering with, the lacrosse playing superstar leapt into action, one thought above all others prompting her on... to save her monarch. Defying gravity, enhanced by a little of her birthright, she somersaulted over an oncoming naga, landing firmly on her feet before realising what she had to do. A distraction, that's what she needed, and she needed it now, because George was almost on his knees, his adversary's evil about to take him out for good.

Bereft of ideas, luck and worst of all... magic, the dragon king was giving ground at quite a rate now prepared to meet his maker, sorry that it had come to this and that the world had gone to hell in a hand basket on his watch. Not wishing even to glimpse those that he loved one last time, arms and palms outstretched, he put everything into lasting as long as he could, but knew that it would only buy him a few moments more.

Enraged, invigorated, replenished and justified all at the same time, the psychotic animal on the other side of the ethereal energy poured everything he had into destroying the being his father, Troydenn, had hated the most, blood lust coursing through him, just the thought of murdering this one hugely arousing, a feather in his cap. In a prime example of the single minded evil that had got him this far in his life, he focused all of his anger, hate and desperation towards the last surviving true monarch of this world, licking his lips at just how delicious his imminent death would truly be.

Wielding the grotesque weapon over her right shoulder in a two handed grip, the rebellious lacrosse playing dragon, still de facto leader of the light-sided force, all the time on the run, flooded her muscles with magic, augmenting them greatly, and in one huge gamble, bounded up through the air. With everything she had, she hurled the spinning blade off into the distance, following in its wake, hoping it would be enough.

Wanting nothing more than to puke his guts up, Peter hoped he'd be able to fight the barking mad she witch as valiantly as he fought off the nausea threatening to overcome him.

Through the fog of madness that had taken her at the sudden death of the familiar she loved, a pinprick of sanity broke through on comprehending the dragon that had landed with a crash... HER SON! Peeling back the madness in her mind, she tucked away her magic, swatted away a new found mental state and remembered her previous thoughts, about her husband and the life they could all have had. Could still have... for both of them, she thought. With an errant salvo of ethereal bolts heading her way, telepathically she ordered all of those under her command out of the immediate vicinity, dropped the ridiculous smile, acutely aware of how nervous it was making him, and took two more steps forward.

Gut telling him that squirting fireballs at her would do nothing more than tickle the sadistic queen, the hockey playing dragon readied the most powerful spells he knew (not particularly vicious in the scale of things) letting tiny blue flashes of lightning crackle between his fingers and across his palm. And although this was the most potent his magic had ever been, he still felt hugely disadvantaged and weak.

"Put it away," she asked, in an extremely civil manner given the circumstances.

"Not a chance," he spat back, thinking that just maybe he had her running scared.

Of course that was never going to be the case.

"It doesn't have to be this way you know," she

suggested, all sweetness and light.

Like a rookie boxer, Peter stood, waiting for the sucker punch. Much to his surprise, it never came.

"Did your grandfather ever tell you about your parents?"

"D... d... d... don't you d... d... dare invoke his name," he babbled, the mere mention of the man he loved causing him distress beyond belief.

"I take it that's a no. Why do you think that was?" she asked, not fully realising that her father and son had only been reunited earlier today in the midst of battle.

All of him shaking, and not just because of the offensive magic he was struggling to hold on to, the anger within forced an answer out of him.

"Both my parents disappeared after they dropped my egg off at the nursery ring, not that it's any of your business."

"Is that so?"

"YES, it is."

"Well," announced Manson's murderous other half, "I'm here to tell you what really happened."

Goosebumps ran riot up and down his arms as his stomach somersaulted like an Olympic gymnast practising, so raw were his feelings on the subject. Figuring it was just another of her sadistic games, wondering why she'd even bother, Peter pondered his next move.

Punching heads, chests, tails and anything else in his way, Hook, one of two rugby superstars heavily involved in the fighting on the battlefield, though of course the only genuine human, had managed to plough his way through the melee to the point of almost reaching the shining gold dagger, just able to see it in front of him in a slight open space on the floor. About to lunge forward and pick it up, pleased with himself at having gotten this far, only then did he spot a dive bombing dragon zeroing in on the precious weapon. Eager not to take on the gigantic prehistoric beast, a huge part of him knew that letting it get away with the dagger was a mistake of epic proportions. Whatever it had allowed Richie and Fredric to do made it powerful, and not just a little. Letting it fall into the wrong hands was not an option. And so on pure reflex, Hook sprinted forward, harnessing all of his rugby training, and as though reaching out with the ball to score a try, threw all his momentum into the mother of all dives. With both beings looking to arrive at the weapon simultaneously, it was anyone's guess as to who would actually get their hands or talons on it first.

Aim true, almost certain to win that prize by a hair's breadth, Hook made his biggest mistake of the day by closing his eyes on impacting the floor, not wanting to see the dreaded creature's scary looking feet as it landed. In doing so, he misjudged where the hilt of the weapon would be, and so instead of wrapping his hand around it, his fingertips just got a touch, spinning it off a few metres out of the way. And then the angry dragon was upon him.

Catching a glimpse of something gold and glittery gleaming through the sea of darkness that constantly wriggled across the ground, the pull and lure of potential treasure temporarily trumped the despotic Manson's diabolical magical orders. Wheeling back around in a long, lazy loop, ignoring some of his comrades as they coughed out vicious fireballs in the direction of their enemies on the ground Zett, as he was known, used part of his supernatural vision to home in on the object that he'd spotted.

'THERE!' he thought, quickly identifying not only its location but the fact that it was some kind of exotic dagger, the hilt dotted with sparkling red rubies, glinting green emeralds ramping up his need to get hold of it. Lifting his tail into the air, he forced his head and body downwards. Bringing his wings in by his side, streamlining his descent, he nose-dived towards his target at quite a rate, ignoring his slippery cohorts all around. Closing fast, he snapped his wings up, flipping his body around so that his legs led the descent, stretched out his talons and prepared not only to hit the ground, but to gather up the loot that was all his.

About to make contact with the dazzling blade, unbelievably an outstretched human hand clipped its hilt, making it spin off into the array of fighting nagas. Angry at having had his prize taken away from him, albeit temporarily, he roared in frustration, flickering flame licking away at his mammoth teeth, squirts of fire peeking out from both nostrils as he did so. Kicking cadavers out of the way in frustration, desperately looking for his reward, the rest of the human that the outstretched hand belonged to bounded into place, from the look of things also attempting to find the dagger. This just enraged him even more. Stomping around, infuriated, he kicked bodies and lashed out with his wings, clubbing more of his comrades out of the way.

Avoiding two very dangerous looking attacks, a flying foot for one, and an angled wing scything through the air, Hook, unsure of whether both were directly aimed at him or just randomly indiscriminate, knew better than to hang around. Clearly the monster was after the same thing as him... the dagger. And he couldn't allow that to happen. So protected by the barrier powered by the necklace, the brave rugby player started to turn over all the bodies in the hope of recovering what he thought was Gee Tee's weapon. Boy has that thing been possessed by a few different beings!

Third time lucky, Hook found the dagger wedged beneath the bloodied tail of what remained of a dark brown naga. Grabbing it with his right hand, he pulled it out, only to be confronted by the very angry dragon, wanting what he regarded as HIS treasure back.

Keen not to use his flame in case he damaged the blade, Zett resorted to a physical attack, striking out with a foot, extending his razor sharp talons as far as they'd go.

So fast that he didn't see it coming, Hook was grateful Richie had cocooned him safely within the barrier as the mighty beast's talons headed straight for him, the invisible magical energy stopping the attack in its tracks, vicious, violet sparks arcing from the point of contact. Frightened that the shield might fail, only then did the rugby player remember his friend's words. Don't stand still. Grasping the dagger in one hand, he set off through the throng of nagas in a totally random direction, not knowing what the hell he was doing or where he was going, hoping all the time to lose the exceptionally disappointed dragon.

All but on his knees, the last of his magic being gobbled up by the inky black blob of writhing tendrils that squirmed and twisted towards him, now only a few centimetres from his face, somewhere deep inside his mind, George had thrown in the towel, already having accepted the agonisingly painful death that was only a split second or so away, goodbyes to those that he loved cast off into the back of his mind. Savouring what he thought of as his very last breath, before he even had the chance to say the words of the renowned mantra he had lined up in his head, from out of the corner of his eye, something moving at speed caught his attention. Not that it was supposed to, after all, it was aimed at somebody else entirely.

Compelling all his supernatural power, urging it on with every last drop of his will to break down the last of the dragon king's ethereal energy, Manson, destroyer of races, cultures, civilisations and worlds was but a moment away from having his blood lust sated, finally fulfilling his father's vendetta. About to finish it with one last push, suddenly something dark and metallic spun into view, heading directly for him. Caught in two minds about what to do, the animal in him desperate to remain and finish off the king, while common sense tried to dictate either some kind of supernatural defence or escape. Both produced convincing arguments, but in the end common sense prevailed, twisting his arm into throwing his body off to one side right at the very last second.

Terminating his magic, the wicked dark dragon leader lunged out of the way before rolling off in the opposite direction to the barely able to stand George.

CLANG, the sword smashed against a massive pile of rubble that had been located directly behind the would-be dictator, bouncing off into the middle of a group of nearby nagas.

Spent, George's exhausted body crumbled towards the floor, ably caught by a certain superstar lacrosse player before it did any damage.

Looking up into that pale skinned, freckled, human face, a mass of curly brown hair poking out from all sides, the king couldn't imagine anyone but her coming to his rescue.

'How fitting,' he thought.

"Thanks my dear. You have a veritable knack of coming to my aid. I hope one day I'll get the chance to repay you properly. You'd better watch out, he's full of surprises as well as some extraordinary unusual magic... naga in nature no doubt."

Showering him with her wicked smile, making everything in the world seem okay for a moment, Richie nodded before speaking.

"Find some cover. I've got a little score to settle with him anyhow."

Wishing her luck, George scooted off to see if he could find an ally or two for protection, wondering what on earth Captain Battlehard and Flash were up to.

Puzzled, confused, emotions heightened by not only the battle but the inquisition about his parents, Peter felt... everything. Wobbling on his feet, facing a being he absolutely hated, loathed and feared, wanting nothing more than to see her very painfully executed, all this talk about what his grandfather had said prodded at the rawest of nerves, and very much like a root canal performed by a dentist, physically hurt, a great deal.

'What really happened,' he thought. 'How the hell would you know? Just because you've spent years torturing my grandfather, somehow you think you know the truth or have the right to frighten me with it before you kill me. Well, screw you. There's no way in hell that I'm playing any game which involves you lying about my family.' And in that moment, in his mind, a decision was made, upholding a longstanding family tradition... TO FIGHT!

Thinking that he'd calmed enough to at least listen to what she had to say, all she had to do now was work out how to phrase it, in an effort to break it to him gently. Of course, they hadn't gotten off to the best of starts (something of an understatement). She was, however, convinced she could turn things around; after all she was his... MOTHER! But much to her surprise, and totally out of the blue, he launched two handfuls of lightning straight at her from only ten or so metres away, forcing her to tumble out of the way, the remaining snakes atop her head hissing and spitting wildly as she returned to her feet. What he'd just done downright annoyed her... no, not annoyed, made her mad. Why did he think it necessary to do that? There was no need. They were after all just talking. If she'd wanted to hurt him, it was easily accomplishable. Her power dwarfed his probably by a factor of fifty, which really was quite pathetic, something she didn't especially want to dwell on right at this very moment. All she wanted was to explain the situation and have a loving family reunion, right here, right now.

Sanity and madness were separated by the thinnest piece of paper in the world, one with lots of tiny holes in that let each side flood ever so slightly into the other, somewhere deep inside her brain. She really had no idea what she was asking him to accept after everything she'd done, not just in the past but here today: threatened to kill him, tried to kill him, attempted to kill his grandfather, and perhaps had actually killed his grandfather, all in the last half a day. Oh yes, I'm sure that'll be fine... you're sorry you say. It was all a mistake and if you could go back we'd have all grown up together as one loving family. As delusions go, this was something of a biggie.

Watching her tumble out of the way with ease, the horrifying serpents atop her head hissing and snapping, scaring the living daylights out of him, the hockey playing youngster tried desperately to think of what else he could do. For some reason she hadn't struck back yet, seemingly wanting just to talk and having unleashed what he regarded as his best shot, something that clearly wouldn't have even grazed her, he needed to come up with a plan and rather quickly, otherwise he'd be joining all the others that had already lost their lives today.

Downdraft scattering nagas dead and alive in a huge circle beneath him, a crimson and green shaded monster of a dark dragon swooped feet first, jagged talons aiming for George's torso in an effort to impale the fleeing enemy king. Realising what was about to happen because of the huge shadow looming over him, the dragon monarch dived to the side and attempted to scramble back up. But it wasn't to be, as a last second adjustment to the beast's landing had him pinned to the ground, his arms straddled by colossal feet, each the size of a desk, the pain unyielding, nowhere else for him to go. Delighted at the quick and easy capture, relishing the thought of one huge bite taking his prey's head off, the primordial beast seemingly had everything under control. Or did he?

Bumping many of the sickly snake-like creatures out of the way with the magical protection that encased him, Hook, fearful that the vengeful dragon whose treasure he'd run off with was still coming after him, abruptly got splattered with a number of extraneous body parts. With a sickly THUMP, thick, gooey blood splattered across his barrier and then started dribbling down in front of his vision.

'What the...' he thought, vision obscured briefly. Wishing for some sort of magical windscreen wipers (how bizarre was that in the situation that he currently found himself in?), peering through a couple of tiny little gaps, he could just make out what had happened, and just like the blood in front of him, his ran cold.

There, pinned to the floor by his arms, from huge feet belonging to a rather happy looking dragon, was the being who'd been introduced to him as the dragon king. With no immediate help at hand and the immense monster looking as though he was about to chomp down on a human shaped snack, there was only one thing the brave rugby playing human could think of to do. Drawing back his right hand as far as it would go over his shoulder, holding the brilliant bejewelled dagger by the hilt, he set up to let it fly. At that exact moment, George turned his head and their eyes locked.

Shockingly, and from out of nowhere, an authoritative voice invaded his head.

"DON'T," it declared.

Somehow knowing that the king of the dragons was referring to him, strangely Hook answered back.

"But why? I'm pretty sure I can hit him right between the eyes."

"We don't have time for questions, but you have trust me. If you're that good a throw, then get that dagger into my free hand... NOW!"

Recognising a command when he heard one, and knowing just how out of his depth he was in the midst of everything going on, summoning up all his strength, courage and agility, he tossed the dagger for all he was worth, hoping he'd done exactly as the king had asked. He had, but with one little twist.

"ARRRRRRRRGGGGHHHH!" cried out George from beneath the dragon, in pain as the metallic blade pierced the middle of his open palm, squirting brilliant red blood across the white marble, much to Hook's horror.

Absolutely aghast, the young rugby player had no idea that it didn't matter, in fact, it was more than the king could have hoped for. Right about then though, Hook's thoughts were directed in a different direction, as a familiar dragon swept a group of nagas out of the way from behind him with his wings, murder in his eyes, his gaze firmly set on his prey, all the time wondering what had happened to his treasure. Zett was back, and he was looking to make somebody pay. Hook gulped and tried very hard not to pee his pants.

Deciding to stop playing with his food, just as his mother had told him, the crimson and green scaled beast opened his primordial jaws wide and stretching out his neck, moved in to bite the head off his quarry, stomach rumbling in ravenous anticipation. Right at that point, a glint of metal caught his eye. Turning, he noticed another human shape, standing there off to one side, looking horror-struck, as though he'd unwittingly committed a crime. A splattering of something soft and sticky across the side of one foot focused his attention back on his snack. Glancing down, he was amazed to find a golden bejewelled blade sticking right out of the middle of the thing's hand. 'Where did that...?' was as far as his thought got before he realised the trouble he was in.

From being downright empty, not even running on fumes, to being, well... not exactly full, but having well over half a tank, the king liked his analogy, having taken a keen interest in the motor cars on the surface, but not having driven one for a few decades. Of course there was that unofficial road trip in the 80's across America, but only a handful of beings knew about that one.

'Goodness me that was something else,' he mused, his mind drifting back to the open roads that made up Route 66, the feeling of the sun on his face, the wind in his not so grey hair, the top down on the cherry red 1965 Ford Mustang that he'd come to think of as his own once the trip had finished, listening to the Eagles and the Beach Boys at full blast. What a month that had been, and well worth ditching his security and the ramifications it had caused. In some ways though, it was the council's own fault. They'd made him have a holiday, implying that he was stressed and overworked. He'd just decided to take it on the surface in his favourite guise, and when they'd tried to reprimand him on his return, he'd given them both barrels so to speak. Really, what he should have done was tell them what an amazing time he'd had. Perhaps then some of the stuck up councillors would have done the same and gained a finer appreciation for all things human and the world above. Of course he hadn't, but if he could go back he would have, and not only rerun his time in the iconic 'Stang', but relive every one of the bar brawls he'd got caught up in from Oklahoma City to St Louis and Chicago... brilliant, all of them.

And so, topped up magically, enough anyway to get back to fighting and restore his confidence, George, with four words alone, cast a mantra that in a heartbeat crushed the windpipe of the monster holding him in place, enabling him to wriggle free and roll out of the way in plenty of time to avoid the beast dropping on top of him. With a huge CRASH the dead body hit the floor, a look of astonishment chiselled in stone across the dragon's face.

Hook, even though protected by the shield powered by the necklace set in place by his friend, knew that he was in trouble as the gigantic Zett stomped forward, eyes fully focused on him. It wasn't so much the size of the dragon that scared the rugby player, but the look on his face. In all his time on this planet, Hook had never seen anything so angry. If that rage remained fully directed at him, there was no doubt in his mind that he'd end up in a world of pain and distress.

Grasping one naga that had tried to attack him with an invisible hand, the current dragon king thrust him up in the air, before stomping him down atop two of his comrades, instantly killing all three. Buying himself a little time, the battlefield seemingly having become less and less crowded because of the great work being achieved by absolutely everyone on the side of light, there and then, he spotted a problem that he was obliged to help out with.

THUNK! With a well timed shot, Zett's humungous, green flecked, scarlet tail came crashing down on top of Hook, the barrier he was encased in sparking and arcing as magic shimmered and flickered, an electrical blue wave shifting in and out of visibility.

Full of thunderous wrath at not having recovered his treasure yet, the frenzied dragon roared in frustration, as he let go with a flaming cone of brilliant bright fire, scorching the rugby player's supernatural defences, the fear from the attack forcing him to try and scuttle away on all fours along the ground. But there was really nowhere to go, and so when Zett's common sense returned, and he again stomped after his quarry, Hook had to wonder if this was really it, how he would end up going, a mere footnote in one of history's epic battles.

Bathed in ethereal energy from the dagger, George, faster than a blur, sprinted through all the corpses which were now piling up more than ever, and without hesitation leapt up and stabbed the crimson and green dragon, the one who'd been about to take down Hook, right through the heart. Instantly the light in his eyes diminished and as the monster attempted to whisper a last word or two in his dying breath, indistinguishable over the other sounds of the battle, its mighty frame slumped to the floor in front of the king and his new found friend.

"Thanks," uttered Hook, totally stunned.

"You're welcome, my young friend, but it's I that should be thanking you. Without your efforts, we'd probably both be dead."

"I'm sorry about your hand. I really tried to get the dagger to land hilt first."

"I know," smiled the king. "What you did was brilliant," he said, thrusting out his hand, showing his palm, which presented as perfect, not a scratch on it.

"What the...?"

Slapping the young rugby player firmly on the shoulder, getting the tiniest of electric shocks for his trouble from what little of the shield around him remained, George shouted over the buzz of magic exploding all around them.

"You need to find some cover, youngster. I suggest you head on over towards Yoyo and his young charges. It looks as though your human friend has made the same decision," he said, spotting Janice, surrounded by the frosty blade of Fu-ts'ang battling their way towards the Australian healer.

"What about you?" yelled Hook, wondering what the king had in mind and if there was anything he could do to help.

"I'm not quite sure, but I can't believe in all this that I won't find something to keep me occupied."

And with that, the dragon king disappeared into the ever diminishing crowd of slippery serpent-like beasts on the ground, leaving Hook to mull over one of the strangest encounters he'd ever had. Was it really possible that he'd just saved the life of the most powerful, most influential being on the planet? The words dream and nightmare came to mind, neither doing justice to what was happening around him. Still, he couldn't dwell on it, not here anyway. Too exposed not to be in danger, he took the king's sage words to heart and at a sprint, hoping the magic around him would provide safe passage, shot off in the direction of Yoyo and Janice, wondering what his other friends were up to.

Bounding to his feet, a little weary from using up so much power in such a short space of time, Manson looked to catch his breath, gather his composure and take in what was happening all around him. Unfortunately for him, a certain lacrosse playing hotshot had other ideas.

Like a hurricane tearing through 'Tornado Alley' in the central part of the United States, Richie was a whirling, twirling vision of death, bright green and blue tendrils of ethereal energy spitting out from her blurred, twisting and turning form, as she crashed into the leader of the opposing force, knocking him to the ground, burning him in over a dozen places, his scorched and charred skin causing instant distress and pain, enough for him to cry out. Briefly that satisfied something inside her, but not nearly enough, not considering what his actions had cost Tim, her one time partner and love. Having been rewarded with a momentary taste of vengeance after killing Troydenn, she was almost addicted to wanting more and in her own inimitable way, was determined to get it by killing Manson and ending all of this here and now.

Caught off guard big time, Earth's other half cursed his stupidity as he scrambled to his feet, the pain from the burns across his body almost too much to bear. ALMOST! Feeling the stupid lacrosse player's consciousness nibbling at his mental defences (yes, without visibly seeing the centre of the twister that had attacked him, he knew it was her, as he could taste the recognisable taint of her magic), his mind reinforced them automatically, knowing that even the slightest breach there would see his body dead in less than a split second.

On the move from one of the few beings here that he actually feared, due mainly to her unpredictable nature and the fact that she'd slain his father, the dark lord of this diabolical force cast nagas out of the way, hurling some into his pursuer's path hoping to gain just a little more distance in an effort to mount a defence, or even better, an attack.

Sprinting after him, deflecting unusual magic out of the way with one hand, zinging off offensive mantras with the other, hoping to get lucky and hit a vital organ, Richie laughed inside at just what a coward he was, fleeing as soon as he recognised that it was her.

'What a gutless cockwomble,' she thought. There was no chance of a change of ownership of the planet while she still breathed. That would only happen over her dead body. Gaining traction, and more importantly momentum, the lacrosse ace poured on the speed, smashing more of the slippery cobra-like beasts out of the way, looking to avenge the one she loved, ready to give everything she had to finish off this monster. If Manson hadn't realised he was in trouble before, he certainly did now.

"Why do you resist?" she hollered. "All I want to do is talk."

"You've had plenty of chances to talk. When I was chained up to Tim in the council building, for example, when you held us both precariously over the drop earlier on, or my personal favourite, when you tried to kill me with your magic. What happened to talking then?"

Totally unable to understand his position, blinded by her madness and convinced the revelation that she was his mother would bring him around to her point of view, she continued, failure not even an option.

"You'll only hurt yourself if you continue to cast mantra after mantra at me. Nobody wants that, do they?"

"What the hell are you talking about, you psychotic witch?" he bellowed, absolutely bewildered at what on earth was going on. At first he'd thought she was just playing with or teasing her prey, making the kill that much more appetising, but something else, something odd was going on with her. For the life of him, he couldn't figure out what it was.

Fluttering one eyelid open was the single most painful experience he'd ever had, and there'd been a lot of those during his career. Things were a blur, whether from some damage to his eye or from the pain receptors across the whole of his body crying out in absolute agony simultaneously. For whatever reason, he couldn't focus in on anything or anyone. But his hearing... well, his hearing was fine, and that was just dandy. Continually blinking his eyelid in the hope that his vision would clear up by itself, using what little control remained, he started to filter out all the noises of the surrounding battle. Magic... that was first to go, with the sounds of explosions, high pitched whines of the supernatural cutting through the air as well as the harsh crackling of much more personal power. Using his mind as the filter, things around him became much clearer after that. Still though, it wasn't enough. Next, the flapping of wings, something that unsurprisingly seemed like the biggest background noise of the lot and considering the number of dragons in the air, was probably about right. After that, the extraordinary had to be dealt with... footsteps, of which there weren't many, the slippery, slithering movements of the nagas, of which there were lots, but that didn't count for much because the noise itself was tiny in comparison with everything else. And finally the harshest regular noise of all, that reverberated like a gong being hit in a cathedral... the clash of blades, no doubt those huge matt black bastard swords that he'd seen most of the enemy carrying, dragons and nagas alike. After that, like an old friend who'd accompanied you everywhere for decades, the quiet ebb of silence softly caressed his earlobes, soothing the throbbing of his head and the aching of his bones. And then suddenly it was all interrupted by a bone chilling voice, one that had haunted his dreams, one that was up to no good, one that he'd longed to rid the world of, the same one that had inflicted all this damage upon him.

"Despite what you think, I don't want to hurt you, and you don't know the truth," Earth went on, the space all around them clear of any enemies, and even the tiniest spark of ethereal energy.

A matter of a few metres behind Peter, shielded by his grandson's dragon form, Fredric's body twitched uncontrollably, his one eye determined to try and focus in on what was playing out, what he was hearing almost driving him insane, already able to guess with whom she was talking... HER SON!

"You're lying!" Peter spat back at her, venom in his voice.

'Good boy,' thought Fredric, 'good boy.'

"I could kill you here and now if I wanted to."

"Go on then," the young hockey player urged.

'Easy son, easy, you don't want to provoke her too much. She's about as mad as a porcupine stuck to a dartboard,' Fredric wanted to say, but was too busy trying to heal up his dire wounds.

"You want me to kill you?"

"That's what you've wanted to do to me from the start, ever since your dick of a husband introduced us. Why not just get on and do it, if that's your intention?"

With the craziness drifting in and out, the mere mention of the word husband had confusion running rife deep within Earth's fragile mind, immediately mixing up Manson with her actual husband, the one who'd died when what remained of the dragon squad pulled him over the side of that cliff on the Welsh coastline all those decades ago.

'How did he introduce us?' she wondered, totally mixed up. 'Surely that's not possible.' Of course it wasn't, and Peter had been referring to the being he hated and feared the most... Manson. With the kind of history that they shared, it wasn't hard to fathom why. What was difficult to come to terms with was how these two deranged killers had got together in the first place.

'Is there an app for that?' he thought. 'Instakiller, Bitter or Psychobook maybe?'

Thoughts of the past and present merging into one, Earth was little use to anyone for the time being, something that benefitted Peter and Fredric given their precarious positions. If insanity and madness rocked up any time soon though, they'd both be in a huge amount of danger.

Feeling a little claustrophobic with the sheer amount of nagas Manson was leading her into, Richie felt as though she needed something to clear the way, and so much like the dreaded new queen of this world, delved back into the past for something that she'd come up with in the time towards the end of her nursery ring stint.

In a lesson designed to prove their mantra knowledge and get them thinking outside the box, the young dragons were tested almost to breaking point. Of course, as usual, it was the young lacrosse playing dragon that had come up trumps, taking snippets out of four mantras, designing one that produced an ethereal flying frisbee that when tossed was large and powerful enough to topple adult dragons if they weren't paying enough attention. Pleased with the idea of invoking something from the classroom, and having already trialled it to destruction all that time ago, sprinting after her chicken of an opponent, she attached most of her willpower, whispered the words in her mind and waited for her new toy to materialise in her hand. Sure enough it did, in the form of a huge, metallic, shiny, silver circle with the letters R.I.B. emboldened brightly on one side. What do they stand for, I hear you ask? Richie Is Best, obviously.

Keeping a mental tether attached, the confident young lacrosse playing dragon added all the resolve she could spare and launched the beast of a frisbee out in front of her, watching as it took the first naga, about to try and stop her, immediately in the throat, throwing him back out of the way with some force, before rebounding off and taking out another, and yet one more after that. With barely a thought, and through an ever changing battlefield, it returned straight to her hand. Rid of three of the enemy in the blink of an eye, pulling her right arm back as far as it would go, ducking her head out of the way of magical missiles and stray bursts of the supernatural, sprinting all the time, Richie once again launched it out in front of her. Again it downed another three, after that four more, after that two more. On and on it went, with the scaredy-cat Manson fast running out of allies to throw to the wolves.

Reversing the glinting golden blade, George stabbed it straight into the neck of the naga that had been about to attack him with a wave of magic that instantly disappeared the moment it died. Watching it slump to the floor, amazed that none of the other beasts were in the immediate vicinity, he took a breath, wondering how they were doing as a force, scared to reach out with his mind for fear of the enemy either intercepting his communication or breaching the fortress of his thoughts. Remaining ignorant of the bigger picture, he glanced around to see what he could do next. Across the way, between the bodies of half a dozen nagas, he saw it and his blood turned cold... the family reunion from hell looked as though it was just getting started, with the dreaded witch facing off with Peter, her unwitting son. And then, lying there beside the hole that the giant column of flame had appeared from, he spotted him, Fredric, his best friend, parts of his body scorched and burnt, tiny wisps of steam rising into the air from the crackling flesh of his exposed arms.

'NOOOOOOO!' bellowed his mind, terrified of losing his brother in arms once again, but that was soon replaced by the cool, calm persona of the king, knowing that full blown panic would not help his pal in the least. He needed a plan, and right there and then he came up with one. It did all depend though, on exactly how badly Fredric had been hurt.

Magically enthralled nagas dropped like dominoes as Richie chased Manson across the battlefield, taking out them, and the occasional dark dragon, in the air with her ethereal frisbee that knew no bounds, able to wound, maim and even on a couple of occasions kill, with exactly the right aim and determination behind it. All the time though, pursuing the evil leader of the dark dragons and nagas, spitting raging lightning from her fingers, attempting to overload his will with hers, peppering his legs with explosive fragments of marble from the ground, willing him to stop, turn around and face her, so that it could be over and done with, she conceded no ground, never gave up, kept on relentlessly coming and coming. But like a child's game of chase, neither knew when it was over, Manson fearful of Richie, especially after having expended a great deal of his gift against the dragon king, the lacrosse star ignoring all the other perils around her, potentially putting herself in danger in the hope of gaining revenge for Tim's tragic death. How long it could last was anyone's guess, but the longer it went on, the more dangerous it became for both of them. Who would outlive the other might well come down more to luck than judgement.

Earth's Surface. The Black Forest, Germany.
Day had turned back into night, the gorgeous body of water only a short distance away taking on a slick, dark, bottomless sheen, the stars barely visible through the canopy of trees. None of that mattered though to the beings there, with only one thought, one mission on their minds... to break into the huge, black cube that they'd been reliably informed was full to the brim with laminium, the most valuable material in the world to any and all dragons because of the supernatural properties it had been imbued with and for what an experienced magic user could accomplish with it.

Working throughout the day, not needing to stop for rest or refreshments, the nagas had ploughed on with their unusual magic scanning and probing, occasionally doing a little more than that, drilling with microscopic filaments of brightly tinged ethereal energy, gauging thickness, strength and capacity. It was painstaking work, but that was why they'd been brought in. Supposedly the best of the best, they would, at least it was assumed, get the job done.

Finally, late in the evening, the disguised reptilians broke off and leaving the cube alone, headed straight for the shadowy cold water, some diving straight in fully clothed, not caring about the consequences, most preferring to strip off before taking the plunge, immediately transforming back into their snake-like bodies as soon as they found themselves beneath the surface. For them it was cathartic, a way to de-stress and unwind, ridding themselves of the unwanted tensions of the day. Some chased fish, wolfing them down instantly on catching their prey, for others it was just a case of enjoying being back in their natural form, a transformation which seemed to happen less and less for most, with their king captured and held to ransom. Doing the evil dragon's bidding was becoming more and more complicated and overwhelming, their race achieving very little else but following the instructions of the mad dragon in charge. And of course lately that had included some of them becoming magically enthralled, an event that had spread through the naga grapevine telepathically, a rumour that most of them had dark misgivings about. After half an hour or so, they all met up on the lake bed, far beneath the surface, each absorbing and enjoying being surrounded by the cool, fresh water, a constant reminder of their true home, something that wasn't wasted on any of them. After a few moments of sharing their complaints about their supposed dragon comrades, some whining about their king never really coming back, they turned their attention once again to the problem at hand... the cube, and how best to break into it.

In the forest, despite patrolling the perimeter, the dark and unruly dragons questioned the loyalty of their naga companions across their closely guarded private telepathic link, concerned by their sudden insistence to go for a dip in the lake. Of course it could have just been blowing off steam, which was understandable, but just perhaps there was more to it than that. Either way, they all vowed to keep a much closer eye on them.

28 BETTER LATE THAN NEVER

Roundabout would be the best way to describe the route that they'd traversed in order to reach the shadowy confines surrounding the blood soaked square that lined the front of the council building in the suburb of Buckingham, numerous cadavers and extraneous body parts from dragons and nagas alike littering the famous plaza.

Looking out from a stairwell cloaked in darkness from beside an abandoned multi-storey building, the dragons and humans of the group remained deathly silent now that they'd arrived at their destination, all of them having been briefed on exactly how dangerous it might be.

Wondering if they'd done the right thing in leaving Salisbridge and coming here, Polo pushed her concerns aside, knowing that it was far too late to back out now and spoke to the human leader, the one known as Garrett.

"What do you think? Do you want to go in?" she whispered. "It'll be all or nothing. There's simply no middle ground on this. There could be a thousand of them waiting for us in there."

A fleeting look at the others told him all he needed to know.

"We're in," he announced. "How do you want to do this?"

"I suggest we go as one group, in as tight a formation as possible. Keep your weapons ready, but please don't fire them unless any of the dragons here engage an enemy. Even with the suppressors on, the guns will still make enough noise to warn the enemy. If we're to have any possibility of success, the element of surprise has got to be our biggest card. Without that, I truly believe we stand no chance at all."

"Understood," replied the 'bald eagle' softly. "Lead the way."

Tentatively slipping out of the shadows and into the square proper, Polo half expected to be either cut down or surrounded in a matter of seconds. Unlike Tank's group earlier on in the day, most of which lay dead in front of them, they seemed to have gained safe passage, with absolutely no other beings around. It was eerily quiet, apart from the bubbling of the lava pools on each side of the humungous steps as they strode up them, something of a challenge for all the humans, not least Garrett himself. Slipping through the giant entrance, the dragons all crouching down, magic readied, the humans having engaged the safety switch on their weapons in case any of the frayed nerves should get the better of them, as a group they crawled along at a snail's pace, Polo and one of the other prehistoric monsters reaching out with their minds in an effort to ascertain where everyone else was. For now it was clear, and so consulting a rather busted monitor to find the best route to the bridge that led directly to the king's private residence, they regrouped and continued their journey, humans and dragons alike totally and utterly terrified.

Much like Polo and Garrett's little group, Gee Tee and those under him were finding it slow going in their efforts to head deeper into the building that housed the crystal node which should hopefully be able to restore worldwide communications as well as reunite them with their friends, Steel, Jar Man and DomCon. Every being so far had performed admirably in staving off the sneak attacks of rogue dark dragons that hadn't been killed by the mantra that had annihilated most of the dreaded naga force, particularly the humans who'd had more than one occasion to use the grenades that they'd held on to since the battle in the Salisbridge market place. Over a dozen so far, that's how many they'd encountered and vanquished, the master mantra maker himself destroying the last one with a quick and deadly psionic attack that shattered the being's mental defences and mashed his brain instantly, waterfalls of blood running out of his eyes, thick puffs of smoke exiting his ears. Not for the first time, the human contingent had to hang on tight to their stomachs for fear of shaming themselves alongside their dragon comrades. It was tough... fighting and killing always were, with the individual battles more unseemly than two groups going at it hammer and tongs. To their credit though, the humans held their nausea in check, and as every moment passed, were going up ever more in the estimation of those with wings all around them. Slowly, they crept forward, Gee Tee figuring there couldn't be many more defensive lines to cross, or fortified gateways to break down. Soon, he knew, they would be at the crystal node and not only would he be able to get the word out to the rest of the planet as to what had gone on here in the capital, but he would also be able to unleash his spell, the one that he and Tank had spliced together on that stunningly memorable night, the one that should neutralise their enemy across the planet both above and below ground. If he could do that, then it might just help his pals, wherever they were and whatever they were up to. If only he knew.

A short way further inside, the three friends, Steel, Jar Man and DomCon had the grim task of checking the bodies of their enemies, making sure that there were no survivors, no surprises waiting to happen. It was something they did as a three, each providing support for the others, each ready to act at the first sign of something untoward. So far it had just been grim... searching through the remnants of the nagas, kicking away severed tails, searching through body parts, trying to give some dignity to those good dragons that worked here and that had been killed at the start when all this had kicked off. Clearly they'd been taken by surprise, not one of them either defending themselves from what they could tell or even having a chance to fight back. Whatever had gone on, it had almost certainly involved a deception of the highest order to fool this number of clever beings all at once. Jar Man wondered what it could have been. Steel focused on checking the bodies, making sure nothing was left alive. Thoughts of revenge circled

DomCon's mind, wanting the chance to find one of them still breathing, knowing exactly what he'd do to them, or at least thinking that he did, because despite his rather tough exterior and dour outward appearance, he was a decent dragon, with a huge sense of right or wrong and honourable to a tee. Almost certainly he would never have followed through on the dark thoughts he was having.

In one giant kick, born of frustration, almost as if converting a try on a rugby pitch, the diminutive dragon punted a sliced up naga tail off into the next room, a trail of blood flicking up the wall beside all three of them, the slippery body part landing with an echoing SQUELCH off in the distance.

"Show some respect," demanded Jar Man.

"WHAT? To these things... NEVER!"

"Not to them... but for the good dragons that were taken away from us here. Look at them all around you. Do you really think they'd want you desecrating this place with their bodies still here? NO! They wouldn't, as well you know. We both understand and share your frustration, but this is not the way to deal with it. Okay?"

"I'm sorry," he mumbled.

"Don't be sorry," added Steel, "you did your job valiantly. Everyone should be proud of what we've achieved. It's just a shame that it's come too late for all of them. Hopefully though, if we can clear things up and get Gee Tee in here, then it might not be too late for the rest of the planet. That's what we have to focus on now, that has to be our main cause for concern."

Both nodding their agreement, the two friends knew that Steel was right. And so they continued on with their checking, leaving no stone or tail unturned, however small.

That might have been the case, but in one last bold move, evil had used its experience and the remainder of its magic to take a seat close to the crystal node and in an extraordinary turn of events, had transformed from a red headed human, into a plain dragon operator at one of the empty terminals. Slumping forward, placing her head against the monitor, Red slowed her breathing and patiently began to wait for her one opportunity to exact revenge. It wouldn't be pretty and she didn't expect to live, but it would be effective and it would damage the enemy force beyond repair, of that she was convinced.

29 A SUDDEN TURNAROUND

Sprinting for all she was worth, too scared to look over her shoulder, all she concentrated on was what was in front, and that was Yoyo and his charges battling in a huge circle, fending off dragons above and nagas below. From behind their defences, Janice caught the eye of one of the youngsters. Immediately a huge smile crossed her scaled face. Noting that she'd gotten her attention, she winked and then inclined her head as if to say,

"This way." The young bar worker didn't need to be told twice, and although already puffing, put on the biggest burst of speed she could and headed towards what she hoped would be safety, however temporary that might be.

Of course Yoyo had seen her coming from some way off. Who wouldn't, with that amount of magic and experience, especially with that devilish, frost enshrouded sword carving her a path, fending off enemies from the front, from the rear and in the air?

'Whatever mysterious force controls that thing should not only be thanked but given some kind of prize or recompense and a title.' Yes, that's right, he could remember a time long, long ago when titles were given out as a reward for great service or immense courage. Not now though, so it could never happen. 'Perhaps,' he thought, his mind wandering, 'the king might like to bring that one back.' On spotting Janice, Peter's friend (there was something else going on there, he was sure, but he most certainly wasn't going to be the one to speak up about it, especially after Fredric's outburst about humans being down here in the first place. It wasn't any of his business and so he remained determined not to get involved) he gave Wiz a gentle nudge, letting her know that she should get the young human back here behind the limited protection of their melded shields, pronto.

And so that's what she did. Blasting a dazzling bolt of

sickly brown magic straight through an attacking naga's right eye, watching it tremble uncontrollably as it slumped to the floor, the cagey young dragon, one of Yoyo's best, dropped her personal magical barrier and stepped aside, allowing Janice to sprint in without changing direction or breaking stride.

"Huh... huhhh... huh... huhhh... huh... huhhh... thanks," declared Janice breathing heavier than a nuisance caller.

"You're very welcome, short stuff," replied Wiz, reassembling her shield just in time to counteract an angry naga, out to take revenge for the death of his friend.

"We're glad you're safe, youngster," said Yoyo from in the middle of them all. "You're lucky to have your friend watching your back. Are you still in control of it?"

"Thanks for taking me in, so to speak," Janice added. "And just to let you know, Fu-ts'ang likes to be referred to as 'he' and is a master weapon smith from many thousands of years ago. While we were linked much earlier on, since he's come back from the dead it would appear that he doesn't need me to guide him on his way. So anything I can do here to help out, please just say the word."

"Amazing!" stated Yoyo, marvelling at Janice's revelation about the frost enshrouded weapon. "Your experience from earlier on in the battle might well prove to be invaluable at some point, my dear, especially given the results that the two of you achieved, something that didn't go unnoticed by us, but for now, if you can keep a look out, whether through your friend's eyes, if that's at all possible, or your own. Anything out of the ordinary or unusual, a sneak attack or some magic we're not paying attention to, just shout it out and as a group we'll get on it. Things, right now, seem to be going much more our way."

'Out of the ordinary,' Janice thought wide-eyed, glancing around, trying to take it all in through the haze and smog of exploding magic. 'Everything that's going on here is... OUT OF THE ORDINARY!' Closing her eyes and reaching out for her flying, scything, ice cold partner, she hoped he'd let her see the battlefield through his eyes once again.

Close by, Vasuki, former Antarctic captive and king of the nagas, was relying on his warrior prowess to take down dozens of his own kind, all intent on killing him because of their supernatural enthrallment for which there seemed to be no cure. Every time he sent one tumbling off into the afterlife it broke his heart, almost literally, a deafening sadness overtaking the whole of his body, the pain so bad, he felt as though it would plague him forever through every moment of his waking dreams. Slithering sideways at the last moment whilst almost doubling over on himself from his chest upwards to avoid what would have been a decapitating strike from one of his own, exerting his powerful will, he crushed his opponent's mind and watched helplessly as the body dropped to the floor with a THUNK, blood and brain matter leaking from the gills on either side. With not even a moment to spare, whirling around full circle to slap another of his kind in the chest with his mighty tail, the courageous naga king whispered a heartfelt, *"sorry,"* deep within the confines of his mind, once again vowing to take down those responsible for this despicable turn of events. Dishing out frost against poison, and lightning against frost, Vasuki, a little of his magic replenished, continued what he regarded as a wicked course of action, determined to do the decent thing by his new found allies, knowing above all, that he was doing the RIGHT thing. How long his resolve could last though, was anybody's guess.

"Watch out!" The words escaped Flash's lips like a butterfly carried on the breeze, gently ebbing through the air towards their intended target.

Adjusting the grip on her sword, kicking away the head of one sneaky naga trying to bite her somewhere below the knee, Amelia Battlehard stabbed at the wings of a dark dragon who'd swooped in from nowhere, looking to blast them with a fireball or two, and replied to her co-

conspirator.

"Thanks... but I've got it. Concentrate on your own targets."

Flash smirked briefly at the formality of the reply, but nobody would or could have picked it up, not in the midst of the fighting and the bedlam. Well and truly told, and loving every minute of fighting alongside her, back to back, however you like to think of it, the ex-Crimson Guard was well and truly caught up in what he was doing, to the detriment of everything else. They were, however, for the first time since this all started, making some headway against the evil serpent-like monsters and their cohorts in the air. It was slow going though.

Sparks flew off her blade as it clashed with one belonging to a golden, green and purpled hued dark dragon that had dropped from the air but a moment ago. Duelling like this was so primitive, or at least that's what she'd been led to believe by all her instructors at the academy, and although there might be something to that, it didn't tell the whole story. Raw and full of emotions, that's how it felt to her, able to feel every slight contact of the blade, even the tiniest of taps and grazes. It felt subtle, even the heaviest of blows, the equivalent of a dance if you like. Turning the protruding cutting edge away with but a flick of her wrist, she dived in, lunging for the beast's kidney, knowing that whatever dark magic the sword had been imbued with would almost certainly pierce the scales protecting the vital organ and inflict a devastating blow. Abruptly her weapon was hacked away in a spirited attack brought on by panic, something she would recognise anywhere. Continually probing her adversary mentally, she steeled her resolve and with a couple of choice words and just a dribble of her magic, yanked the dragon's blade free, sending it hurtling directly into the face of an onrushing naga that had wanted to take her by surprise.

'Amateur,' she thought, as the monster crumpled to the floor. Side on, one foot in front of the other, all that was missing was her free hand on her hip, Captain Battlehard closed in on the terror stricken dragon and distracting him with the tiniest explosion in the world, just behind his left ear, lunged forward and sliced open his belly, looking on as an array of guts and blood splattered all over the floor.

'One down, only another hundred or so to go... great,' she mused, diving in against the next one, all the time intrigued by the ex-Crimson Guard fighting beside her, having heard much about him, most of which was true by the look of things. As the combat continued at a furious pace, their partnership became more dependent, more... personal.

Hidden behind a clump of naga corpses, occasionally batting away stray darts of mislaid magic, often now killing from a distance with but a word or two, George had slithered across the ground on his belly to get a better view of what was going on between Peter and Earth, his thoughts with the young dragon, even if he wasn't. Assuming because there was more of a discussion than a fight going on, that Fredric's grandson would be safe at least for the time being, his mind turned in another direction. Concerned for his newly returned best friend lying on the floor in quite a state, from his position not too far away, he wondered what he could and should do. Despite Peter's body standing between Earth and his grandfather, there was no way for him to get over there without Manson's queen spotting him. And that left... WHAT? He didn't know, but he'd have to come up with something soon.

"My dick of a husband, as you so charmingly put it, will rule the world in ways you can't possibly imagine, running it smoothly, without any fuss and for the benefit of all. Sure, there will be some changes and the humans won't have the same amount of autonomy that they have now, but for the most part they will experience little disruption to begin with. I don't really see what all the fuss is about. Essentially it will be more of the same, with humans now knowing exactly who is in charge instead of all this hiding in plain sight crap. Most of them will probably be glad to have their eyes opened to such things."

Stunned by the words, wondering how any being could be so blind to what was really happening or whether or not she actually believed what she said, deep inside his mind, Peter searched his relatively limited repository of magic for anything that would be helpful or get him and his grandfather out of the sights of the evil woman, dragon, whatever she was, standing directly in front of him. All he knew for sure was that he wasn't moving a muscle. She'd have to get to Fredric over his cold, dead body, something he knew she'd have no compunction about doing.

Coming up short in the mantra department, briefly he wondered whether or not he should shout out telepathically for help. But who could he call? There was no one in his eye line that could help, and he was quite sure, even though the enemy numbers were clearly dropping, that his friends would still very much have their hands full. All he could do for the moment was keep her talking and buy as much time as he could for both him and his grandfather. And so he did.

"It sounds like this has all been a long time in the planning and well thought through..."

Trying to defend and attack simultaneously, whilst squadrons of fire breathing gnats peppered him with stinging, fiery flame, all the time aiming for his eyes, something he sought to protect above everything else at the moment, Tank let rip with a cold mantra, one that had giant icicles crashing down from up above, hoping it would at least buy him some time. It did, working about as successfully as he could have hoped, piercing two of the scorpion men, one straight through the chest, ending his life instantly, the other through part of his thick black body causing him to cry out in pain, all six legs wriggling uncontrollably, not able to go anywhere because the tip of the icicle in question had buried itself straight into the marble flooring.

No time to lose, tumbling head over heels off to one side at right angles to his previous trajectory, the rugby playing dragon thumped a vampiric lizard, mouth wide open, no doubt about to discharge a brilliant surge of lightning straight in the head as he passed, taking it out of the fight, one less enemy to worry about. Unfortunately for him, there were still a great many left.

Out from behind a dark dragon stranded on the ground, due mainly to several rips through his left wing membrane, a target for a number of the mythical creatures, leapt a snarling blue maned wolf baring its fangs, clearly intent on taking down Tank, the smell of the magic wafting off For'son driving it crazy. Slathering uncontrollably and growling with ferocious intent, this was an animal not to be messed with in any way, shape or form, something the consciousnesses of both beings realised immediately.

"*Blast it and run,*" cut in For'son.

"*I might be able to reason with it,*" replied Tank, ever the optimist and dead certain of his ability to empathise and understand anything plant or animal.

"*That won't work!*" stated the mysterious loop. "*This isn't one of your nursery ring projects. These creatures are the worst of the worst the world has ever known. Mythical doesn't do them justice... it should be more like homicidal. You will not be able to negotiate with them, especially if the ra-hoon have any sort of control. Zap them with some magic and let's high tail it back to somewhere safer.*"

"*And just where would that be?*" asked the rugby playing dragon, scanning everything around him.

A brilliant, fluorescent green, sickly salvo of bolts lancing out of her hand tore up the marble behind him in an arc, only centimetres away from his ankle, shrapnel from the floor nicking his lower leg and calf as they continued to run. He had stamina, she'd give him that, but once the young lacrosse player had him in her sights, there was simply no getting away. At some point he'd have to turn and fight, and when he did, there'd be hell to pay.

Panting heavily, even enhanced by his magic, he felt every bit his age as he dodged and weaved through the dark force that was supposedly his to command. Having thrown everything at her, including quite a few of his troops, she just kept coming and coming, like a bloodhound on the scent, seemingly nothing putting her off. And so it was, with his heart pumping like an overworked and under oxygenated car at altitude, his hands and arms shaking and the mother of all headaches thumping across his temporal lobe, he skidded to a halt behind two confused looking nagas, reinforced the magical barrier around him and prepared to unleash everything he had in an effort to wipe the cocky smile off the face of the arrogant lacrosse player that he despised so much. Waiting for her to swim into view, his customary smug expression dominated his features as the nagas beside him readied their unusual magic.

Normally something she only felt on the lacrosse pitch, it was odd that the tingling in her legs and the nagging sensation in her gut should show up here and now. The feeling was one she always listened to when she played, the one that had always led her to personal glory and had never, not once steered her wrong.

'What the hell is it trying to tell me now?' she wondered, applying the brakes just a little, her prey slipping around the corner of a group of nagas all facing the other way. With a split second to determine what was going on inside her now fully human body, the dragon within her roared that she was in danger with an intuition that was hard to ignore. And so instead of flying around the pack of slippery serpents at full speed, she slid to a stop and, crushing a couple of windpipes with only a handful of words and a smidgen of dragon power, momentarily considered her next move.

Standing in the middle of a three, two of his enthralled nagas either side, their dark, devious supernatural power flickering off their tiny fingers, heads weaving this way and that almost in time, Manson knew beyond a doubt they had enough between them to take down the annoying lacrosse player, whatever she countered with. Feeling more than a little arrogant himself, the darkest magic he knew gathered itself in his hands, shadowy swirling tendrils whipping through his fingers, just itching to be released into the air in an effort to seek out their target. Much like the twisted ethereal energy that had destroyed Flash's leg, the one Yoyo had to replace using the mana from the laminium chains, a small part of the sinister power the dark leader had ready had a sliver of sentience to it, and would seek out its objective no matter what. Things were looking up for the dark side.

Wrong and malevolent was how it felt beyond what she could see, and where Manson had disappeared to but a moment ago. Every one of her instincts screamed out not to go in that direction, but the thirst for revenge that had built up inside her since the love of her life had been torn in two by the sadistic monster known as Troydenn was as compelling as it was overwhelming, something she could only rally against for a short time. If it looked like a trap, she thought, and smelled like a trap, then almost certainly it was a trap, but that wouldn't stop her. Taking in her surroundings, the de facto leader and out of the box thinker Richie Rump came up with a plan to get her hands around Manson's scrawny neck once and for all.

Closing off a tiny part of his consciousness so that, hopefully, For'son couldn't detect what he was doing, Tank let his mind flow out towards the snarling asena, sending messages of calm directly at it in the hope of pacifying and reasoning with it. Slowly its growling became less aggressive, its grimace turning to a look of confusion. Overly pleased with himself at having got through and achieved what For'son had said was impossible, abruptly their miniscule contact was broken, the snarl on the creature's face returning with a vengeance and, with a heart freezing growl, the beast leapt towards Tank's exposed neck for all it was worth.

Caught off guard, unable to move, the young rugby playing dragon became abruptly aware of just how much danger he was in as the silky form of the vicious beast hurtled through the air towards him, its blue mane ruffling in the light breeze that meandered through the king's private residence. Thoughts of failure and letting his friends and the world down played through the youngster's mind as the razor sharp claws and gnashing incisors came ever closer.

Suddenly a burst of intense heat from in and around his index finger caused him to wince in pain, almost bringing tears to his eyes. That was nothing to what it had done to the asena though. Using an extraordinary amount of power to directly use a spell, instead of going through a host, For'son had whipped up a laser-like burst of intense heat to carve the mythical monster in two, straight from the metallic band that he was encased in through no fault of his own. The skin around Tank's finger was black and charred and hurt like hell, something that took his mind off the two huge THUNKS as either half of the animal crashed to the ground.

"You're welcome," stated For'son forensically. *"NOW, can we get the hell out of here?"*

Setting on fire a few of the nagas off to one side with an explosive detonation that not only burned hot, but sent sparkling embers shooting out in all directions, spreading panic, confusion and chaos, just as it had been designed to do, Richie reached out with her mind, intent on getting a picture of exactly what was going on all around her, especially in the air. Most certainly quieter now, there were still a good number of dark dragons about, keen to destroy either Flash and Captain Battlehard or the remaining group of King's Guards, off to one side of Yoyo and his charges. And then, out of nowhere, she spotted what she needed... a dark dragon, bathed in brown, tail waving like a giant rudder, banking around, wings outstretched, heading her way, only a couple of metres above her head. Filling her muscles with ethereal energy, whilst at the same time taking down a couple of nagas behind her, severing their vertebrae with but a few powerful words, bending her knees, she crouched down momentarily, waiting for the opportunity that she knew was only a moment or so away.

Giant wings flapping gracefully as it cut its way through the thick, smoky, magic filled air of the king's private residence, the deranged dark dragon that Richie had spotted had its sights set on Flash some way off in the distance, at the cost of everything going on around it. Consumed with rage, desperate to fulfil its pledge, it didn't feel a thing when just the tiniest bit of extra weight attached itself to the talons that were tucked firmly away beneath its streamlined body, as it zipped across the battlefield. Had it been paying more attention, it most certainly would have noticed the delicate, lithe form of the lacrosse playing dragon hitching a ride for but a few seconds, swinging precariously from one of the talons on its right foot, barely managing to hold on by one hand. It was unconventional, inspirational and downright dangerous. But it was all that she had. Would it work? She was about to find out.

Exquisite pain agonisingly tore at every atom of his body, rendering his mind useless, well... NEARLY! If not for his training and experience, that most certainly would have been the case, but over the course of his life he'd come to be regarded, quite rightly, as one of the most powerful beings on the planet. Not for some time of course, due to his unfortunate incarceration, but that didn't change things... oh no. If anything it played to his advantage. Having missed out on so much, he wanted to live, make up for lost time, catch up with those he loved, as well as savour the sweet taste of revenge against those that had captured and contained him, putting the lives of people he cared about in danger. Giving up was not an option, not as far as he was concerned. And so with that in mind, almost on autopilot, his body gave itself over to his magic, letting the supernatural power heal and repair, soothe and restore. Unfortunately for him, because of the terrifying damage his daughter's magical trap had inflicted, it was incredibly slow going, the aching pain unable to be resolved, his mind barricaded against the latest threat to his sanity, a huge chunk of him wanting nothing more than for it to be over. None of this helped his healing efforts, quite the opposite in fact. And the conversation playing out within earshot did nothing but chill him to the bone, once again taking away from his ability to cure any and all of the damage that had been done. Still trying to focus on something, anything, in an effort to get his vision to work, very slowly something fifteen or so metres away swam into view, the strangely familiar blur's features sluggishly resolving into focus. Goosebumps pricked the burnt flesh on his arms, causing indiscriminate pain to flare up inside him, only this time in a good way. For a moment he felt alive, once again filled with hope despite his catastrophic injuries. What had caused this turnaround? The sight of his best friend, the one he regarded as a brother no less, flat on the floor, giving him the mother of all winks. In that instant, he knew he'd get one more chance, knew that things weren't quite over for him. Knowing what he had to do, he plucked up all his resolve and realising that it would cause him a mind bending amount of pain, he closed his eyelid briefly before reopening it, staggered at just how much torture one tiny act could inflict. Withstanding the agony assaulting the whole of his body as best he could, he waited for his friend to act, knowing with absolute certainty that it would be sooner rather than later.

Feeling the chill from the cold, hard marble across the whole of his belly, peeking out from between two naga corpses, his desperate attempt to aid the dragon he thought of as his best friend had brought him to this... hiding amongst all the magical chaos and mayhem exploding across the building that he considered his own. Chastising himself for such thoughts, he once again winked at the being he considered his own kin, despite it not being truly so, hoping that this time there would be some response. Only then could he really act. It would be too dangerous to do so if Fredric's body remained motionless. Abruptly and almost imperceptibly, the founder of the Crimson Guards' head moved ever so slightly, as his left eye opened and closed.

'YES!' he thought, buoyed beyond belief at his friend's strength of will and ultimate refusal to die. Knowing what he had to do, and vaguely amused at returning that which was rightfully his, George crawled to his feet, focused fully on one of his friend's burnt and crisped hands, and using the magic inside him to make sure he got it just right, brought the laminium dagger back over his head, and with exactly the right amount of power and accuracy, tossed it towards his friend.

Bouncing, once, twice, three times before sliding to a halt directly in the grip of Fredric's right hand, the laminium dagger shone like a lighthouse in a raging storm in the dark of night, the jewels in its hilt glinting like treasure at the end of a rainbow.

"Uuuuuuhhhhhhhhh," moaned the founder of the Crimson Guards uncontrollably, his damaged and inert body still hidden from Earth's sight by Peter's dragon form.

Job done, at least for now, George knew better than to remain on his knees in the midst of all the fighting, knowing that somewhere amongst all this, one of his allies would no doubt need a helping hand. Saluting the still sizzling and burning body of his friend, mouthing him a silent, "Good luck," the present king of the dragon domain backflipped out of the way of a swooping dark beast whose talons were meant to carve open his exposed back, blasted him with a salvo of lightning, and without even watching him crash into a crowd of filthy looking nagas, hightailed it back towards the group of King's Guards, hoping to help them defend their position.

Even through rose tinted spectacles, she could sense something was wrong and that the boy dragon, whilst pretending to take an interest in everything that had gone on, was only really playing for time. This irked her a great deal, almost provoking her temper... almost, but not quite. What he was hoping to gain, she had absolutely no idea. Unfortunately neither did he.

"Surely there must be some sort of compromise? Fighting like this makes no sense, for either side," offered up Peter, mirroring Tank's words from earlier, his mind still whirling with all the possibilities, part of it still wondering why the evil witch right in front of him hadn't killed him yet.

"The world needs a change of guardianship. Too many have suffered at the hands of the current regime over millennia," she reflected dispassionately.

"There must have been another way to work out your grievances?" he remonstrated, probably just a little too much.

"What is it you're doing?" she asked, finally starting to run out of patience.

"You wanted to talk."

"I WANTED to tell you the truth!"

"I don't believe you. And you couldn't possibly know anyway. Why don't you go and find your despicable king and kowtow to his demands and do his bidding. You're a poor excuse for a dragon... you and that husband of yours."

Anger pulsed through her veins at being spoken to like that, but again that word... HUSBAND cast her mind off into the past, to better times, thoughts of what could have been swirling around inside her head, confusing and confounding, thoughts of how best to deal with the son she'd never known taking a back seat, at least for the time being. It was an odd standoff, one that Peter was still trying to figure out and make the best of. Even his inexperienced mind realised that he needed help and he needed it quick. Things, he knew, could change in the blink of an eye. But where assistance would come from he just couldn't fathom. As far as he knew, all his friends were some distance away, all doing their best to stay alive in their own personal battles. And so in an effort to distract her a little bit more, attempting to put her at ease, he quickly unlocked the bonds of his DNA in a desperate attempt to turn back into his human guise, something he was much more comfortable in, and he hoped presented as less threatening. It's not like he would have been able to do very much in his dragon form anyway, and at least this way he got to go out in the manner of his choosing. So, as the change occurred, he made one more minor readjustment, something that Tank had taught him in the privacy of his home, a little while after the event with the spider, the one where his friend had sat high up on the wall of the Mantra Emporium and watched him utterly humiliate himself in front of Gee Tee, by taking all of his clothes off before realising it was his human form that was causing offence, not his garments. His change that day had ruined most of what he'd been wearing, something that deeply amused his friend. And so, days later, Tank showed him how he could change between forms and still keep his dignity, and clothes, something that even the ex-Crimson Guard Flash, their friend, clearly didn't know, otherwise he would have used it when Richie allowed him to pass through their shield earlier, when he was carrying the unconscious body of Vasuki, the naga king. By adding just a couple of words, it was possible to add a set of apparel when changing from dragon to human and thus appear fully dressed, instead of very starkly naked. It was a neat trick and something he now nearly always used when transforming back that way, having a particular favourite always in mind... jeans, a light coloured t-shirt, socks, pants and shoes. And so it was now, with Earth, his mother, looking on, he morphed into the guise he favoured most, not really knowing why, but hoping against hope that it might help him in some way.

A boost didn't do it justice. It was intoxicating, mind blowing and familiar. Of course, apart from earlier on in the battle, he hadn't held the dagger that had once belonged to the famous dragon Aviva in many decades, but that didn't stop all the memories returning vividly, the most powerful of which was how he'd come across it in the first place. Visions of open topped jeeps bounding through the desert, careering over giant sand dunes, palm trees and pyramids in the background, crystal clear blue skies, radiant sunsets and the feeling of warm, fine sand trickling between his toes flooded back as the mantras he'd already cast were enacted with a vengeance by the mana that remained in the dagger. Healing dynamically with every second that passed, his body grew stronger and stronger. So did his mind. Egypt... it came to him out of nowhere.

'Of course,' he thought. 'One of the most beautiful and understated countries I've ever visited, and one I'd have returned to reside in if events had played out differently. But for me, they didn't, and as far as I'm concerned, there's simply no going back.' Memories of waking up beside a stunning oasis, cool, clear water quenching his thirst, so good it felt like the first drink he'd ever taken. Then a rush, but a rush to do what? A convoy of jeeps tracking through the desert until they arrived at somewhere... somewhere official. After that, storming a building with the other British soldiers, finding a treasure trove of artefacts being hoarded by those in power, hoping to squirrel away their newly acquired loot for their own devious purposes, paying no mind to the desperate needs of the Egyptian people's poverty or lack of resources. Travesty about summed it up, backed up by the anger and rage that he felt at the time. That came flooding back. An argument... a big one, between those in command of the British and the ever so clever looters who thought they were going to get away with everything. And then out of nowhere, an overwhelming sense of... POWER! Not power over people, or of a financial kind, but the sort only a dragon would recognise. Intoxicating... he could remember just how much. A wanting, no... a needing to have whatever that power was at any cost surged through him, almost knocking him to his knees. Using all his experience and talent, he remained standing, but it was a close call. Employing cunning and deception, he managed to persuade both sides to let him and his men rummage through all the goods... paintings, antiques, valuables in every shape and size. It was a hoard any dragon would have been proud of and one that would have made the dozen or so Egyptian officials wealthy beyond their dreams a dozen times over. Inspecting huge chests filled to the brim with mountains of coins and intricate jewellery, one ropey looking trunk gave him cause to stop. Whatever it was he could feel, it was coming from inside it, he was sure. Scooping out handfuls of gold medallions, tossing them casually over his shoulder, it was only when he caught the red glint of a gigantic ruby out of the corner of his eye that he stopped. Carefully, smoothing coins out of the way with the palm of his hand, he revealed enough of the object to pull it free from the rest of the treasure. Immediately he recognised it for what it was... Aviva's famed laminium dagger. It could be nothing else. With no one watching and using more than a little magical subterfuge, he let the authorities on both sides sort out the morality and finer aspects of what was going on there while he came away with the ultimate prize... the DAGGER!

Crisp, blackened skin shimmered as the change continued at pace, turning instantly pliable and pink, pain swapped for purpose, a return to normal gathering pace. Cells became reinvigorated, muscles charged, hair reimagined as every atom was repaired. It was an epic piece of healing, one that even Yoyo wouldn't have been able to perform, using skills known only to a few. To give you a clue, Flash might have known, depending on just how thorough his training had been. That's right, it was a Crimson Guard kind of thing. With death narrowly avoided once again, there was only one thing to do, and having taken note of everything that had gone on, he felt like now was the right time to intervene. Given that she clearly recognised Peter for exactly who and what he was, no more time could be wasted. It was the precise moment to put an end to this once and for all.

Trying to keep a lid on it had only made it worse, made it thirst to get out, the madness that is. And much like water, insanity will always find a way to leak through and wreak havoc. Here and now it had, and combined with her natural anger, thoughts of bringing her long lost son back on side were crumbling with every second that passed.

"You don't deserve to know the truth!" she spat, the crisscrossing purple lines seeming to stand out on her face as it contorted.

"I have little interest in what you have to say," stammered Peter, knowing that time was running out and that she was about to explode, no doubt with him being the target of her ire.

"I should kill you here and now!"

"Go on then," the hockey playing dragon taunted. "You've already tried once today and failed miserably. What makes you think you'd succeed a second time?"

If ever during the course of events and history there was a wrong thing to say, that was probably it. In a split second, the snarl on her features changed, madness flooded her face, a nervous tick developing above her left eye. Insanity had entered the building and had decided to throw a party.

Dark, dreadful, demonic magic ignited atop her fingertips, swirling, curling and whirling in and around the air surrounding her digits. Peter swallowed nervously, instantly regretting his words. Bravado wasn't his strong suit.

Taking one step closer, all the time playing with her magic, tossing it to and fro between both hands, the devilish witch of a dragon, besieged by lunacy, now wanted nothing more than to snuff out the life of the pathetic little wretch before her, ashamed that he was her spawn, humiliated by the thoughts she'd had of them reuniting and becoming a family. She would kill him here and now, nothing would or could stop her, of that she was sure. But before she did so, he would know the truth, something she knew would tear his insides apart.

"You WILL listen to what I have to say! Not only do I know the truth, but I *am* your truth, something that others have gone to great pains to hide."

'What the hell?' thought Peter, steadily backing away as quickly as he could.

"You've been lied to and manipulated by those around you, those that know what really happened and are too afraid to speak about it. Your grandfather wouldn't dare tell you, and no doubt his best buddy, the king, withheld all the crucial details. I can see now why he valued your life so highly, prized you enough to surrender and let all his defences down. Only you could do that. What a valuable hostage you were. All of this and my betrothed didn't have a clue. He's as much of a fool as you are."

'Mistaken identity,' was all that Peter could think of to justify everything she'd been spouting. Not only didn't he understand half of it, but it just didn't make sense, not to him anyway. And it showed across his naive young face. Well, it would do, wouldn't it? After all, he was as innocent as they come and hadn't a single clue about what she was talking about. Was his world about to end in more ways than one?

Abruptly it finished, the mana from the dagger having done everything asked of it by the mantras cast, with nothing more possible. Closing his fingers tightly around the hilt, his index finger gently caressing a perfectly carved emerald that he recognised from old, Fredric, the king's best friend, former Antarctic captive, founder of the Crimson Guards and of course Peter's grandfather, bounded to his feet, filled with as much supernatural power as was dragonly possible, and vowed to give his all to save his grandson from the nightmare that stood there before him. Up to that point, hidden only because of the proximity of his daughter to his now human shaped grandson, and having heard everything his despicable spawn had said, he figured it was time to announce his presence.

"I FIND IT IRONIC TO HEAR SOMEONE SO FOOLISH TALKING SO BRASHLY ABOUT FOOLS!" bellowed Fredric, startling Peter whilst raising Earth's hackles.

'GRANDFATHER!' thought Peter, relieved not only that Fredric was alive, but that help was now at hand.

Still toying with her dark and deadly supernatural power, Earth sidestepped so that she could take in the being she hated most on this godforsaken planet.

"Weeeellllll... look who it isn't, back from the dead. You have more lives than the luckiest cat. Thankfully you've nearly exhausted them all, of that I can assure you."

Fredric glared, whilst Peter remained almost between them both, now fully aware of two things. If they started to fight... he would be caught up between them, and that there was something else going on. Not sure what, he was aware there was some kind of familiarity that they both shared. For the very first time, there and then, he considered that the dragon witch's words might well not have been totally hollow.

"Isn't this nice?" declared Earth sarcastically, "a family reunion... what fun!"

Using the smallest steps possible, the hockey playing dragon tried to wriggle his way off to one side in an effort to get out from between them, figuring it was just a matter of time before it kicked off. A very tiny and hidden away part of his mind wondered why the hell she was going on about a family reunion. Of course it was... him and his grandfather.

Fury and resentment raged inside him as she laced her words with more than a hint of sarcasm. She'd always been good at that, he knew from firsthand experience, but here and now, he wondered exactly what she was up to. Nothing good, that was for sure. Determined to keep the truth from coming out, he wondered if the madness had consumed her enough that she would hurt her own son. From what he'd heard so far, it seemed that the answer to that would be no. But there were no guarantees, not here, not now and especially not with her, he knew. Readying everything he had, he prepared to intercede, his very first thought to protect the grandson he loved more than life itself.

Arcing wires of all colours sparked and spluttered, hanging through war torn holes in the ceiling above them as they continued on with their journey through the council building. Several times they'd encountered a dead end because of either a collapse of walls and/or floor, needing to turn around and take another route. It was becoming frustrating for them all, including Polo and the other prehistoric shapes, something that didn't bode well because it takes a lot to get dragons irritated, which just showed the stress they were all under. Turning yet another blind corner, on the lookout for enemy troops, they were greeted by one more wall of debris preventing them from going any further in that direction.

"DAMN!" murmured Polo under her breath.

"What is it?" asked Garrett coolly.

"There are several routes that lead out of the building to where we want to go. This was the only one we haven't tried. With our way blocked, I have no idea how to get us into the king's private residence."

Humans fingered the triggers on their NGSARs in total and utter silence, the individuals amongst them all wondering what to do next.

"What if we continue on up?" suggested Nexus.

"With a view to doing what?" asked Polo.

"You took the word right out of my mouth... view," continued Nexus. If we go up, even just a couple of floors, we may not be able to get out and access the private residence, but we might be able to see what's going on and assess the situation. So far we've come across nothing but destruction, but if we can get a handle on what's happening, it makes our position stronger and we might even be able to formulate a plan that will help the others out, should they still be alive."

"I knew there was a reason we brought you along... not

just a pretty face," exclaimed Polo, running her tiny warm hands across her comrade's prehistoric jaw line. "What do you think Garrett?"

"Sound like a plan to me. Anything we can do that gains us more insight would always be welcome."

Accessing the council building plans from her eidetic memory, Polo led the way, softly plodding back around the corner, following the same route they'd come in by, heading for a stairwell in the diagonally opposite corner to the one in which they stood, hoping it would gain them not only some height, but perhaps a sneak peek and a better understanding as well.

With no plan, no leader and no idea what to do next against the most unexpected of attacks, the remaining dark dragons within the crystal node building at Fleet Street had withdrawn into the darkest depths, and not being able to breach the doorway into the room containing the node itself, had decided to lie in wait for their bold attackers, hoping to at least deal them a bloody nose when they arrived.

Somewhere close to the middle of the line, directly behind one of the young humans in fact, Nurse Conscience hugged the shadows down one side of a wall, admiring the guile and courage of their so-called charges from the surface. Heavens knew how they must be feeling, given that she herself was absolutely terrified, and had only gotten this far because of her admiration for the laminium ball captain, Steel, who was supposedly somewhere much deeper in this complex that felt more like a labyrinth, to her anyway. Every chance she had, she flashed her human companions the biggest smile she could, hoping not to intimidate them or appear as if she thought they were lunch. So far she couldn't tell one way or the other what effect that was having.

Abruptly all movement up ahead stopped. As one, the dragons and humans readied themselves for a confrontation. Seconds passed, turning into minutes as they all stayed as still as possible, their breathing shallow, thoughts focused on what they had to do to stay alive.

"What's going on?" whispered the master mantra maker to the experienced dragon at the head of the line, the one that had been doing such a good job up until now.

Without turning, eyes all the time narrowly locked on a point up ahead shrouded in darkness, the dragon replied.

"There's something up there in the shadows, I'm sure."

"Hmmmm..." uttered Gee Tee quietly.

Reaching out with all of his supernatural ability and vast experience, he probed the area in question, hoping to get a sense of what was there waiting for them. NOTHING! Not a thing, that's what he felt. Trying once more, again he came up empty handed.

"I sense absolutely nothing," ventured the old dragon shopkeeper.

"They're there, I assure you."

"I believe you. What would you like to do?"

"Honestly... go home. But I don't suppose that's an option."

"Not really," Gee Tee chuckled softly. "But we could get this done and just maybe the whole of the planet can breathe a sigh of relief."

"Sounds like a plan."

"Why don't we light them up good and proper, and show them that skulking in the shadows is for children?" submitted the master mantra maker.

"I do like the sound of that."

"Shall we?"

Through their collective telepathic link, they informed the other dragons of what they were about to do. As one they steadied themselves, each one bringing the fire in their bellies to the fore. Simultaneously, and much to the human contingent's surprise, the prehistoric monsters they'd allied themselves with all spat out fabulous flaming fireballs, each looking like a comet travelling through space as tails wriggled out behind them through the darkness up ahead. As the fireballs exploded with almighty BOOMS that shook the floor, walls and ceiling, desperate dark dragons, murder in their eyes swooped down, corkscrewing out of the way of the impromptu attacks, dishing out magic and evil of their own, raining down acid, poison and in one case a hail of exploding rock. Allies from Gee Tee's group bounded up to meet them in the air, jinking this way and that to avoid a return volley of fireballs, some skimming the ground, others going head to head, while even more performed a frantic series of evasive manoeuvres. In the tight confines of the stone corridor, dragons thrust each other up against the walls, rammed each other into the floor, blew scorching hot fire into each other's faces, all the time scratching at wings with talons hoping to take away the advantage of flight, as well as throwing all their magic at their adversaries. It was crowded bedlam on an insane scale.

Sheltered behind the monstrous body of Gee Tee, who, with the aid of his vast experience stood picking out targets with his magic, giving his opponents a little nudge into a wall here, turning them into a stone pillar there, deflecting away deadly supernatural hexes from his comrades quicker than the eye could see, the humans of the group were akin to statues, frozen to the spot, barely able to take it all in, let alone follow the action in real time... that was how fast things were happening. Thoughts of using their grenades in the tight, windy passage all but forgotten because they would undoubtedly do as much damage to their own side as they would their enemy, all they could really do was look on and pray that their comrades prevailed. Whether they would or not was yet to be seen.

Working their way back towards the last entrance they'd come through, Steel, Jar Man and DomCon methodically checked all the bodies, from the slippery nagas that had driven fear straight through their hearts, to the innocent operators that had lost their lives through sheer bad luck at being in the wrong place at the wrong time. Depressing didn't really do it justice, with the friends' moods becoming darker with every second that passed.

Suddenly the sound of brutal explosions and magic being wielded to the maximum from the other side of the doorway startled them from their downward spiral of misery.

"It has to be them," shouted Jar Man over the loud and destructive noise.

"We have to get out there and offer support," babbled DomCon enthusiastically, preparing his best one line mantras in his head.

"How do we bring the doorway down," asked Steel thoughtfully, "and in all honesty, should we?"

"What do you mean?" asked Jar Man confused.

"It could be a trap. How do we even know it's them?" growled the enigmatic laminium ball player.

That had them thinking.

"We don't!" announced DomCon.

"What about trying to get through to one of them... Gee Tee maybe?"

"That might work," declared Steel. "Let's each see if we can reach the old dragon. First to do so lets the others know straight away. Okay?"

Both nodded enthusiastically. Closing their eyes, they reached out with everything they had, hoping to confirm that it was indeed their friends and allies behind the reinforced barrier.

Dragons fighting, hurling spell after spell, mantra after mantra, attempting to destroy each other tooth and nail in the most despicable of ways flooded their minds. Pictures of dark dragons biting down on other dragons' necks filled their throats with sickening bile at the revulsion of the act. Dragons clashing on the ground, tearing wings with talons, hurling balls of brilliant red, yellow, orange and blue fire at each other, as well as other unknown dark magic, filled their minds. A sense of chaos and confusion overwhelmed each of them, but at no point could they focus in on anyone that they recognised from the master mantra maker's select force. It was almost impossible to see whether or not it was a trap. That is until quite by accident, Steel stumbled upon something he hadn't been looking for, making up his mind in an instant.

"It's them... let's go," he declared to the other two.

Snapping out of his magical trance, Jar Man asked.

"How can you be so sure? I didn't see anyone I recognised."

"Neither did I," chipped in DomCon.

"I think there's a reason for that," said Steel. "Someone's tampering with our magic, stopping us from seeing exactly what's going on."

"If that's the case," asked DomCon, "then how do you know it's them?"

"Easy," replied the laminium ball captain. "All four of the humans are out there... I can sense them. If they're there, then you can be damn sure that the master mantra maker is with them. He wouldn't go anywhere without them and certainly wouldn't leave them unguarded."

Both friends nodded in agreement.

"Let's get this doorway down and help our friends," asserted Steel.

Taking an absolute hammering, Gee Tee's meagre force battled bravely on in the face of the barbaric acts continually used against them. Nothing was sacred, not necks, heads or even genitals, with some dark dragons clearly targeting all of these in the most hideous ways possible, knowing the psychological effect it would have on their opponents. As prehistoric monster battled prehistoric monster, the shopkeeper did all that he could to aid his side, using wave after wave of mantras, adding all of his experience and willpower to the situation. It didn't look as though it would be enough, not to his trained eye anyway. The longer it went on, the more one singular thought invaded his mind.

'They're just too strong. We've lost!'

And as a rather gnarly old dark dragon chomped through yet another neck, it turned to face the master mantra maker from afar, deciding there and then that he, and the four human faces peeking out from beneath his wings and legs, would be next on the menu. If only there was some ketchup.

Springing into the air, heading straight for the multitasking mantra specialist, a huge blast wave sounding like an atomic bomb going off smashed the gnarly dragon into the nearest wall, banging his head, dazing him momentarily. As he slipped comically to the floor, he glanced back over his shoulder wondering exactly what had happened. Only then did he have cause for concern. As splintered pieces of metal and wood embedded themselves in everything, three hulking great heroes (artistic licence in the case of DomCon) punched through the thick grey smoke and what was left of the doorway, splitting the air, tails swishing, wings pumping, all on a mission to save their friends. Ginge (Jar Man) purposefully bumped straight into two dark dragons trying to tear Nurse Conscience's head off, sending them scattering to the floor, one temporarily winded, the other still up for the fight. Without a thought for his own safety, Jar Man whirled around in pure reflex, his body hissing through the air, and delivered a roundhouse kick with his talons out, straight to his adversary's chest, creating a metre wide slash, through which all of the dark dragon's exposed organs started to leak, spraying bright green blood almost as far up as the ceiling. Knowing better than to dally, the mild mannered ginger dragon took a leaf out of their opponents' book and opening his massive prehistoric jaws, bit down on the winded dragon's neck, immediately severing it in two, a stunned look of resignation still ingrained on the despicable monster's face as its head rolled off into the shadows.

Pumped up, full of adrenaline and now magic, DomCon scythed through the air on an absolute mission, determined to help his allies, disgusted and angry at the scenes playing out before him. With a tiny movement of one finger, he snapped several bones in the right wing of one dragon about to burp out a blazing fireball. Instead of unleashing a fiery hell, he choked on the magic as he spiralled to the ground, crashing clumsily to the floor.

As a group, the dark prehistoric beasts were disturbed by the explosion and the newcomers' arrival, most considering a retreat, should one be possible, the rest having let their guard down enough for their individual targets to get more of a foothold and an advantage, turning things around in the blink of an eye. But not the gnarly dark dragon, he still had his sights set on Gee Tee, determined to take the old shopkeeper and his human charges with him.

Majestically motoring through the hole in the air that had been created by the detonating door, a picture of perfection, one that laminium ball fans around the world would instantly have recognised despite his newly reborn body, homed in on the vicious looking dark dragon that had its sights set on their leader. Tossing his head back in delight as the air washed over his newly reformed scales, Steel rolled axially, running the gauntlet of those other dark dragons all around, only focused on one, ready to do anything and everything to take him down once and for all.

Jinking out of the way of a volley of shadowy dark bolts intent on skewering him, the laminium ball captain stitched the ground with flame, setting alight the sinew and wing membrane of one of his opponents, swiftly knocking him down, rendering him flightless and out of the fight. Streaking past most of the warriors with little time to make up his mind, he opted for the most obvious solution... that of a head on attack. Zeroing in and using all his agility, he kicked his tail out and with little thought of the consequences, darted forward, heading directly for the gnarly dark dragon who'd only just realised he'd become the hunted.

Using all his gained momentum, Steel slammed into the monster just as a crimson barrier of energy appeared around the beast, negating some of the impact, but not all. Both dragons crashed painfully into the wall, sending masonry and brick exploding out in all directions, a thick cloud of dust covering the corridor. Coughing on the fine particles, unable to see momentarily, the laminium ball captain whirled around at speed, kicking out for all he was worth, hoping to catch his opponent with his outstretched talons. But it wasn't to be, with fresh air the only thing slowing down his attack. Confused, quickly he realised trouble was about to present itself. Instinctively, he rolled into a ball and dropped like a stone to the floor, narrowly avoiding a series of deadly dark darts that zipped through the air where his body had been only a moment ago. Feeling the soft rush of air, Steel had a vague idea of where his adversary was and with that in mind, ignited the natural magic that resided within him, savouring the taste of the fire as it travelled up his throat and scratched his bright white teeth. Opening his mouth, he belched out the biggest fireball he could in the direction of his best guess.

Reopening his eyes after having instinctively closed them when the doorway had blown out, on seeing his three friends so ably joining in the fight, he revised his opinion of the outcome, buoying spirits, filling him with hope, the master mantra maker vowed not to lose anyone else. Looking on as a dragon he admired terribly (something he was reluctant to admit) slammed into a monstrous beast that he was pretty sure had just made up its mind to come for him, he wondered what he could do to help. Like Steel, he was unable to see through the veil of dust, and so hoped that his friend's fireball would at least reveal the whereabouts of the beastly monster. It did! The dragon thumped to the ground hard, rolling off to one side before preparing another round of offensive magic to attack with.

'Enough!' was the singular thought that dominated the

master mantra's cunning mind as an unusual wave of anger surged through his ancient body. Instinctively, the old shopkeeper channelled all his fury into an outright mental attack, using his overpowering will to hammer everything in and around the creature's dark, shrouded mind. Feeling a build up of ethereal energy from within him, Gee Tee's spirit found the tiniest gap in its defences and with all his might, flooded it with his most despicable magic. It worked a treat just as the beast was about to cast something dark and horrible. First its nose fell apart, a look of shock and horror smattered into what was left of its face, before brilliant green blood burst free from behind its eyes and streamed from its mouth. The magic that had been brought forth disappeared into the ether, leaving the monster stunned and dying. Without warning, what was left of its head crumpled in on itself, dripping brain matter down its neck, spilling onto its chest. Awkwardly, the rest of its body clattered to the floor. After that, it was all over in a matter of moments, with the rest being rounded up and killed. Gathering in the centre of what was left of the corridor, all of those that remained came together, including the humans that had been sheltering behind Gee Tee.

"It's good to see you, friends. Your appearance was most timely. Thank you," exclaimed the old shopkeeper, puffing frantically.

"It's good to be seen," answered Steel, his thick, taut muscles gleaming with sweat from the workout he'd just received. "I'm just sorry we couldn't get here sooner."

"What's done is done," stated Gee Tee, still trying to catch his breath. "Our mourning will have to wait until another day. There's still important work to be completed. Tell me, did you find the crystal node? Is it still intact?"

"It's still in one piece, although at some cost," reflected Jar Man.

"Then we have to get there now, so that all is not lost. I have two things to do, both of which will hopefully help our friends in their quests to take back the planet. Lead the way."

And so Steel, Jar Man and DomCon strolled off purposefully back through the gateway that only moments ago had been blown to smithereens, with Gee Tee, the humans and what remained of their contingent following hot on their heels.

31 A CULLING OF THE HERD

Through magical explosions turning everything an array of different colours, explosive shrapnel shrieked through the air, peppering beings indiscriminately, flaming fireballs resembling rogue suns crashing down from above, ripping up marble, roasting flesh and searing scales, one being ran for all he was worth, on the hunt for safety having already more than used up all his bravery in saving the rightful king of the dragons. Sidestepping a scything sword cutting through the air in front of him, part of his brain pretended this was rugby training and that the blade was just an opponent trying to take the ball from his grasp. Dodging this way, while ducking the other, lithe for his size, the human jumped over boulders the height of bicycles that traversed his path along the ruined marble floor, flung from some distance off by beings intent on killing each other. Had Hook stopped to take in his surroundings then reality might well have got the better of him, halting him in his tracks, as well as discontinuing the well trained beating heart that enabled him to run at such speed. But he didn't, he kept his focus on the safety some way off, offered by Yoyo, his charges, and now Janice.

Little did he know though, that something had taken notice of his trek across the battlefield, something not recognising his kind, something intrigued and about to disobey the orders that it had been given. Curiosity had taken off and wouldn't be easily shaken. And what was it that had caught sight of Hook and been so intrigued? One rogue nifoloa separated from its swarm, deadly bright green poison dripping from its single, sharp tooth the size of a man's finger, all thoughts of chasing magic nullified, eyes set on a very tasty and unusual target indeed.

Waving frantically at Janice through a torrent of fighting in an effort to attract her attention, the brave human rugby player had little idea that the young bar worker's mind was off somewhere else, chasing Fu-ts'ang's consciousness in an effort to help Yoyo get a better feel for what was going on across the king's private residence. For the time being at least, Hook was on his own, and had no inkling of the danger stalking him.

Deliberately losing all forward momentum, Fu-ts'ang allowed the gravitational pull to exert its force on the whole of his body and dropped like a stone, his will stopping the full extent of his bladed existence about a centimetre from the surface of the ground. Satisfied at avoiding three magical volleys that were intended to rip him apart, his sharp, singularly focused mind took in everything around him and wondered where he could next be of use. Directly in his line of sight, dark dragons were almost queuing up to take shots at Flash, who he'd linked with only briefly, leading to a discovery that he could well be his absolute soul mate and friend in a perfect world. Currently though, the ex-Crimson Guard was forming a deadly combination with a dragon partner, who, much to his surprise was easily holding her own. In an instant, a decision to help out was made in all but a split second. Rocketing off, staying about three centimetres off the ground, freezing pools of slippery blood in his wake, the ancient weapon maker of old, his spirit well and truly imbued in the futuristic looking blade, weaved in and out of corpses, dragon and naga alike, circumnavigated debris, dodging opportunistic attacks, and like a homing missile, closed in on its three targets. THWUMP! Taking them side on, the beings themselves having no idea that they were even in danger, Fu-ts'ang pierced their gills, traversing each of their heads in less than half a second, rendering them dead and out of the fight, their cold, slippery bodies sliding to the floor unnoticed.

About to acquire his next target, abruptly a familiar presence tickled the gateway to his consciousness. Briefly wondering whether it was some kind of trap, it was only then that he concentrated on the aura itself, bathing in its purity and sense of righteousness. It could only be one other being... his friend, Janice.

"Are you in danger little one? Do you need rescuing?" was his first response, despite no immediate sense of jeopardy from his friend's consciousness.

"What... um, no, no... I don't need rescuing, thanks."

"Then what is it child? I'm in the middle of something of a killing spree, trying my best to even up the odds for your friends."

"And I'm grateful, I truly am, but we were wondering if I could share your mind once again to gain a better understanding of the overall picture of what's going on across the field of battle. Yoyo says having a wider perspective will help us strategically and let us know where to pinpoint our attacks."

"Did he now?"

"He did. And don't be like that. He and everyone else are only trying to do what's best. Surely that's all that you want too... for it to be over, and for the fighting to stop?"

"Of course it is, and yes, I'm sorry. Open yourself up and I'll share with you. No more thoughts of marrying that dragon of yours though, otherwise I think I'll puke."

"Is that even possible?"

"NO! But if I had a body, then that's the first thing I'd be doing when you think about that... urrrgghhh, just remembering it gives me the shivers," Fu-ts'ang reiterated, the entire length of his bladed body shuddering.

"Oh... you're funny," whispered Janice's soft, velvety voice throughout his mind as they joined together as one once more. *"Hey,"* she mouthed, *"why are we embedded in all this black gooiness? I need to be higher up with a clear field of vision to see what needs to be done."*

"Yes, Your Highness," replied the ancient weapon, happier than ever to be reunited with his best friend, despite the sorry circumstances. And with that, Fu-ts'ang reversed out of the last dead naga, and sweeping around three incoming pink, magical missiles, angled up and towards the ceiling, all the time taking note of the dark dragons bombing through the sky, thankful that their numbers, to some degree at least, were starting to thin out.

Drawing on his superior fitness, arms pumping furiously, Hook continued on his frantic, one man race to make it safely to the confines of Yoyo's improvised shielded circle, unable to think of anywhere else to go. Instinctively throwing himself into a forward roll, ducking beneath a huge matt black sword that whirled around at lightning speed and would have sliced his head right off had he not seen it coming, he cracked his shoulder hard against a jagged outlying piece of rubble made up of broken marble as he hit the ground.

"Aarrrgghhhh!" he yelled, for all the good it did him, with not a single being able to hear his pain over the racket of the battle, no one paying attention to his plight, well... that wasn't strictly true. One being had locked onto his scent... the nifoloa that desperately wanted to sink its one gigantic tooth into Hook's pale cream flesh was watching with interest, and was now closing in at quite a rate.

Full of cataclysmic sadness as he used his magic to destroy yet another of his kind, one more being that he'd no doubt promised in the past to protect, love and cherish, Vasuki, king of the naga race, didn't know how much more of this he could take. On stepping through the portal that had brought them from the decades old prison in Antarctica to here, the dragon domain capital in the heart of the British Isles, he had at least thought nothing could be worse than being holed up in that mind numbing jail, away from the rest of his race, absolutely no contact with them at all. As soon as the killing had started, and he'd had to renege on his vow not to harm any of his own, he knew that the prison looked a much kinder and happier prospect. Although his species weren't normally full of emotion and didn't suffer the super highs and punishing lows of love and despair that the humans put themselves through on an almost hourly basis, they were for the most part raised well, respectful of others, cherished their family, used their magic sparingly, all wanting nothing but to live in a quiet part of the planet, away from everything else, left to their own devices. They lived and loved, raised their offspring in a time worn manner and relished fishing, swimming and simply the touch of the cold, dark waters they belonged to. That was enough, as far as he was concerned, and always had been, up until the day he'd been lured into a trap by those dastardly dark dragons. That day had changed his and his race's lives forever, and maybe now even the fate of the planet, the singular reason why he was battling here and now, taking the lives of those he loved and cared about, fulfilling his vow to the dragon Fredric who he regarded as a comrade in arms, in an effort to bring about justice and deny Manson the planet he so wanted. Truth be told though, it was hard, the hardest thing he'd ever endured, and that included his time in the Antarctic. Every death nibbled at his soul, destroying a part of him forever. Still he persisted, having more than a vague idea of what was right and what was wrong. Giving in, here and now, might be the difference between the light-sided dragons winning and losing, the difference between how the planet's future would look. But somewhere inside him, he knew that someday he'd be judged by the king of the sea, who wouldn't look kindly on what had occurred this day, or the stupidity he'd shown by allowing himself to be captured in the first place. Felling another of his kind by the use of his huge blue tail, not hesitating to lean down and bite through the exposed neck with his bare teeth, he used a casual bolt of lightning to puncture yet another onrushing naga's throat, with some of his magic having returned, leaving a smoking black hole about the size of a man's fist, and with what reserves he had left, stretched out with his unusual ethereal energy to see what else was going on and whether any chance remained for him to save just a handful of his race. Things did not look good.

Clutching his shoulder for all he was worth, tears from the excruciating pain from his fall gushing down his cheeks, the courageous rugby player stumbled to his feet, managing to leap out of the way of a huge dark naga tail, just as it would have taken his legs out from under him, landing clumsily with a THUD, but remaining upright and balanced, thankfully. Not knowing whether the snake-like creature had its eyes set on him, and not really giving a rat's arse, he took a second or so to get his bearings, caught sight of Yoyo and Janice in the distance, and with as much haste as he could muster, started to jog off in their direction, forgetting all about magic, dragons, nagas and any other threat that might present itself, which was understandable really.

Swerving this way and that, barely able to see beyond the tip of the massive tooth that jutted out in front of its face, the nifoloa chasing Hook drew up short as a huge green and yellow magical explosion detonated right in front of it, sending dust and shards of marble high into the air all around. Zigzagging in between any potentially lethal particles, the monstrous insect of legend dropped at speed towards the surface before pulling up at the very last moment, no mean feat given the weight of the giant tooth. Successfully avoiding flailing talons and tails as well as extreme bursts of heat and fire, its focus wavered for just a second, wondering whether or not it should retreat and reintegrate itself back into the swarm, whose minds it could feel some way off in the direction from which it had come. Just as it was about to acquiesce, it caught sight of its prey, Hook, nursing a damaged shoulder, stumbling on in an effort to reach his friends. That single thought of reaching him before he could get to safety was enough to clear the nifoloa's mind and refocus it back to the task at hand. Leading with the massive tooth, thick, green poison leeching off into the air in its wake, the devilish flying beast flapped its delicate little wings as fast as it could, all the time closing in like a bullet on its intended target.

Hook's mind and body were shot, the pain clouding his thoughts, only his massive strength of will enabling him to put one foot in front of the other in the direction of what he thought of as safety. Unfortunately for him, he was just too far away, particularly given just how quickly one of the mythical beasts from hell was closing in on him. There was only ever going to be one winner, and in this encounter, it was never meant to be the rugby player.

As Fu-ts'ang tore vertically through the air, heading straight up as far as he dared, his beloved friend Janice used her experience from earlier on in the day to take in as much of the battlefield as she could. Instantly her sights locked on a familiar figure bounding between adversaries, heading for his battle hardened group of guards... GEORGE, the current dragon king, looking as though he could defeat the enemy all by himself. Silently she wished him luck. Glancing around, momentarily her heart missed a beat on noticing the dread leader of the dark force, Manson, standing sandwiched between two deadly looking nagas, appearing to be waiting for something, or someone. Squinting, back towards the safety of Yoyo's youngsters, it was then that she spotted what Manson was waiting for, well... not what, but who. RICHIE! And much to Janice's surprise, she seemed to be circumventing the dreaded leader's plans for her, and hitching a ride beneath one of the dark dragons. Right there and then, her admiration for the young lacrosse player, her friend and their de facto leader shone through, alerting her buddy, the weapon's presence.

"Is that really what you think of her? I thought you disliked her a little because of the feelings your would-be partner had for her?"

'It's nothing like that. It was all a mix up. They're only friends. I just think she's amazing... courageous, fearless, outstandingly smart

and not afraid of anyone or anything. I'd give anything to be like her."

Deep rooted laughter echoed up, out and across their telepathic link.

"What's that supposed to mean?" asked the young bar worker, deeply affronted.

"Oh little one, I don't mean to offend you, quite the opposite in fact. Look at what you've achieved here today. You and the young Rump girl are almost identical from where I sit. She might have had to make a few tougher decisions across the course of the hours that have passed, but you're no less brave, fearless or dedicated than she is. In fact, given that you're not a dragon, I would say that you've exceeded anything she might have achieved."

As they drifted high up above everything, the young girl considered all that her friend had said.

"Thank you, I think."

"You're welcome, little one, you're welcome. Make the most of what you need up here, it's nearly time for me to get back to killing our enemy."

And so she did, continuing to scan the chaotic scene below her.

Off in the distance, a curled up ball moving at speed, attracting the attention of everything, dark dragons, nagas, and seemingly other creatures that she didn't recognise, sped to a halt as it slammed into the giant tree trunk like legs of a humungous, wild and insane looking monster. Only then did Janice recognise who had been moving at such a rate. TANK!

'Wow,' she thought, 'boy has he attracted a whole lot of attention, but as is his way, he's seemingly dealing with all of it. Good for him. Go Tank go,' she mused, unaware of his dynamic and powerful partner, For'son. There and then she made a note to tell Yoyo about the other beings that she'd seen.

It was then that a feeling of uncertainty and danger guided her gaze. Immediately she knew why, as she spotted not only her love and the reason she was here, but the deadly witch known as Earth, and Peter's grandfather

Fredric.

'Why the hell is he standing between them?' was her first thought. 'Let Fredric kick seven shades of shit out of her,' was her second. But the more she watched, unable to hear any of the words that were being spoken, the more something sinister seemed to be playing out.

"Focus," echoed a soft voice deep within her mind. *"Do as Yoyo asked and don't get distracted."*

Knowing that her friend the weapon was right, she stretched out again, her mind settling on a pair of beings more than holding their own against overwhelming odds, seemingly working together in perfect unison, that of Captain Battlehard and, of course, Flash. Taking a few seconds, sure that her buddy wouldn't mind, the young bar worker watched the pair batter away all comers, dishing out magic and mayhem, fighting with swords and sorcery, using their minds and bodies to defend and attack, keeping each other safe. Whilst not a reader of people, even she could spot the bond that they'd already formed, one that clearly went deeper than their professional respect for each other.

'Looks like you two might have to get a room,' she thought, oddly wondering if that was a thing that dragons do, which was strange given everything going on around her, and elicited more laughing in her mind from her friend, something that made her blush just a little.

Off to one side, she spotted a sight that nearly broke her heart. Vasuki, she was sure that had been his name, the king of all of the nagas and friends with Flash and Fredric, battled a circle of his own kind, taking them down one by one, almost robotically, clearly against his wishes.

'Yet more pure evil on a day when it just keeps on coming,' she thought as her attention flickered elsewhere.

And then she caught sight of Yoyo and his youngsters, as well as her own body just standing there, eyes closed. Strange didn't do it justice, and she was just about to comment to Fu-ts'ang on that subject, when she spotted him, hurt and alone, staggering ever forward towards her position through the magic, death and danger. HOOK!

'Oh my,' she thought, perturbed by what she saw closing in behind him. Frozen, unable to comprehend how he'd get out of such a predicament, all she could do was watch from the sky and hope for an otherworldly intervention.

Lurching out of the way of a nearby fireball exploding against one of the few remaining pristine parts of the marble, sending glistening, bright white shards splintering everywhere, Hook stumbled across a low slung pile of debris before drawing to a halt, wondering what the hell was producing that buzzing sound continuously assaulting his ears. Ignoring the pain whilst catching his breath, he took a moment to compose himself and in doing so, glanced around over his left shoulder. Both wishing he hadn't and glad that he had, it took a few extra moments for his mind to wrap itself around the reality of what was approaching him at speed. Something wasp-like was hurtling towards him, beating its wings ten to the dozen, sporting a disproportionately huge, white as porcelain, single tooth with brilliant green liquid dripping down from its tip, focused solely on him.

Obviously his idea of danger had changed completely over the last few days. Well, it would, wouldn't it? Dragons, nagas, magic, spells, death, misery and agony clearly redefined someone whose biggest fear had been the odd giant or two on the rugby pitch who'd occasionally caused him harm. And although what was approaching looked nowhere near as formidable as any of the dark dragons or nagas, some kind of danger sense from deep within screamed out at him to be careful and that there was more going on than he could realise.

Almost in range now, Hook, confident that he could take down something so small, turned fully to face this latest threat, much to the surprise of the nifoloa. As he did so though, an onrushing mountain of air from behind and to the left gave him a more immediate cause for concern. Reacting without thought, which given the state of his shoulder was probably a good thing, the rugby playing giant threw himself off to his right, his broad chest taking the brunt of the landing on the hard, scorched marble, sending waves of incredible pain up through every part of his body, almost forcing him to pass out, but not quite. His impulsive actions had probably saved his life, given the size and velocity with which the huge, brown scaled dragon tail came zipping through the air where he'd been only a split second before. Through watering eyes and a body that just wanted to call it a day, his underlying sense of self preservation just had to get up and look, to see if he'd been the target of the dark dragon's attack. As if to answer his unspoken question, a giant brown and green prehistoric head turned to face him, disappointment etched across its scales at having missed the focus of its ire first time around.

'Oh crap,' thought Hook, not knowing which way to turn, scrabbling backwards across the floor, desperate to get away.

But the dragon clearly had other thoughts, and, as it was about to bring its gigantic body around, suddenly it let out a rather undragon-like, "YELP!"

'What in the...?' reflected the human rugby player, barely lucid, unsure if what was playing out around him was fantasy or reality. And that's when he noticed it, perched halfway up the beast's hulking great tail, almost savouring the moment, clawed feet having breached the armour itself, no doubt having caused the beast to shout out. Then, as expected, nature took over and the odd little insect plunged its one pointed, bright white tooth into the dragon, piercing the scale, no mean feat in itself, injecting its venom directly into the massive primeval monster's frame. Hook could only stand and watch, too terrified to move, some small, inquisitive part of him desperate to see how things would play out. He didn't have a long wait to find out, less than a second and a half in fact. That was the time it took for the dark dragon to become paralysed, and given that his last act had been to stomp forward, all of his weight was now over his front foot, meaning that when the toxin kicked in, being off balance caused him to topple over. Luckily, not in the direction of Hook, or the tiny winged, one toothed monster that had immediately unclamped itself and, knowing what would happen, flown away to relative safety.

BOOM! The whole area shook, causing debris and dust to come crashing down on top of the young rugby playing human, his lungs barely able to cope with the amount of filth that he'd inhaled. Nagas toppled or rode the blast wave, while surrounding dragons leapt airwards, unable to work out what invisible threat had taken out their comrade.

Coughing profusely whilst pulling himself free of some minor rubble that had pinned down his bad shoulder and arm, he sat up, his head berating him for doing so as the world around him appeared to spin like the wildest of fair rides. And then, not five metres in front of him, the tiny insect-like beast that we know as a nifoloa, one that was still coming to terms with actual reality, settled down on the only clear bit of floor within his line of sight, its eyes solely focused on him. Swallowing uncomfortably, and having seen what the tiny little monster had done to the colossal dark dragon, Hook began to think that this wasn't how he wanted to go... anything but in fact.

Much like the dragon's magic, both that of his allies and of the magically enslaved dark beasts ravaging the air, Vasuki's unusual ethereal spells had cool downs of different kinds, meaning that for the most part he had to use a succession of different hexes if he were under constant attack, something that was most definitely happening right now. Magically enthralled by something that he just couldn't touch, no matter how hard he tried, and he had, still he continued killing them, for no other reason than it was the right thing to do. Inside, it tore him apart, both as their king and leader and on a much more personal level. Fate, he thought, was a cruel mistress, especially considering his unbelievable escape from the Antarctic prison where, no doubt, he was supposed to die, at least if Manson had anything to do with it. Having already defied the odds with that, the almost alien mind behind his thoughts whirred constantly, trying to find a way to save what remained of his race.

Stretching out his middle finger, moving it in an intricate circular motion, a thick, sturdy icicle appeared out of thin air on a trajectory of his choosing. With barely a thought, one more of his kind approached only to have the gills on either side of her head crushed, killing her instantaneously, as the next in line caught the brunt of the speeding icicle's momentum, taking a hit straight through the top of the chest, yet one more down, but many more to go. And that's when a slight distraction nearly cost him his life. He was, however, the king for a reason, and bounced back using some particularly secret magic that negated all life in a radius of about five metres around him. It was costly in terms of sheer mana used, but it worked a treat, stopping his adversaries' hearts, dropping them immediately to the floor, buying him just enough time to recover and, more importantly, take note of something strange that was happening close by.

Things were getting batshit crazy now, with absolutely no chance of staying still or stopping even for the briefest amount of time. Luckily for him, For'son was constantly replenishing his mana, as well as re-energising his human form's muscles and stamina. Whirling like a rotary washing line in a tornado, Tank's fists, arms and legs, following the guidance of the presence hidden away in the stunning band that he currently wore on one of his fingers, made contact with absolutely everything, the motion and kinetic energy reinforced with an unstoppable supply of magic, dark dragons and nagas finding him the most formidable opponent, something that scattered them, but only enticed in the mythical creatures, whose orders were to hunt that magic down and the cost be damned. Despite the resolute nature of the fight the two of them were putting up, and the huge resource of magical power available to them, the battle that they currently found themselves caught up in dwarfed anything that Manson and Earth had so far come up with. With the war now waging on two fronts, would the distraction and disruption caused by this be the light-sided heroes' downfall?

Witnessing from above the devastating blow the tiny little creature with seemingly just one huge tooth had dealt to the enormous dark dragon, all Janice could do was watch what was about to play out, all the time desperately hoping for divine intervention. She was too far away physically to make any difference, something that very much applied to her mind, sharing Fu-ts'ang's consciousness. Sadness gripped the young woman as she watched someone she'd come to regard as a friend, given everything they'd shared and been through over the last couple of days. At that moment, she'd have given anything, including her own life, to save Hook from his imminent and painful death. Unfortunately, there was absolutely nothing she could do.

You would have thought after all this time he would have been used to it, the death, destruction and chaos that made up this fragile world they all lived in. Goodness knows he'd seen enough of it, and that was despite having been contained deep below ground in Gee Tee's secret storage facility for what must have been centuries, at least. But here and now, this was something new. Feeling Janice's pain at her friend's looming death threatened to tear him apart and send the splinters of what was left of him back to 'the gloom'. Spurred on by thoughts of wanting to help his friend, Fu-ts'ang's mind shot into overdrive, calculating trajectories, speeds, distances, angles and all the other possible variables. No matter how hard he tried, no matter how much out of the box thinking he applied, there was only one real conclusion. There was no way in hell he could get there in time, and that left only one likely result... the death of the injured human, somewhere deep down amongst all of the carnage... one more amongst many.

Pushing the pain from his injuries to one side, Hook stumbled to his feet, much to the amusement of the nifoloa, who it had to be said, liked nothing more than to play with its food. Whilst it had momentarily considered feeding on the dragon that it had just taken down, it knew from watching those it had teamed up with, that getting anything decent to eat out of it would be a struggle given its design and the heavy armour in the form of the scales that encompassed its entire body. Why exert all that effort when there was a delicious snack all but unwrapped here, especially one so fearful of being taken down and devoured.

'Delicious,' it thought.

Ever since arriving in the dragon domain through the side of the rock face in Salisbridge, just before encountering Gee Tee, coming down from the secretive entrance deep within the Poultry Cross from up above, Hook had been wearing his favourite zippered sweatshirt tied around his waist, figuring that if he ever got back to the surface again, then he might need another layer. Plain dark green with a hood, it was warm enough to withstand even the coldest of winter's days, and was the one piece of clothing that he liked above all others. Right now though, his regard for it was headed in an altogether different direction, that is, if he could withstand the pain from his agonisingly bad shoulder.

Without warning, the nifoloa zipped forward, no beating about the bush, straight towards Hook's rough and tumble face, tiny flecks of green poison running down the side of its razor sharp tooth. Immediately the rugby player sidestepped, almost tripping over the tree trunk-like tail of the previously felled dark dragon. His unexpected lurch to the left to avoid the hazardous appendage was all that saved him from being envenomated by the sneaky mythical creature, who, having missed its target the first time, had swung around for another go. During all of this, Hook, having had time to think about it while the petite winged monster had been eyeing him up had managed, through a great deal of pain, to untie the sweatshirt from around his waist, and was now holding it by the arms, the zipper showing.

Liking nothing more than a challenge, the nifoloa circled around well outside the reach of Hook's sweatshirt, preparing to strike again.

Planting his feet firmly on the ground, memories of rugby pitch battles threatening to overwhelm his conscious mind, the heroic human readied himself to swing his sweatshirt in the hope that he could catch the dreaded little beast with the zipper on the end. Knowing it was a long shot at best, he was all out of ideas as to how to extract himself from the situation he was in, and had absolutely nothing else at all.

BUZZ, BUZZ burned his ears as the nifoloa probed his defences, which, given the circumstances, weren't half bad. In a flash, he whipped around the top in a blur of green, the dark zipper whistling through the air on a collision course with the deadly creature's head. BUZZ. As casual as you like, it weaved out of the way, its large and only tooth almost mocking what it saw as a pathetic attempt to ward it off.

BUZZ. It flitted in again, waiting to see what the response would be. This time Hook brought his sweatshirt straight up and over his head, the tip of the zipper scything through the air with great speed, ready to do considerable damage. Again the nifoloa managed to avoid the attack, dodging off to one side at the very last instant.

Not sure whether to be pleased or not that he'd lasted this long, he used the moment to scan for any type of help, wherever it could come from. But none of his friends or any of the light-sided heroes were anywhere near his field of vision.

'DAMN!' he thought only to himself.

BUZZ, BUZZ brought him back to reality, the sweat from his brow running down into both eyes now, something he could seriously do without.

Hovering seemingly without a care in the world, the nifoloa had made its mind up and was determined to finish things this time around.

Sensing a change in its attitude, Hook could feel that a fatalistic point had been reached. Knowing for sure that this would be one concerted attack, the rugby player ignored the biting pain from his other shoulder and prepared to give everything he had in one last effort to bludgeon the little beast to death, deeply aware that if his mother were here, she would probably be saying things like, "capture it in a glass and just put it outside," or "it's more afraid of you than you are of it," none of which was very helpful.

Slinking to one side, the tiny little beast shimmied back the other way before charging forwards at full speed. Knowing that for the time being the floor behind him was clear, all the time walking backwards, Hook swished his top, with the zipper on the outside, this way and that in front of him, hoping with every ounce of his being to strike the deadly monster, knowing that just one hit would most certainly be enough. But it wasn't to be... the nifoloa was just too fast, even for him. And so he retreated further, the burning pain from the muscles in his arm wielding the sweatshirt almost outweighing that of his damaged shoulder. In the end, there was only ever going to be one winner.

With only half an eye on his own situation, Vasuki deflected away a dozen darts of deadly poison that were meant to incapacitate rather than kill, and instead of returning the favour, used the mother of sonic screams to instantly slay his adversary, watching as thick, gooey blood seeped from his attacker's nose and gills. And still they came, unbelievably, now in heavier numbers than before. With the wave of a hand, a section of floor gave way, sending half a dozen at a time falling to their doom, buying him a brief respite, again at the cost of using up more of his limited supply of magic, something that frightened him greatly, having already been totally depleted once today already in an effort to save the rescuer known as Flash. But it had been worth it up until now, because somehow they'd all been replenished. Not knowing how, he was just grateful to have access to any of the defences that he'd thought long gone. Turning away from the next wave momentarily, one of the brief opportunities for redemption that he'd been on the lookout for suddenly presented itself and being the exceptional king that he was, he gladly took it with open arms.

Almost completely out of energy, arm muscles totally burnt out, fingers barely able to grip his favourite sweatshirt any more, Hook's legs gave way as he collapsed up against a slew of dead nagas, the fishy scent of their bodies almost making him puke. At the same time, his fingers instinctively opened, dropping his only available weapon to the ground. Too exhausted and scared to do anything else, he just sat there, mouth agog, waiting for the end. But of course the smart arse nifoloa liked to play with its food, something it would come to regret. In one final fear inducing act, it flew up directly in front of its prey's face and hovered there in triumph, ready to take its prize. And that's when an almighty, forked, zigzagging line of fluorescent blue electricity arced through the air and sliced its head from its body, leaving the air all around it statically charged and smoking, after which a humungous BOOM echoed throughout the chamber. Nearly jumping out of his pale, thin skin, Hook delighted in watching the evil insect's head, weighed down by its oversized tooth, crash to the ground long before its body. Only then did he have the presence of mind to follow the bolt of lightning back to its source. It was, for him, a moment like no other, and one he would remember for the rest of his life, no matter how long that might be. As their eyes met across a crowded and chaotic battlefield, both gave an acknowledging nod to the other, Hook grateful for the save, Vasuki pleased to be of service in his endeavour to at least do something right today.

And that's when sanity, or at least some vague resemblance of it returned, and gathering up his favourite sweatshirt, not wanting anything bad to happen to it, especially not with everything he and the garment had now been through together, Hook stuttered to his feet and as quickly as he could headed back off in the direction of Yoyo and Janice.

With all the exuberance of a dragon a quarter of his age, George, king of everything, at least for the time being anyway, hurled his powerful magic at every enemy that moved in front of him, all the time heading for the group of King's Guards that were so valiantly holding off a wave of nagas on the ground and a flurry of fireballs from the dragons in the air. Although the opposition numbers had come down sharply, they as a force were still vastly outnumbered. They didn't need to regroup, what they needed was a miracle, and although getting this far might almost be seen as one, things were far from looking good for those on the right side of all this.

Dropping acid rain on a squadron of dark dragons in the distance that were dive bombing the group he was headed for, George smirked at the outcome, his ancient dragon DNA taking a great deal of pleasure in their squeals of pain and in watching them drop to their deaths in the most agonising way possible. Knowing you were facing an unavoidable demise in only a matter of moments was not how he would choose to leave the planet.

Drawing the attention of four disappointed nagas who'd figured out where the acid rain attack had come from, suddenly wraith-like, shadowy filaments reached out through the distance between them, homing in on the dragon king, making him fear for his life. Instantly he used his own abilities to snuff out theirs, but it didn't work, if anything enraging the filaments if that was at all possible. Then he tried to nudge other beings, mainly nagas, into their path, hoping to kill two birds with one stone, so to speak. But his opponents countered that with magic of their own, clamping their comrades in place, much to the individuals' confusion. With the shadowy black death in the form of the filaments nearly upon him, with nowhere for him to run or hide, one thought and one alone prompted him into action. If he could kill the individual nagas, hopefully the magic would dissipate... HOPEFULLY!

Long silver locks of hair blowing back over both shoulders, a look of utter concentration ground into his face, he held out both hands in front of him, and in perfect unison, slowly moved all of his fingers down. All four of the enemy looked on in utter bewilderment, and although not quite amusement as they were a serious and studious race, it was probably about as close as they got to finding something funny. Waiting to watch him die a sick and filthy death, abruptly the air above all four of them lit up, forcing them to turn away from their helpless prey. A torrent of huge, flaming arrows, that looked as though they'd been fired from a hundred longbows, all concentrated on their position. Instinctively they all attempted to raise their shields around them, but they did so just a fraction of a second too late, with the first of the deadly projectiles already scything through them. All four died in an instant, followed swiftly by their magic that had gotten within an arm's length of George, and a closer call it was hard for the dragon king to imagine. Wiping the sweat from his brow with the back of his hand, he turned in the direction he wanted to proceed, and snapping the neck of a dark dragon that had just turned to face him with but a few words, he broke into the fastest run he could, leapt over a bloodied naga cadaver and set off for what had been his original goal before he'd been so rudely interrupted.

"Don't you think now's a good time to tell him?" Earth bellowed at Fredric across a much less crowded part of the king's private residence, "after all, he clearly doesn't know."

'What the hell is she going on about?' thought Peter, stuck in between them both, terrified that the murderous magic would restart and he'd be caught in the firefight.

Swallowing nervously, having only just got back to his feet and regained all his wits, the founder of the Crimson Guards looked on painfully at the situation he regarded as of his own making. He should have sorted it out long ago, stamped his authority on her, forced her to change her ways... but he never had, and the longer it went on, the harder it was to do, until eventually the opportunity was lost altogether. And now here they were, reunited in this cauldron of hell.

"Dragon got your tongue, old man?" she scoffed, enjoying every second.

Reluctantly, Peter glanced around behind him at his grandfather. The look on Fredric's face was not what he wanted to see. Difficult to describe, it wasn't so much resignation, as a mixture of pain, longing, love and... anger. How so many emotions could play out on one human shaped face Peter would never know. What that meant though, for the life of him, the young hockey playing dragon just couldn't fathom. Clearly they must know each other, but how or why, just couldn't, or wouldn't enter his thoughts. For most it would have been obvious by now, but being the naive young dragon he was, he certainly couldn't see the wood for the trees.

"ENOUGH!" commanded Fredric, the anger in his face clearly getting the better of all the other emotions there.

"Stand down and then just maybe this won't end in your demise."

Throwing her head right back, the remaining serpents atop it writhing and wriggling uncontrollably, the wicked witch of a dragon cackled a cackle that echoed out across the field of battle, making the hackles of every being there stand on end. Peter's legs froze to the spot. A terrifying knot of trouble stirred in Fredric's stomach.

Lowering her head to face both the beings in front of her, or more precisely, the dysfunctional family that had never been together in this way before, Manson's would-be queen was in no mood to take orders from the being at the top of her hit list.

"As always, you still love the sound of your own voice. And still think you know what's best for everyone. How's that working out for you?"

A jibe, one subtle enough just for him, but he wasn't about to take the bait. Oh, he might have done, had his grandson not been here, but he knew better than to lose control of his temper. The only thing that mattered to him was Peter's safety and wellbeing. Of course he wanted to win the fight, save the world, and do nothing more than hang out with his best friend and grandson for the rest of eternity. Right now though, he'd settle for giving his life to destroy hers, and leave his grandson in the care of his friends, who all seemed more than capable enough. Odd though, he thought, that he should hook up with such proficient and gifted beings. Through all that time trapped in Antarctica, he'd always imagined his grandson would be very much a loner. Of course he'd seen his relationship with the Rump girl and the boy dragon that loved nature, plants and animals so much, but connections and bonds change, friendships break as time goes by. What he must have forged would have been incredibly robust to stand the test of time this long and to still be going strong. Yes... he would give his life to take hers knowing that Peter was in loving and safe hands with those that he'd surrounded himself with. And so with that in mind, he decided to poke the donkey, prod the prey and give back a little something.

"It must be so nice to know everything there is to know about parenting and from such a young age as well. Your mastery of that subject must be all encompassing," scoffed Fredric, fingering the hilt of the laminium dagger.

'What the hell is going on?' wondered the young hockey player caught up in the middle of it all, intrigued and absolutely terrified at exactly the same time as to why his grandfather was having a go back. All this talk of family... was it something to do with that, and if so, what? Confused as he'd ever been, all he wanted to do now that his grandfather had returned, was get to some sort of relative safety, help his friends with their fight, and be reunited with Janice. And with that in mind, he turned in the direction of Yoyo and his young charges, just in time to see the love of his life pull in a deep breath and close her eyes.

'Peculiar,' he mused, that is until he remembered her link with the weapon, Fu-ts'ang and their deep founded friendship. 'Perhaps she's off with him,' was the only conclusion he could draw. 'Stay safe my love, stay safe,' he thought.

Unfortunately, the direction of his brief glance hadn't gone unnoticed, by either of the estranged family members with which he was surrounded, to the great amusement of one, and the absolute horror of the other.

"Oh... this is just so delicious. Please tell me it's so, please tell me," Earth reflected. "The irony is just too much. Dragons always mock humans for believing in karma, which I've always thought is just ridiculous, but I think it might just have come back to bite you on the ass, right here, right now. What do you say... old man?"

Fredric's steely gaze remained firmly locked upon his daughter, the anger he felt inside boiling up like nothing before. More than anything in the world, he wanted to kill her, here and now. Whether that would have been possible without his grandson in the way was debatable to say the least, but with him here, in the middle of things, made it improbable. If only he'd taken her life before then they wouldn't be standing here, letting all of this play out, opening wounds that he'd hoped had long since closed. From the sickening stabbing pains he felt in his stomach, clearly they hadn't, and from the tone of her voice, and the evil in her eyes, the bitter, twisted resentment she'd felt all along still firmly remained. How this played out was anyone's guess.

In the middle of the mayhem, with rip-roaring explosions detonating all around, fireballs howling through the air, beings crying out in pain, some in the last throes of life, one daring young lacrosse playing dragon, stuck in her human guise, dropped silently from the lift she'd just snaffled on the underside of an unsuspecting dark dragon and landed softly on the broken marble surface, her magic primed and ready.

Though chaos reigned all around, his mind and supernatural focus did as it had been trained to do by his petty and abusive father and looked for any and all anomalies, magical and otherwise, no matter how insignificant they might seem. And so, lying in wait to spring his trap on the annoying lacrosse player, Manson's mind flinched ever so slightly as the lightest brush of air played over the back of his head and neck. Knowing that it couldn't be possible, whilst wondering at the same time exactly how she'd done it, a modicum of fear gripped his whole body at the thought of what would happen next. As his instinctive training fought against the terror threatening to not only cripple him but send him to his doom, the tiniest part of him had the greatest of admiration for her.

Monstrous murderous thoughts consumed her mind as she stood behind him, ready to send him and his naga cohorts off into oblivion, the only real question being how to do it? The sole answer she could come up with was: as painfully as possible. With that in mind, the tips of her fingers flickered with tiny forks of the most impressive purple lightning, and in one all-encompassing, deadly strike, she reached out for his neck.

"PETER! Step aside," ordered Fredric, the tone of his voice dour, no nonsense.

Feet frozen to the ground, the hockey playing dragon considered his grandfather's... req... no, order. It made sense on so many levels, the immediate one being that they were no doubt about to go at it big time, once more. And the last place he wanted to be was caught up between them. Even his most powerful magic was insignificant compared with what was at their disposal. But something other than the dread in his legs stopped him from moving. A hunch, intuition, a gut feeling, call it what you will, but it was powerful and although not quite all consuming, it very much had his attention. Turning to face the man he loved dearly, despite barely knowing him at all, he couldn't help but ask.

"What's going on?"

Physically taken aback, his grandfather was surprised not only by the question, but at the child having the courage to ask it. Perhaps he was tougher and more resourceful than he first appeared. That threw something of a spanner into the works.

"Tell him, why don't you? Or do you have something to hide?" suggested Earth, her words enhanced across the distance with magic.

"Oh... you'd like that wouldn't you?" snarled Fredric in reply.

"You bet!" she replied, licking her lips. "As per usual though, I very much doubt you have the courage of your convictions."

Moments of pure and utter truth are few and far between, mostly for good reason, although occasionally the mischievous entity known as Fate gives a subtle nudge in an entertaining direction, entirely for her own means and gratification, usually ignoring the consequences or the greater good. This could very much be the case here and now.

Against the backdrop of absolute havoc, supernatural bombardments, beings trying to rip other beings' heads off, the clash of swords, the swishing of wings and the slithering of cold dark tails, a pivotal point had been reached, not only for these three beings and of course Fate, who liked nothing more that to stir the pot, but likely for the planet at large, that was how potentially important this moment was going to be. The rise and fall of Earth could very well determine the rise and fall of THE earth.

Unable to take his pleading gaze away from his grandfather's face, something inside Peter now knew the importance and significance of what was going on here, and although he didn't know the details, and almost certainly wouldn't want to know, he was very much like a dog with a bone, not wanting to give it up for anything. This was something Fredric immediately recognised, something that gnawed at his very core, having hoped for a long time to have guided the youngster away from any of this, in an effort to not only keep him safe, but to give him peace of mind... but no more. They'd reached a juncture, a tipping point, call it what you will. But there was no turning back, and so, with more venom than any of the nagas around him carried inside themselves, born of decades of anger and frustration, he just spat it out.

"She's your mother!"

Time stopped. That singular heartbeat of a moment appeared to last forever. Despite being in the middle of one of the biggest and deadliest battles the world had ever witnessed, an all encompassing silence shrouded Peter in its grip, his thoughts wandering all over the place.

'You said she was my mother,' he thought, his mind whirring. 'But that's impossible because my mother died, a long time ago. And anyway, how could this... this... *thing* be anybody's mother, let alone mine? What you're saying just can't be true. It just can't be.' And that was the reality of it all, well, at least inside the young hockey playing dragon's head, as the vicious moment continued.

Not sure anything at all was going on, relying on his training and not willing to bet his life on such a thing, still staring straight ahead, Manson grabbed the two nagas either side of him with his mind and threw them at each other behind his back. SMASH! They both collided with something, and it wasn't just each other. Bounding forward in an effort to get to safety, a searing pain plucked the skin at the base of his head and neck, causing him to cry out in agony as he moved. A lesser being would have capitulated by now and lost consciousness entirely, but not him, he had too much to live for, with his plans so close to fruition. No dragon freak stuck in a disgusting human form was going to thwart all that he'd worked for decades for to achieve. The world would either be his, or wouldn't be at all. It was as simple as that. There would be no other outcome. With his bound having turned into a stagger, instinctively he brushed the back of his neck with the palm of his right hand, only to see it soaked in thick red blood, something that was enough to turn his stomach. Not so much the blood, but because it reminded him of the weak, pitiful and disgusting form he'd taken to get the job done, to fulfil his desires, marry his queen and become joint ruler of the planet. Staving off the desire to throw up, figuring he was out of range, he whirled around with much less speed than usual, his head spinning just a little from what he regarded as a cowardly attack from behind... ironic really given how he'd been lying in wait, about to spring his own trap.

And there she was, having been sandwiched between both nagas, the last of the brilliant purple magic that she'd no doubt been trying to embed in his body flickering out into nothingness, the look on her confused face... priceless!

Shaking a little from the shock of the attack, how easily he'd been caught unawares and the throbbing pain from the back of his neck, he turned fully, stretched out his arm and opened the palm of his hand, about to return the favour.

Mirroring almost exactly his thoughts about just how easily she'd been caught off balance, it took only a split second for her nimble brain to respond and gather her composure. With the lightning she had planned having flashed out of existence and the mantra in question having gone into cool down, Richie, The White Dragon, de facto leader and lacrosse superstar sprang into action, banging the two confused nagas' heads together as hard as she could, somersaulting back out of Manson's range before the slippery serpents' bodies had even rolled to the floor. For his part, Earth's other half had only begun to come around to what had nearly happened, the anger and vengeance in his body only now starting to reveal itself. Palm stretched open, a trio of laser-like beams of molten fire erupted in her direction, following her blindingly fast trajectory, ripping up marble from the floor as they missed her lithe, agile and nimble body by a hair's breadth.

Only just coming to the conclusion that she'd really pissed him off, Richie used every part of her athleticism to tumble, roll, somersault, bounce and jump out of the way of the lethal attacks that were coming in her direction.

Purple in the face now at having been outsmarted so easily by someone he regarded as inferior to himself, Manson roared angrily as he changed tactics, fiery laser beams swapped now for rippling lines of shadowy dark energy that shimmered across the gap between the two of them, not caring about possible collateral damage to any of the beings around them or under him.

Weaving in between nagas caught unaware as to exactly what was going on, and bouncing up behind the bodies of gliding dark dragons, the lacrosse player assumed that would at least slow down the psychotic dark force leader, with his own troops in the way. Not a bit of it, much to her surprise, with nagas and dragons alike taking the full brunt of his attacks, some falling from the sky, wings shredded, others exploding into a thousand pieces whilst tails and heads imploded on the ground. Manson's anger and propensity for violence knew no bounds, his sights firmly set on the target of his anger, determined to hunt her down.

After what seemed like a lifetime of holding his breath, of the world spinning off around him, time restarted, much to his horror. He'd have given anything to have stayed in that bubble, avoided the issue, pretended not to have heard those dreaded words, the ones he now had to wake up and face up to. Wisps of magic assaulted his nose, their sickly smells replicating a kind of pollen overload, tickling his nostrils, making his head feel thick and unresponsive. Concussive BANGS made his ears pop and ring, producing an unforgiving pounding right behind his eyes, but that wasn't the worst part. No, that was the look currently ingrained in his grandfather's worn and withered face, something he would never forget until the day he died. Pain, misery, blame, all wrapped up in the kind of hurt no one, not even your worst enemy, deserves to suffer. It was all there, delivered with just one look. Despite being hugely naive, something that most of his friends and those he surrounded himself with found endearing, he knew in that moment that what his grandfather had just said was totally and utterly true. And unlike anything either the magic or Manson had tried to do to him today, this destroyed his very core.

"NOOOOOOOOO!!!!!!" he screamed uncontrollably, as he dropped painfully to his knees, head bowed to the floor, a flurry of irrepressible tears forming rivers down his cheeks.

Fredric took a step forward. So did Earth. Each spying the other, they both stopped, magic sizzling from their fingertips, their grandson and son respectively, kneeling on the floor in between them.

The all consuming cry of exquisite pain that rang out throughout the king's private residence attracted attention from all around, despite the mythical creatures splattering brains and bodies at will, the asag going on an absolute rampage and Manson's prehistoric temper threatening to burn the place down.

Regardless of their precarious positions amid their own personal battles, every single light-sided hero glanced over to where the sound had originated from, unsure of what to make of the scene that greeted them. It was a conundrum given that there appeared nothing physically wrong with the young boy dragon who, up until this moment, had played his own part in leading them. Puzzling frowns abounded, as friends wondered whether they should try and intervene, or whether it was even possible. None could have guessed the source of his pain and grief, apart from one that is. George, king of the domain, and however you looked at it, guardian of the planet, upholder of the truth to some degree at least, had a fair idea of what had just happened, and felt overcome with sorrow at realising Fredric had failed to conceal the truth from the young dragon, knowing just how important that assignment was to his friend. Silently wishing them well, the dragon king skidded to a halt behind a barricade of hissing nagas, despatched them with the kind of ease you and I would turn on a tap, and then slid into place alongside the rest of the battling King's Guards who up until that point could only concentrate on defence. With the newcomer's arrival, it seemed that something slightly more offensive might be in the offing.

Hands and arms shaking uncontrollably, barely able to pull in a breath, the world around him mercilessly caving in, a frightening black blanket of evil had been tossed over Peter's head, one from which there seemed no escape, none whatsoever. Drowning in his own thoughts, visions of his demon mother's horrific looking fingernails drawing blood from his very own neck at the top of them, it seemed for all intents and purposes as though his heart would stop beating and he would die on the spot. But others had a very different idea.

Physical body standing peacefully, eyes closed amidst Yoyo and what remained of his group of young dragons, Janice's conscience stayed high up above the battlefield, entwined with the consciousness of her friend, the weapon Fu-ts'ang. On hearing the scream of horror, she recognised the source instantly... her love, PETER!

"Oh my God, we have to get to him straight away... PLEASE!" she begged her friend.

Looking over everything in his worldly wise, analytical way, using all his thousands of years of combined experience, the soul of the master weapon smith imbued in the blade came to a very different conclusion.

"No," he said calmly. *"That's not the answer."*

"WHAT! You can't be serious. He needs me now more than ever."

"I'm not sure he does, at least, not like that. Us going down there is only going to make things worse, trust me on that."

"Look at him, look at the pain he's in. We have to get down there... NOW!" she screamed, as upset and out of control as Fu-ts'ang had ever seen her.

"Little one, calm down... I need you focused. You're no good to anyone in this state, least of all him. He's not hurt, at least not physically, and he's not in imminent danger, I assure you. Please, centre yourself and find your control. If we are to succeed here today, you of all beings need to be calm, peaceful and in charge of your emotions."

Although only an object, albeit one with a deadly edge and not just a frosty personality, his wise words were not only full of experience, they carried the love, respect and friendship that he felt for her, immediately melting away her panic and alarm at seeing Peter like that, washing away all that flustered her. Moments later, she was back in control, almost as if her outburst had never happened. If the futuristic looking blade could have smiled, then it would have.

"That's better," observed the weapon, grateful for the return of normality.

"We need to find out what's going on, at least," remarked Janice, still keenly watching events play out below.

"I think I might know," declared the weapon, reluctantly.

"You do? Then tell me!"

After what seemed like a deep breath, but couldn't possibly have been because of course he was a weapon, without the biological functions to actually do so, but we'll call it a dramatic pause, the master weapon smith searched for the words to tell his friend exactly what he suspected.

"I think the love of your life has just found out that the monster known as Earth, Manson's would-be queen, is the mother he thought to be long since dead."

"WHAT?!"

"Don't keep saying that, little one, it's very frustrating. You heard my words clearly and correctly."

"I... I... I... I don't know what to say. I'm absolutely gobsmacked."

"Not as much as he is."

"H... h... h... how is that even possible? And wait a minute, does that mean that she's Fredric's daughter?"

"I think so, yes."

"That's absolutely terrible. She tried to kill him right at the start of all of this!"

"I know, I was there."

"Sorry. I'm struggling to think straight. So why did she try and kill him then if she knew he was her son, do you think?"

"I would hazard a guess that she didn't know who he was then. And that perhaps only when he changed back into his prehistoric form, did it become clear."

Back in her physical body and her consciousness here with her friend, it was a lot to take in, and she had so many questions. What had gone wrong between Fredric and his daughter that would lead to this kind of animosity? What could make a father and daughter want to murder each other in cold blood? How was it that Peter didn't know who his real mother was? And was there really any way now to settle this amicably? Her mind was literally spinning, and it had nothing to do with the height from which they overlooked everything. It would seem that her boyfriend's relatives made the Addams family look positively regular. How scary was that?

Lashing, smashing and bashing his way through countless numbers of nagas, the odd dark dragon added in just to break up the monotony of it all, Tank's mind became instantly alert on hearing the scream, not only because it was a sign of danger, but because he immediately recognised the voice to whom it belonged... Peter, his best friend. Still a blur, still trying to outfox and avoid the mythical creatures that were doing everything in their power to hunt down the source of magic that he'd been wielding, he punched with everything he had, performed a serious of roundhouse kicks and then, after buying himself a moment, jumped as high in the air as he could, enhanced in no short measure by a huge amount of his partner's almost unlimited magic. How high, I hear you ask? Pretty damn high, as it turns out, and easily high enough to get a handle on what was going on.

'Phew,' he thought, tumbling back to the ground. 'Although Peter seems to be facing off with Manson's evil other half, Fredric's with him,' and Tank knew above all else, the powerful founder of the Crimson Guards that was Peter's grandfather would die before letting anything happen to his friend. So realising he wasn't needed quite yet, he let gravity take them both, plunged to the ground and picked his next group of targets, all the time knowing that they were running out of somewhere to hide from the strange and unusual creatures that not only fascinated him, but were hunting them both down. Crazy didn't begin to cover it.

Intuitively, Flash turned to face the direction the horrifying scream had come from, easily able to distinguish the owner from all of the other beings there... Peter, it just had to be. Hovering in the air, defending himself with a sword in one hand, plying magic with the other, Captain Battlehard at his back, he knew that all he'd get was one quick glimpse of whatever was going on. If he was needed he'd help in a shot, after all, what were friends for, but he wouldn't leave Amelia exposed and vulnerable to attack. He'd have to wing it and figure something out. As it turned out though, what he witnessed was nothing like what he expected. Peter was on his knees, absolutely distraught, but with no apparent injuries and by the look of it, in no immediate danger, even though he appeared to be caught between Earth and Fredric. Using all his extensive and battle hardened experience, the brilliant ex-Crimson Guard had a decision to make, and only a split second in which to do it. And so he chose not to act, well... to stay and fight alongside Captain Battlehard anyway, knowing that his skills would best be put to use here, at least for the time being. He did however vow to keep an eye on his friend's unfolding situation.

From some distance away, and through a crowd of dragons, nagas, exploding magic and debris falling from the hidden ceiling high up above, a nagging familiarity about the scream that had just pierced the air, ate away at Yoyo. It took him a few moments of realisation, but then he had it... Peter! Instantly he tried to get a bearing on where the young dragon was, but for the life of him, with so much going on, he just couldn't locate his friend. And then he thought of her... Janice, standing only a few metres behind him. Continuing with his healing and offensive duties, he whirled around to take her in, expecting the young human to have seen whatever evil was going on, and be about to rush out and join the one she loved... oh yes, he was one of the few to recognise what was really happening. But instead, there she was, eyes closed, as still as a statue. If her consciousness was still with Fu-ts'ang, and he assumed that it was, she couldn't have failed to miss her lover's scream, and would no doubt act accordingly. The only conclusion he could arrive at was that for the time being at least, things were well in hand.

Running, jumping, slipping, sliding, dodging in and out of any and everyone around her, the light-sided de facto leader had now become the hunted instead of the hunter, and was having a huge amount of trouble staying out of the deranged Manson's clutches, having had more than a few narrow escapes over the past couple of minutes. Worse still, he seemed to have rounded up several of his subordinates, telepathically no doubt, with a horde of them now giving chase and trying to stop her in her tracks. All of that was enough to cope with, and just when she thought it couldn't get any worse, that howling scream pierced her ears, sending shivers up her spine, making her heart beat twice as fast. On the edge of being pinned down and made to suffer a diabolical death, only one thought ran through her mind.

'Peter!' Needing to glean his situation straight away, she picked a random naga facing away from her, sprinted up its dark scaly tail, and channelling all of her magic, jumped as high as she could, making it up as she went along, hoping against hope that one of the many dark dragons filling the sky would come along at exactly the right time. Luckily, one did.

This time, instead of grabbing hold of its talons and holding on for dear life, like she had to avoid Manson's trap in an effort to outsmart the evil leader, her leap skyward, powered by a great deal of magic, had allowed her enough height to get up and over most of the aerial beasts, enabling her to land right on top of one. Surprised didn't really do justice to the menacing looking monster who immediately realised he had an unwanted passenger, the moment Richie's nimble little body touched down on his back. For her, there was probably an even greater feeling of shock, having not really expected to get this far, and certainly not believing herself capable of actually landing smack bang on the back of one of Manson's monstrosities. Now here though, and with the murderous looking beast glancing back over his shoulders at her, what on earth was she going to do? With but an instant to decide, the logical part of her mind reminded her that the tiny lightning bolts she'd only half successfully used on Manson had cooled down, rebooted and were ready to use again. Without any better options, the lightning ignited from the tips of her fingers, and without hesitation, she plunged them into the beast's neck.

Staggered that something would have the utter cheek and audacity to climb up upon him, the homicidal brute of a dragon, about to invert and attempt to shake her off, suddenly found himself unable to think, so agonising was the pain from the lightning burning into him.

"*Do as I command,*" Richie ordered telepathically, "*and just maybe you'll live when all of this is over!*"

Unable to even flap his wings at the moment, Manson's flunky continued to just glide above the battlefield, thoughts shattered, his life barely his own, little choice but to comply.

"*What is it you want? I won't turn over to your side. I'll die first.*"

'Finally one with a little fight and grit, that's a first,' thought Richie.

"*Turn around and do a flyby of everything. Do that and I'll let you go, you have my word.*"

Suspicious to say the least, Croaky the dragon was out of options and so taking the... the what, human, dragon... something else? With the 'something else' having a firm grip on his neck, but having stopped zapping him with vicious tongues of lightning, reluctantly he flicked his giant rudder of a tail in the right direction, altered course and banked, performing a slow loop, coming around one hundred and eighty degrees.

Glad to have somewhat tamed the brutish monster, it was only then that the de facto leader of everything remembered the reason she'd jumped up here in the first place... her best friend! Scanning the ground, looking for some all-out fight to the death with magic raging, strangely she found him kneeling on the floor, in between that wicked bitch Earth and the founder of the Crimson Guards, Fredric. From the vantage point she had, it didn't look as though he was injured at all, although she couldn't be totally sure. Perhaps Manson's other half had struck him down with some of her unusual magic, Richie thought to no one but herself. Wondering whether she should get down there and help and if she should keep her word to the dragon whose back she sat atop, suddenly both decisions were abruptly taken out of her hands as three huge, icy bolts of doom appeared as if from out of nowhere, and ploughed straight into her and the dragon she was riding. Instantly she tumbled off to the side, twisting over and over, spinning wildly out of control.

Done with looking on, Janice was just about to ask her deadly friend to get down there in case Peter and Fredric needed some support, when the slightest of mental nudges got her attention. Wondering what she should be looking for, it then became clear as three icy bolts of magic appeared from out of nowhere, hitting Richie and the dragon she'd co-opted.

'Oh crap,' was all the girl could think, for the first moment or two anyway. After that it was,

"What are you waiting for... get after her."

Fu-ts'ang didn't need telling twice, and in a speeding blur, shot off in the direction of one of the main players of this whole sad affair. Back at Yoyo's fighting group, Janice's body, eyes still closed, instinctively reached out to catch Richie.

'Oh no... I really haven't thought this through,' she

mused, her mind in deep disarray as they sped towards the falling lacrosse captain's body.

"What do you want me to do?" asked Fu-ts'ang questioningly.

Still she fell, wildly out of control, heading straight into a crowd of vicious looking nagas that were all expecting her, as their very smug, and pleased with himself leader, looked on.

"Can she grab hold of you"?" asked Janice as they closed in.

"I wouldn't have thought she would want to. Her hand will be as good as gone almost instantly. That won't work."

"Damn! There's only one thing for it. You're going to have to run her through."

"WHAT?!" screamed the flying super weapon, amazed that anyone would be insane enough to ask THAT of him. *"YOU'RE CRAZY!"*

"Maybe so, but it's the only way. If she hits the ground she's dead!"

And that was the crux of the matter, because Fu-ts'ang knew that what she said was exactly right.

"Any suggestions?"

"I'm no doctor, but what about her right shoulder?"

"Okay... here we go."

Falling faster now, with her back facing the floor, unable to get a grip on her magic, the young lacrosse superstar dragon wished with all her might for the chance to change into her dragon form, the one that had been so abruptly taken from her by the priesthood. Knowing that she must be getting close to the ground now, thoughts of closing her eyes and accepting her fate started to overwhelm her. And then, out of the corner of her right eye, a speeding blur leaving a frosty white trail in its wake came into view, heading straight for her... FU-TS'ANG!

'He must have a plan,' she thought, wondering what it was, knowing that it must be something ingenious. And then, as he started to get closer, without losing any of the speed that he'd built up, panic started to settle in. 'You're going too fast,' she thought. 'Slow down. Slow down!'

But he couldn't, not if he was going to get there in time, not if he was going to save her.

"Little one, you must leave. Warn Yoyo about Richie. I'll bring her to him after I've scooped her up."

"Will do," replied Janice. *"And thank you."*

"You're welcome little one. Now... go."

And with that, she commanded her consciousness to return to the body that was still reaching out trying to catch her friend.

With the glinting metallic, super sharp tip just peeking through the revolving coat of frost now only a moment or two away, it was then that Richie understood what was about to happen. And to say she wasn't pleased was something of a massive understatement. But she didn't have time to dwell on it, and did, in the circumstances, the only thing she could. She braced herself.

Feeling very much like waking up in a drug induced haze... not illegal drugs, but you know, the kind that you take if you've got a really bad case of the flu, the kind that give you some kind of respite and let you sleep a little, that's how it felt to Janice upon returning to her own body. Fighting through the debilitating arrival, she forced her mouth to work, as her legs, which felt strange and brand new to her, clambered over towards Yoyo.

"Yoyo, Yoyo you have to listen please," she stammered, trying to get his attention.

"Yes, yes I know my dear... it was Peter's scream. I assume he's alright given that you're back here with us now."

"No, no... not that, Richie's on her way here, she's in desperate trouble and needs your help."

"My goodness girl, what on earth's wrong with her?"

"She's about to get skewered by Fu-ts'ang, and it's going to be bad."

"WHAT?!" (At this point in proceedings, there was a lot of that going around.)

"I can't explain," replied Janice, "but she'll be here any

second. Please be ready to help her."

"I will child, I will. But this is no joke. If she's been hit by that thing, there might not be too much that I can do."

Turning around to look in the direction of the pitched battle and the area in which her two friends were situated, it was difficult for the young bar worker to see over the heads of the giant snake-like beings Yoyo and his charges were fighting off. Looking to the air, she waited patiently for the special delivery she was sure was now on its way.

'It's going to be close,' thought Fu-ts'ang as he swooped effortlessly beneath a flying dark dragon, shredding its wing sinew on one side as he did so, vaguely aware of the beast spiralling out of control to the ground in his wake. Plummeting into a dive that lasted all of half a second, Fu-ts'ang now found himself able to come at Richie from the floor facing up, which given the millions of calculations every second he'd been doing, appeared to be the optimal course. With the group of nagas below on the ground all baring their teeth in anticipation, they were surprised when a gale force rush of wind washed over them, accompanied by a huge BOOM that shattered most of their eardrums. Worse still was the sight of the most unconventional and futuristic weapon spearing their prey in mid-air, almost within touching distance, before turning and zipping off in the opposite direction. All were in pain, shocked and about to be taught a very harsh lesson regarding failure from their undisputed leader.

Eyes closed, as fearful as she'd ever been, momentarily she wondered if the whole adventure had been a dream or if she'd somehow been rendered in some sort of vegetative state all along. As if to prove her wrong, with almost as much pain as any one being could bear, the super swift, super cool (in more ways than one,) super intelligent flying weapon, Janice and Flash's friend Fu-ts'ang stabbed her through the right shoulder, its hilt jamming up against her pale, white flesh, the ever circling coating of frost freezing her bones, solidifying her blood, immobilising the whole of the right side of her body.

Desperate and in terrifying pain, she cried out, but it was more of a muffled blubber than anything else, with the tears that had instantly been shed the moment she'd been hit now looking like ice encrusted diamonds.

Given their unfortunate physical contact, Fu-ts'ang was now able to speak to the lacrosse playing dragon directly, which may or may not have been a good thing.

"Sorry my friend, there appeared to be no other way to save you. Don't worry, I'll have you in Yoyo's capable hands in but a few moments. Be strong and fight to stay alive. There's still much for you to do, illustrious leader." And with that he cut off all communication, wanting to focus his efforts on getting her to relative safety.

It hurt, more than anything she could imagine... and that was quite a lot, particularly given what she'd witnessed over the last couple of days. Thoughts of Casey's torture, the dragons falling for the 'nagas feasting on dead dragon bodies ploy' on her way here, and of course Tim's body being broken in two by Mason's murderous father. Those were her reference points when it came to pain, and this, having the biting cold gnaw away at her, seemed to eclipse them all. Head spinning, mind wandering, mouthing the word, "help," over and over again, the heroic young dragon who'd done so much already to save the planet looked on the edge of everything as she zoomed high over the head of the pitched battle, seemingly all but forgotten by everyone around her. Well, not quite, because at least two were waiting in frenzied anticipation of her arrival.

"There they are," screamed Janice, over the by now familiar sounds of the raging war unfolding all around them.

"Got them!" announced Yoyo, steel in his voice, not betraying the terror in his heart, unable to countenance losing anyone else, not after Hillier. Pushing away the guilt and sadness that he felt at the loss of his young friend, the healer in him asserted itself, and in its own inimitable way, began calculating what needed to be done.

A sickening blur, tip pointing skywards, leaving a trail of white frost dappled with brilliant red frozen globules of blood behind it, the courageous weapon smith trapped in the blade's body slammed on the brakes and in a superbly accurate piece of showmanship, tumbled hilt over tip, allowing the deathly looking lacrosse player to slide smoothly off his cutting edge, the frozen particles of air passing over her causing her to cry out in absolute agony as she did so. With outstanding timing, Yoyo caught the dragon leader and very carefully laid her down on the ground, much to the surprise of his charges all around, who'd only just come to notice exactly what was going on, each wondering why the weapon that was supposedly on their side had sliced through their commander and ally. Questions that Yoyo himself had yet to have answered.

"Breathe, youngster," urged the healer, "breathe. I'll have you back to your best in a matter of moments."

'I hope,' he added to himself, not fully understanding the extent of her wounds but knowing that a kind word, however false it might be, can on occasion be as good at healing as any mantra or spell.

With Janice looking on and the young charges battling ferociously against the evil elements trying to storm their position, Yoyo sheltered Richie's body with his wings on one side, whilst Janice protected it from the other. Running his flimsy little hands over her entry wound, the healer combined his magic with the power of his mind and his accumulated experience of many, many years in an effort to determine exactly what was wrong. Used to multitasking after the day that they'd all been through, he just had to ask the young human.

"What happened? Why did your friend attack her?"

Surprised at the venom in his voice, Janice was unsure of what to make of the healer's words.

"He saved her life. It was the only way. If he hadn't acted, she would most certainly be dead and we'd all be without a leader. I'm offended that you would think anything else."

Lifting his head up from Richie's broken body to look Janice directly in the eyes Yoyo's cold, hard, serious face broke into a small smile.

"I understand your frustration my dear, I really do. I figured that given all the good he's done us over the course of the battle it would be something like that, but I'm obliged to ask, and I apologise if my words were a little too brisk. That was never my intention. Now help me sit her up, I need to see the exit wound before I can start to heal her."

Swallowing nervously at having got the hump, albeit momentarily, with something massively prehistoric and over four times her size, the young bar worker did as she was told, supporting her friend's head and chest as the healer inspected the damage to her back.

"Hmmm... it's slightly worse than I thought, but not nearly as bad as it could have been. The only concern I have is whether there's anything about her fully human transformation that's unusual or not. We'll have to just hope that's not the case, and that the priesthood got everything right when they wiped her memories."

"Priesthood?" asked Janice. "Why would they do that?"

"I don't know why, youngster. In fact, I've just told you everything I do know. It must have been something serious though. Right! Hold her still. I'm going to attempt to flush out the wound and start to repair all the damaged tissue. She may cry out or try to move. Do your best to reassure her that everything's alright."

Janice nodded in response to the healer's wise words, barely able to imagine anything more unbelievable than what she was caught up in right at this very moment.

"Aaarrrrgggghhhh!" Richie cried, trying to wriggle out of the sitting up position she'd been put into.

"It's okay," affirmed the young bar worker, attempting to calm her friend down. "It's me, Janice. Sit still Rich, Yoyo's healing your injuries. It won't be long now, stay calm."

Through a cloud of pain that wrestled her thoughts and slowed her thinking, the lacrosse playing dragon just about manage to grunt back an, "Okkaayy."

So as Janice knelt on the floor supporting her friend in a sitting position, Yoyo continued with his magical ministrations, for the most part keeping his eyes fully closed, ignoring the outside world as much as he dared given their precarious circumstances.

A numbing agent first, Yoyo thought, easing the pain for the youngster, knowing that even trapped in the human form that she'd gotten used to over time, dragons in any guise absolutely hate the cold. It's their kryptonite and always will be. That done, it was time to mend the bone first, before concentrating on the surrounding tissue and muscles, something that took a little longer than he thought, more so because he wanted to get it right, given who he was dealing with. And then it was finished, almost fifty-five seconds from start to finish, and that was double checking everything. Imagine if human doctors could work like that... the hospitals would be empty, no waiting lists, no queues... it would be quite a turnaround. Perhaps one day, maybe if the dragons ever got around to revealing themselves and sharing their supernatural talents.

"Aaaahhhhhh... that's better," sighed Richie from the ground, pleased to see Janice's smiling face looking down at her.

The young bar worker let go of her friend, now that she appeared to be healed.

"How are you feeling?" she asked.

Nodding her head, their de facto leader answered,

"Much better... thanks for the save. I owe you yet another debt, and Fu-ts'ang. Thank him for me."

"I just did, and he said not only are you welcome, but he's sorry to have caused you such pain. There did seem to be no other option at the time."

"I know," Richie replied, slowly getting up to her feet.

"And you... healer. Thank you. If there's ever anything I

can do to repay the debt, you only have to ask."

"That's very kind of you youngster," Yoyo ventured, "but I was just doing my job. You can help us deal with these pesky nagas though. I know we've dented their numbers, but they still keep coming, it's all we can do to keep up with the attacks."

"Sure thing," declared Richie.

"Hang on," Janice mused.

"Hang on for what?" asked the lacrosse playing leader.

"Fu-ts'ang says he can help with that."

And as those words left her mouth, the heroic, futuristic looking, white frost enshrouded blade leapt up into the air, flew up about fifty metres, inverted and almost faster than a rocket, shot down to the ground, skewering one of the dark, deadly serpent-like creatures through the top of the head, rendering him instantly useless. About three seconds, that's how long it took. And he wasn't finished there either. Reversing back out of the deceased monster, the prolific killer of nagas and dark dragons hovered horizontally for a moment, the rotating cold air around his edge making all the dragons nearby at least a little uncomfortable. Without warning, and quicker than any of those with enhanced magical senses could see, the devilish blade shot off at lightning speed, spearing nagas around the outside of the little circle Yoyo's band of young dragons had formed, murdering not one, not two, not three, but in the end, fourteen of them in one continuous loop, all in under ten seconds. Not only did it give the young dragons a little relief from the constant onslaught, it also made their enemy wary of approaching, at least in such numbers, buying all of the light-sided heroes some respite and if nothing else, a little breathing time.

"He's my kind of weapon," Richie mused. "Tell him that, please?"

"He knows," said Janice smiling.

"Oh my God!" exclaimed Richie. "What about Peter? I forgot to ask you. Is he okay? That's where I was headed when you saved my ass."

"The last I saw he was kneeling down absolutely distraught about something, in between Fredric and that bitch Earth," declared Janice, staring directly into Richie's wide brown eyes. "Do you know?" she asked, very serious all of a sudden.

"Know what?" replied the lacrosse superstar.

"About his mother?"

"No... what about her?"

"Fu-ts'ang told me something, something that might explain exactly what's going on out there. I couldn't believe it was true... still can't in fact, but it does seem to fit all the facts."

"Go on."

"He said that... he said that Peter's mother is that crazed witch... EARTH!"

There was no WHAT this time, only thoughtful consideration about what she'd just been told. It was a shock, that's for sure, but something about it, in some strange way, made a kind of sickening sense.

"So she's Fredric's daughter?"

"Apparently so."

"This is just so messed up. We have to get out there and help him."

"My thoughts exactly," mused Janice. "But how, and what do we do once we're there?"

"Both good questions," replied Richie, "and I have absolutely no idea on either front, so let's have a think."

Right at that point, Hook skipped through a gap in their lines that Yoyo's young charges had opened up for him, clutching his damaged shoulder, looking much the worse for wear.

"What the hell happened to you?" exclaimed Richie, concerned for her friend's wellbeing.

"If I told you, you'd never believe me... not in a million years."

Shaking her head, the lacrosse playing dragon turned to

Yoyo. He already knew what she was going to ask.

"Will you please do the honours?"

"Certainly," the healer answered.

Moments later it was done, and the heroic rugby player was both fully healed and relieved at having made it back to temporary safety.

"Thanks Yoyo... much appreciated."

"You're welcome, my young friend. Try and take better care of yourself in these trying times," the healer said softly with a smile on his face.

Momentarily, they all laughed. And then it was back to business.

Much like Richie on watching the love of her life and the supposed White Dragon, Tim, being torn apart in front of her, Peter was well and truly LOST! Tumbling down a dark, shadowy well into oblivion, his mind was just not designed to take in the news that Earth was his mother. Had any other being on the planet told him so, he would have dismissed it out of hand, but coming from his grandfather Fredric, he knew without doubt that it just had to be true. The consequences were just too terrifying to contemplate in any real detail. He'd watched her kill, relish in other beings' deaths and of course try to murder him, her own son. How such evil existed, he would never know. It was just beyond his comprehension. And part of the all encompassing feeling of wanting to die or be swallowed up, was the taint that it had all painted on his grandfather. Why hadn't he... told him? And did George know? He said that he didn't on the fateful day when Flash was introduced into their lives and the chest was handed over, but looking back, was that a lie? Was he in the loop and just withholding the information from him at his best friend's request? It was all too depressing to think about and although somewhere inside his mind these questions were being asked, the rest of him was almost certainly too lost in everything it meant to have a psychopathic killer as a mother. Ironic in most respects, given he'd always wanted to know about his parents, had spent time during his youth trying to find out, wondering why he missed out on all that love and attention that a lot of the other students at the nursery ring took for granted. And now he knew, knew the truth (well, he didn't actually, not all of it anyway) and it couldn't have been any more brutal. Sobbing pitifully on the ground, all thoughts of the battle, his friends, Fredric, even Janice, all seemingly disappeared, he was a poor excuse of a hu... I nearly said human, but that was never really the case. He was a poor excuse of a dragon, in fact any being, now utterly useless, taken out of commission by only a few words, his naivety and the rose tinted glasses through which he viewed the world his total and utter downfall. Perhaps his mother would come to his aid and put him out of his misery once and for all.

"See what you've done?" yelled Fredric. "This is what it means to be your offspring!"

Serpents hissing and snapping atop her head, Earth snarled at her father, balancing carefully on that fine edge between sanity and madness.

"It's not my fault he's been brought up weak. Your kind turned him into what he is. Perhaps if he were to come with me now, I could toughen him up."

"Over my dead body!"

"As an idea, it's sounding better and better."

"You're an absolute disgrace. You still have no shame, do you?"

"And you're still very much stuck in your ancient ways. You might have thought that your stint in Antarctica would have given you time to reflect on all your mistakes," she smirked, Manson having telepathically revealed something about that to her during the fight.

She was goading him he knew, well... trying to. But with everything going on about them, he'd centred himself, knowing that it was probably the only way he'd survive, even if he brought all his talents to the table. And of course, keep his grandson alive in the process. The only chink in his armour was the fact that he'd let Peter down, allowing the truth, from one point of view, to come out, hurting him in the process. If he had one wish, it would be for that particular secret to never have seen the light of day. But what was done was done, and there was no going back now. All he could do was his utmost to keep the boy dragon alive and hope to hell they all lived long enough to get out of this, and explain fully exactly what had happened. With that in mind, he continued to edge the tiniest bit sideways, hoping to get Peter out of the line of sight between himself and his daughter, because all the time he'd been standing there fingering the laminium dagger that his friend had so judiciously passed to him, an idea of exactly how he'd take her down had been brewing deep within his mind.

"You need to show me where the crystal node is, and quickly. There's something I have to do."

"We know," responded the impressive laminium ball captain, Steel, his chest puffed out, pride at the job they'd done obvious, despite their losses. "Send out a message for reinforcements, after all that is the point of all this."

"Yes, yes," replied the master mantra maker, "but there's something else I must do before all that... something that might improve the odds for those fighting across the planet, almost immediately."

That caught the attention of all those around him, including Steel, Jar Man, DomCon, Nurse Conscience, the rest of the dragons and the human contingent.

"Do tell," asked Jar Man, as they marched swiftly towards their destination, feeling assured of their safety because they'd already checked the dead and dying.

Comfortable amongst friends, which was how he regarded all these beings after everything they'd been through, Gee Tee went on to explain about splicing the mantra together with Tank, much to everyone else's amazement, with all of the dragons there knowing exactly how illegal and dangerous such a thing was, and the humans finding the details of the story absolutely fascinating.

"And you have the mantra here with you?" asked DomCon, more than a little taken aback at what the old shopkeeper had revealed to them.

"I do," replied the master mantra maker, firmly slapping the huge natural pouch circling his massive rotund belly.

"That's quite a risk you're taking, keeping it on you," suggested Steel. "What would have happened, had you been struck with magic? Would it have ignited the mantra?"

"Maybe," said the shopkeeper casually, "I'll guess we'll never know."

All the beings accompanying the legendary mantra

fanatic exhaled in relief, all turning to look at each other, all relieved not to have found out the hard way whether or not that would have been the case, whilst their leader continued without a care in the world. Strange and unusual circumstances they found themselves in.

Stamping in, around, over and in the case of the human contingent, sometimes on the discarded naga and dragon corpses littering the huge stone corridors, careful not to slip in the slick wet blood, Gee Tee's dysfunctional group of heroes neared the exotic looking, even by dragon standards, crystal node, made even more eerie by the lack of lighting and those deceased operators that still slumped against their broken terminals, amongst which sat at least one imposter.

"What do we need to do first?" asked Jar Man, eager to help out.

"We... don't do anything. I... need to check the integrity of the node, make sure there are no traps and then integrate the spliced mantra, after which I can broadcast it worldwide, hopefully stunning all of their kind both above and below ground. There'll be no way of knowing if it's worked of course, but we'll just have to cross our fingers and hope."

"Shouldn't we broadcast the distress call first and let the world know where we are and just what's going on?" observed Nurse Conscience, sceptically.

"We could," Gee Tee reflected, "but as you've just mentioned, we'd be broadcasting where we are, not only to the dragon reinforcements, but to our enemies as well. If they come after us, which I suspect they might, and we don't have time to send out the spliced mantra neutralising the naga threat, then we'll have failed our friends and all those across the planet fighting against the darkness that hopes to envelop us. I think this way round makes much more sense, and hopefully gives us time to escape before the enemy even knows we're here."

"Understood," replied the very shy and retiring nurse, much to the old shopkeeper's amusement.

"It's alright, my young friend," (Gee Tee was the only

being on the planet that could constantly refer to everyone as young, because, as previously mentioned, he was without a doubt, and by quite some margin, the oldest surviving being), "I'm not smiling at you, only at the gusto and enthusiasm with which you live and the fact that you're brave enough to challenge a leader you've only just met. Let me say... well done. You'd be right to question everything you don't understand, and you should... always. Be confident in your decisions, and if everything you do is for the right reason, then you should never be afraid. Speaking up should be a right, an absolute necessity, and something that should never be taken away by either fear or bullying. Mark my words, young dragon, you'll go far with that sort of attitude, and I can see why you were chosen to look after our friend here in his time of need. Keep up the good work." And with that, the master mantra maker turned to inspect the imposing crystal node, wondering where he should start on the checks he needed to make. Before he had a chance to get any further, a familiar voice interrupted his thoughts.

"I can help," suggested Nurse Conscience, buoyed by the old shopkeeper's previous words of encouragement.

"How so?"

"One of my best friends from the nursery ring studied the nodes with a view to becoming one of the network's engineers. She spent over a decade doing just that, and I would often help her revise. I think I know my way around the systems pretty well, certainly well enough to determine if there are any traps or not. I'd be honoured to assist you."

With all of them wondering exactly how this was going to play out, each knowing that the master mantra maker liked not only to have everything under his control, but always to seem to be the smartest being in the room, even though that might not necessarily be the case, they were all surprised when he greeted the help he'd been offered with open arms.

"That would be great," he announced, taking her under

his wing, quite literally in this case. "Let's go and see if we can get started."

Turning to face the others, he had one last order for them.

"Post guards at the entrance to the inner sanctum. Having made it this far, we don't want anyone coming in and spoiling our plans now, do we?"

They all agreed that they didn't, and so with Steel quickly dishing out assignments, as alert as ever, they all rushed off to their posts, eager to stop any of the enemy getting this far. Little did they know that, ingeniously, the last one alive was hidden deep within the bowels of the building.

Inside the gutted and razed council building, amongst the collapsed walls, wrecked rooms and broken corridors, amidst raging fires and thick, cloying black smoke, Polo and her dragons continued to lead Garrett and his human force ever upwards inside an emergency stairwell that they hoped wouldn't come to an abrupt end, unlike the previous ones that they'd tried, where the whole floor above and more had come down atop it, preventing any further exploration in that direction.

With all the humans puffing and panting in the stifling atmosphere, especially their well worn leader, the dragons had not only slowed their pace considerably, but on occasion had taken to giving them lifts on their backs when such a thing allowed in the tight and twisting confines. Although only thirty floors, something all of them should have been able to cope with relatively easily, they were dragon floors, and over three times the height of what human buildings would have considered a storey. Of course they could have flown them nearly all the way to the top, had it not been for the intermittent debris scattered fleetingly about, which made the stairwell simply too tight in places and something of a squeeze for the prehistoric contingent.

Arriving at the next floor, like they had all the others, Polo and the dragons carefully tried to gain access, all of them not expecting to be able to, just like on the previous twenty attempts. But to their surprise the doors opened with ease, granting them debris free entry for the first time on their upward journey. Making their way into the storey, dodging loose wiring, sparking electricity cables, overturned chairs and desks, the dragons led, stretching out with their magic in an attempt to make sure things were clear. Fingering the safety catches on their weapons, nervous as hell, Garrett in the middle of the pack, the group of well trained and utterly gobsmacked humans followed on behind, keeping their own eye on things.

Twenty minutes later, the small group all came together alongside one of the huge bowed, tinted windows from which it was possible to look down onto the chaos of the battle raging below, after having made sure the whole level was free of enemies.

"Wow!" announced Owen, barely able to contain himself on seeing dragons hurtling through the sky, nagas slithering across the ground and a few small pockets of resistance fighting resolutely back.

"Wow indeed," added Garrett, stunned at what they were seeing.

Turning to face his dragon cohorts, the human leader just had to ask,

"Was this what it was like back at the marketplace in Salisbridge?"

"Not on this kind of scale, no," Polo replied.

"I see," said Garrett.

For the next three minutes or so they all continued to look beyond the curved, wraparound window and down into a vision of absolute hell, and that particularly applied when they all caught sight of the asag throwing its huge car sized fists about, punching nagas through the air, some smashing at speed into otherwise distracted dark dragons, others forming rocket-like cadavers, smashing through groups of their own kind. Hell, perhaps, didn't quite do it justice.

"What should we do next? Shouldn't we really go down there?" Garrett asked the one question most of them had been thinking.

"Hmmm..." was all that Polo could reply with.

"I'm still not sure what good it's done us coming all the way up here," ventured one of the other dragons. "Yes... we can see what's going on, but we can't get down there and that's probably where we need to be."

"Can't we just blow the window and fly out?" stated Owen all businesslike.

"The windows of this building are made from polyhexidustron, a metallic carbide created by magic and stronger than almost anything else. Breaking it would be virtually impossible, and that was even if we had something to do that with. Our magic combined wouldn't even touch it."

Rubbing his chiselled jaw for a moment, Owen pondered what had just been said. After considering their dilemma, he removed his huge backpack, put it on the floor and opened it up. A few seconds later, he turned to face the rest of the group.

"We do have these," he announced, holding out some very space-age looking charges in his hand.

"Let me see," urged Polo, snapping up two of the pitch black devices. "How much of a punch do they pack?"

"They'll blow away anything up on the surface," Garrett answered. "They're the best of the best, in human terms anyway."

Momentarily resembling a school playground, the dragons got themselves in a huddle and began rambling on. This continued for two or three minutes, before they separated.

"It might just work," announced Polo. "How many of them do you have?"

"We have three each," observed Owen, knowing exactly

how many they had as he'd been the one to pack all of their rucksacks, intent on keeping one behind.

"If we line them up to form one huge blast, and then use a very exact mantra to channel the energy at one specific point, we just may be able to crack the carbide. If we can do that, it might be possible to break it afterwards. What do you say?" ventured Polo. "Want to give it a go?"

Of course they did, and so under Owen's technically gifted watch, the explosive devices were carefully placed in a circular formation in the middle of one of the gigantic panes of glass-like material. After all eighteen charges were planted all looking like one humongous evil eye staring back out at them, and with the humans' work done, they all retreated to the middle of the room, and started organising desks and chairs as a barricade. A minute or so later, all the dragons came over to find them.

"What are you doing?" asked one.

"We're forming a barricade to shelter behind to avoid all of the shrapnel and debris."

The dragons chortled uncontrollably.

"There won't be any... trust us. The magic cast on it will focus all of the kinetic energy into the window at exactly the middle point. Nothing will escape. You'll be perfectly safe standing right next to it," offered up one of the prehistoric beasts.

"I think we'll stay here," answered Owen, more than a little sceptical and only too well aware of the power the devices packed."

"As you wish... Shall we?"

Pulling out the detonator from his jacket pocket, the current head of security, wondering how the hell he'd found himself here, glanced over to his boss Garrett, who, without hesitating, gave him a nod. Flicking up the safety and really not sure of what was about to happen next, he shouted,

"Fire in the hole!" and then depressed the big red button that all the explosives had been slaved to.

An enormous bright flash followed by a loud, muffled

WHHUMPHH preceded a rippling red energy that, just as the dragons had predicted, contained everything within the blast radius. Impressive really didn't do it justice, with Owen standing there, his mouth hanging open, jaw nearly touching the floor. Immediately Polo strolled right over to the window, Garrett hot on her heels.

Dispelling any remaining magic with just the flick of her finger, Polo wiped away the excess dirt and dust on the glass itself with her hand, and craning her long scaly neck, leant in for a closer look, Garrett right behind her.

"Impressive," she observed, noting the tiniest of cracks in the pane.

"Will it be enough?" asked the 'bald eagle'.

Glancing over at her friends, watching them nod with approval, she turned back to the shiny headed human.

"It should be. Now that there's a weakness in it, we think that we can break it using magic. If you'll all stand back, this might well require your barricade."

Quickly doing as she suggested, the human contingent retreated behind their hastily erected fortification and waited to see what would happen.

One by one the dragons placed their hands against the glass and closed their eyes. Each of the humans was deeply enthralled by all of this, having already seen so much that was new to them... dragons, riding atop dragons, magic, a whole crazy new gigantic world hidden underground, it was mind blowing and more than a little scary. But all were professional, not least Owen, who not only wanted to do his job to the maximum of his ability, particularly in front of Garrett, but was keen to find and help his friend Peter, especially if he was caught up in everything going on down below them.

Last to step up, Polo strode over to the window and setting her hand on the glass, closed her eyes, deep in thought. This time, even the other dragons took a couple of steps back, wary of what might happen.

In total and utter silence, a rainbow of colours played

over the area within which the tiny little crack sat...
NOTHING! But it appeared that the charismatic dragon
leader wasn't done yet. This time a rich blue light shone
brightly almost from within the glass itself, as all of the
others watched, willing it to work... but it didn't! A frown
creeping across her scaled forehead, Polo redoubled her
efforts, as if that were at all possible. A thick, shimmering
dark green pulsed throughout the pane, the reflection
lighting up the darkened room. Abruptly, the tiniest of
sounds echoed out around them, like a small stone chipping
a car windscreen at speed. And then another, and then
another and then... a splintering spider's web of fractures
spread out across the huge panel of futuristic material,
encompassing almost all of it.

Opening her eyes and taking two steps back, her jaw line
twisting into a delicious smile, Polo pointed her finger one
last time and in her mind, uttered one word.
BOOOOOOOOOM! The biggest, the loudest, the most
thunderous noise any of them had ever heard sent shards of
glass flying in every direction, peppering the front of the
barrier the humans all cowered behind. All the dragons
remained safely behind the personal shields that they'd
erected.

As the last few flakes of glass tinkled to the floor, over
the onrushing howling gale from just the sheer height they
were at, each of the dragons dropped down onto their
knees, once more offering themselves up for the humans to
ride upon. Shaking their heads in utter disbelief, and barely
able to comprehend exactly what they were about to do,
reluctantly all the humans boarded their awaiting prehistoric
transports, each of them fingering their NGSARs nervously,
thinking that they had a fair idea of what was going on
down there. They didn't, but they were very quickly about to
find out. Stepping off at exactly the same time, plummeting
into an almost vertical drop, the wind whipping through all
of the humans' hair with the exception of one whose
moustache was getting a thorough cleaning, with biscuit

crumbs from decades ago being flushed right out, each of the monstrous winged beasts yelled exactly the same thing, inside their heads:

"GERONIMO!"

33 A FAMILY FURORE

'Can I? Should I? Or will it make things worse, with the boy never able to forgive me?' were the thoughts winging their way around Fredric's head right at this very moment, concerning the idea he had to rid the planet of his venomous witch of a daughter once and for all. But now there was this slight pause which deep inside he knew might cost him dearly. Because there was one thing he was absolutely certain of: she wouldn't hesitate to take his life, as she'd already shown on more than one occasion. If he didn't use this one chance to do just that to her, it might devastate not only him and his grandson, but the entire world... decisions, decisions.

Taking yet one more step sideways, much to the amusement of his psychotic daughter who it had to be said was smart enough to realise exactly what he was doing, Fredric considered the consequences of what he was about to try and came to the only conclusion he could... be damned with it all. He should have done it long ago for his sake, the world's sake and of course the sake of his grandson, kneeling there on the ground, utterly broken and distraught. As well, any way you looked at it, especially on a lives lost calculation, it was the right thing to do. Choice made, he readied himself for one all-out, gung ho attack.

Honestly, if she'd learnt one thing living under the same roof as him growing up, it was how easy he was to read. A poker face was something he just didn't have. And he hadn't changed one bit during the course of the decades lost in Antarctica. It would almost have been laughable if the stakes hadn't been so high and her son hadn't been caught up in the middle of it all. With the madness pushed temporarily to one side, sanity reigned at least for a while, something of a new experience, with the mother in her knowing she had to do everything she could to avoid confrontation. As her father slowly moved to his right, she did the same thing, mirroring his progress exactly, trying to keep Peter directly in between them, knowing it was as good a way as any to stop him unleashing everything he had at her.

'So that's how it's going to be,' he thought, watching her copy his every action, making what he had in mind hard, but not totally impossible. A surge of sadness washed over him at how he'd always been an open book to her. The fact that it remained so even up until this day, cut like a knife, opening up a wound that he'd long since forgotten was ever there. Kids eh!

Still falling through the darkness, thoughts of anything else drowned out by the pain, sorrow and pity he felt for himself, Peter could have done with his friends all showing up now, that might have been the one thing that could have saved him. Some were on their way but others had issues of their own to deal with given just what was playing out here and now, before they could even focus on him. It was a shame really, because they might have turned the tide, pulled him back from the brink, offered him a glimpse of reality and the happiness that he deserved. But through no fault of their own it wasn't to be, and so he continued tumbling through the air, the thick, cold, dark wind pummelling his face, writhing black tentacles lunging out as he twisted past on his inevitable journey, trying to grab hold and take what little remained of him. Hope, longing, love and any serious amount of fight had been stolen, replaced by a bitter sense of loneliness, resentment and anger that he'd had to wait all of this time to find out. If he'd known before, then he could have distanced himself from other beings, shielded them from all of this and never gotten involved with that human girl. Those were his thoughts and quite against everything cold and dark, he still had some regard for those others in his life. That might just be his saving grace and redemption.

With the brief lull that Fu-ts'ang had brought them, and with Yoyo's young charges watching out for any new attack, Richie brought the others there that were close by into a huddle, in an effort to exchange ideas and work out a plan.

"We need to get to Peter," urged Janice, speaking up before Richie, their de facto leader, even had a chance to open her mouth. "Sorry," she whispered to her friend.

"No problem," replied the superstar lacrosse player. "What she said."

"What about reforming a shield like we had before and crossing the battlefield that way?" suggested Yoyo, not having entirely thought his suggestion through.

"It would take too long," answered Richie. "I don't think he has that amount of time, not from what I witnessed."

"What about sending Fu-ts'ang to pick him up and bring him here like he did with you?" proposed Janice, smiling at the thought that she'd come up with something good.

"NO!" exclaimed Richie.

"NO!" stated Yoyo.

'NO!' declared Fu-ts'ang inside her head.

"Oh..."

"I'm sorry Janice," whispered their leader, "but there's just no way that he'd make it back. I barely did, and unfortunately he's not me. It's a good idea, and that's what we're looking for, but that one is not for him."

"What about one all-out, outrageous, do or die attack?" offered up Hook with more than a hint of sarcasm.

Hook smiled. Janice smiled. No one else did.

"I was joking guys, trying to lighten the mood."

Richie turned to Yoyo and asked,

"What do you think?"

Rolling his head from side to side, the experienced healer began to consider the option in more detail, such as how they'd do it, who would partner who, whether they would have enough magic to get as far as Peter and Fredric and whether the element of surprise would outweigh any pitfalls that might get thrown up.

Hook and Janice looked on in utter horror that is until the young bar worker's face changed ever so slightly.

"Fu-ts'ang wants to weigh in," she said softly.

They'd almost forgotten the legendary weapon was hovering amongst them after the deadly killing spree that had bought them all some time.

"Go on," commanded Richie.

"I could clear a whole swathe of them in front of you. They'd never see it coming. For what it's worth, I think it just might work. What you do after that though, I can't really say. As well, you'd have to get George and the remaining King's Guards, as well as Flash and the dashing Captain Battlehard behind you to have any chance. Whether they'd sign off on it or not is anyone's guess."

Nodding in agreement, their leader could come up with nothing else and although not wanting to throw lives away unnecessarily, bringing some of the pain to the other side and going on the offensive for once, whichever way you put it, sounded very much like something she wanted to do. Opening up her mind with the full force of her magic behind it, she sought to attract the attention of the King's Guards, George, Flash and Amelia, hoping to hell that they would all agree to what she had in mind.

"YOU WANT TO DO... WHAT?!" screamed the current dragon monarch across their shared link. *"YOU'RE ABSOLUTELY MAD!"*

'Nothing like being shot down in flames,' she thought, really not wanting to be any sort of leader or have anything to do with the supposed White Dragon prophecy.

"Hang on a second," declared Flash across the stunning silence that now remained, deflecting away an incoming sword before cutting off the head of the hissing naga it belonged to. *"I think it just might work. As well, we need to get Vasuki on side. His help will be invaluable."*

"Hmmm..." George huffed across the link, clearly

unimpressed. *"What do you think, Captain Battlehard?"*

Continuing to fight back to back with the mountain of a dragon that was Flash, the ex-Crimson Guard, having heard all the stories about the brave protector of the king, carefully she considered his words.

"It's risky, that's for sure, but there is a chance it might pay dividends and get us all to Peter and Fredric unharmed. Whether you all want to take that chance is not my decision. What I will say, is that I'm sick and tired of being on the defensive all the time. I say it's time to make these bastards pay... with their lives."

All of them, Yoyo's young charges and what remained of the King's Guards nodded at this as they continued fighting, approving of not only the words, but the sentiment behind them as well, something that shone through their shared link.

"Well, White Dragon, you seem to have a consensus," admitted George reluctantly. *"If I were you, I'd ask Flash to get Vasuki on side and ready to go. May whatever God is watching have mercy on our souls,"* and with that he cut off his side of the connection.

"You heard him, Flash," stated Richie. *"Ask Vasuki to join us and make sure he knows how important this is. Get back to me when he's ready. I'll give you all as much notice as I can before we start. I know you all will, and that you're the finest of the finest, but I have to stress, you'll need to give everything that you have in this one last push. Let's turn the tables on these bastards and give them a taste of their own medicine. Get ready and good luck."*

"What did they say?" asked Hook having not been able to listen to the conversation, unlike Janice who shared Fu-ts'ang's link to the others.

"We're going to do it," announced Richie.

"What about me, what should I do?" enquired the courageous rugby player.

"Stay just behind me and keep up. I'll protect you as much as I can. Watch our backs for anything we don't see. You'll have to be our eyes and ears. With so much going on, it'll be easy for one or all of us to miss something that might cost lives. How does that sound... Tiny?" she smirked, knowing he'd like that last comment.

"Tiny, indeed. I'll watch your back, lacrosse superstar, but when this is all over, you and I are going out for dinner and a proper drink. Okay?"

Despite thoughts of Tim's tortuous death still fresh in her memory, she had come to really like Hook over the last couple of days. Strong, courageous, loyal with a great sense of humour and although now was sooooo not the time to be flirting with anyone, not with the planet's future at stake, she flashed him her super confident smile, batted her eyelids and agreed to his demand, telling him in no uncertain terms that she would drink him under the table. And that was enough to instil confidence in him and take his mind off what dreadful deeds were still to come.

It took less effort than Flash thought it would to convince Vasuki to join their madcap plan for an all-out attack, with the ex-Crimson Guard knowing the naga king was having a dreadful time. Killing your own race for no other reason than the fact they'd been magically enthralled by a ruthless being, forced into making the wrong choices and being complicit in despicable deeds was, as far as he could see, close to breaking the king of the nagas, and so perhaps going on the offensive might be enough of a distraction to take his mind off it all, at least momentarily.

"I'll watch over you and your kind, youngster," assured Fu-ts'ang in a private conversation with his best friend, Janice.

"I know," she replied, hefting one of the huge black bastard swords over her shoulder with a tremendous effort.

"What's that for?" enquired the master weapon smith.

"I'll need something to take with me, since I'm incapable of wielding any magic."

"You could take control of me again if you like. I'm not averse to it you know."

Nodding, despite the conversation playing out in her head, she truly appreciated the recommendation and had a fair idea of just what it meant for him to say that, given his newly found freedom.

"It's nice of you to offer, but you'll be more effective making your own decisions. Keep it that way and watch all our backs. That will give us the biggest chance of getting through this in one piece. You know that I care about you and that I was devastated when I thought that you had died."

"I do know, and I did die."

"You're kidding?"

"Nope... it's a long story, but your friend Tank and his partner, For'son, brought me back from the dead. If not for them, I would still be there and unable to protect you. I just thought you should know."

'Wow,' was all the young woman could think.

"It's almost time... good luck," ventured the enigmatic blade.

"Good luck to you," she replied. *"Happy hunting and stay safe."*

Having watched his nemesis, the young lacrosse player, being whisked away by the deadly blade that had somehow been re-forged, Manson took out his anger on four of the dumbstruck nagas, all of whom had just stood there waiting for her to fall into their clutches. If they'd unleashed their magic as she fell, they would have achieved their goal, killed one of the best and brightest the other side had, and he could have revelled in satisfaction at a job well done. But no! Once again she'd escaped, avoiding a very painful death. And so he'd made them pay, ripping out the heart of one, making his last act to watch his very vital organ stop beating in the hand of his leader, a sickly smile all the time etched across his face. The next had been sliced in two, precisely halfway down his slippery serpent body, the look of shock burned into his face as death settled in. By the time it came to the next two, he'd become bored as well as full of rage, decapitating them both in one fell swoop, ironically with a spell he'd been taught by one of their own kind. Black viscous energy formed razor sharp ethereal garrottes behind both of them, wrapping around their necks before pulling tight. Against the backdrop of the battle, both their heads tumbled to the blood slicked ground, before rolling off to one side, their filthy dark bodies collapsing on top of one another. Letting out a deep breath, his temper satisfied, at least for now, he glanced around to find his next target and see where he could most be of use, wanting nothing more than to get this over with. In the distance, he could just make out the outline of that whirling blur of an idiot rugby player, who had somehow conned him into believing there could be some kind of truce, when instead he'd managed to restore all of the magic and mana he and his new queen had stolen. It was about time for a little payback, he thought to no one but himself, a lopsided grin appearing across his huge chiselled jaw.

Careful not to catch the eye of the rampaging asag, knowing that even they were vulnerable to its attacks because of the straightforward physicality that it ran riot with, the ra-hoon lurked in the shadows as far back as possible, using the piles of naga and dragon corpses as cover, only ever poking their heads out here and there, keen not to expose themselves to the many on the battlefield that would look to do them harm. Of course, they were practically invulnerable to magic, so that really wasn't an issue. It was more the risk of a dark dragon swooping down from the air and carving them open with its sickly sharp talons that had them being so cautious. Defending against that would have been difficult, if not impossible, and that's why they held a few of their troops back for defensive duties. While the nifoloa, asena, scaled apes, scorpion men, myrmecoleon (an ant/lion hybrid) and two-headed eagles attacked everything that moved, feeding off their innards, releasing their magic, allowing the ra-hoon to inhale as much of it as they could, some of the camaheutos, echeneis, skrikers, gaki, pixiu, conaima, fire breathing gnats and vampiric lizards remained behind as a rearguard, defending the unicorn lookalikes' position, making sure that nothing snuck up behind them, not that it was a real possibility given the wave of death that they were creating across the width of the king's private residence. Only corpses remained in their wake and the lingering taste of magical finality hanging in the air. Urging their troops on, desperate to hunt down that one huge source of magic that they could tell was ever so slowly coming into range, they ignored their losses, revelled in the bloodshed, soaked up what ethereal energy they could and savoured the thought of the biggest feeding frenzy of their lives. If Tank and For'son could have heard what was playing out in their minds, they would have been absolutely terrified. Fortunately for them, they were way too busy to be concerned by that.

"They're slowly corralling us you know," observed For'son all robot-like, deep inside Tank's mind.

"I know," replied the young dragon, *"but I can't see a way out at the moment."*

"It won't be long before we become trapped beside your friends. What are we going to do then?"

"Well... you work on that, while I keep taking down these guys," quipped Tank, more than a little disappointed, wondering what the hell else he could do to appease the distinctly touchy presence.

"I was only saying."

"I know, and I'm sorry if I snapped. I never meant to. It's just with everything going on, giving part of myself over to you, focusing on all these different targets, worrying about my friends and now this brand new threat that looks as though it might eclipse everything else, my head's spinning so badly I don't know whether I'm coming or going."

"You have my sympathy, child," remarked For'son, *"as well as an apology. I'm sorry. You're doing an outstanding job and we'll deal with the mythical creatures when the time comes. If only we could get rid of all these pesky nagas, then that would be half the job done."*

'Perhaps,' he thought, 'there's an upside to Peter being stuck in the middle ground directly between us. Maybe if I can attack her directly with everything I have, unleashing my magic the other side of him from where I am, it's possible that she'll be reluctant to return fire because she might risk hurting him.' But it had never bothered her before... killing innocent beings that is, and that was the gamble with which he was toying, deep inside his head. Could he bet the life of his grandson on his daughter's compunction to see him stay alive? Doubtful at best was the only conclusion he could come to. But something had to give, he knew, and as the battle raged on, and with Manson's murderous monsters looking as though they were winning, continuing to outnumber the pathetic excuse of a light-sided revolt by at least twenty to one, time was running out he knew, and to take her out and join back in with the main force was something that could possibly turn the tide for the good of the planet.

Past dreams of a normal life and having parents that he could go visit at the weekend or even stay with during the week while at the Purbeck nursery ring haunted his further descent into the dark. Throughout his schooling he'd always been jealous of those that had experienced what he liked to think of as a normal paternal relationship. After all, who gives up a child and then just never goes back? Okay, it's more common in dragons than it is in humans, but still, what kind of a being do you have to be for that mindset to take hold? A monster was the only conclusion he could draw, given the startlingly new revelation. Briefly his mind wandered, wondering whether or not because they shared the same DNA, he too had the capacity for unwavering violence and psychotic tendencies. He supposed he had and that it just hadn't reared its ugly head yet... probably because he was still relatively young in dragon terms. Drowning now in the thick, cold, stifling atmosphere, he gasped for breath, but there was none, his mouth gulping like a goldfish swimming ever repeating loops in its bowl, his arms and legs flailing everywhere, making him look as though he were trying to create a snow angel. Thoughts of his friends tried to resurface, but the shadows of doubt, fear and loneliness blocked them out, preventing him from ever knowing they were there. Abruptly and from out of nowhere, he considered taking his own life, using what little magical knowledge he had to implode his own brain, essentially escaping this misery forever. On reflection, some part of him dismissed the idea totally out of hand, but those murky thoughts continued to lurk in the background, ready to surge forward and flood whatever passed for his mental defences right at this moment, adding to his already shady and sinister outlook. With his mind almost lost, would his body last long enough for a rescue of any sort, or would the animosity between father and daughter turn into an all-out battle of which he'd be the very first victim? Soon it would be time to find out.

Apart from the half dozen or so that had disappeared, commanded to guard the front entrance in case reinforcements should arrive, the rest of them, Steel, Jar Man, DomCon and their human friends, all crowded around Gee Tee and Nurse Conscience in the area surrounding the much talked about crystal node, something that during normal times would have been off limits to most, watching with interest exactly what they were doing.

"Check the inverted lattice for any sign of degradation," demanded the master mantra maker in his rough, gruff way, really meaning no harm at all.

Nurse Conscience took it all in her stride with a smile on her face. After all she had experience working with trying individuals, namely some of the doctors back at the medical facility.

"It's clear," she said nodding over at the old shopkeeper. "The monitor reads viability in excess of ninety nine point six percent, well within tolerance."

"Good, good," uttered Gee Tee, almost to himself.

All of the others looked on amongst the carnage of the cadavers and the echoing eerie darkness, hoping they were about to see all of their hard work come to fruition.

"Now," exclaimed the master mantra maker, "is the matrix aligned, and have you checked for foreign bodies of any sort in the capacity drive?"

"I've double checked," replied Nurse Conscience, "and there are no foreign bodies or anything else visible that would cause an overload. And the matrix is fully aligned and ready to be powered up on your command."

Oh... he definitely liked her. She was, in his opinion, just great, so much so, that a job offer to work at the Emporium might just be in the offing.

"Okay," he stated all workdragonlike. "I'm going to switch on the power and bring it up to full, ten percent at a time. If you see it spike, or any indication of a quantum overload, tell me immediately and we'll shut it down. We may only get one go at this, so we have to get it right."

"Understood," she replied.

Using a vertical slider on a touch screen with one hand, whilst controlling the input with a knob on the control panel with the other, all the time monitoring the results on the screen in front of him, slowly Gee Tee brought up the power. In the corner behind them the crystal node pulsed erratically, turning from a dull, blackish green to a much brighter shade of the colour, almost becoming alive. So far, things were going swimmingly.

Swimmingly or not, what none of them realised was that a great white or rather, a great Red, sat all but amongst them, waiting for the perfect time to execute the one last ambush she had planned. Unfortunately for her, there were too many of them crowded around in the confined space for her to be assured of success, and so with time running out, against her best instincts she decided to stay put a little longer in the hope that an all encompassing opportunity would come about. If not, then she would have little choice but to try and take them all on.

With everybody there on edge, the master mantra maker finished bringing the node up to full power without anything catastrophic happening.

"It's in the clear and ready to broadcast," announced Nurse Conscience.

"Excellent. I'm going to set it up to geo locate across the globe, at maximum power, and that should, if I'm right about all of this (or more clearly, if Tank was right, after all, it was his idea in the first place) extend the range of the mantra to include the surface of the planet, hopefully stunning and thus neutralising any nagas no matter what form they are in. It might frighten the hell out of some of the humans as beings across the surface suddenly stop what they're doing for no apparent reason, but it's the best that can be done in a limited amount of time with finite resources."

Moving over to the crystal node itself, looking like a five metre tall, pulsing green Fabergé egg, the wily old shopkeeper searched the pouch around his belly before withdrawing the sparkling, golden sheet of parchment with an array of rainbow colours swirling about on it, looking like a living puddle of oil with the light reflecting onto it.

"Oooohhh..." whispered everyone there upon seeing the precious prize, apart from Red of course who did not know what was going on. Had she done so, then she might well have acted immediately and made the ultimate sacrifice for her leader, probably doing him a massive favour in the process. But she still chose to be patient, something that might or might not yet pay off.

Holding the magical mantra masterpiece up against the crystal node itself, Gee Tee nodded at his accomplice and closing his eyes, put all the will and magic he had left into the multicoloured scroll. As the others looked on, the rainbow almost seemed to come alive, with the words, letters, symbols and numbers moving of their own accord, some writhing in the air, others melting into the node itself. It was spectacular, infusing the air with magic and by now, too late for anyone, including Red, to do anything about.

"It's been successfully transmitted," announced Nurse Conscience, gleefully.

"Thank God," commented the old shopkeeper, utterly spent.

Noting his condition, Jar Man and Steel moved in to guide him to a spare chair, something he was immensely grateful for.

"Thank you, my friends. I feel more exhausted than I ever have. That seems to have taken a lot out of me."

"What about calling for reinforcements?" asked Steel, concerned about getting things back on track.

"We'll need to wait for ten minutes or so for the node to come back up to optimum power," answered his biggest fan, the nurse.

His only acknowledgment was to nod his head.

"We've got this covered," uttered Gee Tee, slumped in his comfortable chair. "Why don't you all see if you can make this place any safer and whether or not they left anything useful behind? Pair the humans off into groups with you. Another ten minutes or so, and then we can consider our jobs done and go about finding out what's happening across the rest of the planet."

Following his instructions, they made it so and groups consisting of dragons and humans set off to explore the rest of the facility, leaving the master mantra maker not quite alone with Nurse Conscience.

Wind rifling through their hair, or buffing up your shiny disco ball head, depending on just who you were, dropping like rocks off a cliff, the six dragons and their seven riders, Polo having once again been the one to take two, Garrett and Owen, nose-dived towards the council building side of the rebuilt bridge, which currently appeared free of any enemies, and offered a considerable amount of cover in the form of huge piles of bedraggled dragon and naga cadavers. Landing with a THUMP, and unbelievably (or not given all the chaos of the battle) unnoticed, the makeshift group immediately hid out of sight behind the mountains of bodies, something they all found grisly and gross. But the alternative, staying out in the open and being spotted by all the fighting factions, was just too bad to even contemplate.

"What do we do now?" whispered Garrett, his heart still beating ten to the dozen, his legs shaking from the daredevil descent that he'd just been part of.

"We wait, figure out exactly what's going on, where we can best be of help, and just maybe make contact with any of ours out there if we can. I think caution from now on should very much be our watchword," answered Polo.

Garrett couldn't have agreed more. And so, from their hidden vantage point, they all settled down to watch and learn exactly what was going on, the humans amongst them breaking out the military grade binoculars, whilst the dragons experimented with the different vision types available to them in an all-out effort to gain more information. From now on in, it was very much a waiting game.

Earth's Surface. The Black Forest, Germany.
After their late night impromptu dip to blow off steam, the nagas were back in the clearing, refreshed and re-energised, their discussion on the lake bed having proved to be something of a turning point, their clear heads coming up with a number of potential solutions to the problems they faced in retrieving the laminium from the ever so puzzling cube. Working in the calm and methodical way they were renowned for, after but a few hours, they all, unusually, became quite excited and started to gather round.

"It can't possibly be this simple, can it?" contemplated their leader, in front of all the others.

"You wouldn't have thought so," replied another, "but perhaps that's the point... to have us chasing our tails looking at it in far too complex a manner."

"Why don't you go ahead and see if it works?" suggested one more of their kind. "That's the only way we're going to know for sure."

Turning back to the encapsulated black box, having done all the so called difficult work, there really was only one thing to do. Placing his human shaped hand (something that thoroughly disgusted him, being in this ape-like guise) against the high tech material and feeding just a little sliver of his ethereal energy into part of the mechanism of the cube they'd been working on since coming out of the lake, on top of the magic they'd already applied, he closed his eyes and hoped they were all right. The tiniest CLINK in the world, only audible because of their supernatural senses, echoed up from where he'd just taken his hand away, and on taking two steps back everything they'd worked for came to fruition all of a sudden.

Silently, all four sides of the black box peeled back, the furthest one away attached to the top of the cube revealing inside exactly what they'd all been told was there... an amazing amount of what the nagas always referred to as 'Dragon's Gold', or as we know it... laminium!

Caught up in the moment, all the nagas started cheering and shouting, alerting their dragon comrades, even those that were sleeping, that something was up. With the exception of those dark dragons that were on sentry duty, the rest of their kind made their way to the cube, utterly astounded that their snake-like cohorts had achieved so much success so quickly. As the dark dragon that went by the name of Oblivion arrived, the overall leader of this particular mission, about to congratulate the celebrating nagas, abruptly their friends from the frozen south, all, to a disguised man and woman, became totally and utterly immobile.

'Odd,' thought all the dark dragons simultaneously, having no clue what the hell was going on, with one or two even prodding and poking their supposed allies. But there was nothing, no reaction, no anything. They were for all intents and purposes still alive, that much was obvious, but they were frozen solid, unable to even blink and proof positive that the spliced together mantra was doing its job to a tee.

Pleased that the laminium had been recovered, and honestly not really ever having had any real regard for the nagas, Oblivion made the only reasonable decision he could and ordered the rest of his dragons to kill the remaining nagas and dispose of their bodies in the lake. Not needing to be told twice, the darkness within the prehistoric beasts flared up immediately, with a little competition going on to see who amongst them could be the most brutal. In mere moments it was over, the most one-sided fight of all time done and dusted, their former adversaries torn apart into bite sized pieces ready to be fed to the fishes. As the competition continued in the form of seeing just who could throw the pieces of their ex-comrades the furthest into the lake, Oblivion took stock of the recovered rare metal, wondering when instructions would arrive and tell him what to do next.

35 STUNNED!

Richie, Flash and Amelia, all communicating telepathically, all still warding off the enemy to some degree or another, were putting the finishing touches to the line up that would, in their minds at least, streak across the battlefield to Fredric and Peter's position, destroying anything and everything in their way. An unbreakable line of attackers who, for a few moments would forget all about defence and who, guided by Fu-ts'ang, himself sweeping across the line from left to right and then back again in front of them, would make their charge, not stopping for anything until they reached their friends. The relatively defenceless humans, Hook and Janice, would stay in Richie's wake all the way there, with the de facto leader and the swashbuckling blade promising to look out for them, both carrying one of the huge black bastard swords each, prised from the dead hands of their enemies. There would be sacrifices, that's for sure, but under the circumstances it was all they could come up with. Although not everyone agreed with the bold plan, the majority did and that was enough to bring the others in line, even the dragon king, George. And so it was that, one by one, Richie contacted each of the heroes, making it absolutely clear to them where they needed to be and exactly what was expected of them, even Vasuki whose strange tongue felt particularly alien and unfamiliar, making the hairs on the back of her pale, freckled neck stand on end. As expected, they confirmed that they understood, and that they wouldn't let her down. The time was close at hand.

Pushing and shoving some of them out of the way, bounding over others, squeezing between yet more, Manson continued heading in the direction he'd last seen the blurring, whirring rugby player, already having planned a surprise in the form of some rather destructive dark magic that would simply rip the smug smile off his face and render inert whatever magic he had available to him. Sensing a commotion about fifty metres in front of him, the dark and dreaded leader brought forth his magic and prepared to wade in and finish off Tank and, unbeknown to him, For'son.

Waning now, despite being fuelled by the almost unlimited supply of mana that the enigmatic band made available to him, for Tank it seemed almost like a mental consideration, and that he'd reached the top end of the number of nagas he could just beat out of the way. Abruptly a whispered warning got his attention above everything else.

"Manson's headed this way, just a few seconds out."

"Okay, what do we do?"

"I'm not sure... he has a lot of unusual magic about him. My guess would be that he's stolen it from the nagas themselves and put his own unique taint on it. Whether we can stand up to it remains to be seen. It might be possible, but it's unlikely given all the nagas around and that snarling pack of mythical beasts trailing us. We might be able to take on two out of the three together, but not all of them at once. Any suggestions?"

"If we stop moving we're sitting ducks and they'll all be on us in a matter of seconds. While I don't fancy taking on Manson, he's a better option than those mythical creatures, I think we can both agree. I say we head in his direction, take him up on his very kind offer, and stay out of range of whatever those ra-hoon have planned for us. It's a shame we can't call up some reinforcements, but most of our allies look busy fighting nagas. If only there was something we could do..."

Knowing they must have sensed his presence by now, he was delighted and more than a little surprised when the Tasmanian devil-like blur that was clearly the rugby playing dragon, started to head in his direction.

'Bring it on,' he thought, still reeling from the lacrosse player's escape and at having the trap he'd been particularly proud of thwarted.

With those around Yoyo and his group of young dragons about to start things off, everybody else fell in alongside them after orders were issued, but before Richie could utter the rallying battle cry she had prepared, something absolutely unbelievable happened.

Across the planet, both above and below ground, time almost stood still as nagas in their natural forms and on the surface disguised as humans abruptly froze in place, turning into complete and utter statues, no matter what they were doing. Some died instantly in car crashes while others stopped in the middle of the street. It was both uncanny and unnerving, with the humans up top having little actual idea of what the hell was going on, as the slippery monsters so realistically blended in, that it just looked like an unusual wave of human deaths.

Below, it took on another form altogether. Across the dragon domain, the dark army was instantly cut in half as the naga contingent became immobilised, neutralising their fighting ability, halting their despicable magic, depleting Manson's fighting force, giving hope to what little dragon resistance remained. Taken by surprise for a moment or two, it wasn't long before improvised troops across the planet took advantage, cutting down the snake-like serpents where they stood. In that one singular moment, hundreds of thousands of nagas below ground were slaughtered, contributing to the biggest single genocide in the history of their race.

Back at the king's private residence, Richie, upon seeing the changed state of their enemies, like all the others, was just about to change the command from CHARGE, to ATTACK!

'WAAAAIIIIIITTTTT!' demanded a voice across the telepathic link that all of the heroes apart from Peter,

Fredric and Tank had joined.

"BUT..." queried the young lacrosse player.

"PLLEEAAASE," begged Vasuki. "JUUUUUUST ONNNNE MOOOOMEENNT!"

"*Give it to him, Rich,*" urged Flash.

"*I think it's the right thing to do,*" added Yoyo.

"*Like this, I could take nearly all of them out in a minute. Just give me the word,*" commented Fu-ts'ang.

While all this was playing out, Vasuki, ignoring those that he'd sided with against the darkness and evil perpetrated by Manson and his dastardly force, reached out telepathically, hoping against hope that this time it would work and that he'd finally get through to those of his race that remained alive. Unbelievably, and much to his surprise... he did! And he could feel not only those in the immediate area all around him, but also his kind in a much larger radius, maybe even the entire continent. With emotions threatening to overcome even his stoic defences, he knew he had to seize whatever slim opportunity he'd been given and do what he'd been trying to do ever since he stepped through the portal of his own creating.

Imbuing his words with all of the magic he possessed, knowing exactly how important this one task might turn out to be, not only for the prevailing battle, but in the survival of his race, he let rip with the mother of all telepathic commands, and hoped to hell it countered everything that had gone on before it.

"*YOU WILL DESIST FIGHTING AGAINST THESE DRAGONS. THEY ARE FROM NOW ON TO BE REGARDED AS ALLIES. THAT IS A DIRECT ORDER FROM YOUR KING, WHO IS NOW FREE FROM THE CLUTCHES OF EVIL. ALSO, NO MORE HUMANS ARE TO BE HARMED UNDER ANY CIRCUMSTANCES. MAKE SURE THIS IS SO IMMEDIATELY!*"

With the effort of neutralising whatever enthrallment had been cast across them, in combination with the magic that had stunned them in the first place, and using just a tad of ethereal energy to make his words as clear as possible, Vasuki, king of the naga race, slumped to the ground, his stunning blue shaded body curling up on the spot, and with the last of his remaining strength, he just managed to say one last thing to his allies.

'Ittt'sss doooone. Theeeeeyyy wiiiillll dddooooo yooooouu nnnoooo mmmmooooore hhhhaaaarmmmm, ooonnnnn ttthhhhaaaat yoooou haaaavvave mmmmyyyy wwwwoooooordddd.'

As those words echoed throughout the telepathic link, a metaphorical bolt of brilliant lightning hit Richie right between the eyes, with her instantly knowing what had happened, or more accurately, who had happened... GEE TEE!

'I bet,' she thought, 'he has something to do with it.'

That same thought had just occurred to the ever moving, oh so full of magic, mini tornado that was his usual partner in crime... TANK!

Having headed in Manson's direction, away from the mythical creatures, downing the odd dark dragon here, pummelling many nagas at a time there, suddenly all those around him became statues, even mid-strike, which was more than a little odd and disconcerting, but something For'son advised him to take advantage of. And so he did, big time, taking out as many of them as he could, until he had the bolt out of the blue that had just hit his friend and realised that his partner, the master mantra maker, must have successfully deployed the rainbow mantra that they'd stupidly spliced together on that unforgettable night. Joy and happiness at his friend's success and the fact that he was still alive and well, lit up every cell in his body, making him feel happier than he could ever remember, perhaps with the exception of learning that Richie hadn't died after all. It was remarkable, unbelievable, and as he knocked the next row of four nagas up into the air, throwing them all at least twenty metres, he came across... MANSON!

Skidding to a halt before falling to his knees and reeling

back like an enthusiastic limbo dancer, the rugby playing dragon dodged the first volley of dark magic meant for him, with it missing his face by about an inch, and with For'son screaming in his ear, set about avoiding the next two rounds which were firmly on their way.

"I've seen some crazy things," uttered Owen to his boss, "but this is absolutely bizarre."

"What is it?" enquired the 'bald eagle'.

"All the monsters that resemble cobras... they've stopped, just standing there, frozen in time, with everything else around them carrying on."

"Really?"

"Yeah... here, have a look if you don't believe me," Owen urged, handing his leader the binoculars.

"He's right," whispered Polo, keeping her usually booming voice in check. "They're immobile absolutely everywhere."

"Is it magic?" asked Owen over Garrett's shoulder.

"Almost certainly, I would think."

"Wow," said the burly guard. "Who would be able to do such a thing?"

"That, my young friend," replied Polo, "is the fifty million dollar question."

"Are you sure?" asked Richie, knowing that everyone's life as well as the planet's survival hung in the balance.

'Ittt'sss doooone. I caaaan feeeeel their commmmppliaaance. Theeere willlll beee nooo moooore reeesistaaance," echoed Vasuki's rough voice through their link.

As each member of the small group glanced across the battlefield in front of them, they tended to agree with the naga king's take on things with all the slippery serpents, to a being, looking as though they were coming around from some drug induced coma, none of them seemingly having any idea as to what had happened, all of them weaving their upper bodies about almost as if drunk, with weapons being dropped and magic dispelled. It was a total and utter turn around. But... the dark dragons still remained, and so did Peter's precarious situation.

"We need to take advantage of this and execute what we had planned. What do you all say?" asked the lacrosse playing superstar.

A volley of yes's greeted her through their shared link. With all of her thoughts turning to the misery of her best friend, and knowing that getting to him was a real possibility with only the dark dragons to worry about, she gave one all important order... *"CHARGE!"*

Instinctively backflipping, Tank had no time to stand still and take in what was going on around him, not with the type of despicable magic Manson was throwing his way. All he knew was that he had to move, quicker than he ever had, because any other action would leave him as the next fatality on Manson's long list. Cartwheeling off to one side, he tumbled over and over, only just able to avoid the naga statues that now littered the area, watching as they took some of the deadly magic that was meant for him. As Manson aimed low, chewing up what remained of the once pristine white marble, shards of which peppered his ankles and calves, he bounded into the air, somersaulting two fully upright nagas who were just coming to, the surprise on their faces at seeing a human tumbling past them at a dizzying speed, obvious had anyone at all been looking. But they hadn't because of course it was only Tank and Manson taking part in this personal one on one, with the exception being For'son, who Manson had no idea even existed. Something that might well be about to change.

Noting the nagas slacking off and not being sure why, as

one, all the dark dragons had the same idea... to take over their fallen comrades' tasks and attack the opposition with a righteous fury burned into them by their very dark and powerful leader. Some swooped down on arcing attacking runs, bursts of huge, primeval flame crackling out in front of them, attempting to torch anything that moved, while others spat out massive molten fireballs from the air, bombarding their positions with showers of onrushing magic, as the remainder dived to the ground before pulling up sharply, most landing with something of a thud, some drawing the crazed black bastard swords most had been given, others choosing to ignite the magic that was their birthright, all now standing between the heroes and their goal.

Bowed over, tears continually dropped straight from his eyes onto the scorched marble, his body stuck on its knees, his mind filled with despair at his family's troubled past. The sheer terror of finding out who his mother was made him question his choices, wondering if he should leave it all here and end his own life. Nothing good could come from being her offspring, not from what he'd seen. She was pure evil, like Manson, and nothing, not even a very special family reunion could change that. Part of him wished that his grandfather would just do it... take her out for good, something he'd been trying his best to do ever since he appeared through that mind blowing wormhole. But so far he hadn't prevailed, something the world might just end up paying for. But what about her? How had all of this happened? Was it one single event, or a series of things that had led her to make a succession of bad choices? It didn't really matter or at least that's what his mind told him, because there was no way to come back from all of this. Wishing for things to move on, for it to just be done, one way or the other, not thinking about his friends, his grandfather, or his love, he remained broken, damaged and stuck right in the middle of things.

With their leader's words or word, ringing in their ears, and with the nagas... what? Neutralised... hopefully, but with the nagas out of the game for the time being, all the heroes, dragon and otherwise, did as they had agreed, and charged with all they had, much to the surprise of the dark dragons on the ground and in the air.

Richie, being in charge, had already made it clear she'd be exactly in the middle of the line and that everyone else would take their lead from her, and so after shouting out the word at the top of her voice across their link, the young lacrosse playing dragon stuck in human form and quite possibly The White Dragon that the prophecy from thousands of years ago had talked about for all this time, turned and with as much human speed as she could, headed straight for her best friend, relying fully on everyone else forming up around her.

Knowing that they'd chosen to go at the fastest human pace because of them, Janice and Hook fell in behind the charismatic young human girl... sorry, dragon, the one they'd followed from the Indian restaurant down into this world full of fantasy and surprises, the one they both regarded as so much more than their friend. Warm, humid air whipping their faces, they both bounded over the uneven, debris ridden surfaces, watching their footing, both knowing how important it was that they didn't fall but kept up with this astonishing group of beings.

Mirroring Zorro's flashing blade, the master weapon smith, friend, confident and futuristic cutting edge sprang into the air to lead the charge in front of the inexperienced dragon they'd all thrown their lot in with, at least for the first few moments. After that, his actions would be two fold. Sweeping across the line in front of those on the side of right, whilst also keeping an eye on both of his friends, Janice and her human companion, the rugby player (whatever that was) Hook. Fu-ts'ang was determined to do his utmost to keep them all alive and help their cause prevail, especially after his close brush with death, or more accurately... the end! Thoughts of retracing his path through 'the gloom' only spurred him on more, not ever wanting to experience such a thing again, although that was probably too much wishful thinking.

Another excuse for charging at human speed was the healer Yoyo, who despite his young outlook and the healthy way he prided himself on looking after his body, was, in dragon terms, quite old, although nothing compared with the master mantra maker, still doing his bit for the cause over in Fleet Street. Not only did Yoyo know this, but so did all of his young charges, having already discussed this privately together and with Richie. And so it was decided that they would form a group around their mentor, friend and of course, father figure, off to Richie's right, outside of her, Flash and Captain Battlehard. Speaking of which...

With all the nagas around them having frozen totally, before then going on to wake up in some sort of daze, the good captain and the fearless ex-Crimson Guard had managed to gain a few moments to have a breather, which was not only much needed, but well deserved given their outstanding heroics.

Gulping in huge lungfuls of air, sweat dripping from almost every part of his body, Flash turned to his fighting companion.

"You fight well Captain, for..." and then he caught himself.

"For... a female?"

Flash laughed a huge belly laugh that seemed almost inappropriate not because of the nature of their conversation, but because of their situation.

"I was going to say," continued the ex-Crimson Guard, "a King's Guard."

"Aahhhh..." sighed Amelia, the scales around her cheeks taking on something of a crimson glow, as her face unscrewed itself from the contorted visage it had started to take on. Inside, she was too busy kicking herself to worry about anything else. Of course he would have meant King's Guard, rather than female, because of the traditional rivalry that had gone on between the two factions over the decades and because he was just that kind of dragon and not sexist in any way, shape or form.

'Damn,' she cursed, wishing she could take back her unruly assumption.

"It's okay... don't worry about it, although I will have to think twice before I try and pay you another compliment."

"I'm sorry," remarked Captain Battlehard shaking her head. "I should have known better. Perhaps if we ever get out of this, you'll let me make it up to you."

"Well," said Flash, "I'm not totally sure my street cred can cope with being seen hanging around with a member of the King's Guard. I have got my reputation to think of you know."

Both of them laughed lightly for a moment or two. As she opened her mouth to say something else, Flash raised his fingers to her lips.

"I know," was all that he said. "Let's get this done for the sake of everyone, everywhere and then we can party well into the night."

"Agreed," she said smiling a huge dragon smile. "I've got your back."

"And I've got yours."

With that, the two warriors prepared to take their rightful places in the oncoming storm.

Using the full force of one particular mantra to rip the wings off a circling dark dragon before snapping the neck of another, George followed the example of the rest of the King's Guards, and in a rare moment without anyone or anything attacking them, he slumped to the ground, and not caring what those around him thought, closed his eyes and inhaled a series of long, deep breaths. It seemed an extravagant thing to do, particularly as they were nowhere near done, with Manson still on the loose, his friend's vicious witch of a daughter still toying with her son, and many, many dark dragons still circling the place, but it was something he desperately needed. He also knew that any second now he'd be required to join in with something that he thought of as utter madness, although now that the nagas had all returned to normal, or regained their sanity, or whatever had happened, the plan might not only work, but it could be their saving grace. Was that dragon lucky, or had she just been The White Dragon all along? No way to tell he supposed, but she was courageous as hell and a born leader, something that sparked the beginnings of an idea that, if they all survived this, might just change the way the world was run. And that was a very big IF.

Helped to his feet by one of the valiant King's Guards, George offered a nod and a smile, and feeling a tiny bit refreshed, prepared to take his place alongside those who had sworn to protect him on the young female leader's left, with him slotting in nicely alongside her. In his wildest dreams, he could never have imagined any of this, certainly not the kind of twist of fate that would put her in charge. But they'd gotten this far, which was quite extraordinary given all of Manson's planning and treachery. If they could just go that extra few metres, neutralise the evil would-be king, do whatever Fredric wanted to with his daughter and regain control of the planet, then the day would be looking up.

Glancing off to one side at the riot of noise his unexpected comrades and rescuers were making, when the time came, and the charge caught up with him, he gladly slid in alongside the exuberant young dragon trapped in human form, whose face alone told him just how much she was relishing turning the tables on the dark force and for once in all of this, taking the fight to the enemy.

'Today,' he thought, 'would be a good day to die.'

'I think you're going to have to turn around and face him. I'll erect the most powerful shield I have, and then we'll hit him with everything we've got," announced For'son, the words ringing through Tank's mind.

It seemed like their only option, because they couldn't go on running forever, and at least not having the nagas to deal with gave them one less thing to worry about. Slipping effortlessly in and out of half a dozen of the dazed serpent-like beasts, the rugby playing dragon slid to a halt beside a pile of debris as high as his waist and turned to face the oncoming dark leader, sweat pouring down his neck, heart beating like a drum, mind taking it all in, including whatever the disturbance was in the direction of his friend... PETER!

Casting spell after spell, his warped and wicked mind working overtime in that department, his mana reserves rapidly diminishing, Manson chased after his prey, determined to make him suffer for what he'd done in somehow restoring all the magic and mana he and his queen had so casually ripped away. If not for him, it would have been long since over, his force would have suffered no more losses, they would all be dead and the planet would now be his. But instead of being the honoured guest at his own party (he could see the banner above the banquet in his mind, 'Congratulations on your first planet', as they all ate) here he was scurrying about amongst his own minions, fighting to survive, yet to put down the opposing force.

'IT ISN'T SUPPOSED TO BE THIS WAY! IT JUST ISN'T,' he thought, in something of a hissy fit.

Zipping around a group of nagas who, unbelievably, didn't seem to be doing his bidding (something he'd get around to punishing after he'd finished with the rugby player) his mind half distracted by thoughts of what should have been, it was only sheer luck that he was paying enough attention to dive out of the way of the attack the slippery dragon had planned for him, tumbling and rolling as far as he could before scarpering out of the way, staying as low down as possible behind all of the confused looking beasts that had up until a matter of moments ago been under his command. That's right... he'd just found out, because he'd given the biggest shout out he could across the ethereal link that bound them to his will, and... NOTHING! Oh... he could feel all of the dragons under him, they were, even as we speak, moving in on his position in an attempt to keep him safe, but the nagas... what the hell had happened there? As flaming balls of fire surged past his shoulder and brilliant, bright blue lightning strikes ripped up what remained of the floor all around him, he ignited his own personal shield and set off a deadly array of explosives behind him hoping that would be enough to keep him safe until his dark dragon guard reinforcements arrived, all the time seething about what had happened to the rest of his troops.

It was right at this exact moment that the very first thought of retreat and living to fight another day, ran through his mind. Not at any other point in the entire process, which had taken decades to come to fruition, had he even considered such a possibility. But with his faith shaken at having over half his horde taken from him in the blink of an eye, and fear coursing through him, the thought of dying suddenly had him back peddling, his confidence shot, in two minds about exactly what he should do. Usually about now the coolness of his egotistical intellect and his unmatched self-belief would kick in and, in his thoughts at least, turn things around. But not this time, with his psyche almost begging his flying force to find him and keep him safe... things had changed, whether for the better or worse would remain to be seen, but here and now, a tipping point on the scales of justice had been reached, one it would be hard to come back from.

Hanging on by a thread, his oh so sensitive mind had

been consumed by the darkness, betrayed by his thoughts, lost without his friends, family being of absolutely no comfort at all, quite the opposite in fact. Afraid of something so trivial sending him down the wrong path and ending up like her, he wanted to end it all and be yet one more statistic in the battle that had been raging for days now. Sure that his life was insignificant, little did he know that what remained of the resistance here, were all on their way to save him, including their leader, his best pal, his soul mate Janice who'd already done so much, and the rest of his friends and true family. Had he known, it might have been enough, enough to rouse him and force him to move out from between the two family members, constant combatants across everything that had happened here today. But as I've already said, he was as lost as anyone could be.

Fingering the hilt of the exquisite laminium dagger, thoughts of the brave dragon agent Aviva flickering throughout his mind, wondering what she'd do in his position, Fredric tried to plan out exactly what he'd need to achieve his ultimate goal here today... to kill his daughter!

Calculations running at a million miles an hour on how best to deploy all the supernatural energy available to him, he knew he'd have to be at his craftiest to stand even a chance of taking her down. Like him, she was good, and potentially even better with the unusual array of dark magic that she wielded, gained, he assumed, from some of Vasuki's nagas, probably under threat of harm to their king. So as they circled, ever so slightly, Peter caught smack bang in the middle of them, each deep within their own machinations, sanity in desperately short supply between all three of them, the creator of the Crimson Guards found himself under pressure like never before to deliver what he'd set out to do.

Serpents snapping and hissing atop her head, collectively rattled at the position they all found themselves in, their presence alone was enough to provide a tingling, deep distracting rapture for the new queen of this godforsaken planet. Totally forgetting all about her new husband's overall mission, having been waylaid by the discovery of her son fighting against her, all the focus she had now was on reforming a bond with the boy and being allowed to spend some time with him, something that, after trying to kill him on more than one occasion, seemed desperately unlikely to work... but not to her. First though, she had to create the right circumstances for such a thing to come about, and she knew that her bastard father was by far the biggest impediment to that. Mirroring not only his every move physically, but mentally as well, thousands of computations about which magic to use and how to set it all up abounded within her, wishing once and for all to end his life and regain the son she'd thought had been lost forever.

Somewhere stuck in the middle, Peter, for his part, had no idea at all as to what was going on, and just wanted things to be over. Whether that was his life, or everything playing out across the planet, he just didn't know, and more importantly, just didn't care.

Mind made up, unaware of anything else, just knowing that this had to be done, and now, Fredric focused and brought forth his magic.

"Factus est ignotum," he whispered internally, directing his attention towards the laminium dagger, the words roughly translating as 'become unknown'. Satisfied that his magic had taken hold, he very deliberately released the restraints he'd had on his temper, and in one all-out, devastating attack unleashed hell on his murdering maniac of a daughter.

Brilliant, bright white icicles rained down on her position, flickering to life from pure nothingness, each leaving a trail similar to that of Fu-ts'ang.

Startled, because she assumed that she'd be the one to instigate things, Earth brought up her almost impenetrable shield, and let the words that were now like second nature to her roll off her mind, as if they were rolling off her tongue. Chains of molten fire appeared mid-air surrounding

Fredric, all with an intelligence of their own, each intent on striking him, each having that ingrained into them.

Ignoring her curious attack, Fredric reeled off more phrases, desperate to force her to move and not stand her ground as she currently was. If he could do that, then just maybe it would be her undoing.

Dark green bolts of brilliantly arcing electricity forked up from the ground around and behind the area she stood on, much to her astonishment. But she knew that it was only enough to tickle her own dedicated shield. It would take much, much more to get her attention.

Acid rain dropped from the air, sizzling as it made contact with her personal protective barrier, followed closely by an all encompassing bright, wispy green cloud of poison that nearly enveloped her entirely. Things were heating up.

Unable to see, she stretched out using just her magic in an attempt to assess his location. Unfortunately, he'd somehow cloaked himself and despite however much she tried, she couldn't find him.

'Damn!' With her son still out there, all alone and defenceless, she wasn't really able to go all-out attack on her father's scaly ass, not knowing exactly where he was. And as more magic shimmered into life all around her, and with her barrier now taking an absolute pummelling, shortly she'd have to decide whether or not to move, something that could have immense consequences.

Giving it everything he had, intense, yellow, orange, blue and red flames surrounded her, the fire, seemingly of its own accord, licking at her shield, probing her defences, providing yet something else to blind her. Wary of not using absolutely everything, just in case, the founder of the Crimson Guards upped the ante even more. Eyes closed, his mind searched for surrounding piles of rubble. Finding them instantly and with just his magical will, he started to toss the largest pieces in her direction, satisfied at hearing them bounce off her magical barricade, all the time being sure to keep everything he'd let loose away from the boy, his grandson, ready and waiting to spring his trap.

It was all too much... well, nearly. But the time had come for a decision to be made, and although not wanting to endanger him in even the slightest way, she knew her father would be having exactly the same thoughts, something he'd already shown, by keeping all his offensive spells as far away as possible from the boy, leaving a huge neutral area next to him. And with her shield still just about coping, she took three steps forward, moving out from underneath her father's dire attempts to harm her and into the space next to her son, keen to get acquainted with Fredric's actual position and return a little bit of the fire he'd laid waste onto her.

'Ha... she's fallen for it. Good for her,' he thought, 'good for her,' moving out from all of his spells into a position where she could easily find him. Not long now, not long at all.

Aware of something different going on all around his physical body and feeling the presence of his mother close by, and his grandfather slightly further away, Peter couldn't shake off the dark, heavy cowl of rollercoaster emotions that had almost fully consumed every part of him. At least, every good part, and that was pretty much most of him. Unable to pull himself out of it, or see a road map that could lead his mind back to any semblance of normality, all he could do was concede defeat and accept the inevitable... that he was like her, and always would be, their paths intertwined, their destinies entangled, merged together for all time. It wasn't what the tiny, logical part of him needed to hear.

Opening himself up further than he ever had before, Fredric let his magic fly, casting spell after spell, mantra after mantra, hex after hex, giving it everything he had, not bothering to hold anything back, knowing that it was now or never, feeling that this, his last chance, would be the one to succeed and take her down for good.

Ethereal energy erupted closer to Peter, attacking the evil

witch from every direction, battering her shield with icy arrows, poison darts, bolts of blistering blue lightning, razor sharp chunks of debris, probing mental attacks, forceful flurries of magnetism, fiery lances of superheated magma, splurges of awesome acid as well as twisting tornados of air, all of which would have given any other being the willies, but not her, well... not yet anyway. It had, however, caught her off guard, something that it was totally and utterly designed to do, a blizzard of magic converging on her location, confusing and confounding, frustrating, maddening and looking to provoke a reaction. Without doubt, it had the desired effect.

Tiny needles pricking away at the restrained madness, her father's attacks pounded her defences relentlessly, testing her temper, making her more than a little hot under the collar. Slowly, she started to forget about the boy, her son, tentatively stretching out with her own supernatural powers, searching for her hidden enemy, desperate to get a grip, preferably around his neck if at all possible.

Shrouded in magic, while attacking her with what was left, Fredric remained between Peter and his daughter, sure that it would provide a little blind spot for what he had planned, something he hoped she wouldn't either see through, or expect. With most of his offensive power currently deluging her position, he pulled out Aviva's laminium dagger, the one that had served him well over the years, the one that he'd cast the mantra on, rolled it in his hands one last time, and using all the focus, concentration and magic he had left, threw with all his might, locking it in directly on his daughter's head. It was something of a gamble because of its laminium nature. If things failed, and she got her hands on it, the world might go to hell quicker than a fox in a hen house, but it should, and I emphasise the should, home in on its target, the mantra surrounding it making it all but invisible until it was absolutely too late. And with the whiteout of magic constantly bombarding the murdering monster masquerading as his daughter, distracting her no end, the hope was that it would finish her off once and for all. As it left his hand, all but a blur even to those with magical powers, all he knew was that it was on target to achieve what he'd set out for it to do. In but a moment it would all be over, once and for all. She couldn't see or sense it coming, its supernatural nature allowing it to bypass her defences. It would, without a doubt... end her!

Exhausted, spent of mana, sick and tired of everything that he'd been involved in during the course of the day, despite gaining what he regarded as some sort of relative freedom, having escaped that Antarctic prison hell, the founder of the Crimson Guards, knowing that he could now die happy, having righted the mother of all wrongs, and saved the grandson he loved from a whole world of pain, slumped uncomfortably to the floor, prepared to savour the moment.

A lot is written about love. How for instance it can inspire us to push ourselves further or faster. He'd run through a brick wall for her. She'd run into a burning building to save him. Love will conquer all. But will it, and if it does, how so? Is there ever a time when all knowing, all feeling, all inspiring love, gets it so wrong? And what does love really mean anyway? Is it a feeling, an emotion... both, or something else? Across time immemorial, men, women, dragons and many other beings have sought the answer to this question, looking to understand what so many others are convinced they feel towards someone close to them. Love is also, very conveniently, and regularly, an excuse for the most heinous of atrocities. "They did it for love," you'll hear in a courtroom afterwards, as if that was some kind of justification. What on earth does that mean? It means love is tricky, undefined, and rarely as simple or black and white as beings often make out. You can love doing a certain thing. I love playing hockey, but I'm not in love with playing hockey, that's something else altogether. Can you love more than one person the absolute same amount? Some would say yes, others would say no, that's utterly impossible. There's no one right answer, and no one single way to measure or define it. Love is something unique and personal to that one particular person at that exact moment in time. Can you stop loving someone or something? Of course, but that's why it belongs in that exact moment. Love can make beings do stupid things, crazy things, romantic things, it can lead them down paths they'd never normally go, change their lives for the better or worse, it can enhance who they are and in some cases it can compel them to make bad choices. And although it can't be measured or seen, we know it exists and we know that because of all of the things it can make us do, it is powerful. But as powerful as what, and can it change the destiny of the planet? Hmmmm...

Blackness crushing his soul, lost and alone, fearful of what he might become now that he knew the truth, naive and kind hearted had been swapped for pitiful and pathetic. He was quite a sight, hunched over on his knees, dark jeans covered in marble dust, his light t-shirt filthy with sweat, a deluge of tears dripping down onto the floor, what little magic he had collapsing in on itself, his very core being consumed by the bitterness of the life he should have had but had been denied by those around him. A sorrier sight it would have been hard to imagine. For all intents and purposes, he was out of it, little use to anyone, his family, his friends, the supposed light side that he fought on against the scourge of evil that even now, was still attempting to take the planet. All in all, a small, shadowy mess, insignificant in every way, shape or form. Until that is, love decided to intervene. Unaware of everything playing out around him, suddenly a totally foreign tasting touch of love unravelled some of his mana, whisking it off into the wider world in an effort to give him just a brief glimpse into what was going on. Magic close by surprised and scared him, as a hint of confusion at stone still nagas some way off addled his brain. The tiniest part of him thought to look for his soul mate, but that was shut down by the darkness immediately. Instead, one single deed, something that shone out like sunlight streaming through the clouds onto a deserted beach on a windswept day, made his mind sit up and take notice, which in turn, prompted his body into the most unlikely of actions.

In one extraordinary act, supposedly powered by love, although truth be told there would be no way of ever actually knowing, the frightened, scared, lonely and confused young dragon did the one thing that Fate, the world, the onrushing rescuers, his grandfather and of course his mother, the psychopath Earth, could never have expected in a million years.

With Aviva's (and now Fredric's) laminium dagger travelling faster than a speeding bullet, literally slicing open the atoms of the air in front of it, about to fulfil a destiny that it could almost certainly have been forged for, and less than the blink of an eye away from carving open Earth's purple crisscrossed head, abruptly the death dealing blade was stopped fully in its tracks as, quick as a flash, a human shaped hand popped up in its way. Quietly, the universe gulped, Fredric, from his spot on the floor, did a double take, while the immensity of what had just happened dawned on his daughter.

Piercing the flesh of his palm with the razor sharp point of its blade, the shining laminium dagger came to an abrupt halt with the bejewelled cross guard unable to pass through what remained of Peter's hand. Thick, red blood sprayed across what little of the pristine white marble remained, the sweat infused, light coloured t-shirt he had on, and across his pale, tear stained face, some of it also running down past his wrist and onto his arm. Surprisingly though, he didn't cry out, as most beings would have. However, his grandfather did.

"NOOOOOOO!!!!!," he bellowed, jumping to his feet,

barely able to comprehend what had just happened.

Shocked to her very core, the varying kinds of hexes that had caused a distraction dissipating all around her, slowly a very smug, arrogant and self-righteous smile crept across her magic infused, damaged face, making her truly look like a superhero's nemesis. She lived, because of him, just like he lived because of her... how ironic and twisted was that? Turning to face the father she hated so much, the one who had just slumped to the ground thinking that he'd finally killed her, one thing was certain... sanity had fled, and the madness was back, that much could be seen from the fire in her eyes. With nothing containing her propensity for evil, and with Peter directly in her firing line, would he even get the chance to realise exactly what he'd done? Probably not, judging by the expression on her face.

Unbelievably, she hadn't seen it coming, not until the boy had thrust his hand up in the air and intercepted it, something that was a surprise to say the least. Her father's gambit had failed, but not because of anything she'd done, having been totally outwitted for the very first time in their feud and this battle, her life spared by some ironic twist of fate. Those were her thoughts as she stared across the divide at him, all the time wondering how the hell she could make him pay, bring him to his knees, devastate his world, just as he'd devastated hers. And with insanity now running rife throughout her mind, and following his outraged gaze, in an instant she knew just how to take revenge and bring things back full circle.

Mind laced with madness, Manson still had a very real understanding of what he was trying to achieve, how that could and should be done, and at exactly what stage of his plan they were at. However, the loss of his naga contingent had blown a very big hole in everything he was trying to do, and his mind was just trying to get its head around that and everything else that was going on, or should I say... going wrong. Playing cat and mouse with the rugby player wasn't helping, with part of him still thinking that things here could be salvaged, the tide turned and the prized planet still be presented as his. That is, until he spotted the extraordinary wave of mythical creatures far in the distance, annihilating groups of stunned nagas and battling dark dragons, taking them down on the ground, in the air, wherever they could reach. And then he caught sight of the giant asag, stomping around furiously, punching dragon after dragon, taking each of them down with just one hit of its giant, car sized fists, none of them able to inflict even the slightest amount of harm to it. That's really when the realisation set in, and he knew, despite not wanting to admit it, even to himself, that retreat was the only real possibility.

'Damn,' he cursed those idiots that he'd put in charge of searching the council building basement, the capture and containment level for all of the mythical creatures. 'How could they get it so wrong?' he wondered, looking straight at his nightmare from hell as the mostly unrecognisable creatures rampaged towards his position. Wanting complete and utter retribution on those who had failed him, it became obvious that if these beings had escaped, then no doubt they'd killed those in charge on the way out, which came as something of a boon.

A surge of real anger ran riot throughout the atoms that made up his body, as immediately he looked for someone or something to take it out on. But the cool, calculating part of his psyche warned him that he had precious little time left, and that if he didn't act now, then he might just be caught out. Glancing back over at the outrageous mythical beasts that were decimating everything in front of them, dragon and naga alike, he knew without a doubt that he had to go now. Searching for his queen, he was astounded to see her taking part in some abnormality that involved the prisoner from the Antarctic and his pain in the arse nemesis... BENTWHISTLE! Wanting nothing more than to join her and finish him off for good, momentarily part of him hoped, from the look of absolute rage and fury on her face, that she'd do it for him. There was, however, not time for him to stick around and see. Opening up his mind, he found her unique intellect straight away.

"Things have gotten too risky with yet more creatures adding confusion to everything going on here. We must leave at once and regroup in the planned place. I'm sorry my love, I feel as though I've failed you... that was never my intention, I assure you. Make haste. I look forward to your safe arrival," and with that, he cut off communication completely.

Punching a naga that was only just re-awakening next to him, straight through the gills, sending him instantly to the afterlife, the dreaded dark leader searched for the words to the spell that he needed to get him out of here immediately. Right at the same time, Tank skidded around a mound of debris in front of him, magic at the ready, the fabled For'son enhancing him in every way possible. It was payback time. Sighing with relief at not having to face the rugby playing dragon who looked to him to be more than a little too tooled up, Manson sarcastically saluted, whilst at the same time whispering the words in his head, attaching all his willpower and considerable magic to them, and right in front of the enigmatic band and the heroic Tank, completely disappeared into the ether.

"What in the hell just happened?" Tank snapped, his magic ready and willing to do his bidding.

"It looks as though their despicable leader has only gone and run off... numpty!"

"What?!"

"Not you... him, for running away."

"Oh... What do we do now?"

"Well... we could start by doing something about... THAT!"

Looking around in the direction For'son had indicated with just a tiny magical prompt, Tank's heart plummeted on seeing the unruly, ungodly and undefeatable mass of mythical creatures heading in their direction. Things had just gone from bad to worse.

Effortlessly slipping together, forming something bigger than the sum of all their parts, the line of light-sided heroes stretched out to almost fill the entire width of the king's private residence as they started to charge from one end to the other, all filling in and around their leader, no... not George, the current dragon king and ruler of not only the dragon domain but the planet itself, but the young lacrosse playing dragon, stuck through no fault of her own in human form, the supposed White Dragon by Peter's estimation, and an unstoppable force for good, caught up in the heart of today's tragic events.

Roaring herself hoarse, Richie screamed obscenities as they attacked the dark dragons they came across in the air and on the ground, the telepathic link they all shared allowing them to coordinate on an unprecedented scale, ignoring the nagas completely, focusing only on all things ancient and prehistoric, ripping off wings, snapping necks, blinding, hamstringing, gouging, punching, kicking and using their combined magic to great effect. Nothing, and I mean nothing, could stand in their way. The greatest heroes were living the greatest moment of their lives, all going absolutely berserk, all in an effort to save two of their own who now faced their greatest challenge.

Hand raised above his head, bright red blood trickling down his arm from the laminium dagger buried up to its crossguard in his flesh, the startling realisation of what had happened still didn't make Peter cry out, with the former darkness maintaining its grip on both his body and his mind, only an overwhelming and shocking surge of love interrupting enough to have made his hand do his bidding and save his mother. For him, his deep seated intelligence hadn't caught up with the reality of what had happened.

On his feet but utterly spent, and now devastated,

Fredric recognised the glint in his daughter's eye at not only what had happened, how she'd escaped the grim reaper by a gnat's genitals and thwarted what he'd had in mind for her, but now found herself in a position of power, which he could do absolutely nothing about. Tables turned, it was time to make him pay. And he could see exactly how she was going to go about it.

"NOOOOOOO!" he screamed. "HE'S INNOCENT... NEVER HARMED ANYONE OR ANYTHING IN HIS LIFE. LET HIM GO. TAKE ME INSTEAD!" he sobbed.

But through the madness and insanity of it all, she could see the pain this was causing her father, hear the desperation in his voice, watch the agony and despair in his eyes, knowing that he was about to witness the death of his only grandson and not be able to do a damn thing about it. And then something familiar came knocking on the door of her mental defences. It was her love, her king, the one and only being she truly cared about on this entire planet. Lowering her cerebral fortifications, she let him in, hoping to hear that the entire world was theirs.

"Things have gotten too risky with yet more creatures adding confusion to everything going on here. We must leave at once and regroup in the planned place. I'm sorry my love, I feel as though I've failed you... that was never my intention, I assure you. Make haste. I look forward to your safe arrival."

Dangerous magic crackling across her fingertips in all colours and varying degrees of fatality, for a few moments Earth was taken aback, frozen in disbelief at the words that had just flooded her mind. At first, her only thought was that it was some kind of trap, but on scanning the battlefield the extent of their overwhelming losses was instantly obvious, with outright winning clearly no longer an option even to her. Secondly, she thought that it just couldn't be. How the hell had all this come about? The last time she looked, which granted, was a little while ago, they still had the upper hand, still massively outnumbered their opponents, and now... THIS! He'd gone, run away, let her down, not even bothered to stick around and make sure she'd gotten out of this in one piece. Just like all the rest of them, he was a letdown and nothing more than a selfish, lying bastard. There, she'd said it.

Heart wrenching guilt tore across her in waves, almost interrupting her connection to the magic that she'd been born with and had, over time, sharpened into the finely honed weapon that she'd become... but not quite. It still remained, flowing out across her fingertips, which were ready to plunge into the exposed head of the being kneeling on the ground in front of her, the one that had caused so much trouble, the one George the king cared so much about, the one her father, the despicable monster that had made her life hell growing up, loved and cherished.

'Well,' she thought, 'if they worship him so much let's make sure there's enough of him to go around and share,' and decided to finish it off and kill the pathetic example of a being in front of her that had saved her life only moments ago. Choice made, she moved to lower her hands, just as the full force of the light-sided heroes pulled up behind Fredric, their combined magical might forming one almighty shield around their friend, Peter, which was impenetrable, even for her. If Earth's face had been angry, unstable and lost in madness before, then that was nothing to the expression the purple crisscrossing lines formed now, with the devil himself scared beyond belief.

Trapped, left behind by her king, deserted and with nowhere to run to, you might have thought that she'd come quietly, but that was never going to be the case, not with all that she'd been through, all that she'd raged against, all the injustices she'd fought to right. Stepping away from 'the boy' as she now regarded him, a peripheral figure rather than her son, her magic flickered and wavered, teased and taunted, hanging in the air like an unanswered question.

"Surrender," demanded Fredric from beside his best friend. "You've got nowhere else to go."

Captured against his will behind an invisible barrier

made up of all the others, dagger still lodged in his hand, blood splattered everywhere, Peter turned to look up into his mother's eyes, longing for that last recognition of love, something, anything even vaguely resembling that emotion, but there was nothing. What had been was gone, gone for good, whether or not it had ever really been there at all. All that remained were dark, burnt out pupils, resembling the heart of a black hole, dying, dead, died. The craziness, in the form of a sickening smile and a nervous twitch across her top lip, gave everyone there the creeps, making them feel at the very least uncomfortable, like they were in the company of a ghoul. In the middle of things, bearing in mind that the battle was still raging, albeit with the nagas out for the count, but with their place having been taken up by the dreaded mythical creatures that had ironically been released by For'son on George's command, back at the very start of things.

"I won't ask again," commanded Fredric. "Give yourself up... NOW!"

Crazed smile disappearing, replaced by something utterly stone cold, she looked him in the eyes from above her son, and spat with as much venom as she could,

"NO!"

About to order his allies to kill her, abruptly a huge POP resounded in and around her and Peter, before sickly green smoke encompassed them both.

Worried that she was trying to get away, but afraid of hurting their friend, the heroes, much to Fredric's dismay, could do absolutely nothing but look on in disbelief and defeat. Slowly the smoke cleared, leaving the young dragon kneeling in the same position he had been for some time, Aviva's dagger still splitting his hand in two, utterly miserable and bereft. Unsurprisingly, there was absolutely no sign of the dark witch, Earth, Fredric's daughter and Peter's mother. Where she had gone, it was impossible to tell. How she'd gotten there was anyone's guess, but no doubt it had something to do with unusual dark naga magic.

With the shield coming down and all the heroes about to be reunited in the most stunning of turnarounds, only then did a loud and familiar voice belt out across their shared link.

"Uhhhh... I hate to be the bearer of bad news, but you guys need to find some cover. I realise that Manson and Earth have fled and that the nagas are of little or no consequence, but we have something far worse heading our way, and when I say... FAR WORSE, believe you me I'm not kidding."

"TANK?" queried Richie.

"Yep," he replied in his own inimitable style. *"And I'm on my way. More importantly though, we have a raging horde of mythical creatures inbound, and they're looking to kill anything even vaguely tasting of magic. Sorry, my friends, but our work here isn't done, and this might very well make the other two and their dark force look like a picnic in the park."*

'Unbelievable,' thought Richie. 'Just ******* unbelievable!'

"Thank goodness... I can see Peter," Owen voiced happily, taking the binoculars away from his face to look his boss in the eyes.

"Let me have a look?" urged Garrett from his prone position behind a pile of naga corpses, the scent of fishy innards really starting to get to him.

Owen handed over the binoculars before commenting,

"He stopped the dagger from hitting that mad woman with his hand and then some kind of foggy haze appeared all around and... POOF, she was gone. Best magic trick I've seen in ages."

"Hmmm..." growled Polo.

"What's up?" asked Garrett.

"Whoever that woman is, or more likely, dragon, it's hard to tell from here, she looks like a whole lot of trouble. If she got away like that, then this thing's clearly not over, not by a long shot. As well, they've got a very different enemy descending on them even as we speak. Watch and learn... we might well be needed."

Heeding the wise dragon's advice, they all waited to see how things would play out and whether or not what little backup they could offer would be required.

Close by, two very similar occurrences had happened within only a matter of minutes of each other, both connected, both of tremendous interest and importance with regard to the future of the planet.

His mana reserves having dropped to just above half way, Manson had few options when the time came to retreat. Using some of the naga magic that he'd become familiar with over past decades, he chose to enact two short teleports, one to the closest point within the council building itself, taking him off the battlefield to relative safety, and then once recovered enough to do so, a short hop to one of the nearby sewers. It worked perfectly, with him finding himself free of any scrutiny and able to go about his business as he liked. Trudging through the thick, reeking sludge, making even more of a mess of the blood soaked trousers he was wearing, he pondered the events that had led him here, wondering what he could have done differently and just how to make them all pay now that they'd taken the planet back from the brief hold he'd had on it. Whatever he was going to do, it would have to be not only spectacular, but cause numerous casualties and a great deal of pain. In the cloying darkness, a twisted smile wormed its way across his face because there and then he knew he could deliver. After all, those two things were his speciality.

Receiving that message from her king, her love, her... what? Seeing that he'd run off without making sure she was safe sure put a different stamp on their relationship, as far as she was concerned anyway. Perhaps there were extenuating circumstances, she thought, trying in some way to justify his actions. Surrounded, outnumbered, about to die a grisly death, barely able to escape with his life, his last thoughts centred on getting a message to her... all not very likely in her personal opinion. But maybe she was wrong. Anyhow, on receiving the message and then having all of the boy's sickening friends turn up to save him, she knew in that exact moment that it was either time to leave, or die. And so she chose to survive, live to fight another day and wreak absolute havoc on them once more at some other unexpected point in the future. First though, she had to see what her king had to say for himself and what vicious plans he had in mind for the exceptionally lucky trouble makers that had just brought their planet a stay of execution, but not much more than that.

Shrouding herself in her magic, she'd used the exact same naga spell that Manson had only a short time earlier, but blessed by a far greater degree of mana she was able to make her escape in one hop, using her considerable power and will to triple the distance that any naga thought possible for the teleportation, landing directly out in front of the council building, on the steps where the whirling pools of lava were located on either side. On getting her bearings, which took but a moment, she fled on foot into the night, seeking refuge in the burning flames and the desolate shadows of what remained of the capital, knowing that for a while at least she was relatively safe, wondering if the nagas that had somehow broken free from their hold could cause her any problems in the future. For now though, she had to move swiftly to join her other half, who would be waiting with vengeful plans of how to take away everything the dragons had won back. How delightful.

Now that he'd freed what remained of his race, Vasuki's link to the nagas under him and close enough to connect was absolute. He could feel their confusion, their worries, their fears and of course... their passing. As the army of mythical creatures stormed across the battlefield, destroying everything in their path, dozens of nagas, maybe more, succumbed to the slaughter, their defences already down, standing no chance at all. He could feel each and every one of their deaths, almost as if it was his own. The souls of lesser beings would have splintered beyond repair, but not him... never him. King for many reasons, one of which was his resilience, he stoically stood fast, remembering each of them, remaining determined to save as many of the others as possible, something he set out to do right away.

Having just about recovered from her expletive laden rant, Richie got her head around exactly what was happening, and more importantly, got it back in the game.

"Form a circle with Peter at the centre," she ordered everybody. *"Janice and Hook, stay in the middle with him and see if*

you can shake him awake. The rest of you know the drill, it'll be shields up when they approach. No one big barrier this time though, I'm not going through all that again. And make a hole for Tank next to me when he arrives. I want him to be able to seamlessly slot right in."

In her mind, she could see them all nodding, which brought a brief smile to her face.

"Fu-ts'ang, please can you take a swipe at some of them just to see their reaction and the defences they put up, so that we have a better idea of exactly what we're dealing with? Don't go too far though, just in case there are any other surprises lurking about."

"Understood," he replied, shooting off in the direction of Tank and the freaky flock that were chasing him down.

Flitting in and out of the statue-like nagas, Tank and his partner finally reached a piece of open ground, and while still being bombarded with fireballs from the dark dragons cutting through the air, made one mad dash for his friends and the standoff that was already in the offing, all the while being chased by a vast array of unusual creatures which all had orders to capture them, no matter what the cost. It was chaos on an entirely different level from what had happened earlier with Earth and Manson, and although that had been frightening, there had at least been some kind of order, unlike this, which looked like one massive free for all, despite the ra-hoon's best intentions.

Resembling a fighter jet, Fu-ts'ang shot over Tank's head, slammed on the brakes pretty quickly, knocking back an attack from a vicious pixiu, slicing through one of its wings and sending it spiralling to the ground, whilst at the same time watching two nifoloa try and stab their giant single tooth into him in an attempt to inject him with poison. Clearly they had no idea what he even was, which was amusing in itself, even more so when they came in contact with his blade and the frost with which it was imbued, because simultaneously both of their single teeth froze, and as they tried to back away, their only weapons started to crack before breaking into a hundred pieces. The look on their faces was priceless. Knowing not to get caught up in the little things, especially on looking around and noting the sheer number and variety of species heading their way, not least the huge, hideous looking rock demon with its terrorising purple stare, something you wouldn't want to be singled out by, the charismatic weapon surrounded by cold reversed direction in a blur and headed back towards his friends, ready to defend them at all costs.

Leaping several small piles of rubble, the young and talented rugby playing dragon skidded to a halt in the perfect Tank sized gap that had been left for him between his best friend and the former Crimson Guard.

"Nice of you to join us," piped up Flash, pleased to see him.

"Well... you know how it is, things to do and all that."

Abruptly, a smart punch on the arm caused him to turn and face the other direction. Slender pale arms fastened around his head as Richie embraced him for all she was worth.

"You didn't miss me then?" observed Tank sarcastically.

"You big lug... you scared the living daylights out of us all. We thought you were dead, and then you appear out of nowhere and restore all of our magic. How in the hell..."

Holding up one giant finger, vaguely resembling one of Hook's sausage-like ones, Tank put it against her lips in an attempt to shut her up.

"Let's just say I had some help in that department shall we, and leave it at that."

"But..."

"No buts. Now is not the time. Fill me in on everything that's gone on."

And so she started to, occasionally being interrupted by Janice hugging her friend, and then Hook getting in on the act, with all of them, apart from the very far away Peter, letting him know just how pleased they were to see him.

Then, from the other side of Richie, George looked over, his eyes focused on Tank's fingers.

"Ahhhh... Your Majesty, I can explain."

A tense moment between the two of them passed, with For'son whispering in Tank's mind.

"Idiot!"

"I don't think that's any way to talk about the reigning dragon monarch, do you?"

"I wasn't referring to him."

"Oh. What have I done now?"

"Don't kowtow to him, boy. Remember, he rejected me and my help. How would we have got out of all this if I'd remained on his finger?"

"I thought it was kind of a two way thing," suggested Tank, rather bravely given exactly who he was dealing with.

"THAT'S NOT THE POINT!" bellowed For'son.

"Sorry," said Tank.

"No, no... it's alright, it's my fault. You were right it was a two way thing. But none of that matters. What matters is that without you, we wouldn't have succeeded. Don't start bowing down to him, and I'll warn you now... do not, under any circumstances, offer to give me back. Do I make myself clear?"

"Crystal," replied Tank.

"Good."

"There's no need for explanations, my young friend," said George, leaving his position in the circle and walking a few paces over to Tank, much to Richie's bemusement.

Fredric followed on behind, having only just been gobbled up by the band of collective heroes.

"I..." started Tank, only to be cut off by the current king of everything dragon.

"No explanations are needed. What you've done, and so quickly, is nothing short of miraculous given our circumstances. We owe you and For'son a great debt, something that almost certainly can never be repaid. But once this is over, we'll try, I assure you of that."

'For'son?' thought Richie. 'Who the hell's that?'

"Did you see or hear anything of Manson?" asked George.

"He disappeared right in front of my eyes, much the same way his wicked queen did here. I have no idea where they've gone, but believe you me, we have more pressing matters to attend to," ventured Tank, pointing back over his shoulder.

"Yes... the mythical creatures. Perhaps, looking back, it was a mistake to release them."

"Hang on a minute," remarked Richie, jumping right in. "You released them? When, and from where?"

"Pheeeewwww..." Blowing out a long breath, the king didn't really think that this was either the place or the time, but he could see that he wasn't getting off that lightly.

"The creatures in question have long since been recovered from across the planet, corralled not only for their safety, but for that of everyone else. Once caught, they were... imprisoned," he didn't like the sound of the word as he said it, which made him think a little more carefully about everything the mythical creatures had been through. He continued, "...imprisoned, in a detainment facility in the basement of the council building, known only to a few, with no chance of parole, but in a magical environment that was designed to provide for their every need."

About to butt in, Richie's protests, despite being leader, were brushed aside.

"I know, I know," continued George. "But before you say your piece, let me tell you this. They were contained in special same species cells, magical in nature and powered by the only source strong enough to do so. They wanted for nothing in these realistic environments, were checked on regularly, and up until I deemed it only right to release them at the start of all this, knew nothing was wrong or any different to what they were all used to. I know you might find it cruel, but myself and my predecessors have always thought it the fairest way to treat these creatures. That's not me passing the buck; I've known about them ever since I became monarch, and chose to keep things the same, for our safety and theirs."

"And theirs?" questioned the lacrosse playing superstar.

"Most of them are valuable, magic wise, in some way shape or form, and could potentially be used for harm, should they fall into the wrong hands. Most would of course have to be killed to extract what they are renowned for. It was a no win situation. At large across the planet, they are some of the top, apex predators, just a few of their species able to decimate the human population, but killing them just didn't seem right. So we did what we had to, in an effort to let them thrive as well as keep them safe. Unfortunately, nothing like this was ever considered. When I released them, it was truly an act of desperation, hoping that we could round them up after we won back the planet, but here we are now and..."

"He's telling the truth," announced Tank, his voice sounding nothing like usual, much more robotic and emotionless.

"Tank?" asked Richie.

"It's not him, it's For'son," stated the king.

"Who the hell is that?" demanded their lacrosse playing leader, getting angrier by the second.

"The presence imbued within the king's ring," remarked Fredric, pointing to Tank's hand.

"Oh..." replied Richie, thinking that she might have some sort of grip on what was going on.

"Since you're here For'son, and with little time to spare, I just wanted to tell you how sorry I am... for everything," declared George. "If I could go back, I would act very differently, of that you can be assured. Stay with Tank, keep doing what you're doing, and guide him as best you can. Good luck my friend," reflected the king, before turning around and heading back to his place in the circle, alongside his best friend.

Shaking his head, appearing to come out of a trance, much like the nagas strewn across the battlefield, Tank stared straight into Richie's eyes.

"I think this is going to be tough, Rich. They're quite

formidable from what I've seen and from what For'son tells me."

"A bit like the dragon himself from what I've heard."

"Oh yes... and just to let you know, he's lapping this up."

"I bet he is," replied Richie.

"Okay... let's get ready. I'd better tell all the others."

With Fu-ts'ang tickling the mythical creatures' attacking edge, probing here, hitting hard there, the bonded group of light-sided heroes formed one big circle, and in their time honoured tradition (well... of the past few hours, anyway) ignited their shields, joining them together, and prepared to face new adversaries they knew absolutely nothing about.

Quietly stalking over to the healing genius that was Yoyo, very gently and cautiously, Janice tapped him on the back.

Turning around, his giant prehistoric face with a huge smile on it, greeted her.

"Little one, how are you? It's good to see you in one piece."

"You too," she replied.

"What is it I can do for you? We're about to go into battle, you know."

"I know," she said nervously, not really wanting to ask. But she did so anyway.

"I was hoping you could take a look at Peter. He's totally unresponsive and won't say a word."

"Ahhh... well, I can heal his hand, that's for sure," Yoyo ventured, his right index finger suddenly spiralling around and around, pointing in the direction of the hockey playing dragon.

With a THWUMP and then a TINKLE, the brilliant, glistening and powerful dagger fell to the floor, which wasn't the most amazing thing that happened as Janice and Hook looked on.

Hand still raised in the air, the blood that had trickled down past his wrist and onto his arm slowly started retreating back up into the wound itself. Globules of thick, red, viscous fluid on the floor shot through the air, reuniting themselves with his body, before the injury knitted itself back together before their very eyes. Amazing!

"Wow!" said Janice.

"Brilliant!" raved Hook.

"Will he be alright now?" asked the young bar worker.

Turning right round to face her, his huge prehistoric monster of a head leaning right down and in, very gently Yoyo whispered to her, trying not to let everybody else hear.

"I've done all I can for him. Physically, he should be fine. What he needs now, almost certainly, only you can provide, given the nature of... your relationship. Do you understand, little one?"

Swallowing nervously, Janice replied.

"I do."

And with that, Yoyo winked once and turned back to face the outside of the circle and the onrushing threat.

"What's going on?" asked Hook, as he and Janice marched back over to Peter.

Turning to face the hulking (to her, anyway) heroic rugby player, she searched for the words.

"Peter and I, we, uh, we uh..." she whispered, not wanting any of the others to know.

Slapping her playfully on the arm, Hook stopped her right there.

"For goodness sake... I know. It's been totally obvious, now that I think about it, even from as far back as the restaurant."

"Really?" exclaimed the young bar worker.

"Of course," declared Hook. "Good for you. Now what can I do to help?"

Wanting a moment or two alone with her love, Janice picked up the pristine gleaming dagger, turned to her friend and said,

"Get this to Richie. She might just need it."

Grabbing it from her hands, he rushed off as fast as he could to find their leader and his friend.

To those that remained alive and were capable of doing so, he ordered a retreat back to the far end of the king's private residence, wanting no real part in a fight that he hadn't picked. Whatever was going on with his dragon allies, this time they were in it on their own... all he wanted to do was gather up as many of his race as he could and get the hell out of there, especially now that Manson and his evil other half had disappeared like rats out of a drainpipe. As far as he was concerned, naga involvement in any of this was over, now being a time to heal and bring what was left of their civilisation back together. And so it was that very slowly, one by one, the slithering serpents that had been duped all that time ago by Troydenn, and then Manson, regrouped around their rightful, king, free at last, keen to hear what orders he had for them.

While they waited for the mythical creatures to stop playing with their food in the form of the remaining dark dragons lighting up the air above them, minor healing was carried out, friends rejoiced at getting this far, and a real optimism about their situation started to circle. It was in this brief respite that Tank told his best friend what he thought he knew.

"If the nagas are down, then Gee Tee must have succeeded in taking Fleet Street," he observed.

"How do you figure that?"

"Some time ago, we... spliced together a mantra, one that if it worked, could be used in conjunction with the crystal node to stun all of the nagas throughout the world. I think we can all agree that's what just happened. If that's the case, and I'm sure that it is, I assume that the node is up and running and reinforcements are on their way."

"YOU SPLICED A MANTRA?!" yelled Richie, forgetting not only who she was, but where she was as well.

"Really?" said Tank. "That's what you took from that?"

"WHO, SPLICED WHAT?" shouted George from across the way, with Fredric looking on curiously.

"Nothing," Tank growled back, hoping it would all be forgotten.

"YOU DO KNOW THAT'S HIGHLY ILLEGAL?!"

"I can't hear you," replied the rugby playing dragon, wishing he'd never opened his mouth.

"So... reinforcements you say," laughed Richie, pleased at having gotten him in trouble.

Looking back, he just shook his head, wondering how his friend and mentor fared across the other side of the capital.

Kneeling down beside him, still marvelling at how Yoyo had healed his hand, the young bar worker leant her head against his, hoping for some indication that he recognised her. Unfortunately though, Peter's form was unwavering, his mind barely able to control its body's basic functions, let alone anything else.

"Peter... it's me, Janice," she whispered, desperate not to give anything away or let any of the others hear what she was saying. Still nothing!

"You need to snap out of it, and quickly. Your friends need your help against another, totally different enemy altogether. Please come back to us and perform some more of your heroics. They need you... I need you. Please... come back."

Still his body remained unmoving.

Her quiet words hadn't gone unnoticed, not by a long shot, something that might well come back to haunt the two of them, should they indeed make it out of this alive.

With those nagas still alive having slithered their way back to Vasuki's rallying point much further beyond the circle of heroes, the mythical creatures had for the most part stopped, some of them grazing on long since dead naga and dragon corpses lying sprawled on the ground, others taking pot shots at, or engaging, dark dragons still roaming the air above. Gradually, those mythical creatures lagging behind caught up, including the ra-hoon, who remained safely tucked away at the back of the pack.

"Can we not either reason with them or put them back in the cells they were so conveniently released from?" asked Richie across the link.

"I don't see how you can bargain with them," observed Tank. *"They're stone cold killers, on the hunt for magic, with very little getting in their way. What would you give them? And how do you know they'll stick to their side of the bargain?"*

Both good points. On the other subject, the king chipped in.

"I can't begin to imagine how you'd get them back in their prisons, which I would guess are now damaged beyond repair. For them to all be here, they must have physically broken out after the magic in their cells disappeared, no mean feat in itself. So those enclosures would need to be repaired, the magic reconnected and then you'd have to lure them back there... three big asks at the best of times, something this most certainly isn't."

"Sorry... I was just thinking out loud, trying to avoid a confrontation if at all possible."

"NEVER apologise for seeking a diplomatic solution to a fight. EVER! Being a leader is doing the right thing, making tough choices no matter how unpopular. We're all behind you and if a fight is unavoidable, then so be it, we'll take them on. But you are RIGHT to consider all available options," and that came from the founder of the Crimson Guards, Fredric, much to everyone's surprise, especially George.

Buoyed by those words, standing between Tank and George, watching as a pack of blue maned asena fought over the guts of a dismembered naga lying curled up on the ground, Richie couldn't help feeling the tiniest hint of failure creeping through everything they did. She had managed to keep them alive, up until this point, anyway, she supposed, but in the process Manson and Earth had escaped, which was heartbreaking considering they'd had them on the ropes.

'How many more beings will suffer because those two still remain at large? And could I, or us as a group have done anything different in an effort to defeat them?'

Gathering some hundred or so metres in front of the circle of heroes, with the ra-hoon carefully taking things in from the rear, the rest of the wild, wonderful and beastly creatures all at least appeared uncoordinated, despite Tank and For'son knowing better. They watched as gaki spun on the spot, their huge blood red and green bulging bellies wobbling like a plate of jelly on top of a washing machine, the three eyes on their cattle-like heads scanning in the direction of the circle, all of which appeared to be for no apparent reason other than to brag about how lethal their body parts were, while camaheutos sharpened their claws on mounds of debris, attempting to intimidate. All the time scorpion men, their bodies the size of a car, clacked their meaty claws in anticipation of what was to come, the noise abounding throughout the private residence, even setting Vasuki and his ragtag bunch of nagas on edge, some way off. As if all of that wasn't bad enough, clouds of fire breathing gnats assaulted dark dragons in the air around them. You would have thought it would have been a totally one-sided fight, but not so, because of two things. One... the gnats were all but immune to fire, their tiny little bodies unerringly able to withstand extremely high temperatures, and two... their ability to seamlessly work together as a group, coordinating telepathically as one, tiny little army. It was an impressive feat that allowed them to decimate beings hundreds, if not thousands of times their size, something they showed off to good effect, targeting the dark dragons' eyes with multiple bursts of small, sharp flames, blinding them almost instantly as well as dashing into their ears, before setting the inner ear canal alight, something on a dragon that offered virtually no protection against fire, unlike the flame retardant scales that covered most of the exterior of their prehistoric bodies. Finally, a squadron nearly always attacked the wings, knowing just how vulnerable the beast would be if it could be grounded, with hundreds of the minute monsters gnawing their way through sinew and membrane, after which it was nearly all over. Impressive didn't begin to cover it, with the heroes taking all of it in, more fearful of them than anything else that they'd faced already that day, perhaps with the exception of Manson and Earth.

Through their psychic link, Richie tried to send an aura of composure and calm, knowing full well, like most there, that all the showmanship going on was designed to undermine their confidence and instil a real sense of fear. As far as Yoyo's young group of dragons were concerned, it appeared to be working a treat, with their nerves becoming apparent even through their invisible connection.

'Easy youngsters, it's all just for show. They're no tougher than the nagas and dragons we've already taken on, in fact, some of them will be a lot easier to take down if you use the cunning intellect you are all endowed with. Work together, cover each other's backs and you'll be fine. Okay?" reflected the Australian healer.

Each sent back a virtual nod, reaffirming that they'd heard and understood everything he said. Richie, for one, was glad that he had spoken up, not just because his words had cooled down his charges, but because she too needed to hear them. Nobody there was immune to the fear the monsters outside were trying to create, even the most experienced warriors amongst them. And so they continued to stand, continued to watch, wondering what on earth would happen next and just how well they would perform when going up against creatures straight out of the annuls of history.

Scaled apes with numerous appendages missing thumped their chests as some of their kind feasted on the entrails of downed dragons, dark green blood, gore and numerous internal organs matting their close shaven furry coats.

Bolts of brilliant blue, green and brown forked lightning licked across what remained of the floor in the king's private residence as vampiric lizards darted about, this way and that, their extraordinarily long tongues tasting the air, their clawed feet scrabbling across the once white, pristine marble surface as some way off in the direction of the council building, the trumpeting of one of the giant elephant beasts, sounding both evil and intense all at the same time, echoed across the air.

With the dark dragon numbers above diminishing, two-headed eagles bravely took their place, flying alongside the fire breathing gnats, the pixiu that resembled winged lions and the nifoloa and their singular sharp teeth, squawking like constipated parrots, their white and brown feathers looking regal and magnificent. Off in the distance, fighting a dozen or so dark dragons all at once, the asag, the giant hideous rock demon, stomped and stamped, its fists flying through the air like a whirling, twirling fair ride, the purple glow in its eyes intensifying the more outraged it became at its clenched hands not connecting with their targets, the quaking of the ground beating to its every footfall. That beast was not under the control of the ra-hoon, although the heroes didn't know that, and in fact both sides were desperate not to attract its attention, for very obvious reasons.

Circling the unicorn lookalikes, forty or fifty echeneis, diminutive twelve centimetre long serpents with ice cold freezing breath that made Fu-ts'ang's frosty blade feel like the brief opening of a fridge, shared the ground with twenty or so conaima, giant were-jaguars, their pacing almost silent due to their soft padded feet, which were doing all they could to avoid the shape shifting venomous snakes that slithered around, under and over everything in the immediate vicinity, one thing on their mind... to protect their leaders, the ra-hoon, at all costs.

Lost as to what she should do, instinctively she grabbed his hand, not the one through which the dagger had passed, for fear that it hadn't quite healed properly, although it looked as good as new. No the other one, and holding it tightly, once again, she whispered in his ear.

"Peter, you have to come back to us. I love you more than words can say, and don't want everything I've been through these last few days to be for nothing. I know you can hear me, and I understand that you've suffered a terrible trauma. But all of your friends are here and not only do they need you, but I truly believe you need them. Focus your mind, return to the present and join us in one last fight to earn our freedom. You being here might make all the difference. I know it will for me at least. Please, Peter, come back."

Amongst the darkness an electric touch to his hand startled him momentarily. Unable to comprehend what could cause such a thing, his mind returned to the resentment, bitterness and futility of it all. Nothing made sense... not his life up until now, his abandonment by his true parents, his missing grandfather, or the way in which he'd become caught up in the plot to steal a vast amount of laminium by that monster Manson... it all seemed like a dream, or more accurately, a nightmare, one from which he couldn't awaken, no matter how hard he tried.

"Please, Peter... come back," resounded into the dark walls of his mind some way off in the distance, the female voice vaguely familiar, although for some reason he couldn't quite put his finger on it.

Abruptly, far, far away, a pinprick of bright white light exploded into view, very much like the end of a tunnel, seemingly out of reach. For a moment at least his consciousness stopped to take it all in, but that's all that happened before it went back on its morose way.

Closing in from behind, not wanting to startle her, he

gently put his hand on her shoulder to let her know that he was there. Instantly Richie whirled round, ready to fight, afraid that one of the mythical creatures had found some way to sneak through their magical defences.

"Whoa tiger, it's only me," declared Hook, taking two steps back.

"Sorry," offered up the lacrosse superstar. "My mind was in another place, keeping an eye on something else."

"No problem. Janice asked me to bring you this. She thought you might need it," he said, offering up the laminium dagger to her.

Mesmerised by the familiar blade's astounding beauty, simplicity and power, it took a few moments for the de facto leader to get her head around seeing the weapon again.

"It makes you more powerful, is that right?" asked Hook, trying to break the silence.

"Something like that, something like that," she answered, her thoughts still elsewhere, the small part of her still present considering whether it was best to keep the artefact or return it to its rightful owner, Fredric, who she was currently keeping a very keen eye on for a number of reasons. Deciding not to return the blade, well... not just yet anyway, she snatched it away from the human rugby player and in a flash stuffed it down the back of her trousers, pulling her top down to conceal it totally.

"Thanks," she said softly, meaning every word. "Please, for the time being, don't tell anyone that you've returned it to me. There's a good reason for me to ask this of you, I just can't explain right now. Do you think you could do that?"

"Of course," he replied, "anything for you."

Interesting words for one so... human, interesting also the effect they had on the young dragon stuck in that form, forcing her stomach into somersaults, sending a shiver down her spine and goose bumps up her arms. How odd. Because of their situation though, and Richie's little... problem that she was hoping wouldn't need addressing here and now, it practically went unnoticed... PRACTICALLY!

Feeling as though she was getting nowhere, and more afraid than she'd been in a while without the company of her friend Fu-ts'ang, and with her lover and soul mate devoid of any kind of emotion, Janice was once again being tested to destruction, this time in an altogether different way, and it was only about to get worse, much, much worse. Although it felt as though she were more alone than at any other time of her life, that was much further from the truth than she could ever believe.

"I KNOW WHAT YOU'RE UP TO AND I'M HERE TO TELL YOU NOW THAT IT WON'T BE TOLERATED UNDER ANY CIRCUMSTANCES. I WILL DO EVERYTHING IN MY POWER TO STOP IT AND YOU. YOUR DISGUSTING EFFORTS TO BREAK THE LAW WILL BE PUNISHED AND YOU WILL BE BROUGHT TO JUSTICE FORTHWITH!" assaulted Janice's mind, the unfamiliar voice almost bringing her to her knees, much like her lover, the words crushing her will, terrorising her spirit.

It was a message and one none too subtle. You might have thought that it originated from somewhere outside their circle, but that was far from the case, with the sender being someone much closer to home.

Wrecked and devastated, the young bar worker's legs started to wobble and her teeth began to chatter as the terrifying words played over and over in her mind, her sanity questioning why on earth she'd ever got mixed up in all of this anyway. Close to being torn apart, feeling lost, alone and surrounded by darkness just like her soul mate, which I suppose was the point, her suffering was profound and utterly undeserved. As tears ran down her stunningly beautiful human face, leaping to the ground like a wingsuit flyer diving off a cliff thousands of metres high, their tiny splashes on the floor by her feet went totally unnoticed, even by Fate herself. Suddenly, she had more to worry about than the sound of teardrops, as once again, the words started up.

"IF YOU PERSIST WITH YOUR SO CALLED SOUL MATE THEN I WILL..."

"ENOUGH!" yelled an

exceptionally familiar voice, one instantly recognisable to them all, and this time not just throughout Janice's psyche, but throughout all of their minds, across the link they all shared.

Because, you see, the callous perpetrator of this cowardly crime, instead of being subtle and directing his anger directly at Janice herself, had carried his words on a vicious wave of hatred that had been pointed in her general direction, something of a mistake on his part, and something that the caring, lacrosse playing superstar leader who would do anything for her friends had picked up on from the off. Despite not knowing the exact reason for what was going on, she was determined at any and all costs to put a stop to it immediately.

Having scared the living crap out of just about everybody there with her harsh sounding word, Richie, her personal shield flickering out of existence, the mythical creatures with all eyes on her, just like everyone else there, stomped out of her place, around George, coming face to face with Fredric, only really chest height to him, her expression one of total and absolute anger. If there was one single being at one single moment in the entire universe that you never wanted to mess with, it was her... here and now!

"What in the hell gives you the..."

Fredric's hand moved faster than the eye could see, attempting to grab the young dragon around the throat, much to the amazement of all the others.

For sure, he was good with all his decades worth of experience and training, but she was on an absolute mission, and more importantly, one of her friends' lives was at stake, and I'm not talking about Peter here, although he would surely have figured somewhere in the equations currently running throughout her mind. Matching his move, she deflected his arm, spun around faster than it seemed possible, used her elbow, with just a hint of magic, to shatter his nose, sending thick red blood spurting out in every direction. Not finished there, she grabbed the fingers on the hand that had tried to wrap itself around her throat, twisted his arm painfully behind his back, forcing him, just like Janice and Peter, to his knees. All done in the blink of an eye, her actions shocked all of those gathered in the circle, about to fight against the mythical creatures.

Tank took one step forward, as did George, no one there knowing what the hell was going on. But she stopped them in their tracks.

"Anybody moves and I'll kill him here and now!"

Immediately they stopped, looking as though the music had abruptly cut out during a game of musical statues. No one there moved as they all waited to see what would happen next.

"Young lady..." George started to say, but she cut him off straight away.

Pulling out the laminium dagger from behind her back, holding it pointing down at the base of his neck, it was clear to everyone there that she wasn't bluffing, and that included Peter's grandfather himself.

"ARE YOU KIDDING ME?" she screamed at the back of his head, "AFTER EVERYTHING WE'VE BEEN THROUGH!"

To a being, everyone, with the exception of those involved glanced around at each other, wondering what on earth was going on.

"Rich..." started Tank. Again though, she was having none of it.

"NO!" she screamed at him, having almost appeared to have lost her mind.

Instantly the rugby playing dragon contacted For'son, asking for his help in disarming her, in an effort to settle things down. But with that much power, magic and responsibility comes a wealth of experience. As well, he'd heard what Fredric had tried to do and had shared that experience with a kindred spirit.

"*You won't help?*" asked Tank, incredulous.

"*I didn't say that. I just think you need to understand her reason. I like her in much the same way I like you. That should tell you all you need to know.*"

'Brilliant!' thought Tank, no closer to getting any answers.

"*TELL THEM!*" she ordered, '*OR I'LL GUT YOU LIKE A FISH!*"

And not one of them there doubted she would be good for her word.

"You don't understand," spluttered Fredric, his shattered nose making his words hard to comprehend.

"I must insist," exclaimed George, "that you tell us exactly what's going on."

Red in the face, angrier than she could ever remember being and that included the recent lacrosse match in which she'd been physically and verbally assaulted, their leader, THE White Dragon, turned to face him, her grip on the dagger still unwavering.

"This scum sucking piece of filth has been telepathically threatening Janice over there, haven't you?" she said, kicking the founder of the Crimson Guards firmly in the back for good measure.

Stupidly, or very wisely, he remained totally silent.

"I don't understand," ventured the king, trying desperately to do so. "Why on earth would he do such a thing?"

"You tell me," replied Richie, hanging on to her temper by a thread.

And despite the confused expression on his face not changing one iota, George had what can only be described as something of a light bulb moment.

From across the other side, Captain Battlehard took a

step in the direction of the argument and the king. Flash held out a wing to stop her going any further, shaking his head in warning, something that raised her hackles more than a little, but knowing his character she chose to obey, for the time being at least.

"I can't believe..." attempted the king, but to no avail.

"You can't believe, you can't believe? Let me tell all of you what I can't believe. I can't believe we're all here, still alive and kicking. I can't believe that humans would risk their lives to travel down into the domain in search of their friends. I can't believe the courage they've shown and the heroics they've performed. I can't believe that without one of their kind, the young blonde headed girl over there, we would all be dead and that Manson and his witch bride, Earth, would-be ruling the entire planet forever. I can't believe that supposedly one of our own would treat HER like this. I can't believe my temper remains in check, because I'll tell you all here and now, just in case it wasn't obvious before, I WOULD DO ANYTHING FOR MY FRIENDS, ABSOLUTELY ANYTHING. AND I WILL NOT HAVE THEM ABUSED IN ANY WAY, SHAPE OR FORM, NO MATTER WHAT THE TIME OR SITUATION... EVER! AND JUST IN CASE YOU'RE UNSURE, SHE, ALONGSIDE PETER, TANK, FLASH AND HOOK IS ONE OF THE BEST ONES THAT I HAVE!"

Well, that left them all in pretty much no doubt.

"Stupid child!" muttered Fredric under his breath.

"You what?" snarled Richie, about ready to stab the dagger through the back of his neck.

"You heard... stupid child."

"I should kill you now. The only thing that's keeping you alive is the fact that you're Peter's grandfather. If not for that, then I'd have already done it."

Tears continued to roll down Janice's cheeks, the fear she now felt at being down here in the dragon domain obvious, her previous bravery having long since deserted her. With Peter's body remaining frozen in place, Hook stepped up and wrapped his huge muscled arms around her, standing fast, one human to another. Although it didn't stop the tears or drive away the terror she felt, it did at least help a little.

"You know nothing of family," Fredric spat angrily. "And as for being in charge, what a laugh that is... White Dragon my arse!"

As the fun and games continued, the mythical creatures looked on intrigued, all the time getting ever closer, inch by inch, hoping their prey wouldn't notice. They didn't.

Enraged beyond belief, part of her wondering how it had come to this, a much larger part not really giving a damn, only knowing what was right and fair, concerned for her friends Janice, Peter, Tank, Hook and Flash as well as the group of humans who'd gone off with the shopkeeper, the lacrosse playing dragon superstar's tempestuous and turbulent emotional side had come to the fore, something that if they'd known all about her, and George did having read all the reports throughout the years, they'd have gone to great lengths to appease.

"Family," she spat back, "you're a joke. But I'll tell you about my family. One dark day I hatched out of my egg, scared and afraid, in a darkened room, all alone... except that I wasn't. There was another being there, the first one I encountered, and despite having never met me, or being instructed to, he showed me total and utter kindness, straight out of the goodness of his heart, even when others might not have. Do you know why? Because that is his nature. And just who do you think that was? Well... turn around and look. The being over there, the one on his knees, lost and alone because he's just learnt that his mother... YOUR DAUGHTER, is that psychopath EARTH, Manson's other half. The first being I ever encountered after I hatched was Peter, and just like Tank, Hook, Janice and Flash, he's part of my family and I'd do anything for them, including laying down my life. For you to try and lecture me on kin is nothing short of pathetic, old dragon. I don't care who you are, what you've supposedly done in the past or who you're friends with, you even attempt to mess with MY family again, and I will kill you where you stand."

"Oh you're full of bluster. I'd like to see you try... human!"

If everyone had thought things had got out of hand so far, that was nothing to what was about to happen.

Confident that he could take her, even with the tip of the laminium dagger almost against the back of his neck, he was surprised to feel a piercing dark cold hammer his chest and rattle his jaw, so painfully that it almost rendered him unconscious.

"Would you like to see me try?" asked a cold, harsh, unfamiliar voice, that none of them had heard speak out loud before, not thinking that he could.

Nervously and very carefully, with the frosty tip of Fu-ts'ang's blade at his throat, Peter's grandfather swallowed, looking much less convincing now that there were two of them.

"Not so ******* clever now, are you?" quipped Richie, cuffing him across the head with her palm, almost pushing it down on to the blade at his throat.

Silence.

"You should stay out of this, weapon smith," Fredric said with malice in his voice.

"Threatening one of my friends could very well be the last thing you do... pathetic warrior. How does it feel to encounter someone of your own ilk? Not quite so tough now you're not picking on a defenceless young human with nothing but good in her heart, are you?"

"I really do think that now isn't the time to resolve all this," put in the king, worried for the safety of his best friend, now quite sure he knew exactly what was going on and just how it had been caused.

"NO!" countered Richie. "I won't stand for this. It gets

sorted one way or the other NOW!"

Eyes locked on one another, George and Richie faced off, neither giving way, both knowing that they were right. Something just had to give, especially given the way in which everyone else there was weighing up their options. Flash considered his position carefully, having loyalties on both sides, but surprisingly ended up favouring the lacrosse playing wizard who he'd seen in action close up in this crisis and admired more than he could ever have imagined. His partner, Captain Battlehard had other ideas, just as you would expect, ready, willing and able to go to the king's aid, after all, that was her job and protecting him had been part of the vow she'd taken. All of the King's Guard to a dragon were ready to intercede on the king's behalf, but currently remained stationary, waiting to see how this played out. Yoyo, with his vast experience, looked on at the mess he saw before him, wondering how on earth all of the battle hardened friends had come to all of this. Whatever Fredric had done, he mused, it must have been all but unforgiveable. A staunch supporter of the king, if push came to shove, he'd have backed Richie all day long, having witnessed at least some of her exploits firsthand. He truly believed, now that it had been explained to him, that she was the fabled White Dragon from the prophecy. If that were the case, then she just had to be followed whatever the cost. Divided, and more than a little sceptical, Yoyo's charges all had a different opinion on events playing out around them, with the vast majority having little respect or love for the monarchy or the king and like their mentor, having seen the spectacular acts that the lacrosse playing dragon had achieved since teaming up with her, and as she'd saved their lives on at least one occasion, they would no doubt fall down on her side should push come to shove.

That left Tank and For'son who, you would have thought, would have been divided on the issue, with the former coming down on the side of his best friend and the latter favouring his former, more legitimate partner. But not so, because having been aware of what was going on, and knowing the details and of course passing them on to Fu-ts'ang, for For'son there really was only one choice, and that was to side with their leader, Richie, and her sound backing of the one they called Janice.

Battle lines drawn in a battle within a battle, the tense standoff continued to escalate, the cunning and curious creatures outside moving ever closer, all trying to understand what they were seeing, whether or not it was a trap, trying to work out if they should be afraid or not. The answer to that last one was most certainly, yes they should.

"Listen to me, young lady..." started the king.

"DRAGON!" declared Richie. "I'm a DRAGON, and you'd do well to remember that."

Prickly didn't begin to describe her character right now, something that George knew all about, that and the fact that she rarely backed down, if ever at all. Looking at the bigger picture, and engaging every ounce of diplomacy that he had, taking a deep breath, he tried again with a different approach.

"Richie," he said softly, "Currently stuck in the middle of a life or death situation like this, is not the time or the place to resolve these issues. Not only are you a formidable leader, but you're smart and savvy, two qualities that serve you well most of the time. Look around you and see what's playing out. No one here wants any of this. As well, you know the creatures are closing in, slowly I grant you, but they are."

In the background, held firmly by Hook, Janice's tears had turned into full on sobbing, ironic really given the heroics that she'd consistently performed since arriving in the dragon domain.

"And just what is it you would have us do... majesty?" Richie scoffed, using the 'majesty' much as Manson had always used the word 'Bentwhistle'.

"Put our differences aside for the time being, come together like we have before, finish up the fight and then sort things out once this is all over."

"NO!" bellowed the low, hard voice of Fu-ts'ang. "I cannot let this go unanswered."

"He's right," announced Richie. "I won't let this slide."

"But..." urged the king.

"Do you even know what went on?" asked the supposed White Dragon.

Stopped dead in his tracks, George had no answer, because of course he didn't know, and neither did most of the others.

"TELL THEM!" Richie screamed at the founder of the Crimson Guards and Peter's grandfather.

Remaining utterly still with the tip of Fu-ts'ang's blade sitting firmly beneath his chin, Fredric knelt, unmoving and unwilling to say a word.

"COWARD!" she yelled, hoping to provoke a reaction.

"BETRAYER!" shouted Fu-ts'ang.

"Rich..." uttered Tank as softly as he dared, fully aware of just how upset his friend was and having the experience to know exactly which way this was likely to go, having seen her in this position a few times before. "We truly do need to turn our attention to whatever's out there. Please, let's just leave this until we've dealt with the creatures."

"And just how are we supposed to do that with someone we can't trust amongst us, eh... smart arse?"

"I will guarantee his behaviour," stated the king, confident that would be a winner.

"Like that's possible," replied Richie, not having any of it. "What, we just get him to promise to be a good boy, and everything's alright?"

"Clearly everything is not alright, but you have my word that he'll behave."

"I'm afraid that's just not good enough... majesty," she sneered, sarcastically. "Especially since he lacks the courage to tell you all exactly what was done. Somebody with at least an ounce of bravery would do that, particularly when they've been so obviously caught out. A coward, liar and traitor... I'd rather fight on my own than alongside somebody that would clearly stab me in the back in a heartbeat."

Knowing that things were going to hell faster than a virus originating in China, George tried one last time to plead with the young dragon. Still though, she was having none of it.

"I can guarantee that he will do no harm Rich," suggested Tank, one of the few here and now that she trusted fully.

"I don't see how that's possible."

"For'son has said that he'll keep an eye on him for any sign of treachery. I assure you, that'll be enough."

Angry, desperate, scared for her friend, wanting nothing more than to protect her and bring Peter back to reality, and of course, well and truly pissed off, the lacrosse playing dragon very deliberately reined in her temper, fully aware of how it could make her act at times, knowing that what she decided here and now affected not only her, but her friends as well. Not seeing that she had any other choice, and knowing that this really wasn't over, she succumbed when she really thought she shouldn't, but with one caveat.

"Fine," she blurted out in Tank's direction. "But if he does anything untoward, it's on you."

Tank, for his part, let out a huge, silent breath, as did nearly everybody there, for once keen to face a horde of demonic creatures who they had no idea how to defeat, that's how desperate their situation had become.

"But I'll tell you now," she said, turning to face Peter's grandfather, who still had the master weapon smith at his throat. "This isn't over, by a long shot. When we're done here, you and I are going to have words, and I promise you you'll wish to hell you'd stayed rotting in that prison cell in Antarctica. Fu-ts'ang, I'm changing your orders. Your number one priority is to guard and protect Janice at all costs from anything you consider a threat. You may use whatever force you think is required. Do you understand?"

"I do, my leader," he replied, wholeheartedly.

"Good. Back to your positions," she ordered despairingly. "Fight with all that you have, I want this over as soon as possible."

A tall order, they all thought, but none of them had the courage to tell her.

Pulling his tip away from under Fredric's chin, frost rotating around the length of its blade, the master weapon smith's futuristic, glistening body hung in the air, seemingly eyeing up the founder of the Crimson Guards. To anyone else it would have presented as a menacing threat, but not to Fredric who just ignored it and strode casually back to his place in the circle. Ready to do whatever was necessary, Fu-ts'ang glided across to Hook and Janice, proud that the young human had stepped up to comfort her when her dragon soul mate hadn't been able to.

And so it was that with everybody back in their original places, personal shields ignited, bonds formed, a fighting stance taken. But things, as you have probably guessed, would never be the same again amongst the heroes. With For'son and Fu-ts'ang keeping an eye on the wayward Fredric, as everyone else focused fully on the approaching enemy, those watching from far off tried to make sense of what they'd just seen.

"It looks like some kind of bust up," observed Garrett, eyes pressed firmly to the state of the art binoculars he held, pleased to see his employee, Miss Rump, still alive and very much kicking.

"She's got some balls on her," mentioned Polo, "arguing like that with the king."

"I do hope not," whispered Owen, so low that he thought he couldn't possibly be overheard.

He hadn't though, accounted for the excellent dragon hearing of those all around him. As chortling and the tickling of flame from a few scaly nostrils abounded, he knew that he'd been caught out... oops!

"Do we need to let them know that we're here yet?" asked Garrett quietly, worried about his voice travelling.

"Not yet," replied Polo. "Contacting them now would be a risk, especially since we don't know the abilities of the strange creatures down there. Clearly there's a magical component of some sort, but if any of them can somehow pick up on telepathic transmissions, it might make us a target very quickly, and believe you me, we wouldn't last very long against them. In fact, the only thing we could really do is retreat, something that doesn't help our friends one little bit."

Nodding in understanding, Garrett returned to the binoculars, keen to see how his people were faring, fearing for the safety of them all.

Across the planet's surface, with the exception of the United Kingdom and the parts of Europe closest to it, individuals were admitted to hospitals paralysed with an unknown condition, put in beds and on ventilators, tests run to determine the cause of their mysterious ailment, their symptoms baffling doctors across the continents. What they didn't, and of course couldn't know, was that the individuals in question were disguised using the most sophisticated and unusual naga magic available, the facsimile forms of the snake-like intruders easily as perfect as those of the dragons who'd sworn to guide and protect their ape-like charges.

For the nagas to be freed from their temporary paralysis, their king, Vasuki would need to use his magic across all the remaining continents of the world. Only then would they stand a chance of returning to any sense of normality.

Without warning, it forced its way into their collective telepathic link, something that really shouldn't have been able to happen, frightening the heroes down to every being there.

"If you give us what we want, we will in turn let you go free," a sickeningly happy voice broadcast across their minds.

"What in the…" they all thought, caught totally off guard.

"The ra-hoon, no doubt," ventured the king, knowing all about their tricks and talents.

"How can you be sure?" asked Richie, putting their past disagreements behind them, at least for now.

"They're famed for their mental abilities, in particular subjugating others into doing their bidding. I don't doubt all the beings over there are under their control to some degree or other. Forcing their way into our link would be child's play for them."

Haunting, happy laughter echoed throughout their heads.

"We need to stop communicating this way shortly," ordered Richie, not knowing what else to do.

Immediately all the other minds in the link pulled back, worried looks on the faces of all those concerned. How would they coordinate their attacks? How would they call for help or healing? How would they let everyone know if anyone was in trouble? All these questions and more were currently being wrestled by the minds of each of the individuals. One thing they all felt though, was that the ra-hoon needed to be taken out first if they were to have any chance of succeeding. How they did that though, was anybody's guess.

One by one, the different species were told in no uncertain terms exactly what was expected of them. Some had to be spoken to twice, their bodies currently fulfilling their desire to be fed, unable to pass up the opportunity to wolf down the sickly, stinking remains of enemies slain in battle. A little mental probing and prodding was necessary on the ra-hoon's part, mixed in with the odd smidgen of pain, an artery pinched here, a vein pricked there, just to keep them in line and continue to let them know who was boss. It worked well, to a large degree, with the occasional individual here and there paying scant attention. But that mattered not with the army of warrior beasts that they had at their disposal.

Over the course of five or ten minutes, assets, as the ra-hoon liked to think of their underlings, were moved into place like strategic pieces on a chess board, with air support and infantry having never looked so strange.

And then it came time to make that one last offer.

"We meant what we said," claimed the still sickly happy voice that, had it been a colour, would have undoubtedly been the pinkest pink that had ever existed. *"Hand over our prize, and we'll let you all live. If we have to come and get it, you'll all be sure to end up dead. Three minutes. You choose."*

And then their transmission cut out.

"What is it that they..."

"For'son!" answered Tank, mindful of saying his name across their shared connection.

"The ring, really... why?"

"Because of the magical power that I wield, youngster," came yet one more unfamiliar voice, again, freaking them all out.

"For'son, a pleasure to meet you at last. Thanks for returning our magic earlier on. I thought we were done without it," Richie replied.

"You would have been," laughed the ring, *"but that's then and this is now. All we seemed to have done is jump from the frying pan into the fire, and I have to say, I really don't want to end up in their hands, more than I didn't want to end up with Manson."*

Tank had a vague idea of just how much that was.

"We'll give everything we have to stop that from happening. Can you tell us anything of value that might give us some kind of chance against them, especially the ra-hoon as they're clearly in charge, and if they can interrupt our minds at will, can they also attack us mentally?"

"I think I have that covered," replied the enigmatic band. *"Tank and I have been talking, and I think I can protect each and every one of you from any mental attacks they throw our way. It won't be pretty, or subtle, but it is doable. They only thing it does mean, is that I won't be able to help out so much on the attacking front, but I*

don't see any other way around it."

"Okay, good to know... Anything else?"

"The ra-hoon themselves are said to be invulnerable to magic of any kind."

"You're joking, right?" enquired Richie, astounded.

"No. You'll have to get up close and personal to take them out, unless you can think of some other way. If you can defeat them, then just maybe we can take the rest down, but it's still a tall ask."

"Something odd's going on," whispered Lotty from behind the pile of rotting dead nagas.

"What do you mean?" asked Polo, keeping her voice down, the human contingent all listening in.

Before Lotty had a chance to explain, the most senior of them, well, age wise anyway, butted in.

"I think something amongst all those crazy creatures down there can interrupt or even take over our friend's telepathic connection," suggested Vion, cautiously.

"Is that even possible?" asked Polo, deeply concerned.

Scratching the yellow and orange scales adorning his jaw, the elderly and experienced dragon considered her question.

"Maybe," he said. "Centuries ago, these creatures might well have roamed out of the way places across the globe, ruling their tiny areas with utter dominance and confidence. But I would surmise that as the earth opened up for the humans, something had to be done about them, at least from the dragon point of view. Over time, there have been rumours of some kind of exotic prison in the basement of the council building, holding, unbelievably, just these kind of species. Perhaps they escaped during the attack and now want either revenge on those that put them there, or their lands back, or even both."

"I did not know any of that," reflected Polo, wondering what the hell to do next. "Do you have any idea which ones could have the telepathic control that we talked about? Taking them out first would help our friends a great deal I would imagine, and allow us to get in touch with them."

"I'm sorry," replied Vion, "I don't."

"Is there any way to find out?" enquired Garrett, who like all the other humans had been listening intently.

"Probably not without giving ourselves away, because we'd have to try and use a telepathic connection."

"Hang on a minute," urged Polo, turning to face Vion and Lotty. "Think about where we are."

"Uh..." sighed Lotty.

Vion got it straight away.

"Oh my God, of course you're right... the king's private library."

"What's going on?" asked Owen politely.

Pointing across the way with one of her wings, Polo told them what they needed to know.

"That tiny stairwell over there is the back entrance to the king's private library. All those floors you can see going up behind the balustrades are different sections of the library itself. If anywhere in the world would have information on all those creatures, it would be there."

"Wow," exclaimed Garrett, more than a little amused at being in the right place at the right time, for once.

"All we have to do though is get past that thing," Polo observed, again pointing, only this time at the gigantic asag, the giant purple eyed rock demon that continued to prowl that section of the residence.

"That's all?" enquired the 'bald eagle'.

"I never said it was going to be easy," smiled their dragon leader.

"Could you fly across?" asked Caren, one of only two females on Garrett's team.

"We could, but I'm guessing it wouldn't go unnoticed by the rest of the creatures. Even one or two of those, and that would probably be it. As well, they'd likely come searching for anyone else, revealing all of us and giving away our best advantage... the element of surprise."

"Okay," said Garrett. "So what do we do?"

Puzzled, Polo carefully considered his question.

"It could be worth at least considering it as an option," George suggested, back in the defensive circle. "Think of all the lives that could be saved."

About to object, his face utterly furious, the need for Tank to do so disappeared immediately.

"We're not handing him over, and that's final. He's part of the team. And don't forget, if not for him, we'd never have recovered our magic and would all be dead. He stays. If you want to hand someone over though, there is one I wouldn't object to."

And without saying his name, they all knew who that would be.

"I just think..." George tried to continue.

"Majesty... I'm in charge. No ifs, buts, ands or whys. That's just how it is. You agreed to it, and so did everyone else. Now please, turn around and get ready to do your part in taking on these beasts. As has already been pointed out, we need to work together to stand any chance of surviving," declared the superstar lacrosse playing dragon.

Without another word the king complied, the look on his face one of great unhappiness, disagreeing with nearly all of this, disappointed with how his friend had been treated, despite not knowing exactly what he'd done.

"GET READY!" screamed Richie to everyone there. "IF YOU NEED HELP, YOU'LL HAVE TO SHOUT OUT. DO NOT USE THE TELEPATHIC LINK BECAUSE THEY CAN PROBABLY GET TO YOU THROUGH THAT. GOOD LUCK!"

And so it began.

A stalking pack of asena, their furry blue manes waving in the faint breeze, crept forward, heading for the shield on the ground, the smell of their prey and the mammoth amount of magic hidden in that direction tickling their nostrils, spurring them on. They were accompanied by support in the air in the shape of waves of fire breathing gnats circling above, gazing down, trying to find any weak points or potential for chaos. Spread out across the diameter of the circle, individual nifoloa flitted and buzzed, searching high and low for any way past the magical barrier that separated them from their targets and the goal they had been so inspired to reach. Poison dripping in huge, green drops from each one's shiny white, massive tooth, they were only too aware of the fear they instigated in others, and continued to do all that they could in that direction.

Through nothing more than an eagerness to get on with it, and still hurting from the death of his brother Hillier, Zebediah closed his eyes, brought the words to the front of his mind and with all his will let go with the mantra, ready to be acknowledged as the first to take out one of these bizarre creatures. But it was never going to be that easy.

Ten or so metres away, a frenzied nifoloa, looking for any weaknesses in their defences and a chance to plunge its tooth into something living, was abruptly aware of Zebediah's bright blue strand of forked lightning appearing almost in front of him. Applying all of its magical instincts, it hovered in the air, darting this way and that, dropping and diving, looping the loop, inverting and doubling back, all in the blink of an eye, successfully avoiding the well planned and executed attack, but now madder than ever. Hackles raised, the tiny little beast went back on the hunt, determined to make them pay and find a way to exploit the dragons' barrier.

Absolutely gobsmacked, Zebediah turned to face his friends, almost as if to say, "What more could I have possibly done?" And, "If this is what they're capable of, just how are we going to win?"

"And that, ladies and gentlemen, is how not to do it," announced Yoyo, much to the youngster's embarrassment. "Now we've seen one of their tricks, use your brains to work the problem. If they can do that, then what is it we need to do? Come on... hurry up, we haven't got all day."

'Yikes,' thought Richie, feeling as though she were back at the nursery ring, the question itself not even having been directed at her. 'He's a harsh task master,' she thought. 'No wonder they're all so good.' Choosing to ignore the lesson being taught, particularly as she already knew the answer, well... she would, wouldn't she, especially given the thing she was the best at on the entire planet, the dragon lacrosse player returned her focus to those in front of her, ever mindful of her three friends in the middle of their circle, concerned for Janice, proud of Hook and afraid for Peter.

"Uhhhh... team work?" suggested Tarko, to Yoyo's question.

"Of course, team work," confirmed the dragon healer. "Work your magic together and give the dreaded little beasts nowhere to go. That way you'll definitely get them."

"But surely that's a huge waste of our mana, isn't it?" asked Monty.

"It's overkill alright, but with something like that able to move so fast, no doubt enhanced by some kind of supernatural foresight, I would suggest there's little option. Some of the other beings you might be able to deal with individually, but with these things you're gonna have to work together, it would seem."

And although the lesson was just meant for his young charges, everyone in the circle heard it, and everyone took note. It was a good warning to them all.

As two asena approached the individual shields all melded into one, three of the King's Guards behind them at exactly that point decided to act in unison and take out the deadly looking beasts. With one of them conjuring up a wall of fire behind and to the sides of them in an attempt to box them in, the others had decided to pound them with poison and pure magma, all three knowing that it should be some show, hopefully giving them a taste of their own medicine. As the air around them turned to flames, instead of the panic the King's Guards had hoped to see crossing the beast's faces, vicious snarls of defiance came into being as they opened their jaws and leapt at the shield. Confident that nothing could get through, all three dragons put their effort into bringing forth the magma and poison. Abruptly both asena jumped at the invisible barrier, and although their bodies couldn't penetrate it, their legs and claws for some reason could, and so they raked two of the dragons across the face, their toxin covered nails making sure to draw blood and pass on their harmful magic. Crying out, more from the surprise than the pain, well... at first, the two stricken King's Guards fell to the floor, their partner in crime adjusting his barrier to cover the two shields that had fallen by the wayside stopping the monstrosities from getting in.

While not witnessing firsthand what had happened, everybody there was aware and immediately adjusted their defences so that they were set up two metres in front of themselves, hopefully a big enough distance for them not to get struck. An unusual ability for sure, and against the backdrop of the shrieking of their colleagues as the infections started to take hold, the remaining light-sided heroes wondered just what other surprises were in store for them.

"Excellent," remarked the ra-hoon across their link which was still very much active, with regards to the good work of the asena. *"Keep probing, we'll keep them off guard and on edge, and when the moment comes, we'll strike with everything we have."*

Knowing better than to disappoint their leaders, having seen in only a short space of time what they were willing to do to those that disobeyed, both asena growled back in understanding.

Very much as Peter had done, not so long ago, Polo's hulking great dragon form folded in on itself and almost immediately reappeared in human guise, dressed in jeggings, a t-shirt, and trainers, all black. She obviously knew Tank's trick as well, coming out fully dressed.

"Are you sure about this?" she asked, still uncertain herself.

"I am. We're going with you," assured Garrett.

"Okay, but I don't know what we'll find when we get up there. It might be nothing but the place could be crawling with nagas and enemy dragons. There's just no way of knowing."

"We understand and we'll take that chance in an effort to help out."

"Okay... we go in two minutes."

"Understood."

Accompanying Garrett and Polo in her human guise was a no brainer for Owen who was determined to keep his boss secure and gain the safe release of his friend Peter from whatever madness was happening below. Before they set out, he gave his second in command, Caren, instructions on what to do in his absence.

"Keep your comms open. We know that at least one of the enemy force can detect the dragons' method of communicating and so it's vital that we have another way of keeping in touch. If push comes to shove, use your common sense in an effort to get our people out and help those fighting against evil. There seems to be a lot at stake here, and so we should try and do our bit. At the moment, only use your weapons as a last resort. If you do use them, be aware you'll attract all sorts of attention and no doubt enemies. Stealth is our friend, and at least for a while we want it to stay that way. Understood?"

"Yes sir," she replied, all formal.

"You'll do great, and I'm sure we'll be back in a jiffy. See you soon."

And with that, they were off, crawling on all fours across the rebuilt bridge that linked the council building courtyard with the king's private residence, using the walls on both sides as cover, as well as cadavers, of which there were many. Reaching the end after many minutes of stop-start crawling and ducking, the three, with Polo in the lead, bolted behind the nearest pile of corpses to catch their breath and assess the situation.

"So far so good," she said softly, their bodies completely shielded from the circle of heroes and their attackers.

"What about him though?" asked Owen, not really wanting to know the answer, all the time referring to the rampaging asag that remained fighting half a dozen or so dark dragons, a few in the sky, others grounded because of the damaged they'd already taken.

"We'll keep doing what we're doing. Stay low, move between any available cover and take our chances when they arise. Hopefully they'll all be too busy fighting each other to give a damn about what we'll be doing," replied Polo, offering up a wink. "You're all much more up for it than I would ever have imagined, and I've spent some time on the surface with your kind. It is truly a pleasure to have you along, and as we dragons like to say... no pain, no gain, and yes, that did derive from us."

Glancing across at each other, the two men shared a look, one that said... "What the hell?!"

Moving off at a fast walk, staying low and keeping piles of deceased monsters in between them and the army of mythical creatures, the three human shapes very slowly made their way across the gigantic room, doing their best not to attract the attention of either the asag or its opponents.

Taking hold of Yoyo's comments and wisdom, four of the young dragons decided to try out their mentor's plan and see if they could in fact destroy one of the huge flying wasps, the ones with the massive exposed tooth, easily the size of a man's finger. Trayrin, the first to go, ignited forked lightning all around it, mirroring pretty much what had been done on that first attempt in an effort to lull it into a false sense of security. Amazingly the first startling revelation was that an insect could look utterly smug, something that none of them would ever have thought possible. Hoping that it was distracted enough, the other three dragons joined in, all adding their magic to their friend's in the hope that overwhelming it would prove a quick and viable route to attack. At first, still with the smug expression on its face, the nifoloa danced and jigged, easily finding a free pocket of air to dart into away from the wicked bolts of lightning, fire, ice and poison. Very quickly though, all the free spaces closed down, with quite a large area around the beast itself being soaked with supernatural power, and not just a little. To let them know they were on the right track, not that they needed telling, the expression on the nifoloa's face changed to one of total and utter fear, something that gave all the young dragons heart, not that they needed it.

Just as the look on the abhorrent insect's face became one of utter defiance, two bolts of sparkling green lightning hit it from either side, eliciting a huge POP, followed by its blazing burning body plummeting to the ground, shrouded in smoke.

As one, all four of them punched the air delighted with their miniscule victory, every last mythical creature looking on, all of them vowing revenge, especially the remaining nifoloas. While they thought they'd struck a very real blow for their side, and to some degree they had, but at quite a cost magically, perhaps all they'd really done was make the opposing force angry, something that might prove to be their downfall in the coming minutes and hours, should they last that long.

Riled up at just how superior the dragons thought themselves, the ra-hoon were tired, weary, still in shock at the day's events and having their world turned upside down, and so with all of this in mind, they took the shackles off and ordered their army to... charge!

All three of them in dark colours, Polo and Owen cloaked in black and Garrett's more formal wear still blending into the shadows nicely, they'd reached the furthest wall and were now hugging it in an attempt to get to the back staircase unnoticed, sneaking up effectively from behind the asag who only had two dark dragons to deal with, one on the ground, wings shredded, the other still tormenting him from the air.

Careful with their footing, they attempted to make as little noise as possible, hoping to dash around onto the staircase and use it as cover in their attempt to get to the library. With only a few metres to go they mentally crossed their fingers and, still hugging the wall, stepped cautiously forward. Right at that very point the dragon on the ground let rip with a stunning orange and yellow fireball that should have done a huge amount of damage, but exactly then the asag shuffled to one side, the fiery attack glancing off what would have been his rib cage, the humungous ball of fire deflected, heading straight for the small group's position.

"Move!" ordered Polo, as quietly as possible but wanting to make sure the other two heard.

They did, and following her example dived directly out of the way.

BAM! The fireball exploded harmlessly against the wall all three of them had been hugging, the consequence of which was to light them all up, something the purple vision of the asag spotted.

Discovered, and with no time to lose now, Polo got the other two to their feet and encouraged them along.

"Come on, we've got to go."

"But what about..." whispered Garrett.

But it was too late. Having dispatched both dragons in double quick time with astounding punches that any boxer in the history of the sport would have been proud of, the hulking great beast turned its attention to them.

"Run!" screamed Polo.

And so they did, with all they had, though because of Garrett's age, he was slow, even at what he considered a sprint.

Polo got past the monster, bounding up the giant, dragon sized steps one at a time, knowing that they would slow the asag's pursuit, should it decide to do so.

Owen, easily as fast as their dragon leader, had stopped, waiting for his boss to catch up. Unfortunately, that made him easy pickings for the rock demon.

"Go," Garrett urged. "Get out of here, don't wait for me."

But Peter's friend and temporary head of security was nothing if not loyal and ignored his words completely. Discounting the staircase, Owen charged towards the creature, ducking under the almighty car sized fist that swung towards him, and picking up one of the many extraneous dragon body parts that remained lying around in a pool of thick green blood, threw it at the asag in an attempt to get its attention. It worked a treat, with the monster howling and stomping, the light from its purple eyes getting brighter in a fit of pique and rage as it turned around to face him, giving the 'bald eagle' a chance to make it up the steps, with a little help from Polo.

With the dragon leader in her human form pulling him along, Garrett turned to face her.

"Stop!" he beseeched, "we can't leave him behind."

"That's exactly what we can do. He did that for you. Don't let his sacrifice be in vain. Come on."

Understanding the full ramifications of what he was about to do, and knowing that she was right one hundred percent, puffing and panting for all he was worth, the 'bald eagle' continued soldiering on up the stairs, determined to get to the top no matter what the cost, sorry to have lost someone he regarded as a friend.

Upon reaching about three quarters of the way up, both Polo and her human counterpart turned as the sound of footsteps from below echoed up towards them.

It was Owen, bounding up the steps in a series of huge jumps. Looking up at them, he waved them on.

And then the enraged asag appeared, stomping and

stamping, rushing as much as it could towards the dragon sized staircase.

Polo and Garrett froze momentarily. Owen screamed up at them, waving them on with his hands.

"Go, go, go," he shouted over the noise of giant fists brushing with marble and rock.

"But..." replied Garrett, not at all expecting what happened next.

Owen smiled, which was odd given the current circumstances and the fact that he was about to be pummelled by the hideous rock demon. Still bounding up the steps, the human security officer opened his previously clenched fist to reveal... a detonator, just like the ones they'd used to break the glass in the upper storey of the building.

"Oh..." mouthed Garrett.

"My..." ventured Polo.

With them looking on, his huge, thick thumb depressed the brilliant red button.

You see, what happened was that Owen had very deliberately kept one last explosive charge behind, figuring they might need it in an emergency, storing it and the detonator in the side pocket of his huge backpack. On drawing its attention away from his boss to give him time to get up the stairs, the young man could only think of one way to fell such a monster. Avoiding a few wild swings from the almighty destructive rocky fists, after already retrieving the explosive, he pulled the plastic off the back to reveal the sticky side, and mustering all the speed he could, dashed straight through the demon's legs, planting the bomb atop its upper left thigh as he did so. And that got them to here.

BOOOOOOOM! In the mother of all explosions, the asag's left leg was torn off in a fury of volatile and unpredictable power, sending a giant crack up its middle, the leg itself remaining almost whole, spinning wildly off into the distance before the hulk of the body fell lopsidedly to the ground, shattering marble, scattering cadavers, making the staircase shake like an earthquake had hit it, attracting the attention of all the beings there, including Vasuki and what remained of the nagas, who were by far the furthest away.

BOOOOOOOOM!

The asag crashing into the ground made more noise than its leg being blown off. All eyes across the private residence settled in on the source of the sound. As the dust scattered through the air, all three of them stood stock still, knowing that they were covered from anyone's line of sight, hidden because they were in the giant staircase itself. Still, it was tense, knowing that everybody was glancing over in their direction. And then things resumed, and they were able to carry on up into the king's private library, with all the other creatures there not knowing about, or expecting their presence. Luck had been on their side. If it could continue that way with the information that they needed falling straight into their hands, then everything they'd done so far would be truly worthwhile.

With the tiniest cones of flame in the world bursting out in front of them, miniscule squadrons of fire breathing gnats bombarded the heroes' defences, probing and prodding, looking for any kind of weakness they could share with their cohorts.

Asena surged forward, clawing and pawing, their jaws crunching and munching desperate to get through the shields barricading their prey inside, blue manes ruffling, their fierce demeanour completed by the blood and guts dripping off their needle sharp teeth. Of course all the heroes had taken a step back, having learnt their lesson with these beasts the hard way, two of their own still down, currently being attended to by Yoyo while he defended and fought with all that he had.

Gaki waddled forward in force, their humungous jelly bellies quivering in time with their footsteps, all three eyes scanning in a different direction, the neon green and red horrors eager to do some damage with their razor blade sharp bony protrusions. With their heads in the shape of various different cattle, it wasn't quite the stampeding herd they'd hoped for but it was in much the same way a nightmare vision of hell.

Waving their huge pincers high in the air above them, the muscular bodies of the scorpion men skittered towards their enemies' circle, their eight frantic legs going ten to the dozen, their long unkempt hair flowing out behind them as they moved, occasionally getting caught up in their stingers that bobbed and weaved at their back, all the time ready to strike.

Two-headed eagles and pixiu landed on top of the dome that had formed around the dragon contingent, pecking and scratching at the invisible shield as if that might make a difference. It didn't, but it did have the effect of putting everyone under the barrier's protection, on edge and off guard. It was quite disconcerting.

Lagging behind the rush to get to the party, conaima padded softly along, their huge sensitive paws avoiding the rubble and debris where possible, sticking to what little flat surface remained, not quite as eager as the rest of them to engage their foes, all coming together through their shared minds in an effort to form the most effective strategy, one in which they all survived... the thinking man's mythical creatures if you like.

Scaled apes jumped wildly, high up in the air as they high fived each other along the way, occasionally beating their torn and bloodied chests, snarling and laughing, living for the moment, eager to carry out the orders they'd been given, keen to be released from under the threat of violence that currently kept them in check and on target.

Announcing itself with the most disgusting and hideously evil trumpet any being is ever likely to hear, swinging its trunk menacingly from side to side, all the other beings giving it a very wide berth, came the giant elephant beast, its hide totally black in colour, only its white tusks and huge, sticky pink tongue standing out. Shaking the ground with each step, it was a monstrosity like no other, and looked as though it was ready to charge the shield. Whether or not their magic could withstand such a thing would soon be put to the test.

With the majority of their opponents heading their way and the adrenaline of battle once again taking over, Richie, their commander-in-chief, shouted the order over the noise of the onrushing horde.

"ATTACK!" she screamed at the top of her voice, clutching the prized laminium dagger firmly in one hand, launching a volley of pink tinged purple magic missiles in the direction of the nearest asena, wanting nothing more than to get rid of those first, given the ra-hoon were out of range for the time being and supposedly unaffected by anything supernatural.

"Any pearls of wisdom?" Tank asked the charismatic band that he wore on his finger, hoping to gain some sort, any sort of insight.

"Try and take down the larger ones first, especially that crazed looking shadowy elephant beast. That looks like a whole lot of trouble. But don't discount the smaller beings. Those things with the single tooth and the tiny flame throwing whatsits could prove to be our undoing. I'm at your disposal."

"Let's do this then."

In an attack of positively epic proportions, For'son and Tank, while the ring all the time protected the force mentally, unleashed a flurry of icicles and a covering of frost at the elephant beast, hoping at least to slow it, if not damage it somewhat. Spectacular couldn't do the attack justice, with it encompassing the enraged creature as well as lots of those around it, including two nifoloa, two swarms of fire breathing gnats, one gaki, half a scorpion man, not to mention a two-headed eagle that had swooped past at just the wrong time.

Arctic could describe the cold down to a tee, with the temperatures low enough to chill even the bravest being's heart. Feathers frozen instantly together, the two-headed eagle smashed firmly into the ground, both its necks broken, a sorry sight for all to see. The nifoloa's limited magical resistance saved both of them, enabling them to circle around and limp back out of range in an effort to recover, both glad that they were able to, especially seeing some of the fire breathing gnats instantly wiped from the face of the planet for good.

Resistance to cold wasn't something that the gaki were imbued with, and so the bright red creature with the head of a cow remained frozen in place, even its jiggling belly, which looked somehow as though it had gained a snow capped peak, while the scorpion man appeared a picture of pain, half of its eight legs frozen to the floor, along with its pincers, head and stinger. However much it tried to break free, realistically it was never going to happen. That left the elephant beast itself, the cool, white frost looking majestic against its dark as night skin. Unfortunately, that was as good as it got, with even the onslaught of icicles not daring to slow it in its tracks. What the giant creature did do though, was trumpet, even louder with a much bigger hint of evil, so much so that most of the dragons had to cover their ears, the reverberation was so fearful.

"Come on, old friend," encouraged George, "let's take down some of those apes, as they seem to mean business."

Glancing back over his shoulder in the direction of his grandson, and the human girl who continued to sob uncontrollably, it was hard for the founder of the Crimson Guards to tear his gaze away, but he did so nevertheless. However, his actions had been noticed by two of the beings there keeping a close eye on him.

"I think I can just about remember how this works. Why don't you follow my lead for a change?" he quipped to his best friend.

Letting go with all their magic in unison, the king was

pleased to see that the dragon he knew was well and truly back with him, and he hoped with every atom of his being that it would stay that way.

Slightly weary of one another after their seamless pairing and the merciless way in which they'd dispatched so many enemies in the final part of the battle against Manson's troops, Flash and Captain Battlehard both wondered whether or not it was time to go solo and work the numbers alone. But with Yoyo's wise words still ringing in their ears, both had better sense than to let their egos and the grudge between Fredric and the others cloud their judgement. So with just a look and a nod, the two of them were back singing from the same hymn sheet, dishing out supernatural justice in the form of flaming fireballs, laser-like rays of boiling hot magma and superheated fiery darts that rained down in their dozens. As winning combinations go, it would have been hard to beat this one anywhere on the planet. Outside the invisible barrier, pixiu fried, gaki were crippled, vampiric lizards scattered in a hail of lightning as the ra-hoon tried to direct events, all the time seething that they hadn't yet got their hands on the source of all that power.

Sighing in relief, having waited at the top of the staircase on the first floor to see if they'd caught the attention of any of the other creatures, they watched in a mixture of sadness and fear as what remained of the asag howled and screeched as it tried desperately to pull its own weight along the ground with just its arms. Both pitiful and a reminder of exactly what they were up against, the three of them came to the conclusion that they shouldn't hang around anymore.

"We'll split up to cover more ground," announced Polo. "You two head off in that direction and see what you can find. I don't know how the library is laid out, no one does, apart from the king himself. We're looking for anything on or about magical creatures, mythical beings or something with 'legendary' in the title. Hopefully the section we need should be obvious. And I don't need to tell you both to keep an eye open. Goodness knows what could be up here amongst all of this. Hopefully it's clear of combatants, but we don't know that for sure. Only fire your weapons as a last resort. Okay?"

Both nodded their head in response.

"Good luck," said Polo, before adding, "and don't worry about coming to find me, stay where you are and I'll find you. As well, if you get a chance, try and have a think about how we're going to get a message across to our friends without using any sort of telepathy."

With that she turned and took off, a steaming blur disappearing off into the distance amongst all the thirty and forty metre high shelves.

"Let's go then," said Garrett.

"Lead the way sir, and I'll cover us," replied Owen, which seemed like a sensible suggestion.

Ever so slowly, they moved deeper and deeper into the strangest library in the world.

Without a care for their own safety, half a dozen nifoloa rammed the defensive barrier with their one single tooth, receiving a sharp electrical burst for their attempts, certainly causing them significant pain but not taking them down by a long shot. It was a concerted effort to pinpoint a weakness of any kind.

Flicking his index finger casually, Tank, reinforced by For'son's wealth of experience, brought to life a huge line of fire directly in front of them, barbecuing a few of the smaller beings, whilst stopping some of the medium sized ones in their tracks, buying them a little respite and time to catch their breaths.

Tarko, Trayrin and Monty had all taken to working together, the first two using tiny tornados of wind to suck up some of the fire breathing gnats that were proving to be a pain with their constant attempts to attack the shield, looking for even the smallest weakness. So the three youngsters had decided to follow their mentor's advice and do something about it. Sucking up the gnats appeared to be no problem, but it was what to do with them after that. At first they'd leaned towards fire, but the damn little things seemed to have some sort of immunity, something they wasted more than a little time and magic on. Next they tried ice, logically thinking that the direct opposite should work wonders. To some degree it was a success, but not the resounding one that they'd hoped for. What they were looking for called for some more out of the box thinking. And so it was that they looked to use their intelligence and magical mastery to warp the forces of gravity itself, something not impossible, but difficult to a very great degree, even for their cunning minds. As Tarko and Trayrin's small but powerful whirlwinds whipped up all around the insidious insects, Monty used his mind to build a tunnel, one that the columns of fast moving air would be drawn into whether they liked it or not. With the crazed bugs looking as though they were being spun around by a blender, Monty would use his magic to close down the supernatural tunnel and fold it in on itself, effectively crushing the death dealing pests into oblivion. It was convoluted, time consuming and mana intensive, but it worked. Two squadrons at a time, as they liked to think of them, were about all they could manage, but they were getting through them, much to the ra-hoon's displeasure.

Working perfectly in unison, having had enough practice to last them a lifetime already today, the remaining King's Guards brought down wave after wave of fireballs onto the battlefield between their defensive circle and the unicorn lookalikes that constantly lingered out of reach amongst the rearguard of their force, with the kind of power and precision you would expect from elite troops fighting to save their livelihood, their king and of course their planet. They were good, that's for sure, but the very different species of magical creatures all seemed to have some kind of supernatural intuition about where and when the strikes would occur, despite there being very little warning because the fireballs were only brought into existence one hundred metres above them in the air, moving at quite a rate. It was remarkable really, and had any dragon scientists been present, the very first thing they would have wanted to study was exactly that trait.

Flash and Captain Battlehard, having brought down the barriers around their trust issues involving Fredric, Richie and the king, had returned to their inspirational symbiotic relationship with the female King's Guard commander grabbing prey with her mind, as the ex-Crimson Guard provided the magic with which to kill it. In a combined effort, Flash would force whatever magic he'd conjured up onto whatever it was that Amelia had a grasp of, and likewise she would force her captured adversary in the direction of her partner's power. It would be safe to say that so far it had worked stunningly well, with the pair of them having taken down a conaima, two asena, three vampiric lizards, a gaki and one scorpion man, although he'd proved to be the hardest to kill, with both of them admiring his determination not to die and his overall resilience, despite him being their enemy.

With one eye on Fredric for her friend Janice's sake, Richie probably wasn't at her best attacking wise, not wanting to hand all of herself over to the red mist and battle rage that had so far today seen her hunt down Manson and kill numerous others already. She continuously probed the different individual creatures out there, searching for any small crack or weakness in their mental armour. And, unbelievably, she kept finding it, having been able to crush the wills of two nifoloa so far, the dreadful beasts dying instantly, and one of the distracted scaled apes, leaving his mind in tatters and what remained of his body broken on the ground, dribbling like an idiot. Regarding her haul as quite decent, it was about as far as she wanted to go with her trust in Fredric totally shot away, and concern for her friend paramount.

Genuine fear and grief tinged with just the tiniest amount of anger crept over him as his body lay paralysed and broken, shrouded in darkness. Surprisingly though, those feelings weren't his, but belonged to someone close by. Why was he feeling them if they didn't belong to him, what did they relate to and who was this mysterious being nearby were all questions he asked himself, despite not really wanting to know the answers. But his psyche was a little bit curious, or at least part of it was, and so stretching out with what little magic it still had access to, slowly it looked to gain a foothold on the situation in an attempt to find out what on earth was going on around it. In yet another round of surprises, it found that a raging battle was taking place with creatures it somehow recognised fighting for their lives and best, or worst of all, depending on how you looked at it, the being whose shattered emotions he seemed to be sharing was none other than the love of his life, his soul mate and partner, the young bar worker Janice who now stood, comforted, in Hook's arms.

'Is it me?' his internal voice asked, thinking that's what had upset the young human girl. 'Is she so distraught because she thinks I'm not coming back?' Something in the deepest, darkest recesses of his mind told him this was wrong, urging him to fight back against the surrounding black depression and retake control of his destiny. But whatever tiny voice had been doing so, was almost immediately crushed, forced back into the shadows, shut down in no uncertain terms. And the fighting, what was going on there? In some sense he could recognise the feelings of beings that he was supposed to know, but with his head in the state it was, he couldn't remember their names or anything of consequence about them. It was a shame, because if he had, if his consciousness had connected the dots and retained the information it already knew, matching names with faces and faces with memories, which might have been enough to raise the shadowy curtain of doom that had fallen over him. Unfortunately, that was not to be.

Stealthily, Owen and Garrett padded through the great library, one of the finest repositories of magical knowledge on the whole of the planet, each gobsmacked not only at the sheer size of the thing, but of the categories and information it contained. Planning and Design (dragon and human); Infiltrating the Earth's Surface (what kind of a category was that? wondered Garrett wanting to stop and look, fully aware that another chance like this might never come along). Plants (above and below ground); Underwater Entities; Historical Battles; Redacted Files; Innovative Power Solutions; Law; Transportation; Council Minutes (Copies); Geography; Weapons Through The Ages; Origins; Betrayals; A Magical History, and many, many more, none of which helped them at all. Staggering, overwhelming and utterly fantastic, the place was mindboggling and if you were a scholar, the ultimate place from which to learn.

Reaching the end of one aisle, Owen stuck his head out first to make sure the way forward was clear. It was, and they proceeded with Garrett regaining the lead, all the time scanning the huge shelves for a clue as to what they contained. Alchemy, Witchcraft... the amount in these two sections alone was stunning. Mind full of rough calculations, Garrett, good with figures, estimated that there must have been between five and ten thousand books, scrolls, and weathered, dusty old tomes for this one portion of the shelves, let alone aisle or even floor. It was just staggering. And then he noticed it... the next set of shelves, disappearing up into the air, almost higher than he could make out. The bookshelves themselves all had noses carved into, or extending out from them. Some were tiny, others stuck out more, some human, some dragon, crooked, wonky, large, small, perfectly formed, squashed. Witches' noses, wizards' noses, cats' noses, dogs' noses, cute little mouse noses, donkeys' noses, every which way of nose that ever existed. It was... weird. Wanting to stop and inspect, Owen whispered that they should continue and keep moving, knowing that time was of the essence.

Well aware that what his friend and employee had said was correct, they both furtively continued to move along, that is until the 'bald eagle' held out his arm to stop Owen in his steps.

"Look!" he whispered, pointing up to one of the shelves on his right hand side.

Subheading... underwater cities, jungle islands, and then he saw it in big bold letters: **Creatures, magical, mythical and legendary.**

That was it, just what they were looking for. Slinging his weapon back over his shoulder, the big burly guard asked,

"Where do we start?"

Scratching his stubble ridden chin in reflection, Garrett considered Owen's question.

It needed to be something obvious, something outstanding, otherwise they'd never narrow it down and would probably be here forever. There were too many flying insect-like things, as well as a considerable number of wolf and tiger-like beasts. Something original, that's where they needed to begin, and then it came to him.

"The unicorn things with two horns... we'll start there. There can't be too many of those, and if we're going to find something about anything, it'll be them."

"Okay," replied his friend. "You take low and I'll take high."

And so they did, blowing thick layers of fine dust off the ancient covers as they worked their way along the shelves, all the time hoping to uncover something, anything of use in the quest to help save their friends.

Glancing over her shoulder at her comrades Yoyo was attempting to heal from the asena's first strikes, Wiz took her eye off the ball so to speak with regard to her spatial awareness, nearly taking a strike from yet another asena's long legs, the toxin infused claws missing her thigh by barely a centimetre. Lurching back in fear, the minor distraction caused her to lose focus at exactly the wrong instant. It was however, enough, and quite a long time relative to any insect, especially the nifoloa who prided themselves on taking their opportunities... and so one did, zipping through a sizzling weakened part of her shield, delving its one huge, poison soaked tooth straight into the left side of her face, forcing her to cry out in agonising pain, attracting the attention of all her friends and allies.

Living up to his name, Flash was the first to react, freezing the deadly little bug before crushing it using a linked up pressure spell that saw it smashed to smithereens, but the damage was already done.

"WIZ!" bellowed Yoyo, bounding straight over to her, immediately forgetting about the two King's Guards who were on their way to being mended. Before he could reach her, she slumped to the floor, clutching her pierced cheek, scratching away blindly at it, hoping no doubt to be rid of some of the pain.

"Stay calm, my dear," commanded Yoyo's familiar voice in an effort to stop his young charge from going into shock, thoughts of Hillier's recent demise still fresh in his mind.

Ignoring the fuss from off to one side, the two best friends, Fredric and George, used all their formidable experience to synchronise their attacks and maximise the harm they could inflict. While the king pummelled the crazed creatures with a multitude of cold mantras... flurries of damaging magical snow, slippery patches of ice, freezing fog and blistering bolts of brilliant icicles, his best friend lit all of that up with a huge spread of forked lightning in every different colour... blue, green, white, yellow and even red on occasion, stopping their enemies' hearts, frying their bodies as well as burning their heads. It was outstanding, impressive and above all... deadly!

Aware of what had gone on with the young dragon Wiz, Richie drained a little of the power from the laminium dagger and, stretching out with her magic, filled in the gap that had temporarily appeared within the ranks of their shield, determined to make sure none of the other nasty critters sneaked through their lines and did any more damage. Catching sight of Fu-ts'ang executing his orders and protecting Janice, Richie nodded an acknowledgement to the ancient weapon smith, and although he didn't have a head or eyes, his whole body tilted forward in response.

'There's a being I can trust,' she thought, doubts about putting him to use that way surfacing in her mind. 'Think of the damage he could do out there. How wasted is he in here, doing very little?' Knowing it was true and that as one of the most valuable resources they had, his effectiveness was being squandered, didn't change her mind because of the value she placed on her friend Janice, someone who'd been through so much and had in her own way got them all to this point. Wasted or not, he stayed with her for now. She could of course always change her mind at some point in the future, something she reserved the right to do.

In the middle of the King's Guard line up, three giant scorpion men attacked, their huge crab-like pincers constantly snapping at the invisible barrier, as the occasional probing attack by their stingers kept the dragons alert. Caution seemed to be the watchword for those that had survived Manson and Earth's devastating attack, which kept them on their toes so to speak, and meant that when some of the poison from one of the scorpion men's stingers squirted through their magical defences, they were to some degree ready for it, even though it did come as something of a shock.

Three of the dragon guards stepped back, all the time extending their invisible shields out in front of them, each doing their best to negate the sickly, thick grey poison that had been launched at them, knowing above all else not to get near or touch it. Who knew what other surprises it held?

Remaining cool on the outside so as to project a facade of calm and not appear too outwardly worried, inside his emotions were a seething mess, with his mind doing all it could to fight off the fear of losing yet another one of his own. The professional part of him brushed all that aside, working quickly and logically through a list of mantras he hoped would help. About three quarters of the way through it and NOTHING, so far, appeared to make even a sliver of difference. Time was running out, Yoyo knew, and he had no answer to the nifoloa's deadly injected poison.

Groggy, still recovering and lucky to be alive, thanks only to Yoyo's quick thinking ministrations, the two King's Guards scrambled to their feet, a look of surprise and worry furrowing their brows on seeing the injured Wiz lying on the ground in front of them. Knowing that now wasn't the time for regret or sympathy, with their team mates needing them to join back in, both slipped into their previous positions and ignoring the weakness and constant pounding in their heads, they got on with their business, which was of course destroying as many of the enemy as possible, something they were now even more glad to do after what they'd both been through.

Picking books up from that section at random and scanning through their indexes seemed to be the only way to go about the search for the relevant information they required, and so that's what both Garrett and Owen currently found themselves doing in the most magical library on the entire planet. The only places that came even vaguely close were the repository in Rome and Gee Tee's hidden vault beneath the Mantra Emporium, which although lacking in capacity, did at least have some of the rarest scrolls, one off mantras and unique literary masterpieces to be found across the dragon kingdom.

Trying not to cough as he blew dust about two centimetres thick off a burgundy book cover entitled

'Masquerading Monsters', Garrett's worn and wrinkled fingers flicked through the pages to the index, before his eyes started to scan all the information there.

Sirens

Mermaids

Medusa

Bucca

Eloko

Karina

He didn't recognise the words, let alone what creatures they were related to.

'Damn!' he thought, getting more and more frustrated at wasting time. None of the indexes in any of the books made any sort of sense. They weren't in alphabetical order, very rarely provided a description, and even if they did, it was beyond vague. How were they supposed to find any of the creatures that were attacking downstairs, if the information compiled was so... unreasonably set out? Shifting his hands, ignoring the cloud of dust that sprang up into the air, he opened the book a bit wider and started flicking his fingers through the pages as quickly as possible. It didn't take him long to find exactly what he was looking for... a drawing in the middle of one of the double spreads.

'Great,' he thought. Some of the books had illustrations, so perhaps the only way to do this, was to inspect the pictures in each book and go from there. In his mind it seemed a little backwards, but they didn't have time to read each one. And so he told Owen about his change of tack, and with both of them doing the same, they hoped they'd soon come across something they would recognise.

Abruptly the invisible barrier rippled as if a stone had been thrown into a pond, as a wall of freakishly malevolent noise battered against it, although from quite some way out, as the black as night, mighty elephant beast trumpeted again, only this time using the sound as a weapon, aiming it directly at the shield around where the King's Guards were congregated. You might think as supernatural attacks go this one was a little more lightweight than all the others. But that was only because of how far away the beast was from the personal shields all linked together, and even then, it took seven of the remaining King's Guards to reinforce their colleague's mind, that's how fierce it had been. Had the goliath brute been any closer, there wouldn't have been anything they could have done, and their defences would have been well and truly breached, a worry on so many levels.

The ground shook, the earth moved (not like that!) rocking the friends, the strapping rugby player maintaining his balance for both of them with everything going on. Face soaking wet from the stream of tears that had flooded her delicate face, the blonde bar worker sniffled profusely as she looked up into Hook's browbeaten face, pleased to see the smile that was nearly always there.

"Thanks," she sniffed, wiping her eyes with the back of her right hand.

"Not a problem," he whispered back softly. "Are you okay?"

"I... I... I... I'm not really sure, of anything at the moment."

"What happened? Why did Richie get so worked up?"

"I don't really understand what's going on," she replied, glancing over her shoulder in the direction of Fredric, who had his back to her, fighting away alongside his best friend, the king. "One minute I was tending to Peter, trying to catch his attention, the next... there were all these horrible words echoing around my mind in a voice that I just couldn't recognise."

"It was your love's grandfather," Fu-ts'ang spoke compassionately, concerned for his friend, worried what effect it might have had on her.

"Why would he do such a thing?" asked Hook, thinking that things couldn't get any weirder, talking to a futuristic weapon hovering there in the air in front of him.

"Why does anybody do what they do?" answered the weapon in a melancholy way.

"I can't understand it. There was all that stuff after he awoke when we first recovered him... all about humans being here in the dragon... now, what did he call it... that's right, dragon domain. But I thought everybody including the king had gotten over that. Perhaps it's something to do with that?" she offered up.

"Doesn't sound like it though, does it?" observed the rugby player.

"No it doesn't," added the weapon smith in agreement. "Unfortunately though, we have more pressing matters to deal with."

Senses starting to come fully back to her, Janice fully took in her surroundings and exactly what was going on.

'Same shit, same place, different adversaries!' was her exact thought.

"What can we do?" she asked Fu-ts'ang, still sniffling but wanting to help out, the natural bravery within her starting to shine through once again.

"I don't know," said the revolutionary blade. "My orders were just to protect you... nothing else. And without magic yourself, making a difference outside our little bubble here is all but impossible."

"Why don't you see if you can get through to Peter again?" suggested Hook. "If you can shake him out of whatever he's caught up in, then there's at least one more magic user on our side to add to the fight."

"You're right, of course," agreed Janice, standing up on tiptoes to kiss the courageous rugby playing legend on one cheek.

Smiling in response, his cheeks just a little redder than usual, he told her that he and Fu-ts'ang would watch over her while she did whatever was necessary to bring Peter back from the dark place he currently found himself in.

It was enough to instil just the tiniest smidgen of hope

that they might all yet get out of this and back to some semblance of normality, whatever that looked like.

Polo, sprinting along at super speed, enhanced by the supernatural powers she all too often took for granted, darted through aisle after aisle, inspecting all the sections as she went, not getting even close to finding what they were looking for.

'Hopefully,' she thought, 'the humans are having more luck than I am.'

Discarding the next book onto a pile he'd made on the floor, in too much of a hurry to even put them back in the correct places, wondering if some gigantic dragon librarian might roast him over hot coals at a much later date, Garrett picked up another book, blew the thick, musty dust off the front of it, revealing a dull yellow leather cover, and started letting his fingers do the walking. Flicking through the pages with all the speed he dared, wanting to be as thorough as possible and not miss anything pertinent, he dismissed pictures of hippo-like creatures, wolves... that seemed to be a common theme, but they weren't anything remotely like the creatures his friends were battling down below, something that appeared to have the body and legs of a lizard but the head of a feline, various giant yetis, some covered in thick fur, others not so much. Winged creatures abounded, more bat-like than anything downstairs. Continuing on at breakneck speed, he came across more elf-like creatures, snakes, sea serpents and then a... unicorn. Stopping in his tracks, he scanned the picture to double check that it just had one horn... and it did.

'Bugger! But hold on, what's that next to it?' he thought, unable to read any of the text in the whole book, not recognising it at all. Although not a huge linguist, he was fluent in at least five different languages, almost essential for all the work Cropptech did overseas. The scrawl, as that's what it looked like, resembled nothing he'd ever seen. And while the picture only showed a unicorn, in the bottom corner of the page, part of the text was emboldened and looked like some kind of warning. Perhaps it was about whatever those creatures down there were, staying out of harm's way at the back of the fighting, seemingly controlling and guiding the others. But how could he possibly tell?

Stopping Owen from what he was doing, the 'bald eagle' explained his theory.

"It does look like a warning," mused the security officer. "But how can we be sure?"

"We need Polo. Do you think we should shout out?"

"Hmmm..." considered Owen, "it might be a little risky. She did say that she'd find us, but when or how I have no idea. Do you think that if we just spoke a little louder than normal that she would hear?"

"Maybe... let's give it a try. Polo... can you hear me. We've found something, it's not much, but I think you should take a look. Ahhh... thanks, Garrett."

'That was awkward,' thought the Cropptech owner, feeling as though he'd just left a tongue-tied message on a stranger's answer phone. Oh well, fingers crossed.

Ninety seconds later, a black speeding blur zipped around the corner, pulling up just short of the two humans.

"What have you got?" asked the female dragon.

Handing her the book, Garrett showed her.

"Great work!" she exclaimed.

"Is it what we're looking for?"

"It is."

"Sorry... it's just that we couldn't read it."

"Oh... of course, how silly of me."

"No problem."

"Would you like to see it now?"

"Really?"

"It's easily enough done. Open your mind and focus on the bold part of the text."

Whilst Unicorns themselves are shy, sometimes inquisitive, with their coat and horn providing an assortment of remedies and magical enhancements, you should beware. Reports from Southern Asia, Mongolia and China suggest that it has a black hearted cousin known only to a few as the ra-hoon. Typically having two horns where the unicorns only have one, these creatures ideally live in a dry, arid environment. From what we can ascertain, ra-hoon are invulnerable to magic of any sort. Their key offensive skills tend to revolve around their mental prowess. More than capable of asserting their will over another, they're known to be able to control many beings at once, as well as interrupting other species' telepathic communications. Although they graze physically in much the same way as their distant cousins, local dragons from the regions concerned swear that these conundrums hunt and feed on magic itself. Although it sounds like something of a tall tale, I've interviewed enough dragons to know that there must be at least some foundation to such gossip. One rather grizzled old beast told me that as well as their mental acuity, they could also use the supernatural abilities of others to power attacking mantras, spells and hexes of their own. No such proof of that exists, but rest assured that these beings are apex predators and have the potential to control and dominate whole communities over large areas. It would be hard to see how these monsters could be readily rounded up, given that they're spread far and wide and can only be subdued with physical violence.

If I hear of anything else I will be sure to add it in the margins or to the next book that I'm working on.

Scrawled across the margin were two notes that seemed to have been added much later on.

Due to their rarity and the abilities they possess, the dragon council have just passed a bill that will grant ra-hoon special protected status. From now onwards they are not allowed to be either hunted or killed. Experimentation might still be possible, with the correct licence.

After having been invited onto the team that have been studying the ra-hoon under magical quarantine, today we had something of an occurrence. One female accidently had both her horns torn off while fighting, getting them both stuck in a tree. You would think they might regrow or that she'd just fit back in with the rest of the community. NO! It appeared as if after the accident, she couldn't communicate with them at all, making it look as though the source of all her telepathic abilities is in fact both horns on her head. Whether this is correct or not remains to be seen. Will update further as soon as we have validated this theory.

Although it implied that there would be more entries, there was in fact absolutely nothing else, leaving it at just that.

Blown away by Polo's ability to change something so incomprehensible into full blown English with just her mind, the 'bald eagle' tried to get his head around everything... the library, the fighting, dragons battling a cadre of mythical creatures, some of whom were even bizarre by their high standards.

"Wow!" stated Garrett to the dragon leader before them. "It would seem that this is just what we're looking for."

"Quite so, quite so," reflected Polo, her thoughts clearly somewhere else.

"What are you thinking?" asked Owen.

"We need to get back to the others and tell them what we've found. We, and when I say we, I mean all of you and your fancy projectile weapons may all yet have a part to play in this."

"You mean in taking out the ra-hoon?"

"Yes... it would seem that they might be the key. If we can kill them, then those battling down there can re-establish their combat link, making fighting that much easier. If we do manage to get rid of the ra-hoon, I would guess that the remainder of the beings won't be nearly so coordinated and might just think about surrender, which would save a lot more bloodshed and potentially many more lives."

"That sounds like a worthy goal. Why don't we get started right now?" asked Cropptech's owner.

"We need to go back and tell the others. I can't use my telepathic abilities in case it attracts the attention of the ra-hoon."

"We can contact our people ma'am," suggested Owen, "using our comms. We'll let them know what we've found and they can set up there with line of sight on the deadly beasts. And if we," he indicated all three of them, "set up on this level on the overlooking balcony, the ra-hoon will be caught in crossfire and won't know what's hit them."

Nodding, all the time running things through her head, Polo mulled it over for a few seconds.

"Sounds great," she said. "It's just a shame we've no way to contact any of the fighters down there. If we had, we could get them to engage all the creatures, even the ones milling around at the back alongside the ra-hoon. If they could be encouraged to move forward, that would make sure all of us are protected against attack, and we could take out those damn unicorn lookalikes at will."

"Hmmmm...," mused Garrett. "I think I might have an idea about that."

Things were getting crazy... I mean, crazier than they already had been.

Two-headed eagles dive bombed the very top of the defensive dome that they'd created, bouncing off with a kind of wet SPLAT. The remaining squadrons of fire breathing gnats followed suit, along with the odd nifoloa or two, all spurred on by the ra-hoon's control over them. Winged pixiu raked their claws along every magical surface, trying to find a way in or any kind of flaw that would let them harm their adversaries in some way, shape or form, motivation once again being provided in the form of the ra-hoon in their heads, confusing and baffling, laying down orders that just couldn't be disobeyed.

Neon bright green and red gaki took turns to run up against the shield, bouncing at it with their huge wobbly bellies before using their bony protrusions, sharp talons and horns in an all-out whirlwind of an onslaught, spinning and whizzing around at such a rate that it seemed impossible to sustain. But they did... somehow.

Armoured apes leapt atop the dome and, avoiding the incoming barrage of fantastical flying bombardments, thumped their chests to intimidate before pounding, stamping and in one case, head butting the top of the invisible barrier, much to the horror of those beneath it, particularly Hook who had little else to do now except think about all the different ways in which he could die... GREAT!

With the asena still striking furiously, desperate to claw at any and all enemies, the conaima still padding softly around, using their sensitive noses to sniff out even the smallest hint of magic, and the approaching shadowy giant elephant beast slowly hammering forward, crazy had just teamed up with daft, foolish, unwise and downright dangerous in an effort to get more hands on. For the dragon and human heroes all once again sheltered behind the invisible, magical barrier, things did not look great. What it would take to get them out of this was anyone's guess. Luckily, a group of beings close by had something of an idea.

"So they know to protect my people?" Garrett asked once again, just wanting to make sure.

"They do. When the shooting kicks off, they'll do all they can to keep your squad safe from any of the creatures that the ra-hoon order to come after them. Hopefully providing fire from two directions will help confuse and hinder their actions."

"Indeed," added the 'bald eagle'.

"And if you can get our friends down there to draw the rest of the creatures surrounding the ra-hoon into the fray that will be an even bigger bonus. Do you think it's possible?"

"Let's see, shall we?" put in Garrett, pulling out his mobile phone. "You said you think it'll probably work because if anywhere down here will have reception, it's the council building, is that right?"

"I'm no expert, but I would have thought so," replied Polo.

Swiping through his contact list that was nearly a thousand people long, he arrived at the appropriate one, touched the screen, held the phone up to his ear, and hoped for the best.

One eye on Fredric, the other on Janice, Hook and Peter, the daredevil lacrosse playing dragon still had time to implode the mind of a pixiu that had dropped its guard somewhat, over the cacophony of explosions, magic dealing and flying debris. Suddenly, through the chaos of it all, something she hadn't heard in a while caught her ear.

'Oh my God,' she thought. 'It's my phone. Who in the hell is calling me right now?'

Pulling the very latest hi tech mobile from the pocket of her tattered and worn trousers, she glanced down at the screen. On the vibrating and ringing handset, the words 'Unknown Number' appeared in big bold letters.

Knowing that she didn't have time for whatever kind of cold call it was and that her focus needed to be one hundred percent on what was going on around her, she hit the big red cancel button, before returning it to her pocket, her thoughts briefly turning to the four friends that had disappeared off to Fleet Street in an effort to get word of a rescue out. Perhaps the call had been one of them, was something she briefly considered, but it didn't seem very likely. So redoubling her concentration, she attempted to pull the wing off a murderous looking little nifoloa and returned to keeping an eye on the friends that were with her.

"Damn!" swore Garrett, pulling his phone away from his ear.

"It doesn't work?" enquired Polo disappointedly.

"No, it's not that. It rang and rang, but then it got cut off."

"Well... they are kind of tied up at the moment," offered up Owen.

"Hmmm..." mused Cropptech's owner.

"Well... that's that then," reflected Polo.

"Let me just try one more thing," ventured the 'bald eagle', once again flicking through his phone.

Downstairs amongst the rubble and corpse strewn battlefield that was the king's private residence, the air hummed with magic as a mixture of monsters all attempted to bring down the invisible barrier that their enemies cowered behind.

Frustrating, was how the fifteen or so ra-hoon in charge viewed everything going on. They were so close to the big payoff... the huge accumulations of mana, magic and experience that lay just out of reach amongst those that would stand against them. It should be going better they knew, but their enemy was experienced, fearless and cautious in the same breath, not really falling for any of the traps that they'd set, preferring instead to stay safely tucked away behind that damn shield. With that the case, they'd tried to encourage the one being that had escaped from the basement which they didn't have total control over, to march over to the barrier and bring it down... the giant elephant beast. But despite its sheer power and raw ferocity, it was reluctant to get any closer, recognising a true threat when it saw one, knowing that it might have almost met its match in the form of their kind. And so the cunning, crafty, invulnerable to magic, unicorn lookalikes carried on doing what they were doing, sending wave after wave of attacking creatures at the weary dragons, hoping to grind them down and trick them into some unforced error.

Igniting a football sized sphere of flame between the jaws of one of the conaima, setting its lips and tongue firmly on fire, causing it to "YELP" with displeasure, turn on its tail and head back in the opposite direction, Richie smiled at the thought of doing damage to something so dangerous and deadly. A miniscule buzzing and a slight vibration from her pocket got her attention.

'Not again,' she thought, starting to get deeply disappointed. But that was curtailed quite quickly by the same thought that she'd had last time. 'What if it was one of her friends attached to Gee Tee's force?' Delving deep into her pocket, she pulled out the handset, determined to find out exactly what was going on. This time it was a text message.

PICK UP THE PHONE. WE'RE HERE TO HELP. BUT WE NEED TO SPEAK TO YOU FIRST!

'Odd,' thought the young dragon leader, scrutinising the words for a second time to make sure she'd read them right.

And then the phone rang again.

Amongst the chaos, confusion and death, she wondered whether or not to answer. What if it was a trap? She couldn't see how, but it was possible. But the message sounded, or at least... implied that it was from friends, someone she knew. In the end there was little choice, and so, very tentatively, she answered.

"Hello?"

"Miss Rump... it's so good to hear your voice."

'What the ****?' she thought, convinced she was dreaming.

"Garrett!"

"Yes, my dear. I meant what I said. It's good to hear your voice."

"Ummm... I'm really sorry sir," said the lacrosse playing dragon, "but now's not really a great time for me to speak."

The very last thing she expected to hear down the phone was a mixture of glee and uncontrollable laughter. What on earth was going on?

"Glance over to your two o'clock, Miss Rump, and then look up."

'What?' she thought, utterly confused. But she did as he said, scanning across the private residence to roughly two o'clock, and then started looking up at the balconies belonging to the floors above. What she saw sent goose bumps up her arms and a cold shiver down her back.

"What in the...?"

Knowing that he'd caught her attention amongst everything going on, Garrett gave her a brief wave before ducking down out of sight behind the balustrades of the balcony.

"How... what... why... I don't..."

"It'd take too long to explain, my dear, but needless to say we've brought some help. I'm going to pass you over to a very kind dragon called Polo who I believe you've already met. Good luck."

And with that, he passed the phone to his dragon friend.

"Ahh, my illustrious leader... how the devil are you?"

"Have we met?"

"Yes... back at the marketplace in Salisbridge. My name's Polo and I was one of the ones left behind to take care of the dead and watch out for anyone else coming our way."

"And why aren't you still there?"

"Because more of your friends from the surface arrived, armed to the teeth, looking for those humans that disappeared, determined to find you. After much consideration, all of us left in Salisbridge decided it was wise to try and help, so here we are, having eventually tracked you down... and not a moment too soon by the look of things."

"What do you mean?"

"The reason we're talking by phone is that the ra-hoon, as they're called... you know, the unicorn looking things with two horns, can, as you've no doubt already experienced, block or hijack telepathic communications and even mentally subjugate others. And that's on top of them being invulnerable to magic of any sort."

"Tell me about it," declared Richie.

"They are, however, physically vulnerable, and that brings us back to your friends with the weapons. My best guess is that they have enough ammunition, if their shooting is accurate, to take down all the ra-hoon."

"Nice!"

"But you and your force need to do something for us."

"And what's that?" asked the de facto leader, inquisitively.

"You need to pull all of the species guarding the ra-hoon off them and in your direction, otherwise we might get swamped and with only a handful of us, well... let's just say I don't think we'd last too long."

"Okay... consider it done. Where will you be shooting from?"

"Don't worry about that, it won't be from just up here on the balcony. We should be able to catch them in crossfire and stop them from getting away. We just need the others out of the picture."

"I'll get right onto that. As soon as we engage them, feel free to fire at will. Good luck."

"And to you."

With that, the line went dead.

'Rescued by Garrett and the Cropptech crew... whatever next?' the young dragon mused, wondering exactly how she was going to get to the ra-hoon's bodyguards. It was then that she was interrupted.

"You alright Rich?" asked her best friend, showering her with the biggest, dopiest smile he had.

And that gave her an idea.

"Why on earth are you mucking around with your phone in the midst of all this?" he asked.

"We've gained some unexpected aid. Is For'son listening in?"

"Of course."

"Good. I need your help," she said referring to both of them.

"How so?"

"All of those creatures guarding the unicorn things... the ra-hoon. I need to attract their attention and then lure them away. Do you think you can make it happen?"

"I... er... I... er... I don't really know. But anyway, why would you want to do that? It sounds like madness."

"If we can do that, then I'm pretty sure I can take out the ra-hoon, which means we can restore our telepathic communications, get all the other creatures out from under their grip and just maybe stand a chance of ending all this insanity. What do you say... help a girl out?"

"I've let the others know what's going on and they've said they'll all be ready," assured Owen, as he lay down a thin mat on the cool, light, marble floor of the library, setting up his NGSAR (Next Generation Squad Automatic Rifle), aligning the sights before setting it down and getting all the spare ammunition clips from his backpack and placing them on the floor beside the mat. "When it all kicks off," he continued, "we'll be ready to spray those ra-hoon bastards with everything we have. If they're not vulnerable to magic, then I assure you they will be to these."

"Good enough," replied Polo, really not wanting to kill the ra-hoon, especially not given their special protected status, but unable to think of any other way of getting around the problem.

And then something occurred to her.

"How accurate are your weapons?" she asked Owen.

"Very," he replied. "The rounds they shoot have the power of a battle tank and can easily tear through protective armour of any kind. Up to at least six hundred metres or so, I could take the hairs off Garrett's moustache, one by one."

"Impressive," stated Polo.

"Let's not put that to the test," added the 'bald eagle'.

"The reason I ask," Polo continued, "is that I wonder if it's possible for you to take out the horns on the head of the ra-hoon first, before attempting to kill them."

"Why?" enquired Owen confused.

"These beings are valuable and their lives are not to be taken lightly. I fully understand the situation and exactly what we're up against, but capturing them alive would be not only the best thing to do, but the RIGHT thing to do. Destroying their horns should decimate their telepathic abilities and neutralise the main source of the threat. I think with that done, we might be able to end all of this."

"You don't know for certain that it'll work. What about if the note in the book was wrong? There never was another entry. If that dragon didn't know what he was talking about, what do we do then? We'll have given any advantage that we had away for absolutely nothing," Garrett remarked.

"I know, and I'm aware of the situation your friends find themselves in. I just think that if there's even the remotest chance, we should at least give it a go."

"Of course," said the 'bald eagle', not at all happy with the situation. "You are in charge and know a damn sight more than we ever will about all this. We will happily defer to your judgement."

"Thank you."

"Boss?"

"Do as she asks, Owen. Inform the others as well. Shoot for their horns first, and then we'll see what happens and decide on the hoof what to do next."

"Yes sir," replied the security guard, immediately getting on his comms and informing the others of the revised plan.

"We're going to WHAT?" Tank bellowed, well... in his mind at least.

"It'll be okay," assured For'son calmly.

"You're bloody kidding me. It'll be okay for you perhaps... you probably can't be harmed. But you want me to sprint out there, kick and punch the living daylights out of all the creatures that surround these ra-hoon type things, all the time pretending I'm there for them, and then run off in the hope that they chase me... not a chance in hell!"

"It will be okay. And if this neutralises those unicorn lookalikes, then it will all be over in a jiffy. Isn't that what you want?"

Oh he did, and it was impossible to calculate just how much, but it was a lot. A bit like being quarantined for months on end, not being able to go out, visit the sea, the forests or eat at a favourite restaurant... he wanted it sooooooo much. But this plan didn't sit well with him. Unfortunately though, he couldn't come up with anything else that would meet Richie's requirements. Once again, she'd got him right up to his neck in it. He really should know better by now.

"Okay... let's get on with it," he said, all the time shaking his head at exactly how easy he was to manipulate and at just

how stupid he was to agree.

"I'm ready!" he told Richie.

Still multitasking on an extraordinary level, keeping an eye on Fredric, Janice, Hook and Peter, as well as what was going on inside and outside the shield, she leaned in, kissed him firmly on the cheek, told him how brave he was and wished him luck.

Grinning inanely, he winked, turned away and almost faster than the eye could see, sped off out into the utter chaos and magical mayhem, hoping that his friend stuck in the confines of the ring would protect him.

"Whatever they're going to do, they'd better do it soon," declared Garrett. "Their position looks almost overrun."

"And there they go," Polo commented.

"Where?" asked Owen and his boss simultaneously.

"Oh, I forgot... sorry. You can't see it yet, because your mind can't make head nor tail of anything moving that fast, but keep an eye on the creatures surrounding the ra-hoon. You should see more than a little disturbance. And Owen, please keep your weapons ready and be prepared to order your team to fire. This will hopefully be it."

Staring down at the ra-hoon, constantly pacing about at the back edge of the huge group of mythical creatures, both humans wondered what they should be on the lookout for. And then it happened. From out of nowhere, a blurred thickening of the air tore through the grouping, smashing camaheutos in all directions, kicking echeneis along the ground and scattering myrmecoleon and the shape shifting venomous snakes everywhere.

'What in the...?' was as far as the two humans' thinking got, before they noticed the man sized gap next to Richie, with the stocky, blonde haired guy who had been there only a moment ago missing from the party. Or not, as the case may be.

Caught off guard, not a single creature of any species

there had expected one of the enemy to storm out from behind the invisible barrier and start assaulting some of their own. Where was the logic in that? But one had, and to great effect.

Fuelled once again by For'son, Tank moved at a blinding rate, so much so that his friend and ex-Crimson Guard, Flash, would have been proud of him, zipping in and out of gaki, avoiding their monstrous, brightly coloured stomachs and whirring body parts, weaving between the stalking asena and conaima, and most satisfying of all, sliding beneath the gesticulating black trunk of the giant elephant beast, avoiding not only its destructive blast of sound, but the stamping of its massive feet. Dodging beneath some of the flying predators, namely the nifoloa, two-headed eagles and the pixiu, Tank closed in on the ra-hoon's position, trying to get their attention and that of the surrounding menagerie of guards, in the hope that he could raise their ire and, in general, piss them right off.

Scooting over a little to cover the gap that her friend had just left, she used her mind to extend out her part of the barrier, making sure there were no exposed fissures or breaks anywhere. Wishing him luck, and hoping that Garrett was good for his word, she went back to cracking heads and exploding minds.

Throughout the circle, Tank's disappearance hadn't gone unnoticed, with most wondering what the hell was going on. Without their telepathic link, something she hoped would be restored soon, Richie wasn't able to tell them or keep them updated, but that didn't stop one of their own desperately trying to find out.

"RICH!" shouted Flash over the dissonance.

Barely able to make him out, despite her only slightly enhanced hearing because of being stuck in human form, the superstar lacrosse player glanced his way, pleased to see that he was okay and dishing out as much misery as usual.

"He must be mad going out there. What's going on?" thundered the ex-Crimson Guard.

"He'll be okay," she bellowed back. "He's gone to put a stop to things."

THAT got everybody's attention, including a certain former Antarctic prisoner.

"How?" yelled Flash

"Hopefully, with a little help from our friends."

Trying to guide the sensible and yet reckless young human was becoming more of a challenge with each second that passed, at least that was For'son's experienced opinion, having already given up on yelling instructions into the dragon's head, well... almost.

"Go for their 'nads," he urged, manically.

"What?" answered Tank, momentarily distracted.

"Their genitals... go for their genitals. That'll make them mad enough to chase us and leave the ra-hoon."

"Oh... I see what you mean."

And so he did, kicking, punching, gouging (yikes... that doesn't sound very pleasant at all), beating and pummelling any of them that moved, ignoring the monsters in charge, just as he should do, hoping to get one hell of a rise (not like that!) out of all the surrounding beings. From the homicidal looks on their faces, it was beginning to work. Now what?

Compelled by magic, their time since having their will enslaved by the mysterious ra-hoon relatively unexciting, only expected to hang around just in case some threat presented itself, for the camaheutos, echeneis and myrmecoleon, life was all good, although not as good as the replicated prison in which they'd lived for many, many decades, unbeknown to them. There was no fighting to be done, and an all you can eat buffet at almost every stop of the road. Yes, life was still good, or at least it had been up until about fifteen seconds ago, when some absolutely deranged dragon in human form had come tearing through them all, kicking, punching, screaming, not only making a right mess, but going for their... well, you know... their importances. And if there was one thing every species hated, it was that. It was time for retribution.

37 ONE LAST SURPRISE

Keeping an eye on the time, waiting for the invaluable crystal node to come back up to optimum power, Gee Tee remained slumped in the chair that Jar Man and Steel had procured for him, utterly spent, feeling every one of his centuries' worth of service, barely able to finish this latest adventure. As he sat, Nurse Conscience checked displays, aligned components, using all her experience to make sure they'd be able to send out a request for reinforcements when the time came. Things were going swimmingly and the shopkeeper, despite his fatigue, was happier than a dragon in lava.

Twenty metres away, disguised as one of the apparent dragon corpses, head slumped against a busted monitor screen, the epitome of evil that had overseen events here remained motionless and alert. Bitterly disappointed that she hadn't been able to react before now, having heard what they'd supposedly done... stunning nagas in all of their different forms across the world, both above and below ground, no mean feat to say the least... Red was still just biding her time, making sure that the other dragons and (just the thought of them made her want to spit on the ground) humans, had indeed gone off into the rest of the facility. Once she was sure it was just these two, she could carry out the dastardly finale she had planned and put even more of a spanner in the works than she already had.

With Angela and Emma having gone off with Jar Man and DomCon, Steel remained in the company of Sam and Taibul, two very capable young humans in his opinion, given what he'd seen of them so far on this epic adventure. Wandering through the dark corridors, flickering light fixtures occasionally giving off enough radiance to see where they were going, all three of them slowly gathered their wits and took in their decimated surroundings. Already having achieved what they'd set out to do, the laminium ball captain and regular hot shot should have been ecstatic, but was instead mired in self doubt and the thought that somehow, somewhere, he'd missed something of vital importance. Trying desperately to shake off the negative thoughts that were coming thick and fast, he instead decided to try and concentrate on the here and now and in an effort to do so, tried to engage his companions in some small talk.

"So, Taibul, what is it you do on the surface of the planet?"

Startled by the sudden noise breaking up all the silence, it took the youngster a few moments to process the question.

"I... I... I work at my father's restaurant and I play hockey regularly."

"That sounds interesting," whispered the laminium ball captain. "What sort of food do you sell?"

"Traditional Indian cuisine."

"That's making my stomach rumble just thinking about it."

"Have you tried some?"

"As a matter of fact I have, and it was utterly delicious."

"Where was that... on the surface?"

"No, I'm afraid not. Being a laminium ball player, one of the many things we have to sacrifice is the ability to venture above ground. Those are just the rules and enforced vigorously, I'm afraid."

"Then where?"

"Even though I can't go above ground, I can still, how would you say, order take out. In fact, because of how revered laminium ball players are throughout our society, I can ask for pretty much anything and those in charge find a way to get it to me."

"What did you like best?"

"Hmmm... let me think. Lamb korai was easily my favourite, washed down with some naan bread, popadams and a plateful of onion bhajis... mmm, heaven sent."

"Did you try any of the chicken? That's our speciality."

"I did try some... chicken tikka and tandoori chicken...

both very nice, but as a dragon, I'm not too keen on white meat, usually preferring something a bit darker... I'm sure you can understand."

"Of course, of course."

"And you young Sam, what is it you like to eat?"

Brightening up at becoming part of the conversation, for Sam it was an easy answer.

"My favourite is Chinese," he said. "You can't beat crispy shredded beef in hot chilli sauce or aromatic duck with hoi sin sauce... hmmmmm."

"Ooooh... I've tried all that as well. Definitely the steamed pork and prawn dumplings... they were just melt in the mouth."

"I would have thought most things for you were... melt in the mouth," replied Sam, deadpan.

"Apart from humans, Sam... they tend to need a little ketchup to make them more palatable."

Swallowing nervously, wondering just how serious the mighty dragon was, it was only when Steel's bright white, razor-sharp teeth shone through in the form of one humungous grin, that Sam knew for sure he'd been played.

It took a few seconds for Taibul to catch up, (catch up, not ketchup) something they continued to rib him about as they moved ever forward.

The conversations had let them all ignore the elephant, or dragon, or more accurately, dead bodies in the room, easing the depression slightly, taking them out of the shadows and slightly into the light. Something still hung over the laminium ball captain though, niggling away at the back of his mind, important and yet ignored, forgotten and yet there, just out of reach.

In the opposite direction to Steel, Sam and Taibul, Angela and Emma trailed Jar Man and DomCon, marvelling at just how much the two dragons resembled an old married couple. Arguing about the most meaningless of things, talking over each other, occasionally snapping back and then in the blink of an eye making up with a laugh and a joke, one playfully pushing the other into... rotting corpses lying on the floor. Perhaps not quite like an old married couple then. Continuing to scour the place for anything of use, what that actually meant, Angela and Emma had little real idea. All they were looking for was anything out of place, again something hard to tell since so much of the architecture, styling and contents, to them at least, seemed utterly alien. Holding each other's hands behind the other two, they continued on their merry way.

Only a couple of minutes to go now. The crystal node looked to be recharging at its normal rate, Nurse Conscience having expressed exactly that on a few occasions. Lounging in the chair, long scaly tail tucked firmly through the purpose built hole in the back, not quite touching the floor, the master mantra maker's mind was some way away, considering the words he was going to use when they sent out the message. Something like:

"London under attack from a plot that extends out across the planet. King alive but still in grave danger. Please send help."

Something short and sweet like that seemed appropriate, especially since the communities of dragons that received it would no doubt have their own problems to deal with in the form of sabotage and maybe just outright attack. Part of him thought it wise not to send the message at all, leaving those across the world to clear up their own mess, with the ones remaining in London grouping together and finishing off Manson and his cohorts. But everything pointed to the planning of this having taken years or even decades, with no eventuality left unconsidered. If that was the case, then the earth might already be lost. Falling back to the capital might well be the only option, even if it sounded like a last resort. Settling on the words, the old shopkeeper's thoughts turned to the dragon he thought of as a son, hoping that he was still alive, still putting up a fight with his friends, turning back the tide of evil, using all the knowledge he'd gained working at the Emporium throughout the years. Briefly a smile brightened his face as he relaxed in the chair.

In only a matter of moments, that would change forever.

Knowing from listening in on the pair of them that the crystal node would be recharged enough to send out their message requesting reinforcements in only a matter of moments, Red knew that there was no time to lose if she wanted one last shot at causing as much chaos as possible. Eyes closed, head slumped firmly against the damaged monitor, she hadn't been able to get a look at the two remaining dragons left behind to put out the call for help. She had though, been able to hear what was going on all around her and use just a touch of her dark magic to get a feel for everything. Her conclusions... a pitiful, weak, inexperienced female dragon with barely the skills to operate the node, accompanied an ever weaker and infirm, much older dragon that needed to sit down to recover enough energy just to send a message. Luck couldn't have been much more on her side, she thought, knowing that taking out these two might be a task that lasted as long as five, maybe even six seconds. After that destroying the node would be child's play, and then they'd see just where their reinforcements would come from. So about twenty metres off to one side of where the master mantra maker currently sat, the dark, evil wraith of a dragon that had often made the colour red her own, steadied her mind and prepared to act, knowing it would all be over in a matter of seconds and that after she'd obliterated their precious crystal node, she'd take as many of the others with her as she possibly could.

With Sam and Taibul barely keeping the contents of their stomachs down, and even the mighty dragon Steel doing all he could to stop himself from gagging profusely due to the blood and guts splattered all over the place, the sickening smell seemed to permeate every single room the three of them entered. Despite all of this keeping their minds occupied, not wanting to trip over and fall into any of it, or miss something important during their search, that nagging sensation at the back of the laminium ball captain's mind continued to persist like an itch that just can't be scratched, almost driving him crazy. In the lead and about to step over two halves of a deceased naga that had obviously been brought to an end by some very explosive magic, exactly at that moment it hit him... right between the eyes.

'RED! Oh my God,' he thought. 'She was the most dangerous, the most twisted and sadistic of them all, and we haven't found her body.' Worse still, they'd all just left Gee Tee and Nurse Conscience alone with the crystal node. There and then, he knew that if he was Red, and still alive somewhere in here, then he'd do everything he could to destroy that thing. Not wanting to leave the humans here alone, but knowing there was simply no other way, he told them that he had to go and that they had to make their way back to the node, before telepathically trying to contact Jar Man and DomCon in an effort to warn them. Turning on his heels, he used all his magic to enhance his speed in an effort to get back to both dragons he now regarded as friends.

Would he be fast enough, and had he realised in time?

Like a bullet being shot from a rifle, that's how explosively fast her reactions and magic were. It took Red a moment or two to exert her will over the falsehood of a body that she'd fashioned at short notice, especially since she'd had to dull her heart rate, making it appear as though it had been killed in the original attack. The surprise and viciousness, she knew, would make up for any momentary lag.

Pleased with the words he'd devised for the message that was about to be sent out, without any notice at all, a screaming sense of danger reverberated around his head, all thoughts of words disappearing completely. Turning, or at least attempting to, he hadn't got more than a quarter of the way, when it felt as though the back of his head had been split in two by a sledge hammer. Mind ablaze with the most vicious pain he'd ever encountered, through a distorted blur he looked on as the sickening vision of a dragon he recognised as being dead, from a few monitors along, let go with a spinning kick that caught Nurse Conscience directly in the face, drawing copious amounts of blood and sending her spiralling to the floor. Barely able to draw breath, let alone think about defending himself from this new found threat, didn't stop the master mantra maker from attempting to get to his feet. But that's all it was... an attempt.

Pinning him firmly to the chair, one hand clasped around the worn scales of his throat, the attacker, emblazoned hatred in her eyes, squeezed with the full force of a human excavator, relentless in her savagery. For the very first time in his life, which was quite something given the scrapes he'd found himself caught up in over the years, he genuinely feared that he would die, here and now, unable to say goodbye to those he loved, in particular Tank, whose companionship he'd come to adore more than anything else. Oxygen starving his innovative and crafty mind, like a candle running out of wax the light inside him began to dull, about to be snuffed out for one very last time.

Sensing just how near death her victim was, a smug snarl, something that didn't seem at all possible, became etched across Red's face, the pleasure at taking the life of another always, for her, the ultimate thrill. Lowering her face so that it was level with his, she looked straight into his bulging eyes, wanting to let him know that she'd bested him in every way possible, before he left this realm for good, something she'd done before, more times than she could remember. But this was no ordinary being or even dragon that she was dealing with, the old shopkeeper renowned across the centuries for his stubbornness, something that reared its ugly head here and now, not wanting to die, full stop, especially not like this. With time running out and his vision failing, he did the only thing he could... he lashed out!

It wasn't brilliant, beautiful, effective or creative, because, simply put, his mind hadn't had a chance to think, that's how quick the attack had been. All he'd been able to do was scramble some words together and put all of his will and what remained of his magic behind them. It did surprise Red however, because in her mind, she was already celebrating his death and her victory.

Fiery lightning was how best to describe what he'd come up with, something that the world had probably never seen before and would probably never see again, effective only because of their close proximity. After all, he'd used up most of his mana and supernatural ability sending out the spliced mantra to neutralise the nagas in conjunction with the crystal node only a short time ago. Five to ten minutes was not nearly enough time for him to recover in any way, shape or form. He was much too old for that. Although more than a little weak and insipid, it did burn her hands, face and eyes, and more importantly it surprised her, something she wouldn't have thought possible from a dragon so old and decrepit.

Rolling back onto the floor away from the chair and the shopkeeper, flooding her hands, eyes and face with cool healing magic, a surge of spiteful, malicious and venomous anger boiled Red's blood, infusing every atom in her body with fury, giving her a thirst for vengeance and punishment like she'd never felt before. And don't forget who we're talking about here, Manson's chief fixer, his go-to torturer, the one being he liked to watch inflict pain, because she was so good at it. With her eyesight returning and the ache from her injuries becoming almost manageable, she set her sights on bringing down this one dragon and inflicting more hurt and misery on him than she ever had on any other being in her life. Gee Tee was about to wish he were dead.

Cheeks, nose and at least one eye socket broken, a whole river of blood running down the back of her throat, head ringing, her mind failing to understand what had just happened, Nurse Conscience was in quite a state, strewn out across the floor below the main control panel of the crystal node. Attempting to get her head around the situation, her mind couldn't process any of the information properly. All that it knew was that they'd been attacked, how, or from where, who knew? But it was imperative that she got back up, that much was a certainty. If she didn't, it could not only be the end for her, but her companions as well, and she just couldn't let that happen.

Barely regaining his wits, she came back at him, the full force of her cruelty powering her on.

Pure logic alone told his mind to raise the personal shield that he hadn't used in what seemed like forever, but in times of absolute stress, things don't always go the way we hope or plan. Needless to say it didn't.

Punching him full on in the face, part of her hoped it hurt him as much as it did her throbbing hands, the extent of the fiery lightning still taking its toll on her soft, supple, scaly skin.

The stinging contact across his jaw confused his mind, the words he was hoping to bring forward flying all over the place like a flock of bewildered seagulls. And the pain only got worse.

Furious at being caught out, forgetting all about destroying the node and taking care of the other dragon there, Red's red mist descended as she exploded into action. A fair fight it most definitely was not, far from it in fact. A centuries old dragon depleted of magic, on his last legs, taken by surprise, against a dark prehistoric presence who had no compunction about using violence as a tool when it was needed, having enjoyed every ounce of pain she'd ever inflicted, the addiction to impose more a compulsion that she could never fight back against... ironic really.

One swift punch with a twinkling of her magic behind it, and CRACK, Gee Tee's sternum broke in two, the old shopkeeper crying out in pain through tear filled eyes. Not stopping there, the fiendish female spun around on one foot again, almost as if it were her signature move, this time snapping the master mantra maker's right leg, incapacitating him totally, firmly gluing him into the borrowed chair.

Prostrate on the floor, head spinning, the agonising pain from her face almost forcing her into unconsciousness, the only other person there, Steel's biggest fan, tried frantically to figure out what was going on. Something had appeared, as if from nowhere, attacking them both, just as they were about to use the crystal node for a second time.

'But who and why?' she asked herself. Her mind couldn't wrap itself around the questions, screaming at her to get up and fight or be parted from this world forever. Spurred on by the thought of the laminium ball captain she admired so much, knowing exactly what he'd do in this situation, she groggily stumbled to her feet, all the time wondering what on earth she could do against such a violent, psychotic and experienced adversary.

'So many things to do,' his brain thought. 'Ease the pain, heal the wounds, form some kind of defence that would buy some time, formulate some kind of plan to go on the offensive, call for help,' were all conscious thoughts the old shopkeeper's brain was having. But the moment it focused on one, BOOM, the most excruciating pain would blossom out from wherever he was struck next. A crushed sternum, bruised ribs, a broken leg and arms as well as acute damage to both wrists and an ankle. And that was just up until this point, his brutish attacker still raining down blows on his defenceless, prehistoric body as if it were some kind of scaled punch bag, and she were the boxer warming up for a big fight... unfair, uneven, unending. That is until, through brilliant green blood soaked eyes, he caught the slightest hint of movement behind her.

BAM! She head butted him in a fit of pique, causing a great big gash to open up and blood to flow freely, an unbearable throbbing right across his forehead assaulting his mind. Thinking had become almost impossible as he hung on to his life by the tiniest of threads, the friends and mistakes he'd made across all the centuries of his long life, peeking into his subconscious in what felt like his final moments.

Taking a step back to catch her breath, Red figured she'd broken enough of the old dragon's bones to make him suffer and that now was the right time to fry him with a little magic, and she knew just what to use.

Calm and clear headed with most of the pain from the fiery lightning expunged, the damage all but healed, the calculating torturer figured she'd go all-out in putting the old dragon out of his misery. Weaving a series of complex patterns with her wiry looking fingers, half a dozen sumptuous plum coloured bolts flashed from her digits, drilling directly into his already broken chest, lighting up his scales, passing through some, setting fire to others. Writhing in misery, screaming out for his life, the master mantra maker's shrieks of exquisite agony acted like an aphrodisiac for Red, making her want more and more, and yet more.

Tears filled his eyes now, making everything a blur, his square plastic glasses having long since fallen to the floor. It was pain unlike anything he'd ever experienced, with every part of his prehistoric body feeling on fire... bones, scales, sinew, muscle and all his vital organs. The one thing he regarded above all else, the one thing he was renowned for, loved for, valued for... his mind, was almost in tatters, barely able to operate or function, that's how bad things were. Just when he thought it couldn't get any worse, she drilled a shaft of crackling red velvet coloured ethereal energy straight into his genitals, making his thoughts implode and causing his vision to explode in a halo of bright white.

Having got to her feet, the pain from her head and face forced Nurse Conscience back down to her knees, landing with a huge CRACK on the disjointed floor of the building. Unable to concentrate, and feeling guilty at not living up to Steel's high standards (she was sure he would have vanquished the despicable interloper by now, had he been here) it took all her resistance against the nausea inducing pain that threatened to overwhelm her, not to throw up.

Unfortunately for her, Red's attuned senses had heard her drop back down to her knees, and now knew that she had another being to finish off. Ramping up what she considered her very last attack on the old shopkeeper, she launched everything she had at him, showering him with nightmarish, freaky, black shadowy tendrils that cut through his scales and flesh with sizzling coldness, breaking his heart, his intellect and his very soul, just as it was meant to. Scorched, burnt, cut, battered, bruised and unequivocally broken, Gee Tee's huge dinosaur-like head sagged forward, his chin hitting his ruined chest with a bump, eyes open, completely unmoving, his broken limbs stationary across the great big chair. Heartbreaking and horrendous, it had at least been all over quickly, the whole thing taking less than twenty seconds. Mind still clouded with rage, and only half a job completed, Red turned to face the fallen dragon nurse, preparing something equally vile and disgusting, and started to step forward.

As she turned away from his dead husk of a body, something within him recognised what she was going to do... kill Nurse Conscience and in one death knell scream that sounded something like, "NOOOOOOOOOOO!!!!" what remained rallied against the inevitable and found the words to the one mantra he thought he'd never, ever use. Accepting that it was over and all that came with that particular thought, cunning, guile, skill, bravery and courage raged in what would be his one last act. Before he left this plane of existence, there was no way in hell that he was going to let that bitch harm anyone else. In one last goodbye he said the words that had been stored at the back of his mind for so long. Across the fire damaged, blackened, smoke filled, ravaged, desolate, devastated and plundered dragon domain, one of its brightest lights went out forever, in one last blaze of glory.

"TEMPUS FUGIT!" he roared deep within his head.

Roughly translated as 'time flies', in this sense its meaning was tinged with irony, because unlike almost any other mantra that had ever been created by dragons throughout history, it did exactly the opposite of its true meaning.

Red and black wisps of hot, deadly magic streaming from her fingertips, the thrill and ecstasy from taking yet one more life in a list of many written all over her face, Red turned her back on the dragon corpse and took one step in the direction of her next victim, who was only a moment away or two from joining her comrade. And then it happened, springing up all around her, with surprise and fear having a track race through every molecule of her makeup, her mind having a fair idea of what had just happened, her body not quite paralysed, but it might as well have been for all the good it did her.

Shuffling back on her knees, knowing that she was as good as dead, Nurse Conscience offered up little resistance, her mind unable to bring forth any of the mantras that she knew might help, confused because of her physical injuries, distraught at seeing what had been done to the master mantra maker, unconsciously she accepted that the same fate was meant for her. And then right before her very eyes, an epic, fluid, translucent teardrop the size of a truck sprang into life from absolutely nowhere, stopping just short of her body and encompassing both her friend the old shopkeeper, and the murderous dragon that had so brutally taken his life. Standing up, still fearful, not having yet flooded her face and body with the healing energy she was so useful with, she did a double take, wanting to touch the smooth, liquid outer layer, but quite wisely not daring to. On closer inspection, she acknowledged that she had been wrong, and that things inside the giant teardrop weren't frozen, because she could see the strands of volcanic red and dark as night magic blazing from the top of the dragon's fingertips moving, ever so slightly. As well, Gee Tee's body was... ON FIRE! Not in a big burst of flames kind of way, but gazing across at him intently in the hope that there was something she could still do, it immediately became clear that there was no opportunity for that. But on doing so, she could see that a few of the scales around his neck and chest had started to combust, and were, at an epically slow rate, burning themselves out of existence.

Like the superhero Flash, only somewhat quicker, a streaking blur whooshed around the corner, drawing to a halt next to the massive bubble resembling a tear. It could only be one other being... HER HERO!

"What the...?" Steel exclaimed looking as flustered as she'd ever seen him, his heart well and truly broken, obvious from the look on his face.

"I... I... I... I..." she tried to get the words out, to explain what had happened, but they just wouldn't come, no matter how hard she tried. To some degree it didn't matter. He was pretty sure he knew.

Glancing into the teardrop, offering up a stare of pure evil to the murderous monster that had spent all that time torturing him, knowing that she probably not only recognised him, but the trouble she was in, he peeked back towards the brave female dragon that currently looked in quite a state, the one that had done so much back at the medical facility to nurse him back to health. Acting on instinct, he flooded her with all the healing magic she needed and more, instantly knitting her face back into its prehistoric best and dissolving all of her pain, well... physical pain, anyway.

Relieved to be able to think straight once again, instinctively, she threw herself at him, more in shock and terror than anything else. Of course, being the dragon that he was, he caught her, wrapping his arms and huge wings around her entire body, giving her the physical reassurance that she so desperately needed. A few seconds passed before he had to free himself, take a step back and ignite his magic as two more speeding blurs zipped around the corner from the opposite direction. Halfway through igniting a rather potent looking fireball, the need to do so disappeared, along with his magic.

"What the...?" growled DomCon.

"Oh crap!" declared Jar Man, summing up everything they were all thinking.

"Do you know what it is?" asked Steel, the sorry look on his face obvious for all to see.

"I believe I do," acknowledged his friend.

And then they both mouthed the words simultaneously.

"Tempus fugit."

"I don't understand," announced DomCon, echoing the good nurse's sentiments.

"It's one final hurrah," noted his friend crestfallen, "designed to be used by those with little or no magic left in tragic circumstances. Known only to a few, you'd have to be some dragon to pull it off."

Which of course described the master mantra maker down to a tee, they all thought. Before his friend could ask his next question, the ginger dragon continued where he'd left off.

"It slows time, trapping enemies within its grasp, sometimes for hours, days, even weeks, depending on the individual that ignited it into existence. From the look of it, I'd say our friend there is one of the more powerful dragons to ever have given it a go. Might be a week or so until that bitch in there could move the few paces she needs to, in an effort to start to get out."

"That's not going to happen," snarled the laminium ball captain ferociously.

"If he had no mana left, how on earth could he cast it?" DomCon asked, puzzled to say the least.

"Tempus Fugit is something that's set up well in advance of time, sometimes a few hours before battle, sometimes weeks in advance, occasionally decades or even centuries. Clearly the master mantra maker had it down in case he ever needed to use it in anger, determined not to go out alone. And to answer your question, it's powered by the residual magic that resides in the cells of every dragon that's ever lived. If you look closely, you can see some of them slowly burning."

"What will happen to him?" asked Nurse Conscience having never heard of the mantra they were talking about.

"It depends," put in Steel, a keen study of everything dragon and mantra related, often found at the library in Rome during his free time. "It might be that he remains that way and continues burning until there's nothing left."

"Oh my," added the nurse, tears starting to bubble up in both eyes.

"But in some rare cases, a talented individual has been known to key the spell to their enemy's life. And when that enemy is slain, the mantra disappears completely, leaving whatever's left of the castor."

"Do you think...?" she put in, but her hero was already on it.

"Let's see shall we?" he said in a low, guttural voice.

Striding purposefully over to one of the dark dragon corpses across the way, the laminium ball captain knelt down and through all the guts and gore, seized one of the huge black bastard swords that the majority of their enemies had carried. Marching back over towards the glistening teardrop, he raised the weapon over his right shoulder in a two handed grip.

Without having been asked to, Jar Man and DomCon ushered Nurse Conscience about five metres back, where the three of them just stood, stared and waited to see what would happen.

Staggering and unbelievable were words that filled her head as she contemplated the impossible. She was paralysed and yet not, because her mind was fully aware of everything going on. It was just her body and all that was associated, her magic included, which wouldn't move, despite how much she willed it on. And yet it did seem to be moving, she thought, watching the tiny tendrils on the top of her fingertips extend out, but only by a fraction of a millimetre over the course of perhaps a minute. What the hell was going on, she wondered. Of course magic was involved, and if she'd been facing the other way and could see the cells on the dragon she'd just dispatched starting to burn up then her vast intellect might have been able to comprehend. But as it was, it just couldn't. Then to her surprise the dragon ahead of her climbed to her feet, and as if that wasn't bad enough, a familiar looking form pulled up beside her.

'HIM,' she thought, 'that son of a bitch I was torturing only a short while ago, the one who mocked me and resisted me, something that I'm really not used to.' In one of the very last moments of her life, they locked eyes, just briefly, with her instantly able to recognise the roiling anger and fury that had ignited within him. In a fit of panic, she started trying to cast all the spells she knew, including the teleportation spell they'd all been trained in, stolen from the nagas themselves. But time had all but stopped, and anything she tried was just wasted, with her magic failing to ignite behind her words and will. And so it was that she just stood there, helpless and alone, for once in her life sharing the feeling of those that she'd so heartlessly dispatched and tormented. Looking on from somewhere out of sight, Fate cackled at the turnaround in her fortunes, as the abrupt ending neared.

Powered by the anger and ferocity of losing a friend and someone he cared about, despite the fact that he'd only known the shopkeeper for an incredibly short time, but realising that none of what they'd achieved would have been even remotely possible without him, the brave and courageous dragon sports superstar put all of his energy, both magical and otherwise, into swinging the matt black monstrous sword. Cutting through the air, powered by righteous rage and the vicious venom of revenge, recognising the dragon inside the teardrop as the torturer that had inflicted so much pain on him, despite her prehistoric guise, the blade felt little resistance when it sliced through the small part of the teardrop, scales, muscle, sinew and bone of her neck. With an almighty THUMP, her surprised and still alive and conscious head bounced onto the floor. The second that happened, the magic born into existence out of desperation came to the realisation that the enemy it had been keyed to had ceased to exist and disappeared completely.

As Steel dropped the sword with a desperately loud CLANG, all four of them ran over to what remained of the master mantra maker, Nurse Conscience seeing if there was anything at all that she could do for him. But nothing could be done. As the cells of his body that were already on fire continued to burn, all four of them knelt down in front of his broken and battered form, each saying a few words in their own minds in recognition of what the famed shopkeeper had done, each keeping their own counsel. As they rose to their feet, four sets of human footsteps converged on their position, drawing to a halt some way back.

"Oh my God!" screamed Angela quickly grasping the seriousness of the situation.

"Oh no," sighed Sam.

"Please tell me it's not so," urged Emma.

Taibul, young, naive and having never seen anyone he knew die, just stood there, taking it all in, a dark fist of grief squeezing at his heart deep inside him, unable to comprehend what he should do and what would happen next.

Turning to address them, the decapitated head of the tortuous bitch staring up, eyes wide open from next to his giant right foot, Steel tried to be of some comfort.

"He died saving lives, possibly more than he could ever know. A braver, fiercer, more loyal dragon and friend I can't imagine. And he thought the world of all four of you. I know you might find it hard, but I can say with absolute conviction that he wouldn't have wanted you all to mourn his passing. Instead, at some future point, we'll all celebrate his life. But for that to happen, we need to all do our jobs for a little bit longer."

Glancing over at his biggest fan, he really needed her to

snap out of the daze she currently found herself in. Kicking the sickly stinking head off into the miserable darkness, he tried to regain her attention.

"Before he died, did he get the message off?"

"Uh?" was all that the good nurse could reply with.

"Gee Tee. Did he get the message for reinforcements and help out, through the crystal node?"

"Uh... no," she shook her head.

"Can you help me do that now please? It's of vital importance."

Distracted by the sound of her hero's voice, reality returned for the nurse that had given so much.

"Of course, of course," she said, sliding back into the chair beside the crystal node's control panel. "Tell me what you want to say, and I'll broadcast it worldwide for you right now."

Without nearly as much thought as the old shopkeeper, Steel racked his brains for the right words. Eventually, they came to him.

"The kingdom as you probably know is under attack. London has suffered severe losses, with the king remaining in danger. To any and all of you that can help, please make your way here with as much haste as is dragonly possible. Our small force is located at..." that made him think a little. Revealing their position through something that could probably be intercepted by the enemy was not a smart idea he knew, and so he decided to opt for something else. "...located at the king's private residence. Converge on that point and let's do our best to give these bastards a bloody nose. Out!"

Glancing over her shoulder, having typed everything into the console, she said only one word.

"Done!"

And that's exactly when the silence was broken by one of the humans, Angela in fact.

"Damn!" she declared. "We need to get hold of TANK!"

38 A RISKY RESCUE

Real resentment and anger stirred in their fairytale bodies at the way the hunt for the magic they so desired was turning out. They'd assumed they would have had it by now, but this group of dragons were stronger than they appeared despite their obvious disagreements and differences which had shown up right at the start of the fight. What they'd fallen out over behind their pathetic little shield was anyone's guess, because they'd kept it all to themselves, but they would pay, on that all fifteen ra-hoon could agree one hundred percent. With one of the insane dragons having left the respite of their supernatural defences, something they couldn't get their heads around at all, viciously attacking all the creatures that had been guarding them, the ra-hoon, as one, backed away even further from the battle, knowing that they were all still well within telepathic range of their so-called army, still able to dish out orders and dominate wills. And so that's what they did, ordering an all-out onslaught of the group of dragons, compelling on those under their command to find a way to breach the defences, no matter what it took or the cost in terms of lives wasted. For them, their ragtag army was just a means to an end and not something to be valued or worried about. So the fighting intensified as the desperation, desire and hunger to finish things off increased tenfold.

Unable to think of anything but breaking into the shield and getting hold of the powerful ring, not realising it was actually a great deal closer than that right now, groups of scaled apes took it in turn to charge different sections of the invisible barrier, some bouncing at it chest first, others taking a run and jump before hitting it with their feet, even more attempting to punch the living daylights out of it with their fists, all having little success so far, only really freaking out those behind the shield with the sheer determination and venom behind their attacks.

Much the same for the scorpion men, their conscious wills almost totally suppressed, they too threw themselves at different parts of the magical barricade, skittering into it, their huge claws snapping and clacking, the giant stinger of a tail they all had, constantly darting in trying to penetrate the ragged looking magic that kept their enemies safe. Just like the scaled apes, they knew their attacks were having an effect, even if it was only to keep the enemy off guard.

From above, two-headed eagles shared the space with their cohorts the pixiu, the winged lions having mostly settled on top of the defensive barrier, clawing, scrapping and gnawing at what separated them from their enemies, while the freakish birds pecked with their beaks and raked with their talons. Again, it was unsettling, especially if you were below.

The remainder of the fire breathing gnats circled some way off, their numbers having been decimated by Yoyo's young dragons who'd managed to take out about seventy percent of them. Angry, scared and frightened, their minds in total disarray because of the ra-hoon's hold over them, they were more than a little confused, with the only consensus they could reach being to back off for the time being in the hope that it would keep them safe. It had so far, but only because other targets had become much more of a priority.

Grey, brown and green shaded vampiric lizards scurried around the circumference of the circle. spitting their vile multicoloured lightning at anything, hoping against hope that some of it would get through, their huge oversized eyes constantly on the lookout for an opportunity to exploit.

Excruciating howls of pain from the not quite dead asag reverberated around the field of battle, sending goose bumps up limbs, a chill down backs and filling stomachs with a knot of twisted energy. Even in the throes of death, the hideous rock demon was still one of the scariest things there.

Piling in between the scorpion men, scaled apes,

vampiric lizards, the asena and all of the aerial threats, bright blood red and brilliant neon green gaki probed the shield with their sharp talons, sometimes bouncing their bellies against it while crying out in the voices of all sorts of cattle, hoping to rattle their enemies and feed off their souls. Apart from the giant elephant beast, they were the most fearsome and disturbing foes the light-sided heroes faced.

With their trust issues still up in the air because of the spat between Fredric and Richie, Flash and Captain Battlehard had gone back to fighting together, albeit not quite as effectively and efficiently as before, when they'd been combating Manson's troops. Something unsaid remained between them, each knowing that they might yet end up on opposite sides depending on just how things were resolved between the king, his best friend and of course their de facto leader. It was complicated, and would at some point need to be resolved, that is, if they managed to defeat the overwhelming horde that continued to try and get at them. Amelia grabbing one scaled ape with an exotic telekinesis mantra, Flash using something similar to pick up a gaki, both of them, with just a look, threw their prey at each other's, the resulting collision killing both beasts instantly, and although not quite as symbiotic as before, the coordination of their attacks was a massive boon to all the dragons fighting for their lives.

Through the monstrous, magical mayhem, the fighting and the team work, the worry, fear, sorrow and regret, one of the most experienced dragons there fought with all his might, wit and intelligence to save the life of one that he loved. Using all of his vast wealth of knowledge, he tried tirelessly to stop the poison the nifoloa had injected into Wiz's cheek from spreading out into her body, knowing exactly how much harm it would do. Try as he might though, his supernatural attempts were not having nearly the effect that he'd hoped, with a couple of them having made things worse. As he knelt down beside her, her impressive dragon body started to convulse, and there wasn't a thing in the world he could do about it. Out of ideas, having tried everything that he knew, all he could do was comfort the young dragon and hope that somehow her own body fought off whatever was ravishing her on the inside. This he continued to do for about ninety seconds, until she half sat up, cried out, gave one last gasp, and then flopped back to the floor, still as a statue, forever to remain that way. Tears flooded the healer's face as his will continued to question the point of everything.

'One more lost,' was all that he could think, 'and it's my fault, after all, I got them mixed up in all of this.' Only the cry of his name from one of his other charges startled him out of his self pity, unable to resist the compunction to use his given gifts for good on those all around him. Saying a brief farewell to one of the charges he considered his own, salty tears still blurring his vision, he crawled back to his feet and once again started to render aid.

With the famed blade Fu-ts'ang and the heroic rugby player Hook watching over her, the brave blonde haired human once again knelt down beside her love, this time hoping to get through to him, not just for her sake, but for all of them, knowing that adding another ally to the cause could well be the difference between winning and losing. But how to do such a thing, that was the question. If what her friend the mighty weapon smith had said was true, how could she hope to bypass that kind of trauma and make Peter feel the love she had for him?

Looking out beyond the creatures, keeping an eye on what one of her two best friends was doing, and whether or not he was having the effect he was hoping for on the monsters surrounding the ra-hoon, a little tickle of her psyche drew Richie's attention off in another direction, namely that of Fredric. In the middle of all the violence he and George were spreading with their powerful ancient knowledge, he had turned around to glance in the direction of his grandson, and more importantly as far as she was concerned, her friend Janice. Over the founder of the

Crimson Guards' shoulder, the lacrosse playing superstar locked eyes with George himself, who was just realising what his best friend was doing. It was a look that seemed to last an age, although in reality it was only a moment, but telling because of the king's reaction. Not mad, angry or upset, he appeared calm, more accepting, as if he had come to realise the full extent of whatever was wrong. At the end, there appeared just the tiniest of nods, almost an acknowledgement that he'd made a bad call, an apology if you like. Not swayed one way or the other by the virtual olive branch that had supposedly been offered out, the de facto leader of them all turned back towards the ra-hoon, hoping that Tank was making good progress in pissing them off. The sooner they got this done, the sooner everything else could be resolved.

"I know you can hear me Peter," whispered Janice's soft voice in his left ear, unsure really of why she was whispering given the racket going on all about them and the enhanced hearing of all the dragons amongst them, including, she thought... Fredric!

But she had to try, and wanted to sound as kind and caring as she ever had in the hope that it might sway her soul mate to somehow find his way back to her.

"I can imagine how shocked you are at what you've just found out. I'd like to say that I know how you feel, can relate to your pain and have all the right answers for you, but I don't and perhaps never will. What I will tell you is, that like all of your friends here, Richie, Tank, Flash, Hook, Yoyo, George and..." she hesitated to say it because of what had happened, but thinking it might make the difference, proceeded anyway, "Fredric, your grandfather, I care about you a great deal. No... more than that. I love you with all my heart. Meeting you changed my life beyond measure. If I died in this moment, something I hope a great deal doesn't happen, I'd die happy because of you and what we've been through together. I don't care that you're an entirely different species, all I care about is the time we've spent together and the time to come. I see in you a kindred spirit, one I'd love to spend the rest of my life with, have children with if that's even possible, grow old and infirm with. Please my love, whatever it is, we can make it right together. Come back to me. Come back to us all."

Compelling words indeed, but would they make a difference?

Out of the corner of his eye, the darkness parted just a little, like curtains on a stage being pulled back slightly to see the audience, letting just a tiny amount of light flood through. Peter's psyche, so lost and alone, got his first glimpse of the hope he'd thought lost, of the opportunity to put things right. Memories of his friends that had been pushed off into the deepest recesses of his mind came flooding back, all of them... Richie, Tank, Flash, Hook, Yoyo, George, his grandfather Fredric, and of course, most importantly of all, the love of his life... JANICE! Dreamlike would best describe the tangled mess of his psyche, darkness attempting to taint everything, including the memories of those he loved. Not knowing which side to come down on, light or dark, far off in the distance he could faintly make out someone speaking, presumably to him. That was just enough to turn the tide, push back the shadows, let in the unencumbered light. It wasn't so much the words that had done it, but the voice itself and who it belonged to. She was there, waiting for him, and after all that she'd been through, entering the dragon domain, fighting deadly dark monsters, being captured by Manson, finding solace with Fu-ts'ang and then almost being killed again before making it this far, there was simply no way that he could run away from that, not now, not ever. And so in a biblical sea of blinding light, his conscious will returned to his broken body and, exhaling a long deep breath that startled his soul mate, given that she'd been whispering in his ear all this time, he returned and in one fell swoop, wrapped his arms around her neck and held her as tight as he could.

"My love," he ventured, so full of joy to be back.

"Oh sweetheart," she replied. "I'm so glad you returned. Promise that no matter what, you'll never do that to me again."

"I promise."

And that was that, except for the snarl that Richie couldn't help but notice on Fredric's worn and weathered face, something she would make sure to wipe off once all of this was over.

Glad for the sake of his friend that her soul mate had returned from whatever fresh hell his mind had been lost in, knowing that she remained at least as safe from the founder of the Crimson Guards as she could do, for the time being anyway, the master weapon smith in the guise of the ultramodern blade drifted through the air to a point behind the lacrosse playing dragon's back, awaiting her attention which he knew he'd got from the cold coming off him. It didn't take long.

"Has his mind returned?" she asked.

"Yes," the blade replied, frost and an undisputed chill filling the air all around it.

"Excellent."

"Where can I help?"

Without even another thought, she knew exactly where she needed him.

"Tank's gone out to try and rid the ra-hoon of the constant presences of the species surrounding them. If you can help there, that would be great. If we can isolate the ra-hoon, then I'm pretty sure this will all be over in a few moments."

"Really?" enquired the enigmatic cutting edge.

"It'll take too long to explain how. Just trust me... please?"

"Always! I'll go and find your friend and see if I can stir up a bit more trouble in and around the ra-hoon."

"I'm grateful for your company Fu-ts'ang," she said, meaning every last word of it. "We all are, in fact."

Brightened up by her sincere words, feeling as good as he had in a while, the cold infused weapon bowed in an effort to convey his thanks, and as fast as he could move, shot off tip first in the direction of Tank and For'son who were valiantly trying to provoke a series of deadly species into a fight.

Reluctantly releasing his grip on the love of his life, Peter was suddenly enveloped by a massive human frame that towered over him. And instead of it being the usual rugby player, it was a slightly different one this time.

"Hook... my friend. How are you?"

"All the better for your return buddy... are you okay? You had us all quite worried."

Pulling in a deep breath, shaking his head, all the time taking in his new surroundings and of course... attackers, he answered his friend's question.

"I think so... not really sure what hit me. Whatever it was, it's gone now. Um... can I ask, what the hell is going?"

"Long story," replied Janice, "but I think you might be needed. You can slot right in there next to Richie and take Tank's place."

"Where on earth did Tank go in all of this?" Peter asked.

Not knowing the answer, and not wanting him ending up next to his grandfather, the young bar worker just ushered him forward until he slid in beside his best friend.

"Evening," she stated sarcastically, implying that he was somewhat late, "nice of you to join us."

"Well... what can I say, other than, I like what you've done with the place."

"Of course... you've been gone so long a completely different enemy now has us in their sights. Thanks for that!"

"Pleasure," ventured Peter, a big cheesy grin chiselled into his face at being back alongside his best friend, despite the circumstances.

"Where's Tank?"

"Don't ask," she replied shaking her head, her enhanced vision searching for the rugby playing idiot she considered the other one of her two best mates.

As if it wasn't bad enough that you and your kind were being kicked, punched, gouged, a vast array of magic shot back at you, especially towards your valuables (and I'm not talking about your purse, wallet, phone or watch) the more than somewhat cheeky dragon... yes, they knew that much, despite its outwardly human appearance... had now taken to mocking them with an assortment of hand gestures and facial appearances as he sped dizzily around in a circle. Unbelievable! Despite the ra-hoon's considerable and powerful protests, most of the surrounding creatures had gone off the reservation completely and were in the midst of hunting down Tank and his cohort, For'son.

The echeneis, although only twelve centimetres long, were proving to be the hardest to draw out and combat, because every time he and For'son sped into their little nest, they all blew out a freezing breath, with several of them having nearly captured Tank in their trap already. The rest of them, well, their temperatures were already ramping up, almost at boiling point, following the partners for what it was worth, trying to catch up, getting close but not quite near enough. Every time they thought they'd caught Tank, he just managed to slip out of their grasp, usually doubling back towards the echeneis in an effort to get them to take the bait and leave the ra-hoon on their own... so far though... no luck. But all of that was about to change.

'Hi guys... need some help?' asked a familiar voice spanning both Tank and For'son's minds.

'Fu-ts'ang!' they thought simultaneously.

'Do you want me to take care of those frosty little cockwombles?' asked the master weapon smith, having heard some of the others use that word and liking it a lot, especially in this situation.

'That would be great,' replied the rugby playing dragon. *'We'll allow this lot to follow us on a wild goose chase. If you can draw those...*

cockwombles," (Tank was embarrassed to say the word, even in his mind) *"out and away from the ra-hoon, it should be mission completed for us."*

"On my way," replied the frosty blade. *"Good hunting!"*

With lightning speed, the revolutionary weapon zoomed into the nest of echeneis and protected against their attacks because of his resilience to cold and, without warning, did exactly what the enigmatic band For'son had suggested not long ago, stabbing them right where he hoped their genitals were located. Surprisingly, it didn't take long to find out whether he was wrong or right. Luckily for him, he was right on the money, raising their ire instantly, with every single one of them following in his wake as he tried to scarper, slower than his normal pace of course, just to make them think they could keep up. It shouldn't be possible for something that small to look that incensed. Because of their size though, and despite being as angry as any being could ever get, their idea of irate still came across as quite cute in spite of their deadly, demonic nature.

And so it came to be that the ra-hoon were left on their own (self isolating... that gives you a clue to when this was written) for the most part, not having realised what had gone on and just how they'd been duped.

"On my mark," whispered Owen into his comms. "And don't forget take out both horns on your main target before moving onto the secondary. Five... four... three... two... one..."

Disguised by the background noise of the magical melee taking place in and around the heroes' makeshift defensive circle, a quiet, sharp POP, POP, POP could be faintly heard, the suppressing rounds leaving Garrett's squad's NGSARs. Although having never seen actual combat, the human members of the tiny squad led by Owen were not just good, they were the best, with all of them decimating both horns on their primary ra-hoon targets first time, before readjusting the sights on their weapons and acquiring their secondary objectives.

Watching from a distance, disappointed at the assault by those species under them taking so long, about half their group simultaneously cried out in agonising pain in a sort of cross between a sharp neighing sound and an abrupt snort, triggering absolute chaos in their ranks, some of them riding up on their hind legs, lone ranger style, others galloping around in circles trying to locate the threat.

With surprise having played its part dutifully, something much more like pot luck started to kick in, as the fast moving mythical creatures came to realise that something was wrong and a number of unknown assassins were now targeting their position; all they could really do was keep moving in the hope that would be enough to stay safe. Without both of their horns, having had their telepathic powers ripped away in the blink of an eye, all those ra-hoon affected collapsed on the ground, the shock too much for them, the voices of the others in their minds deathly silent, feeling like an amputee that had just lost a limb. Cruel, painful, unforgiving, but necessary and it was much better than the alternative... DEATH!

Even though they were great, what was expected of them now was nothing short of impossible. Of course they had enough ammunition to keep trying over and over again, but the fact that the crazy creatures were constantly on the move made what was asked of them beyond difficult.

POP, POP, POP, POP resounded through the air, the bullets kicking up pockets of marble and tiny little wisps of dust as they missed what they were aiming for. One or two rounds accidentally felled a couple of raging ra-hoon, bringing them to a standstill, knocking them to the ground. Once this occurred, all the shooters in both locations trained their scopes on the horns of the incapacitated creatures, immediately ridding them of their powers, what remained of their bony protrusions tumbling off onto the floor, howls of exquisite pain accompanying the act.

Across the comms, Owen and the other shooters agreed that the only way to proceed was to aim for the bodies of the ra-hoon whose bony protrusions remained, in the hope of injuring them just enough to take them down and then be able take the shots. It was a dubious plan, one that Polo herself acceded to, with no guarantee it would work. But it was all that they had and so they got right on it.

Sprinting up towards the huge white marble steps of the king's private library, camaheutos, myrmecoleon and shape shifting venomous snakes, that even as they moved transformed on the run into monstrous yeti-like creatures, Tank, having almost come full circle could see the chaos and confusion of... what? If he'd had to guess, he would have said gunshots, but that would be impossible wouldn't it? Who in the domain would have guns? Certainly not dragons, and that left... what? He had absolutely no clue. Unfortunately he didn't have time to dwell on such things, given how close the creatures chasing him were, despite For'son swelling his magic and guiding some of his actions.

'Damn!' thought Richie, watching with interest from a great distance away as the ra-hoon got what they deserved, at least that's what she thought was happening. On closer inspection however, it looked as though Garrett's shooters were, for some unknown reason, blowing off their horns, and with it happening across the board, it must have been a very deliberate ploy.

'Oh well,' she thought, 'they must be doing it for a reason, however daft it might be.'

Reversing roles in a diabolical twist of fate, the super smart, super brave, futuristic blade Fu-ts'ang had used the extreme cold that constantly revolved around his blade and supported his life essence, or soul as some like to think of it, freezing all of the echeneis to the floor off to one side of where the ra-hoon were. Currently, he just hovered in the air, trying to get a grip on the situation and assess where he could best be of use. It took him a few moments to realise what was going on, with the projectile weapons all seeking out the horns on their deadly adversaries, he supposed to nullify their threat without actually killing them, which was rather indulgent given the circumstances, he thought. But whoever they are, they must have a good reason to be doing it that way.

With only one ra-hoon left with both of its horns intact, the others having all been shot off, their owners left lying on the floor, confused, dazed and most certainly out of the fight, the master weapon smith watching as bullets ricocheted everywhere, made the decision to help and wrap things up once and for all. Streaking in towards the central site of the ra-hoon, tip first, a frosty trail hanging in the air in his wake, Fu-ts'ang hugged the ground on his approach, whipping up dust and debris, weaving in and around the cadavers of dragons, nagas and numerous mythical species that he just didn't recognise.

Approaching the rampaging unicorn lookalike from behind, the last one with two horns intact, his gut instinct telling him just to skewer it especially after everything it had supposedly done in controlling this whole fiasco, the master weapon smith took a moment of deep contemplation as he travelled, before making his decision. Slicing through the air, Fu-ts'ang followed the contours of the ra-hoon's head as his blade delicately sliced off the base of both horns, as a chainsaw would with a branch. Slamming on the brakes, pulling a full one-eighty, the resplendent weapon gazed down at his work as the bullets stopped and the monster collapsed sideways onto the floor.

Across the board, the attacking horde of mythical creatures suddenly started to act erratically, those flying nearly crash landing, managing to avoid a costly collision at the last minute, those on the ground taking a second look at where on earth they currently were, the ones chasing Tank and For'son momentarily slowing before once again catching up. Even the giant elephant beast had stopped, seemingly considering his next act.

'Oh you little beauty,' thought Richie, having keenly

observed everything that had happened, more impressed than ever with Janice's bladed friend. But that would have to wait... there were things to do, the first of which was to re-establish the main telepathic link, now that it was safe to do so.

"All of you... listen up. It's me, Richie, your leader. It's safe to open up your consciousnesses. The threat to our link and your safety has been neutralised. Join up so that we can coordinate our attacks better. That's an order."

Rather reluctantly they did so, and several things became obvious all at once. First... Yoyo and the effect of yet one more of his charges dying on him coursed through their bond, his feelings of loss, grief, failure and regret clouding their senses. Not a single one of them couldn't feel his pain, with one or two of his young charges not having known that Wiz was even dead, something that didn't play out well across their link. Morose and depressed, a shadowy dark cloud hanging over all of them, the decision to join minds looking like it might cost them dearly, suddenly a cry for help from one of their own caught all their attention, moving the subject on completely, focusing them on something else.

"Uhh... everyone, if you could lend some assistance, it would be much appreciated," urged Tank, more than a little on edge.

As one, all the heads safely hidden behind the transparent shield turned in his direction, off in the distance to one side of where the ra-hoon had fallen, Tank was currently being hunted down by an array of different creatures, his magic and speed barely holding them off.

Mind in crisis because of her friend, Richie could think of nothing else to do but to sprint out there and try to help, but before she could the strong grasp of a time worn hand clasped her arm tightly. As a surge of anger threatened to explode within, she turned to face the last being she wanted to, knowing that they still had a score to settle.

"Sorry!" said George, immediately removing his hand and regretting his actions.

Scowling at him viciously, her temper remained frayed as her body lingered, her decision not quite made.

"There's another way," he assured her.

"Let's hear it!" she snapped back.

Not letting it bother him, knowing that the fallout from before had yet to be resolved, he filled her in on his idea.

"Now that the ra-hoon are out of the equation, it might be possible to get all the other species to surrender. I suggest you ask them."

"And just how do we do that... send them an email?" she replied sarcastically.

This time it was his turn to hold his temper, not used to anyone speaking to him in such a way. After all, he was still the reigning monarch of the domain and the planet as a whole.

"Get Tank to do it through For'son. It was his presence that contained the creatures for so long. Just maybe they'll recognise his touch and be reassured by that. Tell him to cut whatever deal would see them willing to go back to their secure cells. If they agree, some of the King's Guards can escort them, and then this damn mess will all be over."

It was a good plan, she knew, and one that could hopefully reduce the risk of any more lives being lost... if it worked. Without hesitation, and still trying to out-glare George, she filled Tank in on exactly what he needed to do.

"Can you do it?" he asked, his thoughts only half there, the other half concentrating on not stumbling or making a mistake and allowing the crazy creatures in pursuit a chance to get their teeth, fangs or claws into him.

"I can try, whether they listen or not is something else altogether."

"Do it, do it, do it," he urged, running out of patience and puff.

Using a considerable amount of the magic stored within him, For'son splayed out his mind across the king's private residence, attracting the attention of all the mythical creatures, including what remained of the ra-hoon, although because of their lack of horns, they were unable to answer back or do anything that required magic or mental acuity.

'Listen carefully,'' his telepathic 'voice' boomed across the open channel, knowing that he had the attention of every being there. *'Enough is enough. You cannot win, not now your despicable leaders have been so harshly dealt with. We mean you no harm, quite the opposite in fact. Up until today, you've all led peaceful lives, coexisting with your own kind in worlds set up to suit your biological make up perfectly. Not once have you ever starved, been without water, heat, light or prey. And yes, your existences were held in check magically which would have not only been a shock but an affront to some of you. But for numerous reasons it had to be this way, and... it could still be again. I'd like to propose that you consider going back. We can make some alterations to include practically whatever you like. But this has to end. And I think all of you know that the winning side won't be yours. Of course, you could cost us a lot of lives still, but only at the expense of every being on your side. Please, let's stop any further bloodshed and go back to how we were. You have exactly one minute to decide and give us your answer!''*

'Wow,' thought Richie, 'he doesn't mess about. One minute? Surely that's not long enough?' But it would have to be, because the presence behind the mighty, magic filled band would not give a second more.

With those attackers chasing him having stopped as a group, Tank skidded to a halt next to a huge pile of rubble, wondering what on earth he should do now. To get back to the safety of the circle and his friends, he'd have to go through what remained of the force of mythical creatures, and given that some of them hadn't stopped to consider his partner For'son's demand, including the giant elephant beast, that presented a risk he really didn't feel like taking right now, especially if they agreed to surrender, something he supposed all the species were talking about telepathically at this very moment.

With a natural pause in proceedings, everyone there stopped to catch their breath.

Janice and Hook hugged briefly before pulling away. The only two true humans there, they were just grateful to have survived thus far and still remain standing.

Yoyo's young charges swarmed all over him, whilst still leaving their shields up, the loss of Wiz deeply affecting them all, much as Hillier's death had. The outpouring of emotion had the Australian healer in bits, not in the least concerned with any sort of fight that might or might not resume any time now.

Flash and Captain Battlehard took a breath, both utterly exhausted and sweating profusely. Neither said a word, which was a shame really because they had so much in common and would have got on like a house on fire. But with the Fredric debacle still hanging in the air, they might yet find themselves on opposite sides of the debate, something neither of them wanted, and that wouldn't bode well for future relations.

George and Fredric embraced, both relieved to have a few moments of respite, despite their sticky situation, the founder of the Crimson Guards looking over his friend's shoulder at the grandson he barely knew, hoping against hope... no! Vowing there and then, not to let history repeat itself, no matter what it cost him.

The remaining King's Guards savoured the moment, keeping the shields in place with the enemy still milling about outside, hugging and back slapping their friends new and old, hoping against all odds that finally this might be over.

Richie and Peter embraced, two best pals having fought off injustice and death what seemed like a dozen times over in only the last few hours, their camaraderie as strong as ever, united as one until the end of time. It was just a shame that Tank wasn't there, because that would have made it perfect.

"Are you really alright?" she asked him.

"I'm not too sure," he replied. "But I think I will be with all my friends around me. Sorry to worry you."

Playfully slapping him on the arm, she continued the assault.

"You should be, you know. We were all really concerned. You do that again and I'll turn you into a spider... permanently. Got it?"

"Yes," he replied grinning.

"Pete," she said, turning all serious. "There's something else you should know."

But before she could continue, he held up his hand to stop her.

"You're talking about what my grandfather tried to do to Janice?"

Surprised to say the least, wondering how the hell he knew all about that, she was just about to ask him when instead he got there first.

"I can remember being far away, smothered in black, barely able to feel or see, but for some reason my hearing wasn't impaired. And although I don't know what he actually said to her, I know what happened, how upset she was and just how angry you were. Thank you, your love and understanding is valued now more than ever. I can't express how much it means to me that you would stand up for Janice," he said, tears welling up in the corners of his eyes. "I love her Rich, I truly do, with all my heart. That conversation we had all that time ago, it makes sense now, it really does."

Smiling sympathetically, she reached for his hands and looked him in the eye.

"Standing up for Janice was not only the right thing to do, as leader of everything it was my duty to do just that. But it wasn't about that, or even your love for her. And you should listen when I say this, alright."

Peter nodded, wondering where this was all going.

"She's my friend, and I truly mean that. You might think you know most of the stuff she's done since she's been down here, but I assure you that's not the case. I've never met someone so brave and so selfless. I find it hard to believe there's a more courageous and valiant being out there, and as far as I'm concerned, you couldn't have chosen any better. But I warn you now, when it's safe to do so, your grandfather and I are going to have a rather uncomfortable conversation... well, for him, anyway."

Leaning in, he planted a huge kiss in the middle of her freckly forehead, before saying,

"You're my hero, and always will be. Like the rest of the beings here, I would follow you anywhere. Who else could lead the current dragon monarch? It could only be you. Stay safe."

And with that, he turned and strolled across to Hook and Janice, keen to see how they were doing.

Hovering only a few metres away from the shivering and pathetic bodies of the emasculated ra-hoon, Fu-ts'ang made himself as tall and proud as he could, hoping against hope that For'son's ploy brought a premature end to all the hostilities, knowing that his friends, the ones behind the huge circular shield across the way, needed to rest and regroup as a matter of urgency.

And then for all the beings, with the exception of Vasuki and his group of nagas, across the king's private residence, loud words resonated throughout their minds as For'son once again spoke, with the authority his centuries of experience afforded him.

"IT'S TIME! CHOOSE!"

Pure unadulterated silence flooded each and every consciousness linked to the enigmatic band's words. No being there moved, including the giant elephant beast, each and every one of them aware of the pivotal moment that had been reached. Would it be more magic, explosions, deaths and an all-out race to self destruction, or would common sense and self preservation prevail? Futures hanging by a thread, it was time to see.

"We accede to your demands, but we have a few of our own," submitted a gruff voice of one of the remaining scorpion men.

"Such as?" asked For'son, eager to get the details of this tied up and for it all to be over, though his voice didn't

reflect any of that, still all business.

"Twice yearly meetings outside the cells for all the leaders of each species with more of a say about our environments, development, diet, prey and perhaps the chance to feel some real sunlight on our backs at some point, the place to be determined by your good selves."

'Hmmm...' thought For'son, 'not unreasonable at all, considering.' And he had been given carte blanche in negotiating a settlement.

"You have a deal, right here and now, providing you all agree to be magically bound to stop fighting the dragons and humans and agree to go straight back to your cells. Once you're there, I'll power them up and we'll get some of the dragons to make repairs as soon as possible. What do you say?"

Again, more silence, perhaps thirty or so seconds of it.

"We can do that," announced the scorpion man, seemingly in charge.

"Okay then. Gather around the ra-hoon immediately, and we'll get started."

And so they did. In a matter of minutes it was over, every creature there, including the giant elephant beast and the disabled ra-hoon, agreeing to be magically enthralled so that they couldn't harm another dragon or human ever again, in return for a say in the important decisions about their future once back in their enhanced bio containment cells. For every being there it seemed like a win, with the King's Guard escorting what remained of the mythical creatures back off to the basement of the council building, while the rest of them just collapsed to the floor, soaking up the relief at it being all over and of course remaining alive. For some, Yoyo and his charges, the grief of losing Hillier and Wiz was all too much to take, with them all collapsing in on each other, tears and hugs aplenty.

Flash and Amelia embraced awkwardly, their true feelings held firmly in check by loyalty and duty, but both barely able to believe that they'd seen the day out with everything that had happened.

Peter, Janice and Hook all embraced, doing a little jig as

they did so, absolutely ecstatic at the fighting having stopped, amazed to all still be in one piece after the adventure of a lifetime.

Tank, with For'son still firmly wrapped around his finger, marched over, Fu-ts'ang hovering alongside him, both chatting away, now that the master weapon smith had found his external voice, each pleased to see their friends intact and alive, the ring's presence barely able to believe it hadn't fallen into the hands of either Manson or Earth, pleased at finding a new, exciting and compatible partner.

To the surprise of nearly everyone, although it shouldn't have been given the way most of the ra-hoon were taken out, Polo, Garrett, Owen and the rest of their troops met up at the bottom of the library stairs amidst what remained of the lifeless asag and casually strolled over to what had been the circle, but was now just indiscriminate clusters of friends, all doing their own thing. Some were explaining super amazing battle moves from somewhere along the day, others were just embracing, more overcome by emotion, with one or two solitary figures just sat on the floor, trying to take it all in.

"Oh my God!" exclaimed Peter, leaving Janice and sprinting over towards the newcomers. "Al," he cried out, "Owen!"

Smiling, the two humans caught him as he leapt into their arms, so utterly pleased to see them.

"What the hell are you doing here?"

"Saving your arse, once again," quipped Owen, smiling.

"We couldn't let you have all the fun, could we now?" observed Garrett, relieved to see his young employee safe and well.

Over strolled Richie, offering out her hand to Cropptech's owner. Not bothered about the inappropriateness of it all, Garrett pulled her in for a huge hug, holding her tight, something she appreciated a great deal and unbelievably she held on to him in excess of ten seconds before pulling away.

"Al," she remarked, "it's good to see you, and even better that you could provide us with that save. And Polo, yes I do remember you," she said, turning towards the female dragon. Thank you for all that you've done. Without you, we'd have been in a shed load of trouble."

"Your thanks aren't necessary, leader. I think the courage and valiant fighting that you and those under your command have shown has made for a resounding success, if that's what it can be called," she said, gazing out across the body strewn battlefield.

Richie just nodded, not knowing what else to say. But then her eyes caught sight of Fredric and George, and the fire within her reignited.

For two of the parties, there was still the matter of the unfinished business from earlier. It hadn't been forgotten, far from it in fact.

A small sense of satisfaction at leading those still left alive through all this, when for a time it looked as though they'd all be decimated by the evil villain Manson, was curtailed by the need to confront her best friend's grandfather over his actions during the middle of the battle. Sights set, anger coursing through her, knowing exactly what her opening line was going to be, she started to stride purposefully in the direction of George and Fredric. All of those left spotted what was about to happen and immediately became silent, unable to take their eyes off what was about to play out, knowing that they might just have to take sides, something none of them were keen to do.

Half way to them, ready to fight if necessary, Richie's steps were suddenly interrupted by the dulcet tones of a mobile phone ringing.

Blushing profusely, the strapping rugby legend Hook reached into the pockets of his jeans and in one swift move, pulled out his phone and answered it, stopping the lacrosse playing dragon in her tracks, much to her disappointment.

"Hello," he remarked.

In total silence, the waft of death warming their delicately soft noses as they eyed his every action, each one of them watched the tough and courageous hero's face go from rosy red, to the palest of ashen whites in only a few moments. And that wasn't the worst of it, because a tiny trickle of tears had started to seep from both of his eyes.

With everyone looking on, wondering what the hell could have had that effect on the man mountain of a rugby player, he turned to face one individual in particular, his lips quivering uncontrollably.

"What is it?" asked Tank, the person he'd turned to face.

"It's Angela on the phone. She said it's Gee Tee... he's, he's dying."

Not all of them there knew who the master mantra maker was, but most did. Of those that did, to a being they all wondered how on earth that would be possible. If any mortal on the planet could ever continue to cheat death, surely it would be him. For a few seconds, nothing happened. And then like a sprinter out of the blocks, the dragon whose first love were his two friends, followed swiftly by the human sport he'd come to adore, tore off at speed towards the bridge that spanned the gap between where they were and the council building.

"TAAAAANNNKKKK!!!!" she screamed, louder than she ever had in her entire life, knowing that her buddy was not only in danger, but in need of a friend.

Peter followed suit, aware of just how his pal was feeling, wanting to go with him.

"TAAAAANNNKKKK!"

But their comrade didn't even break sweat, not looking over his shoulder or anything. About to give chase, only then did she realise just how fruitless it would be, because there was simply no way that she could keep up with him, stuck in her human form. On the run, faster than the humans could see, the brave, heroic, courageous saviour of them all, along with his partner For'son, rippled just slightly, and in an act that the humans could see, transformed into his magnificent prehistoric guise. With one flap of his gigantic wings, he lifted off over the bridge, and circling in a spiral vortex, disappeared inside the entrance the nagas and mythical creatures had used to exit the building. He was gone, and with no one there to console or protect him. Well... not quite.

A cold, familiar hand startled her as it landed on her shoulder. Turning around, tears flooding her eyes, she came face to face once again with George, the reigning monarch of not only this domain, but what was left of the world itself. Instead of defending his best friend which she assumed he was going to do, he tried to offer some soft words of comfort.

"It'll be alright... he's not alone. For'son will keep him safe and make sure he arrives at Fleet Street in one piece."

And that, right at that second, was enough to console the lacrosse playing superstar who, at a cost, had led them to a stunning victory, saving not only all of them, but the planet itself... for the time being, anyway.

39 ONE LAST REUNION

Storming out through the front entrance of the council building, atop the steps which led down to the bubbling pools of lava on either side, without any fuss, his hugely muscled legs powered his enhanced leap into the air, and with his tail guiding him in the right direction, he caught the biggest updraft he could and disappeared through a narrow gap between two buildings, heading in the general direction of Fleet Street, knowing exactly where he was going and not worried one iota about being attacked by any stragglers still remaining in the rubble and ruins of the capital.

As the smoky haze from two dozen fires washed over his aerodynamic body, making him look like a racing car being tested in a wind tunnel, his tucked away arms shivered, not from cold but from the emotion he struggled to contain, his throat red raw from all the screaming he'd let out whilst continuing to move through the council building, despite knowing that it might give away his location to any enemies in the vicinity, his vision blurred through so many tears. Nothing short of an absolute mess, it would have been funny had the situation not been so tragic, with the young rugby playing dragon more distraught than he'd ever been.

During the course of their time together at the start of the battle in the king's private residence earlier on in the day, he'd been deliberately mean in an attempt to find out the character of the dragon he'd been dealing with, one he somehow vaguely recognised from another time... which was strange in itself. Something that had in the past, lasted weeks or even months when monarchs died only to be replaced shortly afterwards by somebody he didn't know. He didn't take great pleasure in it, quite the opposite in fact. But he did consider it necessary, because you never really knew who or what you were dealing with until the chips were down. And this one... Tank, For'son knew, without a doubt after everything that they'd been through over the course of just one day, was one of the finest and most courageous dragons he'd ever had the pleasure of joining up with. When all his probing and testing had taken place, he'd gotten a sense of the kind of relationship and bond that he shared with the master mantra maker, and from that alone, understood just how devastated he was inside after getting the call. For once (he really couldn't remember any other time that he'd done this) he stayed totally silent and still, concentrating all of his powers in an effort to look out and avoid any enemies should they still be around, knowing that what few words he could offer would never be enough to console his young friend.

Avoiding the worst of the thick plumes of sickly black smog, most originating from massive pyres of broken and beaten dragon cadavers, Tank glided this way, before cutting back that way, all the time attempting to take the shortest route to where they were going, his body on autopilot, his mind slowly breaking apart, lost in the past.

Strangely, memories of being berated and told off swarmed the inside of his head first of all, the master mantra maker always having been a harsh task master even from day one.

After receiving news of a successful interview, he was informed by a telepathic letter that he was required to start the next day. More than a little flustered, having expected the whole hiring process to take at least a few more weeks, he could recall feeling unprepared and more than a little nervous as he stepped across the threshold of the Emporium one Tuesday morning in the early autumn, the bell above the front door ringing in his ears as he did so. Making his way swiftly and efficiently to the front counter, he was surprised to find it totally deserted despite the early hour. Keen to get started, he wondered just what he would be up today, his mind then harking back to a nursery ring visit by a rather attractive and exotic female dragon by the name of Cat. That's what had inspired him to focus his studies in this direction and do so well in his exams. Being taken on at the Mantra Emporium had been his goal for decades, with the confirmation letter being the pinnacle of his life so far. Little did he realise he was about to be brought back down to earth with a very sharp bump.

Standing propped up against the counter, giant dragon rucksack slung over one shoulder, a healthy and hearty dragon sized lunch along with everything else he thought he would need contained within, the rugby playing hero, who at the time hadn't quite found his niche with the sport that he would go on to adore, was surprised to abruptly get called through to the workshop by none other than the shop owner himself, Gee Tee.

"Close the door," insisted a gruff dragon voice from behind a set of tall metallic filing cabinets, "we don't want the world seeing, now do we?"

Slightly flustered, but striding on through anyway, full of false confidence and wanting to impress, the newly graduated nursery ring student put his rucksack down on the table, eager to get on with things.

"Come on, come on now, I don't have all day," urged the voice around the corner, more than a little grumpily.

Not knowing what else to do, Tank headed in that direction, wondering what all the mystery was about. On turning the corner, he got the biggest single shock of his life, right up until this very moment.

There, facing away from him, hands, head and wingtips touching the floor, huge scaly dragon arse high in the air, pointing directly at him, nothing left to the imagination, was the gruff old shopkeeper in whose employ he'd only just started. If he could have burnt his own retinas there and then he would have done, but the only burning done on that day was into his memory... forever!

"Uhhhh..." he started, wondering what the hell was going on, assuming it was part of some first day prank.

If it was, it had already gotten way out of hand.

"What have I already told you?" the shopkeeper voiced from his almost upside down position. "I haven't got all day. Just stick it in and get on with it. What's the problem?"

'Stick it in and get on with it?' Tank could remember thinking, feeling as embarrassed as he ever had across both his time in the domain and on the surface.

"LISTEN!" barked the master mantra maker harshly. "As I've already explained, I'm on a bit of a tight schedule... okay? I just need you to check my prostate doc, like we agreed, and get the hell out of here. I've got some snot nosed newbie starting today, that I'll no doubt have to babysit and spend months breaking in, not something I really want to be doing, but there's nothing else for it. For sure there will be lots of, oh... look at my exam results, and oh look at how I can cast a level four mantra with all the bells and whistles on, well all I can say is... I don't care! If it were up to me, nobody else would be taken on and I would just rehire all those that have already left. But it's not, and I can't. So I'm told I just have to make do. So please doc, just hurry up, stick your finger up there and get this all over with."

To say an awkward silence encompassed the room was a huge understatement, with Gee Tee remaining in his assumed position, whilst Tank's hopes and dreams became crushed beyond recognition.

"Ummmm... I think there's been something of a mix up. I'm not here to... you know, stick my... up your..."

"WHAT?" exclaimed the shopkeeper jumping up to his feet, before turning around to face the newcomer.

Instinctively Tank backed away, the look on the old dragon's face enough to scare anyone.

"If you're not the doc then..."

And with the newly graduated youngster cowering in front of him, the penny finally dropped as to exactly who he was.

"Ahhhh... you're the 'snot nosed newbie' that I had so

much to say about," quipped the master mantra maker chuckling ever so slightly.

Not knowing what to do or say and just wanting to grab his rucksack, run out of the Emporium and never return, it was left to Gee Tee to clear things up.

"Not the most auspicious of starts to the day for either of us," he remarked, wondering where the hell the new doctor he was waiting for had got to. Ironically, just as he thought this, the bell above the entrance to the shop rang, well... it would, wouldn't it?

And that was their first encounter, something that normally made Tank blush just thinking about it, but not today, because right here, right now, zooming through what remained of the dragon domain capital, he'd give anything to go back and be with his friend, even if it meant having his arse shoved in his face.

In spite of the dire situation and his devastating feelings, a small smile crept across Tank's prehistoric jaw line as his tail swished through the air, the breeze brushing the whole of his body, the blazing fires from across the capital reflecting a fierce yellow and orange off his shiny scales, his thoughts still caught up sometime in yesteryear.

Visions swam before his eyes of the time he'd nearly raised what could potentially have been an army of undead Romans with just a misspelt word on a one off mantra instead of creating a protective cloak that would have deflected away any projectile aimed at it. A close call even by the shopkeeper's standards, he'd had the mother of telling offs that day, demoted to just washing mantra brushes and cleaning the workshop for over two weeks his punishment, barely a word said between the two of them over the course of all that time. During all of it though, even the early days which had tended to be worse, he still knew deep down that the master mantra maker, his friend, cared for him and just wanted to pass on everything that he knew. Doing it in his own inimitable fashion was simply a quirk that he had to put up with. And he had, for the most part, getting them both in equal amounts of trouble on occasion.

There was the time they were both working their way through a set of old mantras, wondering whether or not they should keep them or bin them. Employing all the usual safeguards, and having worked through five or six in quick succession, one popped out in Inuit that looked most unusual. Remembering the nervousness he'd never really seen in the shopkeeper before, against HIS better judgment, the old dragon cast it and... a nightmarish vision from hell in the form of an ice salamander dropped into existence from out of nowhere. After successive attacks that eventually split them up, with him out on the shop floor, his partner in crime, the master mantra maker cowering in the workshop, it was only the timely arrival of Peter and Flash that allowed them to defeat the cunning monster and banish it back to where it had come from. That, he remembered, was one of their closest calls, but still he looked back on it with fond memories.

Wheeling high above buildings and columns of raging fire, off in the distance he spotted his destination and hoped that his friend's force had not only taken it completely, but wiped out any sign of resistance in their wake. Dropping sharply momentarily, his huge wings tucked in by his side, he pulled out of the dive, pinwheeled, levelled off and then yanked a slow loop, pointing himself exactly at the entrance to the main Fleet Street building, having been there numerous times running errands for his boss. The very thought of him turned his mind back to their latest adventure, one that might just, had it been enacted as he suspected it had, have saved millions of lives, if not the entire planet.

What was the grumpy old dragon thinking? Working so tirelessly night after night was always going to take its toll, even on a young dragon, something he most definitely wasn't. Thinking the webcam in his bedroom might at least slow him down, he really should have known better, because if any being was ever crafty and cunning enough to get around such a thing, even though he didn't understand the technology, it was of course... Gee Tee, owner of the famed Emporium. And so it proved. Luckily though, he had a partner that not only cared for him, understood how his mind worked and looked out for his welfare, but knew the extent to which he would go in an effort to do the right thing and keep beings safe. And that's why HE was able to sneak in and surprise the old dragon.

Increasing his smile just barely, his watery eyes letting him know he was still on course to land right in front of the main entrance to the Fleet Street building that housed the crystal node, he could remember the exact words that he'd spoken on exiting the shadows, like it was only yesterday.

"And there was me thinking you were fast asleep!"

Watching his friend scatter scraps of paper everywhere and nearly jump out of his skin was slightly mean, but pleasurable nevertheless, with a short, sharp lesson handed out to Gee Tee on how he'd gone about things and more importantly, left him out. Caught red handed in the midst of something highly illegal, he knew that the shopkeeper was glad to finally come clean and to have some company on that very long and tiring night. Splicing mantras together, something so dangerous that it had long since been outlawed, seemed like the perfect way to cement their complicated and delicately balanced relationship. And it had, affirming it in a way nothing else could, the results of which might well have saved the planet from being under Manson and Earth's control, even as we speak. From surprising his friend, to the laminium rivets to the prized golden sheet of parchment, the litany of rainbow colours swirling about upon it like multicoloured rivers all merging at the entrance to the sea, that was one heck of a night and one he would certainly never forget.

Landing with one hell of a bump, having come in much too hard and fast, he didn't really care as he marched stoically through what had been the main entrance where the door hand once been, tattered remnants of its outline littering the outside courtyard. Taking a deliberate decision not to fly, even though the building accommodated such things, he chose instead to run, enhanced by as much of the magic his friend For'son would allow him.

"I need your assistance For'son," he asked, communicating through their telepathic link.

Having stayed purposefully quiet, the enigmatic presence trapped in the extravagant band wasn't sure whether contact now was a good thing or a bad thing, but he would most certainly help out his friend.

"I'm ready."

"Can you guide me to the crystal node?"

There was a pause before the ring answered.

"I can feel it pulsating throughout all the magic here. I'll have no trouble in directing you to it."

"Thanks," said Tank, feeling dejected and lethargic.

"No problem."

"There's one other thing, that I'll need the best of you for," Tank ventured.

"Don't worry... I'll be ready. Whatever we encounter, I'll stop them and get you through to the node, on that you have my word."

Well... that was quite an offer. Unfortunately, that wasn't it.

"It's not that," the rugby playing dragon answered, confident he could reach his destination unharmed. *"But when I ask, please be on hand to assist."*

"I'll certainly try my best," stuttered For'son in reply, wondering what on earth all that was about.

But there was no time to worry, because with his slim little arms pumping by his side, Tank, drawing just some of For'son's extra magic, sprinted off into the depths of the Fleet Street building in an effort to not only find his friend, but to save him as well.

"Shouldn't we do something?" asked DomCon.

"What do you mean?" replied his friend, Jar Man.

"I mean, shouldn't we cover him up or something. It seems odd just to leave him like that."

"Given our situation, it's hard to know what to do with him," chipped in Steel.

"Tank will be here soon," urged Angela. "He'll know what to do."

"That's if he can get here," Sam reflected. "Who knows what they're all dealing with and just what the situation is between here and there? We don't know if he's coming or even when. It might be now. It might not be for days."

Swallowing nervously, Angela went with what felt right.

"He's on his way here, probably breaking every record in the process. I'd bet my life on it."

Good call.

As a speeding blur winged its way around the corner in front of them, the dragons amongst them lit up their magic, ready to fight once again, each thinking that they'd missed another one, all hoping it wouldn't cost them so dearly again. But as the speeding image resolved itself, all four of the humans in a valiant attempt to make things right, jumped between them, knowing that their friend was the new arrival.

"STOP!" ordered Emma, just beating Angela's open mouth to the command.

Magic still out, ready to be used at a moment's notice, the three dragons at least looked less concerned, but still a tad wary.

"This is Tank. He's our friend and the one we told you about. Tell them Tank?"

Storming forward, the young rugby playing dragon didn't have time for all this and just ordered them out of the way.

Complying (after all, what else could they possibly do with a huge prehistoric monster stomping in their direction?) all of the humans positively leapt out of his path.

Taking two steps back each, Steel, Jar Man and DomCon looked on alert, ready to strike if need be. But it soon became obvious that the dragon before them only had eyes for one thing, or should I say... one being. GEE TEE!

Dropping immediately to one knee in front of him, just from his expression the others could see how horrified he was.

"Oh my God!" he exclaimed. "What the hell's happened?"

Before the others could interrupt with any sort of answer, Tank spoke out loud, confusing them all.

"For'son... heal him!"

More of a command than a request, it was unlike the rugby playing dragon to do such a thing. But he was hurt, in pain, with nothing else in the world mattering to him right at the very moment than his friend, the master mantra maker.

Knowing now what Tank expected of him, the ring's consciousness was as conflicted as it had ever been, recognising instantly what was laid out before him. Realising it was a waste of time, but doing it anyway knowing that he would be asked or ordered to, he scanned the huge dragon body that sat slumped back in the chair. Seconds later, he had the confirmation that he did not need, but in fact dreaded. Now all he had to do was tell his partner. Deciding that he and his friend might well need the support of the others all around them, he ignored their mental link and spoke out loud.

"I'm sorry... there's nothing I can do. He's gone!"

"WHAT?" bellowed Tank, bringing his hand up to his face and glaring at the extraordinary piece of jewellery wrapped around his finger.

The others had not a clue what was going on or who or what For'son was, especially when a voice out of nowhere replied to the dragon's question, with the exception perhaps of Jar Man who thought he might have recognised the ring.

"I have scanned him," replied the enigmatic band, "even though I didn't need to. It was obvious to me, and I suspect to you, from the moment you set eyes on him that he was gone. Using Tempus Fugit is a one way journey, something he clearly knew on igniting it."

"And I suspect," added Steel, "that he didn't do it lightly. It must have been the worst of circumstances, but he did at least deal a killer blow to the enemy that did this and in turn saved this," he pointed towards Nurse Conscience with the tip of one wing, "lovely dragon in the process. You should be proud of what he's achieved here today. I very much doubt any other dragon across the world could have pulled this off. He was exceptional."

It was odd, standing in front of the four humans, the three unfamiliar dragons (although something in the back of his mind screamed at him to look at the one that had spoken, the one with the supple and almost new scales) and Gee Tee's deceased body, hearing all about what had been accomplished. None of it mattered, not now, not at all. The only thing of any concern was that his boss was gone, never coming back. At that point, the anguish and sorrow all became too much for Tank to handle and as the tears started to pour from his eyes, he dropped to both knees in front of the chair what remained of the old shopkeeper sat on, and buried his head in the belly of his friend, his mentor, what felt like his... father. Sobbing profusely, arms and hands shaking uncontrollably, the rugby playing dragon had never felt so afraid and alone, even a short time ago when the presence in the ring, For'son, had gone about testing him by withholding his magic and making him feel as isolated as possible. Inconsolable, tears dropping off his prehistoric chin, landing in the middle of Gee Tee's scaled belly, abruptly a magical chain reaction started to happen.

From around the edge of the master mantra maker's bulging stomach, glittering golden particles of magic shimmered into being, sparkling and dazzling, floating in the air unhindered. Assuming something bad, Steel took one step forward looking to pull the youngster back off the shopkeeper's body. But Jar Man, wise beyond his years, intervened, blocking the laminium ball captain, understanding that whatever was happening was something predesigned and destined to take place between the two of them, and certainly not a threat.

With his face buried into his friend and his eyes closed, wringing out the tears, Tank had no idea that anything at all was going on, let alone anything magical. By now, more and more particles had appeared, dozens had turned into hundreds, and then hundreds into thousands, specks of golden dust hanging in the air, perfectly still now, almost as if deciding what to do next. And then as one they moved, achingly slow at first, but getting faster all the time, almost as if the decision had been made. In one burst of golden light, they swarmed all over Tank and, much to his surprise, and those surrounding him, buried their way into him.

"Uhhhhhh..." he cried out.

Steel, figuring his friend had been wrong, leapt forward in an effort to see what he could do, but just as he did so, the rugby playing dragon and Mantra Emporium worker started to glow a bright yellow all over. Again Jar Man pulled Steel back, whispering in his ear as he did so.

"Whatever it is, it's meant to be. Leave well alone. It's not anything bad, I assure you."

Glancing over at his friend, he followed his instructions and stepped back out of the way, letting whatever process was taking place continue.

In one all encompassing bright yellow and orange blast, Tank glowed as if he were on fire, so bright that everyone else there had to close their eyes, and then abruptly, it was gone, all the golden magical particles having drilled their way inside the rugby playing dragon's young, scaly body.

Rising to his feet, tears having stopped, at least appearing outwardly well, Tank brushed himself off, before glancing around at those that were there, taking them all in for the very first time.

"Are you okay?" asked a concerned Steel.

"I am Steel... thank you."

"How do you...?"

"What just happened, it was a message meant for me, from my friend. How, I honestly don't know. I've never heard of such a phenomenon, but one thing's for sure, he liked his surprises. I'm assuming he must have recorded it after he ignited the Tempus Fugit mantra and that it was keyed to my specific DNA. I'm only guessing by the way, but it does seem logical."

"What did he say?" asked DomCon, eager to know.

"A brief explanation of what you've all done, who you are," he said pointing at Steel, one of his all time heroes, "just how much he loved me, my friends and all of you, and some instructions to do with the Mantra Emporium. If it helps, he says he owes you all a great debt, was proud of how valiantly you all fought, especially all four of you," this time he nodded in the direction of the humans, "and that he couldn't think of a better way to leave this mortal coil. His last words though, Steel, were directed at you."

"ME?!" exclaimed the laminium ball captain.

"Yes. He said... good job with the sword."

Steel, Jar Man and DomCon all smiled at that. Clearly their friend had put those words down as Steel was about to decapitate that evil bitch Red and must have watched in some satisfaction as he did so. He died knowing that his death had been avenged by his friends, something that consoled the three of them no end.

Turning away from the dragons and humans, Tank stepped back up to the dragon that he thought of as his father, stretched out his arm and reached into the huge hidden pouch that circled his humungous belly. After a little rummaging around, he pulled out an intricate looking key. As he did so, it started to glow a golden colour, just as those magical molecules had only a short while ago. Smiling, he secreted it inside the hidden pouch around his waist.

"Do you have any news of what's happening elsewhere?" asked Jar Man, eager to know what was going on, but not wanting to interrupt the newcomer's grief.

"I do," he said, and proceeded to tell them all everything

he knew.

40 A MAJOR DISAGREEMENT

Face ravaged by tears, torn up inside at seeing her friend rush off to be with the master mantra maker, the thought of him dying almost too much to handle, her mind turned to everyone there and then settled in on one in particular, and the related unfinished business from earlier.

Knowing that he meant well and had only tried to console her, Richie's anger at the world was back, increased by her worry for Tank, the concern for all her friends, especially right at this moment Gee Tee, and the ache in her false human body after what she'd put it through over the last few days. With all that in mind it was no surprise then that she abruptly shook off George's grip on her shoulder and whirled around to face him, the metaphorical red mist descending right before her eyes.

Surprised at her reaction, George, trying to be the peacemaker in all this, and having put the pieces together as to why his friend had done whatever it was he'd done, took a couple of steps back, familiar with the snarling look on her face.

"Let's do this then!" she sneered. "Where's your friend? Get him over here now!"

'Oh boy,' he thought, 'this is not going to go well. What on earth can I do to defuse the situation?' Suddenly stepping out from behind him, Fredric's huge frame cast one massive elongated shadow over both of them.

"I'm here, child. Exactly what is it you think you're going to teach me, stuck in that mockery of a form? If you were a true dragon like all the rest of us, I might have some respect for what you have to say, but, like that, not so much."

That was never going to calm her down, was it? Quite the opposite in fact.

"You two... just settle down, alright," ordered the king, trying to get a grip on the situation.

Almost imperceptibly, all around them, with the

exception of Yoyo and his young charges who were all mourning Wiz's passing, different factions slipped ever closer to those that they supported, wondering how this had all gone sideways so fast and whether or not they'd have to go up against beings that only a few moments ago had been their allies. Captain Battlehard edged away from Flash, hoping deep down that they wouldn't be on opposite sides. The remainder of the King's Guards became alert, sidling over towards their monarch, offering up their support, much to Fredric's amusement.

Peter, Janice and Hook, already standing beside Richie, stayed where they were, backing her to the hilt. Flash moved in to join them, his eyes firmly locked on Fredric's, wondering what the hell this was all about and just how it could be resolved to everyone's satisfaction. Garrett and the rest of his human contingent casually edged closer to the Cropptech employees, all of them fingering their NGSARs apprehensively.

Polo and her dragons, caught in two minds having pledged their allegiance to Richie back in the Salisbridge market place, were not thrilled about the prospect of standing against their king and so stood perfectly still where they were, desperate to remain neutral.

Fancying his chances totally, given just how much they outweighed their opponents, despite his grandson opposing him, it was then that the smug smile on Fredric's face was wiped away as the last member of Richie's little force floated into place by her side, a cold frost whipping around its blade, the shining metal that made up its terror inducing body looking as formidable as ever... Fu-ts'ang!

While before it might have been possible to take the ragtag bunch of humans and dragons by force if necessary, with the blade joining their ranks, both George and Fredric knew that there was absolutely no chance of that now, not having seen the weapon smith's abilities close up, and knowing the passion and friendship he shared for and with the young human girl, the one that Fredric blamed for all of this trouble.

Given everything that all of them had been through that day, and survived, this was a turnaround of epic proportions, one that nobody could really have seen coming, nobody able to predict how it would end.

With the king in between them both, Richie stalked forward, driving him back, getting as close to Fredric as possible.

"Come on then," she goaded. "Come and have a go if you think you're hard enough!"

Things were very quickly getting out of hand.

"Out of the way, my friend," the founder of the Crimson Guards urged his pal. "She needs to be taught a lesson, one that she won't easily forget."

"A lesson... that's a laugh," mocked the superstar lacrosse player for all to hear. "It's you that needs a lesson... a lesson in manners and how to behave. Most here don't know what you've done. Why don't you 'dragon up' and let them know, and then see if they side with you."

Silence reigned as everybody continued to watch, unable to look away, despite desperately wanting to.

Without warning, fire flickered atop Fredric's fingertips, his magic bursting into life, ready to have a go.

Losing herself in the moment, Richie yanked the king out of the way with one flick of a finger, and enhancing her speed with a little of the magic from the dagger she still had, charged forward, on top of her adversary, Peter's grandfather, in the blink of an eye, knocking his hands out of the way, head butting him straight in the face, a resounding CRACK of epic proportions echoing around the residence, both factions alert and ready to support their leaders.

Crawling to his feet the king wondered what he should do, but by this time things had already gone too far, with his friend bleeding plentifully from his face, his nose once again splattered, already fighting back, applying what looked like deadly force to each one of his swirling, whirling kicks that missed their target by millimetres in some cases, which in some ways let him off the hook, because if he'd hit her she would have fallen, perhaps never to get up again.

Mind ablaze, working overtime, her magical instincts heightened beyond anything that had happened previously, Richie knew without doubt that he was trying to take her down permanently. Unable to understand why the king would let that happen after everything that they'd all been through, these thoughts only reinforced her will and determination to succeed in overpowering Fredric and exposing him for what he was and had tried to do to her friend Janice.

Channelling her anger and sense of righteousness into her fighting, Richie ducked, tumbled and jumped out of the way of his blurred limbs, narrowly avoiding the worst of the assaults, her senses almost able to envisage the strikes before he'd even thrown them. Not even really a decision to make and having already backed off, she blocked two of his precision attacks with her forearms and moved in close, socking him under his chin, rattling his teeth as she did so, before walloping him in his kidney, the look of pain on his face scant reward.

In two minds as to whether she'd done enough or not, the question was answered when brilliant green forked lightning shot out from his fingers, catching her full on in the stomach, causing her to cry out in agonising pain, but not dropping her to the ground as he'd somehow expected. Through watery tears she turned to face him, a snarl of extraordinary proportions etched into her beautiful, pale, freckled face. With everyone around them ready to take sides and fight, the moment had come to decide. It looked like everything they'd been through had been for nothing. What was the point of saving the world, if the world ended up looking like this?

Magic ignited, targets locked, friendships forgotten, all of the heroes had chosen, believing in their cause steadfastly, whether for the king or the impromptu leader who was supposedly The White Dragon. With so much loss of life today already, could the planet really afford for this to happen?

Only a moment away from all hell breaking loose and something happening that there would be no coming back from, one above all others who'd fought as valiantly and courageously as anyone there, without whom they wouldn't have got this far, stepped forward and intervened.

"ENOUGH!" screamed Janice at the top of her voice, determined to be heard.

Hook and Peter nearly jumped out of their skin, having been standing right next to her.

Successful in getting everyone's attention, she marched over and placed herself right between Richie and Fredric, absolutely terrified by the way in which Peter's grandfather looked at her, determined though to get to the bottom of things. There was too much at stake, she knew. Manson and Earth had both escaped, Gee Tee was, as far as they knew, in dire trouble and the world both above and below ground was hurting badly. Whatever this was, it had to be settled and it had to be done quickly.

Supernatural energy fizzing, sparking, arcing and threatening to erupt, and with looks of pure murder on the face of the two main protagonists, the young human bar worker stood amidst it all and instinctively tried to do what was necessary.

"Stop this now!" she ordered, looking around at everyone. "Haven't we all been through enough today? Instead of fighting, we should be celebrating coming out of this alive, mourning our losses, helping those that are hurt, turning our thoughts to rebuilding and if I'm not mistaken, hunting down the escapees, Manson and Earth. Let's put aside our differences and work together. Too much has been lost already. Please... no more."

'That's me put in my place,' thought the king, knowing that it should be him in between the two of them speaking those eloquent words.

"What he did to you was wrong," announced Richie, tiny wisps of dark grey smoke rising up around her head from the lightning inflicted wound that hurt like hell.

"I know, and I thank you for caring enough to do something about it. But you should let it go... it really isn't worth it. Look around... friends and allies taking sides against each other, after the events of today... that's just tragic. Let's move on and deal with more important issues."

A look of murderous thunder ground into his face, the hatred boiling off him was hard to ignore. That said, Fredric, thanks to the young girl's words, assumed that he'd got away with it and that they would all move on. But he hadn't figured on the courage, commitment and passion of those on the other side, including that of his grandson, Peter.

Striding forward to stand next to the being he thought of as his soul mate, Peter stopped, standing face to face with his grandfather, albeit a head or two shorter.

"I want to know what you said, grandfather. And I want to know why," he ventured, surprising everyone there.

With only the sobbing from Yoyo and his group piercing the air, it was tense stuff. Peter's intervention had moved things along considerably.

As the outlier magic users calmed down, dispelling anything that had been ready, not quite relaxing but taking a step back and a breath or two, things really did boil down to those individuals deeply embroiled in all of this... Fredric, George, Janice, Richie and Peter. With none of them willing to back down, it was hard to see where this was going. With exceptional courage already shown by the human bar worker, something that everyone there no matter what side they'd chosen was willing to acknowledge, it looked as though it would take someone else to step up to the plate for things to move on. Following Janice's example, something he should have done before, the one true king of this realm butted in.

"Whatever you've done, my friend, you need to explain

your actions. I can speculate and probably deduce why, but these beings here, they need and deserve to understand your reasons. I think it's time everything was made clear."

Fredric's stony face turned on his one true friend, sporting a look of pure and utter loathing, their reunion now tainted in his eyes. That didn't stop the king from carrying on though.

"Your grandson, the thought of whom you've already admitted to me kept you going through all of those decades of incarceration in Antarctica, his friends, one of whom is almost certainly The White Dragon from that damned prophecy and has led us all to safety, Flash, a braver and more courageous Crimson Guard it would be harder to find, no doubt modelled on you, as well as the humans and all the other beings here today, all deserve to know. They've all risked their lives for you, all had your back during the course of today's events, including the most stunning piece of weaponry I've ever had the pleasure of fighting alongside, and something I've yet to say thank you to," he said, acknowledging the frost enshrouded blade hovering just out of the way.

"As I mentioned before, 'it' is a 'he', Your Majesty," mused Janice, "and has a name... Fu-ts'ang."

"Good to know," said the king. "Good to know. Thank you Fu-ts'ang. You saved my life on a few occasions, and everyone else here I'm sure. I will make certain that history applauds your contribution."

Drifting a little bit closer through the air, the master weapon smith came to a stop.

"I'm not interested in being part of your history. I'm only concerned with protecting my friends and the truth. If it doesn't come out here today, there will be a reckoning, and I can guarantee you that it won't go well for those under your command."

A threat, and to the king as well... looks as though it was back to squeaky bum time.

Ignoring the animosity, hoping it wouldn't spark any sort

of riot, George faced his friend and urged him to come clean, fully understanding just how hard it would be and the toll that it had already taken on him, sure that, once out in the open, redemption might just be a possibility. It was a big ask.

"So, what happens now?" asked DomCon, addressing the sad group of humans and dragons that had been bolstered by the rest of their force from within the confines of Fleet Street itself.

"We have to get back to the king's private residence," declared Tank. "Have you sent a shout out for reinforcements?"

"We have," answered Steel, "but we've had no reply, not that we were necessarily expecting one. We told them to rally outside the council building."

"Makes sense," observed Tank, caught up in his own thoughts.

"What about..." Jar Man asked reluctantly, pointing to the chair and its unmoving occupant, "what about the big dragon?"

"He's coming with us," insisted Tank, making no bones about it. "There's absolutely no way we're leaving him here."

"Agreed!" said Steel, not that there was ever going to be any real debate.

"We'll help carry him," Jar Man said, offering up his and DomCon's services.

"I'd like to as well," observed Steel.

"The four of us can carry his remains as we fly back then," Tank decided. "Perhaps some of you would assent to carry the humans on your back?" he said turning to address the others there.

Immediately he had four volunteers.

"How dangerous is it going to be crossing the city?" a voice from the crowd asked.

Pausing for a moment to think, trying desperately to remember the journey here which was more blurred than anything else, especially given that most of his mind had been elsewhere, he tried to answer the question as best he could.

"The nagas have been neutralised across the world by Gee Tee's actions in conjunction with the crystal node. You all made this possible. How many lives you've saved today, no one can count, but lots, dragons and humans, so that side of the threat to our journey has been greatly decreased. Are there still dark dragons out there wanting revenge? Undoubtedly. But not in great enough force to present a threat to all of us, particularly now that I have this," he held up his right hand and as expected, there was a collective sigh of owwwws, every single one of them recognising the amazing ring that they all normally associated with the ruling monarch.

"So what's the plan then?" Steel enquired.

"We carry Gee Tee's body respectfully back outside. The four of us," he said, indicating himself, Steel, Jar Man and DomCon, "carry him through the air to the plaza outside the council building after which we switch back around and walk him through to the king's private residence. It might take a while as the council building is a poor shadow of its former self, but it is doable, as I've proved by getting here. It will mean all of us doing our part, and making sure the humans amongst us stay safe. You and I know that's what the old fella would have wanted."

To a being, they all nodded, knowing what Tank said was totally and utterly true.

Before they could leave, there was something Tank had to do. Taking two giant steps, he stomped on over to the four humans and leaning down, craning his neck in towards them, he ignored his grief and spoke.

"I'm glad to see that you're still alive. All of us have been thinking about you and hoping that you were safe. Because of what's gone on here, I can't spare the time I wish I could to spend with you. But know this. Gee Tee was proud of all of you, I know, because he told me so. And believe you me, that kind of praise was never forthcoming from the old dragon. So take it as the compliment that it was meant to be. And know as well, that your friends are alive and as safe as they can be... Richie, Hook, Janice and Peter. That's where we're headed now."

About to turn away, it was Angela that said what all of them were thinking.

"We're sorry for your loss. If there's anything we can do..."

"That's very kind of all of you. We need to get him back to the others. After that, we'll see."

With Tank leading the way on foot, Steel, Jar Man, DomCon and the humans falling in behind, with Gee Tee's giant husk of a corpse held up on the shoulder of six of the remaining dragons, carefully they made their way through the debris ridden and corpse strewn tunnels of the building, leaving four of their kind behind to guard the node, promising to send reinforcements at the earliest available opportunity.

Half an hour later, they were outside and ready to take what would be the master mantra maker's final flight. Respectfully swapping over, four dragons, one in particular that meant the world to the old shopkeeper, raised up his body, and as one, leapt into the air.

Heartbreak, sorrow, regret and anger were just some of the myriad of emotions that wrapped around his heart, preventing the outside from getting in, and his insides from getting out. It had been that way for such a long time that he knew little else, even more so during his enforced confinement in Antarctica. Thoughts that he desperately wanted to keep under wraps... no, not so much thoughts as the facts of the matter, ones that he never wanted revealed, bubbled to the surface of his consciousness, ones that he'd wondered for some time whether not his friend knew about. He figured he did, pretty sure that during the time of his illness he'd blurted it all out, with neither one of them saying a word, either confirming or denying what had gone on. Perhaps they should have done, after all, a secret shared is a burden halved.

Studying the timeworn lines that had ravaged his grandfather's face, he found it impossible to imagine everything that the warrior in him had gone through, and that was just the little he knew about him. From gallant knight travelling and fighting alongside George, to founder of the Crimson Guards to being incarcerated in that dreadful place for so long, that toll alone would surely have been excruciating. But that didn't excuse his behaviour now, not in Peter's mind, and never would. An attack on Janice whether because she was human or because THEY were having a relationship, there... he'd said it, well... in his mind anyway, after what she'd done, after what she'd been through on their behalf, was nothing short of inexcusable and not something he would stand for. With Richie at his side, as well as the rest of his friends, now was his time to stand up and be counted, and although more afraid than ever with the king and everybody else looking on, he threw caution to the wind, attempted to batten down his fear and, for the love of his life, attempted to do the right thing.

"You should never have said those things, grandfather," he suggested in a voice much calmer than he actually felt.

"You know little of what you speak, Peter."

"I know the difference between right and wrong, good and bad, all of us and the evil trying to be perpetrated here today."

"Hmmm..." mused the founder of the Crimson Guards, as everybody else looked on.

"What I don't understand is how you can come to our rescue like that, through a hole in space/time, or whatever it was, act so daringly, so selflessly and then... do something like that. For the life of me it makes no actual sense. Of course seeing HER must have hurt. Battling HER must have caused no end of suffering, distress and regret, but to take it out on an innocent, and a human, one that had proved herself a dozen times over in battle, and that's just what you would have witnessed, is nonsensical. I don't understand. They," he spoke, pointing around to everybody else there, no matter whose side they were on, "don't understand, none of us do, apart from our glorious monarch," he said sarcastically, "who seems to know more than he's letting on."

Disappointed with how he was name dropped into events, George decided he had to speak up.

"I'm sorry you think that way, Peter. I'm not entirely sure I know the facts to which you think this all pertains, but even if I did, it's not my story to tell. And so I'll leave it at that."

Ignoring the king's bluster, not for one second taking his eyes off his kin, like a squirrel with a honking great nut just before hibernation, he couldn't let go.

As proud as she'd ever been of her best friend, the lacrosse playing superstar, still leader of this rabble, as far as she was concerned until told otherwise, watched events unfolding, ready to intervene should it become necessary, ready to defend her friends, not so much Peter, more the humans in her care, the ones she'd dragged down here from the Indian restaurant, the ones she felt wholly responsible for.

Thumb hovering nervously over the safety on his NGSAR, Owen, standing next to his boss, Garrett, had no clue what they were talking about, but could tell that his friend, who he now knew to be a dragon in human guise, was cut up about whatever was going on and so in true friend style, was ready to raise his weapon in an effort to protect him if need be, even against powerful, magic wielding dragons. That was how much he meant.

With sweat trickling down the back of his hot, shiny, sticky dome, the temperature in this environment not doing him any favours at all, Garrett found it remarkable with all they'd been through, that it had come down to this, whatever this might be. Some kind of family squabble was all that he could really gather, but he assumed it was much more than that. He would, of course, have Peter's back no matter what, some time since having gauged the measure of the... he nearly said man, but what he meant to say was... being. Whatever... he would have his back.

Secrets that resided on this planet, he knew better than most, were always meant to come out and most likely at a time least desired. It was the way of things and had been for millennia, in his experience anyway. Having seen his share of them across many, many lifetimes, he had little desire to see any more, but he would not shy away from what was happening here, because his friend was in need of his support, perhaps in more ways than one judging by how things were going, and there was just no way that he would let her down, not after all she'd done for him. He hovered close by, between the sly and snarly founder of the Crimson Guards and the delightful human bar worker who he knew he could count on in times of crisis and was proud to call his friend. If things went south, then he would be ready to act against whoever proved a threat, no matter who they were, even the dragon monarch himself should such a thing come to pass.

"I want to know, grandfather, NOW! Tell me why you would do such a thing, to the woman that I... LOVE!"

There it was, he'd said it out loud and be damned. What the others there would say he neither worried nor cared. In the end he knew that his true friends wouldn't think any less of him, in fact they'd probably be proud that he'd finally come out and said it, got it out in the open, no more messing about, with most of them already having more than an inkling about what had been going on. Out of the corner of his eye, he just managed to catch her smile, reassuring, like the sun peeping through the clouds and hitting you on an overcast day.

"Peter, what you've said is absolutely forbidden under dragon lore..." started the king, in an effort to distract from the real issue here, but the young dragon wasn't having any of it. Neither were his friends.

"I think, currently, that's beside the point," suggested Flash, his huge prehistoric face eyeing the king suspiciously.

"I'd have thought you'd have more sense than to comment on a matter like this, Dendrik," mused George, trying to send the ex-Crimson Guard a subtle message, but that only riled him more.

"If you've taught me one thing, Your Majesty, it's that truth and friendship are two of THE most important things in the world, no matter where they lead. Here and now, I KNOW that I'm on the right side of things. I wonder if you can say the same?"

Like the cold from the cutting edge of Fu-ts'ang's blade, that hurt... probably because there was more than a reasonable amount of truth buried in the words.

"I would expect jobs to be hard to come by in this tortured new world turned upside down by what has happened," retorted the king. "Perhaps holding your tongue and sticking with the one you have might serve you well in the future."

Flash smiled at the thinly veiled threat.

"How unbecoming of you, sire. I thought you had more

class than that. I'm good right where I am, thank you very much."

And that exchange had one steadfast dragon caught in the middle of it all, conflicted beyond belief, but determined to do her duty, changing her mind, and against all odds, switching factions for something that she believed, something that she'd been part of, even though it might well mean her downfall.

Not short of the required courage, something that had been on display during the course of today's harrowing events, Captain Battlehard made her decision, and in a surprise to them all, and in some ways to herself also, strode coolly and casually across to Flash, sidling up to him, her intentions clear.

"Captain?" enquired the king.

"I'm sorry, Majesty, but if fighting alongside you today has taught me anything, it's that you have to be true to yourself. I admire, respect and even love you as a person, with the oath I've taken in service to you meaning everything to me. But on this matter, after all that's happened, I'm afraid to say you're wrong. Look at yourself, threatening Flash after everything he's done. You can't tell me for one moment that it's the right thing to do. You know that it isn't. So why do it? You're conflicted and emotionally compromised by your friend there. And I understand that, I really do. But your behaviour is unbecoming of your status and I'm afraid to say, I just can't support you in this sire, even if it means charges being brought against me."

Not giving anything away on his exterior, inside Flash smiled, recognising the courage and passion of the talented captain, as well as the loyalty, dedication to the truth and devotion they both shared. Having already realised she was something special, his heart started beating double time at the thought of what it would mean to be with her.

"This is your doing," said the king, his comments aimed directly towards Richie.

Hackles raised, temper simmering but not quite boiling over, she knew exactly how to respond, having perfected it hundreds of times over. Lolling her head slightly to one side, she gave him the biggest, cheekiest grin she could manage, and in her mind whispered,

'Stick that where the sun don't shine.' While it was nice to get the support of more beings and to have some help in standing up to the king, Peter, well aware they were all going off topic, attempted to get things back on track.

"I want to know... grandfather. And you owe everybody here, after all that they've done for you, an explanation. Spit it out!" the hockey playing dragon demanded.

With the hurt on his grandson's face burning into his very soul, thoughts of unburdening himself bubbled up into his consciousness, the conflict of doing so playing out in his head, much as it had throughout his confinement in that blessed prison for all that time. With all eyes on him, even those of his best friend who, not unsurprisingly, had risked everything to stand up for him, the only conclusion his mind could reach was to tell the truth, however ugly that got.

Huge, fat teardrops plummeted from his eyes, splashing onto his timeworn cheeks, before making their way down towards his chiselled chin, leaving a shimmering trail in their wake for the light in the residence to reflect off. With nobody making a sound and everybody there watching and waiting, he took a long, deep breath, and searched for the words that he needed to bring events to life.

"In the mid 1930's I was based in Europe, given a huge degree of autonomy and loving my life more than ever. I had everything a dragon could want... a beautiful partner and a daughter that had excelled at everything the nursery ring had thrown at her. First in most of her classes, the third in her year to take flight, perfect marks on her human impersonations, a wicked imagination that could lead to magical incarnations of every different sort, the long and the short being that she was a superstar in the making, one that only came along in a nursery ring every generation. We were so proud," his voice shuddered, breaking as he whispered those last few words.

"Graduation led to a flood of offers as to what to do next. Politics, business, espionage, engineering, you name it, somewhere along the line they'd been in contact. But none of it mattered, not at the time, as she'd decided, as was her wont, and like most students of a certain age, to take a year out, enjoy life and figure out what the future had in store.

Loving Europe, with Germany being a particular favourite of mine, we settled in dragon domain Berlin, enjoying the party atmosphere, the deliciously unique food and the welcoming attitude of all of our new neighbours. It was a highlight, that was for sure and after long days at work for me, it made a change to come home to somewhere vibrant and so alive. For a time, we were the happiest dragon family on the planet, with my work turning out to be mundane. The pinnacle was travelling to London once a week to update my leader in person on our ongoing investigations," he observed, glancing over at his friend George, the tears still dutifully flowing.

"Anyhow, one evening I returned home to find both mother and daughter conspiring, in the good way that they do. When I enquired what was going on, my daughter told me that she'd like to take human form and go to the surface. Knowing that she had the experience of past nursery ring field trips to fall back on as well as the talent and ingenuity to pull such a thing off in spades, it did beg the question as to why she should want to. And so I asked. Her reply was simple. She just wanted to explore, get to revel in the culture, take in all the scenery, bask in the pure, bright sunlight, sample the human experience for herself in an attempt to see where her future lay. Not unreasonable at all, I remember thinking, in fact quite the opposite. With both of them as giddy as teenagers, I gave her my blessing, actively encouraging her to travel to the surface across Europe and get to know the different people and cultures better. Whilst it's possible to get a feel for it in the nursery ring, it's always much better to have practical firsthand experience I told her, meaning every last word.

While I tracked across the continent, fulfilling my duties, working in the shadows, returning home later and later of an evening, the apple of my eye spent most of her time above ground, doing exactly as she wished, while her mother studied, cooked and attended to all the dragon crafts that kept her so happy. Separate but together I always liked to think, the three of us almost always catching up late at night. Not ideal you might consider, but we made the best of it. I believe I can safely say that all three of us were content in our own little way," he contemplated, swallowing nervously.

"Some time along the way though, that all changed. I found myself having to travel more, sometimes not coming home for days at a time. Caught up in work, it meant catching up with my family became harder and harder, my focus almost entirely on the job, not realising that anything was amiss at home. I suppose my first clue was after two days of hard graft tailing suspects both dragon and human, I arrived at home just before what would have been in local time, 5am, only to spot my daughter sneaking into our dwelling via an unlatched window at the back of the house."

Sniffling like a snot nosed toddler, wiping his eyes with the back of his arm, the former Antarctic prisoner tried to continue.

"Taking a few days off, when she was there I subtly tried to probe her for information as to what she'd been doing and where she had been going. But she was good and gave little if anything away, her mother always brushing things aside and making excuses for her. What worried me most at this point was her attitude, something that had changed noticeably. Before she would have been polite and respectful, something we'd brought her up to be, but now she'd become secretive, guarded and wilful, thinking nothing of answering back or being rude, almost as if her personality had changed completely."

The wobble in his voice during the retelling of this part of the tale made even his staunchest opponent's heart bleed, the compassion and love for his daughter utterly evident, the sadness compelling.

"And then one day I arrived home unexpectedly, about late afternoon to find my daughter in her human guise, sitting at the table with her mother and another being disguised as a human. Tired from working so hard, I'm the first to admit I was surprised and caught off guard to find an apparent blue eyed boy, supposedly about eighteen years of age, sporting a mop of wispy blonde hair, speaking almost perfect German and English, something that should have rung alarm bells but didn't. Eager not to upset the applecart, and to appease my wife, not wanting any sort of a war between myself and our daughter, I played the doting dad, kind, considerate and generous, never going too far, but just interested enough. Truth be told, I knew something was up there and then. While it was obvious this was no human before us, it didn't feel like your normal run of the mill dragon either, seeming more alien than anything else. If I had to say, looking back on things with everything I've experienced now, I would guess at it having been a naga, but it was long ago in the past, the feelings and memories are hard to pinpoint and get right."

Burying his head in his hands, Fredric had to take a small break to compose himself, the toll that spilling his guts was taking evident to every being there, most feeling sorry for the ancient dragon, but not all.

"Eventually, much later on in the evening, the boy left, my daughter escorting him back to the surface, why... I don't really know, but there was no chance to argue with it, besides, I had much more on my mind. You see, as the afternoon and the evening had worn on, my partner, whose name I don't particularly want to mention, had started to act... strangely! Odd little things had become apparent... shaking hands, forgetfulness, the dropping of glasses and a distinct lack of spatial awareness, clumsily bumping into doors and walls, something that in all the time we'd been together I'd never seen her do once. And my concern didn't end there. By the time we retired that night, she was slurring her words, had a shortness of breath with the occasional cough that sounded as though she was hacking up a lung. So worried that I didn't sleep a wink, I watched over her all night as she tried to get some rest. By the morning, as you can probably guess by now, things had taken several turns for the worse. She could barely see, her speech was hardly understandable and walking, while possible, appeared to cause her the utmost pain. Thinking on my feet, I called in the only person I could, one of the medics attached to the Crimson Guards and somebody I trusted totally."

"Arriving in double quick time, he took one look at her and said what I'd been thinking... that she'd been poisoned, and badly."

Clutching his head, hands and arms starting to shake uncontrollably, Fredric slumped to the ground, arse first, landing with a BUMP. So great was the dragon's apparent pain that Peter wanted nothing more than to go and hug the hell out of him, but before he could, an outstretched arm in the form of his best friend stopped that from happening, Richie wanting to see what would happen next and just how this would play out.

Knowing the next part of this, George bowed his head, sorry for his friend's pain, wishing he could go back in time to the moments that Fredric had been talking about and alter history in a fashion that would see his partner and his daughter's mother live a long and productive life. Alas, that could never be so. What was done was done and would remain that way forever.

"The long and the short of what happened next was that my partner died, within twenty four hours, with my daughter not at her bedside or even knowing," he continued. "Of course I tried to get hold of her telepathically, even had squads of trained Crimson Guards out hunting for her, but much as they tried, and they did, under strict orders from me, they could not find hide nor hair of her. It was only two days later that she appeared back at the property we'd been renting, walking in without a care in the world, when I had to explain what had happened, asking her where she had been. As you might expect given her turnaround in attitude, things... did not go well. In fact, you might say that was something of an understatement. Although she never said as much, it became apparent that she blamed me for her mother's demise, why... I'm not entirely sure. On my part, well... let's just say I didn't do as much as I could have to help the situation. Looking back, I think there and then we stopped being father and daughter, only going on to share a house more out of practicality than anything else. I'd like to say we only became distant, but it was as if our relationship was nonexistent, all of which made my dark and sombre mood spiral out of control. In the aftermath of all that, my training and paranoia got a choke hold on my heart. Convinced that the being she'd invited into our home had something to do with my partner's demise, I ignored all my duties and took to following my daughter wherever she went. Boy, was I in for a surprise, because the first three times I tried to tail her, she evaded me completely on each occasion. It wasn't because of the grief, of that I can assure you. But to be able to do just that to me, with all my training and experience meant only one thing... somebody had schooled her in espionage. The question in my mind was of course the one you're all thinking... WHY?"

Breathing raggedly now, his long unkempt hair sticking firmly to his neck and shoulders, he looked quite a sight, resembling a homeless vagrant rather than one of the most powerful and experienced fighters on the planet. With the exception of perhaps Richie and Fu-ts'ang, most there pitied the dragon veteran for everything he'd gone through. But unfortunately, there was still far more to come.

Having joined hands and said what Yoyo considered to be a sacred prayer, something that not all of the youngsters agreed with, after closing their friend's eyes, and much consoling of each other, the healer and his contingent of young charges turned to see what was going on, all remaining respectfully quiet on seeing the others listening so intently.

"Eventually," Fredric continued, "I got the hang of tracking her, using some unusual magic that she most certainly wouldn't have known about to aid my secretive journeys. What I found out broke my heart in more ways than one. The young man, the one that she'd brought to the house, was a member of quite a famous organisation on the surface of the planet at the time. I say famous, what I probably mean is infamous because you see the group in question was the Hitler Youth."

Everyone there, including Yoyo's unschooled dragons and the humans who clearly weren't as educated as all of their prehistoric counterparts, had heard of the Hitler Youth, a partial paramilitary organisation that started off around 1922, underground (not literally), clandestinely spreading Nazi ideology, indoctrinating teenagers. Starting out with only a few hundred, the movement had over twenty five thousand followers by 1930 and over one hundred and eight thousand two years later.

Sighs and gasps of shock abounded at what the founder of the Crimson Guards had revealed, nobody there, perhaps with the exception of the king, knowing where all this was going.

"Ironic really," reflected Fredric sadly, "because you see, one of my ongoing missions was to monitor and study the Hitler Youth because of unspecified reports of dirty dealings, rogue dragons and magic being used to coerce members into joining. Let's just say that when I found out, I was utterly gobsmacked, more so than at any other point in my life. Anyhow, back to Jurgen, that's the blonde haired, blue eyed boy that had gained the affection of my daughter, and just for the record, what a little bastard he was."

That caught them all off guard, a bolt from the blue for

some of the young dragons and humans, but not for the rest of them.

"Through a series of covert encounters using magical manipulation to hide my true identity, I learnt a lot about him. First off, that he had many women on the go at once and that his relationship with my daughter was more of a mission than anything else. Second, that he had no respect for anyone else, least of all females of any sort and often resorted to violence so as to, as he liked to refer to it, 'keep them in line'. And thirdly, that he reported in to some higher power, something I never could get him to reveal, no matter how hard I tried. And I did! On that subject, I'll say no more, but needless to say, by now, they well and truly had their little hooks firmly into her, making her sing their brainwashing songs and read the associated literature. She was gone... a lost cause, no matter how hard I tried, and once again, yes... like any father in my position, I tried... all to no avail."

It was, so far, a moving tale, on that they could pretty much all agree, with a pattern starting to develop that could very well connect the dots between it, and what he'd so stupidly put Janice through.

"Somehow, and I don't know how, she found out that not only had I been following her, but that I'd... let's just say, had a fair old go at her sweetheart, something that doesn't quite do it justice. Boy did we argue, with me banning her from having anything to do with that particular movement, and her screaming blue murder at me for killing her mother, the reason for which I could never truly figure out. Her mother's death was as much a mystery to me as it was to the Crimson Guards doctors and specialists that were brought in to investigate. Needless to say it all fell apart, with us becoming more estranged over time, with her even going on to try and kill me outright, which in part led to my incarceration in the Antarctic, something that's only recently come to light. And that's what's led us to today, and trying to kill each other on more than one occasion. We're both screwed up by what's happened, one more than the other... who knows? But you've seen how dangerous she is, the destruction and loss of life that's she's caused. If not for the young dragon with George's ring showing up, she'd have taken sickening pleasure in ending your lives and as far as I'm concerned, she deserves to be put down once and for all. As a wise being once told me," he said, glancing across at his friend, "you can choose your friends, but not your family."

Bowing his head, resting it on his exposed knees, sticky, matted hair flowing down either side of his tear stained face, Fredric started to sob openly, shaking as he did so. But he wasn't quite finished.

"So you see, my opinion of dragons having any sort of forbidden relationship with humans or anyone else is somewhat clouded and negatively slanted, given everything that's happened to me. I don't want my grandson suffering the same kind of trauma and heartbreak that I have. Those rules, as far as I'm concerned, were put there for good reason."

Shocked, dismayed and utterly taken aback at what he'd been told, Peter despite the situation, desperately wanted answers to some other questions.

"How did I come about?" he asked. "How did you find out, and what about my father?"

"All good questions, my boy," he sniffed under the gaze of those all around, some with their minds made up about the heroic dragon, others reserving their judgement for the end.

Sitting up straight, wiping away the tears with forefinger and thumb, Peter's grandfather wondered just how to tell the boy dragon what he knew.

Landing as gently as a soft, floating feather drifting back and forth numerous times before deftly settling on the grass, Tank, Steel, Jar Man and DomCon touched down in what would have been total silence, if not for the bubbling pools of brilliant bright lava, wriggling and gurgling, popping and hissing, swirling around as if nothing unusual had taken place, despite the heinous events of the last few days. Tenderly, they lowered the broken and battered body of their friend to the cold cobbled ground of the square overlooked by the gigantic modern buildings, thoughts sombre and respectful as they did so.

Equally quietly, the rest of their squad dropped out of the sky after what had been a short and uneventful flight, with only one incident that had threatened their safety, a trio of dark dragons leaping off a building after them, determined to wreak vengeance on whatever had been done to their slippery naga comrades, taking them out of the fight, before flipping their allegiances right around. But it had been child's play for For'son to act, dismissing them easily from this plane of existence like annoying flies or some other tiny insects.

Looking utterly thrilled from yet another dragon ride, the four humans, Angela, Emma, Sam and Taibul, all dismounted with the grace of a professional horse rider, each softly thanking their individual mounts, all of whom offered nods of appreciation.

With Tank and the others stoically watching from halfway up the steps, six of the other dragons carefully drew Gee Tee's body up, holding him aloft. Satisfied with the care and dignity that had once again been shown, the young rugby playing dragon, with For'son remaining totally silent behind his thoughts, turned and started off towards the main entrance as the others followed in his wake.

Inside it was a mess, more so than when he had left, as far as Tank could remember, but that wasn't much of a surprise given exactly where his mind had been at the time. Unable to recall how he'd gotten out, it had been agreed between the four at the front that they would move cautiously through the building, taking the most direct route to the courtyard that opened up onto the bridge linking the stunning council building to the king's private residence. On the way they would move any rubble, debris and broken fixtures and fittings either physically or with their minds, working in unison to clear a path to their friends.

"I don't know a great deal about your father, but I'll tell you what I do," declared Fredric, having stopped shivering, sounding more like himself. "During the second world war, your mother and her partner, a British fellow, or so we thought at the time, your father, carried out over a number of years, numerous missions for the Nazis. Starting off small, the two of them soon became the next big thing, using their supernatural abilities, that's right, he was a dragon of some sort, to trap and murder allied agents across Europe and maybe even further afield. Using my position, I sent out multiple teams in an attempt to thwart their efforts, with almost all of them failing, most not even coming close."

To nearly all there, those words came as something of a shock, each finding it hard to imagine throwing their lot in with such an evil and corrupt group, incapable of seeing how any dragon could do such a thing. But to three of them, Peter, Richie and of course George, the news came as little surprise, with the paper cutting from the trunk that Fredric had left to Peter swimming immediately into their visions. Scratching the harsh hair that adorned his checks and chin, the founder of the Crimson Guards gathered his thoughts, tried as hard as he could to order them, and continued.

"They committed atrocious crimes over and over again that not only harmed key individuals, heroes of the allied forces, but actually prolonged the war by... I don't know, maybe years. But their efforts didn't go unnoticed and on one occasion, they were both actually captured and detained," he remembered, "but magical forces working in their favour broke them free before I had a chance to get my hands on them. After that particular episode, they disappeared, at least for a while."

It was as he'd feared all along, thought Peter. His parents were not only Nazi sympathisers, but actually working in cahoots with them to try and help them win the war. Not really wanting to know, he wondered if there could be anything more disturbing and brutal about their nature? Crestfallen, he waited for his grandfather to continue.

"Having pulled something of a vanishing act, the squads that I'd engaged to find the pair of them searched fruitlessly for quite some time, occasionally picking up leads, almost always coming away empty handed. This continued for a matter of years, until one day we received a tip off that the pair of them had been spotted in a small town on the southern coast of England in the area above Purbeck Peninsula. Raiding what was thought of as their home, the dragons under my command must have missed their departure by a matter of minutes, their trail once again going cold after that. On a hunch, and it was just that, I myself checked out the records for the nursery ring there. I'm not sure exactly why, it just seemed like the right thing to do. And I found absolutely nothing of interest or anything that would connect them to that place. About to turn away and leave, for some reason it occurred to me to see if my name was mentioned anywhere in their files. Low and behold, they found reference to me with regard to an egg that had been dropped off only a matter of weeks before, handed in by two individuals in the middle of the night, matching the exact descriptions of your mother and father. It made mention of me, specifically ordering that I was not to come near said dragon for the entire duration of its stay in the nursery ring. With the rules on such things being totally black and white, and laid down for very good reason, there was no way that even I with such power, and the ear of the king, could change that decree. Discovering all this broke my heart, but not the will to love, protect and look out for the dragon I subsequently found out was my grandson."

Following his grandfather's lead, Peter slumped to the floor, choosing to sit cross legged and slightly more upright, too tired and emotionally drained to stand any more.

Lost in the tale, eager to hear more, Richie glanced across at the young human bar worker, her friend, wondering what the hell she was making of it all.

"Years passed and with the war over, the dragons under me were assigned to more pressing matters, the two individuals concerned having been all but forgotten about, but not, as you can imagine, by me. Of course they were still wanted individuals, if for nothing else than the crimes they committed throughout the war and for escaping custody, but no one was out there actively searching for them. And then one day we got a tip off, like the one about the coastal town in England, only this time from a dragon that had been, how shall we say... expelled from the domain. Untrustworthy and unreliable, we did at least send a couple of our best to check things out. Surprisingly, what she said turned out to be true and through a total and utter fluke, we once again found ourselves firmly on their trail. Unable to go myself, three squads of Crimson Guards, five in each, were dispatched to bring the couple to justice."

Shaking his head, unable to look up, the founder of that particular group had clearly reached another poignant part of the story, one he looked as though he almost couldn't carry on with.

Remembering being told about this with absolute crystal clarity, the king, head bowed, waited to see if his friend could continue, hoping that once and for all, solace could be found for all those involved.

"To say it didn't go well would be the understatement of the century. All the dragons were lost, and I don't just mean simply killed, but brutally murdered in the worst way possible. It was a bloodbath like none ever witnessed before, or at least that was the report laid bare by the investigators who, acting on all the evidence that they could find, felt that my daughter and her husband had killed all the dragons present, quickly and viciously. But it had come at a cost, because as far as they were concerned, only one being walked away from all that murderous mayhem and chaos."

Looking straight into his grandfather's eyes, Peter said,

"My mother!"

"That's right."

"What about her partner?"

"Well... that's where it all gets a little tricky. They'd got a good idea of what had happened, following the evidence and using all the forensic methods available to us at the time to back track movements and the like. It would seem that to start with the two of them fought together, after which they split up. Why, it was impossible to tell, but the best guess would be that one of them, and they seemed to think it was your father, had been injured and so headed for higher ground. Anyhow, however the battle went down, it appeared as though one of the Crimson Guards, no doubt on his death bed, dragged him over the edge of the cliff, causing the death of both of them. Unfortunately that could never be proven beyond doubt, because while all the dragon bodies, or what was left of them were recovered, the body of your father never was. Dubious DNA samples collected next to, and on, the dragons at the base of the cliff certainly indicated that another being had gone over the edge with them, but without a corpse it was difficult to determine exactly what had happened. An indentation in the stone strewn sand remained next to the unfortunate dragons on the beach, but it was determined that the tide had been right in at least once, potentially washing away the victim. What happened for sure, nobody knows, perhaps not even your mother given the state we believed her to be in after the fight. In hindsight, this might have been the moment of truth that led her further into the darkness, to a point of no return. Losing someone close like that would do it, of that there is little doubt."

Letting out a deep breath, the burden finally shared, more so than he would have liked, it did at least feel as though a weight had been taken off his shoulders.

"And that's it... all there is to know. You're part of probably THE most dysfunctional family that has ever lived. For that youngster, I'm truly sorry."

A tragic tale, but would they all forgive him for what he'd done to Janice? It would all become clear in short order.

Cloaked in her magic, pissed off, angry and scared, the she witch known as Earth, Fredric's daughter and Peter's mother, had hightailed it away from the council building and its surrounding district as fast as possible, eager to rendezvous with her king despite their change in circumstances, knowing that he probably had something else up his sleeve, some other way to make the dragons pay. Whatever it was, she would be part of it, wanting nothing more than to bring what remained of the world down on top of them, especially her father, the being she loathed and despised the most right at this very moment. Interestingly, all thoughts of her son had long since been forgotten, the madness within choosing what to hide and what to retain.

Reaching a locked wooden door at the top of the black metal staircase, of which she'd lost count of the number of floors that she'd climbed but it must have numbered into the hundreds, Earth, panting heavily, stopped to catch her breath momentarily, convinced she wasn't being followed, sure that nobody else knew about this long forgotten exit to the surface. Upset, defeated, desperate for a drink after having inhaled so much of the dirty smoke that now engulfed quite a lot of the domain and missing the serpents from around her head who'd once again disappeared, she wondered exactly where this route would bring her out on the surface, knowing only that she was somewhere south of the river.

Using a custom made mantra that acted like a set of lock picks, her supernatural abilities soon had the door open.

Searching ahead with her magic and finding it clear, she slipped across the threshold and delved into the shadows of the night.

Lewisham was where she'd come out, not far from the centre in fact, somewhere that she was at least vaguely familiar with. Only a few kilometres from the Royal Observatory at Greenwich, it was somewhere she'd plied her illicit trade many times before, something that at least instilled a little hope and confidence in her after the painful defeat that still felt like a series of physical kicks to the gut. Pushing her feelings to one side, focusing on achieving her goal and meeting up with Manson, she knew that to travel above ground, there was one thing she had to do first. Sticking to the dark, concealing her face at all costs, she made for a road that ran along the back of all the high street shops, looking for the rear entrance to one of them in particular. It didn't take her long to find it, and even less time to break in using her unique set of skills.

Superdrug, as the store was known, was one of the few places she knew would have exactly what she needed. And what was that, I hear you ask? Makeup! You see her face as it was would be an instant giveaway to her identity. And having tried over the years almost all the magical spells and mantras that she knew in an effort to remove or disguise the stunningly bright, purple crisscrossing lines that adorned it, all to no effect, the one thing she had been able to master, out of necessity, was the ability to combine a smidgen of her ethereal energy in conjunction with some human cosmetic products to at least create a believable disguise. So, having disabled the alarm, and with just the ambient light from the high street coming through the huge plate glass window to guide her, Earth made her way to the makeup section of the shop, knowing exactly what she would need, determined just to get it and get out.

Filling her pockets with copious amounts of concealer, foundation and primer, totally ignoring the vegan makeup, knowing that it wouldn't coalesce with her magic nearly as well, the last thing she took was a tidy black compact, knowing that she'd need the mirror inside to help apply everything and check that it had worked. Flicking it open in almost virtual darkness, she noticed it came equipped with a battery powered light running around the mirror's circumference, something of a surprise, not at the light itself, but at the humans' ability to add more and more useless crap to everything that they touched. They really were a piss poor race, she thought, determined to make sure they received their comeuppance. Gazing at her reflection and the raised purple lines that stared back at her, an unexpected memory that had been unknowingly suppressed flickered to life behind her eyes.

Momentarily she was back in that German hotel, sitting on the foot of the bed, applying makeup with the help of a damaged old compact, the mirror inside cracked in a couple of places, resembling tiny little spider webs. Just really a fine brush up, it was noticeable then just how much the concealer didn't work without the touch of her magic, almost sliding off the painful purple lines that marred the once beautiful face that her husband had admired so much. Patiently covering every millimetre, after fifteen minutes it was done, and with the help of her supernatural abilities, nothing of the hideous lines showed through, in fact, she looked very much like the younger version of herself, the one that had been so carefree, attentive and loving, before her mother had died. That thought stuck in her head, hard to shake, as she gathered her black leather bag, the one with the pistol secreted inside. Not even bothering to pull it out, because it clearly wouldn't be of any use against her father, she stepped out into the corridor, locked the door behind her and made her way downstairs, sure that it would all be over shortly. It would be, but not in the way she envisaged.

Back in the present, slipping the compact in her pocket with all the makeup that she'd stolen, not bothering to hide her tracks or reset the alarm, Earth headed out into the night to find a secluded spot to apply all her goodies and continue on with the deception.

Simultaneously, grandfather and grandson climbed to their feet amongst the bodies strewn across what was left of the cold, white marble floor. At that exact moment, it was hard to know who needed a hug more, the young dragon that had already been through so much today, perhaps more mentally and emotionally rather than physically, or the Antarctic escapee who'd just bared his soul in front of a group of strangers. In all honesty, it was a coin flip. Unfortunately for both of them, it didn't get that far. With everyone silent and still, absorbing the details, the raw emotion, all trying to understand just how that would affect you, had you suffered through it, movement came from the unlikeliest of sources.

Striding purposefully past her love, Janice, sweat soaked blonde hair gripping her forehead, the muscles across the whole of her body aching like there was no tomorrow, walked straight up to Fredric, purposefully invading his personal space.

Feeling the tension all around, Richie and Fu-ts'ang on guard, ready to act, planning out every move in their minds as to how they might intervene in what could well mean the end of everything that had been forged over the last day or so.

Confused and conflicted, as well as having retreated somewhat into his shell, after plucking up the courage to make his grandfather reveal the truth, all Peter could do was stand and watch, all but powerless to get involved.

A long, intense silence swept across the place as the tortured falsehood of Fredric's body stared stoically into Janice's wide eyed, delicate, gorgeous face. For her part, she gazed back, almost as if getting a glimpse into his cold, dark soul. Seconds turned into something longer, with the time not quite reaching a minute before it occurred. And it was not what any of them expected. In a roll of the dice, and following the kind and caring instincts that had taken her this far in the adventure of her life already, she threw herself at the broken human form that she knew to be a mighty dragon and gripped him for all she was worth.

"I'm not like the beings your daughter got involved with. I swear on my own life, I would never harm your grandson... EVER! And you should know, he's as much part of me, as I am of him," she whispered, hoping that only he could hear her words.

Ha... of course that wasn't true, not with all the enhanced magical senses listening in. With the humans being the only ones that hadn't realised what had been said, with even the master weapon smith taking an interest, he would tell anyone that asked, to make sure nothing bad was happening to his friend, those gathered there waited to see what the response would be from the founder of the Crimson Guards.

Hope barely visible, drowned out through watery eyes, Peter looked on, astounded at how his soul mate had dealt with the predicament, having, like most of the others, heard every word, optimistic that only one outcome would play out.

Tears flowing, Fredric enveloped her in his huge muscled arms, pulling her in tight, burying his head on her slender shoulder as he did so.

"I'm so sorry for what I did. I'm a stupid old dragon and should have known better. Just what little I've seen of you today should have taught me you were different, and not just a little. A more courageous being I don't think I've ever met. My assumptions and prejudices are just that, and should in a just and fair world, not reflect on you or anybody else. And although it's been quite a day for me, as it has for everybody else here, I would never use that as an excuse. I am so sorry, my dear. With everything that's gone on, I feel more than a little thrown. I hope you can find it in your kind heart and forgiving personality to excuse me and let me have another chance. I promise to try and throw off the shackles of the past and embrace this brave new future that no doubt will be defined by you and Peter, and of course everyone else here. What do you say?"

What could she possibly say? There was, of course, only ever going to be one answer.

Pulling his head down towards hers, she kissed him gently on one of his weathered cheeks, ignoring the hairs that threatened to tickle her nostrils.

"Of course, and let me assure you, I meant every word of what I said."

"I know," he replied, "I know."

The vast majority of those watching exhaled, not having even realised that they'd been holding their breaths, each and every one of them finally relaxing their guard, with the chaos, murder, machinations and mayhem of the day all put behind them.

BOOM, a crashing noise came echoing across the residence from inside the council building itself. Instantly ready to fight, to a being they answered the call to arms.

"ASSEMBLE ON ME!" Richie yelled from her mouth and across their minds, wondering what fresh hell could be coming for them now.

They all did just that.

Hood of the dark green sweatshirt that he'd stolen pulled up over his head, sitting on the most uncomfortable bench... well... a metal monstrosity supposedly sculptured to comfortably conform to the human shape, the red beast was the least relaxing thing he'd ever had the displeasure to sit in or on, depending on how you looked at it. But given the early hour, five past four in the morning to be precise, and given he was waiting for the station to open properly and start running trains, he had little choice as to where he could wait, out of the way. Wondering exactly what his next move should be, aware of the agreed rendezvous with his queen... hmmm, that didn't sound quite right, not given the previous day's events, an illicit liaison with her, his lover, friend, confidante... all of those things, it was more the bigger picture that played on his mind at the moment. Could he come back from his failed attempt to take the world? It seemed unlikely, and if it could be done, it would be decades at least before plans could be put in motion, something that didn't improve his ill mood to say the least.

'If not that, then what?' he wondered, darkness clouding his brain, one idea above all others directing his thoughts. And what was that I hear you ask? It went something along the lines of,

'If I can't have it, then neither can you.' Can you guess what he was referring to? That's right... THE PLANET! And unfortunately for every other living being that shared it with him he had a plan, something that involved the stolen laminium currently residing in the Black Forest in Germany and the procured nuclear submarine that lay undetected somewhere off the southern coast of England.

Closing his eyes, pretending to be asleep, hugging his backpack on his lap, well... not exactly *his* backpack, it had actually belonged to one of the three youths that he'd encountered on making it to the surface unscathed, all of whom had attempted to jump him in a bid to do him harm. With the sort of day he'd had, you can imagine just how badly that went for them. After handing them their arses on a plate, and ignoring their disfigured and blood dripping corpses, he rifled through their clothes and belongings, picking up anything that could be of use and/or help to disguise his appearance. If he were to make a successful escape that would be the key, he knew. Shoes, slightly ill fitting jeans and the exceptionally comfortable hooded top, as well as the backpack containing two different phones, money, two debit cards, snacks and drinks as well as a notebook and some pens, accounted for everything stolen. There were a few other items, but they'd gotten soaked in the boys' blood, something he was too tired and cranky to deal with at the moment. So he left with what he had, figuring it would be enough until something else caught his eye. Stepping onto a nearby bus, covering as much of his head as he could, trying to walk as normally as possible given the lack of his missing cane, he knew that right at this very moment, nobody was looking for him... later... maybe, but not right here and right now. Boarding the bus, which felt a bit like Mos Eisley, a hive of scum and villainy at that time of night, he eventually disembarked at London's Victoria railway station and finding somewhere out of the way to sit, vowed to consider his next move very carefully, all of which had led to him ending up here.

Furious, disappointed and absolutely spent, Manson closed his eyes in an effort to get half an hour's sleep before things in and around the station started to get cracking. As he lazily drifted off, his mind pondered all the things he still had to do. Unlock one of those phones so that he could get a message out to not only Germany, but the sub as well. That couldn't be for another eighteen hours he knew, as the damn thing had only prearranged to come up and check comms once every twenty four hours. Angry at that, looking back, it had seemed like the right thing to do at the time. He'd also have to work out where it could pick him up, no mean feat considering its size and exactly what it was. Part of him was tempted to head back to Purbeck and join it in exactly the same way that he'd disembarked, but that presented too many risks, and as well, getting down there from here was not an easy thing at all. Other options included any number of points on the south coast, Portsmouth, Worthing, Hove, Brighton, but none were as perfect as the quaint town of Swanage had been with its enclosed little bay. Knowing that he'd have to make the decision soon, because he'd have to choose exactly what train to get on, with endless possibilities running around his brain, he really couldn't make up his mind. Drifting off now, one other thought occurred to him, a much more worrying one. Briefly, just before he'd left the domain for good, he'd tried to get a feel for, and to contact Red. Surprisingly, when he tried, there was absolutely nothing, no sign or sense at all of her, something he thought really didn't bode well.

Pulling back before placing a strong, comforting hand on her shoulder, the founder of the Crimson Guards looked the young human female full on in the face and said,

"Stay behind me... I'll protect you," before turning to face whatever this new threat was. Something of a turnaround given everything that had already gone on, I think you'll agree.

As magic in all its forms, shapes and colours sprang into life against the backdrop of loud booming noises emanating from the council building, Richie, Peter and Flash beside her, stepped up to face the threat head on, like all the others there with the exception of the humans, who stood behind the dragon ranks, swallowing nervously, all having hoped that by now it was over. Glancing across at the founder of the Crimson Guards, having heard his story and what he'd just said to her friend Janice, Richie pulled out what had once been Aviva's dagger, and with a nod in his direction, threw it straight at him. Catching it one handed, hilt first, he bowed his head in her direction, acknowledging the trust she'd just placed in him. With that, the biggest BOOOOOOOOM of the lot blew out the side of the wall that exited on to the courtyard adjacent to the council building side of the bridge.

Expecting Manson and many more of his goons to have returned or even another hideous giant rock demon... yes, some of them had caught a fleeting glance of the asag before it had been so expertly put down by the fearless Owen, through the dust and the debris of the explosion out strode a sombre looking Tank, followed by a whole host of beings, some of whom they recognised, some of whom they didn't. One thing was for sure though... they all knew the corpse being carried along in their wake by six strong dragons and, as one, their hearts sank.

Virtually unnoticed and not bothered what anyone else there thought of him, the vision of his friend arriving like this became all too much for George, who gently bowed and began sobbing uncontrollably. Although for some time they'd become estranged, having only really relatively recently made up, the present king of the dragon domain regarded the old shopkeeper as one of his best and finest friends, especially given the shenanigans they'd got up to across the centuries. If not for his help, George knew, he'd never have been crowned monarch and would probably have died with not even a footnote in history's tome to mention his existence.

After everything today had held for him, Peter would have sworn that it just couldn't get any worse. How wrong he was. Seeing the master mantra maker's cold, dead form carried on the shoulders of the six dragons felt like a knife twisting in his gut. At that moment, he'd have given anything at all to bring the old dragon back to life... ANYTHING! But there was no way that could ever happen. Locking eyes with his approaching friend, noting the look on his face just trebled the terrible feelings that he felt. A needless waste of the most heroic, knowledgeable and selfless dragon he'd ever met, was all that he could think, and remembering the night just the two of them had messed about in the Emporium workshop drinking the Peruvian mantra ink, reminded him of exactly what he would be missing, reinforcing the fact that there was now a small gap somewhere inside him that could never be filled. Parched and dehydrated, it shouldn't have been possible for him to shed any more tears, but he did, and rightly so.

For one being there you might have thought the sight of the old shopkeeper's huge broken body being carried across the rubble would have been something of a delicious irony, his spirit now captured forever, unable to taste the freedom he'd so valiantly fought for. As someone who'd had the shackles very much put on them by the master mantra maker, captured and held prisoner in his own magical junkyard for all that time, Fu-ts'ang had a perfect right to gloat and feel smug about the demise of the old dragon. But he didn't, not at all, fully aware of the part Gee Tee had played in their compelling victory, even in a sense granting him the freedom he'd longed for by placing him in the hands of the courageous young human, when he didn't have to. Tilting forward on his axis, the master weapon smith bowed out of not only respect, but friendship as well.

Closed eyes still hidden behind those ridiculous plastic glasses made the mighty dragon and somebody she considered a friend look all the more sad, along with the ruffled wavy grey hair that peeked out from behind his neck. Not one to have made friends easily across her short life span, Janice regarded those that she did with a special bond, one not readily broken or given up on. To see one of those that she regarded as such, deceased and carried with so much dignity given the situation, made her shoulders drop and her brave, optimistic heart skip a beat. He'd been the first dragon she'd ever seen, the first she'd been introduced to. As well, he'd given her Fu-ts'ang, although that probably wasn't wholly his choice. And then of course there was the save, at the market place, slowing lots of the fierce enemies down with... now, what did he call it... that's right, some kind of mantra, using up so much magic or energy, or both, in the process that it pretty much knocked him out. As if all of that wasn't enough in itself, there were his words to her about Peter, something that no doubt were meant to inspire and encourage her, something they did, in spades. Bowing her head, in her mind she paid tribute to the old dragon, wishing him well in whatever afterlife he was currently experiencing.

The sight of him like that... carried aloft, his still, bruised, battered and broken body out in the open for all to see, felt very much like she imagined being hit by that hideous rock demon would have felt... only trebled. Not convinced she could take or give any more, the de facto leader of everybody found her legs starting to tremble and shake, threatening to give way, her heart broken, soul firmly crushed at the death of the being that had changed the course of events, stood firmly on her side, supported, respected and even cajoled when necessary. As tears streamed down her face, zigzagging in and out of her cute, brown freckles, the thought of the crafty old shopkeeper dropping to his knees back in the marketplace in Salisbridge flooded her memory. At the time it had been a shock, something she thought of as a spur of the moment reaction. On reflection though, it was anything but, his highly trained, cunning old brain working overtime, forcing the issue with very little chance of any other outcome than the one that he wanted.

'Damn you,' she thought, smiling, knowing that his actions had been warranted and that he'd been right all along, even, and she didn't want to admit this, especially to herself, about The White Dragon part. In one sense she envied her friend, having worked with the erratic and unpredictable genius day in, day out, spending all his time walking amongst the bookshelves of the famed Emporium, tasting ancient and unusual magic, the likes of which might never be seen again. But seeing his face, here and now, the look of utter crushing despair burnt into his features, that envy quickly fluttered off into the ether. With the master mantra maker still on his knees in her mind, bending the issue of leadership to his will, instinctively she did the only thing she could, even though it wasn't especially respectful. She did know though, beyond any doubt, that Gee Tee wouldn't have minded. With the human speed she only usually reserved for the lacrosse pitch, she tore off in the direction of her friend, eyes only for him, wanting nothing more than to throw herself into his gigantic, prehistoric body. Arriving but a moment later, she did just that, Tank gladly catching her as she did so.

Mirroring his pals' dismay at the sight before them, Flash felt like he'd been royally kicked in the teeth at not only the demise of the old shopkeeper who'd managed to keep him alive when nobody else could, including the best of them all, Yoyo, but at Tank's look of utter regret and resignation. For one that had accomplished so much here today, including saving them all and restoring their magic, with of course more than a little help from For'son, the young rugby playing dragon looked broken and lost, a mere speck of the former self that had left here in such a rush on learning the news that his friend had been hurt. Able to sympathise with him, he wondered if there was anything he could do. As those thoughts caught up with him, memories of the master mantra maker came flooding back.

Drifting in and out of consciousness, aware of lots of beings all around him and an unfamiliar dragon with... strange glasses, of all things, looking over him... odd, was the word that he most associated with that experience, the one where he'd negated the poison from the nagas' attack in Antarctica and saved his life at the cost of being stuck in human form for the rest of his days. Briefly, and it had been for about two seconds, a surge of anger directed solely at the shopkeeper had consumed him, but that's all it had been, because it had taken him that long to realise that he'd rather be alive and continue serving his king and the domain stuck in an ape shape, than die and no longer be of any use. After that moment had passed, and recognising the guilt the master mantra maker felt at what had happened, he considered them firm friends. Then there was the night he hooked up with Peter and they travelled up to London to the Emporium. Boy did that get the adrenaline pumping. Entering the shop to nearly be blown away and find that the pair of friends had conjured up some kind of demonic ice salamander queen that they couldn't get rid of was laughable looking back on it, but at the time had been savagely brutal and had nearly cost him his life. How they'd survived, he wasn't sure, but it didn't matter because that evening had just reinforced his friendship and bond with the old dragon, amongst all of them. Finally, a vision of Salisbridge marketplace meandered into view, Tank hanging bloody and broken from the concocted metal gallows, the unconventional rescue brokered and led by the late dragon himself, saving them all with a fancy mantra that had nearly killed him with the mana it had consumed. Of course it had worked, and was the main reason why most of them were standing here now. As big blobs of salty tears splashed to the scorched marble of the floor beneath him, the ex-Crimson Guard found it hard to come to terms with his friend's passing, knowing that it should have been anyone but him, there and then, he would have gladly given his life to save that of the master mantra maker's.

Although not his biggest fan, with them having had almighty arguments and disagreements over the centuries, it upset Fredric more than he would have thought to see Gee Tee's cold corpse arrive on the shoulders of the six strong dragons. After what he'd heard had gone on, it appeared that the shopkeeper had more warrior in him than anyone would have figured. That much he admired, admitting to himself that perhaps his judgment on this matter in the past had been clouded and wrong. Bidding him farewell from deep inside his mind, he wished him a safe journey onwards.

Polo and the dragons under her command, loosely speaking, on seeing the corpse of the old dragon that had done so much to save them all back at the Salisbridge marketplace, immediately dropped to one knee and bowed their heads, all they could really think to do to honour his memory and show the respect that they had for him, given everything he'd done.

Not knowing what was really going on, Garrett and his crew of humans recognised the tragedy playing out before them and just how upset dragons and humans alike appeared to be at the sight of the humungous prehistoric corpse being carried aloft. Unsure of what was appropriate, on seeing their dragon protectors drop to one knee, they immediately followed suit, as it seemed like the right thing to do.

Cold, numb and all but totally broken, reeling from the

death of yet another one of his young dragon charges, Yoyo wouldn't have thought it possible for the grief and loss that he felt to get any worse, but on witnessing the battered and broken body of the master mantra maker raised aloft at the back of a makeshift procession, his insides twisted, almost as if on fire, the pain blossoming out to encompass all of him. It was yet one more devastating blow in a day of them, one that had cost them all dearly. Although he hadn't always seen eye to eye with the old shopkeeper, appalled on their first meeting as to just how fast and loose he was willing to be with Flash's life hanging in the balance, he did recognise the dragon's knowledge of all things magical which was second to none, his selfless actions towards others, which were for the most part hidden by bluster and misdirection and the shared love of the young dragons that surrounded him, something they both had in common. As guilt and grief collided inside him, yet more tears were shed. Watching the others kneel, it only seemed appropriate for him to do the same. Out of respect, his young charges followed suit.

On seeing the old dragon and his plastic glasses, thoughts of the heavy water backpack immediately sprang to mind for Hook, the battle for Salisbridge still fresh in his memories, the wonder at meeting a real dragon now tempered by the consequences of everything they'd all been through. And then, through the ranks of those that followed, a sight for sore eyes made him sprint into action, following Richie's lead. Nodding to Tank in commiseration as he passed, Steel, Jar Man and DomCon making way for him, without thought he grabbed hold of the four human friends who he hadn't seen hide nor hair of since they'd left the Hampton Court nursery ring, what seemed like a lifetime ago.

"Thank God... you're all okay. We've been so worried," he declared.

Throwing themselves at the huge rugby player, it was a relief for all of them to see him fit and well, along of course, with the others.

"We missed you so much," cried Emma, hugging him tightly.

"Good to see you safe, man," added Sam.

"Oh Hook... what an adventure," declared Angela.

"Glad you're okay," ventured Taibul, pleased to see the big rugby player as well as everyone else, including... PETER!

Stepping forward with the authority of his station, wiping away tears with the back of his hand from bloodshot eyes, looking more noble and regal than he had done in days, with a swipe of just one hand George magically cleared the area all around them of bodies and bloodshed, leaving only the blemished and scorched remains of the cold white marble behind. Using just his index finger, he indicated to those who carried Gee Tee's corpse that they should put it down to rest right there in front of them. Slowly and carefully, they did just that.

With everyone gathered around the gigantic prehistoric body of their legendary friend, it came as no surprise that nobody knew what to say. Dragons and humans alike could not find the words to express how they felt, sadness reeling in their tongues, heartache and sorrow keeping their lips firmly closed. Taking responsibility, just as he should, the king acutely, aware of the relationship between the master mantra maker and his former apprentice, approached Tank.

"I'm sorry for your loss, youngster. I know just how much he meant to you."

"Thank you," replied Tank, Richie's arm still clinging hold of his huge dragon form tightly. "I know how fond he was of you, despite how on occasion it might look otherwise. I'm sorry for your loss."

The king nodded, pretty much unable to do anything else.

From underneath her friend's mountain of a dragon body, the distraught lacrosse player scanned the new arrivals, absolutely delighted to see all the friends she'd started out on this adventure with. About to rush over to see them, something utterly impossible caught her attention, and she just couldn't let it go. Releasing her rugby playing best friend, she marched across to those dragons behind him and asked the question more than one being there was thinking.

"It can't be true! I watched you die!" she announced in front of everyone.

Startled out of their reverie, all and sundry turned in her direction, wondering what the hell was happening now.

"It's a long story," whispered the laminium ball captain sombrely, hoping to change the subject at this most unhappiest of times.

"Briefly!" she ordered, still believing herself in charge.

And neither he, nor any other being there, was going to argue with that at the moment.

"Mind and remnants of my physicality pulled from the lava, using magic and the most advanced technology available, a new body grown from a single preserved scale and boom... back in the land of the living with the help of some exquisite medical care. That about covers it!"

"But you are HIM?" she asked, already knowing deep down the truth.

"I am," Steel replied, much to the wonderment of all the dragons there.

"And you fought alongside Gee Tee?"

"We all did," answered the laminium ball captain, sweeping his hand across all those behind and beside him. "He saved all our lives on multiple occasions, especially mine," he remarked, eerily reminded of the torture Red had so harshly inflicted upon him.

"It's a pleasure to meet you, all of you," ventured Richie. "Welcome to what remains of our meagre force. What you've done will go down in legend, be sung about in songs, your names resounding through history."

"But before that all happens," interrupted the king, "there are a few more things that need to be settled first.

Namely capturing that bastard Manson and his despicable queen, the still wanted criminal that goes by the name of... EARTH!"

Having got their attention, and pleased to take it away from The White Dragon herself, the king's moment didn't last nearly as long as he thought it would.

"But first," Tank observed, indicating his mentor and friend, "we honour HIM!"

And nobody there could disagree, well... apart from one.

"Uhhhh... I'm not too sure that now's the appropriate time," suggested George fretfully.

Tank, unable and unwilling to hide his face full of pain, took three steps over to stand in front of the king, and lowering himself so that his prehistoric body and the king's human form were level, told him just how it was going to be.

"During all of this, Gee Tee saved us on at least half a dozen occasions, and those are just the ones I know about. You yourself have already admitted in front of me that you owe him your life. While he could be fussy, stubborn and downright pigheaded, he was as heroic as they come, and sacrificed his life so that the rest of the world could live. I don't care about anything else, but before we go on, we WILL be honouring his memory. Do I make myself clear?"

Practically the whole world gulped as the young, rugby playing, plant and animal loving, wouldn't-harm-a-fly dragon stood there intimidating the king himself, the unseen threat clear from just the tone of his voice.

Struggling to come up with a suitable answer, and more than a little shocked by the mild mannered dragon's brazen reply, George could only really stutter,

"The... the... the bereavement grotto couldn't possibly be ready in time. They need at least five days to get things in order."

With Tank's piercing blue eyes tearing away at his soul, the king didn't know what else to do or say. In the end, it was Captain Battlehard that came to the rescue.

"I'm sure, Majesty, that given the unusual circumstance we all find ourselves in, that those in charge could speed things up, just this once. While we gather intel and await reinforcements in an attempt to rid the rest of the capital of the remaining dark dragons, the grotto could be prepared and made safe, ready for a fitting tribute for a dragon to whom we all owe our lives."

'Wise words indeed from someone so young,' thought Flash, more and more intrigued by the intuitive and inspiring captain.

Glancing around, it took George a moment or two to work out that nobody objected to what was going on, quite the opposite in fact, with all of them, by the look of things, vehemently supporting what was proposed. With no other choice, the king confirmed that's what would be happening, and with more than a little apprehension, sent Captain Battlehard and Flash off to check on the royal bereavement grotto and set events in motion for the mother of all endings.

With that done, George, unofficially back in charge, knew that he had to get things back on track if they were to stand any chance of catching up with Manson and Earth, after they had all paid their final respects to Gee Tee. And so with the exception of Peter, Richie, Tank and the human contingent, who couldn't have helped with it anyway, he had the dragons at his disposal working together to clear the residence of corpses, checking of course that there were no dark dragons hidden among the dead ready to enact mischief of any kind, and using a fond favourite in terms of mantras to reduce the biological waste to absolute zero, they went about clearing up the mess, step by step, body part by body part. After that, he showed them how to repair the marble and make the whole residence as good as new.

Aware that it would boost morale for him to join in and be part of the team, he stepped in beside his friend to do just that whilst enjoying Fredric's company at the same time, but as he did so, the founder of the Crimson Guards turned abruptly and began walking away.

"Where are you going?" shouted the king towards his friend's disappearing visage.

"I've just been summoned... start without me. I'll be back soon."

Excused of duties by the king, Peter, Richie, Tank and all the Salisbridge residents embraced each other in a big huddle, Tank having reverted to his human form now that any immediate danger had passed, in an effort to make his friends from the surface more comfortable. Truth be told though, it wasn't really necessary, not given everything that they'd been through, having now become almost accustomed to seeing and travelling with full-on prehistoric monsters in their natural dragon forms. Of course they were all delighted to see each other with some more shocked than others as to who was there and how they'd arrived.

With Tank, Hook, Sam and Taibul sitting off to one side, quietly consoling each other over the death of the master mantra maker, they watched as Angela and Emma recounted their exploits to Richie, adding huge, extravagant hand movements to enhance their tales, not that they really needed to do so. It was the lull after the storm, the tide retreating after a massive, unexpected wave, quiet introspection for nearly all, ahead of what was to come, something that nobody, not even the monarch, knew.

In the furthest corner of the king's private residence, a gathered group of nagas nursed their wounds and tended to their injured, with no thoughts of anything else, not paying the slightest bit of attention to any of the dragons, something of a complete turnaround given their previous enthrallment. Towering over them all, sharing his magical abilities and energy, the naga king stood out majestically above all others.

Seeing his comrade in arms in charge put most of his fears to rest, although Fredric would be lying if he said that he was totally at ease with the situation. The mere sight of that many nagas after what they'd all been through raised his inner alert level, almost to the point of bringing his magic to bear, but not quite.

Approaching from behind Vasuki, he waited patiently until the king of the nagas had finished sharing some round of magic, eager to know what this was all about.

"My friend, thank you for coming over. I have much to tell you," remarked the king of the nagas.

Confused, Fredric's worn and weathered face contorted into a vague resemblance of itself.

"What's happened to your voice, if you don't mind me asking?"

Smiling, which just looked wrong on a creature that alien, Vasuki put away his needle sharp teeth in an attempt to put his friend at ease.

"My... how would you put it... speech impediment has been cured by one of the others here in thanks for saving her life. It seems things in this regard have moved on a great deal during the course of our incarceration. I fear that everything has changed and that I will no longer be able to keep up."

"There are no doubt, things both of us will have to try and get our heads around. It won't be easy, but then what worthwhile cause ever is?"

"True words spoken by one full of experience... I'm sorry for the loss of your dragon friend. I assume from the look of things that he was a being of standing?"

"To most he was. For me... I barely knew him, but he was a brave and courageous soul and for that he should be commended."

"Too many of those have died here and elsewhere today."

"Agreed."

"I asked you over to tell you that we're leaving," Vasuki whispered, his voice seeming odd without the usual impediment.

"Do you have to go now?"

"We do, I'm afraid my friend. Our race has been decimated by what's happened. I can't be sure how many lives we've lost in total but it's on a scale never witnessed in the history of our kind. Rebuilding might be possible, but I think it's highly likely we won't come back from this. And maybe that's the just thing," said the naga king, sadly.

"Don't talk like that," urged Fredric. "None of this was your fault. Like all of us, you were manipulated by Manson, an expert at such things, specialising in the dark arts of lies and deception as well as unusual magic."

"And we're, I'm told, responsible for some of that as well," fumed Vasuki. "Some of the supernatural things he's capable of stem from my kind. They were forced into sharing spells or mantras as you would call them, magic forbidden from being passed on to strangers, in exchange for supposedly sparing me. Never in my life could I imagine my kind being influenced in such a way as to put the rest of the planet in danger like this. I'm so sorry, my friend, for the dragon world and the humans on the surface."

It was a poor sight for Fredric to see, knowing full well what a brave and honourable creature Vasuki really was, having spent decades in his company as a prisoner, witnessing him on a daily basis unable to be broken, even when constantly tethered to those draining chains, and of course having fought valiantly by his side through the course of their escape and the rest of today's events. Watching him talk like this, seeing just how guilty he felt about what had happened was a crying shame and one the founder of the Crimson Guards wished he could turn around. Unfortunately it looked as though the naga king's mind was fully made up. There would be no reversing that decision.

"Where will you go, if you don't mind me asking?"

"We can transport ourselves in one go, in very much the same way we escaped Antarctica, out of here into the North Sea. After that, I think we'll make for the Arctic and try to regroup. We have outlying posts and settlements there where nobody could ever find us. Back to basics would be the best bet, staying well away from dragons and humans. Whether or not we'll be able to rebuild remains to be seen, but it's something I'm willing to spend the rest of my life trying to oversee."

"A noble cause," added Fredric.

"Indeed."

"So this is really it?"

"It is, but I wanted you to be able to contact me should you ever need our help. If not for you and your friends, the world would now be in the hands of that maniac, I'd be dead, with the rest of my race following shortly behind. That much he told me. Throughout our history, we've always paid our debts and I intend to honour that with you. We have a beacon, located around the equator. If you would open up your mind to me, I'll show you how to access it."

Not in the least bit sceptical or afraid, Peter's grandfather cleared his thoughts, lowered his natural defences, and waited to see what would happen.

Reaching out with one small scaly hand, Vasuki, more than a little drained of magic after everything he'd been through, touched his comrade in arms gently on the forehead, and with only the power of his psyche, showed him in graphic detail where the beacon was, how to access its abilities and the nature of the messages it could send. Done, he removed his hand and watched as his friend slumped forward.

"Do you understand?" asked the king of the nagas.

"I do," replied Fredric.

"Only to be used in emergencies."

"Understood, but I will send word to you with a way to get hold of me should you need to. It will be via the human world, and again should only be used in dire need, but I will need time to set it up, after having been away for so long."

"Good to know. Farewell Fredric. It has been an honour to know you. I only wish it were under better circumstances."

"So do I, Majesty, so do I."

"Perhaps you could do me one last favour?"

"Anything."

"Convey my gratitude to the one they call Flash and the other dragons that rescued us from that prison. They should know that they will always have a special place amongst my kind should they ever need it."

"I will do just that."

"Thank you... so long."

Turning away to face the rest of his kind in various states of distress, Fredric could see that his friend was clearly speaking to them telepathically, no doubt rounding them up before they left. Letting out a long, deep breath, because it had been that sort of day, once again he watched as the king of the nagas weaved his own extraordinary supernatural magic. In the blink of an eye, much quicker than their exit from Antarctica, a raging portal of liquid energy appeared before them, this time full of furious reds and deepest purples. As what remained of his race here dived through head first, the two former prisoners shared a moment, a bond forged of camaraderie and hardship, friendship and a will never to give in. And then it was over, and without another word, Vasuki turned and, just like those before him, dived headfirst through the portal... gone for good. With a mighty WHOOOSHING sound, the magic disappeared.

Looking across at his best friend, he wasn't surprised to see him talking solemnly with the leader of the nagas, Vasuki, who had, as far as he was concerned, performed admirably during the course of the battle. What did surprise George though, along with everyone else there, was a huge portal similar to the one through which their Antarctic rescuers had arrived earlier on that day, opening up, and through which those nagas left alive piled through, including the naga king himself finally, leaving Fredric standing all alone. It felt surreal and in some ways incomplete, especially with Manson and Earth both on the run, but George supposed he couldn't blame them, not after what they'd all been through. Turning his mind back to the task at hand, applying more of his ethereal energy, he vanished more corpses both dark dragon and naga, and with just a hint of satisfaction, returned what was left of the marble beneath them back to how it had originally been.

Through the gore and the bloodshed of what remained of the king's private residence, Yoyo and his young charges, helping out at the king's request had, before getting involved, carried out their own grim task. Splitting off into two groups, with none of them wanting to, under the Australian healer's supervision, they set about moving the twisted dead bodies of their friends, Hillier and Wiz, carefully carrying them over to lie beside the master mantra maker Gee Tee's cadaver. Heartbroken and as cut up as it was possible to be, none of the youngsters had ever experienced bereavement up close, and so had little idea how to deal with it. Yoyo, in his usual knowledgeable way, got them back on track by joining the clean up routine, sure that it wasn't something they wanted to do, but trying, as always, to do what was best by them. Only then did he remember something he should have done as soon as the fighting had stopped. Rushing up to George, he thought it best to ask permission instead of just getting straight on and doing it.

"Yoyo."

"Majesty."

"Something on your mind?"

"I... I... I really need to use the crystal node to get a message out," said the healer as cryptically as possible.

"You know that it's locked down at the moment, used for only the most critical of information."

Crestfallen was how the Australian dragon looked, so much so that it made the king take notice.

"What is it you need, my friend?" George asked sympathetically.

"It's my wife... I need to let her know that I'm safe.

She'll be worried sick. I wouldn't ask, but..."

Stopping him there, George knew that the very least he could do was grant the heroic healer a brief conversation with his... wife, well, that was certainly unusual... a dragon wife; to his knowledge, there weren't many of those about. Sharing with him the access code that Jar Man himself had locked down the crystal node with before heading this way, he did at least ask that he be brief in whatever it was he had to say. With the world still getting back on its feet and shadowy dark forces still at large, there was no telling what they might yet be facing.

Close by, something similar was going on.

Addressing all the humans gathered there with them, Garrett let them know just how much they were being missed and exactly how much distress and anguish they had caused their loved ones.

All forlorn and upset, he assured them he would get a message out at once. All buoyed by that, there was one thing they were keen to do.

"We need to stay for the funeral," observed Emma. "I'm not going back until we've said goodbye to him properly.

In unison, all the others agreed. Wondering exactly why he'd bothered, Garrett shook his head before coming up with something of a compromise.

"What about if I get a message back to all of your loved ones saying that you're all safe and will be back in Salisbridge in the next twenty four hours?"

"You can do that?" asked Taibul, pleased as punch.

"I can, and I'll do it right now, if you'd like me to."

Surrounded by a gaggle of nodding heads, the 'bald eagle' pulled out his phone and dialled a familiar number.

"Mrs Green... it's me, Al," he spoke, calmly into the handset.

"Oh Al, we've all been so worried. Are you okay?"

"I am yes. I'm sorry but I don't have very long. Could you do me a favour please?"

"Of course, anything," she replied, concerned, their

complicated relationship all but coming out over the line during the duration of the short call.

"Could you please get in touch with the relatives of the missing Salisbridge residents and let them know that their loved ones are safe and well and will be back home within the next twenty four hours."

"You've found them! That's brilliant Al... good for you."

"Can you do that for me?" he asked softly.

"Of course, I'll get straight on it."

"Okay... thanks, I've got to go. I'll see you when I get back."

"O... o... o... okay, she stuttered awkwardly.

"I miss you," he added. That brightened up her tone of voice.

"I miss you too."

And then the line went dead.

"Thank you," said Emma, a weight lifted off her mind, knowing that at least her family would know that she was safe.

All the others followed suit, except Angela and Janice who didn't really have anyone to get in touch with. In Janice's case, the person she loved and cared about the most was here with her, in fact, the reason that she'd come on this adventure in the first place... that damn hockey playing dragon.

With dragons placed outside on the steps of the council building, watching and guarding, waiting for any and all reinforcements, those inside finished the cleanup. Six hours later it was done, the king's private residence looking immaculate with not a drop of blood of any colour visible, the shiny white marble with the intricate writing absolutely perfect.

In groups ranging from half a dozen to numbering in their hundreds, the reinforcements answered the call, armed to the teeth, magic raging, desperate to lay down their lives for their king. As thousands gathered inside and out, platoons were formed and under instruction from Captain Battlehard, were dispatched into London to mop up any remaining pockets of dark dragon resistance. The nagas themselves, at least those remaining alive, had already answered their king's call and headed off somewhere into the North Sea.

As numbers swelled, reports came in about events across the planet and just how Manson's coalition of dreaded beasts had tried to cause chaos both above and below ground. What they hadn't counted on though, was the dragon ingenuity and strength of will, with those that had been targeted never giving up... not once, saving dragons and humans alike. Breathtaking stories of selfless heroics were whispered throughout the residence, with the groups of reinforcements all trying to outdo each other with their tales. It was a triumph over adversity and despite the desperate circumstances, something the king was proud to listen to and be a part of.

With so much going on and being organised, carefully the three remaining dragon corpses of Gee Tee, Hillier and Wiz were moved off into the corner below the back staircase that led up to the library. There, Yoyo's young charges sat watching over their fallen comrades while, resting against his former boss's huge belly, Tank contemplated what kind of life remained in store for him. The sad and sorry sight was given a wide berth by all the new arrivals, not knowing what was going on, but sure that it was the right thing to do to stay out of it.

During all of this, word arrived that the royal bereavement grotto would be ready to honour the three fallen warriors in only a matter of hours, news that provoked little reaction one way or the other from the rugby playing dragon.

Sitting halfway up the giant marble dragon steps, watching over their grief stricken friend and the bodies of the dead, Richie and Peter sat either side of Janice, all three wondering what lay in store for them next.

"What's going to happen after the ceremony?" asked the young human bar worker softly, barely able to take her eyes off the master mantra maker's corpse and Tank's soul destroying sadness.

"I don't know, my love," declared Peter.

"I do," announced Richie, attracting the attention of both of her friends.

"You do?" asked Peter surprised. "Has the king spoken to you?"

"He doesn't have to. Whether he likes it or not, I still have a huge say in where we go from here."

"Rich... I'm really not sure that's the case, and I'm pretty certain he doesn't think that way."

"He might not, but as you've already informed sooooo many beings, I'm The White Dragon and like it or not, that carries more than a little weight, what with the prophecy and everything."

"What are you going to suggest they do?" asked Janice politely, interrupting her love's train of thought and negating any kind of argument before it had even started.

"I'm not going to suggest anything... I'm going to tell them. We're going after those two psychopaths whether they like it or not, and we won't stop until this thing is finished. Nothing like this will ever be allowed to happen again."

"And just what do you expect them to say?" Peter asked.

"I'm pretty sure that plans and intelligence gathering are already in motion to find out where they are or might be. Let's face it Peter, I'm not the only one who thinks this way. The king, Flash, your grandfather... they all want this done and over. Only then can the planet be healed and repatriated."

Sitting four giant steps up behind the three friends, the rest of the humans, looking pretty glum, chatted about their adventures, shared stories and looked forward to returning home to see their families on the surface. Garrett and his squad watched over them all like hawks, making sure they were okay, sharing some of the rations they'd brought with them from the surface, determined to keep the youngsters safe until his promise had been fulfilled.

Quiet and introverted, something that in itself would have been unusual, Hook sat silently, listening to the adventures his friends had got up to, feeling their pain and sorrow as they described pyres of dead burning dragons and floors slick with blood, all the time his thoughts elsewhere, mainly on the lacrosse playing dragon that was now permanently stuck, from what he could make out, in human form. Did that make her a human, a dragon, or something in between? He had no idea. What he did know though, was that he wanted to spend more time with her, find out more about her. She intrigued him, she... hmmm, he didn't know what. But his thoughts remained firmly on her and that odd feeling she provoked in him, setting his stomach alight and making his mighty legs wobble uncontrollably. Perhaps sometime down the line, that date they'd talked about might become a reality.

Without warning, from somewhere high up, a dragon touched down on the steps above where Garrett and his squad were sitting. Reaching instinctively for his NGSAR, Owen quickly realised it was one of their prehistoric friends who they'd travelled up from Salisbridge marketplace with.

"Hi," said the 'bald eagle', giving the beast a personable nod.

"Hi yourself," he replied. "Mr Garrett, the king needs to see you at once. If you would like to climb onto my back, I'll take you to him."

"Ughhh... sure," he replied, not knowing what else to do, feeling like he was back at school and being taken to the headmaster's office.

Owen got to his feet to accompany him.

"That won't be necessary," observed the dragon firmly. "It was only Mr Garrett's presence that was requested."

Signalling with his hand for Owen to sit back down,

slowly and very carefully, Cropptech's owner mounted the smiling beast, and in something not totally unfamiliar, hung on tight as it leapt into the air above all the humans, and instead of flapping its wings, it glided gracefully to the far end of the main floor of the private residence, landing adjacent to an exposed doorway that Garrett hadn't noticed before. Lying as flat as it could, the dragon allowed its passenger to gently dismount. On doing so, all Garrett was told was to follow the twisting path and that the king would be waiting. All sounding a bit cryptic for his liking, the human, not wanting to disappoint the dragon leader (well you wouldn't, would you?) marched calmly through the entrance, wondering what the hell was going on.

Everything up until now had been a shock, but this, well this was something else altogether. The room he'd just walked into must have been half the size of a football pitch, a very bright red fabric sofa about the size of a tennis court the centrepiece. Trying to get his head around the sheer scale of things, the experienced human continued to glance about the place, as you'd expect, noting an abundance of human literature on fantastic shelves carved into most of the walls, marvellous works of art, some that he recognised, some that he didn't, huge, gently flapping tapestries that looked antique to say the least, as well as black and white pictures of rock and pop, movie or television celebrities, perfectly framed, all sharing the camera lens with one familiar face... the dragon king, in his human guise... how odd.

"Aaaahhhhh Mr Garrett, there you are. Please, won't you come and join me?" urged the dragon king from near a small human sized desk set back right in the furthest corner of the room.

Blown away by everything here, Garrett marched on over, a journey across one single living room never having taken so long.

"Please, have a seat," offered George.

Garrett sat.

"First of all, I'd like to say thank you for what you and the rest of your group did. It was exceptionally brave and without those actions we might well not be sitting here now. You have my heartfelt thanks and the dragon domain's gratitude."

"Thank you, Majesty," extolled the 'bald eagle'.

"Now, the main reason you're here is that I find myself in something of a predicament and hope that you might be able to help me out."

"I'd be honoured to do so if I can."

"Good, that's... very kind of you." Taking a deep breath, wondering what the hell he was about to get himself into, and aware that the minutes were counting down until they all had to be at the bereavement grotto, George, not one to hold back, got on with it.

One of the first to arrive back at the king's private residence, surrounded by some of those from her home town, having been on holiday visiting her parents in Norway when the crisis broke out, Madeline, the king's private assistant, now in her pink, purple and blue dragon form, looking quite lovely I might add, carried a massive pile of material in a myriad of colours, the stack almost reaching her nose, plodding around to individual dragons, ones that would be attending the bereavement grotto, having raided the king's closet to acquire as many cloaks as she possibly could. Reaching Yoyo's rather solitary looking young dragons, she cheerfully made them look at each offering, filling their minds with wondrous stories of dragons gone by, lighting up their eyes, well, a little anyway, letting them know just what an honour it was to be given passage to the next world via the royal bereavement grotto here in London. Choosing cloaks from an almost impossible number at least took their mind off their fallen comrades, something that Yoyo was grateful for as he looked on, well aware of what Madeline had done.

"YOU WANT TO DO WHAT?" bellowed Garrett, so loudly that at least two dragons poked their heads into the king's living room. Immediately the monarch waved them away, savouring the surprise on the human's face.

"YOU'RE KIDDING, RIGHT?!"

"I know it can't all be done at once, and that a phased approach would almost certainly be better, I just think that now is not only the right time, but the only time. All the events, both on the surface and down here below ground in the dragon domain seem to be guiding us in this direction. Yes... it'll be a shock, and not a small one. But if we don't use what has happened for good, to reunite, to get it all out there, things will go back to the way they were and all of this will be forgotten. And while I admit to being more than a little sceptical, afraid and nervous, I think in this case it would be wise to take one giant step, rip the band aid off, and get things out there. Humans, in my experience, are much smarter and more courageous than they are ever given credit for, as has been proved over the last few days, and much more willing to accept the truth and face the future than most of us like to admit. The more I think about it, the more the dragon inside me tells me it is time. Will you help?"

Richie had already refused a cloak despite being offered one, after all, what the hell was she going to do with it, stuck as she was in human form, almost certainly forever... the damn thing would have wrapped her whole body up twenty times over. If it was a picnic blanket that she wanted, that would have been perfect, and could have accommodated at least two lacrosse teams, including all the officials, and still had room left for a couple of cars. No... no cloak for her, despite wanting one in order to do it properly, but, with all the humans going, Richie knew she wouldn't be alone. She'd just overheard Peter tell the king's private assistant, Madeline her name was, that he'd be going in his human guise to support his friends from the surface and make them feel more comfortable.

With Peter off chatting to Owen, no doubt catching up on everything Cropptech, The White Dragon herself was surprised when her young human friend, the bar worker, wrapped her arms around her shoulders and tenderly asked,

"What will you do when this is all over?"

Smiling, hugging her back, the pair of them having become best buddies during the course of all their exploits together, she considered the question before replying.

"Honestly," she said, puffing out her cheeks, trying to look to the future, "I can't see anything beyond all of this."

"Not at all?"

"Nothing whatsoever, no Cropptech, no lacrosse, no going back to Salisbridge... nothing! It all seems totally alien. Of course I miss all of it, and the friends and teammates that aren't here with me. But I can't think beyond the here and now and that involves taking down Manson and Earth, once and for all."

"Will he let you do that?" Janice asked nervously.

"Who... the king? He'll have little say in the matter, even if I pursue them on my own."

"No," whispered Janice, "I meant Peter. Will he let you do that?"

Smiling, a bright moment in a sea of lacklustre, the young lacrosse playing dragon meant no offence.

"You do know that he can hear you, right?"

"What," replied Janice, "from all the way up there?"

"Yep!"

"Oh!"

"Anyhow, he'll be just fine... won't you?" said Richie really quietly, messing with the both of them.

Glancing down at the pair of them, having turned away from Owen momentarily, Peter fun-lovingly poked out a tongue, causing the two females to giggle hysterically, something this place hadn't seen in some time, which was a marked improvement against the background of angst and sorrow.

"This is an absolutely monstrous step," stated Garrett, attempting to get his head around everything George was proposing. "Is it really doable... to let all of the humans on the planet in on your very well kept secret?"

"I was hoping that we could see together."

"What would the rest of your kind say about such a thing, especially since you've remained hidden for so long?"

"I imagine there would be uproar, but at a time like this they would no doubt rally around their leader. We dragons are after all, if nothing else... pragmatic."

"What would need to happen...? I mean on my part," asked Garrett, getting more and more sucked into the idea presented to him by the king.

"There are dragons in and around the most powerful men and women on earth. It would be relatively straight forward for them to set up a meeting between you and their boss. Of course it wouldn't be everyone, how could it be? I'm talking something along the lines of the G7 at first, perhaps moving on to the G20 somewhere further down the line. After that, maybe some kind of formal announcement to go worldwide, but not any time soon. It would be months before that could happen, and everything would have to be agreed and just right."

"I understand," replied Cropptech's owner, but truthfully he didn't, well... not fully. But he was willing to give it a go and try to broker some kind of deal to bring the dragon race out of the shadows and into the light.

Right then, a loud horn echoed throughout the building, startling each of the humans, the dragons looking very nonplussed about it all.

"It's time to attend the ceremony. What do you say, will you help put it all together?" asked the king, rising from his chair, content with being in his human form.

"The chance to help make history with the most amazing beings I've ever met?" observed Garrett, smiling, his huge hairy moustache doing the hokey cokey all on its own. "I'm in!"

"Great news," added George. "And once it's all done, there'll be no more cloak and dagger stuff and we'll be able to purchase all your laminium above board."

"Hang on," reflected Garrett, stopping the monarch in his tracks. "That's you... you buy all the laminium?"

"Of course," replied the ruler, smiling. "Who else would it be?"

Both shaking their heads, the two of them wandered off in the direction of the bereavement grotto, the king grabbing a huge piece of material that looked as though it were made up of a dozen of the gaudiest Hawaiian shirts ever made, but was in fact the cloak that he intended to wear, Garrett just content to be part of events.

Throughout the residence, those dragons and humans that had played their parts both here and during the encounter at Fleet Street stumbled to their feet, all queuing up before a door that was pretty much unnoticeable, unless of course you were looking for it, underneath and off to one side of the main staircase that flowed regally up to the first floor of the king's private library. With his friends looking on, making sure not only was he alright, but that he was coming along, Tank was the last to get to his feet, his muscles aching from having sat next to his friend, mentor and father figure for so long, his mood not having improved one iota. Together, they joined the end of the queue, with all of them in their own sad way hoping to find some sort of closure. Once they'd disappeared off into the darkness, ornately decorated dragons dropped down from the air above, and very gracefully and respectfully gathered up the three corpses, whisking them back up into the air, disappearing off into who knew where.

Not having the time, knowledge or patience to hack the phones in his procured backpack, Manson decided there and then at the station, on another course of action. Walking towards one unsuspecting female at the end of the platform with her phone to her ear, knowing that the train he needed to board would be arriving in only a matter of moments, with just the turn of his index finger he created a distraction in the form of an almighty BANG two platforms across, and with everyone looking that way, hit the woman who was holding the mobile with a surge of blue and white electricity, catching her full in the stomach, forcing her to double over, sending her phone spinning off through the air as she did so. Catching her body with one arm and the handset with his other hand, the former major, or at least that's how he liked to be known, instantly slipped the electronic device into his pocket while gently laying her body down on the platform, calling out for help, stating that something had happened to her. As people from the huge crowd swarmed in to see if they could assist, knowing that he'd avoided the security cameras, Manson subtly slipped off into the chaos and a few seconds later, when the train he was expecting arrived, slid into the front carriage and, with consummate cheek, pulled the stolen phone from his pocket and set about disabling the password so that he could use it at will. Job done, he slipped it back into his pocket and resting his head back against the seat, waited for the train to depart, having opted to travel towards Ramsgate in Kent rather than towards the more crowded south coast destinations of Southampton or Portsmouth. In some ways it was a pain, because meeting up with his beloved in either of those places would have been much easier. But to get to the sub there, given just how busy Southampton water and the area around the Isle of Wight was, made things extremely difficult. Opting to go further east appeared to be the least worst choice, not ideal, but something he would have to adjust to on the move.

Knowing all that he could do now was wait for the once a day opportunity to contact the submarine's commander, he hoped that his love remembered just how to get in touch with him in time of need. Again, switching their rendezvous point wasn't brilliant, but he did deem it necessary. And then he stopped to wonder for the first time whether or not she made it out of that blessed building and all of the fighting.

'Of course she did,' he thought, berating his mind for its nonsense. She was a warrior... his warrior and would always fight to the very end and could easily outwit those simpleton dragons. Closing his eyes, hoping to get more sleep on the journey, he felt safe to do so because his stop was at the end of the line. With plans and machinations whirling through his mind, he dropped off into a very deep slumber indeed.

In the form of a huge curve, a light coloured rock shaped plinth, jutting out at a jaunty angle some fifty metres in length was reached, feeling more like a reception desk at a fancy new office block. Lit by subtle blue and green lighting, the how of which wasn't really obvious, with those that had never seen it before assuming magic was involved, two elderly, distinguished female dragons with dark blue tattoos depicting star filled galaxies across both cheeks, courteously greeted them with a bow of their heads and warm wide smiles. All the humans were asked to relinquish their weapons, but this really only applied to Garrett's squad who, still armed to the teeth, were reluctant to give up their high tech and valuable NGSARs, even for a short while. It took the intervention of the 'bald eagle' himself to make it happen, and even then the humans involved felt less than happy.

Moving along in single file, for that's really all there was room for in the tight fitting corridor, dragon wise anyway, the humans still able to walk side by side, every single being there, on reaching the end of the plinth, came across an array of huge glass horns laid out across a massive, black as night cloth. Encouraged to take a horn each by yet another graceful, elderly female dragon, again bearing similar tattoos to the others on either scaled cheek, it was only when the first of the human contingent arrived, Sam in fact, that a much smaller and reasonably sized horn was found for him. Mirroring the much larger, dragon sized variety, the glass had clearly been fashioned in much the same shape with the same adornments in gold leaf, having been created in only a matter of hours, one of the many reasons for the delay in proceedings. Picking it up as cautiously as possible, with it looking impossibly delicate, the young human turned it around in his hands trying to make out the intricate depictions that graced its circumference.

"If you're wondering, it depicts the signing of the prophecy, one of the most historically important events in the history of our kind. If you look closely you can just make out the Basilisks, the Hydra Queen herself, the Manticores and the Heretics of Antar."

Taken aback and more than a little confused, the only real thing Sam could appreciate was the work that had gone into making it, the characters glistening in the blue and green light almost seeming to move on the backdrop of crystal glass which although feeling strong, appeared almost wafer thin. Sure to hold it in two hands, the young sportsman shuffled on after the dragon in front of him, wondering how he'd know when to use the aforementioned item. It would soon become obvious.

Before he could move on, the female dragon cleared her throat, making sure she had the attention of all of them, which of course she did, before announcing,

"All of you in your human forms, even the dragons amongst you, need to stay in the seats behind the transparent shielding. This has been specially provided to protect you from the intense heat given off. If you do not follow the instructions you will suffer catastrophic burns. Please take heed."

Nervously, and rather pale faced, they all nodded their agreement to the sweet talking dragon.

Following on at the back, making sure that Tank was coping, showing him their support in his time of need, Peter and Richie each chose a glass horn, nodding to the dragon handing them out as they did so, before walking ever forward into the darkness.

Clearly these moments are always destined to be sad and filled with grief, how much probably depends on who the departed was and just what your relationship to them is. And so although mournful, every single being at that ceremony should have recognised what an honour it was to take part in a rite held in those surroundings. Normally only reserved for the reigning monarch, and only ever used in respect of the incumbent royal family, in its history, this tiny little hidden enclave had been used thirty-two times, for twenty four kings, the remainder their direct relatives. Those invited were nearly always council figures and relatives of the deceased, so not only was it the first time ever that humans had set foot in here, but also for dragons outside the council and the royal bloodline. Rules were being broken across the board during this latest skirmish, something that was likely to continue if George's plan to announce themselves to the humans proved fruitful.

Turning a sharp corner, only visible because of the blue and green lighting playing out across the raggedy cracks of the dark wall in front of them, on doing so, it was like pulling away a dark curtain to reveal a magnificent light show, which in this case was made up of the roiling, boiling, orange, red and yellow swirling lava, constantly moving below them in an ever shifting lake of molten magma that provoked different reactions for all of them.

For Steel, it screamed two words at him... LAMINIUM BALL! Since all this had started, it was the first chance that he'd really had to miss his sport, all of his friends and teammates. The intoxicating, quite deadly mass of writhing molten liquid gave him a sense of being, made him feel stronger, invincible, like he was born to be part of it. Visions of knocking down 'teeth', tormenting the opponent's mouth guard, intercepting the laminium ball, having his abilities enhanced even further, sent shivers up his spine. Abruptly his thoughts turned to his teammates, wondering whether they'd managed to stay safe through all of this and if they knew that he were still alive. Boy... were they in for a surprise if they didn't, he thought, sitting down in the seat he'd arrived at, his huge, powerful tail slipping snugly through the specially designated hole in the back of it.

On entering the light, memories of the last time he'd been here all those decades ago to mourn the loss of the daughter of the reigning monarch of the age caught up with him, making him once again reflect on all his time imprisoned in Antarctica. About to spiral off into that dark place again, he was saved by something so straightforward and ordinary that it nearly made him smile... the astronomical heat that assaulted his throat and hammered his scales, something that took a few moments to adjust to, but once done, felt like heaven personified. Dragons absolutely adore heat and none more so than this one, here and now, especially after all his time confined in the cold. Closing his eyes, lost in the ecstasy of it all, his mind said his last goodbyes to the shopkeeper.

Jar Man and DomCon proceeded respectfully along until they reached their seats, after which they sat down, honoured to be there, absolutely exhausted by everything that had gone on. And although having only known the old shopkeeper for an exceptionally short time, both felt like they'd been firm friends with him and that they owed him their lives, something they were determined to thank him for during the course of this ceremony.

The cadre of King's Guards that had been a constant throughout the battle made their way in, tired, bleary eyed, run ragged after all the recent events, including, for them, having convinced all the mythical creatures to willingly go back inside their cells, after of course they'd been fully repaired. No mean feat, even with For'son's help in not only powering the magical environments, but promising them the newly agreed rules would be obeyed to the letter. A tough day to say the least, but any further tragedy and many more deaths avoided.

George plodded behind all the others, having transformed back into his dragon form on the way in, knowing that tradition needed him to do so, despite the fact that he'd rather maintain his usual human charade. Following some of the King's Guard that had fought valiantly in front of him, well... for a short while, without too much warning, he disappeared off down a neatly concealed set of steps towards the lava floor itself when about half way along, no doubt something to do with the details of the thing. But two beings there did notice, both of whom were following in his wake: Captain Battlehard and Flash.

Similarly quiet, both fierce dragon warriors had their minds on the state of the intelligence gathering going on somewhere above them in the king's private library, both to some degree or other shielding not only their thoughts but emotions as well, knowing that nothing good could come of them breaking down, not with so much work to be done, with Earth and the deadly Manson still to be rounded up.

Following their leader and mentor, Yoyo, the sad and grief stricken young dragons, all holding their glass horns, scuttled into the royal bereavement grotto with about as much enthusiasm as a chicken crossing a KFC car park. Occasionally holding one another's hands for support, they took their seats alongside the Australian healer who was still having difficulty coming to terms with what had happened.

Although he'd managed to guide his body here, somewhere so renowned, he thought he'd never see the inside, it had been pretty much on auto pilot, his legs doing the walking, his brain, and more importantly, thoughts, somewhere far, far away, the gist of his thinking something along the lines of...

'Why on earth did I get them involved? They were barely old enough to graduate from the nursery ring, had such a thing been available to them. If only I'd done something different...' It was tragic, not only what had happened, but his thinking as well, because part of his mindset locked away somewhere in that fantastic head of his certainly knew that if he hadn't got them involved, then without doubt the world would be lost, every dragon here would be dead, the humans and surviving dragons would be enslaved, all of which there would be no coming back from... EVER! But because of the missing holes where Wiz and Hillier used to fill his heart, his mood and his mind were gripped by shadows, the kind that only time would be able to heal. Glancing across at his remaining charges, he offered up the best smile he could, and doing his best to hold back the tears, stared straight out ahead into the bubbling cauldron of sizzling hot lava.

Leaving the first five seats behind the heat resistant transparent shields free as he'd been asked to do, Garrett dropped into the next one, transfixed by the movement of the molten magma lake before him, looking like a cross between a river and a violent sink hole, as well as the sheer volume, the resounding noise was just monumental. Wiping his shiny forehead, the sweat continually building, he wondered what it must be like to experience the heat without the dragons' thoughtful protection.

Sidling in next to Garrett, Angela, Sam, Emma, Taibul, followed closely by Owen, Caren and the rest of their squad all took their seats before watching the others come past, the last the oddest of them all.

Richie, followed by Tank, Peter, Janice, Hook and then with the air changing from hot to ice cold being the giveaway, Fu-ts'ang, they all strode purposefully in, remaining in that order across the five seats that Garrett had left free, the master weapon smith in his chilly fear inspiring form choosing to rest upright, gently between Janice and Hook, keen to pay his respects also.

In front of the constantly moving orange, red and yellow eddies and whirlpools, Richie and Peter both grabbed one of their friend's hands, holding on just tight enough to show him their support, and the love for the master mantra maker that they'd come to know over the last few years. Staying totally silent, experiencing every ounce of pain his partner currently felt, For'son had been here enough times that he knew what would happen off by heart, always vowing never to return. For the most part though, he had little choice about the matter. Some of the kings throughout the ages he'd liked and had gone on to be friends with. Most... he didn't get on with, something that neither mattered that much or bothered him. The being whose hand he currently sat on felt like more of a friend than all of them. There and then, he would have done anything to take away the pain he was feeling. Unfortunately, even his powerful magic couldn't do that.

Without any warning, the lights that most hadn't realised had even been on in the ceiling above the lake of lava and in and around the seating area, all flickered out, leaving the molten magma itself as the only illumination. A beautiful spectacle in its own right, it was only a shame that death tainted the moment. From off to one side, movement of a darker kind captured everyone's attention, as the female dragon that had handed out the glass horns they all held, came hovering across the lake from some unseen position, a plain old rock her chariot, splurges of thick, gloopy molten orange liquid trying to capture it as it passed. Reaching a point in the middle of the seated crowd, directly out in front of them, the elegant female dragon stood tall, and announced,

"Please be upstanding for the current incumbent monarch of the dragon domain."

As one the crowd stood, Tank a little slower than everyone else at getting to his feet. Even Fu-ts'ang moved forward, becoming more upright.

As the female dragon was whisked back off in the

direction from which she'd arrived, George appeared on another one of the hovering rocks, feet apart, wings spread wide, sucking up the heat, letting it enhance and invigorate him.

With the exception of the bubbling and effervescing brightly coloured lava not a sound was heard, all of them waiting for him to speak, most wondering just how this goes.

Having deliberately made them wait, hoping to focus their minds on contemplating the very reason they were here, taking a deep breath, enjoying the searing heat licking at his throat, the king began.

"For most other bereavement grottos across the planet, it isn't customary for someone to speak. In this one it is, and I'm afraid you're stuck with me."

Trying to lighten the mood, he soon realised just what a tough crowd he was dealing with.

"Normally," he said, continuing on, "this sacred place would be reserved for royalty and members of the dragon council, but not today, and rightly so. You may all now be seated."

As one, the crowd returned, with the exception of Futs'ang who remained unmoved, the chilly white frost still circling his blade in total contrast to the brilliant red sea of lava out in front of them.

"In these troubling times, it's difficult to know where to start," suggested the king, "but I will do my best to express my feelings for those we've lost. Hopefully that will stir up the memories inside each of you which best reflect your feelings towards those we're here to honour."

Without warning, it started in the pit of his stomach, an unavoidable reaction to previous events, brought on by what was happening here and now. Rallying against it did no good either, his defences torn apart by the wave of love and compassion he felt for the friend who was like a father to him. As tears flowed freely from his eyes, all he could do was lower his head and squeeze his friends' hands tighter, wishing it would all go away.

Caught up in their own little worlds, only when the pressure increased on their hands did they notice the trouble their friend was in, recognising his pain instantly, afraid and unaware of what to do to quell it.

Caught up in her own swell of grief, Janice glanced over at Peter for some support, only to find his head turned towards Tank, a steady flow of teardrops raging from his eyes, the rugby playing dragon's sadness and hurt visible for all to see. Only then did the young human bar worker wonder what it would be like to love someone that much.

Struggling to find the words, as he knew he would do, dealing with the death of his friend more than a little upsetting, the king, as was his wont, pushed through for the sake of others, particularly Tank and Yoyo.

"Hillier and Wiz, I'm afraid I didn't know," declared the king "not until they burst through that supernatural wormhole and saved not only all of us, but the planet itself. Brave, fearless, selfless, inventive and loved by all those around them, in essence they were my kind of dragons. I understand that Hillier was always up to mischief, the class clown if you like, making everyone laugh and smile, something that can go a long way in a tight knit group. As for Wiz, a more gentle soul, I'm told, it would be hard to find. With a love of growing plants and reading, she was constantly there for her friends and always the first to stand up for what was right. They will both be sorely missed, by all of us, but we will carry them in our hearts for as long as we live. Truer heroes it would be impossible to know. However, a piece of them will live on in this the most sacred of places, next to royalty, prestige and power, sharing the importance of our ancestors, basking in not only their own glory but that of those that have preceded them, and might I say, it's only fitting that they should."

As you can imagine, by now, Yoyo resembled Tank, tears flowing freely, as did all of the other young dragons under the Australian healer's command, proud at what their friends had achieved and just how they'd given their lives. It was perhaps the perfect place for them both to end up.

"Please," urged the king, "bring out their bodies."

Dropping down through a concealed hole in the centre of the ceiling, two ornately decorated male dragons, each holding on to one of Wiz's arms hovered to a halt some thirty or so metres above the boiling and popping lava, edging just off to one side to make room. Seconds later, the same thing happened, with three more dragons appearing, only this time the body in the middle being held by either arm was Hillier's looking stone cold serious. There they hovered for another thirty seconds or so, giving their friends one last chance to say goodbye. And that's what they did, in their minds, wishing them a safe and speedy journey to whatever destination their life forces had chosen.

"Please remove that which will serve as a reminder to their bravery, honesty and integrity," ordered George, still facing the audience.

Each of the dragons on the left hand side of the departed reached in around their hidden belly pouches, and simultaneously pulled out a pair of diamond edged cutters, the ancient design of the tools making them look a little like secateurs from an old garden shed. Stretching around to the back of the neck for each of their particular corpses, in one swift move, the largest of the scales there was cut off and caught in an outstretched palm. Leaving the dead bodies held in place by just one of their kind, the scale snippers turned around and sedately flew across to a wall above a series of rocks that poked their heads out above the lava, seemingly immune from its devastating effects. Concentrating, each of the dragons put their particular scale against the wall, and chanting something that nobody there could understand, let go of it. In a blur of blue and red shimmering light, the scales merged with the rocks, something the entire audience could now see had happened all around, now that they knew what they were looking for. That, however, wasn't the only surprise. Right in front of where the scales had been placed, a magical hologram flickered into life, producing a real life representation of each of the dragons, a perfect replica in every last detail. Not only was it eye wateringly cool, but a stunning tribute, one that could and should last for all eternity and something that had utterly amazed all those looking on, pleasing Yoyo and their friends beyond belief. Watching the audience look on in utter fascination and with both the dragons having returned to their cadavers, with a flick of his fingers, George gave the command.

Moving off slowly to start with, the two groups of three, Wiz and Hillier secured in the middle of each, started to circle the lake of lava, not quickly, but not slowly either.

Right at that very moment, Peter had a flashback to the bereavement grotto at Honister Pass Boulders in Cumbria when he'd attended Mark Hiscock's ceremony, the sad loss of yet another of Manson's victims threatening to overcome him. Bravely, he fought it off.

With none of them there able to take their eyes off the moving assortment of dragons, the audience's mouths for the most part hung wide open, until after the third pass, after which all six dragons returned to the middle of the chamber. What happened next was inevitable.

Without any fuss or further ado, both sets of dragons that had been holding their corpses in the air let go, and like lead balloons, what remained of both beings dropped unceremoniously into the lava, causing two almighty splashes that sent brightly coloured molten magma spraying up all the walls. With two sharp gurgles, both prehistoric bodies disappeared beneath the lava, returning back to whence they had come. Upsetting for some watching, a relief for others, the conclusion of it all finally hit home.

Breathing heavily now due to the heat, fumes and his age, the king, focusing his thoughts on what he had to do, ignoring the desperate need he felt to get back to searching for the wicked creatures, Manson and Earth, swallowed nervously, hoping nobody would notice and set about doing his friend justice.

Thoughts of what they'd just seen burnt into their minds forever, it was only when the king started to speak that they give him their full and undivided attention.

"It would seem evil's work is never done, with it being time to induct yet one more dragon into the ranks of the self-sacrificing, brave, courageous and noble beings that already line these walls," bounced the king's voice off the rocky sides of the secluded chamber.

Sad at the death of two of the beings that had appeared out of nowhere to save them, humans and dragons alike felt as though their hearts had dropped from a thousand kilometres up, crashing with a force like nothing else into a body of water, crushing all their organs, especially their hearts, making them feel as though every atom of their being was on fire. Having forged all sorts of friendships across his long and brilliant life, the remnants of the fire that had been used by the shopkeeper to do so, now burned scorching hot, out of control, searing and scalding all those on the other end of the flames, causing them no end of pain and sorrow.

"Where can I start with the master mantra maker?" the king mused, looking as though his thoughts were somewhere else. "We've known each other for centuries, due to a chance meeting in a tavern somewhere in the middle of nowhere. Having caught him in the grumpiest of moods, yes, I know, whenever was it any different? Anyhow we went at each other hammer and tongs, both of us unable to admit to the other that we loved every second of it. Soon after that initial meeting, we became firm friends. After that, well... I would pop round to the Emporium on a weekly basis, pretending I needed something or other, when in fact all I wanted was a chat and to spend some time in his company."

A familiar feeling resonated within Peter, recalling many of the trips to see the master mantra maker for exactly the same reason, which elicited the very first tears from him,

Tank by now sobbing like a lost baby, barely able to hear the king's words.

"Eventually we became best friends," George continued, "with me hanging out all the time at the Emporium, and Gee Tee providing me with more and more useful mantras for the dangerous work I found myself caught up in. It was a match made in heaven, that is until, politically, things got a little too hot, and I suppose if you like, he... got burned. Not deliberately on my part, but he got offended and I suppose I could have handled things better, with the long and the short being we became distant, estranged even."

As he had on opening up the ceremony, the king let the silence linger for effect, hoping those there might take note and remember his tale for the future, avoiding the same sad consequences.

"Recently," he started up again, "our friendship reignited, due in no small part to some of you here today. For that I'm exceedingly grateful. Just to have another chance was both rewarding and cathartic, something that to me anyway, means a lot, despite his sometimes odd and chaotic behaviour. That aside, he was always my hero. I can't tell you the number of times he saved my life. I was thinking about it earlier, trying to put a casual estimate on it. My best guess concluded that it was anything between nineteen and thirty times that he'd genuinely saved my life. If you included all the half hearted attempts that he prevented, it was easily the other side of fifty... I mean fifty, what the hell?"

The words they heard, well... kind of. They fluttered about on the baking hot breeze, whispers on the wind, there but not, some of them offering up meaning, others just a vague distraction off in the distance somewhere, all of which applied to almost all of the friends, Tank, Peter, Richie, Janice, Hook and the rest of them. And although the king meant well, the meaning of what he said seemed to get a little lost in translation.

"But now I suppose we should turn our attention to

more recent events," George continued, his heart broken inside at the loss of his friend, barely able to get the words out, seeing with his own two eyes just how distraught all the others up on the balcony were, part of him determined to put a rush on the rest of it in a fruitless attempt to curtail all their sorrow and suffering.

"While I don't perhaps know every detail of everything that he did, I do know enough, enough to know that without him, our exploits over the last few days were doomed to fail, with the lives of so many faltering. The rescue attempt at Salisbridge, in conjunction with our fearless human friends, only succeeded due to his input and his magic. Without that, Flash wouldn't have been able to get to Antarctica and save the prisoners there, which in turn would have led to no dramatic rescue for us via the magical wormhole. I'm pretty sure all of you don't need me to spell out what that would have meant. And that's before we even get on to his spell in charge of infiltrating Fleet Street, a Herculean effort that was accomplished exceptionally well and, on its own, might well have saved the planet. The long and the short of it is, probably every being in the world currently owes him their life. I don't think I can put it any more bluntly or pay any more importance to his death than that. What a dragon, what a being, what a friend. He will always be sorely missed from my life, and I know you all feel the same," snuffled the king, tears now plummeting from his eyes, hissing violently as they dropped towards the lava.

Without having to say anything else, just a tiny gesture with his right index finger, every being there in the audience looked to the ceiling, in the direction of the concealed entrance they now knew to exist. Sure enough, flanked by two hulking great dragons, both bejewelled to the hilt in gold and silver, Gee Tee's body slowly revealed itself, stopping some thirty or so metres above the bubbling and steaming lake of scorching hot boiling lava.

"NO!" Tank sobbed, overcome with emotion, not

wanting it to be so, the finality of it all just too much. Jumping out of their chairs, his two best friends embraced him for all they were worth, trying to suck all the pain out of him, not that such a thing were possible, even for them.

Hearing the poor boy's cries, recognising them for what they were, George struggled to compose himself, needing everything he had just to push forward. Not daring to stop for even a moment, fearing that he'd be unable to go on, telepathically he gave the dragon to Gee Tee's left the order, and let him do his thing.

Producing an identical set of diamond edged cutters, he reached around and in one quick and precise SNIP, the largest scale of the lot came away, expertly caught as it did so. Leaving the master mantra maker's huge frame in the capable hands of his colleague, the dragon that had taken the scale glided on over to part of the rocky wall slightly further along from where Wiz and Hillier's scales had been placed. Using the sacred magic oath known only to a few, passed from generation to generation, he implanted the last piece of the shopkeeper's DNA into the rock and let it take effect.

Springing to life all around him before he'd had the chance to retreat back to his role at the body, the master mantra's lifelike holographic appearance came in at twice the size of Wiz and Hillier, much to everyone's surprise. With just a telepathic nudge, the king sent the dragons holding the body on their way, Peter and Richie making sure their friend Tank took it all in, soaked it all up with his eidetic memory, knowing that in the future, he'd desperately want to refer back to this moment.

Head uncontrollably lurching forward, plastic glasses still attached to his face, through the use of magic no doubt, the one thing all of those there would say in the coming days was that the old shopkeeper looked at peace. Whether through magic, design, chance or just because it was true, it did at least bring a little comfort to those watching. Laps finished, the mass of dragons glided towards the centre, the realisation of what was about to happen not lost on anyone in the audience.

And so without any formality or order, the two dragons on either side of Gee Tee relinquished their grip, allowing his huge prehistoric body to tumble down into the molten magma. Hitting belly first, like a school kid's first inexperienced dive from the top board at a swimming pool, a disaster in all but name, the pain exquisite, the only difference being that the school kid would resurface, something that had no chance of happening here. The old shopkeeper's plastic glasses drifted slowly down after him, dissolving instantly on making contact with the bright orange surface as they did so.

As the master mantra maker's scales sizzled black before disappearing into nothingness, frantic sobbing throughout the whole chamber could be heard, for the first time in many decades. Leaving it a minute or so, which seemed to him like a week, the king decided to call it, and in time honoured fashion started to bring the glass horn up to his face in an effort to end the ceremony. Before he did so, and got everyone else there to follow on, a few sad words escaped his parched lips.

"I wish you a fiery farewell, my friend."

The adventure continues in book 6, Evil Endeavours. Read on for an extract...

"We don't have to do this," he said warmly, "not if you're having second thoughts."

She wanted to, more than anything, and with him, but the fear of the unknown continued to hold the young lacrosse playing dragon in its grip, making her more than a little hesitant.

"It's not that, it's..."

And that was as far as she got before squeezing her eyes closed and shaking her head in what looked like pain.

"Rich?"

"Oh crap!"

"What is it?" enquired the strapping rugby player from his position next to her on the sofa.

Grabbing his arm, she jumped to her feet, pulling him up on the way.

"We need to go... NOW!" she duly announced, dragging him down the hallway, past the front door and out onto the pavement.

"But..."

Instinctively her first thought was to transform so that they could fly there, him on her back. Immediately, her permanent change in circumstances hit her like a shovel to the head. That was impossible now, the dragon guise she'd grown up in and loved so dearly, gone forever. If not that, then what, she thought, the magic of her birthright starting to bubble to the surface.

Using her grip on his arm to pull her around to face him on the pavement directly outside the house, Hook gazed longingly into her eyes, concerned at the worry that was clearly evident.

"What's wrong?"

"They're in trouble... BIG trouble and need our help."

"Uhhh... okay!"

"How long can you hold your breath?"

"WHAT!"

"How long?"

"Uhh... I don't know... a minute, perhaps a bit more."

"Take a deep breath!"

"Rich..."

"NOW!" she ordered.

Willing to do absolutely anything for her, including this, Hook did as he was asked and pulled in the biggest breath he could.

"HANG ON!" she cried.

Knowing there was no other way, she slammed the front door closed, redoubled her grip on his arm, and in a ball of multicoloured lightning that radiated out with her at the centre, both of them tore off out of the city heading north, their combined mass not concerned with roads or pathways, her brilliant and instinctive mind avoiding obstacles such as trees and fences, choosing the most expedient route to their goal, a massive speeding blur so fast that the humans they passed couldn't recognise it for what it really was... two heroes on a rescue mission.

ABOUT THE AUTHOR

Paul Cude is a husband, father, field hockey player and aspiring photographer. Lost without his hockey stick, he can often be found in between writing and chauffeuring children, reading anything from comics to sci-fi, fantasy to thrillers. Too often found chained to his computer, it would be little surprise to find him, in his free time, somewhere on the Dorset coastline, chasing over rocks and sand in an effort to capture his wonderful wife and lovely kids with his camera. Paul Cude is also the author of the White Dragon Saga.

Thank you for reading...

If you could take a couple of moments to write a review on either Amazon or Goodreads, it would be much appreciated.

CONNECT WITH PAUL ONLINE
www.paulcude.com
Twitter: @paul_cude
Facebook: Paul Cude
Instagram: paulcude

BOOKS IN THE SERIES:
A Threat from the Past
A Chilling Revelation
A Twisted Prophecy
Earth's Custodians
A Fiery Farewell
Evil Endeavours
Frozen to the Core
A Selfless Sacrifice
Christmas in Crisis

www.ingramcontent.com/pod-product-compliance
Lightning Source LLC
Chambersburg PA
CBHW060935190726

48286CB00005B/1287